United We Stand

Four Complete Novels Demonstrate the Power of Love During WWII

Joan Croston

Jane LaMunyon

Darlene Mindrup

Colleen L. Reece

BARBOUR BOOKS

An Imprint of Barbour Publishing, Inc.

C for Victory © 2000 by Barbour Publishing, Inc.
Escape on the Wind © 1997 by Barbour Publishing, Inc.
The Rising Son © 1997 by Barbour Publishing, Inc.
Candleshine © 1992 by Colleen L. Reece.

Cover photo: ©PhotoDisc, Inc.

ISBN 1-58660-523-2

All Scripture quotations, unless otherwise noted, are taken from the King James Version of the Bible.

Published by Barbour Books, an imprint of Barbour Publishing, Inc., P.O. Box 719, Uhrichsville, Ohio 44683, www.barbourbooks.com

 Member of the
Evangelical Christian
Publishers Association

Printed in the United States of America.
5 4 3

United We Stand

C for Victory

Joan Croston

To my husband Lee;
my daughters and sons-in-law,
Kelly and Darren Kalthoff, Jenna and Erich Harris;
and my friend Jan Shy.
Thanks for your help, encouragement, and proofreading—
and for keeping me from being devoured by the computer!

Chapter 1

Ruth Sinclair tucked a strand of wavy brown hair under the red-and-white bandanna tied around her head and slipped into her coat. "Can you believe it, Grandma? The Nakamuras forced from their home! Raw egg thrown all over it—inside and out! How can anyone be so hateful?" She grimaced and gave a shudder. "Cleaning up the slimy mess over there is an awful job, but if you let it dry, it sticks like glue!"

Alma Peterson chuckled as she put the last of the dishes away. "Getting squeamish on us, Ruth?" she teased and hung up the dish towel.

"I didn't mean it that way, Gram," Ruth answered softly. "Cleaning up the mess is nothing compared to what the Nakamuras are going through."

Alma shut the cupboard door with a sigh. "And it's certainly no laughing matter, either. A community couldn't ask for better neighbors than the Nakamuras—and then to treat them like this! Shipped off to an internment camp by the government and their home ransacked by hoodlums!" She shook her head as she grabbed the broom and tackled a dusting of flour that lay like a skiff of snow on the brick-patterned linoleum.

A cold spring wind whistled and whined around the corners of the old farmhouse. Inside, Alma's kitchen was warm and cozy as a fire crackled in the wood cookstove, and the fragrant aroma from her morning's baking lingered in the air.

Ruth buttoned her coat and glanced at the familiar clutter. A flour sifter and measuring cups were waiting to be put away, and oatmeal cookies and loaves of fresh bread had been set out to cool. She smiled, remembering how a cookie and a hug had soothed her hurts over the years. *But that won't be enough comfort in this war,* she thought sadly.

She reached for a cookie, then paused as a plaintive *moo* drifted into the kitchen. A moment of silence followed, and it started again. "If it's not one thing, it's another." She sighed and stepped to the window to check on the heifer standing in the backyard. "I've chased that cow all over the place 'til I see hamburgers every time I look at it!"

"You'd better go before she wanders off, Ruth." Alma came up behind her and peered over her shoulder. "Grandpa's working at the back of the Nakamuras' house, replacing more of the windows those hoodlums broke. Tell him he needs to hurry home and get that cow back in the pasture. She won't mind anyone but him." She rested her broom against the wall and picked up the dustpan.

Ruth nodded and patted her coat for the Nakamuras' key, finally finding it in the pocket of the brown slacks she wore. "While I'm there, I'll stay and do more scrubbing, Gram. At least the kitchen's done. That was the worst. All those broken dishes!"

"Just do what you can, Dear. The Ladies' Aid will be out next week to finish cleaning." Alma emptied the dustpan and hurried to assemble a package of cleaning supplies.

Ruth picked up a cookie. "How can this be happening in America, Gram? Since Japan attacked Pearl Harbor, I know people are afraid, but we can't start turning on each other."

Alma handed her the supplies and patted her shoulder. "People aren't trusting the Lord, Ruth. They've let fear get ahold of them."

Ruth opened the door and stepped out to see the fawn-colored Jersey staring at her across the lawn. "Just wait. Grandpa'll take care of you!" she threatened. It bellowed and gave a frisky leap as she descended the steps.

Alma followed Ruth out on the wooden porch, wiping her hands on her blue-flowered apron. "I'll keep an eye on her 'til he gets here. At least she's happy with the grass in the yard for now."

Ruth hurried down the driveway and turned onto the gravel road, stepping carefully to avoid puddles left by the night's rain. She shuddered as the April wind tore at her coat, then whipped through the Douglas fir trees swaying beside the road.

Ahead, the Nakamuras' white farmhouse stood silent and empty against the gray sky. "It looks as gloomy as something out of a Gothic novel." She stared at the house as the wind tugged at her bandanna. "Lord, what's happening to our world?" she whispered.

Since the past December 7 when Japan had bombed Pearl Harbor, nothing had been the same. Lives had been disrupted as men went off to war and families moved to work in the war industry. Fear stalked everyone. As a result, the government had issued Executive Order Number 9066, requiring that all persons in America of Japanese ancestry be sent to internment camps. People were afraid the Japanese Americans might spy or signal the enemy. When a Japanese submarine fired on a petroleum complex near Santa Barbara, California, on February 23, their worst fears seemed to be confirmed. Though no evidence was found, fear pointed to spies and Japanese espionage.

Ruth turned off the road and started up the driveway to the house with a sigh. "I wonder where they are n—"

A car roared up behind her and screeched to a halt. She whirled around to see an old battered car idling on the roadway. The driver thrust his head out the window, his face an angry red above a black, scraggly beard. He shook his fist in the air as he screamed at her. "We don't need no Jap lovers around here, Teach!" he shouted. "We drove them traitors off this place. Git back home and decide which side of this war yer on!" He gunned the engine, and the car sped down the road, careening around the bend and disappearing from view.

Ruth stood stunned. "Who was that?" she whispered. Her heart raced and prickles of fear ran down her arms. In the distance, she could hear a car coming toward her. She caught her breath. "I hope he's not coming back!" Quickly she turned down the muddy driveway.

She took a step and glanced toward the sound. As her shoe hit the slippery mud, her feet flew out from under her and she fell backwards, catching herself on her hands. "Oh, no! Fine time to be clumsy, Ruth Sinclair!" she moaned aloud as she glanced up to see a late-model green Plymouth driving toward her. *At least it's not him,* she thought with relief. But what a place for the local teacher to be on display! She made a futile effort to stand, muttering at the mud covering her shoes and coat.

As the car reached the driveway, it suddenly swerved to the side of the road, skidding on the gravel until it came to a halt. The door flew open and a tall, well-built man jumped out. A quick jolt of fear ran through her as she stared at him.

"Are you all right, Ma'am?" the stranger called out over the top of the car with an air of friendly concern.

Ruth could only nod. She looked carefully at the dark-haired stranger and hesitated. He was well dressed in a business suit and topcoat. Not the type to be a threat. "Just stuck in the mud," she finally answered.

The man stepped carefully to the driveway and reached out to pull her up. "No, my hands are too muddy," she protested. "You're dressed up. I can make it." She attempted to stand and slipped back down.

He smiled warmly, his dark brown eyes showing the hint of a tease. "When a lovely lady keeps falling at my feet, the least I can do is help her up. Here, grab hold. I'm washable." He pulled her to her feet and handed her a handkerchief to wipe her hands.

"Hey! You! What's going on out there?" George Peterson rushed around the corner of the farmhouse, a pitchfork in his hands. "You okay, Ruth?" he called out as he hurried toward them. He eyed the stranger warily, holding the fork in front of him.

She nodded and took a deep breath. "I slipped on the mud, Grandpa. This gentleman stopped to help me." She shook some of the mud off her shoes. "Did you hear what that man shouted? The one who roared by in that old car?"

George lowered the pitchfork, his eyes still on the stranger. "Heard it clear back there."

The man kept his eyes on the fork and stepped back to the edge of the road, one hand jingling the coins in his pocket. "I saw the lady had slipped on the mud, Sir, and only stopped to give her a hand."

He let out his breath as George jabbed the pitchfork into the ground and said, "Appreciate that."

"Did something else happen here?" the stranger asked, glancing from Ruth to George with a puzzled look on his face.

Ruth related the incident. "I didn't recognize the man," she concluded.

George thrust a hand in the pocket of his overalls and turned to the stranger. "This is the Nakamura farm. We're neighbors. Promised to look after their place while they're gone." He leaned on the pitchfork but kept his eye on the stranger.

Anger flared in Ruth's eyes. "Can you believe it? The Nakamuras were hauled away with two days' notice. No trial. No checking their loyalty to this country. Just because they're of Japanese ancestry. They're American citizens, but it didn't mean a thing! They were appalled at Pearl Harbor." She sighed as her angry tirade cooled.

The stranger watched her intently and smiled. "The world sure could use more like you, Ma'am." He reached up quickly as the wind tugged at his hat.

"We're cleaning up the damage so the place will be ready when they come home," she explained. "As soon as the government finds out they're loyal citizens, they should be released. After all, this is America." She lifted a muddy shoe. It sloshed and she smiled sheepishly. "Looks like I'm the one who needs to clean up."

"A mud bath's supposed to keep a lady beautiful." The man winked at her. "Don't mean to be impolite, but I'm late for an appointment." He opened his car door and turned. "Be careful, both of you. Anti-Japanese sentiment is strong right now. Too many people think every Japanese helped plan the attack on Pearl Harbor personally. And they don't take kindly to those who befriend them." He touched his hat as he climbed into the car and drove off.

George pulled the pitchfork out of the ground. "Don't remember seeing him around here before." He looked at Ruth's muddy appearance. "You'd better go clean up, and I'll get back to work. Nak and Suzi were good friends and neighbors. Those hoodlums won't scare us off."

"Oh, no, Grandpa; I almost forgot. Grandma needs you at home. A cow got out, and we couldn't get it back in the pasture."

George sighed. "That's Britches again. Too smart for her own britches!" He chuckled and winked at her. "You staying here?"

Ruth nodded and retrieved the package Alma had given her. "I brought supplies to do more cleaning." She glanced down at her muddy shoes and coat. "Myself included!"

"You'll be okay here by yourself?"

"I'll be fine, Grandpa. They're too cowardly to try anything in the daytime. Besides, at twenty-four I can't act like a baby when there's work to do."

"Feed Billy's pigeons, too, will you?"

Ruth nodded and he hurried away.

She turned toward the two-story house, trying to shake off the fear and sadness the incident had brought back. As she remembered the day the Nakamuras were forced from their home, Suzi's parting words echoed in her ears. "Don't worry, Ruth. The Lord will be with us in the camp just as He was with us here. And think of all the people we can tell about Him. He's giving us a mission field." Her faith had shone through the tears in her eyes.

Lord, I wouldn't see opportunity instead of anger, she thought as she approached the farmhouse. *I wish I had Suzi's trust.*

A gust of wind blew scraps of paper across the yard and banged the screen door against the house. She picked up a paper as it tumbled over her feet and stared at the 100% she had marked on Amy Nakamura's math paper. March 23, 1942. She shook her head and ran her finger over the date Amy had written only a month ago. Now, to many people, this gentle Christian family had become the enemy.

She stopped at a faucet on the side of the house and washed the mud off her hands. "But there's no hope for my shoes or my coat," she muttered, scraping her muddy shoes on the grass.

"Meow."

She started at the sound, then laughed as a small orange cat bounded out from under the porch to chase a paper blowing by. "You startled me, Fluffy! It's so quiet here I'm getting jumpy." Ruth picked up the cat and walked to the porch steps. Fluffy purred loudly and snuggled against her. "Let's get out of this wind. You're supposed to stay at Grandpa Peterson's while Amy's gone. Why do you keep coming back home?" She scratched Fluffy's ear. "Mice taste better here?"

She slipped off her shoes and coat, then pulled the key from her pocket and reached for the door. Stains of spattered egg and anti-Japanese graffiti were still evident even after all the scrubbing they'd done.

At her touch the door swung open. She hesitated, looking around. "Anyone here?" Only silence answered her. "I'm sure I locked up after we cleaned last time. I hope no one broke in again." She poked her head through the doorway into the kitchen. Her heart skipped a beat. "Doesn't look as if anything's been disturbed, Fluffy." She held the cat closer. "Big help you'd be, but I feel better having something alive with me."

The cozy kitchen was clean and tidy again and waiting for the Nakamuras to gather around the large oak table. Books were back in order on shelves extending along the east wall. And above the stove Suzi's beautifully stitched motto declared the faith the family lived by: "The Lord is my Shepherd."

What a mess this was! she remembered. Eggs had been thrown inside the house, too. Windows broken. Glassware destroyed. Furniture overturned and smashed. Books torn and scattered everywhere. The Ladies' Aid had attacked it with mops, brooms, and scrub brushes while Grandpa Peterson and the men worked on the damaged furniture.

Ruth filled a pail with soapy water and carried it to the dining room. "It would be so easy to stay angry," she said aloud, "but Suzi wouldn't want that. 'Look for the Lord's nugget of gold in your troubles,' she'd say. 'He always hides one in there, but remember, if you're angry, you'll miss it.'"

She scraped at a hardened chunk of egg yolk and hummed one of Suzi's favorite songs to counter the anger she felt at the senseless damage. "'Count your blessings; name them one by one,'" she sang softly as she worked. "'Count your blessings; see what God has done.'" She stepped back and checked her work. "This war's bringing so many woes right now, it's easy to forget the blessings."

She picked up the bucket and carried it to the sink to dump the dirty water. Suddenly she froze as footsteps moved across the porch and the door rattled.

"Yoo-hoo, are you in there, Ruth?" Marge Evans's voice sounded from the porch as she rapped on the kitchen door.

Ruth let out her breath in relief. "I'm in the kitchen, Marge. Come on in," she called out as she rinsed the pail and set it down, her heart still pounding.

Marge stepped into the room, patting her blond windblown hair and pulling her coat back in order. "I declare, Oregon's not a state for women and hairdos!"

Ruth laughed as she wiped her hands and surveyed her friend. "I don't know about that, Marge. Looks like the wind raised your pompadour another inch. You'd never have managed that hairdo on your own," she teased.

"I'll ignore that!" Marge tossed her head and glanced around the room. "What a difference! I haven't seen it since you ladies cleaned it up." She ran her hand over a chair. "Your grandpa did a great job repairing the furniture, too."

Ruth nodded. "A lot of work, but it's getting there. We want to have it ready when the Nakamuras come back. Hopefully soon."

"Oh, did you hear?" Marge took off her coat and laid it on a chair. "The latest rumor says Leland Hinson and a cousin of his were part of the gang that ransacked this place."

Ruth hung up the towel. "Grandma Peterson says it's hate looking for an excuse to land somewhere."

"It sure landed here. What they wrote on the door was awful!" Marge declared.

Ruth put the cleaning supplies under the sink. "Here on the West Coast people are afraid we'll be bombed or invaded by Japan. And some just want an excuse to hate." She described to Marge the incident she had experienced on her way over. "I don't know the man who stopped to help me, but I'm glad someone was there for me, embarrassing as it was." She wiped the bucket and hung the rag to dry. "Are you going to the community meeting at the school this afternoon? It's about the war effort on the home front."

"That's one reason I stopped by," Marge said. "To see if you were going,

I mean. Your grandma said you were over here cleaning and feeding Billy's pigeons."

Ruth leaned against the counter. "Grandpa and I promised Suzi and Nak we'd look after the place for them, and that includes Billy's pigeons. Grandpa took most of the other animals to his place, but it was easier to leave the pigeons here."

Marge put down the package she carried and leaned over a book on the table. "Ruth, look at this. I can't believe they left their Bible behind. They read it all the time." A large Bible lay open in the center of the table.

"They took a small one with them," Ruth explained as she joined Marge at the table. "They always left this one open to the chapter they were reading. Suzi wanted it to stay at the center of their home while they're gone." She peered at the book—Psalm 23. "Be their Shepherd, Lord, and keep them safe wherever they are," she prayed softly.

"Amen to that!" Marge added. She reached into the package. "I brought supplies so we can start repairing the books that were damaged." She took out glue and tape. As she sat down, her toe hit an object that slid out from under the table. "What in the world. . . ?"

"Ben-Hur!" Ruth bent to pick up the book. "So that's where it was. Suzi wanted to take it with her, but she couldn't find it." She adjusted Suzi's bookmark and laid the book on the shelf.

"Here you go." Ruth carried a pile of damaged books over to Marge and sat down. "Our local librarian to the rescue." She smiled at her friend and handed her a book. "Your expertise in book repair is greatly appreciated."

"Glad to help. I had to work the day you ladies cleaned." Marge concentrated on the torn spine of the book, then glanced at her friend sideways. "But now let's get to important things—like matters of the heart!" She put the book down and looked at her friend intently. "So, tell me, what's been going on with you and Harold since he went overseas?" she pried. "I've been gone so long; I'm way behind on the life and loves of Ruth Sinclair. Rumor says he was injured in combat. What's happening?"

Ruth pushed a strand of dark brown hair from her face. "I'm not sure, Marge. Pilots stationed overseas are too busy to write these days, I guess. His mother says he's been in the thick of the fighting. His plane was hit and barely made it back to the base. According to her he wasn't badly injured, but I haven't heard from him in ages."

"I don't understand." Marge looked up and frowned. "I know we haven't had time to talk much since I moved back here, but we were best friends, Ruth Sinclair. There's trouble in paradise and you didn't tell me?" Marge pursed her red lips. "You have some explaining to do!"

Ruth's fingers traced the red-and-white-checkered patterns in the oilcloth table covering. "Marge, when Harold and I dated in high school, I was sure

13

we'd get married someday, but we drifted apart in college. Afterwards, when he moved back here and we started dating again. . ."

Ruth sighed. "I thought my dreams were coming true 'til I found out he was running with a wild crowd. I couldn't believe some of his language or the parties he wanted to go to. And he hardly ever went to church anymore. I tried to talk to him, but. . ." She took a deep breath.

"But trying to save him from himself didn't work, I guess," Marge ventured softly as she reached for a book.

"Once we got back together, I thought he'd be the guy I'd always known." Ruth shook her head. "But, no, it didn't work."

"You should have settled this before he went overseas. You know, talked it out and decided one way or the other," Marge declared firmly.

"I tried, Marge. I told him I couldn't spend my life with someone who didn't have the same values I did. We had a big fight, and then he told me he was leaving to be a pilot for the Royal Air Force in England. He thought of it as a big lark and said this would get the adventurous spirit, as he called it, out of his system. It was so dangerous over there; I didn't have the heart to insist we were through for good."

"I'm confused." Marge frowned as she applied glue to the book spine. "Did you promise to wait for him or what?" She peered up at her friend as glue ran down the book and onto the table. She quickly reached for a rag.

"No, not exactly. Actually, I'm not sure what I promised, Marge. He begged me to write him. He said it would help to have a girl back home when he was in the thick of things." Ruth twisted a strand of hair between her fingers.

"A girl back. . .Ruth! He's just trying to keep you on a string while he lives as he pleases over there. You need to tell him to take that string and go fly a kite instead!" Marge drummed her long red nails on the table.

"Dear John letters are so low, Marge; how could I? There he is risking his life and even getting injured. Besides, maybe the war will wake him up. According to the few letters I've received, so far it hasn't worked at all, but he should be home on leave soon, and we'll settle it then."

Marge laid the book aside and put her hand over Ruth's. "I'm sorry you and Harold ended up like this, Ruth, but it's time for you to move on. Harold has!"

"But, Mar—"

"Ruth, face it. It's over!" Marge patted her hand. "But you're not alone. I'm here, and I'm putting myself in charge of your future!" Marge's eyes twinkled. "What you need is someone new in your life, and I'm the one to help you find him. No one's better at matching up couples than Marge Evans," she declared smugly. "Remember how well I did with Tom and Betty and Mark and Ellen? And Jack and me, of course." The diamond on her finger sparkled in the light.

"Marge, I don't need your help. I'm not looking for anyone right now,"

Ruth protested. "I have to settle things with Harold first."

"That's why you need me. I'll save you from yourself!" Marge put the repair materials back in the package. "It's a good thing ı got this job at the library and moved back here, or who knows what would have happened to you!"

"Marge, I. . ."

"Remember this, Ruth. Harold tied you down here, knowing your sense of loyalty. But if I know the new Harold, he's having a wild time over there while you just sit here. I won't allow it!" Marge shook her finger in Ruth's face.

Ruth grabbed her friend's hand. "I know you mean well, Marge, but I can't. This has to be settled the right way. Dad always taught us to stand by our word no matter what. I have to wait 'til Harold comes home and settle this face-to-face."

"You can't keep me from trying, Ruth Sinclair. It's for your own good!" Marge raised an eyebrow at her friend. "Hmm, let's see now." She looked Ruth up and down. "Medium height. That's easier to match. Slim, very pretty—that helps." She reached for a piece of Ruth's shoulder-length hair. "All you do is part it on the side and pull it over with a clip. Now if you had a pompadour. . ."

"Marge!" Ruth looked aghast. "I'm not a horse on an auction block!"

Marge calmly ignored her. "And your clothes are too plain. You need some color and fashion zing. Now if. . ." She paused to study her friend.

Ruth finally exploded. "That's quite enough, Marge Evans! I'm not looking for someone, and I don't need to be analyzed!"

"Temper, temper. It's for your own good," Marge insisted, ignoring her protests. "I'm a matchmaking success because I analyze and plan carefully, Ruth Sinclair. You just wait. You'll see." She sat back and thought a moment. "Now let's see. Who's single around here? There's Warren Bowman and Herschel Owens and. . ."

"Herschel Owens! Marge! He's old! He must be at least thirty-five, and he lives with his mother! Besides, he's strange. He always makes me feel uncomfortable. I'm not looking for anyone, and there's no one around here even if I were. That's enough of that!"

"I'm just taking inventory, and I have to be thorough." Unperturbed, Marge glanced at her watch. "Lunchtime. Gotta run. Want to go to the meeting together?" She put her coat on and picked up the package of supplies.

"If you start behaving yourself!" Ruth threw Marge a scowl. "Grandpa's driving over. We can stop to get you on the way. That'll save your hairdo," she teased as she put the books back on the shelf.

Marge wrinkled her nose at her friend, pausing at the door to button her coat. "Thanks. With both my parents working at the shipyards, there's never a car available. See ya."

Ruth tidied the room and nudged the cat sleeping on a rug by the door. "Let's go, Fluffy. You can't stay in here."

Outside, she put on her muddy shoes and coat and hurried out back to the pen where Billy Nakamura kept his prized pigeons. Fluffy trotted alongside. As Ruth opened the wire cage and poured grain into the feeder, Fluffy made a leap for the open door, missed, and clung to the edge of the cage.

She grabbed the cat and quickly fastened the latch. "To you they're just ten tasty meals, Fluffy. There had better be ten pigeons here when I come back, or you're in trouble! Come on. Let's go home."

She picked up the cat and started toward the path leading to her grandparents' farm. "We'll go this way. It'll be soggy, but there's no use chancing another run-in with that man."

At the edge of the field, Ruth paused to gaze at the world she loved. Fields carved out of the woods. Vine maple and dogwood trees. Wildflowers peeping up in the field. Douglas fir trees towering over everything. It all looked so peaceful. "I never dreamed this could be threatened by war," she murmured, "but I can't deny it. Our country's at war with Japan and Germany, and it affects all our lives."

Fluffy gave a wiggle and leaped to the ground, bounding after a robin hopping across the field in search of a worm. "For you, life's easy, Fluffy. Home is wherever there's a bird or a mouse." The robin flew off safely, and the cat bounded back to her. "My world's all turned around. Mom and Dad have moved to work in the war industry. I'm living with Grandma and Grandpa. Bud's in basic training." She shook her head. "I can't imagine my brother in the navy!"

She picked up the cat. "And then there's Harold. Always ready to go when there's a hint of adventure. He had to head for England to help the Royal Air Force, danger and all." Fluffy snuggled up under her chin, purring loudly. "I do worry about him, Fluffy, but things are so different between us now."

She started through the field. "Lord," she whispered, "the world's falling apart. We need You."

Chapter 2

A large sign posted on the side of the school gym announced the afternoon's event:

Fir Glen Community Meeting
"The Home Front"
Speaker: Jim Griffin,
Community Coordinator of Civilian Defense

"The whole community must be here," Ruth murmured, peering on tip-toe over the crowd at the door as she and Marge edged their way into the gym behind George and Alma Peterson.

The old building felt comfortably warm from the large woodstove at the side of the room. Chairs and benches were lined up in rows facing the stage. People milled about, warming themselves and chatting in small groups.

"Hey, Miss Sinclair!" A short, blond-haired boy dressed in army-style boots, rolled-up jeans, and a khaki shirt bounded toward her, working his yo-yo and looking eager. "Think our class'll get to do some stuff to help win the war?"

"Tim, be careful with that or you'll hit someone," Ruth warned, putting out her hand to stop the yo-yo. "The community coordinator's here to tell us what's planned. I'm sure there'll be some way you kids can help."

"Maybe he'll have so much for us to do we won't have time for English and spelling anymore." Tim raised his eyebrows and looked hopeful.

"No such luck." Ruth laughed and patted his shoulder. "If we're that busy, we'll have to start school earlier."

"Oh, no!" Tim wandered off, groaning at the prospect.

"Take your seats, everyone. We need to get started." Joe Duncan's voice boomed over the buzz of conversations. Ruth led the group to four empty seats. Conversations died and attention shifted to Joe Duncan on the wooden stage at one end of the gym.

"I got this job because I can talk so loud." The audience chuckled and nodded. "Don't have much to say, so I'll turn this meeting over to our community coordinator of civilian defense." Joe's voice boomed through the gym. "You all remember Jim Griffin. Went to school here in Fir Glen. After college, he went off to work in California, and now he's back to help his dad run Griffin's Container Company. Got himself appointed coordinator of this-here civilian defense. Jim, it's yours." He gave a sigh of relief and returned to his seat.

A tall, dark-haired man in the front row stood and walked to the stage. Wind rattled the windows and whined mournfully around the corners of the old gym as the people watched curiously.

"I remember him," Marge leaned over and whispered to Ruth. "He was three grades ahead of us. All the girls thought he was so good-looking. He still is!" She paused. "I didn't realize he'd moved back here." She glanced at Ruth sideways. "Beth Marshall heard he's single. Hmm. . ."

"Shh, let's listen." Ruth scooted in her seat so she could see around the woman in front of her. She looked at the man carefully and nudged her friend. "Marge, that's the man who stopped to help me this morning." Ruth settled back in her seat as the speaker began.

"It's been awhile, but I see a lot of familiar faces out there." Jim Griffin smiled and scanned the audience. "When I went to school here, Fir Glen was a community of friendly people always willing to help someone else. I'm counting on that now. The war effort needs the help of all of us, young and old."

"Kids, too?" Tim Henderson piped up, then ducked as his mother leaned over to shush him.

"Yes," Jim nodded seriously, "kids, too. We have a big job ahead of us." He looked out at the crowd. "I'll be coordinating the defense and war-related efforts for Fir Glen. That includes air-raid drills, blackouts, scrap drives, volunteer projects, rationing—whatever it takes to help the war effort and keep us safe."

He shuffled through the papers he held. "First, I want to introduce volunteers who will fill important posts. Bob Miller will be our air-raid warden. You all know Bob, owner of Fir Glen Market across the road."

Bob jumped to his feet, proudly waving a hand in the air and beaming as the audience applauded. He hooked his thumbs in his suspenders and rocked forward on his toes. "I'm in charge of air-raid drills and the blackout," he announced. "You'll hear from me if there's any light showing from your windows at night. Keep them blackout curtains closed!"

Marge nudged Ruth. "We're in for it now. That authority'll go to his head for sure!"

Ruth smiled and nodded. "He reminds me of Grandpa's bantam roosters—cocky and always strutting around." She watched Bob's suspenders snap back into place as he removed his thumbs.

"Bob's also volunteered the lot behind his store for our scrap drives, starting with tires and any rubber we can scavenge," Jim continued. He looked at his papers. "Next volunteer is Joe Duncan." Joe bobbed up and down, ducking his head shyly at the applause. "Here on the West Coast we have to be prepared for a Japanese attack at any time," Jim declared seriously.

A murmur ran through the crowd. People looked at each other, fear reflecting on their faces.

"Joe will head up the Ground Observer Corps. Any comments, Joe?"

"We need volunteers. See me after the meeting to sign up," Joe called out. "You'll be trained to identify any enemy aircraft you see and phone in the information. The observer post will be set up on the feedstore roof. We need to keep that post manned!"

"And," Jim added, "scrap paper can be dropped off at the feedstore. You kids will have a lot of collecting to do." He looked over at Tim, who grinned at his classmates and waved at Ruth.

Jim paused and looked out at the crowd. "Now to the part you've been reading about in the *Oregonian*. We'll have to make sacrifices to win this war. That includes rationing. Tires were rationed back in January. The next item will be sugar."

"Oh, no!" A groan broke out spontaneously from the younger generation scattered throughout the room.

Jim continued. "On May 4 through 7, you'll register here at the school so every individual can receive a sugar book, as we call it. One person from your family can register for the entire household. Each month you'll be allowed about two pounds of sugar per person."

A lady in the third row stood. "Most of us bake and can our own fruit. How will we get by?" She sat down to a murmur of agreement throughout the audience.

"This threatens my sweet tooth, too," Jim admitted, "but I know you'll all join me in making any sacrifice to win this war." He smiled and patted his waistline. "And think how slim and trim we'll be without all those desserts!"

The crowd chuckled and nodded.

"When you go to the market, you'll turn in stamps from your ration book in order to buy sugar," he continued and held up a sample booklet. "No stamps, no sugar. And," he warned, "the stamps must be torn out of the book in the presence of the store clerk, or they become void."

He paused and looked around at the crowd. "To prevent hoarding, the stamps are coded so they're good for about a month. After that they'll expire. In order to get the next ration book, you'll be required to turn in the old one, so don't throw the book away when it's empty or expired."

People in the audience glanced about uncertainly as Jim explained the regulations.

"And be sure to check your sugar supply before you come so you can tell us how much you have on hand," he added. He looked over at Tim and his friends. "Since we'll register all day on May 4, the school board has canceled classes for the day."

A buzz of excitement ran through the children 'til frowns from their parents silenced them.

Jim added, "The rest of the week you can register after school."

Ruth watched the speaker. *Marge's right,* she thought. *He is good-looking. Dark hair. Maybe six foot. Friendly, with an easy confidence.* She heard him mention teachers, and her thoughts turned back to the speech.

"Our dedicated teachers," Jim was saying, "will be in charge of the registration, with help from our local women's club. Could we have the teachers stand, please?" Ruth blushed and rose to her feet along with three other women.

"Ah, yes, Mrs. Foster. Our favorite first- and second-grade teacher." Mrs. Foster nodded to the group and smiled.

Jim continued. "Mrs. Christianson. It's been a long time. For you, probably not long enough. As I recall, I wiggled my way through third and fourth grades."

Mrs. Christianson laughed and protested. "But you were still a good student, Jim."

"And Mrs. Hastings. By the time I was in your seventh- and eighth-grade room, we had become a little too well acquainted in your principal's office, I'm afraid." As the audience chuckled, he turned to Ruth. "And this is. . ."

"That's Miss Sinclair," Tim announced. "She's my teacher."

Jim smiled at her and paused.

He recognizes me, Ruth thought. *He wouldn't dare explain in front of everyone!* She shifted uncomfortably, and the room suddenly felt extremely warm.

"I know I wasn't in your class. Glad to meet you, Miss Sinclair." Jim smiled at her as she blushed again and gratefully sat down with the other teachers. "I'll meet with you ladies this week to brief you on the registration procedures. Is Tuesday after school okay?" His glance rested on Ruth while the other teachers nodded their approval.

"Now let me call your attention to the posters." Jim pointed to the array on the gym wall. "You'll see these all over. They're to remind you and inspire you." On one, Uncle Sam pointed and declared, "I want you," while another promoted war bonds.

Arlan Anderson stood up. "With so many people working at Swan Island Shipyards, we need to pay special attention to these." He pointed to a cluster of posters: "Loose talk kills." "A slip of the lip may sink a ship." "Don't tell secrets." "You never know who might be a spy these days, so be careful what you say!"

"Good point, Arlan; one we need to take seriously," Jim commented. "I guess that's it for now. We'll post announcements at Bob's market and the feedstore. Check their bulletin boards often." He paused and looked out at the audience. His eye caught Ruth's for a moment, and he smiled.

"One more thing. I think I should say this straight out and get it over with. Many of you have a brother, uncle, son, or husband in the service." Heads nodded here and there. "I'm doing all I can here because the service wouldn't take me. Too many ear infections as a child, and I ended up with a broken eardrum. But I promise to work hard on this end to keep us safe. Now let's have Pastor Cameron lead us in prayer for our country, and then we'll close with 'God Bless Our Native Land.'"

As the singing faded and people rose to leave, a small figure pushed through the crowd. "Hey, Miss Sinclair, I'm gonna collect papers and catch some spies! Me and Charlie are starting a detective club!" Tim bounded up, looking thrilled.

George chuckled. "What are you going to do? Knock 'em out with your yo-yo?"

"Hey, good idea, Mr. Peterson!" Tim grinned and wandered away with his friends, whispering plans for detecting spies.

Alma chatted with neighbors as they worked their way to the door. George followed patiently behind his wife.

"He noticed you," Marge whispered to Ruth. "Did you see it? Jim Griffin kept looking right at you. He's interested in you." She spoke excitedly. "You need someone new in your life, and he'll be perfect."

"Marge!" Ruth ignored her and peered ahead to see what was slowing their exit. By the door she saw Jim Griffin meeting the people as they left the building. She felt a nervous flutter. As they approached the door, Marge nudged her. She scowled back.

Jim held out his hand and grasped hers warmly. "Ah, the new teacher. I'm glad to meet you—again." He smiled and continued to hold her hand.

Ruth smiled back. "Thank you again for your help, Mr. Griffin." She pulled her hand away and moved on.

As they stepped outside, Marge gushed, "He's even better looking up close. How can he still be single?" She muttered under her breath, "Jack, Jack, Jack," and winked at Ruth. "Just reminding myself. If there were to be a temptation, that would be it. But I do love Jack, so I'll leave Mr. Griffin to you."

"Enough of you, Miss Matchmaker. You know the situation. It's not right."

"You two ready?" George interrupted as the wind tore at his hat. "The car's this way."

"If we can tear Ruth away," Marge teased.

"In the car with you." Ruth opened the door for her friend. As she waited for Marge to get in, she glanced toward the building where Jim was greeting the last of the crowd. He was shaking old Mrs. Benson's hand and patting her shoulder.

"And you said there was no one around to get interested in," Marge said smugly as Ruth climbed in and shut the door. "Once I'm on the job, look what turns up. What did I tell you? Matchmaking's a gift I have!"

21

Chapter 3

The bell of the white country church resounded throughout the community the next morning, each bong echoing an invitation to come. Ruth stepped into the church entry, clutching her Bible and pulling on her white gloves. She straightened her hat, feeling all askew after an hour in the basement with her fifth- and sixth-grade Sunday school class.

People stood around chatting in small groups as they waited for the service to begin. Spying her grandmother's flowered dress and small black hat, Ruth walked over to the cluster of ladies gathered around Alma Peterson. "We'll meet here in the basement on Tuesday mornings," Alma was saying. "Bring your scrap material and supplies."

She turned as Ruth walked up. "There you are, Dear. The Ladies' Aid is going to make quilts for English refugees bombed out by the Nazis. Those poor people need anything we can send them. They've lost everything."

"When school's out, you'll have to join us," Hazel Ellison added with a giggle.

Ruth smiled to herself. A better-hearted woman couldn't be found, but she was unique. Whatever Hazel said was accompanied by that giggle. And her hats! A pile of flowers swayed atop the hat as Hazel giggled.

"Ten o'clock Tuesday morning, ladies," Alma reminded them and took Ruth's elbow. "Grandpa's saving us a seat. We'd better sit before people think we're the choir marching in. Wouldn't they be sorry!" Alma bustled away to join her husband.

As the congregation sang the opening hymn, Ruth looked around the sanctuary. The old pews were worn from worshippers who had come faithfully over the years to praise God and pray. Again they came on this morning to beseech God's help for their country and to thank Him for His blessings. She studied the people. With the world at war, what would happen to their lives? What sacrifices would they be called to make? Her mind drifted to people in the war zones and the extreme sacrifices they were facing.

She was drawn back to the service as Pastor Cameron stepped to the pulpit and looked out at his congregation. "My friends," he began, "we live in fearful times. Each day's news is worse than that of the day before. The Japanese have taken Guam, Manila, and places most of us had never heard of before the war. We read of horrors like Bataan and its death march."

A child dropped a hymnal, and the congregation jumped.

"Fear grips our land," he continued. "A cruel and inhuman evil strides through the world. Is Satan winning? Will he be victorious?"

The congregation grew quieter. Even the children were still. Ruth glanced around at the people she had known since she was a child spending summers at her grandparents' farm. Good people. Not perfect but good-hearted and hardworking. As her eyes moved down the rows, she saw Jim Griffin sitting with his parents, intent on the pastor's words.

"In the months ahead, you'll be hearing about V for victory." The pastor held up his hand in the victory sign. "Victory gardens. Victory homes. We must all do our part to stop this evil and defend our human freedom, but can man by himself defeat evil?"

Ruth could see heads firmly shaking.

"Never!" the pastor continued. "Our men in the service are paying a price to contain evil, but they cannot defeat it forever. Only God can do that. He, too, had to pay a price—the life of Christ, His only Son. On the cross Christ defeated death, Satan, and evil with His life."

Heads of the congregation members nodded their agreement. Ruth could see Hazel Ellison's flowers bobbing.

"V for victory? Yes, but for us it's C for victory—Christ's victory. We must all do our parts, but our main battle must be on our knees in prayer."

Ruth glanced over at Jim. His face was serious and his head nodded in agreement.

"So I implore you to join in the war effort every way you can, but I implore you above all else to pray without ceasing. Remember, the only true victory is in Christ. Amen." He shut his Bible. "Let's close with 'Onward Christian Soldiers.'"

As the hymn faded, the congregation rose. "He sure got to the bottom of it," George Peterson commented as they left the pew. "If people hadn't left God out of things, we wouldn't be in this mess."

"Prayer is the only way," Alma agreed.

As Ruth followed her grandparents, a deep voice sounded to her left. "Hello again. Miss Sinclair, isn't it?"

She turned to see Jim Griffin smiling at her. "Yes, I'm the teacher you didn't have," she replied and smiled. "The one who takes mud baths in public."

Jim chuckled. "My loss, though I am glad to meet you now instead of as a student. As for the mud baths, you're a living ad for their effectiveness. Say. . ."

"Hey, Miss Sinclair!" Tim Henderson pushed his way through the crowd and shook her arm. "Mr. Griffin's gonna coach our youth softball team. I'm gonna play first base! C'mon, Mr. Griffin. The guys are waiting for you. We need to plan our first practice." He tugged at Jim's sleeve. "C'mon, Mr. Griffin."

"I guess I'm needed for critical defense planning. I'll see you Tuesday at the meeting, Miss Sinclair." He winked at her as Tim led him away.

Ruth took a deep breath and followed her grandparents out of the church.

"He's a nice young man," Alma commented. "And he's in church on Sunday, too." Ruth knew her grandmother's comment referred to Harold's infrequent attendance.

Outside, worshippers hurried to their cars in the blustery April wind. Ruth and her grandparents escaped to their car as a gust swirled around them. "I got the repairs done on Suzi's lamp table," George said as he pulled out of the church parking lot. "I'd like to drop it off at the Nakamuras' on the way home. Do you have the key with you, Ruth?"

She fished around in her purse. "It's right here, Grandpa. I keep it with me."

George nodded and turned toward the Nakamura farm.

As they pulled into the driveway, Ruth again felt the emptiness of the place that had been so full of life such a short time ago. Sunday dinners had been great times here, discussing the sermon and talking about the season's garden or new crochet patterns. Afterwards, Suzi loved to adjourn to the living room for a session of gospel songs around the piano.

"Don't be long. I have a roast in the oven," Alma warned as George parked by the back porch.

"Here, I'll help you, Grandpa." Ruth jumped out and held the trunk lid as George removed the small table. "Let me get the door open." She hurried up the porch steps as a gust tugged at her coat.

They stepped out of the wind into the tidy kitchen. "I'll put this where it belongs and be right back," George said as he carried the table to the living room.

Ruth walked to the kitchen table and stared. "How did this get here?" She frowned at Suzi's copy of *Ben-Hur* lying on the table. "I thought I put it back on the shelf yesterday."

She glanced around the room. The door had been locked and the windows repaired or boarded over. Everything seemed to be in order. She took a deep breath. "Where's your common sense, Ruth Sinclair?" she chided herself. "Books don't hop around a room, and the house was locked up, so no one could get in."

She paused and felt goose bumps on her arms. "Could someone else have a key? No, that can't be. I have the only one. Either I'm getting old and forgetful, or Marge left it there and I didn't notice."

She shook off the uncomfortable sensation and picked up the book. "Suzi promised I could read it after her. She'd be happy to know I'm taking care of it while she's gone." She tucked it under her arm.

"Talking to yourself again, Ruth?" George teased as he appeared in the doorway. He glanced around the room and nodded in approval. "Looks mighty good after the ladies tackled the mess." He shook his white head. "Sure too bad what those hoodlums did. Well, let's go home to dinner. I'm ready for Grandma's roast!"

★ ★ ★

Ruth looked up from *Ben-Hur* to find the afternoon's light fading. George was finishing his chores while Alma crocheted a doily for the center of the dining room table. The old country home George and Alma had built forty years earlier was warm and cozy. A fire crackled in the fireplace, adding a homey touch as well as its warmth. The wallpaper was faded and old-fashioned, but to Ruth it meant something in the world stayed the same.

"Time to close the blackout curtains, Grandma, or Bob Miller will be after us." Ruth got up and wrinkled her nose. "Such a cheery color." She pulled the opaque black curtains closed, making sure no light escaped around the edges.

Alma chuckled. "Bob does get carried away, but he's right. We don't want our lights to make us targets for Japanese bombers."

Ruth picked up *Ben-Hur* and looked around for Suzi's bookmark. Not finding it, she absently reached for a piece of paper to mark her place. "I wonder where Bud'll be stationed, Grandma. The censors cut so much out of his letters sometimes that you can't tell what he's saying." She held the book tightly. "I hope he isn't assigned to one of the battleships in the Pacific. That's so dangerous."

Alma nodded. "And that reminds me. I need to get material to make a banner for our window to show someone from our family's in the service. We're proud Bud's serving his country." She reached for a piece of paper and a pencil. "Let's see. It takes blue for the star, white satin for the background, and red felt for the border." She busied herself determining the material she'd need.

Ruth got up with a loud sigh. "I'm going upstairs to correct some papers, Gram."

Alma looked up from her calculations. "You sound sad and lonely tonight, Dear. This war's brought so many changes to our world. Adjusting takes time."

"I know, Grandma, but I miss everyone the most on Sundays—Bud, my folks, the Nakamuras. Remember the wonderful Sunday afternoons we had together?"

Alma patted her arm. "I remember, Dear. They were good days."

Ruth hugged Alma and touched her cheek gently. "I love you, Gram."

Upstairs, she plopped down on her tall feather bed and looked around. "This was Mom's old room. I wonder if she sat here dreaming and trying to understand life, too." Ruth looked at the pink-flowered wallpaper and the dark dresser with its oval mirror. She imagined her mother sitting there primping for a date with her father. Her mother patted her hair, then skipped down the stairs to greet her date. Her father looked handsome and smiled at her as she took his arm. Ruth sighed.

She pulled her knees up to her chest and rested her chin on them. "Why do I feel so lonely on Sundays?" she asked aloud. She sat up and reached for the math papers she needed to correct. "I guess because Sunday is a family day, and that's all changed now. I told Marge I wasn't looking for anyone. It's true, but I guess I'm missing someone—and I'm not sure who it is."

She turned back to the papers, but again her mind wandered, and she pictured herself peering through the living room window at her parents as they left on their date. They smiled into each other's eyes, unaware of anyone else in the world.

With a sigh, she put the papers aside and reached for her journal. She opened it and stared at the blank page as she nibbled on the end of her pencil. Slowly, words flowed onto the page. She took a deep breath and sat back to read.

LOVE

It came and it went
Like the time that I spent
In my dreams that were all about you.

Time came and time left
Like the hope that I let
Fill my heart and my soul about you.

Love came and love's gone
Like the words in a song
That I listened to thinking about you.

It came and it went
Like the time that I've spent
In these words that I've written about you.*

She put the journal down and ran her hand over the cover. *Time and love are slipping away*, she thought, *and I can't seem to grasp either one anymore.*

---

*poem by Kelly Croston Kalthoff, 1989.

Chapter 4

"Class dismissed!" The words were barely out of Ruth's mouth before the children hurried to the door.

"Hey, Miss Sinclair, I'm gonna go collect newspapers. Then me and Charlie are gonna look for spies." Tim raced for the door.

"It's Charlie and I, Tim. Don't forget your spelling book. There's a test to-morrow," Ruth reminded him.

Grumbling, he returned to his desk.

"So this is the fifth- and sixth-grade room," Jim Griffin spoke from the doorway. "It hasn't changed much since I spent two years in here." He looked at the penmanship examples along the front blackboard and the pictures of presidents on the side wall. The desks were in straight rows, one desk attached to another.

"You went to school here, Mr. Griffin? Wow, I didn't know the school was that old! Well, see ya." Tim ran from the room, his spelling book under his arm.

"How's that for a quick aging?" Jim grinned. "Just call me old man Griffin."

Ruth laughed. "The kids think we're fossils." She picked up her notebook. "The meeting's in Mrs. Hastings's room. Shall we go?"

"Ladies," Jim began as he addressed the four teachers, "these are the forms to be filled out so each family can receive its ration books. Take a look at them, and we'll discuss your questions."

The teachers read over the forms, and Jim explained the regulations. As the discussion wound down, he pushed back his chair. "Remember—it's very important to note how much sugar they have at home. They'll be allowed a small amount without losing any stamps from their sugar books. Now, if there are no more questions, I'll be here with the materials bright and early Tuesday morning."

He gathered his papers together. "Oh, one more thing. The government doesn't provide any help for the community coordinator, so I'm looking for a volunteer assistant. I thought one of you would be a good choice. Anyone volunteer?"

Mrs. Foster spoke up quickly. "Three of us are busy with families. I think Miss Sinclair would be the logical one. Don't you ladies agree?" She looked around at the other teachers, who nodded their approval.

"Good idea," Jim interjected quickly. "That's four votes yes. Miss Sinclair it is." He looked at Ruth. "You do volunteer, don't you?"

"A rather heavy-handed approach, I must say," Ruth replied good-naturedly, "but, yes, I'll do it. I've wanted to get more involved in the war effort, and this could be a good way."

"Great." Jim collected his papers. "I'm late for an appointment. I'll get in touch with you later in the week about your job." He grabbed his briefcase. "It will be a pleasure working with you, Miss Sinclair." With a wink he hurried from the room.

★ ★ ★

"Red light, green light!" a child called out as Ruth watched the children enjoy their recess on a sunny spring morning. The air was clear and fresh, and a robin warbled from a nearby tree.

"Do they still play King of the Mountain and Mother, May I?"

Ruth turned to see Jim Griffin standing with his hands in his pockets, enjoying the children's play.

"I loved this old school at recess. The trees and the creek ditch were great places for hide-and-seek," he reminisced.

"Yes, and they still play tag, jump rope, and softball. Oh, and red rover, red rover. . ."

"Send someone right over," Jim finished and laughed as shouts sounded from the ball field.

"Tag him, tag him!"

"He's out!"

"No, he's not!" Voices rose in argument, then play resumed.

"Those were good days," Ruth agreed.

Jim looked over at her. "I stopped by to see if we can get together after school to discuss the work you'll do. How about meeting at Sandy's Café for an ice-cream soda to inspire us as we talk? At, say, 3:30?"

Ruth nodded. "That's fine with me. Oh, there's the bell. Recess is over. See you at Sandy's." She smiled and turned toward the building. Jim gave a wave of his hand as he walked away.

★ ★ ★

At 3:30 Ruth entered the café and sat down in a red-and-chrome booth by the window. An array of war-related posters covered the walls. "Uncle Sam wants you" seemed to point right at her.

"I'll never smile again until I smile at you," Frank Sinatra crooned from the jukebox. Memories flooded over her. All those times she and Harold had met in this café. She could picture him sitting across from her, his blond head tilted in that special way as he smiled at her. It seemed so long ago.

If he hadn't changed, what would my life be now? she wondered. But he had.

She shook her head to clear out the memories and picked up *Ben-Hur*. *Jim's late,* she thought, *but that's never a waste for a bookworm.* She found her place and tried to read, but her mind wandered. *When Harold's so far away, it's easy to forget how much he changed. And I do miss the way he used to be. What will he be like when he comes home? Will the war wake him up?*

When she looked up, she saw a man staring at her intently. He seemed vaguely familiar. Who. . . ? The man in the old car! The one who had shouted at her the day she fell on Suzi's driveway. Why would he be so interested in her? She moved uncomfortably, then looked up quickly as a voice sounded beside her.

"Hi. Sorry I'm late. We had a problem at the plant." Jim smiled warmly at her as he stopped beside the booth and took off his overcoat. "I'll get the sodas and be right back. What kind would you like?"

"Strawberry's fine," she replied. As Jim turned to get their order, she looked toward the man at the counter. He was slumped over a cup of coffee. She studied him carefully, remembering the words he had shouted at her.

"Best fifteen-cent sodas around." Jim returned and set two ice-cream sodas on the table. "Now, first things first." He settled into the booth. "I never work with someone I don't know, so tell me about Miss Sinclair. I'd prefer to call you Ruth, if you don't mind."

"No, that's fine," Ruth replied and took a sip of her soda. "There's not much to tell. I went to the teacher's college down in Monmouth. My dad's an engineer, so my folks moved to help set up the war industry. With housing so tight, it wasn't fair for me to take up a whole house. They leased it out, and I moved out to Grandma and Grandpa's farm. And you?"

"University of Oregon. Business major. I always planned to take over for Dad at the factory." Jim peered around her soda. "I don't see a ring on that finger. Unattached?"

Ruth twirled the soda glass back and forth in her hands. "I've been dating Harold Ramsdale on and off for several years. He's a pilot with the Royal Air Force."

Jim raised his eyebrows. "Any commitment?"

She shifted in her seat. "Harold has to get his fill of adventure before he settles down, but he thinks. . ." She hesitated. "I promised to write," she finished lamely. She looked down at the soda. *It's true,* she thought, *but why didn't I explain?*

Jim smiled. "That's encouraging. You're not taken then. So how about joining me for dinner?"

She took a deep breath. "I can't, Jim. Harold and I are still together—sort of. For me there are some big problems, but he's over there risking his life. It wouldn't be right." She was surprised to feel a stab of disappointment.

Jim was quiet a moment. He looked at her and nodded. "I understand. Actually, I admire loyalty, especially to someone over there, fighting, while I have to sit home." He smiled. "So, friends?"

Ruth nodded.

"Friends—unless there's a change in your status?" He cocked an eyebrow hopefully.

"You're an impossible flirt, Mr. Griffin."

"This doesn't mean it's back to Mr. Griffin."

"Okay, Jim."

He reached for his briefcase. "Now, about the job. We can't talk much here." He pointed toward a poster that warned the enemy is listening. "Right now I need someone to do paperwork for me—file, type, post notices—that kind of thing. How does that sound?"

"I'm not the world's best secretary, but I can handle that. When do I start?"

"Anytime this weekend. I need these notices typed and posted at Fir Glen Market and Joe's Feedstore." He handed her several pages.

"No problem." She put the papers with her book. "Jim, do you know that man at the counter, dark-haired with a beard, slumped over his coffee?"

Jim turned around. "I've never seen him before. Why?"

"He was the one who shouted at me the day you helped me out of the mud. He keeps staring at me."

"Maybe he has good taste in women but bad manners," Jim teased.

"No, seriously, Jim, he's very anti-Japanese. He let me know in no uncertain terms what he thought of their friends, too."

"Let me know if he gives you any problems." Jim rose from the booth. "Since you won't go to dinner with me, I'll let you go home and write your letters. Isn't that what girls back home do on Friday nights?" He opened the door, and they walked out.

"Well, well, out on the town, I see." Marge walked up, smiling smugly.

Ruth turned to greet her friend. "And what are you doing out of your library, Marge Evans?"

"Meeting Beth Marshall for a Coke." She looked at Jim. "Don't I get a personal introduction, Ruth, or are you trying to keep him all to yourself?" A mischievous smile played at her mouth.

Ruth shifted the papers she carried and made the introduction, giving Marge a sideways scowl.

Jim reached out his hand. "Glad to meet you, Marge Evans." He raised his eyebrows. "So this is where the good-looking women of Fir Glen congregate."

Marge grinned. "Umm, Ruth, you didn't tell me he was so charming, too." She glanced at the frown on Ruth's red face, enjoying her friend's discomfort.

Ruth changed the subject. "I can't stay and chat, you two. Grandma's waiting for me at the church. Call me, Marge." She thanked Jim for the soda. "I'll get these typed and posted right away."

She hurried to her car. As she took out her keys, the papers she held slid to the ground. She quickly bent to retrieve them as the wind scattered them under the car next to hers. Crouched between the vehicles, she could hear

Marge's voice from the distance.

"Good to meet you, Jim. I'd better let you hurry home to get ready for your Friday night date."

Jim sounded sheepish. "I just got turned down. My luck to meet a girl with a guy overseas."

Ruth froze where she was. *Oh, no, Marge, don't you dare!* She could hear her friend pause.

"You mean Ruth?" Marge laughed. "It's not the way she makes it sound, Jim. Her heart's not tied to Harold anymore, just her ethics. She won't write the cad a Dear John letter. She insists on waiting 'til he comes home to break up."

"I thought they. . ."

A car started near Ruth, drowning out Jim's words.

"But he changed. . .played on her sympathies. . ." Snippets of conversation drifted over to her. When the car pulled away, Marge had headed for the café, and Jim was getting in his car.

She held the papers tightly. "I know what you're trying to do, Marge Evans," she murmured, "but it won't work." She got in the car. "I've got to do what I've got to do, whether you understand it or not!"

Chapter 5

Thaat's all the sugar we have on hand, Dear," Alma called from the pantry as she estimated the number of pounds and put the containers back on the shelf.

Ruth jotted down the information. "I hope everyone remembers to estimate their sugar supply before the rationing registration tomorrow," she commented as she closed her notebook.

"It'll be a challenge to cook with less sugar, but we'll be healthier for it." Alma came into the room, wiping her hands on her apron.

Ruth watched her and smiled. *Except for church, Grandma always wears a full, wraparound apron. It's her uniform—and her hand towel,* she noted fondly. *And I've never seen her do anything slowly.* Alma bustled about the kitchen, clanking the dishes in her haste. Ruth glanced at a cup on the table with a nick in the rim, another result of Alma's fast pace.

★ ★ ★

The next morning Ruth arrived at the school gym to find Mrs. Hastings taping signs on the tables while Mrs. Foster tacked a poster over the entrance that read: "Sugar Rationing Registration Here."

"Good morning, ladies," Jim Griffin called out as he entered the gym carrying a large box. "Here you are. Straight from the county clerk's office." He set the box down and began to unload registration forms, sugar books, and pencils. "Are you ready?"

"If we can get the children to add and spell, we can register the adults, Jim," Mrs. Hastings responded firmly as she distributed the supplies to the registration tables and assigned each teacher her place.

"Is this where we register?" A man and woman stood in the doorway, looking around uncertainly.

"It sure is. Come on in." Jim greeted the couple and ushered them to a registration table. He turned to the teachers. "I'll leave you ladies to your duties. My dad's a stickler about getting to work on time. I'll drop by at noon to see how you're doing."

Ruth sat down at one of the tables as a small elderly woman approached her.

"Is this where I sign up for our ration books? We have three pounds of sugar at home. That's all." The woman stopped in front of her and smiled. Her well-worn gray coat hung loosely, and a small black hat perched on her head.

"Yes, Ma'am. And this is the information we need." Ruth smiled warmly as she laid two forms in front of the woman and started to explain them.

"Oh, no, I can't. I can't do that. I can't read, you see, and I don't write." She clutched her purse in both hands and stood in front of Ruth, waiting.

Ruth picked up the forms. "I'll fill them in for you. Just give me the information and we'll do fine." She smiled at the woman kindly and bent over the forms, asking the required questions. "So far, so good. Now, we need to know your husband's height, Ma'am."

"He's about that much taller than I am." The woman spread out her arms and smiled at Ruth.

Ruth stared at her. "How much is that in feet and inches, Mrs. Albers?"

The woman stared back. "You're the teacher, Dear. You'll have to figure that out." She smiled and waited.

The briefing hadn't told her what to do in situations like this. Ruth squirmed in her chair.

Mrs. Foster leaned over from her end of the table. "I know them, Ruth. Mr. Albers is about five feet ten inches."

Ruth smiled her gratitude and continued with the form. "We're done, Mrs. Albers. Remember, you can't buy sugar without the ration stamps. Do you understand?" She handed the woman two sugar books.

"Oh, yes, Dear. Thank you." Mrs. Albers smiled as she walked away, looking through the ration book.

Ruth glanced over at Mrs. Foster and shook her head. "Would you believe that!"

"Mrs. Albers had very little schooling. She was the second of thirteen children and had to stay home to help her mother," Mrs. Foster explained, then turned to help the couple approaching her table.

A steady flow of people came through the gym all morning. "We'll go to lunch in shifts so someone will be on duty at all times," Mrs. Hastings announced. "Mrs. Christianson and Miss Sinclair may go after they finish their next people. And, remember, the Women's Club will be here to relieve you at three."

Ruth turned to a man in bib overalls standing before her. She smiled. "Good morning, Sir. How many people are there in your household?"

"Two, Ma'am, but I need three sugar books," the old farmer stated firmly.

"You only get one book per person, Sir," Ruth explained as she laid two forms on the table.

"I need three," he repeated. "Need a sugar book for Josephine, too." He stood with his hands in his overall pockets.

Ruth looked puzzled. "Is Josephine a daughter who lives with you?"

The old man chuckled and slapped his leg. "Josephine's my daughter! That's a good one!" He chuckled again. "I need one for Josephine, too. She's not my kin."

"Is she someone who lives as part of your family? You can't register for other than your own household," Ruth repeated patiently.

He chuckled again. "Josephine's my mule."

Ruth's mouth fell open. "Your mule? You want to register your mule?"

He nodded seriously. "She don't do no work unless I give her sugar. Got to keep her going to get the farmwork done. I need a sugar book for Josephine."

"But, Sir, I can't do that." *What do I do now?* Ruth thought. *He's dead serious and not budging.* Out of the corner of her eye, she saw Jim Griffin enter the gym and beckoned him over to her table.

"Sir, Mr. Griffin is our community coordinator. He'll explain this to you." She turned to Jim and smiled sweetly. "A problem for the expert." She quickly straightened her table and said to Mrs. Foster, "I'll be in my classroom if you need me." As she hurried away, she could hear Jim trying to convince the farmer that Josephine didn't qualify.

Jim entered her classroom a few minutes later. "A mighty quick exit there, Miss Sinclair. Thanks for leaving him to me. Stubborn as a mule he was. I wasn't sure which was Josephine!"

"Give me a classroom of kids any day!" Ruth replied. "You can't believe the stories people came up with or the problems they had with the form."

Jim sat down at one of the desks. "After that episode, I can imagine."

"There was the lady who claimed she had a drawer full of sugar. She had no idea how many pounds were in it or its size. And then there was the one who had about six sugar bowls full." Ruth shook her head.

"Many of these people didn't have much formal education. I run into this all the time at the plant."

Ruth unpacked the lunch her grandmother had prepared and laid it out on her large oak desk. "Join me? Grandma insists on packing my lunch so I'll eat right, and she sends enough for a farmhand. I'll get fat if I eat all this."

Jim cocked an eyebrow at her. "I can't have you ruining that perfect figure, now can I? I'm honor-bound to help out." He reached for a piece of fried chicken and sat back in the seat.

The classroom clock ticked steadily on the wall above the blackboard. Across the room a wall of long, narrow windows gave light to the room. Jim touched an ink bottle set in the small well in the desk and ran his finger over a name carved in the desktop. "If I look, I might find my name carved on one of these desks, too." He grinned sheepishly. "I spent some time in Mrs. Hastings's off.ce for that bit of mischief!"

"Jim, I'm shocked! I expected you to be well behaved!" Ruth exclaimed.

"I wasn't really bad, just mischievous—until my dad got ahold of me, that is!" He chuckled as he got up to put the chicken bone in the wastebasket. "These wooden seats were mighty hard sitting for awhile after he got through with me!" He glanced at the clock. "Gotta run. Thanks for the lunch." With a wink he left the room.

Ruth returned to the gym, where people arrived in spurts throughout the afternoon. As she waited for the next person, Ruth heard a voice to her right. "Miss Sinclair, had I realized you were on duty I would've registered with you." Ruth looked up to see the large figure of Herschel Owens smiling broadly.

Oh, no, she thought. "Mr. Owens," she answered briefly but politely.

He was looking at his sugar book. "No sacrifice for the war is too much, Miss Sinclair. We must give our best for our country, don't you think?"

A lady stepped up to the table and waited impatiently for Ruth to help her. "I must get back to my duties, Mr. Owens." She turned to the woman in relief as Herschel ambled away. *Marge better not be trying to set me up with him!* she fumed to herself.

"Finally!" Mrs. Foster sighed. "Relief's here. The Women's Club just arrived." She reached out to tidy her table.

Ruth gathered her belongings and hurried from the gym. As she rounded the corner of the building, a green Plymouth drove by. Jim gave a honk and waved. She felt an odd flutter as she smiled and waved back.

The power of suggestion, she thought. *Marge's suggestion. Just ignore it, Ruth,* she told herself and hurried home.

★ ★ ★

"How'd the registration go?" George Peterson looked up from his newspaper that evening. He was comfortably settled in his favorite deep blue, overstuffed chair.

"You wouldn't believe it," Ruth said. She sat down and related incidents from the day.

"That will seem easy compared to the gas rationing registration in a few weeks. People won't like having their driving restricted." He put the paper down. "How about a game of checkers, Ruth?"

She saw the gleam in his eye. "Think you're going to beat me again, Grandpa? Not this time." She got out the board and set up her side, enjoying the warm atmosphere of her grandparents' living room.

"Do you have plans for the summer, Dear?" Alma asked as she knitted socks for the men overseas.

"Helping you with the garden. Keeping up the Nakamuras' place. And I'll be busy helping Jim Griffin, I'm sure."

"He's such a nice young man. Goes to church every Sunday. Works so hard to help out. He's the settled-down kind." Alma's knitting needles clicked.

"Your move." George sat back smugly.

Ruth looked over the board. "Oh, Grandpa, you did it again. I'm trapped. If I didn't know better, I'd think you conspired with Grandma to divert my attention. Okay, you win again."

"Concentration. That's the key." George got up. "Got to check on the calf."

"How's your work with Mr. Griffin going?" Alma asked. She looked up at Ruth.

"There's not much to do so far—typing mainly. When school's out I'm sure there'll be more."

"No word from Harold?"

"None." Ruth could sense the direction of the conversation.

"Harold's a nice enough man, but I wonder about his faith, Dear." Alma stopped her knitting. "Fun and success seem more important to him than the things of the Lord. You need to think about that if you're going to spend your life with someone."

Alma laid her knitting aside and leaned forward. "Could I ask you something personal, Ruth? Were you really serious about Harold? He didn't seem very settled."

Ruth's fingers played with strands of hair as she paused. "Harold was a lot of fun, Grandma," she answered evasively. "Maybe the war will make him take life more seriously."

"Fun isn't the basis for a solid marriage, Ruth. If God isn't the foundation of your life together, you won't survive the hard times. And, believe me, they'll come."

Ruth sat quietly. "I know you're right, Grandma."

"Tell me about this Mr. Griffin. I think he's interested in you." Alma peered over her wire-framed glasses.

She blushed. "We're just friends. Even if I am rethinking my relationship with Harold, I won't let someone down who's risking his life for his country." She looked at her grandmother. "Jim's a great guy. If there were no obligation to Harold, who knows? But there is. I have to see that through first."

"Talk to the Lord about it, Ruth. He doesn't want you making a mistake. Read Psalm 127. The Lord knows what's best for us." Her knitting needles clicked rapidly.

"I know, Gram." She stood up. "I'm going upstairs to finish some lesson plans for tomorrow. I love you." She hugged Alma. "Thanks for caring."

Upstairs, Ruth took out her Bible and turned to the psalm. " 'Except the Lord build the house, they labour in vain that build it,' " she read aloud. She looked up from the Book. "I do want You to build my house, Lord," she whispered, "but I'm confused. I know You're in control, but with the world in such a terrible mess, it doesn't look like it. Didn't people in the war zones have faith and pray, too? The Nakamuras did, and look where they are. You'll have to help me, Lord. What I believe doesn't seem to fit with the world's reality anymore. Intellectually I know what's true. It's just harder to have the same trust when evil seems to be taking over."

She put the Bible down and picked up a reading text. "Everything seemed so much simpler six months ago, even my beliefs." She opened the text and began to plan the lesson.

Chapter 6

The spring breeze was soft and mild as it whispered through the evergreen trees. Sunny dandelions glowed from the lawn, and primroses poked their heads through the soft earth by the porch. "Finish weeding along the house there, Ruth, and then go inside to do your work. I'll get these weeds and branches picked up," George instructed as they worked in the Nakamuras' yard one afternoon.

Ruth looked up. "What will happen to their fruit trees, Grandpa? Nak took such good care of them. His cherries and apples were so excellent, they always got top prices."

George stopped, his arms full of trimmings. "Men from the church'll organize work teams to take care of the orchards, and we'll have some family workdays when harvest comes. Pastor Cameron set up an account for the profits so the Nakamuras'll have something to use when they start over."

Ruth nodded. "That's only right. They were always the first ones to help someone else."

"Won't be bad with everyone pitching in." He turned toward the pile of trimmings he had accumulated.

Ruth pulled the last of the grass from among the rhododendrons and azaleas. She stood and brushed dirt from her hands. "I'll be inside if you need me."

She let herself in the house and went to work on the kitchen, enjoying the warm atmosphere and humming as she worked. She pushed the mop over the kitchen floor and turned to dust carefully around the Bible, then stopped to stare at it.

"You about done?" Her grandfather stepped through the kitchen door.

"Almost," she answered. "Come over here, Grandpa. This is strange. Every time I come here, the Bible's turned to a different page. At first I thought it was the wind, but the door and windows haven't been open. No one else has been in here. I'm the only one with a key."

George leaned over the table.

"See." Ruth pointed. "It's open to Numbers 2. When Suzi left, it was Psalm 23. And it's been open to other books. I can't see that anyone's been in here. Besides, who would break in to read the Bible?"

George shook his head. "It's a mystery to me." He glanced around. "Things look okay in here." He moved to the door. "Fluffy around?"

"She stays at our place since Grandma's been feeding her so well."

"She's well fed all right. Something got three of Billy's pigeons, and it was probably Fluffy. Don't know how she got in or out, though. The cage was all locked up."

"I hope no one's playing pranks. People still have it in for this place—and anyone connected with it."

"We'll keep our eyes on things. Let's go home, Ruth. Men from church'll finish up."

★ ★ ★

As they walked into the kitchen, Alma looked up from the stove and wiped her hands on her apron. Enticing aromas rose from kettles bubbling on the stove. "I need one of you to run down to Bob's market and pick up a few items for me. If you want supper, that is."

"Smells good enough now," George said as he raised a lid and sniffed.

"No, you don't, George Peterson. Keep the lid on that kettle!" Alma quickly took the lid from him and replaced it.

"But I'm a good taster, Alma, my dear. Such torture you put a man through."

"If you were out in the barn where you belong right now, you wouldn't be tortured. Out!" Alma winked at Ruth as she attempted a scowl at her husband.

George left the room, rubbing his stomach and sniffing the delicious aromas.

"They say the way to a man's heart's through his stomach. Sure works with George," Alma declared with a twinkle in her eye as she checked her kettles.

"I'll go, Grandma. What do you need?" Ruth asked and reached for her car keys.

Alma handed her the list and money. "Enjoy the drive, Dear. We'll be walking everywhere once gasoline is rationed."

★ ★ ★

The bell above the door jangled as Ruth entered Fir Glen Market. All the spare wall space in the small country store was covered with war-related posters. "Man the guns. Join the navy!" a poster declared. "It's a woman's war, too! Join the Waves." A new grouping encouraged their efforts on the home front: "Conserve everything you have. Raise and share food."

"What can I do for you, Ruth?" Bob Miller stood behind the counter in the large grocer's apron that enveloped his small frame.

Ruth selected the items on her grandmother's list and placed her purchases on the counter. Bob rocked back and forth on his heels and pursed his lips as he surveyed her selections. "Where's your empty toothpaste tube?"

"My empty what?" Ruth asked, puzzled.

"Toothpaste tube. Can't let you buy any more toothpaste unless you turn in your empty tube. They're war materials now, you know," he informed her smugly. "Government regulations."

"I hadn't heard about that one." She put the toothpaste back. "Next time."

38

She scanned the list. "How's the job of air-raid warden?" she asked, making conversation.

"Well," Bob said as he rocked up on his toes, "most people are pretty careful about covering their windows at night, but I've got some I'll have to get tough with." He stuck his thumbs under his apron straps. "Old man Jones is one. Sneaks around, too. Makes a guy wonder what he's up to, especially with spies around." He jerked his head toward a poster that declared "The enemy is listening."

Ruth was relieved to hear the bell jangle as Marge stepped into the store. A bus could be heard pulling back onto the road. "If it isn't the hardworking librarian, home after a long day's work." Ruth went to greet her friend. "After next week, we'll all be riding the bus instead of driving."

Marge wrinkled her nose. "It's better than walking, but I'd rather drive. What's up?"

"Just picking up some items for Grandma—and being caught up on local gossip." Ruth jerked her head toward Bob. "A side benefit of shopping here."

"Know what you mean." They walked over to the counter. "I get off early Monday," Marge said. "Want to meet at Sandy's for a Coke after school? My folks are so busy at the shipyards, no one's ever home. Mom's been promoted to. . ."

"Ahem, ladies," Bob interrupted, pointing to a poster. "Enemy agents are always near; if you don't talk, they won't hear," it read. "We must be careful what we say these days." He reached under the counter and pulled out a newspaper. "See this ad?" He held it up. "Even the FBI wants our help in catching suspicious characters. Think they'd have that ad if spies weren't everywhere?"

"We'll be more careful, Bob," Ruth assured him as she picked up her groceries and winked at her friend. "I need to get these home to Grandma. See you, Marge."

★ ★ ★

On Monday afternoon, Ruth erased the penmanship examples from the blackboard and turned to the class. "Put your pens and ink bottles away," she directed, "and pass your papers to the front." A bustle of activity followed. "And remind your parents that the picnic on the last day of school is a potluck. That's next week." She looked at the class. "You're dismissed."

"Hey, Miss Sinclair, think I'll pass spelling this year?" Tim Henderson said as he hopped over to Ruth.

"If you study instead of collecting newspapers and chasing spies. You have all summer to do that."

"No, I don't. I have to pick strawberries and beans and all that stuff. My parents said so. Hey, I've made three dollars on the papers I've collected. Haven't caught any spies yet, but we're on their trail. Me and Charlie saw lights flashing around Mr. Griffin's plant. When school's out we'll find out what it is. See ya."

Ruth smiled. *I should turn Tim loose on the mysteries at Nakamuras' place,* she thought. She put together the papers she needed to take home and added

Ben-Hur to the pile as she left to meet Marge.

★ ★ ★

The two women settled into their favorite booth by the café window. "So, have you seen Jim lately?" Marge pried as she sipped her Coke.

"Not for the past week," Ruth answered and shifted in her seat. "He's busy at the plant, I guess."

"He likes you, I can tell." Marge grinned at her friend.

"He's just a flirt and a tease." Ruth twirled a strand of hair between her fingers and looked down at her Coke. "I am over Harold, Marge, but I can't send him a Dear John letter now. Just because Jim's here and attractive doesn't make it right to dump Harold that way."

Marge raised an eyebrow at Ruth and shook her head. "You protest too much, my dear." She wiped her mouth with a napkin. "Not to change the subject, but I need to do some shopping. Want to meet me in Brookwood Saturday? I go to lunch at 12:30. We can eat and look around a bit. I need some new lipstick." She pursed her pink lips. "Something bright."

"Sounds good." Ruth picked up her papers and followed Marge out the door. As it started to close, a man shoved past her. Ruth staggered sideways, trying not to fall. The papers went flying, and *Ben-Hur* skidded across the ground. The man grabbed the book and dashed behind the café.

Ruth regained her footing and stared after the retreating figure. "Marge, that's the man who hollered at me for being at Suzi's. Why would he steal a book?" She started to reach for the nearest papers.

"My, my, you need to be more organized, Miss Sinclair." Jim came up behind them and bent to pick up the papers. "Or is this a new way to grade papers—throw them out and the closest ones get As?"

Ruth frowned. "Actually, it's not funny, Jim. A man pushed past me, knocking the papers and a book out of my hands. It's odd, though. He grabbed *Ben-Hur* and ran off with it."

"A literary thief? Doesn't he know we have libraries?"

"He's the man I told you about—the one who hollered at me for being at Nakamuras'. The book was one I borrowed from Suzi."

Jim walked around the back of the café, and Ruth and Marge followed. "No one here." He bent over and picked up *Ben-Hur*. "Either he's a mighty fast reader, or he didn't like the book." He handed it back to Ruth.

"It's another attempt to intimidate me because I'm helping my Japanese friends," Ruth declared firmly.

"I've been so busy at the plant I've neglected our defense work, I'm afraid," Jim commented. "But gas rationing and scrap drives are coming up. I hope you're ready for a busy summer, Miss Sinclair."

"Once school's out, I'll have plenty of time, Jim. Just let me know." She smiled at him.

"You can count on it. Nice to see you, Marge." He touched his hand to his hat and entered the café.

"Ruth, you're crazy. That man is handsome, charming, witty, successful— you name it. And he obviously likes you. But you insist on staying loyal to a guy who doesn't even deserve it." Marge hit her palm against her forehead. "The teacher needs to go back to school."

"Come on, Miss Dramatic. You've spent too long in the romance section of your library. A walk home will clear your head." Ruth pulled Marge toward the road, but her mind was still on Jim retrieving her scattered papers.

Chapter 7

Alma bustled about the living room doing her spring-cleaning. The windows had been stripped of their lace curtains and sparkled after Alma's thorough scrubbing. She removed the cushions from the sofa and stacked them on the floor. "We'll have to take these outside and beat the winter's dust out of them."

Ruth collected doilies from the end tables and added them to the pile of curtains. "I'll get all these washed and starched, Gram. Where do you store the frames to stretch the lace curtains? I'll put them together for you."

"In the. . . Ruth, is this your bookmark?" Alma held up a strip of paper that had fallen under a sofa cushion.

She looked up. "It's one of Suzi's. I wondered where it went. It fell out of *Ben-Hur* awhile back."

Alma inspected the bookmark before handing it to Ruth. "She wrote Bible verses down one side." She chuckled. "Suzi knows the Bible better than this. There's no Psalm 638:42. And there's no Amos 34:14 either. Hmm, maybe Amy wrote them." She turned the bookmark over. "Ruth, these are lovely." Tiny colored sketches of flowers, animals, and angels covered the strip of paper.

"Suzi loved to make them," Ruth explained. "The whole family liked to read, so she made a supply of bookmarks they could all use. I felt bad to lose this one."

Alma handed it to her. "Take it upstairs, Dear. And check your cake on the way. It smells mighty good. Be sure to let Grandpa know it's for the school picnic tomorrow. You know how much he likes chocolate cake!"

★ ★ ★

The next morning Ruth balanced her cake in one hand and books in the other as she approached the school, where Mrs. Foster was unlocking the front door. "Here, let me help you." Mrs. Foster hurried to let Ruth into the building. "Mmm, yummy-looking cake. Can you believe this is the last day of school? Where has the year gone?" she chatted as she walked down the hall with Ruth. "I'll hold your cake while you unlock your classroom."

Ruth pulled the door open. "Thanks, Mrs. . . Oh, what's happened?" Books were strewn all over the floor in front of the bookcases.

"Oh, my, who would do that?" Mrs. Foster set the cake on a desk and stared at the mess. "Some of them have been damaged. Mrs. Hastings needs to know about this. I'll take care of that for you."

"Thanks." Ruth took a deep breath. "I'll have a word with my class, but I'm sure it wasn't one of them." She bent to pick up a book with a broken spine. "I know I locked the room yesterday. I had to unlock it to get in this morning. How did someone get in?" She stared at the mess.

"Hey, Miss Sinclair." Tim bounded into the room. "I came early to help you get the class booth ready." He stopped when he saw the mess of books. "Hey, why are all those books on the floor?"

"I have no idea, Tim. They were there when I came in. Do you know anything about it?"

"Uh-uh. Nobody in our class would do that, Miss Sinclair." Tim's face brightened. "It's a mystery. Hey, me and Charlie'll be on the case." Tim got down on the floor and looked carefully among the books. "I'm looking for clues, Miss Sinclair."

"I feel better now, Tim." Ruth smiled and glanced at her watch. "I need to set up our class booth. When you're done, come out to the gym and help me. We'll clean this up after Mrs. Hastings looks into it." She turned to straighten her desk.

"Sure thing." Tim got up and inspected the door, then moved to the windows at the side of the room. "Hey, Miss Sinclair, this window's not closed! See!" He pointed to a middle window that was slightly ajar.

Ruth stared at the window and shuddered. "That's how someone got in! But why?" She looked at the mess again and shook her head. "We'll take care of this later. I have to get to the gym. Don't disturb anything until Mrs. Hastings has been here."

Tim nodded.

Ruth hurried to the gym to find it transformed into a school carnival. The PTA had draped streamers and set up booths along the sides where the classes would sponsor games. A fishing booth offered prizes for the younger children while a ball toss was set up for the older ones. Near the piano, chairs were arranged in a circle for a cakewalk. A bingo game and the ringtoss completed the games along that wall. Down the center of the room, the Women's Club had added three booths that offered prizes for tossing buttons into saucers, dropping clothespins into bottles, and pinning the tail on the donkey.

There was a bustle of activity in the room as Ruth walked over to the ringtoss booth. "Milk bottles, rings, the sign, box of prizes. It's all here." She spaced the milk bottles around the table.

"Hey, Miss Sinclair, is our class doing the ringtoss?" Tim bounded over, picked up a ring, and tossed it toward the glass bottles. It ricocheted off and dropped at Ruth's feet. She bent to pick it up.

"A fifth- and sixth-grade tradition, Tim. Here, help me put up our sign." Ruth held one end while Tim grabbed the other.

"Hey, Mr. Griffin," Tim waved and called out as he spied Jim coming into the gym.

Jim looked around at the array of activities and waved back. He stopped to chat here and there as he walked over to them. "Mighty impressive booth you've got there." He picked up a ring and tossed it. It spun around the neck and settled on the bottle. "So, what do I win, Miss Sinclair? How about dinner Friday night?" He glanced at her and grinned.

"Enough of you, Mr. Griffin. I'll have to put you to work to keep you in line." She put the ring back and shook her finger at him.

Jim put his hands up in defense. "Actually, I'm leaving, but I need to borrow your assistant. I'm in charge of the softball game, and I need Tim to show me where the equipment's kept. Okay, Tim?"

"Sure thing, Mr. Griffin." Tim bounded out of the booth. "Oh, hey, I found a clue to the crime."

Jim's eyebrows shot up. "Crime? What crime?" He looked from one to the other.

Ruth explained the situation she had walked into that morning.

"I'm investigating it," Tim declared. "Me and Charlie are solving mysteries. We're checking on the lights around your plant, too, Mr. Griffin."

Jim frowned and jingled the coins in his pocket. "What do you mean, Tim, lights around the plant?" He stared at Tim intently.

"Me and Charlie saw lights—like flashlights—blinking around your plant. I live down the road from there, you know. Me and Charlie play outside after dark, and we saw the lights. When school's out, we're gonna see if it's spies."

"You'd better let me handle it, Tim. I'm glad you told me." He ruffled Tim's hair. "Come on; let's get set up before the bell rings." Jim walked off with his arm around Tim's shoulders.

Ruth tidied the booth and hurried back to her classroom as the tardy bell rang and the children made a noisy dash for their seats. "Class, quiet down. I need to talk to you." She looked around at their faces. She knew them all well. The boys could be noisy and mischievous, but not one would cause any damage. "When I came in this morning, all the books were out of the bookcases and on the floor. Does anyone know anything about it?"

They looked at the mess on the floor, at each other, and then back at her. Heads shook no.

"If you hear anything, let me know."

They nodded and wiggled in their seats, anxious to get on with the morning's activities.

"Before we clean up, I need a word with the Junior Volunteers. Over the summer, you'll have a lot to do to help the war effort. Tim will be your captain. He'll notify you about meetings and what needs to be done. Be sure to wear your badges so people will know you're official." She looked around the room. "Any questions?"

Mike raised his hand. "What'll we do?"

"Continue to collect newspapers. Also, the government needs milkweed floss to use in life preservers. It looks like this." Ruth held up a sample from the display Jim had given her. "And you can collect foil from gum wrappers. You'll be paid fifty cents for a large ball."

A buzz ran through the room. "Fifty cents! Wow!" John exclaimed.

"Take all this to the feedstore," Ruth concluded. "Now, let's clean out the desks. Mrs. Hastings investigated the problem of the bookcase, so Tim and Charlie can put the books back on the shelves. Cynthia, Betty, and Alice will clean the back cabinets. I'll be by to check your desks."

The room was a bustle of activity as the children packed up their belongings to take home for the summer, and the wastebasket grew full of old papers. Finally, Ruth clapped her hands. "Take your seats, class. The room looks great."

With a noisy scurry, the students returned to their desks and sat impatiently. She nodded at them. "You're excused to the gym for the carnival." As they dashed for the door, she called out, "Don't run!" They slowed to a fast, long-strided walk. Ruth followed with her cake. "Slow down, John!"

"That's like telling a hurricane to slow down, Miss Sinclair," Jim commented as he met her at the door. "Umm, cake looks good." He reached his finger toward the frosting, and Ruth slapped at his hand. He feigned a hurt look. "What's the agenda for today?"

"The carnival 'til lunch. Afterwards, your softball game for the older kids and outdoor games for the younger ones." She waited while he opened the door.

"Sounds great. I'm on my way back to work. See you at noon. I don't want to miss the picnic!"

"If you promise to keep your fingers out of the frosting, would you drop my cake off at the grove on your way? I need to get to the gym."

"Only if I get the first piece. The way to a man's heart, you know." He winked and grinned as he took the cake and walked off.

Ruth hurried to the gym and the class booth, where a line of children had already formed, waiting impatiently for her arrival. The games began, and the morning passed quickly as the children enjoyed the booths and the prizes they won.

As she waited for more customers, Ruth overheard a group of boys arguing nearby. "Our side'll beat you. Mr. Griffin showed me how to pitch."

"Uh-uh, will not. He coached us good. We can hit that ball clear out of the field."

"Mr. Griffin said. . ." The group ambled on to another game.

She smiled to herself. *Jim's certainly made a hit with the boys around here. He's been a strong Christian influence on them, too.* She sighed. *If I hadn't made that promise to Harold, what would my life be now?* She watched the buzz of activity around her. A small girl squealed and jumped up and down at a prize she'd won. *I'd be dating Jim Griffin; that's what I'd be doing,* she said to herself. *Why did I give in when Harold told me he was going overseas? Would breaking up then really have been worse? When I compare Harold and Jim. . .*

She glanced at her watch. Her head was ringing from the piano tunes Mrs. Foster had been playing all morning for the cakewalk and from the noisy chatter and squeals of the children. "Tim," Ruth called out, "would you be in charge of closing down our booth? Get some others to help you. I have to help set out the food." She brought out boxes in which to pack the items.

"Sure thing, Miss Sinclair," Tim replied and went to round up some classmates.

She hurried to the grove of fir trees behind the school, where picnic tables were set up, and began cutting cakes and pies. Mothers were setting out an array of food on long tables—mounds of potato salad, platters of sandwiches and fried chicken, and bowls of shimmering Jell-O.

"The war hasn't affected the potluck spirit, I see," Jim commented as he approached the tables laden with food and eyed the enticing selection. "I do love potlucks!"

"These pies and cakes won't be as sweet as they used to be, but I doubt there will be much left anyway." Ruth cut the last cake and set it with the other desserts.

The noon bell rang, and, with shouts and whoops, the children raced to the grove, shoving and pushing to be first in line. She watched as Jim stepped over to the line and stood with his hands on his hips, staring at them. The roughhousing ceased, and they settled down to wait their turns.

He walked back to Ruth as she finished cutting the last pie. "Join me for lunch? I have a few things to bring up about civilian defense." He began to fill his plate, taking some of each dish 'til his plate overflowed.

Ruth nodded. "My feet will be thankful to rest awhile."

They found a place at the end of a table. Jim put his plate down and bowed his head briefly, then tackled his food. Ruth sat a moment in surprise. *Harold would never have done that in public,* she thought. *Why do I keep comparing the two?*

"You're not hungry?" Jim asked, bringing her back to the meal. "This is tremendous!" He smiled at her warmly.

And this is crazy, she thought. *I'm blushing. I feel as silly as Cynthia Richards when Billy Benton chases her. Calm down, Ruth. You're a teacher, not a kid.* She looked around. Certain her red face was obvious to everyone, she bent over her plate. "Starved," she replied. "I was just thinking about the year. So much has happened since last fall."

Jim put down his chicken bone. "The war sure has changed the world," he agreed as he tackled his dessert.

Ruth ate the last bite on her plate. "Now, what is the civilian defense business we need to discuss?"

Jim finished his piece of cherry pie. "Tart is good," he muttered through puckered lips and pushed his plate away. "This really is business and not a date. Scout's honor. A week from Saturday there's a civilian defense meeting in Portland. It's important we both be there."

"What's it about?"

"Rallying community support for the war effort. There's a lot of activity coming up, and we need to be prepared. So, it's a date? No—sorry—wrong choice of words. You'll go?"

Ruth nodded. She picked up her plate and reached for his. "But right now I have to help clean up, and you're wanted on the ball field."

A group of boys rushed up to their table with bats, balls, and mitts. "Come on, Mr. Griffin. Time for the game!"

Jim rose to his feet, groaning. "Don't I get time to rest after all this food I ate?"

"Nooo," the group chorused. "Play ball!"

Ruth carried the plates, her heart pounding. *This is not a date,* she reminded herself. *Get your mind focused on the reality of your situation, Ruth Sinclair, and get your heart back in control. You'll only cause it a lot of pain.*

She watched Jim on the ball field, surrounded by an excited group of boys. *They've found a great hero. He may not be overseas risking his life, but he's sure making a difference in the lives of these kids.* She fought a stab of sadness as she watched him start the game. Her mind drifted to the defense meeting. A whole day together. . . She shook her head. *Come on, Ruth, get busy with the dishes. You got yourself in this pickle. Now you'll have to live with it.*

Chapter 8

The aroma of fresh bread filled the kitchen as Alma took a loaf from the oven. "Mmm, smells good, Grandma." Ruth entered the kitchen and sat down at the table. "Got your list ready? I'd better get going, or I'll miss the bus and be late meeting Marge for lunch."

Alma wiped her hands on her apron and looked over her list. "The material for the banner, thread. Oh, and some seeds. We need to get the rest of the garden in." She jotted down the items she needed and handed Ruth the list.

"Walking and riding the bus will take a bit of getting used to." Ruth picked up her purse. "With gasoline rationing, our lives aren't the same." She paused at the door. "Well, I'm off. I'm thankful we're only a half mile from the bus stop, Gram."

★ ★ ★

As Ruth waited for the bus in front of Fir Glen Market, she looked around at her world. It looked the same, but it wasn't. Joe's Feedstore on the corner was now used to spot enemy planes. Arlan's gas station on the other corner was rationing gasoline. The school across the road organized children to collect materials to fight the war. "And beyond the school is the Griffin Container Company that produces cans for Bird's-Eye Foods and brought Jim Griffin back home to complicate my life," she muttered aloud.

A horn beeped in front of her, and she looked up to see the bus waiting. She handed the driver her ticket and took a seat toward the front. *Even the bus is a reminder of war,* she thought as she noted the men in uniform, accounting for most of the passengers. The bus pulled into the depot in Brookwood where groups of servicemen waited for buses to their destinations.

I'll get Gram's material before I meet Marge, she said to herself and headed down the block toward Penney's.

Her heart gave a funny turn as she watched the couple ahead of her. A bobby-soxer in plaid skirt and saddle shoes walked with her little finger linked to that of a guy in a letterman's sweater. That had been Harold and her. As the couple turned into the malt shop where the high school crowd still gathered, she wondered what the future held for them—and for her.

In Penney's she paid for her grandmother's material, then headed for Woolworth's and lunch with Marge. As she entered the five-and-dime store, a hand waved at her from the lunch counter.

"What are you having?" Marge asked Ruth quickly, then twirled her stool around to give the waitress their order. "I'm so excited! I got a letter from Jack. He's stationed in California now, you know. He misses me terribly and wants to get married as soon as he comes home on leave. You'll have to help me plan the wedding!"

The waitress brought their food, and Marge nibbled on her hot dog as she chatted about dresses and flowers. "You'll be my maid of honor, so I need your honest opinion. What do you think of that combination? Ruth, are you listening?"

"What color was that?" Ruth asked. "I was daydreaming, I guess." She took a bite of her sandwich.

"Umm, telltale sign. You never did that 'til Jim Griffin came around. I see signs of infatuation, Miss Sinclair," Marge said smugly. She glanced at her watch. "If we get going, I have time to buy some makeup. You done?"

"All set; lead the way." Ruth collected her package and purse and followed her friend to the makeup section.

Marge picked up a tube of red Tangee lipstick. "I love these bright colors! Or do you like the shade of this Maybelline better? I can't decide. See if you can find a sample." They rummaged through the tiny samples for the right shades.

"We probably won't see these samples much longer if the war continues," Ruth remarked. "Every week some item becomes scarce."

"Speaking of scarce, if you see any bobby pins, let me know. They're hard to get now. Rolling my hair up on rags just isn't the same." Marge wrinkled her nose as she made her selections and got in line to pay for them. "Waiting in line is becoming another national pastime," she grumbled. The line inched slowly toward the cash register.

"So, Miss Sinclair," Marge pried, "how are things going with Jim? Any progress?"

Ruth felt herself blush and looked down quickly so Marge wouldn't notice. "We're just friends, Marge. Now that I'm on vacation, defense work will pick up, I'm sure."

"Good, good." Marge grinned. "I was afraid I'd have to work at getting you two together, but this way I can just let nature take its course." She found herself at the cashier and put her items on the counter. "Do you ever get bobby pins in anymore?" she inquired.

The cashier stopped, put her hand on her hip, and stared at Marge. "Don't you know there's a war on?" she snapped. She slowly rang up the purchases, handed the change to Marge, and smacked her gum before turning to the next customer.

"I remember when clerks were helpful and had manners," Ruth commented dryly as they walked away. "It's the war again. Not enough workers to go around, so nobody worries about getting fired anymore."

Marge glanced at her watch. "Gotta run," she declared. "The library waits for no one. Thanks for coming in, Ruth." She checked her purchases and hurried away.

Ruth shifted her parcel. *Only seeds to go,* she thought and headed for the garden supplies. *Why am I feeling so melancholy? Snap out of it, Ruth. Think how blessed you are to be in America, safe and sound.*

Back on the sidewalk, she passed a record shop filled with high school kids listening to the latest songs. A melody drifted out the door. "There'll be bluebirds over the white cliffs of Dover. . ." She paused to listen. *The same English cliffs Harold's been flying over with the RAF,* she thought. *Fighting the Nazis is so dangerous. I pray he's safe.* She walked on and stopped at the end of the block to check the traffic.

As she crossed the street, Jim Griffin stepped out of the county clerk's office. Her heart gave a funny thump as she walked up to him. "Hi, Jim. Busy on defense business?"

His face brightened into a smile. "The teacher on vacation! Just the person I want to see. We have lots of work ahead of us this summer." He cocked his eyebrow in the way that had become so familiar. "We'll have to spend hours and hours working together. I like that idea—friend." He chuckled.

Ruth shook her head. "You're impossible."

He glanced at her packages. "I see you bought out the town."

"No, just some material and seeds for Grandma. I had lunch with Marge."

A fine mist began to drift down softly but steadily. "Good old Oregon mist. We'd better find some shelter. Did you drive in?" he asked.

"With gas rationing? You must be checking up on me. No, it's these feet and the bus from now on, I'm afraid." Ruth held a package over her head as the mist came down.

"Then I'll offer you a ride home. I'm on official business, and you work for me, so the gas is provided." Jim smiled at her warmly.

"I gladly accept, Boss."

"This way." He took her elbow and led her to his car. The mist continued as they got in and headed out of town.

"So, how do you like being back in Oregon and working at the plant?" Ruth asked him.

"It's good to be back. I knew I'd run the plant one day, so I wanted a chance to be on my own for awhile first. When the war started, it was time to settle down and do my part." Jim looked over at her. "And you. Where are you heading in life, Ruth? What's important to you?"

The mist came faster on the windshield, and the wiper blades moved with a rhythmic *whish* and *thump.* "I enjoy being a teacher and guiding the children. It's like a calling, I guess."

Jim nodded. "I know what you mean. That's what I feel in working with the youth at church. God has done so much for me; I need to pass it on."

"Have you always been a Christian, Jim?" Ruth looked over at him.

"I was raised in a Christian home, but in college the world seemed pretty attractive. When I moved to California, I felt God could wait for a later day. I wanted my version of fun and success first. It was the war that got to me. That and John Kensington, a guy I worked with."

"What do you mean?" She looked puzzled.

"John was a strong Christian, but his faith wasn't just some beliefs he memorized or a list of rules." He paused. "The way he lived made his faith seem so real. He was what he believed."

The mist turned to a steady rain, running in rivulets down the side windows.

Jim drummed his fingers on the steering wheel. "For a long time, I had wrestled with the way God runs the world. It didn't make sense and wasn't how I'd have done it. And I didn't like someone telling me what to do, even if He was God. Then I met John and saw it all differently. He got me into Bible study, too. I even took some classes at a Bible college."

He pulled up to a stop sign and shifted gears. The car was quiet for a moment before he continued. "I have to admit I didn't take God seriously when I was younger. It was just something I did. But when the Japanese attacked Pearl Harbor, I really woke up. You see, a good friend of mine was killed in that attack. I realized how fragile life is and who's ultimately in control."

"You didn't get bitter at the Japanese, like some people around here?"

Jim shook his head. "No, God deals with us as individuals, so that's how I have to deal with people. I'm not perfect, and God still loves me; so I have to give others that, too. And not all Japanese are against America."

He turned down Woodland Avenue, and they rode in comfortable silence. "Here we are," Jim said as he pulled into the Peterson driveway. He reached into his briefcase and took out several papers. "Type these for me?"

"Sure thing, Boss." Ruth took the papers. "I'll drop them by the plant when they're done." She put the packages over the papers to protect them from the rain.

"Thanks for all your help, Ruth. I appreciate what you do for me—and for our country. I. . ." Jim paused and put his hand over Ruth's. "I. . .uh. . ." He seemed to be searching for the right words and squeezed her hand gently. "I'm glad you volunteered for this job," he said softly.

Ruth looked away from his tender gaze, not trusting the emotions stirring in her heart. She took a deep breath and opened the car door. "Thanks for the ride, Jim. See you later." She closed the door and dashed to the house as the rain poured down.

The house was quiet when Ruth stepped inside. She left the packages for her grandmother on the kitchen table and walked into the living room, stopping at the window to watch the rain. "I've done it," she said out loud.

"I'm falling for Jim Griffin. He's everything I want and admire in a man, but I feel so guilty. Even though I think he's what God would want for me, I wasn't brought up to dump someone who's risking his life in a war." She paced the room.

"God, what do I do? I feel so torn. This rain is me inside." She cried softly. With a sigh she sat down and bowed her head. "Lord, I feel trapped. Show me Your will and direction for my life. I don't want to go back on my word to Harold or hurt him when he's off fighting for his country, but my heart isn't with him anymore. Please help me!"

Chapter 9

Ruth woke to the sound of pots and pans banging in the kitchen. She dressed quickly and hurried downstairs. When she poked her head through the door, Ruth saw Alma was noisily putting the utensils back in the cupboard. "Is this your new alarm clock, Grandma?" she teased as she walked in.

Her grandmother paused. "Morning, Ruth. Sorry I woke you so early. I couldn't sleep any longer." She plopped into a chair with a sigh, wiping her hands on her apron. "It's that Velma Miller. Nobody gets under my skin like she does."

Ruth chuckled and poured two cups of coffee. "What's she done this time?" She placed one cup in front of her grandmother.

Alma's fingers drummed on the table. "Her women's club does a lot of good; I'll grant you that, but she has to run everything. As you know, our Ladies' Aid is making quilts and collecting clothes for the English refugees. We're sending them through the church's relief agencies. Now Velma's gone and promised it all to the Red Cross without asking anyone. And she didn't even help us. If she'd come to church more than once or twice a year, she'd know what's going on."

"She does have a lot of nerve." Ruth got up. "Come on, Grandma. You need to work out your frustrations." Ruth opened the back door and looked out. "The rain's cleared, and it's a perfect day to plant the rest of the garden. I'll help you." She stepped outside into the crisp morning air.

Ruth collected the rake and hoe while Alma retrieved the seeds and string. "We'll start over here where I left off," Alma said as she surveyed the garden. She bent over to pull a weed.

"Ouch! I still can't do that, Gram." Ruth watched as Alma bent over, legs straight and hands to the ground. "That makes my legs ache!"

Alma laid her hands flat on the ground and grinned up at Ruth. "Don't tell me you're too old," she teased. "Must be my second childhood that does it." She straightened and stood with her hands on her hips.

"I couldn't do that in my first childhood. Must be Dad's side," Ruth declared as she picked up the hoe and dug a shallow trench for her grandmother's seeds.

The air was fresh after the rain. A robin hopped along the ground, looking for worms, and a meadowlark warbled from a nearby tree. "I think heaven must be an eternal spring, Grandma; it's so lovely." The fragrance of spring blossoms wafted on the gentle breeze that rustled the leaves. Ruth breathed deeply and turned back to her work.

Alma scanned the garden, planning the remaining rows in her mind. "I want several plantings of beans. Let's leave room here for another row later." She bent to drop seeds in the row Ruth had prepared. They worked quietly, enjoying the chorus of birds in the nearby trees.

"You ladies do a fine job," George called out as he stopped at the end of the garden. "I could watch you work all morning."

Alma straightened and put her hands on her hips. "If you have that much spare time, George Peterson, you can clean the henhouse!"

"Nope. Been working with Joe over at the Nakamuras' and came to get a saw. Say, Ruth, it's odd. Went to feed Billy's pigeons and now there are ten. Did you have a talk with Fluffy and get her to put those three back?"

"I'm afraid not, Grandpa." Ruth frowned. "Someone's messing with things over there. The community was so upset when the place was ransacked; maybe someone's resorting to more subtle mischief instead. Anything to get back at us and make us uncomfortable over there."

"As long as nothing's hurt, I guess there isn't anything we can do. It's odd, though." He turned. "I'll get what I need and go back over."

Alma picked up her string. "That's enough for now, Ruth. I have bread rising and need to get back to it. And the Ladies' Aid meets this afternoon. We're sorting clothes we can repair for the refugees."

She walked to a round seedbed and bent over to pull a weed. "Flowers are slow coming up this year. Must be all the rain. The zinnias and marigolds are so colorful when it's brown and dry in the summer. I hope they do well."

Ruth collected the rake and hoe and put them away. "I'll get cleaned up and walk down to Bob's market, Gram. I have a couple notices to post for Jim. We can finish the garden this evening. Need anything while I'm there?"

Alma shook her head and headed for the house.

★ ★ ★

The morning sun had warmed the air when Ruth left for the market. "God's nugget," she murmured. "Walking isn't as convenient, but I'd have missed this beauty if I'd been driving." Fields along the gravel road were a carpet of green. Wildflowers poked their heads up here and there, adding an array of color to the scene.

The bell over the door jangled as she entered the store. "Good morning, Mrs. Edwards," Ruth greeted a customer and walked to the bulletin board. Bob hurried over to read the notices Ruth was posting.

"Got to keep track of what goes up here," he said. "This is an official board, you know." He lowered his voice. "I think old man Jones is up to no good. Someone said his neighbor's cousin saw him sneaking around the Nakamura place. He's always been the sneaky sort. Won't cooperate, either."

"What's he done?" Ruth's mind tried to imagine old man Jones pulling the pranks at Suzi's. It didn't fit.

"It's them chicken houses of his. Won't keep the lights off at night. Says he's allowed to keep 'em on so his hens'll lay. Uses 'em to signal the enemy, I say." He rocked back on his heels, his thumbs hooked in his suspenders. He leaned closer and looked around. "Rumors are the Griffin plant's been converted to war production. Don't know what they'd make instead of them cans. Bullets, maybe? It's all hush-hush. Arlan says a lot of trucks come and go, and they have a guard now."

The bell clanged as a woman entered the store. Bob stood back, his finger to his lips. "Keep an eye out for old man Jones. He's up to no good." He turned to his customer. "Hello, Mrs. Wilson. May I help you?" he asked cheerily.

Ruth removed an expired notice from the bulletin board and slipped out the door while Bob was occupied with his customer. "Shopping at Bob's is always an experience," she muttered as she hurried around the corner of the building and ran headlong into a large figure.

"Oh, I'm sorry. I didn't look where I was going!" she exclaimed and looked up to see the smiling face of Herschel Owens. *Oh, no,* she thought with a sinking feeling as he continued to smile at her.

"No harm done, Miss Sinclair. And how are you this fine day?" He pulled a grayish handkerchief from the pocket of his rumpled jacket and wiped his brow.

She stepped back, mumbled a "Fine, how are you?" and tried to edge around him.

"Fine, fine," he responded as he tried to pull his jacket together over his large waistline. "Mother and I haven't seen you in our store, Miss Sinclair. Being single and all, you should come in to consider some of our furniture. We have some lovely new pieces. Mother selected them herself, so they should suit a lady like yourself."

Lovely furniture, my foot! she thought. *Trader's Corner is full of old junk no one would want.* She forced a smile. "Greet your mother for me."

"I will, I will. She felt poorly this morning, the dear soul, but she insisted on helping at the store, weak as she was. Wouldn't you say that's a fine mother's love?"

Fine mother's love, ha! She'd be more at home running a chain gang! Ruth grumbled to herself. "I need to be on my way, Mr. Owens," she responded briefly. She stepped around him and tried to hurry away.

"Herschel, my dear; it's Herschel to you." He continued to smile at her, then turned and walked to the door of the market.

She heard the bell jangle as she headed for the road. *There's something about him—oily, I guess I'd call it.* She gave a shudder and hurried toward home.

★ ★ ★

Alma looked up from her ironing as Ruth walked in. "So, what's new from gossip central?" She unplugged the iron. Without waiting for an answer she went on, "Ready for lunch? Grandpa's not back yet. We may as well eat."

Ruth took a loaf of bread from the drawer. "Sounds good. I'll make a couple extra sandwiches and take them over to him. He gets so busy he forgets to stop. I need to check on the house anyway. I worry about what's going on over there." She sliced the fresh loaf. "About the rumors. With Bob you never know how much is fact. He says the Griffin plant is producing war materials and even has a guard. His latest target is old man Jones. He thinks he's a spy." She placed thick slices of home-cured ham on the bread.

"That poor old man. He is a bit odd, but he's no spy. Since he lost his family in a house fire years ago, he hasn't been the same. I've always felt sorry for him," Alma said as she put the ironing board away and joined Ruth for lunch. They ate quietly, remembering the tragedy that had occurred down the road from them.

"Suzi looked out for him when she was here," Ruth added. "I don't think he talked to anyone else." She got up and cleared the table, then wrapped the sandwiches for her grandfather. "I'll be back soon, Gram."

She crossed the field and followed the sound of her grandfather's saw to the orchard where he was pruning limbs. "Time to eat, Grandpa. I brought some sandwiches." She put the basket down. "After lunch I'll haul those branches away for you."

"Appreciate it." He sat down on a stump and took the sandwich Ruth offered. "Things sure grow up if you don't keep at 'em. Joe had to run, but other men from the church will be over later. Thought I'd get a start. Kind of enjoy it." The smell of sawdust and damp earth hung in the air.

"I wonder how Suzi and her family are. I try to imagine how I'd feel in their situation." Ruth shuddered.

"They'll be okay. God gives strength at times like that." George took a bite of his sandwich and looked around at the peaceful orchard. "Newspaper says our men sank four Japanese carriers at Midway Island. Maybe this war's turning around." He stood up and wiped his brow. "Well, back to work. After you clean up the branches, go in and check the house while I finish trimming."

Ruth hauled the last of the branches, then headed for the house. She unlocked the door and went in. "I wonder if. . . Oh, my, what's this?" Books lay scattered all over the floor. She hurried to the porch and hollered, "Grandpa, come here! Something's happened!" She returned to the kitchen and stared at the mess.

George rushed up the porch steps and yanked open the screen door. "What's the matter?" he called out as he hurried into the room.

"Look!" She pointed to the books. "Just like at school."

George looked around and shook his head. "Everything else looks okay. Someone up to pranks, is all I can say." He stared at the books scattered over the floor.

Ruth picked up several books and began returning them to the shelf. "Someone doesn't like our friendship with the Nakamuras, and they're not letting us forget it," she declared. "They want to make us so uncomfortable here and scare us away. Remember the man who hollered at me from that old car a few months ago?"

George nodded and turned at the door. "It's a puzzle, all right. Keep your eyes open, Ruth, and be careful. I'll mention it to the sheriff. Maybe he can keep an eye on the place." He stepped out on the porch and paused. "But we won't desert our friends." He left to collect his tools.

Ruth put the rest of the books back on the shelves. "How do they get in?" she fussed. "I'm supposed to have the only key. If they want to mess things up, why do they break in so carefully? It makes me uncomfortable. Maybe that's what they want. A lot of people are looking for empty places to live these days. Housing's scarce. If they can scare us away, they'll have a place to live. But as Grandpa said, we won't be scared off!"

She locked the door carefully and joined her grandfather for the walk home.

Chapter 10

"You wait and see. Don will ask Beth Marshall to marry him before he goes overseas. I just know it. Matchmaker's instinct," Marge declared firmly. She and Ruth sat in their favorite booth at Sandy's Café, sipping their Cokes. "Ruth, don't you think so? Oh, Ruth." She waved her hand in front of Ruth's face.

"I guess so," she answered flatly and continued to stare at her glass.

Marge tried again. "Summer's whizzing by. We're over halfway through June already." She paused, then put her hand over Ruth's. "What's wrong? Something is; I can tell."

Ruth twirled her Coke glass with her hands and evaded Marge's prying.

"I'm not doing well on your love life, that's what," Marge declared. "And for the umpteenth time, I didn't talk to Herschel Owens about you. I have better instincts than that; I hope you know."

"The problem's not my love life, Marge. I just feel melancholy. I don't know why. It must be the war. There's such terrible news on the radio every day."

"Have you seen Jim lately?" Marge inquired.

Ruth shook her head. "He's been busy."

"That's it! I'm a regular Dorothy Dix at solving people's problems. Think I can get my own advice column, too?" Marge looked smug. "I told you it was your love life. No Jim Griffin around and look what happens to you. Now, what can I do to get you two together?"

"Stop it, Marge. I can't get interested in Jim right now, and you know it. Besides, we're attending that civilian defense meeting in Portland Saturday, so you don't have to cook up something."

Marge brightened. "Great! You need a pick-me-up. I'll come over to help you get ready." She studied Ruth carefully. "Let's see. What should you wear? I'll look through my clos—"

Ruth interrupted her. "It's not a date, Marge. You don't need to fuss."

"Just try to keep me away!"

★ ★ ★

"No, no, that dress is too plain," Marge declared as the two rummaged through Ruth's closet Saturday morning. "You want to look businesslike but with a zing to it. This is Jim Griffin you're going with; may I remind you!"

Ruth pulled out a two-piece navy outfit. "For the last time, this is not a date, Marge," she insisted and hung the outfit on the closet door.

"Then why are your cheeks red and you all in a dither? Tell me that, Ruth Sinclair." Marge plopped on the bed.

Ruth tossed her head and hunted through the closet for her shoes. "I just don't want to look inappropriate."

Marge rolled her eyes. "Sure, sure." She picked up a hairbrush. "Now about your hair. Let's see if. . ."

"Oh, no, you don't. I can handle that myself, Marge. If you want to do something, get the bottled stockings for me, will you? Over on the other dresser."

Marge wrinkled her nose. "These war shortages. What I wouldn't give for nylons!" She sighed and picked up the container. "Two years ago if someone had told me we'd put stocking-colored liquid all over our legs and draw a seam down the back with an eyebrow pencil, I'd have laughed my head off!"

Ruth finished dressing and put the final touches on her shoulder-length hair. "That about does it."

Marge stood back to check Ruth's appearance. "Nice, but I wish I'd brought my new lipstick—Passion Red, it's called. That would be the touch you need."

Ruth laughed. "Passion Red doesn't sound like a civilian defense meeting, Marge. Now, along with you. I don't need a chaperone."

"I'm going, I'm going. I get the hint. But you have to call me as soon as you get home."

"Out!" Ruth ordered. "It's not a date!"

The screen door slammed, and Ruth walked into the living room to wait. *I'm nervous*, she thought. *This does feel like a date, though I'd never admit it to Marge.* A knock sounded at the door. She opened it, and Jim stood there, handsome in a dark blue suit. *Just like a guy picking up a date*, she thought. *Get ahold of yourself, Ruth.*

"Ready?" Jim stepped inside as Ruth grabbed her notebook. "Mm, I'll have the best-looking assistant there." He looked her over in obvious admiration.

Ruth flushed. "You're too much, Jim Griffin."

"Just honest." He opened the car door for her, got in, and pulled out onto the road. "If we're lucky, we'll miss the shipyard traffic. That gets nasty, even on Saturday." He smiled at her. "So, how's vacation?"

Ruth settled back and relaxed. "Busy. The Victory Garden, typing for my boss, keeping up the Nakamuras' place—that sort of thing." She glanced out the window as they turned onto the highway. "Oh, look, Jim." She pointed. "My favorite Burma Shave signs." She stared out the window at the series of small signs, each with part of the rhyme that advertised Burma Shave Shaving Cream.

She started to read the first sign, and Jim joined in:

"Past
Schoolhouses

Take it slow
Let the little
Shavers grow.
Burma Shave"

Jim laughed. "That's my favorite, too." His fingers drummed on the steering wheel as he glanced at her sideways. "So, how's the rest of your life going?"

Ruth ducked the question. "Just fine. No problems. Life's busy. This war keeps the days packed with things to do," she rambled.

He cleared his throat. "Inside of Ruth, I mean. You look distressed; I guess I'd call it."

She looked down and didn't answer.

"I don't mean to pry, but I get the feeling you and God have a cooling between you."

She turned quickly and frowned. "How can you say that, Jim? I'm in church every Sunday. I teach Sunday school, do my devotions. Are you implying I'm a heathen?"

He laughed. "Of course not. But I can sense you lack peace in your heart."

"With a war on, who does have peace anymore?" she replied with a touch of sarcasm.

He continued. "I can tell because I had the same thing, the same bit of sarcasm and feeling of helplessness. God's not running things the way I think they should be run, so I'll back away from Him."

"No, I . . ." She stopped. She stared out the window at life going on around her. People walking into shops. Cars whizzing by. All as if there were nothing wrong. No evil destroying lives and cities. No hearts in a jumble.

A car honked behind them, jolting Ruth from her thoughts. "The world shouldn't be this way, Jim. You're right. I do want God to hurry and fix it."

Jim nodded. "I know the feeling. But we seldom give up the need to do it our way unless we have to. When life gets bad enough and we can't fix it, we finally let God do what He's been waiting to do all along. Make sense?"

Ruth shifted in her seat. "Of course. I could have told you that if you'd asked, but knowing and doing are two different things. It's the doing that's getting me." She ran her fingers over the notebook in her lap. "My mind knows one thing, but my feelings want something else."

Jim slowed as the traffic thickened. "That's why God often works best in life's difficulties. We're forced to stop and listen when we can't do it all ourselves. Let God work in your life, Ruth. Trust Him."

"Sometimes it all looks so bleak, Jim. The awful war news. Worry about Bud and others I know over there. The Nakamuras. It's hard to trust when people are suffering. And on top of it I feel guilty that I don't trust."

His fingers tapped on the steering wheel as he waited at a stoplight. "Did you ever think God may be able to get more of that good stuff done if we got out of the way—or were willing channels He could use? We're too busy trying to force things our way."

She was quiet and then nodded slowly. "How can I ask God to do His will when at the same time I'm demanding He do it my way? It's hard for God to work when His own people work against Him, even in their good intentions." She nodded her head in understanding.

Jim smiled over at her.

"How did you get so wise, Boss?"

He took a deep breath. "A broken heart," he said softly.

"You? Never! Not break-their-hearts Griffin."

"Yep, me. Back in California. A girl I knew there. Very pretty. Fun. Lots of parties and dancing. Then I met the friend I told you about. The Christian guy I worked with." His voice sounded far away as he remembered. "I started to change. Went to church and Bible study. She didn't like it. She wanted the parties and fun. So she told me it was God or her."

"I'm sorry, Jim," Ruth said softly.

"Talk about a struggle. I wanted God to change her—and right away. Why couldn't I have both her and Him?" He leaned his shoulder against the car door. "Lately, I think I see why He didn't let me have my way." He gave her a penetrating look. "But God still works with me. I've had to accept the reality of Harold."

Ruth was flustered. "Jim, I, uh, I . . ."

"Remember this, Ruth. Our faith is often like a greenhouse plant. It's strong only as long as the environment stays just right. When evil's on the march, it becomes a time of testing, and we see the shallowness of our faith for what it is. But instead of a disaster, this is God's opportunity to strengthen and deepen it so it can survive anywhere. That's what God's doing with you."

"Hm, an opportunity instead of a failure. That's encouraging, Jim."

He smiled. "The world you've known hasn't included the horrors of war and gross evil, Ruth. It's been a shock to you and confused your trust."

She nodded thoughtfully. "I agree. Because I think the world should be straightened out, I assume that God wants to correct it my way, instantly, with a wave of His hand, too. But He may have other agendas." She smiled at Jim. "My mind sees this, but it may take awhile to bring my heart and feelings in line. The two seem to pull in opposite directions from my head these days."

"Keep trusting Him, Ruth. God doesn't promise to prevent all the evil in the world, but He does promise to be with us in it and see us through it. We're never alone in our troubles." He turned down the block. "Now, it's a gorgeous day. There'll be a lot to learn, and we can help our country."

"Thanks, Jim; that helped." She smiled at him. "Now, let's have a good day."

He pulled in the hotel parking lot in Portland and found an empty space.

Ruth looked around. "For instance, I could spend the day shopping at Meier and Frank's Department Store while you take notes on the meetings. No? Oh, well, it's Saturday, so I'm too late for their big Friday Surprise Sale anyway," she teased.

Jim took her arm and steered her in the right direction. "You're not getting away from me today, Miss."

Inside the hotel, they were directed to the registration table and received their agendas. "Session 1," Ruth read. "Rallying Community Support (scrap drives, rationing), Room 135, or Air Raids and West Coast Evacuation Procedures, Room 142." She looked at Jim. "Now I know why I came along. I go to one while you go to the other."

Jim nodded.

She continued. "Session 2: Civilian Defense Officials, Room 128, or Campaigns and Rallies (war bonds, rally days), Room 102."

"But it's also the company. Can you imagine if I had to spend the day with Bob Miller?" Jim wiped his hand across his forehead in mock relief. "I'll go to the sessions on air raids and civilian defense. You go to the other two. When the sessions are over, meet me back here." With a wink he walked down the hall to his session.

The afternoon sped by as Ruth filled her notebook with ideas and information. The last session ended, and she headed back to the lobby, where Jim waited for her. "Learn anything, Teacher?" he greeted her.

"My head's swimming. I filled a notebook with some great ideas I'll tell you about on the way home."

They hurried to the car and pulled out into the traffic. "How were your sessions?" Ruth inquired as they were swallowed up in the mass of buses and cars filled with Saturday afternoon shoppers.

"Informative, but that's all I can tell you. Secret stuff, you know." He winked and turned out of the traffic snarl.

As they headed out of town, Jim suggested, "How about grabbing a bite to eat? I'm starved. Traffic should be thinned out by the time we're done, too."

"Um, sounds great. All that thinking's made me hungry," Ruth replied as he drove into a restaurant parking lot and helped her from the car.

"No business talk while we eat," Jim said as they were seated. "When I have dinner with a lovely lady, I never spoil it with business." He picked up the menu. "Try the chicken with me? It's delicious." She nodded, and he gave the waitress their order.

This isn't a date, Ruth repeated to herself as she twisted the napkin in her lap.

"And you are lovely, you know," Jim was saying. "Yes, I know—just friends—but I can still admire a lovely friend, especially one with such deep blue eyes."

"Thank you, Sir." She gave a nod of her head.

The waitress arrived with their dinner, and Jim bowed his head briefly. He picked up his fork. "So what have you seen of Tim since school's out?"

"Actually, I haven't seen him. He's been picking strawberries, so the paper collecting and spy catching have slowed." She smiled. "He's quite a character. And such an avid detective. I may have to put him on the trail of all the odd things happening at the Nakamuras." She took a bite of her dinner. "Um, this chicken is delicious."

Jim looked serious. "Back to the Nakamuras'." He put down his fork and leaned toward her. "Odd things? Like what?"

Ruth related the varying number of pigeons, Bible pages turned, and books scattered. "Grandpa says it's a prankster. I think it's someone who hates the Japanese and their friends and wants to irritate us enough that we'll quit working over there. Bob Miller would say it's old man Jones."

Jim was quiet and ate slowly. "Keep your eyes open, but don't let your suspicions carry you away. There's probably a logical explanation."

On the way home, Ruth related the information she had picked up from the sessions. "We're to hold scrap drives for metals, rubber, grease, and paper. And we're to push war bonds and stamps. They want us to hold a special rally day with a parade and lots of flags and banners, and we could get some trucks to haul scraps to Bob's lot to kick it off. I thought maybe the Fourth of July. With a big picnic. What do you think?"

Jim remained quiet and lost in thought. "Jim?"

"Oh, sure, sounds great. Go ahead with your plans for it." He drove in silence 'til they pulled into her driveway. He turned toward her. "Thanks for coming along," he said. "I can see you're going to be a great help." He reached for her hand. "Be careful, Ruth. I care a lot about—my friend." He looked at her tenderly, then got out and opened her door. "Hurry on in now, before I forget this was business and there can't be a good-night kiss."

She paused, hoping he'd forget, 'til the guilty stab came back. "Good night, Jim," she said softly and hurried inside. She closed the door and leaned against it, her heart pounding.

Chapter 11

Alma carried a bowl of fresh strawberries into the kitchen and set it down by the sink. "They're beauties this year."

"And endless," Ruth added as she filled her bowl with more berries to clean. "We'll have a big supply canned and in the cellar for winter. Even the birds can't eat them fast enough."

Alma chuckled. "Speaking of birds, did you see the Armstrongs' scarecrow? They painted a Hitler-style mustache on it, cold beady eyes, and that dark hair combed across the forehead. Even the birds should know how scary that looks!"

The screen door squeaked. George came in carrying the morning paper and plopped it on the table. "Take a look at that!" He pointed to the large black headline for June 22, 1942: JAP SUB FIRES ON OREGON.

Ruth gasped. "Oh, no, are we being attacked? What did they hit?" She quickly scanned the article as Alma looked over her shoulder.

"Praise the Lord," Alma whispered. "Nothing was hit."

"They fired seventeen rounds at the mouth of the Columbia River—Battery Russell." Ruth looked up from the paper. "Do you think they'll attack here, Grandpa?"

"We'll pray not." George sat heavily. "Thought I was too old, but I'm signing up with Joe Duncan to be a plane spotter. These old eyes should be good enough for that." He pounded his fist on the table. "We need to keep that post manned!"

"Grandma. . ." Ruth turned to see her grandmother with her head bowed, praying. She could sense fear even amidst her grandparents' faith and shuddered. Suddenly the war was more than projects and what happened "over there."

"Ruth, are you all right?" Her grandmother looked up, concerned. "The Lord hasn't forgotten us, and He's still in control, but we have a lot of praying to do."

"I'm okay, Grandma. It's just a good dose of reality." She took out a paper and pencil. "And this is a good time to rally community support for the war effort when everyone's had a scare."

George stood up and grabbed his hat. "I'm heading to the feedstore to talk to Joe." He stopped at the door. "Keep praying."

"Oh, my, I almost forgot the berries in all the confusion." Alma sat down and began to hull strawberries, putting the stems in the bowl with the clean berries and throwing the berries in the scrap bowl. She looked up at Ruth writing furiously. "Slow down, Dear. Frantic effort won't win the war." She looked at the bowls. "Oh, my, I should talk!" she exclaimed as she saw what she had done.

Ruth sighed and returned to her plans. "Right now, it helps to keep busy. Besides, I have some great ideas." She picked up the paper and turned to Alma. "And I think I can help you out, too, Grandma." She had a mischievous twinkle in her eye. "I've been planning a Fourth of July Rally Day to build support for the war effort. I'm putting Velma Miller and her women's club in charge of decorations and war-bond sales. And I'll have her round up musicians for a band." She jotted down the note.

Alma stopped her work and looked hopeful.

Ruth looked at her grandmother smugly. "That'll keep her so busy she won't have time to take over your Ladies' Aid project for now. Just see that you get your shipment out to the church relief agency by July 4!"

"Ruth Sinclair, that's good thinking. She'll be so busy she won't bother about our church project." Alma chuckled and looked relieved.

Ruth raised an eyebrow at her grandmother. "If I see to the program, will you be in charge of the food?"

"If you'll help me finish these berries." She handed Ruth a bowl. "This is the last we'll can for winter. Any more goes to Pastor Cameron's food drive."

"Grandma, do you think. . . ?" The doorbell rang. "I'll get it," Ruth said as she put her bowl down. She opened the door to see Tim Henderson looking very official. He handed her a pamphlet that read "What to Do in an Air Raid."

"Hey, Miss Sinclair. I'm here representing the air-raid warden," he recited. "Read these instructions and be prepared for an air-raid drill at any time. The signal will be the school bell tolling. Cars will drive up and down the roads honking—uh. . .uh—three long blasts—no, three short blasts and one long. That means V for victory." Tim caught his breath after the long spiel.

"That's quite a speech, Tim," Ruth commented. "We'll study your pamphlet and be prepared." She smiled at him and swatted a fly with the pamphlet. "Now that strawberry picking's about over, we need the help of the Junior Volunteers. We're preparing a big Fourth of July Rally. Can your group put up posters for us and be victims for the Red Cross demonstrations?"

"Victims—hey, that sounds fun, Miss Sinclair! Well, gotta go. Got lots of houses to do." He jumped down the steps and took off on his bike.

Ruth sat down in the living room to study the pamphlet. "What is it, Dear?" her grandmother asked as she came into the room.

"Information on air-raid drills. At the signal, we're to lie flat under a solid table, it says. And we're to be sure we have no lights showing." She handed the pamphlet to Alma.

"Looks like that Japanese attack yesterday got Bob going," Alma commented. She put the pamphlet down. "Let's get these berries done and clean up the kitchen."

When they had finished, Ruth sat down at the table with her notebook. "The Red Cross will put on a first-aid demonstration. Jim will speak on what needs to be done. I'll get trucks lined up and organize the parade." She sat back, pleased with the plans. "I need to be sure people are doing their jobs, and then we're all set."

★ ★ ★

The next morning she completed her phone calls. "I need to ask Pastor Cameron to have a prayer," she said aloud. "Oh, and check with Tim to see if he has volunteers for the first-aid drill. And I need to round up some scraps to start off the drive." She made a note.

The day flew by. Plans were going well, and the volunteers were doing their jobs. Ruth walked into the kitchen. "Helping you with dinner will be a relief after all that. I'll peel the potatoes, Grandma."

When George came in from his chores, dinner was on the table. "It's good to sit awhile." Alma sighed as she bowed her head for grace. She looked up and passed the mashed potatoes. "I'm sorry dinner is so late. This has been quite a week."

As they finished the meal, Ruth brought out Alma's strawberry shortcake. "Mm, Alma, my dear, you're a wonder. No one would know there's any rationing; we eat so well." George smiled fondly at his wife as he relished his dessert. He patted his stomach. "I'm not sure I can even make it to my chair to finish the paper. If you ladies will excuse me, I'll go see if the world's still here." He headed for his paper and favorite overstuffed chair in the living room.

"I'll clean up in here, Grandma. Go in and sit with Grandpa. You deserve a rest after all the canning you've done."

Ruth had cleared the table and put the last of the dishes away when she heard the *bong, bong* of the school bell followed by a loud honking of car horns. She hurried into the living room.

"What in the world. . . ?" George began.

"It's an air-raid drill!" Ruth hollered above the noise. "Turn off all the lights and lie flat under the dining room table. I'll go under the kitchen table." She hurried about switching off lights and crawled under the table.

The school bell fell silent, and the car horns sounded farther and farther away. "How long do we stay here, Ruth?" George called out.

"Till the all-clear signal. It should be anytime."

The minutes ticked by in the dark and silent house. A mild evening breeze rustled the curtains at the open windows and blew gently through the screen door to cool the house, still warm from the day's canning.

After twenty minutes, she heard her grandfather moving about in the living room. "That's enough of that," he declared. "I don't hear any bombs, so. . ."

Pow! Pow! Rapid gunfire followed by breaking glass and angry shouts sounded through the open front door. Ruth hurried into the room.

"You don't suppose this was the real thing, do you?" Alma froze in confusion.

George dashed to the front door, following the direction of the sounds. "It's across the road and down at old man Jones's place."

They clustered on the dark porch. Flashlights winked in the darkness, and the angry shouts continued. "I can't understand 'em, but at least it's English, so we haven't been invaded by the Japanese," George said in relief. They could hear footsteps hurrying their way.

"Good evening, Mr. Peterson." Jim's voice came through the dark as he walked up the driveway. "Don't worry. There's no danger. Just a drill gone awry."

Alma let her breath out in relief. "What's going on, Jim?"

"That was Bob's first bungled air-raid drill, that's what. Bob forgot to give the all-clear signal because he was so busy running around checking to see that people followed orders." He chuckled. "There he was in his white helmet and whistle, checking every house he could to be sure lights were out and everyone was under a table."

"But what was that ruckus all about?" George asked.

Jim shook his head. "Old man Jones had lights on in his chicken house and wouldn't turn them off. Bob was going to teach him to follow regulations, so he went over there and shot out the lights. A neighbor called me. I had to pull rank and tell Bob to settle down."

"Old man Jones can't be too happy about it," Alma commented. "He'll be mighty peeved if his hens got so scared they won't lay."

Jim sat down on the steps. A peace settled over the evening as the crickets chirped and frogs chorused in the background.

"Trouble is, after that fiasco no one will pay much attention to the next drill," George said. "I'm going back to my paper. Come on, Alma. Sit with me awhile." He patted his wife on the back tenderly and opened the screen door.

Jim moved to the porch swing beside Ruth and sighed. "Sometimes you wonder who's the enemy in this," he said dryly. He looked over at her. "How are plans for the Fourth coming? I've been thinking about my speech."

She explained who was involved. "This has been done on short notice, but I think it will turn out okay. People are enthusiastic and willing to help. With gas rationing, they'll stay around here for the Fourth, and this will give them something to do."

Jim moved the porch swing with his feet. It added its creak to the chorus of crickets and frogs. "I chose the right person for an assistant even if I did mess up on air-raid warden." He shook his head. "I still can't believe that drill. Bob was supposed to clear it with me and we'd go over all the details first, but he wanted the authority to do it on his own." He put his hand on hers. "Thanks for all you're doing. I get so busy I don't tell you how much I appreciate you." His look was warm and tender.

Ruth was sure her heart could be heard over nature's chorus. It would be so natural to move closer and put her head on his shoulder. . . *Stop it, Ruth,* she chided herself. She gave a shiver.

"You're getting chilly out here. I'd better let you go in." He stood and helped her to her feet. "Good night, Ruth." He gently touched her nose, turned abruptly, and walked into the dark.

Ruth sat down and moved the swing slowly, enjoying the romantic moment.

Chapter 12

A large banner fluttering between two trees announced the Fourth of July Rally Day. "Over here!" Ruth called out as Marge walked across the school grounds to the grove of fir trees. The Women's Club was busy draping red, white, and blue bunting around the bottom of a raised platform that would serve as a stage. Tables were set up in the shade for the potluck at noon, each decorated with small flags.

"A perfect day," Marge called back as Ruth teetered on a ladder, fastening one end of a banner.

"You're just in time to help, Marge. The girls in the skit will be here any minute. I need you to get them ready." Ruth's mind was on her list of things to do. She climbed down. "The Red Cross is preparing for their demonstration over there. And that's the war bond booth," she explained and pointed.

Joe Duncan drove up in his feed truck. "Where to, Miss Sinclair?"

"Over on the ball field. I'll be right there." She turned. "Come on, Marge. Help me get the trucks ready for the parade." She grabbed several banners and headed for the ball field. "Take the other end, Marge." She held the banner to the side of the truck, and they taped both ends.

"Scrap Metal Drive," Marge read as she stepped back from the decorated truck.

"That's the first one." Ruth surveyed their work, hands on her hips. A small flag fluttered above each fender.

Another truck pulled up and was soon decorated with its banners and flags. Ruth walked back to the feed truck. "Joe, here's the agenda." She handed him a paper. "Just announce each item."

"Miss Sinclair, I. . ."

"You'll do fine, Joe. No one else has a voice loud enough to get people's attention out here."

Joe nodded.

"It's almost time. Let's go." She hurried back to the stage. "You get the girls ready, Marge. I need to find Jim."

Families milled about, talking in small groups and laying out blankets to sit on while children played tag nearby. Ruth searched the crowd. "Jim, there you are," she said in relief as she walked up to him. "I thought you'd skipped out."

"And disappoint a pretty lady? Never! Is everything ready?"

"We'll know in a minute. Here we go." She motioned to Joe, who climbed up on the small stage.

"Attention, please," his voice boomed over the noise of the crowd. "Welcome to our Fourth of July Rally Day. We're here to raise support for our country at war and our men fighting overseas," he read. "Let's open with a prayer by Pastor Cameron."

With the amen, Joe continued. "First on the program is a skit by girls in our school."

Six girls rushed to the stage in red, white, and blue outfits, whispering and giggling. Cynthia Richards gave her recitation flawlessly, followed by the girls' patriotic songs and a short skit. As they finished, the audience clapped and cheered.

"Next we have a first-aid demonstration by the Red Cross," Joe announced.

Ruth motioned to Tim, John, and Charlie. They ran to the edge of the stage while the Red Cross director described the first-aid classes to be offered at the school. "Now we'll demonstrate some things you'll learn. Boys," he said.

Charlie hopped up on the stage. "Our first boy has a head injury caused by debris from a bomb explosion. We'll demonstrate how to treat it 'til help arrives." Charlie fell to the ground, clasping his head and moaning. The audience roared with laughter. At this his cries grew louder, and he flopped about the stage. Red ketchup oozed over his forehead, and girls squealed in disgust.

"Lie still, young man. We can't treat you unless you're still," the director hissed. Charlie gave a dramatic flop and lay still while the bandages were applied.

"He's quite the ham," Marge whispered to Ruth.

"It wasn't planned that way," she replied dryly.

Tim and John climbed on the stage as Charlie miraculously recovered. "The next boy was injured in the side and his friend has an arm injury," the director continued.

Tim grabbed his side and with a loud moan fell to the floor. "I'm hit! I'm hit!" he shrieked as the audience doubled over laughing.

John moaned and held his arm, staggering to the side of the stage. He gave his last moan, clutched his arm, and stepped off the edge of the stage. With a cry he tumbled to the ground. "My arm!" he cried. "It really hurts bad!"

"More!" a voice called out.

"Good acting, John!" the crowd shouted.

The director rushed down and helped John to his feet. "My wrist hurts bad, Mister." Tears ran down his cheeks. "It hurts so bad. It's not pretend."

The crowd grew silent as the director helped John to the steps while two Red Cross nurses and his mother hurried over.

The director stepped back on stage. "This was not planned, but our nurses will show you how they treat a real sprain. Let's give a big round of applause for our fine actors and a special hand for John." Tim and Charlie jumped up and bowed to the whistles and cheers, and John managed a wave with his good hand.

"After all that excitement, you must be hungry. Lunch is waiting," Joe announced. "During the break, be sure to visit the war bond booth and buy some bonds. Kids can meet out on the field for games when they're done eating. We'll continue the program after lunch." The crowd swarmed toward the tables laden with food, then returned to their blankets to enjoy the lunch.

Ruth plopped down with her plate of food. "That was more excitement than we planned. I'll be glad to settle down for awhile," she said to Marge.

"May I join you ladies?" Jim asked as he seated himself. "Good crowd. Congratulations to my assistant for a well-organized event. And your actors were superb. I'm not sure the Red Cross appreciated all their antics, but the audience loved them. I checked on John and he'll be fine. A mild sprain."

Ruth took a bite of potato salad. "The boys got carried away, I'm afraid. That wasn't planned." As they ate, Ruth watched families enjoying the day. Shouts and squeals came from the field where children played a game of tag. A soft breeze blew and the sky was clear.

"Ruth, oh, Ruth. Come back, Ruth." Jim waved his hand in front of her face. "No one's allowed to daydream and look so content when I have to worry about being the next speaker." He stood and picked up his plate. "Now, if you'll excuse me, ladies, I need to go over my notes."

"And I need to get the parade lined up." Ruth got to her feet. "Take over, Jim. We'll be waiting for your directions." She hurried to the platform where the musicians were tuning their instruments.

"We're not a large band," Arlan said. "Couldn't get more than two trumpets, a trombone, and the drum. If we play loud, maybe no one will notice."

"You'll do fine," she reassured him.

"Ladies and gentlemen," Joe called out, "we're ready to continue our program. Please be seated." He waited 'til the crowd was quiet. "Next up is Jim Griffin."

As Jim started his speech, Ruth gave the parade units last-minute instructions.

"The war industry needs our help," Jim continued. "They need materials to make the arms, ammunition, planes, and submarines defending our freedom—freedom to gather as we are today. We can help keep America strong and free!"

A cheer broke out from the crowd.

"Our parade today is the official beginning of Fir Glen's scrap drive. We call it Scraps for Freedom." Jim turned to the band and raised his hand. A drumroll followed, and Wallace Coulter drove Joe's feed truck past the platform with Ruth's "Scrap Metal" banner on the sides and several pieces of scrap metal stacked on the truck. "One shovel will make four hand grenades." Jim held up a shovel, and Tim ran to put it on the truck. "Search your barns and

71

basements. Bring your scrap metal to Bob's lot."

Jim raised his hand again and the drumroll sounded as Bob Miller drove forward, his banners reading "Scrap Rubber Drive." An "Air-Raid Warden" sign had been added below it. "This man wants your old tires, rubber boots, hoses, raincoats—anything rubber. One B-17 bomber requires a half ton of rubber. Keep our men in the air. Bring your scrap rubber to Bob's lot."

Bob honked his horn, leaning out the window, waving and pointing to the "Air-Raid Warden" sign he had added to his door.

At the third drumroll, Velma Miller and Charlotte Hunt marched past the stage carrying a banner between them reading "Grease Collection." In the other hand, each lady held aloft a can of kitchen grease.

Suddenly the truck in front of them gave a loud blast of its horn and jerked to a halt. Bob jumped out and dashed to the back of the truck, grabbing a rubber garden hose that was falling off, one end dragging behind. As he gave a yank, it curled between Velma's feet. With the next jerk, Velma's feet flew out from under her, her grease can sailing through the air.

A collective gasp came from the crowd. "Oh, no!"

"Watch out, Bob!" hollered a bystander as the can headed straight for Bob. With a thud it struck his shoulder. Grease flew into the air and all over Bob.

Joe helped Velma to her feet. She straightened unsteadily, moving her legs carefully as a Red Cross nurse led her away for observation.

The stunned crowd recovered to see their air-raid warden head to toe in grease. A ripple of laughter started in the audience and spread 'til it became a roar. Men doubled over and slapped their legs. Women laughed so hard they wiped their eyes.

Ruth threw up her hands and hurried over to her grandparents. "Grandpa, would you drive the truck, please? Grandma, will you take Velma's place?" she pleaded. "What'll happen next?"

Bob ran his hands over his greasy, dripping clothes.

"Nice aftershave there, Bob," a voice called out. "That fragrance makes me hungry."

"You won't have to use hair oil for awhile," someone else teased.

Bob's face turned an angry red. "After all I've done for Fir Glen, this is the thanks I get." He stomped his feet to shake off a chunk of lard.

"We're only funnin' you, Bob," a man called out.

As Bob stomped off, Joe quickly took the stage. "Let's get back to our program. Jim, it's yours." The crowd quieted.

Jim continued. "Bring your cooking grease in metal containers to Joe's Feedstore."

"Not to Bob!" a voice shouted amid snickers.

"Collection dates will be posted on official bulletin boards. The grease is used to make ammunition." Jim paused.

At the fourth drumroll, Tim and Charlie marched into view, carrying their banner: "Kids, Too!"

"Our young people have been collecting paper and milkweed floss. They'll also be asking for foil from gum and cigarette wrappers," he announced.

Jim looked out over the crowd. "And now to your part. You were asked to bring at least one scrap item to contribute today. The band will lead off, followed by the trucks and marchers. We ask you to place your items on the trucks, join the parade, and march with us to deposit this material at Bob's lot. Then we'll close by singing the national anthem. And as you go, be careful not to slip on the grease."

As the crowd followed Jim's instructions, he came over to Ruth. "Don't look so downhearted. It's a big success."

She shook her head. "First John gets hurt, then Velma falls down, and Bob goes off mad and covered with grease. People won't take this seriously. They'll think it's just a comedy of errors."

"Wrong, Miss Sinclair. You've created a spirit of unity, and they had fun, too. They'll remember what they learned longer than if it had gone perfectly smooth." He took her elbow. "Come on. Let's join them."

The band attempted to play "Stars and Stripes Forever" but quit with a squeak and switched to a simpler tune as the crowd marched to Bob's lot.

"Excuse me a minute, Ruth." Jim hurried over to talk to Joe Duncan. As they reached the lot, Joe raised his hands at the crowd.

"Ladies and gentlemen," his voice boomed, "before we deposit the scraps and sing the closing, we want to thank all who participated. And let's give a special thanks to Miss Sinclair for organizing it all!"

Jim beamed at her as the crowd applauded wildly and cheered.

"Great job, Miss Sinclair!"

"Best Fourth we ever had."

"I'll go home and see what scraps I can bring."

"I'm joining the first-aid class this fall."

Comments swirled around Ruth. "Thank you. I appreciate it." She smiled.

"I liked the funny parts. Speeches get boring."

"I'll remember that. I don't think Bob will volunteer again, though." She chuckled.

As the last strains of the anthem faded and people drifted off, Jim grinned at her smugly. "See, I told you."

"Okay, Boss, you were right. I don't look forward to my next trip to Bob's market, though," she said with a grin. "But it seems to be successful in spite of everything. I'm so tired, but in a good way."

"Let's go see about the cleanup. Then you deserve a ride home." Jim took her arm and led her toward the school. The cleanup crew was busy returning tables to the school building and dismantling the decorations when Jim and

Ruth got to the grove and joined the effort.

Ruth picked up the last scrap of paper. "That's it. I'm ready for that ride you offered."

"Car's over here." Jim led the way, carrying the box of supplies Ruth had brought. She climbed in with a sigh and laid her head back on the seat. Jim chuckled. "Looks like we wore out my assistant today."

He pulled into the Peterson driveway and turned to her. "I appreciate all you did, Ruth." He reached for her hand. "We make a good team." He looked down. "I'm sorry it has such limitations." He looked at her tenderly but sadly and said softly, "But I respect your stand. Good night, Ruth—and thanks again."

Chapter 13

The morning sun shone through the bedroom window, giving the room a golden glow as the rays danced on the flowered wallpaper. Ruth stretched and lay back, listening to the birds warbling in the tree outside her window.

"The Lord must love mornings. He made them so beautiful," she said aloud. She swung her legs over the edge of the bed. "Lord, thank You for a safe new day." She completed her morning devotions, dressed, and went downstairs.

"Good morning, Sleepyhead," Alma teased as she folded the clothes she'd brought in from the clothesline. "I got up early to get these done before it gets hot."

Ruth poured a cup of coffee. "All the summer's activity finally got to me, I guess, Grandma. You shouldn't let me sleep so long."

Alma folded the last towel and added it to the pile. "Do you feel like a trip to town today? Emerson's Grocery in Brookwood has a sale on. We need coffee and a few essentials."

Ruth nodded. "What time?"

"In about an hour. I need to check my grocery list against my ration books and the ads to see what I can buy."

"I'll be upstairs cleaning. Call me when you're ready, Gram."

★ ★ ★

An hour later, Ruth turned into the parking lot beside the grocery store. "Here we are, Grandma. Ready for the big adventure?"

Alma sighed and picked up her pocketbook. "I don't look forward to this. Shopping is so hard with the shortages and ration stamps. I'm just thankful we can grow so much of our own food."

They entered the market and wandered down the aisles, looking for specials. Out of curiosity, Alma picked up a can of applesauce. "Can you believe it? Sixteen cents! When we get home, I'm going out to sweet-talk our apple trees!"

Ruth chuckled. "I'm sure you will, Grandma."

Alma peered at the meat display. "Hamburger—forty-three cents a pound. Grandpa's butchering soon. We'll wait." She walked on. "We need to check on Maxwell House Coffee. They may have a good special to celebrate their fifty years on the market. Let's head for that aisle. And keep your eye out for sugar. I need to use my stamps before the end of the month, but there hasn't been any in stock."

With several items in the basket, Alma stopped to check her purchases and her ration books. "I'm too old for this, Ruth. Let's go." Alma reached the cashier and counted out the required ration stamps and money. "Grocery trips wear me out these days." She sighed as they headed for the car.

"You get in and sit down. I'll load the groceries," Ruth directed. She could feel the day's heat bearing down.

She put the last of the purchases in the trunk. As she looked up, she saw Jim coming out of the county clerk's office across the street. Her heart gave its usual extra thump. Then she looked again. Someone was with him. A blond woman. Young and very pretty. The woman smiled up at Jim as she talked.

Ruth slammed the trunk lid and climbed into the car. *That odd feeling can't be jealousy,* she chided herself. She started the car and was turning around when Alma exclaimed, "There's Jim Griffin. Say, who's that woman with him?"

"Probably someone from the county clerk's office. As community coordinator he works with various government departments," Ruth responded casually, making a strong effort not to betray her feelings.

"That doesn't look like business to me. She's holding his arm. Oh dear, I was hoping you'd become interested in Mr. Griffin. He's such a fine Christian man."

"You never cared for Harold, did you, Grandma?"

Alma hesitated. "I never disliked him. I just didn't feel he was a sincere Christian or very settled. I wanted only the best for you."

"I know, Gram. When Harold comes home, that's something I have to settle."

"Don't wait too long, Dear. Mr. Griffin's an attractive man. He won't wait forever. There's that woman. . ."

Ruth laughed. "You're impossible." *But right,* she thought. *I never expected Jim to find someone else before Harold came home.* An uneasy feeling crept into her heart. She backed out of the parking space and took one more look toward the county clerk's office, but Jim and the woman were nowhere in sight. With a sigh, she pulled out of the parking lot and headed home.

Ruth turned into their driveway and pulled up by the back door.

"Let's get these groceries put away. This heat isn't good for them or me," Alma said as she got out of the car.

"I'll do it," Ruth insisted. "You go inside."

Alma sighed. "In this heat you don't have to push much. Shopping and heat wear me out." She paused at the round bed of zinnias and marigolds ablaze in blossoms of yellow and orange, red and purple. The flowers drooped in the day's heat. "I have to get these watered today, too. Don't let me forget, Ruth." She headed for the house. "I'm glad Oregon doesn't have a whole summer like this."

Ruth set the groceries on the counter and paused to fix her grandmother some cold juice. "Take this and go sit in the living room. You rest while I get all this put away. That's an order."

Alma patted Ruth's shoulder. "Thank you, Dear. You're good to me." She took her cold drink and walked to the living room.

"You deserve it," Ruth called after her. She turned to put the groceries away.

"Ruth! Oh, no, Ruth, come here. What's happened?" Alma called out.

Ruth's heart gave a lurch. "Lord, let her be okay," she whispered as she rushed to the living room with a sinking feeling. "Are you all right, Grand—" Ruth stopped and stared at the mess as she entered the room.

"Look at this," Alma whispered. Books were torn out of the bookcase and scattered over the floor. George's desk was a mess of strewn papers. "Someone was in our house while we were gone." Alma sat down heavily. "What could they want? We don't keep money here." She stared at the mess and shook her head. "Grandpa's working with some of the men out in the Nakamuras' field. We can't get ahold of him. Oh, my, what do we do, Ruth?"

"I don't know," Ruth replied, "but I'm calling Jim. This is the third bookcase ransacked—and someone got in our house."

Jim arrived ten minutes later.

"The same thing happened at school and the Nakamuras'," she explained. "What does someone want?"

"Have you seen anyone suspicious around here?" he asked.

Both women shook their heads. "And nothing's been taken that we can see. It's just a big mess," Ruth replied.

Jim looked among the books. "When you clean up, check carefully to be sure nothing's missing. I'll tell the sheriff, but as I said before, he wasn't very concerned about the two previous incidents. With a war on, he's got other things to worry about, he says."

"What bothers me is that someone was in our house," Alma said softly.

He was quiet and looked concerned. "I don't like it, either, even if these are pranks, as the sheriff seems to think. Maybe someone's still upset about your friendship with the Nakamuras. Anti-Japanese sentiment is strong in some people." He looked sharply at Ruth. "Don't take any chances. Be sure to lock your doors. Let me know if anything else happens, however small."

Alma shook her head sadly. "What's the world coming to when we distrust others and have to lock our doors? I never thought I'd see the day."

Jim picked up his hat. "I'll speak to the sheriff, but since I've been here, I'm sure he won't send someone out." He looked at Ruth soberly. "Be careful." He turned to Alma. "Don't worry, Mrs. Peterson. I'll see what I can do about it." He smiled at Ruth and was gone.

"We're blessed compared to people in Europe, but I still feel invaded when someone has been in our home." Alma sighed, sat back in her chair, and fanned herself with a paper.

"Drink your juice and rest. I'll get all this cleaned up. Grandpa can check his desk," Ruth said as she began to put the books back.

"I think I'll lie down a bit." Alma got up and walked to the hall. "The war seems closer today—all the ration stamps and now this. After lunch I want to work on the banner for our window. We're proud Bud's in the service defending our country." She paused. "And we're blessed we can put up a blue star for Bud. On the way home today, I saw a banner with one gold star and two blue. Can you imagine—three men in that family in the service and now one killed or missing in action. We need to talk with the Lord a lot, Ruth." She turned toward her room.

Ruth plopped down on the sofa, trying to sort out her thoughts. *Someone was in our home!* She paused as she thought of the scene in their living room and Jim's quick effort to help. *I've come to rely on him a lot,* she admitted. Finally with a sigh she got up and walked to the kitchen. *This won't get the work done or solve the problem.*

She had put the last of the groceries away and tidied the room when Alma walked in. "You were supposed to rest," she chided her grandmother.

"I'm better now, Dear. When I've had a talk with the Lord, I'm rested." She got out the material and started on the banner for their window. Ruth joined her as she measured and cut the material. "It's looking good," Alma commented later, "but I need to stop and knit awhile, Ruth. The Ladies' Aid wants to ship our batch of socks overseas soon, and I'm behind on what I promised to make." She folded the material and straightened up. "Knitting's a quiet thing to do on a hot day."

"Good. It'll make you sit still and rest awhile, too," Ruth said with satisfaction as she got up. "I'm going for a walk in the woods, Gram. Will you be okay here by yourself? I need to think."

"No one will bother me, Dear. Those hoodlums only come when nobody's home. Run along, but be careful for poison oak."

Ruth walked across the yard and headed for the woods behind the barn. A narrow path left the pasture and wound into the trees. The warm air was fragrant with the smell of fir needles, and insects buzzed as she wandered down the path. Oregon grape brushed against her legs.

She came to a moss-covered log and sat down. *My thinking spot,* she remembered as she looked about the small clearing covered by a canopy of leaves. *I've come here so many times over the summers.* A breeze lazily moved the vine maple leaves above her.

When I was little, I pretended this was my house, and the moss was my carpet. It was all safe and secure and special. I even imagined my dolls could come to life here. I miss that innocent world. Anything was possible, and everything was exciting.

A fly buzzed about her head. She swatted at it. *But the world's not like that.*

An innocent world is the one that's pretend. Even here there are bugs to bite you and plants to make you itch. She turned at a rustling in the underbrush. *It's that way out there, too. But I want to nestle into a world where everything's good and safe and happy. I don't like it when evils and troubles intrude.* The fly buzzed around her again. She gave a sigh. *They've intruded in a big way this time.*

She sat on the log swinging her legs. *I'd like to return to Eden, but I can't. There's sin in this world, and all our efforts and longings won't make it perfect. Only God can do that.*

The woods responded with chirps and buzzes and the soft breeze rustling the leaves. A squirrel stopped in its run up a tree and chattered at her intrusion into its world.

She stood and dusted off her slacks. *Well, now Jim's a worry, too. Has he found someone else?*

A spider made its way along an almost-invisible strand of web. She ducked and started on the path back to the house with a sigh. *And I never dreamed I'd be harassed because of a friendship, either, but that's what's happening. We're being threatened because we won't desert our Japanese friends.* She stepped over an old log and moved a small branch out of the way with her hand.

Helpless, that's how I feel. Jim said I had to grow out of my greenhouse faith. Is that what this is all about, Lord? Are You trying to teach me to have faith when life's hard and out of control as well as when it's good? A long, briered vine tugged at her pant leg, and she stooped to release her slacks from the sharp thorns.

She left the woods and walked through the pasture in the late afternoon sun. The cows rested in the shade, and ahead Fluffy was stretched out on the porch. "Your world looks peaceful today, Fluffy," she said to the cat as she climbed the steps and reached to open the screen door. "Mine's not so peaceful. I have two new worries. Who broke in our house? And is Jim giving up on me?"

Chapter 14

Ruth climbed the wooden steps of the old feedstore and breathed deeply. *Mm, the smell of hay and feed is pleasant,* she thought. *It reminds me of the fun Bud and I had playing in Grandpa's barn when we were kids.*

"Hi, Joe." She smiled at the owner as he unloaded sacks of grain from a truck. He raised his hand in greeting. "I'll need five sacks of chicken feed before I leave today. I brought Grandpa's pickup."

"Sure thing, Miss Sinclair." He put the sack down on the pile. "You can have your grease collection over there." He pointed to the end of the long wooden loading dock where two metal barrels were located.

"Thanks. I'll put my poster up on the wall behind them, if that's okay."

Joe nodded.

She walked to the end of the dock and inspected the poster she had lettered: "Grease Collection Here. Save Waste Fats for Ammunition!" She held the poster to the wall and fumbled in her purse. "Oh, no, I forgot the thumbtacks." She lowered the sign. "Joe," she called, "I'm going over to Bob's store. I'll be right back." She grabbed her purse and hurried across the road.

The bell jangled above the door as she entered the market where Bob was on a ladder putting up a Royal Crown Cola poster. "I'm looking for thumbtacks, Bob."

"Can't get 'em now," he replied. "War shortages, you know. You'll have to use tape. It's down that aisle and on the left." He climbed down the ladder and stood with his thumbs hooked in his suspenders. "I guess you heard the news." He looked around to be sure no one else was there and lowered his voice. "A shipment from Griffin's factory was broken into." He nodded his head smugly.

"Who did it?" Ruth was shocked.

"Spies, that's what. Found out about the shipment and broke into it. Has to do with lights people see around the plant."

"This is terrible!"

Bob nodded eagerly. "Those Nazis have been sinkin' our ships off the East Coast. I say spies are signaling 'em our ships' locations. If they're doing it on the East Coast, you can bet we got spies out here, too." He pursed his lips and rocked up on his toes.

Ruth tried to grasp what she was hearing. "How could they do that without being noticed?"

"Plow signals in the fields. Bonfires. Them little lights. They're clever. Got to keep your eyes open. Keeps me busy checking on everyone."

Ruth shuddered. "I have to run, Bob. Grease collection at the feedstore." She paid for her purchase. "Thanks."

No wonder I haven't seen much of Jim lately, Ruth thought as she hurried back to the feedstore. She arrived to find two members of the Fir Glen Women's Club waiting.

"I had to go over to Bob's for tape." She put her purse down on a feed sack next to her notebook and *Ben-Hur.* "Mrs. Olson, if you'll hold that end of the poster, I'll get it taped up."

She applied the tape and stood back to survey their work. "Okay, ladies, we're all set. To our posts. Actually, to our barrels," Ruth quipped with a smile.

The women glanced at each other. "You look, uh, comfortable, Dear, in those slacks. I would never wear them myself, of course, but I suppose they are handy in some circumstances, though for a teacher in public. . ." Mrs. Archer stood primly in her well-cut suit and matching hat, carrying white gloves.

Ruth's face grew red. "This can be a messy job scraping grease out of cans and buckets. No use splattering good clothes."

"To each her own," Mrs. Olson snipped. "I intend to keep records for this collection, so I dressed appropriately for that." She turned to her fellow club-woman, similarly dressed. "Mrs. Archer, you see that everyone stays in line and give them directions. This must remain orderly," she directed. "You never know what kind of people will be here."

Ruth felt her anger rise. "Then who will man the second barrel?"

The women looked at each other. "If you didn't think to arrange for some-one, I guess you will have to do both, Dear."

"But that's why you're here," Ruth protested.

"Dear, you can't expect us to scrape grease out of cans into a barrel. If it splatters, our clothes will be ruined. We have bridge club later."

"That's why I wore. . ." She stopped. *Okay, Ruth,* she told herself, *admit it. You've been had.*

"I hear our first contributors coming now," Mrs. Olson said briskly. "Mrs. Archer, you direct them to me. I'll record who they are and how much they brought, then send them on to Miss Sinclair."

A line of children and a few adults soon formed, each carrying a metal container of lard or grease. Ruth poured what she could into the barrel and scraped out the more solid form. The line seemed endless, and the smell of bacon grease grew nauseating in the summer heat.

"This looks exciting." Ruth looked up to see Jim watching her. He glanced around. "Why are you the only one at this end of the line? Those ladies don't seem to be doing much."

"Because I'm a chump. I dressed for it. They cleverly didn't. At this rate we'll be here all day."

Jim took off his suit coat and rolled up his shirtsleeves. "Your hero to the rescue, Ma'am."

"Jim, you can't. You're dressed up," Ruth protested as he winked at her.

"Do you think I'd leave a lovely damsel in distress?"

"Oh, Mr. Griffin." Mrs. Olson bustled over. "You shouldn't be doing that— you, the community coordinator, and in your good clothes."

"We do what we can to help out, Mrs. Olson," he said evenly. "No job is too small or too messy. Miss Sinclair needed help, and there didn't seem to be anyone else willing, so I volunteered."

"Well, I—we—didn't expect, I mean. . . ," she sputtered, turned briskly, and walked back to her records.

"Next time, I'll request help willing to dress for the part and work where needed," Ruth said wryly.

"After this, we should send them over to Bob's to sort messy, empty toothpaste tubes." Jim chuckled as they waited for the next contributor.

Ruth smiled. "I haven't seen you around. Things busy lately?"

"Problems at the plant. You know how business goes," he replied evasively. "I have such an able assistant; she carries on when I'm otherwise occupied."

"Half an hour to go. Our line's thinning out," Ruth observed. "I won't be sorry when this is over."

"Oh, Mr. Griffin." Mrs. Olson hurried over. "Our women's club would like to have you as guest speaker at our next meeting." She smiled sweetly. "We'd be honored to have you speak on the war effort."

Jim glanced at Ruth and sighed. "To help the war effort, what can I say? Let me know the time and place, Mrs. Olson."

"I'll have my daughter get in touch with you. She's a secretary in the Brookwood mayor's office, you know. Being single, she has more time than I do. She'd be here today, but she's working." Mrs. Olson smiled proudly.

"Fine. And, thank you, ladies, for your help. We've taken up too much of your time. I'm sure you have things to do." He ushered them to the steps and smiled. With a wave of their white-gloved hands, they were gone.

"Well, Mr. Griffin, Fir Glen's society has its eye on you for its daughters. Do you like teas?" Ruth teased.

Jim grimaced. "Spare me, please." He looked around. "Is there much left to do?"

Ruth shook her head. "The truck will be here to pick up the barrels any minute. I think it went well." She turned to a pile of grain sacks, picked up her notebook, and hunted around.

"Missing something?"

"My purse. I left it here with my notebook. Now it's gone." She looked behind the sacks. "*Ben-Hur's* missing, too."

"I'll check down here," Jim said as he searched the length of the loading dock. "Nothing there."

"I left them with my notebook. Nothing's ever stolen in Fir Glen."

"You seem to attract the strangest problems, Miss Sinclair. Ransacked bookcases are one thing, but a stolen purse is a matter for the sheriff. I'll make a call and be right back." He turned toward the feedstore office.

"Miss Sinclair, are you still here?" a voice called from the end of the dock. Jim stopped. "She's at the other end. Come on up."

Cynthia Richards approached and held out a brown purse. "Is this yours? I found it around the corner by some bushes. The stuff was scattered all over the ground. I put it back in."

Ruth took the purse. "Yes, it's mine. Thank you, Cynthia. I was looking all over for it." Ruth let out her breath in relief.

Cynthia beamed. "Well, gotta go. Glad you have it back."

Ruth poured out the contents and reorganized the items. "That's odd, Jim. Nothing's missing."

"You're sure?"

"Positive. These incidents have to be pranks. Otherwise, something would be missing—other than *Ben-Hur*, that is. I feel so bad about Suzi's book. This is a message aimed at me because of my friendship with the Nakamuras. Loud and clear it says, 'Don't befriend any Japanese.' Remember the man who hollered at me last spring when I fell in the mud? That was my warning!"

Jim stared at the purse. "Keep your eyes open, Ruth, for anyone suspicious." He stood, reached down, and lifted her chin with his finger. "Stay safe. I'm late for an appointment. Can you finish up on your own?"

Ruth nodded and he hurried away.

She sat down on a feed sack, catching her breath. *That man can leave me breathless and limp as a cooked noodle,* she admitted to herself. *Why do my head and heart have to pull in opposite directions?*

★ ★ ★

An hour later, Ruth arrived home and climbed her porch steps with a sigh. "That was a long, hot day," she said aloud and opened the back door. As she put her notebook down on the table, an envelope caught her eye. "A letter from Harold! It's been so long."

She took a deep breath. "You won't find out what it says by staring at it, Ruth Sinclair." She picked it up and went into the living room. "Opened by Censor" was stamped across the front. "Oh," she grimaced, "that means the censor will have cut out half of it, and it won't make sense."

She sat down and took out the paper. "I'm nervous," she said out loud. "If he's coming home soon, I'll have to face some hard discussions."

"Dear Ruth," she read, "I'm. . .after two weeks. . ." *This is irritating. Is he coming home in two weeks? I don't know what he's saying.* She continued the letter.

"We've been friends for a long time now. I wanted you to be the first to hear my good news. By the time you read this I'll be married. . . ."

Ruth's hand dropped to her lap. A jolt of shock went through her, and her mind couldn't grasp what she had read. She slowly picked up the letter and read the words again. "By the time you read this I'll be married. She's a wonderful girl. You'll love her. She works in. . . We've been dating awhile and with life so. . .we decided, why not? When I get home, I'll come by and introduce her. I know you'll be good friends. Got to go. Take care. Always, Harold."

She sat back in the chair trying to get her breath. *I feel as if the wind's been knocked out of me,* she thought. *Harold married! "We've been friends for a long time."* A wave of anger swept over her. "I worried about breaking up, when to him we were only friends. How could I have been so stupid?"

She looked at the letter. *"We've been dating awhile. . ."* All the dates she'd turned down with Jim to be loyal, and Harold was dating someone else—and seriously. She threw the letter down and got up. "I'm supposed to be crying my eyes out, but I'm too mad," she fumed.

The phone rang three times before she recognized the sound and picked it up. "Hello. . .hi, Marge. . . Do I know a young blond woman—pretty—tall? I don't think so, why. . .? She and Jim ate at the café and left together? Probably business. . . No, you would think any close, personal conversation was romantic, Marge. I. . ." Ruth's anger melted as she remembered the woman she had seen with Jim in Brookwood, and she suddenly found herself crying.

The phone slipped from her ear and dropped toward the floor, bouncing at the end of its cord as Ruth covered her face with her hands and sobbed.

"Ruth, what's the matter? I didn't mean to upset you. Ruth. . . Ruth. . . Oh, my, I'll be right over. Stay there." Marge's voice could be heard from the dangling receiver. The phone clicked. Ruth stood there listening to the buzz as she wiped at her wet face.

She finally put the receiver back on the hook and sat down in the chair, trying to piece together what was happening. How could the world fall apart so completely in a couple of hours? She jumped up as loud pounding sounded at the door, and she opened it quickly to see Marge with her fist raised to pound again.

"Are you trying to punch me in the face, Marge? Come on in. I've already had all the punches I can take for one day."

"What's going on, Ruth? You're white as a sheet." Marge frowned with concern as she hurried in and stared at her friend.

"You'd better sit down." Ruth led her to the living room couch. "Read this. It came in the mail today." She handed Marge Harold's letter and leaned back as Marge read.

She looked up at Ruth quickly. "He's married? I don't believe it! Is this a joke?"

"Read on, Marge."

"Just friends? He's going to bring her by? And you've been sitting here turning down dates with Jim Griffin and. . ." Her face registered her sudden awareness of what she had said earlier on the phone. "Oh, Ruth, I'm so sorry. Me and my big mouth. Jim and that woman probably just had some business to discuss." Marge stopped, not knowing what to say next.

"I've seen them together myself, Marge. After my big mistake in judgment with Harold, I don't think Jim was ever interested in me. He's just a flirt, and I fell for it. Get that look off your face, Marge. Yes, I admit it. Like a fool, I fell for Jim Griffin."

Marge nodded. "I knew it, but I sure don't feel any satisfaction in an 'I told you so' now." She shook her head in disbelief. "This is my first failure as a matchmaker."

The room became quiet, and the clock ticked louder and louder. "Will you be okay, Ruth? I need to go."

"Run on home, Marge. I'm so mad at my stupidity, but I'll be okay. I need some time to think before Grandma and Grandpa come back anyway. Thanks for being here for me."

The screen door slammed, and Ruth began to pace the floor in silence. "Lord," she said finally, "I know this seems small compared to what people in the rest of the world have to suffer from the war, but it still hurts—badly. This could have been an answer to my confusion, but I waited too long, and Jim found someone else. What do I do now? How do I work with him? At least he doesn't know the latest about Harold or my feelings, so maybe we can go on without embarrassment."

She sat down and put her face in her hands. "Please help me, Lord. I feel so alone tonight."

Chapter 15

The next morning Ruth sat across the kitchen table from her grand-mother as they drank their morning coffee. "We got home late last night, Dear. Your light was out. We didn't want to disturb you." Alma took a sip of the coffee. "Grandpa helped the Ericksons with their wheat harvest, and I went along to help Cora with the cooking. Everyone got to talking, too, so it took longer than we figured."

Ruth sat quietly with her hands around the cup. Alma looked at her sharply. "Did you get your letter?"

Ruth nodded.

"I guess it wasn't good news," Alma ventured.

"It makes me feel like a fool." She reached into her pocket, pulled out Harold's letter, and handed it to Alma.

Her grandmother put her cup down and adjusted her glasses as she began to read. "Oh, my, I can't believe it!" Alma exclaimed as she looked up from the letter.

"I know what you just read, Gram. Read the rest."

Alma finished the letter and shook her head. "I'm not pleased with something that hurts you, Ruth."

"And that's not all. Jim's seeing another woman. The one we saw him with in Brookwood. I took so long, he gave up—if he really was interested. If I could be so wrong about Harold, I was probably wrong there, too."

"No, Dear, I. . ."

"I feel like such a fool, Grandma. Twice. I was just starting to admit I cared for Jim. I never thought I'd end up an old-maid schoolteacher."

"That's taking this a bit far, Ruth. You're young. God knows who's right for you. Take this to Him and let Him handle it."

Ruth pushed her chair back and glanced at the clock. "At least I have plenty to keep me busy. I meet with the Junior Volunteers this morning at the school." She wiped her forehead. "My, it's warm already."

Alma agreed. "It'll be another scorcher. August never goes by fast enough for me. This heat'll bring on the beans again, too. Canning is so hard in the heat."

"You rest today, Grandma. I'll pick the beans early tomorrow morning, and we'll try to get them done before it gets hot." She picked up her notebook. "At least in Oregon we don't have too much of this heat. Grandpa says the rains always start with Labor Day. Cooler weather will be here soon. And so will school," she added. "While I'm at the school, I'll stop by my classroom. Staying busy will be good for me right now."

"I feel too old to be much help at a time like this, Ruth." Alma patted Ruth's arm and fanned herself with a paper. "Talk to your mother about it next time she calls. She'll know what to say."

"You've been wonderful, Grandma. You keep me focused on the Lord and remind me He's in control. That's what I need." She gave Alma a hug. "I won't be long."

Ruth hurried to the school yard to find a group of children waiting under the shade of a tree. "Hey, Miss Sinclair, you're late! It's five minutes after ten." Tim was gleeful. "Miss Sinclair is tardy," he chanted.

Cynthia began to imitate Tim. "Hey, Miss Sinclair," she taunted. "Hay, hay, hay. Straw is cheaper; grass is free, Tim Henderson."

"What do you know? You're a girl," Tim retorted.

"Okay, kids, that's enough. We have work to do," Ruth reminded them.

The children sat down on the grass. Charlie yanked the back of Carrie's hair. She started to yelp, but a look from Ruth quieted them.

"You've done very well this summer collecting paper and foil. Oh, yes, and milkweed floss," she complimented. "Now we need your legs and your bikes."

Eyes grew big. "You need our what, Miss Sinclair?" Tim squeaked. Sunday's paper had featured a soldier who had lost a leg in the war.

Ruth burst out laughing, realizing what she'd said and how they'd taken it. "No, not to put in the scrap drive," she said as she looked at their horrified faces. "I mean we need them to go collecting. People have metal and rubber junk in their basements, barns, and attics they could contribute to the scrap drive. We need you to go door-to-door and ask people to give all they can. If they can't get the scraps to Bob's lot, a truck will come by to pick them up. Can you do that?"

Heads nodded enthusiastically.

"We need to get this done before school starts. Tim will be captain again for the next school year. We'll use the same organization as last time so we won't miss any houses. I'll go by the places that are too far for you to reach on your bikes. That's all I have for now."

As the group wandered off, Tim and Charlie walked with Ruth toward her classroom. "Me and Charlie told Mr. Griffin about the lights around his plant. We've been checking on spies all summer," Tim informed her. Charlie nodded. "And we're checking the lights at Billy Nakamura's, too. Me and Charlie and Billy used to play in the creek by their place. Me and Charlie were down there last week and saw the lights there, too."

"What are you doing down there at night?" Ruth asked as they stopped outside the building.

"I have to pick beans all day. We're building a raft after I get home. And we saw old man Jones snooping around there, too. Mr. Miller says we need to keep an eye on him. He's susticious," Tim declared.

"Suspicious, Tim," she corrected. "You boys be careful. Let Mr. Griffin and the officials know. This doesn't sound like something for two boys to handle."

"We will. Bye, Miss Sinclair. We gotta go get our aluminum so we can get in the movies to see Roy Rogers. It's an aluminum matinee. Charlie doesn't have any money. If we take aluminum to give 'em, we get in free. See ya."

Ruth smiled at the two and let herself into the school building. She paused and looked around. *Maybe this will be my life—school, teaching, kids. Could I be happy with only this? Do I have a choice?*

She opened her classroom and stepped in. "I'll take home last year's plan book and my teacher's manuals," she murmured. "And these." She picked up two books. "I'll have to plan special work for Tim in English and spelling."

As she added the books to the pile, a strip of light cardboard floated to the floor. She reached down. "Suzi's bookmark! I wondered where it went." Suzi's beautiful drawings of flowers and birds covered the edges of the paper, with angels in the center. "Now if I had her copy of *Ben-Hur,* I'd feel more comfortable." She tucked the slip in the material for Tim and locked the door.

The sun's rays were hot as she crossed the school yard and headed for the road. "The traffic gets busier by the year," she observed while she waited for cars to pass. She noticed two people come out of Bob's market across the road, then looked again. "That looks like Jim—and the woman." She watched as they walked to Jim's car, laughing and chatting easily.

Ruth sized up the woman. *Pretty. Blond. Tall and slim. Stylish. Looks outgoing and very confident.* She sighed. "Well, that's that. I can't compete with her. I'll put Jim Griffin behind me and get on with life. I'm glad I wasn't too head over heels before I found out."

The traffic cleared and she crossed the road, watching Jim's car disappear.

★ ★ ★

"How was your meeting?" Alma inquired when Ruth got home. She was rolling out a piecrust. Flour and ingredients were spread over the table, and Alma had a white dab of flour on the end of her nose.

"Great. The Junior Volunteers work hard," she replied. She carried her books to the stairs as the phone rang, and she picked it up to Marge's hello. "Shopping. . . ? I guess so. I do need to buy some things before school starts. . . . I'll meet you at the bus stop at nine." She hung up and walked over to Alma.

"Marge and I are going shopping in Portland Saturday. There's time to do some sewing before school starts if I get the material now. And this will keep me too busy to pine away."

★ ★ ★

Sunday morning Ruth was adjusting her new hat in the hall mirror as Alma came out of her room dressed for church. "That hat looks lovely, Dear, but how did you resist the fancy ones with all the fruit and feathers piled on top?"

"Easy, Grandma. You wouldn't believe the prices. So I settled for a plain and practical navy with a ribbon around it. I do like the wider brim, though."

"That'll be good for gardening. And birds won't be trying to eat it or make a nest in the feathers," George commented as he came down the hall in his Sunday suit.

"Grandpa, where's your sense of fashion?" Ruth teased as she carefully thrust the hatpin into the hat.

"Makes no sense to me. You don't wear your food on your head or put feathers up there if you don't want birds making a nest in 'em."

Alma took her husband by the elbow. "Go on, George, get the car or we'll be late for church. What women wear makes no less sense than that piece of cloth you men wear around your necks and call a tie." Alma winked at Ruth as George went out the door.

On the way to church, Ruth wondered if Jim would bring the woman to the service. As they pulled into the parking lot, she scanned the groups of people. *I just don't want to be caught off guard,* she thought.

The three entered the sanctuary and sat down in a pew. Ruth settled back, then turned as a movement in the aisle caught her eye. She looked up to see Jim escorting his parents—and the woman—to a front pew. *Why do I keep being surprised and hurt?* she thought. She joined in the singing but soon found herself staring into space, seeing the woman holding Jim's arm. She gave her head a shake and prayed, *Lord, help me clear my thoughts. I'm in a turmoil.* When she looked up, Pastor Cameron was closing his Bible and announcing the closing hymn.

The congregation rose to leave. "Miss Sinclair." Tim Henderson's mother came up behind Ruth as she tried to edge through the crowd before the Griffins made their way past her.

Trapped, she thought and turned.

"Tim will be in your sixth grade this year. I know he struggles in English and spelling. If he can have some extra work, I'll see that he gets it done." Mrs. Henderson spoke earnestly.

Ruth nodded. "Good, Mrs. Henderson. I'm working on special lessons for him now. If we keep in close touch, I think we can help him out this year."

Mrs. Henderson agreed and moved away. As Ruth waited for the crowd to disperse ahead of her, she heard the familiar voice that made her heart race.

"You need to ask Miss Sinclair about that, Stan," she overheard Jim saying to Stan Evans.

"Aw, please, Mr. Griffin. Miss Sinclair just got dumped. She won't want to," Stan wheedled.

She could hear Jim pause before he asked, "What do you mean, she got dumped?"

"That guy Harold she wrote to. He up and married some lady in England. I heard my sister Marge talking about it. He sent her a letter or something," Stan explained. "Please, Mr. Griffin."

"I'll let you know, Stan."

Ruth could feel the rush of embarrassment flowing over her. She looked quickly for an escape, but Jim had seen her and made his way toward her. The woman stood chatting with his parents.

She put on a smile and chattered quickly, "Hi, Boss. The Junior Volunteers are organized to canvass the neighborhood before school starts."

"Good, good." He didn't return her smile. Instead, he handed her a paper. "I need this typed and posted by tomorrow. Sorry it's such a rush, but it's very important it be up as soon as possible."

She took the paper and looked at it. "No problem. I can get it done."

He looked down a moment and then closely at her. "Ruth, life's not always what it seems. I. . ." He appeared uncomfortable. "I can't say more, but just remember that. Please." His eyes pleaded with her. "I've got to go. Thanks for your help."

At least he's uncomfortable for being such a flirt and leading me on, Ruth thought. *Life sure wasn't what it seemed around him. Maybe he was seeing this woman all along, and I was just a diversion. How could I be so dumb?* She looked down at the paper. *In this small community I can't avoid him. I can't quit the war work. It's too important.*

She walked out the door and toward the car, where her grandparents waited. *Just push it all away, Ruth, and grow up, just as you tell your students to do when they have a hopeless crush on someone.*

Chapter 16

P attern pieces and brown gabardine material were scattered across the dining room floor. Ruth crouched, pinning patterns, her lips holding the pins.

"That will make a sensible skirt for school," Alma commented as she came into the room. "Will you get it done for the first day of class?"

"Umm, uh um," Ruth mumbled through the pins. She sat back and took the pins from her lips. "Sorry, Gram. I hope so. I'll have a good outfit for fall when I get the blouse made, too. And it'll stay in style longer than the new military look that's coming out."

"One thing about getting old. You worry less about clothes. A few house-dresses, a nice navy, and a flowered dress for good, and lots of big aprons. That does me just fine," Alma declared.

Ruth folded her material and patterns. "We have our first teachers' meeting at 11:00 this morning. Planning the school year and dividing up duties. Then some time in our rooms getting ready for the first day." She put her sewing away. "The summer certainly flew." *Thankfully, the next weeks will be too busy to worry about Jim Griffin,* she thought. *I'm safe except for the Friday night Bible study Jim's starting. I'm sorry now I promised to help out.*

★ ★ ★

The four teachers gathered around the table in Mrs. Hastings's room, discussing schedules of recess duty, music, and lunch hour. "Ruth, would you inventory the playground equipment? With a war on, we'll have to repair and make do."

Ruth nodded as a sharp rap sounded at the door. Mrs. Hastings hurried to open it. "Come in, Mr. Griffin. We're at a good place for a break."

Ruth shifted uncomfortably in her chair. *Just what I needed today—facing Jim Griffin!*

Mrs. Hastings turned to the group. "Ladies, Mr. Griffin has asked to brief us on civilian defense policies that concern the school. Please take notes so we'll make no mistakes in procedures."

Jim took a seat at the table and smiled at the teachers, his gaze lingering on Ruth. Her heart gave the familiar nervous thump.

"I want to discuss monthly air-raid drills and the procedures to use," he began. As he went through the steps, Ruth's mind flitted back and forth between what he said and how good he looked dressed in his dark brown business suit.

I'm just like the kids, she thought. *What I can't have is the most appealing.* "During air-raid drills, practice getting the children to the basement as quickly as possible," he stressed as he finished his presentation. "Their safety depends on it."

"Thank you for coming, Mr. Griffin," Mrs. Hastings concluded. "Ladies, we'll break for lunch and come back to finish up at 1:00."

Jim stayed at the table when the teachers rose to leave the room. "Ruth, may I see you a moment?" He was quiet and sat looking at the papers in front of him. "I have a few things to be typed." He seemed uncomfortable instead of the flirting, teasing Jim she was used to.

"What do you have for me to do?" she finally asked.

He looked up and stared at her a moment. "Type these two, if you would. And mail them as soon as possible." He looked down and fingered the papers. "Ruth, I. . .uh, I. . ."

She couldn't stand the tension and his obvious discomfort around her. She picked up the papers. "No problem. I'll get them done right away. Please excuse me, Jim. I have some things to do before we meet again at one." She turned away abruptly as Jim said a soft thanks.

She entered her classroom. The door closed behind her, and she leaned against it. Tears finally came. Tears for the Harold she had once known. Tears for Jim, who no longer cared.

★ ★ ★

When Ruth arrived home, Alma was straightening the house and setting out teacups and plates of cookies. "Hazel Ellison and Grace Schumaker will be here any minute, Ruth. You're welcome to join us."

"Sorry to miss your party, Gram, but I'm off to notify people about the scrap drive—ones living too far out for the kids to reach on their bikes. I need to get it done before school starts." She headed for the door. "Have a good time."

She got in the car and checked the list of names. "Womacks are the closest," she said aloud as she pulled out onto Woodland Avenue and headed north, turning off on a dirt road that wound through the wooded countryside. A small white house, its paint flaking and peeling, came up on the left, and she turned into the driveway. In the backyard she could see the rusting remains of old bedsprings, an icebox, and a car that had died long ago. Chickens wandered about the weedy yard, and a goat stared at her over a fence as she got out of the car.

"Uh-oh!" she exclaimed as two geese gave loud honks, lowered their heads, and came at her. She raced for the porch, then jumped as a dog raised up on the steps with a howl, sniffing at her suspiciously as she climbed the stairs.

"I'm not sure this is safer," she muttered, looking around. The sagging porch was covered with an old mattress on which slept a cat and six kittens. Old newspapers were strewn about. Flies buzzed, flying in and out of a screen door that had more screen torn and hanging than attached to the wooden frame. "You'd think they could fix it," she criticized, "and clean up the mess."

She knocked loudly and soon heard footsteps scuffing across the floor. A woman's face appeared in the doorway, her long, dull brown hair stringy and unkempt, and her faded dress hanging like a sack on her very thin frame. On her feet she wore old blue slippers.

"Mrs. Womack?" Ruth inquired. *The woman looks as neglected as the rest of the place,* she thought as she stared at the figure before her.

The woman nodded as a small girl came up from behind and grabbed her around the legs. Ruth stared at the thin, shy child. A baby could be heard coughing and fussing in the background.

"I'm Ruth Sinclair, Ma'am." She went on to explain the reason for her visit. "I noticed a pile of metal scraps in your backyard. Would you be willing to contribute?"

The woman shifted uncomfortably. "Ben's not been well. Don't think he could get the stuff hauled. Truck died anyhow," she answered shortly.

Ruth watched the forlorn-looking pair before her. "I can send trucks out to pick up anything you're willing to contribute, Mrs. Womack. And the government will pay you for it, too."

She could see the woman considering the offer and the small glint of hope that lit in her eyes. "Pay us? For junk?"

"Yes, Ma'am. Haven't you heard of the country's scrap drives—metal, rubber, paper, and old cloth?"

The woman sighed and shook her head. "Don't take the paper no more and don't have a radio. Electricity's off anyhow." She looked defeated. "Ben's been sick and the baby, too, but we can't afford no doctor. Sure could use some money."

Ruth took a deep breath. A wave of guilt came over her for the quick judgments she'd made as the Womacks' situation sank in. "The government will pay you well for all you can give," she explained as she thought quickly. "And since you don't have a car, maybe the men could take your husband to the doctor when they pick up the scraps. If he can get some help, he could be able to work again."

The woman picked up the little girl and stepped out on the porch. "There's lots more junk down in our gully. Old cars and tires and stuff rustin'. You can take it all." She pointed to an area beyond the pasture where Ruth could see the tip of a large pile of rusting metal. "People from all over dumped their junk in there for years. Never thought it would be any use."

"It is now, Mrs. Womack. If you sell it, you'll help your country and your family." Ruth smiled at the little girl who had buried her face in her mother's shoulder and peered at Ruth out of one eye.

"Times have been hard," Mrs. Womack explained. "Things went bad when Ben hurt his leg. And then he got sick. Only had the garden and animals to keep us fed. Don't know what we'll do when winter comes." The grim, tense look returned to her face.

"With so much scrap material to sell, I think you can start getting back on your feet." Ruth stopped to slap at a fly buzzing about her. "If you agree, I'll have the men out here this week."

The woman nodded.

Ruth smiled at the girl. "Your folks'll get paid for the scraps, and then I'll have some ladies from our church give you and your mama a ride to the grocery store."

The woman took a deep breath. "My grandma took me to church when I was a girl. Church had a piano, and we sang so nice." A longing came into her voice. "It's been so long. Ben weren't never one for church."

"If you want to go, I'll see to it," Ruth assured the mother quickly. "Someone can pick you up on Sunday. We have a piano, and the people love to sing."

Mrs. Womack smiled for the first time and looked at Ruth with tears in her eyes. "I been prayin' for help. Didn't think we mattered enough He'd bother, though." She wiped at her eyes. "Maybe He does care." Tears rolled down her cheeks as she hugged her little girl tightly.

"God cares, Mrs. Womack," Ruth assured her. "He led me here. I know He did." She blinked her eyes and walked carefully down the sagging porch steps. "I have to get to the other houses around here. Expect the trucks out tomorrow or the next day. I'll arrange to have someone take you to town, too." She waved at the two as they watched her leave.

She got in her car and sat there. "Lord, forgive me for judging before I knew anything about them. And thank You for using me to give them hope in spite of my attitude. I take so much for granted in my life." She sat a moment, then went on to finish her calls.

★ ★ ★

That evening Ruth described her visit to the Womacks. "I almost cried, Gram. They'd lost hope."

Alma shook her head. "I'll get the Ladies' Aid out there tomorrow. We'll bring food to get them by and some supplies to help clean up. And we can certainly spare some of the clothes we've collected so they're decently dressed." She got up and turned. "The Proctors live out that way. I'll see if they can give them a ride to church." She headed for the phone to make the arrangements.

George sat quietly in his chair. "Sounds like they got so far down they couldn't see up," he said finally. "I'll get some men out to look at Ben's truck. Could be they'll need some wood cut, too, if Ben's laid up. Lord expects us to help when we can."

"It's all set," Alma said as she came back into the room. "The ladies will be out tomorrow. I'll go see what I can put together. Trucks can't get out there for the scraps 'til day after tomorrow so we'll get them through 'til then."

Ruth nodded. "They're a good family. Just down on their luck. With a little help they'll get back on their feet. They couldn't have made it much longer, though." She stood. "The first day of school's almost here. I'd better get busy, or it'll be here before I'm ready!"

★ ★ ★

On Monday afternoon Alma was stirring a kettle bubbling on the stove as delicious aromas filled the kitchen. "How was your first day of school?"

Ruth sat at the table with her shoes off. "Not bad. My feet hurt and I'm tired, though. It takes getting used to every year. I have twelve fifth-graders and eight sixth. One new student. Basically they're a good group." She nibbled on a slice of Alma's fresh bread. "How did the scrap collection go at the Womacks'?"

Alma turned with a big smile on her face. "Wonderful! They got paid well for all the scraps. Ben and the baby got the medicine they need. Grandpa found the parts for Ben's truck, and the men'll be out to help fix it. They'll stay and cut a bit of wood for them, too." She stopped to check a kettle.

"Hazel and I took Mrs. Womack and Lizbeth Ann to church for some clothes, and then we went to the grocery store. Mrs. Womack was so pleased she could buy food for the family herself. The Ladies' Aid stocked their cupboards, though. They'll need plenty of good food to put on some weight. My, they're all thin!"

"And the Proctors will give them a ride to church Sunday?" Ruth inquired as she wiped crumbs from the table.

Alma nodded. "They were glad to help out. Pastor Cameron's been out to see them, too. Mr. Womack hadn't had much to do with church, but he sees all this help as an answer to his wife's prayers. His heart's open, and he's anxious to attend, too. She could never get him in a church before."

"Our actions can preach better than a dozen sermons," Ruth commented as she stood up. "I'm going to work on my blouse, Gram. Call me when I can help with dinner." She went into the dining room.

As she pinned a pattern piece on the material, she heard her grandmother's voice. "She's in the other room, Marge. Go on in."

"How's school, Teach?" Marge asked as she came in the room. "I stopped by to see if you survived the first day."

"I have no real troublemakers, so it should be a good year." She laid another pattern on the material.

"So, anything new with Jim?" Marge asked.

"Only an awkward meeting last week." Ruth stopped and recounted the teachers' meeting. "Now that he has someone else, why am I still so hung up on him? I've prayed about it and gotten after myself."

"You've never admitted how hard you fell." Marge paused and looked thoughtful. "I've seen Jim and that woman together around town. They're an odd couple. She clings to his arm, but he doesn't seem too thrilled. He's too serious. Not the old friendly, teasing Jim."

Ruth nodded. "I've noticed that, too, but I thought he was just uncomfortable because he led me on."

"They don't seem like a well-matched couple. Unlike Jack and me." Marge grinned and flashed her ring.

Ruth sat back on the floor. "Jim's Friday night Bible studies are coming up soon," she said with a sigh. "I don't look forward to an evening with him— or maybe even him and her—but after I called all the people and urged them to come, how can I back out? Don't forget you promised to come with me, Marge. I don't want to face it alone."

Marge wrinkled her nose. "I'm not that much into Bible study. Sunday morning's okay, but. . ."

Ruth gave her friend a fierce scowl. "No excuses, Marge. It'll be good for you—and for our friendship!"

Chapter 17

What a perfect fall day to get the place ready for winter!" Ruth declared as she and George pulled into the Nakamuras' driveway. "Indian summer for sure." The sky was deep blue with white fluffy clouds. The air was mild with a hint of coolness and the smell of burning leaves.

She looked around. "People from church have helped keep the yard looking nice this summer."

George nodded. "And we had a good fruit harvest, too. With everyone's help, we had a handsome profit to put in Suzi and Nak's bank account." He picked up the box of cleaning supplies and followed Ruth to the porch. She unlocked the door, then jumped back and screeched as something leaped at her.

George chuckled. " 'Fraid you'll get eaten by Fluffy?"

"She startled me!" Ruth exclaimed indignantly. "What in the world were you doing in there, Fluffy? How did you get in? You were at our house for dinner last night."

"She's not talking." George smiled. "Must have a way to sneak in. Check the windows while you're in there."

"There's nothing open. Someone had to let her in," Ruth insisted. "I tell you, strange things are going on here. If someone's trying to irritate us, it's working! But it makes me even more determined not to give up!"

"We won't solve it standing here, and the sheriff's not concerned," George replied. "Let's get to work."

Ruth went through the house, checking all the windows, and found nothing open. She shook her head in irritation as she pulled a sheet over the sofa to protect it from dust.

Her thoughts drifted to the Bible study and on to Jim. *Does everything in life have to be a puzzle? Now Jim's one, too. He and that woman don't match. Or am I wishing?*

George appeared in the doorway. "It's odd. Last time I checked there were five pigeons. Now there are ten!"

"I keep telling you strange things are going on here, Grandpa."

"Don't know what it's all about. Someone's trying to rattle us, I guess." He shook his white head. "I'm done back there. You ready?"

She nodded and closed up the house.

"Where do you think the Nakamuras are, Grandpa?" Ruth asked as they climbed into the car for the drive home. "I was sure they'd be back by now."

George cleared his throat and paused, glancing at her. "Gabriel Heatter's broadcast the other night said all Japanese have been relocated off the West Coast—Utah and Wyoming and places like that—so they can't spy or signal the enemy. Grandma didn't want to upset you."

"Oh, no," Ruth whispered. "I've been so busy I haven't been catching the news. How can this be happening in America?" She slumped down in her seat.

"People are afraid. They don't trust the Lord. But the Nakamuras do. We need to, too," George said as he pulled into their driveway.

★ ★ ★

On Sunday morning, Tim bounded into the Sunday school classroom where Ruth was going over the attendance list. "Hey, Miss Sinclair, you teaching our class?" he asked as he looked through the pile of lessons she had set down on the table.

"Yes; Mrs. Everett got sick and can't finish the quarter," Ruth replied and picked up the lessons before Tim mixed them up.

"This isn't real school, so I don't have to watch my English here," he declared. "We learn about God stuff. I like the story about David and Goliath best. Me and Charlie wanna make slingshots and practice with stones, like David. Then we'll be ready to catch spies!"

Ruth let the comment slide as she placed a lesson at each child's place.

"Hey, Miss Sinclair, did you know Mr. Griffin's plant has trouble with spies?" Tim chattered on. "They're bringing in the army and the sheriff. Me and Charlie are on the case, too. We'll give 'em our clues!" He sat down and placed a book on the table in front of him. "Oh, yeah, we found this book by the plant. Charlie says it's yours. Here." He handed her Suzi's copy of *Ben-Hur*.

Ruth took it in surprise. "You found it outside Mr. Griffin's plant? What was it doing there?" She turned it over in her hands. The cover showed only slight damage from the damp ground.

Tim shrugged. "We just found it on the ground. We were looking for spies, and Charlie stepped on it."

"Thanks, Tim. I'm very glad to get it back. I borrowed it from a friend and felt so bad I'd lost it. Tell Charlie thanks, too." She paged through it. *Someone's been marking in it,* she noticed. *I'll have to get that erased.*

The door opened as several children walked in and clustered around Tim. Ruth put the book with her purse and turned to start the class.

★ ★ ★

On Friday night, Ruth and Marge entered the church basement for Jim's Bible study. People milled about, talking in small groups as they waited for the class to begin. Ruth could see familiar faces here and there.

"I'm surprised to see so many people," Marge commented as she looked at the group.

"Times are hard. They're looking for answers," Ruth replied and glanced around the room.

"She's over there. By the kitchen," Marge whispered.

Ruth turned casually and took a good look at her competition. *Wearing slacks and a blouse cut a bit too low,* she observed. *Very pretty, but she looks out of place here.* The woman was surveying the crowd and caught Ruth staring at her. When she smiled confidently, Ruth looked away quickly.

Jim walked over to the circle of chairs set up at one end of the room. "Please take a seat and let's get started," he called out over the conversations. People turned toward the chairs and found places to sit.

"This way, Marge." Ruth hurried for seats that wouldn't be directly across from Jim. The woman sat down next to him, a Bible in her lap.

"I'm pleased to see so many here tonight. Since we have people from all over the area, let's go around the circle and give our names," Jim said after an opening prayer.

Ruth listened carefully as the woman's turn came and she said, "Carolyn Samuels."

Jim opened his Bible. "Our topic tonight is one that's affecting all our lives right now—fear."

"You said it, Jim!" Tom Adams piped up. "Everyone's scared with this war on. All those people gettin' killed overseas. . ."

"Yeah," Bill Smith interrupted, "God says He answers prayer and helps us, but people over there prayed, and look what's happenin' to 'em anyway. A guy'd be crazy not to be scared." He slumped back in his chair.

Jim smiled. "I can see this was a good topic to start with." He paged through his Bible. "First, let's see what God says about fear. Turn to John 14:27."

Pages rustled as the class hunted for John. Ruth turned quickly to the chapter, then watched as Carolyn Samuels fumbled with her Bible. She opened it to the front and looked around at the group. Noticing they opened it past the middle, she began paging through the book. *She doesn't look as if she's ever opened a Bible before,* Ruth thought with surprise.

"I'll read it," Delores Fuller volunteered. " 'Peace I leave with you, my peace I give unto you: not as the world giveth, give I unto you. Let not your heart be troubled, neither let it be afraid.' "

Jim glanced around the circle. "What does Jesus say here about fear?"

Mary Brown raised her hand. Her white hair framed a gentle face. "Jesus says not to let our hearts be troubled or afraid," she answered softly. "Even in this war, Bill. In Matthew 28:20, He promises He'll always be with us." She smiled at him kindly.

Bill looked sheepish. "I know, but I'm still afraid my friends will be killed overseas or my family bombed here. I want God to protect us, not just be with us. I don't feel like I can count on Him to do that even if I ask Him." He ran his fingers through his hair, leaving strands sticking up here and there.

"Me, either," Tom agreed as he fingered the cuff of his blue-plaid flannel shirt. "If I can't trust Him to keep awful things from happening, how can I help being afraid?"

Murmurs buzzed around the circle. Ruth glanced toward Jim to see him listening intently to the comments.

"I think the answer lies in what we're trusting Him for," Jean Preston spoke up. "Do we trust Him only to do what we want, or do we trust Him just because He's God?"

"That first part's me," Tom confessed. "Trust is hard for me because I don't really believe He'll always do what I want."

"Whew!" Bill shook his head. "I'm afraid if I trust Him to do what He wants, He'll make me do something I won't like—sort of like having to eat liver and onions." He shuddered. "It's supposed to be good for me, but, ugh!"

The class chuckled. Ruth glanced at Carolyn to see her stifling a yawn, and she remembered the woman Jim said he stopped dating in California because she wasn't a Christian. *His beliefs haven't changed,* she thought. *I don't understand why he's with someone who seems so uninterested in God.*

Jim leaned forward with his arms on his knees. "Remember, since the Fall, there's sin and evil in this world. Believers live in the world and feel the effects of that evil. We'd like God to put a wall around us as soon as we believe, so nothing bad will touch us, but it isn't that way."

"The lives of the disciples certainly illustrate that," Jean declared firmly as she smoothed her skirt. "They suffered for the gospel."

"They did," Jim agreed. "Now turn to John 16:33." Pages rustled as he continued. "Jesus tells the disciples that in Him they can have peace, whatever happens. He says in this world we will have tribulations or troubles, but we're to be of good cheer because He has overcome the world."

"So, Jesus is saying the world will always be a mess." Tom sounded discouraged.

An elderly man sitting next to Carolyn cleared his throat. "Jesus gives us His peace," he began quietly. "Not the way the world tries to by winnin' wars and treaties and gettin' lots of money and such." He looked around. "It's by trustin' Him with our lives because He's God that we can have peace in our hearts no matter what happens." He kept fingering one side of his mustache.

The room grew quiet as he continued. "I've lived a long time, and I've seen people try a lotta things to get peace." He shook his white head. "Doesn't work. People just waste their years trying to find peace on the outside. Trusting Jesus with our hearts. That's where peace is." He sat back. "Didn't mean to say so much."

The quiet continued as his words sank in.

Bill squirmed in his chair. "Guess I got it all backwards. I wanted life to be peaceful all around me, and then I'd get peace inside. Sounds like God works from the inside out." He looked around for confirmation.

Ruth nodded. "You're right, Bill. If we don't trust Him and His will, we'll never have peace in our hearts. But it isn't trust when I ask God to do His will and then tell Him how He's to do it. It's hard to give up insisting that things be done my way, especially in a war, but to me that's what trusting God means. But it's not an easy lesson to learn," she admitted.

Jim smiled at her warmly and held her gaze. "We've come to that critical point where we all have to struggle every day of our lives: Trust God to do as He sees best, even if things aren't going the way we want at the moment. It's not easy to accept that, especially in bad times like this, but it's something we have to grow in if we want peace inside instead of fear. We learn it best in the hard times. God makes good use of them. In the hard times ahead in this war, there will be many opportunities to grow in trust and leave our fears behind. Don't let them slip by." He glanced at his watch. "On that, we'll stop for tonight. Let's close with prayer."

After the amen, Ruth pulled on Marge's arm and whispered, "Let's go before Jim comes by."

As they hurried from the room, Marge looked puzzled. "Did you see that woman with Jim? She didn't know where the Book of John was. And when we were reading, she looked as if she couldn't believe intelligent people would actually swallow all this. I don't get it—Jim and her, I mean."

"I thought it was just me," Ruth agreed.

As they walked to the coatrack, Marge continued. "I thought Bible studies were boring talks about living way back when people were living in tents and wearing robes and riding camels. This applies to us now. It has to do with our lives. I'm surprised." She handed Ruth her coat.

"That's the beauty of the Bible," Ruth replied. "No matter when you live, it speaks to you. God wrote it that way."

"I guess I've never really read it. We learned stories in Sunday school, but my folks weren't into reading it, so I thought it was for kids and sermons on Sunday. Not for getting along in the world." Marge paused to rebutton her coat correctly.

"When we think we can handle life, we put God on a shelf, Marge. When it gets rough, we're willing to take a look at what He has to say to us." She remembered her conversation with Jim on that topic. "I'm a good example of that."

"You? How?" Marge asked, puzzled. They stood in the entry talking as voices floated up from conversations downstairs.

"I worry about my life and where it's going. About Harold, my feelings for Jim, the war. I'm afraid my faith and trust have been very shallow."

"Then where does that leave me?" Marge looked concerned. "I still think He should straighten out the mess this world's in—and Jim and that woman."

"He's just waiting 'til we realize we can't handle things so we'll listen to Him. I struggle here. Especially since I can't seem to get Jim out of my heart," Ruth declared with a tone of discouragement.

As they stepped from the church, George drove out of the parking lot and pulled up to the door. "Just like taxi service," Marge quipped and got in the car.

"How was Bible study?" Alma inquired as they pulled out onto the road.

"Excellent." Ruth related the evening's discussion as they drove to the Evans's and dropped Marge off.

"We had a lovely time at the Hoeffers'," Alma commented. "She's a wonderful cook and even makes war recipes taste delicious."

"I agree there," George concurred and pulled into their driveway. "Um, that pie! But, Alma, my dear, your crust is flakier." He winked at Ruth as he climbed the steps and opened the door. "I didn't want to sleep in the barn tonight," he whispered.

"I heard that, George Peterson." Alma followed him into the house.

George chuckled and whistled down the hall to their room.

"That man!" Alma smiled at Ruth. "I pray you'll be as blessed someday! Good night and sleep well, Dear."

Chapter 18

The steady tick of the clock echoed in the otherwise silent kitchen. Ruth placed her Bible and purse on the table, sat down, and put her head in her hands. "Lord, so many strange things are happening." Tears ran down her cheeks. "I admit it, Lord. I've fallen in love with Jim Griffin, and now it's too late. This lesson in trust is a hard one. Help me."

She sat a moment, wiped her eyes, and got up. *A good sleep will help*, she thought as she climbed the stairs to her room. She pushed the door open and turned on the light. "Oh, what's happened?" she gasped. Books lay scattered all over the floor. Dresser drawers were ransacked and clothes strewn about the room.

She ran to the top of the stairs. "Grandma, Grandpa, come up here! Something's happened!" she hollered.

Lights flicked on below as her grandparents hurried from their room. "What's the matter, Ruth?" George called as he rushed up the stairs.

"Are you sick?" Alma followed behind.

"Someone's been in my room and torn it up." Her face was white and her hands shook. She pointed through the doorway. "Look! I walked in and found it like this."

George and Alma stood frozen in astonishment at the mess in Ruth's room. "This is no prank. I'm getting the sheriff's men out here," George said grimly. "Don't touch anything." He hurried downstairs.

Ruth and Alma stood in the hallway, staring in disbelief at the mess.

George came up behind them. "His men'll be right here." He shook his head at the disaster.

"I don't understand," Ruth spoke dazedly. "I don't have anything worth stealing. I haven't done anything to anyone. Why would someone do this?"

At a sharp rap on the front door, George hurried down the stairs.

"I'll go put the teakettle on. A cup of hot tea will do you good. Will you be okay, Dear?" Alma asked. Ruth nodded.

"She turned on the light and found the room as it is," George was saying as he escorted two officers up the stairs. "This is my granddaughter, Ruth Sinclair." They nodded a greeting. "We were out for the evening. It happened while we were gone. And we locked the doors before we left."

The two officers stepped into the room and looked around. One gave a low whistle. "Some mess!"

George put his arm around Ruth. "Go down to the kitchen for something warm to drink while the officers do their job." Alma met them at the top of the stairs. "You go with her," George said. "I'm staying up here. I want to be nearby in case they have any questions."

Alma followed Ruth into the kitchen and bustled about preparing the tea. They could hear the men talking and moving around upstairs.

"This house has always seemed so safe from the dangers of the rest of the world," Ruth said as she sat down. "Someone's taking that away."

Alma poured two cups of tea. "We have to learn it over and over, but there's only one safe place, one secure refuge, and that's the Lord."

Ruth nodded. "I'm getting that lesson, but no more homework on it, please." She smiled weakly.

One of the officers appeared in the doorway. "May I use your phone, Ma'am?"

"It's in the hall," Alma directed.

Ruth sipped her tea. "First it was the bookcase at school, then the one at Suzi's and all the strange things happening there. Someone stole my purse and *Ben-Hur*, and now this. I have nothing valuable to steal, nothing secret. It has to be harassment, Gram, because I won't desert my Japanese friends." She searched for some logical answer.

"Miss, you can go up and straighten your things. We need to check out the downstairs and talk to your grandparents." The officers came into the kitchen with George.

"Go ahead, Ruth. You'll feel better with your things straightened up," Alma urged.

Upstairs, she looked at the jumble of clothes and books. As she began sorting out the clothes and putting them back in the drawers and closet, she could hear a rap at the living room door and someone hurrying to open it. The voices moved to the steps, then footsteps came up the stairs and stopped at her doorway.

A familiar voice uttered a soft "Oh, no," and she looked up to see Jim standing there. Her mind stopped in confusion. "What are you doing here?" she blurted.

"The officers called me, and I came right over." He jingled the coins in his pocket, his face showing concern and anger as he surveyed the mess.

She looked puzzled. "But why would they call you for this? The sheriff's men are here."

"We run everything unusual through civilian defense these days," he replied evasively. "Are you okay?"

She nodded and joined him in the hall. "I don't understand, Jim. Why are all these strange things happening?" She began crying.

Jim reached out and pulled her to him. "It's okay. Have a good cry." He held her close and stroked her hair. The fears and dangers melted away as she nestled in his arms. She closed her eyes.

"I have to talk to the officers. You finish straightening up here, and then we'll talk." He held her away from him. "Will you be okay?" He raised her chin with his fingers and looked in her eyes. She nodded numbly and could only stare at the concern and caring in his eyes. Time seemed to freeze.

"Jim, could we see you down here?" an officer called up the stairs, breaking the spell.

"Be right there," he returned. To Ruth he said, "Gotta go. Check carefully to see if anything's missing. We need to know."

Ruth continued putting her possessions back where they belonged. "Nothing's damaged. So far nothing seems to be missing," she muttered. She placed the last book back on the shelf and walked to the doorway. "As far as I can tell, it looks the way it did when I left for church. What was I doing before I got ready? I wrote some letters—they're on the table downstairs—and then I read *Ben*. . . Where's Suzi's book?"

She went to the bookshelves and searched through the titles, then checked under the bed and found nothing. "That seems to be all that's missing." She looked around. "Why all the fuss about that book? If they wanted the book, why did they tear up the rest of the room when the book was on the bed in plain view?"

"Ruth, could you come down here? The officers need to speak with you before they leave," Alma called up the stairs.

Downstairs, she recounted what she knew of the events.

"There's evidence the door has been jimmied," one of the officers explained. "Keep a lookout for any strangers. We'll call if we have more questions." The officers stood. "Good night, folks. We're sorry this happened."

"Appreciate you checking on this," George replied. "We'll keep things locked up and our eyes open."

Alma got up from the table. "We're heading for bed. If you have any more problems, Ruth, call us."

"I love you both. Thanks." She hugged her grandparents and put the teakettle back on the stove.

Jim searched her face with concern. "I want to know everything strange that's been going on. I know you've told it all before, but maybe something new will come out. It's important."

She poured the hot tea and sat down. "You know most of it, Jim." She recounted the events that had occurred over the past months.

"Nothing else?"

She sipped her tea. "The varying number of pigeons at the Nakamuras'. Oh, and Fluffy getting locked in their house."

"Go on."

"Jim, the strangest thing is *Ben-Hur*. I borrowed it from Suzi's. It's the only thing missing upstairs. But it was on the bed in plain sight. If someone wanted it, why was my room torn apart?" She cupped her hands around the mug and thought a moment. "Oh, I forgot to tell you. Charlie and Tim have been hunting for spies and saw the lights outside your plant. When they checked on them, they found *Ben-Hur* lying on the ground beside the building. Tim brought it back to me."

Jim's head jerked up. "You should have told me."

Ruth shrugged. "It didn't seem important. What's going on, Jim?"

He took her hand. "I can't tell you much. You've heard rumors our plant has been converted to war production?"

She nodded.

"It's true. And we've had some shipments broken into. We want to find out who's doing it, not just scare them off so they move on to cause trouble someplace else. What connection the book has to all this I don't know. We'll try to find out."

"Don't get in any danger, Jim." Her hand tightened on his.

"I can take care of myself, but I'm worried about you. If you get the book back again, let me know right away. I want to see that book." He sat quietly looking at her hands. Then he spoke carefully. "Because I'm civilian defense coordinator for Fir Glen and because of what our plant is doing, I've gotten involved with—uh—certain parts of the government and military."

He looked down at the table. "Ruth, there's so much I'm not allowed to say. Please trust me and don't take things as they seem. I know this doesn't make sense, but it's all I can say for now." He slammed his fist into the other palm. "I feel so helpless and frustrated. I . . ." His voice drifted off. He lowered his head and shook it slowly from side to side.

"I'm sorry you have problems of this kind at the plant," she said softly. She stared across the room. "You've been a good friend, Jim. I appreciate it."

A low groan came from his lips. "Ruth, friend is a word I'm coming to dislike." He stood abruptly. "Be careful. Keep your eyes open and let me know anything unusual." He grabbed her hand and pulled her to her feet. "Get some sleep."

He looked down at her tenderly, then leaned over and kissed her cheek quickly. "I've got to go. I need to go by the plant yet tonight. I'll be praying for you." And he was gone.

"Whew!" Ruth plopped down in the chair. "That man makes my head spin and my heart pound right out of my chest, even if it's hopeless."

She stood and cleared the table. "After everything that's happened, all I can say is I'm more confused than ever."

Chapter 19

The October air was clear and balmy for the season with just a tinge of invigorating crispness. White fluffy clouds floated in the blue sky, and in the distance Mount Hood stood tall and majestic with a thin mantle of new snow. Fall was putting on her annual show, painting the vine maples, dogwoods, and birches with brilliant reds, purples, oranges, and yellows.

"I do love fall!" Ruth declared as she helped her grandparents harvest the last of the vegetables from the garden.

"You said the same thing about spring," Alma chuckled. She pulled the remaining carrots in the row and shook the dirt off the roots.

"If we had just those two seasons, it would be fine with me," Ruth replied. "Spring's exciting and fall's cozy and lovely. Until it's time to pick walnuts and filberts, that is. They stain and tear the fingers so badly."

"The church'll be out to harvest Nak and Suzi's nuts soon. Then we're done over there for this year," Alma reminded her. "Your brown fingers will be right in style."

"Weather report said cloudy with showers today, so enjoy this while you can," George commented as he loaded the last pumpkin into the wheelbarrow. "We'll get these in just in time. Rain's coming."

Ruth laughed as she put a crisp head of fall cabbage in her bucket. "You could predict that every morning in Oregon and be right 90 percent of the time, Grandpa."

"Now, Ruth, you know we wouldn't have this beautiful green state without all the rain," Alma chided. "Here, help me get these turnips and carrots to the house."

Ruth carried a bucket of vegetables to the faucet at the side of the house and washed off the dirt. As she walked to the porch, the wind whipped around the corner. "Grandpa's right. Something's brewing," she murmured as leaves scudded across the yard. Fluffy rubbed against her legs and purred loudly. "Head for the barn, Fluffy, or you'll get that orange fur wet."

Inside, Ruth helped her grandmother with the produce. "Grandpa will get the vegetables to the root cellar if you'll take the trimmings to the compost pile, Ruth. I'll sit a minute, and then I think I'll do some baking." Alma sat down at the table. "But first I have to see how much sugar I can use."

Ruth dumped the scraps in the compost pile behind the house and looked around her. *Such a beautiful place! Like a little bit of heaven—or at least Eden.* The tall green fir trees swayed amid the brilliant colors of fall. She looked up to see the sky overcast and the clouds darkening. *It'll be a cozy day inside. I can get some sewing done this afternoon,* she thought.

"Better head for the house before you get wet." George came up behind her, looking concerned. "My turkeys are acting strange. Piled in a big huddle. They spook easy. Storm's coming." He hurried off.

Big drops of rain began to fall as Ruth ran to the house. "Grandpa was right. It's raining," she said as Alma put a pan of cookies in the oven. "Can I help you, Gram?"

"No, Dear, go ahead with your own work." She turned to knead her bread, and soon the aroma of fresh bread and cookies filled the house.

Ruth finished cutting out a winter dress and began to sew. The wind moaned around the eaves and rain pelted the windows. She looked up as the lights blinked. Wind was blowing hard, rattling the windows and whipping the trees. She heard her grandfather come in the back door, and she joined her grandparents in the kitchen.

"I got the animals in and tied down what I could. This storm could get bad. The rain's coming down hard, and that wind's strong. Better get the lamps and candles ready."

The phone rang shrilly in the hall. Alma answered it. "For you, George. It's Wallace Coulter. He sounds anxious."

George hung up the phone after the conversation. "Wind's trying to take Coulter's chicken house roofs. He needs help. I'm loading up and heading over. Call all the men you can and get them over there right away." George pulled on his boots and donned his rain gear.

"If this lasts awhile, send the men over here for sandwiches and something hot to drink. I baked today," Alma directed.

George nodded as he hurried out the door.

"You call neighbors, Ruth, and I'll get the food ready. The men will be cold and hungry."

Ruth hurried to the phone and soon had a crew of men lined up. She went to the living room window and looked out at the storm. A dark afternoon would soon turn into a black night, and the storm raged on. The lights flickered again and then went out, leaving the house in an eerie dusk. Ruth joined her grandmother in the kitchen.

Alma was laying out cookies and sandwiches on the table. "I'm thankful I kept my old wood cookstove alongside the electric one. It warms the kitchen and is a blessing at times like this." The room was comfortable and cozy in the lamplight.

The stomping of boots sounded on the back porch, followed by a tap on the door. "Come on in," Alma called out. Three men took off their dripping rain gear and entered the kitchen. Ruth looked up in surprise as Ben Womack stepped through the door.

"Sure feels good in here," Joe Duncan said as he rubbed his hands together over the cookstove. "Nasty out."

"Sit and have some food. I'll pour hot coffee." Alma bustled over to the stove. "How's it going over there?"

"We're stacking sandbags on the roofs to hold 'em down, but the buildings are long. Takes a bunch of 'em," Arlan replied. "A lot of men turned out, but it's still a job."

"George is sending two or three of us over at a time to get a break and warm up. Sure appreciate the food, Alma. We missed supper." Joe tackled another sandwich. The three warmed their hands around the hot coffee cups.

"Cold out there," Ben spoke up, "but sure feels good to do for someone else after people was so good to us." His face looked red and chapped but healthy and filled out.

"Well, we'd best get back and let the next bunch come over. Thanks, Alma," Arlan said as he stood and walked to his rain clothes.

Shifts of men came in and out of the warm kitchen throughout the evening. "Am I thankful I baked today! The Lord sent company but a day early," Alma commented as she refilled the sandwich plate.

"Anything left for us?" The door opened and George came in followed by Jim.

"What were you doing? Playing the hero out there, George Peterson? You'll catch your death of cold. Sit down. I'll get some dry socks while you eat. Ruth, pour the men some coffee." Alma picked up a candle and hurried from the room.

"A dry shirt sounds good, too," George added. "Be right back."

Jim gave a shiver and sat down at the table. "That stove sure feels good. It's raw out there." He reached for a sandwich.

Ruth filled his cup with steaming hot coffee. "How bad is it?" She paused by the table.

"We're saving the roofs, but there'll be damage to repair. At least the chicken houses weren't blown away and the chickens with them." He helped himself to another sandwich. "Most of the men around are helping. Takes a lot of sandbags for all those long chicken houses."

Ruth looked at his wet, tousled hair, his streaked face, and damp shirt. She turned quickly for more coffee. *All I want to do is hold him close and take care of him,* she thought. *But that's not my place.*

She poured the coffee, and he looked up at her. "Thanks," he said softly. "I'll feel warmer out there remembering you like this."

She turned back to the stove. *Sure you will, Jim. Good line. I only wish it were true. But I won't fall for it again,* she thought.

With a quick rap on the door a man burst into the room, dripping water all over the floor. "Mr. Griffin, someone's broken into the plant!" he gasped, struggling to catch his breath. "It's so dark and wet I couldn't see everywhere. Jerry didn't stay for guard duty. Had to save his barn. I couldn't cover his post and mine, too. Coulter said you were over here. Phone lines are down."

Jim was on his feet and grabbing his coat. "Tell your grandpa I had an emergency." He rushed from the room.

"That feels better," George was saying as he and Alma came back into the room a few minutes later. He stopped. "Where's Jim?"

"The plant was broken into, and the guard came to get him. That's all I know."

George sat down and sipped his hot coffee. "Guess whoever it was took advantage of the weather—the lights out and all the men working on the chicken houses." He finished his sandwich and reached for his coat. "Sounds like the wind is slowing down. We may be done soon."

"Let's have a cup ourselves, Ruth. We need to sit a bit." Alma poured two cups of hot coffee and sat down with a sigh.

"I hope Jim's not in any danger." Ruth stared into the cup she was holding.

Alma looked at her sharply. "You still care, don't you, Dear?" She reached for a sandwich. "I can't figure out why he's with that woman. She's not his type." They ate in silence.

"George was right. The wind is down and the rain's let up. I think the worst is over." Alma sighed and took a sip of her coffee. "Sure warmed my heart when I saw Ben come through that door. What the Lord has done in his life! He has a job at the shipyards now. And Hazel says he has a fine voice and is joining the choir."

"Thank the Lord!" Ruth declared.

"Every morning we need to ask Him to help us see the opportunities He puts in front of us," Alma said firmly. "When I think what would have happened to that family if you hadn't stopped by. . ." Alma shook her head.

As they cleaned up, the kitchen door opened, and George stepped into the room. "We saved 'em. I'm going to change out of these wet clothes and then come back for some hot coffee." He picked up a candle and left the room.

Alma was pouring three cups of hot coffee as George came back in dry clothes and sat down to recount the evening's work. "We thought we'd lose one roof," he related. "There'd have been chickens and feathers blown from here to the Cascade Mountains, but the sandbags held it down." He shook his head. "Wind 'bout blew us off the roof, and rain came in our faces so hard we couldn't see."

There was a light tap at the door, and Jim stepped into the warm kitchen.

"Everything all right?" George asked as he looked up between sips.

Jim pulled up a chair. "Someone broke into the office and went through the files. There were papers all over the floor. We don't know what they found, but we'll have to alter our shipping schedules and put on more guards." He ran his fingers through his hair. "I came over tonight because of this." He placed *Ben-Hur* on the table.

"Where did you get it?" Ruth was astounded.

"It was found on the floor of the office. Apparently, it was dropped and the papers scattered over it." He looked over at Ruth. "I need to keep it for awhile. It's time we found out why there's been so much fuss over this book—and why it was at our plant."

Ruth nodded. "It's Suzi's, but you can keep it for now."

"Did you have much damage?" George inquired. He wrapped his hands around the hot cup.

"No damage. Just a mess of papers. There are people interested in what we produce and where we ship it. With a war on, the enemy wants to know the country's military and industrial output." Jim paused and looked at a napkin he folded as he talked. "I'm not at liberty to explain much. War restrictions."

The other three nodded.

"The way things are today," George commented.

"I was disturbed to find the book dropped by whoever broke into the plant." Jim turned the book over in his hands. "It was probably the same person who ransacked your bedroom, Ruth, and your classroom and Suzi's house. We don't know the connection yet, but if I keep the book, they shouldn't bother you about it. They know where they lost it."

"Why would someone want that book?" Alma asked. "It's a religious story."

"I don't know yet." He leaned back in his chair.

Ruth commented, "The only other person connected with the book was that dark-haired man at the café. He stared at me that day while I read it. And then he grabbed it and ran off with it. But if he wanted it so badly, why did he throw it down? Remember, Jim, you found it."

Jim nodded. "You never discovered who he was?"

Ruth shook her head. "I haven't seen him since. He's probably not around here anymore."

"It's late." Jim stood up. "You people need some sleep, and I have to get back to the plant. There's a lot to do so this can't happen again." He picked up his hat. "The war's complicating life everywhere."

"But the Lord's with us," George said softly. "The world may be going crazy, but there can still be peace inside for believers."

The room was quiet as his words sank in.

"We need to pray and trust the Lord," Jim agreed as he put on his hat and opened the door. "Good night, all."

★ ★ ★

On Friday night, Ruth rushed around dusting the living room furniture and plumping the pillows. "Thanks for letting us hold the Bible study here tonight," she said as she straightened the doilies on the end tables.

"Church basement'll be a mess for awhile yet," George commented. "That wind took the shingles right off the roof, and then the rain poured in. Takes time to dry out."

Alma brought in another chair. "I worry there won't be enough seats for everyone, Dear," she fussed.

"We'll have enough. Some of the people canceled. They had to clean up their own storm damage," Ruth explained.

A rap on the door sent Alma scurrying to admit Jim and three other class members. "Come in and have a seat," she urged as she took their coats. They sat down and chatted about the storm as a few more drifted in.

Ruth's heart gave a skip when Jim greeted her, and she hurried to the kitchen. Marge entered the room as she was piling Alma's corn-syrup cookies on a platter.

"There you are, hiding out in here," Marge teased. She picked up a plate of cookies and carried it to the dining room behind her friend. "He's here by himself again," she whispered. "Carolyn's missed the last two Bible studies. I told you she looked bored."

"Shh," Ruth whispered back. "Someone'll hear." She put down the plates of cookies.

"Okay, let's get started," Jim called out. "Our group will be smaller tonight, so we won't wait any longer." The class settled down and attention turned to Jim as Ruth took a seat next to Marge.

"This week we're going to talk about choices," Jim announced. "Let's start by taking a look at the first choice mankind faced and the decision that was made. Of course I'm referring to Adam and Eve. God gave them a choice. What was that choice, and what did they do?"

Art Fuller piped up. "They chose a Red Delicious apple! I saw it on the front of my Sunday school lesson when I was a kid," he joked. "Made me scared to eat apples for years!"

The class laughed.

"Reminds me of the apple the wicked queen gave Snow White in my daughter's storybook," he continued. "It was poison!"

Jim chuckled along with the group. "Actually, you're not far off, Art. Their choice was a poison we call sin, and it did cause death. But turn to Genesis and let's go back. . ."

Ruth watched the faces in the group as they eagerly responded to Jim's discussion. *Choices—great!* she thought. *A fine topic for me! Seems like I've been making wrong choices this whole year. If only I'd told Harold. . .* She glanced at Jim as he listened intently to Jean Preston's comment. *He made a choice, too—and it wasn't me! I hope Carolyn realizes how fortunate she is to have a man like Jim. But why can't he get her to Bible study anymore?* she wondered.

She could feel Jim looking at her. "And what do you think, Ruth?"

Her face grew warm as she tried to remember what they were talking about. "Would you repeat that, Jim?"

"You looked so deep in thought I was sure you had some words of wisdom." He smiled at her and reviewed the last comment. "Mary said our choices are important because what we choose can affect the spiritual lives of others. Can you elaborate on that?"

Ruth swallowed hard. "The world's full of darkness today," she began uncertainly, hoping she was on the topic. "In our choices, we can either contribute to the darkness or be a light shining for Christ. We must choose to stay close to the Lord so He can shine through our lives to others."

"Sounds like a tall order to me," Art admitted. "Don't think I'd be a very big light, dark as the world is now."

Ruth nodded. "Me neither, but that's where the whole church comes in. One candle doesn't give a lot of light, but a whole bunch of candles can make a great light. That's what the church is to be—a lot of little reflectors of Jesus making a light big enough to dispel the darkness. Staying close enough to Him that we reflect Him—that's a very important choice."

"Yeah," Tom Adams added. "Guess if more people had followed God, we wouldn't be in this awful war. Sure makes me think about how careful we need to be!"

"You've wrapped it up well. Remember, when we choose to read the Word and pray or not, when we make a choice to obey or disobey God, it makes a difference. Ask God to help in what you choose." Jim closed his Bible and smiled at Ruth. "Let's close with prayer."

As the group rose from their seats, Alma called out, "Help yourselves to cookies in the dining room."

Ruth waited as the line formed. A sudden rap at the door jolted her, and she hurried to open it. There stood Carolyn Samuels smiling at her.

"I'm sorry to interrupt, but I need to speak to Jim," Carolyn was saying as Ruth looked at the lovely woman before her. Her hair and clothes were the latest style, and everything about her was modern and immaculate. Unconsciously, Ruth patted her simple hairdo and looked down at her worn shoes.

"Come in. I'll get him for you." She closed the door behind Carolyn and worked her way through the group to Jim, a sinking feeling settling over her. *I hadn't seen Carolyn for awhile,* she thought. *I guess I hoped. . .*

"Jim," she said as she approached him, "there's someone at the door to see you." She watched him glance that direction and a knowing look come over his face. He nodded and hurried to the entryway where Carolyn waited. They talked a moment; then Jim headed for the pile of coats and rummaged through for his. He quickly thanked Alma for her hospitality and followed Carolyn out the door.

Ruth gave a shiver. The room suddenly seemed empty.

"What was that all about?" Marge came up behind her.

Ruth shrugged. "I guess she came to pick him up."

"Don't look so down, Ruth. I'm still working on your love life, but it's hard these days with all the men going off to war." Marge stepped to the doorway and hesitated. Her face grew serious. "Pray for Jack and me, Ruth. I'm so scared he'll be shipped overseas when he gets his new orders." She blinked her eyes, then quickly slipped out the door.

Chapter 20

Alma plopped into a kitchen chair on a fall Saturday afternoon. "My, it's good to sit down!" She rubbed her sore fingers stained brown from the walnut harvest at the Nakamuras'.

"We picked a lot of nuts. Glad so many people from the church showed up to help," George commented as he washed up.

Ruth busied herself putting away food left from the noon potluck that had fed the pickers. She looked around. "Gram, where's the roast? I don't see it here."

"Last I saw, it was on Suzi's stove in the roaster. Hazel was cutting it into sandwich meat. There was plenty left, though." She looked at George. "Anything more in the truck?"

"Nope," he replied. "Brought it all in."

"Fine day to be forgetful," Alma sighed. "With all the work we did, I thought it would make a quick and easy supper."

"I'll go get it, Grandma. The walk will be a good way to unwind." Ruth slipped into her coat. "You two rest while I'm gone. You deserve it. In fact, I hear those overstuffed chairs in the living room calling you."

Ruth ambled down the path, humming as she crossed the field. The late afternoon sun cast long shadows across the ground in its descent behind the fir trees bordering the field. *A lot of sore backs today, but it feels good to know we didn't let any of Nak's crops go to waste this year,* she thought as she enjoyed the glow of fading sunlight.

As she approached the farmhouse steps, Fluffy let out a meow and bounded to meet her. "Just because you got lunch here today doesn't mean there'll be supper here, too. You have to come home with me for that," she said to the cat as she mounted the stairs.

The screen door gave a loud squeak as she pulled it open. The door stood ajar. "I should have checked it before I left," she scolded herself. "Good thing I came back." She pushed the door open and walked toward the stove, pausing at the table.

"Who did this?" she demanded. On the table lay Suzi's bookmarks, a strip of paper with a listing of Bible verses, and an open book. "I told the kids not to play with these this morning, but someone didn't listen. Suzi's bookmarks are too special to be used as toys." She crumpled up the strip of paper and stuffed it in her pocket. "And look. They marked all over Suzi's book." She picked it up along with the bookmarks. "I'll take it home and get these marks erased."

"Well, well, well, if it ain't the teacher," a deep voice spoke behind her.

A jolt of fear ran through her as she turned to see a dark-haired man with a scraggly beard coming into the room. "I told ya to git back home once, but ya didn't listen." He glared at her. "Can't you learn nothin'?"

Ruth opened her mouth, but no sound came out.

The man strode to the table. "Leave our stuff alone." He grabbed the book and bookmarks from her. "The paper, too," he demanded as he held out his hand. "Git in here, Leland," he barked toward the hall. "We got work to do."

Leland Hinson slinked into the room and slid into a chair at one side of the table.

"Sit!" the man ordered Ruth. "We don't have no time to bother with you now. Boss'll be here soon." He pulled a tiny piece of paper from his pocket and reached out to turn the pages in the Bible. Then he took one of Suzi's bookmarks from the pile and started to write on it.

"No, you can't do that! Those aren't yours." Ruth was shocked to hear the sound of her own voice.

The man glared at her. "You gonna stop me?" he snarled. "Shut up! We got coding to do. Leland, git out and see if the last message is in. We need it to git this done."

Leland soon returned with a tiny capsule. "Last bird was in," he said as he handed it to his cousin.

A wave of fear hit Ruth. "You're the ones who took the pigeons," she gasped. "You're spies!"

"Smart lady. Leland, the teacher can add two and two," the man said sarcastically.

Leland glanced at the clock on the wall. "Boss'll be here soon, Bert." He shifted nervously in his seat. "What'll we do with her? Boss won't be happy." He licked his lips, and his eyes flicked from Bert to Ruth. "Boss gits mean, real mean, if things ain't right."

Lord, Ruth prayed desperately, *help me. Show me what to do. Bring someone to help me. Please!*

Bert picked up the book and began underlining words here and there.

She caught her breath. "You're the one who marked in *Ben-Hur* and kept stealing it!"

Leland snickered. "Boss was sure mad 'bout that Ben book. Had the code list on the bookmark in it, too. Told Bert to git 'em both back or else. But Bert's dumb. Threw the book away the first time just cause the bookmark warn't in it. Boss was in a fit!"

"Shut up, Leland." He glared at his cousin. "You're the one lost the book twice."

"Bert's got a nasty temper. Tears things up. Boss was mad he left a mess looking for it. Made people suspicious."

Ruth squeezed her shaking hands together.

"Boss'll pay us soon," Leland rambled. "Can git my farm back. Chase them foreigners out, and there'll be room for us real Americans." He rambled on as Ruth sat terrified.

Keep him talking, she thought. *Stall for time. Someone will come looking for me if I'm gone too long.*

"Spies must get a lot of money," she managed to squeak out.

Leland nodded and grinned. "Easy work, too. Just sneak around and find out what's goin' on. Bert met Boss in Califorony. Boss said we could make a lot of money if we helped. Government ain't done me no good, and I sure could use the money." He glanced at the clock again.

Greedy and scared. I wonder if he knows how much trouble he's in. An idea formed in her mind. "You must be very brave to be a spy," she ventured.

"Nah, just sneak around. Easy."

"But it's so dangerous. If you get caught you could be executed, you know." She forced a look of concern.

Leland frowned and his eyes got bigger. "Bert said spies don't git no more 'n a few days in jail. No big deal."

"The government caught eight German spies on the East Coast this summer. They executed six of them on August 8 and two went to prison." Ruth watched his face carefully.

"Tell her, Bert. Spies just get a few days in jail." She could hear the fear creeping into his voice.

"Don't pay her no attention," Bert growled. "We ain't gittin' caught. Leave me alone. Got to git this coding done."

Panic crossed Leland's face. "I ain't gittin' killed, Bert, and I don't wanna go to prison. All I want's my farm back," he whined and swallowed hard.

From the look on his face, Ruth could tell he saw the same movement she did. Their eyes stared at the window.

"I saw something out there, Bert. Like a face," Leland whispered.

Bert snorted. "Dumb cousin. You believe in ghosts?"

As he glanced at Leland, a face flashed by the window, vague in the deepening dusk. Bert shoved his chair back and dashed out the door, searching around the house, then storming back in. "Nothin' there. Just gittin' spooked. Now leave me alone." He looked at the clock. "Got to hurry this. Boss'll be here." He settled back to work on the coding.

Leland jerked his head toward his cousin. "Bert can do a lotta things. He can break in anywhere. Best counterfeiter in these-here parts, too. He. . ."

All three heads swung around as footsteps sounded on the porch. Then there was silence. Bert rose and moved stealthily to the door. He stepped outside and searched around.

"Didn't see no one. Musta been the wind. Gittin' spooked." He frowned as he returned to the table.

Leland's face had turned pale. "Can't be the boss. Boss won't come while we're here. Have to signal when we leave. Maybe someone's onto us." He shoved his chair back. "Don't want no money, Bert. You can have it all. Don't want to git killed. I'm outta here!" He rushed to the door and out into the night before Bert could react.

Ruth watched tensely as Bert glanced at the clock and swore. "Dumb cousin. No help anyway." He looked up again at the window and grabbed the papers to finish his coding. As he put the items away, the bookmark he had worked on slid to the floor and under the table. He placed the book and the rest of the bookmarks back on the shelf.

"I ain't gonna worry about you. Leave that to the boss." He took out a piece of rope and pulled her hands behind the chair. He tied the knots tightly, then tied each ankle to a chair leg. "You're not runnin' off and bringing the sheriff to ruin my deal." He gave the rope a yank as Ruth flinched in pain.

"Teachers talk too much. This'll keep you quiet." He pulled a rag out of his pocket and tied it around her mouth. "Always wanted to do that when I was in school." He smiled grimly and glanced around the room. "That's what ya git for not listenin', Teach." He picked up his flashlight. "Time to signal the boss." He slipped out the door and was gone.

Ruth was left in silent darkness as she fought a wave of panic. *Why hasn't anyone wondered where I am? Why hasn't Grandpa come to check on me? I've been gone far too long.* She tried to move her arms, but the ropes were tied tight. *Lord, please send someone before the boss gets here. It'll be too late then. I'm so scared, Lord.*

Her heart pounded as another wave of panic rushed through her. *They know I can identify them. Lord, give me strength no matter what happens.*

A noise on the porch sent a jolt of fear through her. The boss. . .

The door opened quietly. In the dusk she couldn't see who it was. The footsteps came toward her and stopped behind her chair. The figure squatted down and grappled with the ropes binding her hands.

Who is it? Her mind tried to understand. "Umm uh um," she mumbled as loud as she could and shook her head.

The figure stood and reached for the knot on the gag. As it fell away, Ruth took a deep breath. "Thank you." She tried to peer at the figure. "Who are you?"

The figure stared at her silently, then mumbled a reply. "Jones." He squatted and went to work on the ropes holding her wrists.

"Mr. Jones, am I glad to see you! We have to hurry. Those two men were spies. Their boss will be here any minute, and then we're both in trouble."

He pulled and worked at the ropes, but the tight knots wouldn't budge.

"Get a knife from Suzi's drawer over there and cut them. Please hurry, Mr. Jones."

He brought the knife and bent to saw at the ropes. As the first one fell away, the door opened. Ruth's heart stopped, then pounded as if it would burst through her chest. Heavy footsteps entered the room, and a flashlight beamed its light, first on her and then on Mr. Jones as a large figure walked toward them.

"Why, Miss Sinclair, what are you doing here in these circumstances?" a voice inquired.

She peered toward the figure. That voice. Who. . . ? "Oh, Mr. Owens," she exclaimed in relief. "I'm so glad it's you! Leland and his cousin are spies! Bert went to signal the boss. He'll be here any minute. We all need to get out of here as fast as we can!" She spoke rapidly as she stared at Herschel's dark figure.

Herschel ambled toward them. "Now, now, Miss Sinclair, don't you fret. You say there are spies around here? That's hard to believe, but maybe I should take a look. Mother always told me to be a good citizen. I'll just see if I can find out what they were up to, and then I'll take care of you." He walked directly to the bookshelves and searched through the titles.

"What are you doing way out here, Mr. Owens? It's so late." She watched his movements as his hand stopped on a book. His face looked eerie above the small beam of light directed toward the bookshelves.

"Why, I heard you had a nut harvest out here, Miss Sinclair. When the store closed, I came right over to see if I could help, but everyone appears to be gone."

An uneasy feeling rushed over her. *Why isn't he helping me first?* She watched as he picked up a book and looked through it, then walked to the table and peered at the Bible. He searched around, muttering angrily as he looked for something. How had he known where to look? How would he know about the book and the Bible? She gasped. No, it couldn't be!

"You're the boss!" she blurted out. "You're looking for Bert's codes!"

Herschel continued his search. "Now, Miss Sinclair, I'm deeply offended to have you accuse me like that. Mother would be so hurt if she knew you called *me* the boss." He slammed the book on the table.

As he searched frantically, his coat fell open, and she could see a gun tucked in his belt. She heard Mr. Jones catch his breath and stiffen behind her. He placed a hand on her shoulder and spoke up in his soft voice. "Saw Bert out at the pigeon coop when I come in. Might be he left something out there."

Herschel turned and the hard look on his face changed into his broad smile. "Why, I appreciate your help, Sir. If I'm to solve this riddle, I need all the pieces. You both sit tight, and I'll be right back. Then I'll see to you." He gave Mr. Jones a hard look above the beam of light. Ruth could hear the scraping of wooden legs against the floor as he picked up a chair and slipped out the door. She heard him jamming the object under the handle on the outside of the door; then his footsteps faded away.

Mr. Jones quickly bent to saw at the ropes with Suzi's dull knife. Both froze as voices and shouts sounded outside. The door burst open, and they were instantly blinded by a mass of bright lights. In a flurry of activity, Ruth could make out men in police and military uniforms rushing about—and Carolyn Samuels. Ruth's head swirled as she tried to take it all in.

An officer hurried over and quickly cut the remaining ropes binding her. "Are you all right, Miss?" She rubbed her wrists and nodded, then watched, confused, as Carolyn Samuels checked the table and bookcase carefully. Officers were searching the house, and she could hear others moving about outside.

"You do get in the biggest messes, Miss Sinclair." She heard that familiar voice behind her as Jim reached out to help her to her feet. "Are you okay?"

"Oh, Jim, I. . ." She longed to go to him for comfort—but there stood Carolyn Samuels, two feet away. Suddenly her legs felt weak, and she reached out to steady herself. She felt dazed and dizzy.

Jim grabbed her arm quickly. "Sit down. You've had quite a scare."

"The boss," she began. "He's out at the pigeon coop. It's Herschel Owens. Don't let him get away! He has some of the codes with him."

"The officers picked him up as he tried to escape in the dark," Jim reassured her.

Ruth looked around. "Where's Mr. Jones? He was helping me."

"Taking Tim and Charlie home. I'll explain later," Jim answered. "Right now these officers want a word with you. Then we need to get you home."

Two officers sat down at the table with Jim and Ruth, and Carolyn joined them. Jim introduced the officers. "And you've met Carolyn Samuels, government expert in codes and spies. She's been a big help." Ruth was so astounded she couldn't say a word. Carolyn smiled at her and shrugged.

"Now, Miss Sinclair, tell us what happened here today." The officer nodded to her, and the table was silent.

She took a deep breath and told all that had happened that afternoon. "Leland and Bert took off before you came," she added.

"I'll have our men out looking for them," the officer assured her and turned to speak to one of his men.

Jim shoved his chair back from the table. "She needs some rest, gentlemen," he said protectively. "This has been a rough day." He helped Ruth to her feet.

"We'll get in touch with you soon, Miss. We'll have more questions," the officer said, "but they can hold till you've recovered. I—"

With a slam the door burst open, and George Peterson dashed into the room. "What's going on?" He looked around at the officers. "Why are all these men here? Ruth, are you okay? What's happened, Jim?" Fear and confusion showed on his face.

"Ruth's okay, Mr. Peterson," Jim assured him. "We caught one of the spies who had been using this place. Right now we have a lot of work to do here. Take Ruth home, if you would. I'll be tied up here for quite awhile."

George shook his head. "Alma and I sat down to rest when Ruth left. We were so tired from the walnut picking we fell asleep in our chairs. When we woke up, it was dark and Ruth wasn't home yet so I hurried over here." He looked around at everyone. "It was only an hour or so."

Ruth came up and hugged her grandfather. She felt so safe tears finally came. George patted her shoulder. "I'm so sorry, Ruth. If anything. . ."

"I'm okay, Grandpa." She wiped her eyes and picked up the roast from the stove. "The Lord took care of me. Let's get home so Grandma won't worry." She paused at the door. "Thanks again to all of you."

★ ★ ★

As Ruth and George pulled into their driveway, Alma rushed out to meet them. "Here's the roast, Gram. Now we can have dinner." Ruth handed her the roaster and got out of the car.

"Not 'til we find out what happened to you. We were so worried, Ruth." Alma followed her up the stairs.

Over a warm cup of cocoa, Ruth related the afternoon's events. "Oh, Ruth, to think. . . The Lord was good." Alma stood up. "Now to bed with you. We'll talk more after you've recovered."

Chapter 21

The bedroom was dark when Ruth awoke. She sat up quickly in confusion. "What day is this?" She shook her head to chase away the cobwebs. "Why is my room still dark? Isn't it morning?"

Slowly her thoughts began to clear, and the frightening events came flooding back. "Oh, no," she said aloud. "It can't be true." She reached over to turn on the lamp beside her bed. Ten o'clock! She stared at the alarm clock on her dresser. "It's still Saturday, and all these terrible things happened only a few hours ago? Or was it just a nightmare?"

Grandma and Grandpa will know, she assured herself and headed for the stairs.

Below she could hear voices that sounded like Jim talking to George and Alma in the kitchen. Words and phrases drifted up to her. "Spies. . . Herschel. . ." Jim's voice faded, then returned. "Carolyn. . . ," he was saying. "Worked together closely. . .engaged. . .friend. . .Ruth."

She grabbed the stair rail to steady herself and sank down on a step. *So that's the way it is. The nightmare did happen, and Jim and Carolyn are engaged.* She tried to breathe, but her chest was tight with a terrible ache. She couldn't seem to catch her breath. *All this in one day! How. . . ? How can I. . . ?*

All her hopes and fears and dreams jumbled about in the turmoil inside her. As the ache in her chest threatened to stifle her, she bowed her head. "Lord," she whispered, "this is so hard, but You saved me this afternoon. I know I can trust You with my life. And I know You have a purpose for me, whether it's with someone else someday or teaching children. I'll always have You." She took a deep breath. "If it's Your will for Jim and Carolyn to be together, I trust You and ask You to bless them and to heal the ache in my heart." A quiet peace settled over her.

She sat there a moment. "Lord, I've been a slow learner when it comes to trust. And it took something terrible to teach me." She nodded. "Jim was right when he said You often get a lot done in the bad times." She got up and headed down the stairs.

"Having a party without me?" she quipped as she walked into the kitchen. George and Jim rushed to pull out a chair for her. "Here, sit, Ruth," George said as he grabbed her elbow. "Jim's been telling us what happened."

A plate of roast beef sandwiches sat in the middle of the table. "We never did get around to having supper tonight. After all the trouble you went through,

I thought we could at least have sandwiches." Alma passed the plate to her. "Here, Ruth. You need to keep up your strength."

"They look delicious, Gram," Ruth said as she reached for one.

"We feel so bad we fell asleep and didn't come looking for you sooner." Alma placed a cup of tea in front of Ruth.

"The Lord took care of me. Someone could have been hurt if Grandpa had burst in earlier." She smiled calmly and took a sip of tea.

"I came over tonight to see if there's more information you three can give us." Jim stared at his cup and turned it in his hand. "You know the most about what's been going on. We're hoping you can add some missing pieces so we can get this cleared up." He looked up at them sharply. "Whatever we say here tonight is not to leave this room. I hope you understand."

The three nodded.

"Wartime necessity," George agreed.

"Good." Jim sat back. "Now that you've had a rest, Ruth, tell me again what happened today, especially what Bert did and in what order."

Ruth recounted the evening, then paused to think. "About Bert. As I remember, first he took a tiny piece of paper from his pocket, and Leland brought him another that came in a capsule the pigeons had carried. Then he turned to someplace in the Bible and wrote on one of Suzi's bookmarks. I think that's the one that fell under the table."

"We found it," Jim said.

"He took *Ben-Hur* and underlined words in it, then wrote on another bookmark. Oh, yes, there was a strip of paper with some writing on it, too." She looked over at Jim. "What's it all about?"

"Carolyn thinks they were attempting a complicated communication system so no one could tell what they were doing," Jim explained. "The Nakamuras were religious and liked to read, so the material was all there— and with the pigeons they were all set to send and receive information. Our experts are working to figure it out. Shouldn't be too hard. They weren't geniuses." Jim took a sip of the tea. "We do know Bert and Leland were part of the mob that ransacked the Nakamuras' house. They must have seen the possibilities and passed the idea on to the boss."

"The boss!" Ruth sat up straight. "Was I shocked to find out it was Herschel! I'm so glad you got him."

Jim smiled. "We caught Herschel Owens and the boss, but Bert and Leland are long gone. Leland didn't even take his things. Just ran. Bert must have seen the police descend on the place. He's gone, too."

Ruth nodded. "It figures. Leland was really scared when he found out spies could be executed or sent to prison." She frowned. "But what did you mean, they caught Herschel Owens and the boss? Herschel was the boss."

"That's what we thought at first, too," Jim said, "but when the officers searched Trader's Corner, they found the whole setup and the identity of the real boss—his mother!"

Ruth sat back astounded. "His mother!" She nodded slowly. "Yes, it makes sense. I always said she'd be more at home running a chain gang than being the loving mother Herschel talked about."

"This isn't the first trouble she's been in," Jim added. "The government's been looking for her for several years."

"Oh, my!" Alma exclaimed. "I hardly knew her, but here in our own community. . ."

"Those two had quite a racket going. In the storeroom they were getting ready to print counterfeit ration books to sell. The furniture store, if you can call it that, was just a front for their various illegal activities," Jim explained.

"That fits. Leland told me Bert was the best counterfeiter around." Ruth finished her tea and set the cup down.

George leaned forward. "Every time Ruth and I went to the Nakamuras', we found a different number of pigeons. They took 'em to send messages, appears to me." He went on to explain what he and Ruth had seen at the pigeon coop over the months.

"You're right, Mr. Peterson. We found pigeon droppings all over their storeroom."

"Why did they tear up all those bookcases and Ruth's room?" Alma looked puzzled. "What does that have to do with this?"

Jim shifted his chair as Ruth got up to pour more tea. "It appears Herschel and his mother were hoping to sell information about our war production and used Bert and Leland to collect it. The pigeons brought the Bible references that gave Bert messages from the boss, Carolyn assumes, and then Bert relayed their information through words he designated in *Ben-Hur*. She thinks the bookmark and the strip of paper had master codes written on them."

"Remember the bookmark I found under the sofa cushion, Ruth?" Alma asked. "The one with the chapters and verse numbers not in the Bible? That must have been one of the code lists."

Ruth poured the tea. "The boss was desperate to get the book and bookmark back because they were incriminating evidence. Bert tore up my room even though the book was lying on the bed because he also needed the bookmark with coding on it." She sat down and related the rest of Leland's ramblings that afternoon. "And Bert was the one who could break in anywhere. He used a skeleton key to open the Nakamuras' door."

"But looks like they got careless sometimes. Left the door open and even let Fluffy get caught inside," George commented.

"I don't understand. If Bert and Leland hate foreigners so much, why would they help them by spying?" Alma looked puzzled.

"They wanted money," Ruth explained. "They worked for the boss and didn't see themselves as part of the war or helping either side, just themselves. They were anti-Japanese and tried to use that to keep us away from the house. When it didn't work, they went ahead anyway." A memory came back to her. "Mr. Jones. He was trying to help me when you came, Jim. I want to thank him."

Jim smiled and looked over at her. "You have three heroes to thank."

Ruth frowned. "Three heroes? I don't understand."

Jim sat back in his chair. "Tim and Charlie were down at the creek, building a raft, late that afternoon. Old man—er—Mr. Jones was helping them. The three had become good friends and worked together on the project. Mr. Jones came up to the Nakamuras' to find a rope they needed to secure the raft for the night. When he went by the window, he saw you with Bert and Leland."

"That was the face we saw!" Ruth exclaimed.

Jim nodded. "He knew those two had caused trouble before, so he went back to get the boys. The three hurried to check out the situation. You heard their footsteps on the porch. Mr. Jones sent the boys to tell me you were in trouble while he stayed to keep an eye on things."

"But when Bert checked, no one was there." Ruth was puzzled.

"They ducked under the porch. He didn't look there. Bert and Leland aren't the brightest. I called various authorities right away. We arrived in the dark and saw a flashlight over at the pigeon coop where we picked up Herschel. Then we came to find you."

George shook his head. "I should have taken it more seriously when Ruth told me about the strange goings-on, but the sheriff wouldn't listen, and there was nothing else to do."

"The sheriff has an anti-Japanese attitude, so he didn't really care what happened over there—or to any of their friends," Jim explained.

Alma sighed and sat back. "Now that you're safe, Ruth, I'm suddenly very tired. It's been a hard day. Ready for some sleep, George?"

"Don't have to ask me twice. My back's letting me know I did too much bending for a man my age." He stood. "The Lord's been good to us today." He patted Ruth's shoulder tenderly as he left the room.

Ruth poured two more cups of tea. "Thanks for all you did, Jim. I have so many questions, I don't know where to begin." She took a sip of the hot tea and set the cup down.

Jim was quiet.

And I know why, she thought, *but I'm at peace with it. I trust the Lord's plan for each of us.*

Jim finally looked up. "Ruth, I'm not sure where to begin. This has gotten so tangled."

"It's okay, Jim, I know. . ."

He reached out and put his hand on hers. "Let me explain. Please. There's still much I'm not allowed to say, so I have to choose my words carefully, but you deserve the best explanation I can give. I'll probably say more than I should." He paused and considered his words.

"You knew I worked with my dad at the plant," he began. "What you didn't know is how I'm, uh, also connected with the government. Since I couldn't get in the service, I became involved with other departments that have to do with national security. The plant was not only a good cover for my special activities but also useful to the war effort. We knew Swan Island Shipyards could become a target for spy efforts, along with any converted industry like our plant. As community coordinator, I'd be in a good spot to keep a handle on things. And here on the West Coast we had to get defense efforts going as soon as possible."

Ruth was surprised. "I had no idea, Jim. I just thought. . ."

He nodded. "You were the last person I wanted to put in danger, so the less you knew the better; and all this had to stay quiet. We wanted to get the big guys behind the scenes, not just the small fish like Bert and Leland." He lowered his head and shook it. "Then I messed up big-time."

Her eyebrows went up. "Were you in danger?" she asked with concern.

"Not the way you mean, but my whole future was in jeopardy." He put both hands around hers. "Ruth, I know about Harold and what happened. You can't imagine how terrible I felt."

"No, Jim, it's. . ."

"Shh." He squeezed her hands. "Let me explain. We needed to get Carolyn Samuels into the Fir Glen community without raising suspicion. She's highly trained in detecting spies and breaking codes. So when they suggested she pose as my girlfriend, I went along with it. You were still being loyal to Harold. I thought it might make you jealous." He looked at her sheepishly.

Ruth's mouth fell open, and she sat speechless.

"Only a couple of weeks later, I learned the truth about Harold, but by then they couldn't let me out of the plan."

"You mean you're not engaged?"

"Engaged? Where'd you get that idea?"

"When I came down the stairs awhile ago. I heard you talking to Grandma and Grandpa about Carolyn and being engaged."

He let out a breath. "Carolyn's engaged—but not to me. To a guy overseas."

"Then you mean. . ."

"I mean I'm not attached in any way to anyone—yet. Now I'm afraid I'll never be. I'm afraid I've blown it with you completely." He glanced at her sideways. "I'm afraid to hope." He looked miserable. "I've been in love with you ever since I helped you out of the mud in the Nakamuras' driveway last spring, and now. . ." He shook his head hopelessly.

She caught her breath and sat up, trying to grasp his words. The room was silent, and the clock ticked loudly as relief washed over her. She straightened in her chair and looked over at Jim. "I will say this has affected our friendship, Jim," she said with as serious an expression as she could manage. "As you recall, we're just friends unless. . ." She raised an eyebrow at him.

He sat there, not sure he had heard right. He blinked and looked up as he caught her meaning. Then he leaned back in his chair, that mischievous smile spreading over his face as he took a deep breath in relief.

"So, Miss Sinclair," he teased, "you're not engaged?"

She shook her head.

"No commitments?"

"None."

"You've promised to wait for someone?"

"No, Sir."

"Then one more thing we have to clear up. Do I have to take you out on a first date before I ask you to marry me?" The old Jim was back. "With a war on, there's no time to wait on formalities."

"No moonlight and roses?" she teased back.

He stood and held out his hand. "My lady, would you do me the honor of accompanying me on a date to your grandparents' living room? The moon's not out tonight, and the rose season has passed, but I have many sweet nothings to whisper in your ear."

Ruth stood and gave a small curtsy. "Offer accepted, Sir." She took his arm. They walked to the living room and sat down on the sofa. He put his arm around her and pulled her close.

"Remember the old high school rule, Jim. No kiss 'til the third date."

"Since you're already home on date one, I'll ask you out on dates two and three right now."

"I accept," she murmured as he lifted her chin and kissed her. She caught her breath and nestled in his arms as all the months of heartache melted away.

Jim stroked her hair. "Someday I'd like to shake the hand of the woman who ran off with Harold."

She touched his face tenderly. "You already had my heart, Jim, but I'm glad we don't have to wait 'til Harold comes home," she agreed.

"So, if I promise to protect you from spies, keep your bookcases safe, and never buy you pigeons, will you marry me, Ruth Sinclair?"

She gazed into the love in his eyes. "Yes, Jim, spies and all." His tender kiss left her weak and breathless.

"So, how about tomorrow?"

She frowned. "Tomorrow for what?"

"To get married, of course. With the war, everything's escalated, so no use wasting time here, either."

"Oh, no, Jim Griffin; there may be a war on, but you're not depriving this girl of time to plan the big day!" She smiled at him sweetly. "Speaking of plans, we have a lot to talk about—like what date and our colors." She excitedly chattered on about ideas for the wedding and their life together. "Of course Pastor Cameron will marry us."

Jim shook his head. "Women. . ."

A loud crash in the kitchen sent a bolt of fear through both of them. Jim froze for an instant before he dashed to the kitchen. Sounds of hurrying footsteps came from her grandparents' hall.

"What's going on?" George switched on the light as they rushed into the room.

The four of them stared at the table. There stood Fluffy with a piece of roast beef in her mouth, a broken plate, and sandwich remains on the floor.

"How in the world did you get in here?" Alma demanded of the cat.

Jim took a deep breath. "That may have been my fault," he said sheepishly. "When I came over tonight, she was by the door. I didn't pay any attention to her as I came in. She must have sneaked by."

George nodded. "We were too worried about other things to notice."

"Now that you two are up," Jim began, "I have something to discuss with you. Since Ruth's parents aren't here, Mr. Peterson, I'll ask you for Ruth's hand in marriage. And I warn you, Sir, I won't take no for an answer."

Alma's hand flew to her face. "Oh, my, thank You, Lord. You've answered my prayer!"

George beamed and reached out to shake Jim's hand. "With pleasure. You have our blessings, Son."

Alma hugged them both. "When is the big event?"

"Tomorrow morning?" Jim suggested hopefully.

Ruth wrinkled her nose at him and rolled her eyes. "Men!" She looked at Alma. "December will be best, don't you think? Mom and Dad will be home for that month."

"That's such a short time. There's so much to do," Alma said. "We'll have to. . ."

George interrupted. "Get used to it, Jim. The women are taking over already. Time for some sleep, Alma. Leave the planning to them." George put his arm around her shoulder and turned her toward the hall. He stopped. "Housing's tight these days. You always have a home with us if you need it."

Ruth looked at Jim. "We talked about it and decided we'll stay at the Nakamuras' for now. Suzi would be so pleased, and we can keep a better eye on the place."

Alma gave Ruth a hug. "The Lord knew what was right for you." She looked fondly at her granddaughter. "The best I can wish is that you be as happy as I've been."

George beamed and gave a cocky strut. "These women sure know how to find the best, Jim." He winked at him and sashayed down the hall.

"That man!" Alma declared. "I thank the Lord you're as blessed as I am, Ruth."

When they were alone, Jim took her hands. "This was not planned for tonight. I don't have a ring to give you."

"As long as I have your heart, that's all I need." She reached up and kissed him tenderly.

"I'd like to announce this in church tomorrow. I'm taking no chances on your backing down."

She laughed. "Don't worry. You're stuck, Jim Griffin. There's no getting out of this now!"

★ ★ ★

The next morning the four entered the church and found a pew. At the end of the service, Pastor Cameron paused and looked out over the congregation. "We have some joyous news to share this morning. Jim Griffin will tell you about it."

Jim stood and pulled Ruth to her feet. "I need to finish something I started, and what better place than among God's people. Last night I asked Ruth to marry me. It wasn't planned, so I didn't have a ring."

Across the room Marge let out a gasp.

He reached in his pocket. "Ruth, in front of these dear people of God, will you accept this ring and build a life with God and me?" He slipped a beautiful old-fashioned ring on her finger. "It was my grandmother's."

Her heart was so full all she could do was nod. Tears came to her eyes as she beamed at him.

Friends quickly milled about them, offering congratulations. Marge pushed her way through the crowd. "I'm so happy for you!" She hugged Ruth. "And you've saved my reputation. I'm a matchmaking success, after all!"

"You need to circle our date on your calendar, Marge. I'm counting on you to be my maid of honor."

"You bet! I never dreamed you'd beat me to the altar, though!"

As the congratulations ebbed, Ruth saw Tim, Charlie, and Mr. Jones standing at the side of the room. She pulled Jim by the hand and went over to them.

"Hey, Miss Sinclair, we helped solve the mystery," Tim whispered. "But we're not supposed to tell. War secrets, you know. Maybe we'll get a medal when the war's over."

Charlie beamed and nodded.

Ruth patted Tim's shoulder. "You probably saved my life, boys. Jim and I thank you with all our hearts."

She turned to Mr. Jones. He was dressed neatly in an old-fashioned suit. She held out her hand. "Thank you, Sir," was all she could say. She squeezed his hand tightly.

"Suzi was good to me. I look out for her friends and her place," he said with a slight bow. He glanced at Tim and Charlie. "They're my friends."

"We brought him here, Miss Sinclair. He doesn't know much God stuff, but we're teaching him. I told him about David and Goliath."

Charlie nodded.

"We're proud of you boys." Jim smiled at them and ruffled Tim's hair.

"Let's go." Jim directed Ruth toward the door.

They stepped out of the church and headed for the parking lot. Jim got in the car beside Ruth. "I'm taking you to dinner to celebrate, Miss Sinclair." He reached for her left hand. "Mm, that ring looks good on your finger. Too bad all our parents are out of town on business. Mine were thrilled when we called them. Mom was the one who suggested I use Grandma's ring." He paused. "But if you want a new one all your own, we can look tomorrow."

"No way! You're never getting this one off my finger, Jim Griffin."

Jim drummed his fingers on the steering wheel as he waited for a car to pass, then pulled out onto the road. "I have a question." He paused a moment. "You went through a terrible scare yesterday, then thought I was engaged to Carolyn. Yet when you came into the kitchen, you were so calm and at peace. What happened?"

Ruth stared out the window and smiled. "The Lord looked out for my life yesterday afternoon. I let go and trusted Him with my heart and my future, too." She looked over at him. "Remember Pastor Cameron's victory sermon the first Sunday you came to church last spring?"

"Hmm, so you noticed me way back then?" He nodded and grinned. "I was hoping you fell for me the day we met."

Ruth rolled her eyes at him. "When I thought you were engaged, I sat down on the steps and let God have control of my life. And I had peace." She smiled. "I like the phrase Pastor Cameron used—'C for victory.' That's where peace comes from—not from winning wars or getting our own way but from Christ's victory in our hearts."

Jim nodded and squeezed her hand.

He pulled into the restaurant parking lot. "Ready, Mrs. Griffin? I wanted to hear how it sounded."

"Mm, I like it."

He opened the door and took her hand. "Just want you to get used to it. That'll be your name for at least the next fifty years!"

JOAN CROSTON

Joan was born in Oregon, the setting of her first novel, *C for Victory*, but she currently lives in Missouri where she and her husband are restoring a 100-year-old farmhouse. They have two married daughters. "To me good Christian fiction is theology in action," Joan says. "In experiencing the lives of fictional characters, I live the Christian life the author portrays, and when I'm done I carry some of that Christian living away with me. That's the experience or message I would like to leave my readers."

Escape
on the Wind

Jane LaMunyon

This book is dedicated to my husband Jim, an aviation expert,
who never tired of answering my questions about planes and flying techniques.
It is also dedicated to three of my relatives whose names I found in Jerusalem's
Yad Vashem's records of those taken to Nazi concentration camps:
Elias van der Noot, 8–4–17 to 8–27–43, Auschwitz;
Hans Jack van der Noot, 9–28–42 to 8–27–43, Auschwitz;
and Louis van der Noot, 5–16–10 to 3–26–43, Sobibor.

Chapter 1

September 2, 1934

After Amanda's birthday dinner, Stanley, the servant, cleared away the crystal water goblets, then pushed a linen-covered cart to the table between Amanda and her father. Stanley removed the white linen to reveal a pile of brightly wrapped presents, then moved back to stand beside the door.

"Thank you, Stanley," said Amanda's mother. Her blue eyes sparkled in her round face as she cast a satisfied look at the dinner guests. The double circle of braids crowning her head glowed softly in the light from the chandelier.

With a dimpled grin, Amanda's sister Victoria said, "Open them! I can't bear the waiting!" Her two aunts nodded fondly in agreement.

Amanda opened her presents, thanking her family for the lovely items, some of which were clearly meant for her hope chest. The French linen tablecloth with Battenburg lace edging from Aunt Edith brought admiring sighs from the guests, but Amanda wondered if she'd ever have a use for it as she quietly folded it back into its box. Aunt Emma's gift was a dozen matching napkins.

Her father presented her with a leather-bound first edition of Stendhal's works. She gasped in pleasure, running her hands over the gilt letters of the top book *Lucien Leuven*. "Oh, Father, you remembered. Thank you!"

Her father nodded brusquely. "Hm. Yes. You always did favor those French writers."

Soon there was a pile of wrapping paper on the floor beside her chair, the boxes stacked neatly on the tray. "Thank you all," said Amanda. "I am—"

"Wait!" Delbert pushed his chair back and stood. He flashed a smile at the seated guests, then took Amanda's hand, drawing her to her feet. "I haven't presented my gift yet."

Amanda looked at him with some confusion. She glanced at her father, leaning back in his chair, looking smugly satisfied, then at her mother, who clasped her hands with anticipation.

"Amanda, we've grown up together," Delbert began. "Everyone here knows how I feel about you."

Amanda could feel her face coloring.

Delbert's brilliant dark eyes glittered as he continued. "On this auspicious

135

occasion, and before these beloved guests, I offer this, a token of my love and esteem." He pulled a small box from his jacket pocket and presented it to her.

She almost recoiled from it, a premonition shouting warnings in her head, but she held out her hand and he laid the box in her palm. *Let it be a locket,* she prayed silently as she slowly lifted the lid.

But it wasn't. A large marquise diamond, flanked by two smaller ones in a graceful setting, winked up at her. She stared at it in shock.

"Will you marry me, Amanda Chase? Say yes, and make me the happiest man in the world."

Taking a deep breath, her cheeks burning, she looked away. Her father didn't seemed surprised. The image of him and Delbert in deep discussion last week filled her mind. Now her family eagerly watched for her reply.

Delbert flashed a bright, confident smile.

She pushed back a flush of anger with a small laugh. Her aunt Emma smiled and wiped her eyes with a lace handkerchief. With iron control, Amanda said, "I'm speechless! Delbert, this is such a surprise; I don't know what to say."

She could almost hear the silent group saying, *Say yes; say yes.*

She closed the lid over the sparkling diamond. "I'm too overwhelmed to answer right now." She set the box on the table. "Thank you all, and please excuse me." With her head held high, she walked out of the room.

Her heels clicked on the parquet floor of the hallway as she fled. Mrs. Heathman, the cook, pushed the swinging kitchen door open. "Happy birthday, Miss!" she said.

Amanda glanced back, a tight smile hurting her face. "Thank you." Continuing on through the parlor, she made a quick decision not to go upstairs to her room and went out the front door.

The cool night air did little to dampen her hot anger. She stomped her way past the two cars parked out front, through the posts lighting the driveway, over the grass to the knoll. She took a few deep breaths to calm herself. Holding onto a low branch, she looked out over the lights of Boston below.

How could Delbert humiliate her? Sure, they'd been friends for the last two years, but that's all it was—friendship. They'd talked about marriage, and she'd explained that marriage and family weren't in her plans right now. He contended that *settling down* was what a woman must do—take care of home, family, and her man.

That's fine for Mother, Amanda thought. *But not for me. Not yet.* She sighed with regret, thinking of her mother's and aunts' looks of bright anticipation. To them there was no higher call than that of wife and mother. *But there must be something more,* thought Amanda. Some warm, even passionate, feelings. And there should be spiritual agreement. Delbert always shrugged when she brought up God, as though the topic wasn't important to him.

As she tiptoed through the wet grass to the stone bench, she heard the front door close and Delbert calling her. She glanced back to see him walking down the driveway behind the post lights. She felt her indignation rise in response to his approach.

It's time to take care of this, she thought. "I'm here!" she called.

Peering through the darkness, he loped across the grass toward her.

Knees pushed into the stone bench, hands gripping its back, she watched him approach. His long legs took the distance quickly. He looked perfect in his three-piece suit and tie, his dark hair neatly combed back.

"Sweet girl, are you all right?" He came around the bench to her side. She looked away.

"What?" he asked, his eyes clouding with concern.

"I'm fine, Delbert." She sat and slipped off her shoes, setting them beside her. He sat, too, the shoes between them.

He reached into his pocket and brought out the ring box again. "I may have made a mistake, Darling. Maybe you'd rather I asked you privately to marry me."

Leaning forward, he presented the box again. Putting his right arm along the bench back, he stroked her neck slowly. "Will you, Amanda? You know how much I care for you."

She stared into the bright luster of his eyes. "Delbert, you and I are too different to ever become one." She folded her hands in her lap, ignoring the box.

"I know your job is important to you, but my company is doing well, and I make more than enough money to support us." He continued to hold the box toward her. "You can go to church, but you'll be so busy with other things, you won't have time for much else."

"It's not going to church or my job, Delbert." She paused for a second, then asked, "What 'other things' would keep me busy?"

"Oh, the running of our home, our social engagements, and—you know—being my wife."

"You're asking me to give up everything to take on the job of making your life easy?"

"It's a big responsibility," he said.

"And what I do now isn't?"

He looked baffled. "Sure it is. I'm proud of your little newspaper stories. But someday you'll have to stop examining other people's lives and settle down to a real life of your own, you know—your own home and family."

She froze, her words coming out in icy chips. "I have a real life. And my work is more than 'little newspaper stories about other people's lives.'"

He lowered the box, resting it in his lap. "You want that more than a loving husband and home of your own?"

"Delbert, you're a good person, and you're doing well in your profession. But I don't feel any more for you than I would a good friend. I do know that

I couldn't love anyone enough to give up my beliefs and my life's work."

An expression of pained tolerance swept over his face. "I'll go to church with you, Sweetheart."

She expelled her breath in aggravated surprise. "You don't understand! Going to church isn't the same thing as being a Christian."

With a confused expression, he stared at her. "What do you mean?"

"I mean, it's more than walking in the church door, more than just *saying* you're a Christian. It's a whole new life; it's being born again."

"You're talking in riddles, my dear."

"No. I've told you before, and you've heard it when you went to church with me. It's believing that Jesus is the Son of God, that He was born of a virgin and died on the cross for your sin, that He ascended to heaven and sits at God's side. It means that you look for Him to come again as He said He would."

"Well, that's a lot to think about." He thrust the ring box back toward her. "Keep this, and think about our engagement."

She jumped up and slipped her shoes on. "We've never really communicated, have we, Delbert?" She walked away. There was nothing more to say.

He followed her back into the house. Her aunt, uncle, and two cousins were leaving. "Here are the lovebirds!" said Aunt Joan, reaching for her left hand. "Let me see the ring!"

Amanda pulled her hand back. "I'm not wearing it."

"Yet." Uncle Mark put his arm around her shoulder and winked at her. "He's a prize, Girl. Don't let him get away."

Amanda slipped her arm around her uncle's waist and held out her hand to her aunt. "Thanks for coming, all of you."

After all the guests had gone home, Amanda's father took her arm and said, "Come with me. I want to talk to you." He led her to the study. Victoria followed them, eyes wide and curious.

"Maybe Victoria should go on up to her room now," said her mother, with an appeal in her glance to her husband.

"No. Victoria is part of the family, and she'll learn something."

Still strong with the resolve to hang on to her career, and the feeling that she'd been right to refuse Delbert's proposal, Amanda closed the study door and turned to face her father.

She'd always liked this room, with its wall of books, the smell of leather, and the solidarity of the huge mahogany desk where her father worked with his gallery accounts. He stood beside it now, resting one hand on the edge. Her mother sat with her back erect in the leather chair beside the fireplace and folded her hands in her lap, waiting. Victoria leaned against the bookshelf, her slim legs crossed.

Her father stared at Amanda beneath heavy eyebrows. "I'm not going to beat around the bush with small talk. Tonight we celebrated your twenty-fourth birthday, and I want to know why you didn't accept the proposal from that decent young man."

Before Amanda could answer, her mother spoke, her words coming rapidly as if she could no longer hold them back. "I can't imagine what you're thinking! You're twenty-four years old! Twenty-four! And you're still a spinster. When I was your age, I'd been married for five years and had a child. Delbert's a good man with a successful business, which, as you know, in these times is a miracle. I know you like him. How could you turn him down? And in front of everyone!"

Amanda carefully took a deep breath to stay calm.

Victoria chuckled. "Spinster?" She wrapped a blond curl around her fingers, smiling at the odd idea.

"What your mother is trying to say," her father said, "is that we gave you the best education money could buy—how many girls study at the Sorbonne in Paris these days? You've traveled the world, had all the right social connections, and for what? Here you are, still single at an age when most young women are taking care of their own households and husbands."

Her mother nodded her head. "You don't visit your friends lately. They *are* married, and you don't have much in common with them anymore."

"My career. . ."

"Your what?" Her father glared at her. "Is that why you're so often late for dinner? Were you out making headlines for that rag? Were you scooping Walter Winchell on the Boston Ladies' Sewing Guild luncheon? You call that a career?"

Amanda answered with quiet firmness. "The *Boston Chronicle* isn't a 'rag.' It's a reputable newspaper."

Victoria's hands flew to her mouth to cover a smile, and Amanda hastily added, "Beating Walter Winchell to a story has never been my goal." Today she had covered the South Boston Women's Croquet tournament. That morning in the seedy part of town she took notes and talked to people for a feature story on the plight of the depression's abandoned children. But she wouldn't give her father the satisfaction of either laughing at her trivial croquet story or berating her for the danger of consorting with "undesirables."

"All right. So you don't want to be a better reporter than Winchell. That puts us back to my original question. Just what *do* you plan to do with your life?"

Her mother leaned forward in the chair, her blue eyes pleading with Amanda to agree with her. "Her goal is the same as any normal young woman. A home and family—eventually. Am I right?" To punctuate her point, she added, "After all, you're not getting any younger."

Amanda gazed down at the familiar scrolled pattern on the Turkish rug and girded her resolve. She looked up at them. "Mother, Dad, I've always done my best in what you've asked me to do. I went through school earning honors, and I was valedictorian at college graduation. Should all that knowledge go to waste while I plan menus and entertain the hoi polloi for the benefit of some man?" She cast an affectionate look to her mother. "You're a wonderful wife and mother, but I'm not you. I'm just starting my career, and it's important to me. I'm sorry if I'm a disappointment to you, but I can't give up my life to some man and never know what I could have done or been."

She looked her father right in his eyes and struggled to keep from trembling. "I must devote my life to improving this world in the best way I know how, by documenting and exposing society's goodness and evils. If I can make someone understand this world a little better and change a life because of it, then I will have been successful. That's my goal."

"Poppycock! Most people glance over headlines, find the comics and crossword puzzles, then wrap their garbage in the papers. The poor wretches sleeping on park benches cover themselves with it, and I hear that they even slip them inside their shoes to cover the holes. We're in a depression right now, and I don't know how that rag stays in business."

Amanda bit her lips together. This was as frustrating as the scene she'd had with Delbert. She hadn't communicated the inner flame, her passion for her career. They didn't understand.

"What you're going to do is wake up and do what's right. I won't support this hobby you're glorifying into a career. You resign and either marry Delbert or start seeing other men, with the intention of being a real woman and settling down."

Stunned, she stared at him. "I am a real woman, Father!"

His gaze never wavered. "We'll do all we can to help you. But if you don't take your responsibilities seriously, I'll be forced to take steps to persuade you to comply."

Her mother leaned forward, her elbows resting on the chair arm. Her face lighted up with joy. "Think about it, Amanda. We can have a gala engagement affair; we'll invite everyone who is anyone. It'll be the event of the season, and—"

"Oh, I do so adore parties," said Victoria, looking into a scene only she could see. "I can see the Chase sisters turn this town on its ear!" She frowned as Amanda moved her head slightly from side to side. "Oh, don't be so dreary. It'd be such fun."

Amanda kept her eyes locked with her father's. "What steps?"

"Face it, Girl. Your job is taking you nowhere. If you persist, you'll never find a man to take care of you; and you'll grow old, living at home. That would be detrimental to you and an embarrassment to us. I'd be a poor father to allow that to happen. There is no option. You must give up this notion of saving the world and face reality."

"Or?" Amanda's voice was so low, she wasn't sure her father heard her.

"Or I'll have to curtail your allowance and speak to your editor and resign for you. Then you'll take the proper responsibilities of a young woman."

She tried to read regret or hesitation in his eyes, but she could detect neither. His gaze hid any emotions he might be feeling.

She was no longer a child he could order to take a certain class in school or dictate who she could and couldn't visit. But she knew him well enough to know that approaching her editor was no idle threat. Cold fear clenched her stomach, but she resisted it with every ounce of energy she could muster, lifted her chin, and said, "I've planned my career, my life. I told Delbert I can't give up my plans for him or anybody." She broke her gaze with her father to look at her mother, who was staring at her with stunned disbelief. "I'm sorry," she said to both of them.

"I know this is hard for you to understand," said her father, "but I am doing what's best for you. I'll give you a week before I take action. Do you understand?" She nodded. "Good. You're a smart girl. I fully expect by next week you'll be back on course toward a full and happy life."

★ ★ ★

Later, she paced restlessly in her room. Although her father still didn't believe her, for the first time in her life she had defied him. It was scary, but she had to do it. She planned on being independent eventually, before the shadowy idea of marriage and family became a reality. In these modern times, lots of women had careers. She mentally tallied up her material assets: her savings account, her annuity, which she'd received from Grandpa Morganstern when she turned twenty-one, and her meager pay from the *Chronicle*.

She pushed the balcony window open and stepped out into the cool night air. Hugging her shoulders, she looked up. "Oh, God, what am I going to do? I feel a restless urge toward something; I don't know what." A breeze trembled through the oak tree, and after another minute she went back inside. They thought she couldn't take care of herself? She vowed to prove them wrong.

Chapter 2

Curley Cameron's eyes snapped open. The rain had quit. A drop of water snaked down the closed window as the predawn light glowed feebly into the barracks room. Curley pushed off the heavy cover, shivering as he crossed the room to the window. He slid it up and leaned out into the coolness with his hands braced on the sill.

Wildflowers bloomed nearby, and their fragrance surrounded him. The clouds were mostly gone, the wind was light, and he knew if he got high enough he could see for miles. "Hot dog!" he said to the new day, quickly dressing.

He stuffed his few belongings into his duffel bag and took a last look around before quietly closing the door behind him and tiptoeing past closed doors; most of the airmen were still asleep. In the latrine, he splashed icy water on his face, shaved quickly, and left for the mess hall and a cup of coffee.

He saluted to the officer of the day, who was also up early for his duties. Avoiding puddles of leftover rain, Curley scanned the horizon over the airstrip, and with long happy strides, walked faster. Flying weather at last! The reveille bugle pierced the air as he went inside the warm mess hall. Chow wasn't ready, but the cook gave him toast and jam with his coffee.

Back outside, he slipped the catch from the hangar door and pushed it sideways. It was still dark inside, but dawn light glowing behind him touched the propeller with a gentle gleam. "Hello, Sweetheart," he said, patting his DeHaviland Moth. "We're going up today!" He pushed all the hangar doors to the side, opening it up.

He circled the plane, checking for loose bolts, feeling for uneven wing surfaces, and looking for anything else that could cause an in-flight problem. When he finished, the sky was fully light, and he could hear guys moving around on the other side of the wall. He stuck his head outside to see two men pushing a P-26A out of a hangar down the line.

By 6:30 A.M. the hangar doors were all open but one, four planes had already taken off, and Curley had gotten assistance in pulling his Moth out onto the tarmac. He stowed his duffel bag in the back and fueled up, then pulled his clipboard out from under his seat and stood beside the struts, studying it.

He'd mapped out his route to California three days ago, before the rains slowed him down, and he had studied it every day, marking airfields he'd touch down in. Nevertheless, he checked the flight plan once more, memorizing the route.

His concentration was interrupted by the warmth of a soft body pressed to his back and smooth white arms circling his chest.

He lowered the clipboard to his side and turned. She held on so tightly he had to lift his left arm over her head. He grinned down at her. "Ah, Jenny! What brings you out so early?"

Her lips puckered into a lovely pout. "I think you're leaving without saying good-bye."

"Honey, you know I have business to take care of."

Her chocolate-colored eyes gazed at him wistfully. Then she stood on tiptoe and put her head on his shoulder and nuzzled his neck. "Stay one more day," she murmured.

He stepped back and took her face in his large hand. "It's time. I have to go."

Her eyes narrowed with sudden anger. "You think you can just toss me aside like an old shop rag?" She looked down her nose at him under half-closed eyes. "I have other fellas calling on me, you know."

"I know that, Sweet One. You're much too fine a girl for the likes of me." He rubbed her chin gently with his thumb.

She stared over his shoulder at the airplane. Not meeting his eyes, she said, almost to herself, "You won't be back." She turned her compelling eyes on him, and he had to force himself to pull his hand away from her soft cheek and step back.

He shook his head slowly. "Don't think about it. Turn around, walk away, and forget about me."

"But we. . .I. . ." She looked around in desperation as if searching for the answer to a confusing puzzle. "You can't just leave!"

He shook his head. "I go where the Army Air Corps sends me. That's the fact of it."

"But—"

He put his finger on her lips, not wanting to prolong their good-byes. Holding the clipboard at his chest between them, he gave her a light kiss on her cheek and said, "Good-bye, Jenny."

She stared at him for a moment, then raised her chin and defiantly informed him, "In two weeks—in two minutes, I'll have forgotten you, like this!" She snapped her fingers and walked away without a backward glance.

Curley watched her walk away, feeling admiration for the way she turned the situation around to seem as if she were leaving him instead. *Women!* he thought. They craved rose-covered cottages and forever-afters. He never met one who didn't either hint or downright talk openly about it. Why were they always in such a hurry to get themselves tied down?

He glanced at his flight map, then walked back to the hangar, thinking of how dependent women were, needing a man to complete their lives. *Bless them, though; they sure make life a lot more interesting,* he thought, smiling.

His thoughts were interrupted by a summons to the base commander's office.

He entered the colonel's office, saluted, and said, "Reporting as ordered, Sir." He stood at attention until the commanding officer said, "At ease, Captain." The colonel tapped the papers on his desk with his pencil. "Captain Cameron, I have orders here that you are to depart immediately and report to General Franklin in Washington."

"Sir?" Curley eyed the official envelope under the colonel's fingers. "I'm geared up and ready to report to Muroc Air Base."

The colonel handed him the sealed orders. "Report to the general at eleven-hundred hours."

"Yes, Sir." Curley took the envelope, saluted, and left the CO's office, wondering what this was all about. He'd been looking forward to going back to California where the only family he knew waited for him.

He pushed his plane back into the hangar. As he approached the CB-5 he'd fly to D.C., the mechanics and pilots he'd worked with wished him well.

The minute the wheels left the runway, as always he felt as though a weight holding him to the ground snapped free, leaving him to float on the air, climb the currents, and ride the sky. This was where he belonged. Everything below seemed unreal. This was reality. He soared into the heavens, his plane merely an extension of himself, and then dipped the left wing, heading in a northerly direction toward Washington, D.C.

★ ★ ★

Amanda drove herself to work Monday morning, with Delbert following. He'd come by to pick her up, but keeping her goal in mind, she had insisted on driving herself.

Her father's threat worried her. Would Mr. Mitchell fire her at her father's request? He certainly wouldn't want trouble from one of the most prestigious families in Boston. And her stories hadn't exactly been banner headlines. But she didn't get the plum assignments, either, and there was only so much she could do with the topics she covered.

Her hands gripped the steering wheel as she drove through neighborhoods that had once housed families filled with dreams and hopes. With the Great Depression, they faced the terrible loss of work, and few managed to keep their homes. Grass and weeds stood tall in the small yards in front of the row of forlorn-looking houses. Downtown, the employment office was besieged by a crowd, waiting for the doors to open. For every rare job offer, a hundred hungry people applied. She didn't notice until she arrived at the

Chronicle building that Delbert was no longer following her.

Inside, the smell of paper, ink, and pencils settled over her like a familiar cloak. Noise filled the room: the clatter of typewriters, ringing phones, and the hum of the fan which didn't efficiently rid the room of cigarette smoke. Her coworkers glanced up from their work and smiled as she passed.

She stood over her desk, checking for messages. She was relieved to see a note from Mr. Mitchell, asking her to come to his office as soon as she arrived. She wanted to see him right away, too.

She tucked her croquet tournament and abandoned children's stories under her arm and made her way through the desks to the glassed-in corner office. Behind his desk, Titus Mitchell leaned forward, clutching the telephone in one hand. With the phone's earpiece in his other hand, he gestured her to come inside.

She paused inside the door, but he motioned her to sit; and she perched on the edge of the chair, her stories on her lap. Mitchell paced behind his desk with restless energy, still connected to the phone. In his dynamic presence, Amanda felt her resolve shrinking.

He finally hung up the phone and smiled at her. Glancing at the papers in her lap, he said, "Croquet story?"

"Yes. And a feature on the plight of homeless waifs."

He grimaced. "Too depressing. I don't—"

"There's a group of people trying to help. This is an upbeat story, with hope."

"Well, lemme see it, and I'll let you know." He held out his hand, and she placed her stories in it. He'd barely glanced at the top page when Eileen, his secretary, opened the door.

"The battle between hired goons filling strikers' jobs in Pittsburgh is getting bloody. Details are starting to come through on the ticker tape," she said.

"I'll be right out." He looked at Amanda and said, "I want you to interview Edith Barnett about the Women's Works Program."

"Yes, Sir."

"And see what you can find out about the Boston Relief Committee's plan to distribute food to the poor."

"We did a story on BRC last week."

He shrugged. "Then find a new angle."

"Mr. Mitchell, I . . ." Amanda's fingers tensed in her lap, and she chided herself for tending to stammer.

Mitchell, now standing at the door, glanced at the activity in the newsroom, then turned his gray eyes on her. "Yes?"

She sat straighter in her chair, gathering her courage. "I'd like to do a big story. Something that will be different from anything the *Chronicle* has ever done."

"And I assume you have that big story figured out?"

"As a matter of fact, yes," she said. "Many papers, even ours, have run stories about Germany's prosperity and growth since they elected Adolf Hitler. Clean streets; happy people, all with jobs; and order from the chaos they used to have."

"Yes, so? That's not news."

She leaned forward. "It's not true." She saw that he was going to argue, so she quickly added, "Not all of it."

He hardened his mouth around the word, "Propaganda?" He stepped closer to her. "We don't print propaganda!"

"No, of course not," she agreed. "I think we just don't have the complete story."

"And you, I suppose, can get this complete story?" He looked at her as one would at a child who'd just said she'd had breakfast with President Roosevelt.

With quiet but firm resolution, she said, "My mother's sister and family live in a small town near Berlin. They're Jewish, and from their letters I know it's not all peaches and cream there. I intend to bring back the real story."

"Girlie, you're good at what you do. Stick to fashion and society news. If there are sinister happenings in Germany, it'll get back to us. Besides, if what you say is true, it could be risky."

"I know there's a story there, and I can cover it, because I have sources the correspondents there don't have. I'll write a story that will touch our readers' hearts."

He craned his neck to see if the Teletype story had started coming. "No Germany trip. You don't even have an expense account. You think I'd send you on a wild goose chase halfway across the world?" He turned and shook his head in disbelief.

"I'll cover the expenses myself, and when I bring you my story, I want a byline and better assignments."

He laughed. "Amanda girl, you just want a vacation."

She stood as a crowd gathered around the ticker-tape machine. He left to get the tape as it came ticking out and didn't look back at her.

Amanda stomped back to her desk. He'd laughed at her! This was the last straw. She found a paper sack in the supply closet and began dumping her personal belongings from her desk. After several phone attempts, she found a boat going to Europe in two days. She'd have to share a cabin, but that was fine with her. She typed a letter to her aunt Esther to tell her she was coming and a note to Mr. Mitchell.

She went home to pack, vowing to bring back a story that would knock the socks off Mr. Titus Mitchell, make people think, and earn her a headline and a place on his reporting staff. There were respected women journalists in this world. It was time for the *Boston Chronicle* to enter the twentieth century.

As she drove up the curving driveway at home, she braced herself for the scene that would follow when she told her mother and father her plans.

★ ★ ★

Curley touched down at the airfield near Washington at 10:15 A.M. and taxied to a parking area as directed by the ground crew. He shut down the engine, grabbed his duffel bag, and climbed out onto the tarmac. The flight-line sergeant asked, "Any problems with this ship we need to look after?"

"No. No problems. She's a good little plane."

A soldier drove up in a pickup truck, leaped out, and saluted. Curley tossed his duffel bag in the back and they drove to the flight operations building, where Curley logged in, then to the headquarters building.

In the latrine, he took off his flight suit, put on his uniform, and combed his hair. A quick look in the mirror told him he was presentable.

In the general's anteroom, he waited on a stiff wooden chair. Finally, the secretary announced that General Franklin would see him. Curley took a deep breath and marched into the general's office. He saluted and said, "James Lee Cameron reporting as ordered, Sir."

In his early forties, General Franklin had close-cropped hair with a touch of gray at the temples, and a thick mustache covered his upper lip. Curley stood, legs spaced apart, hands behind his back, watching the general scrutinize him with the eye of a man sizing up a new team player. "Captain," he said, "drag up a chair and make yourself comfortable. How about a cup of coffee?"

"Thank you, Sir."

General Franklin touched a button, and before Curley got the chair pulled toward the large desk, his secretary rushed in, then out again to fetch the coffee.

The general settled back in his chair. "Captain, I have a mission that requires a special man. You're one of our best pilots; you know as much about the planes as the mechanics, and you've shown yourself to be, shall we say, adventuresome. I've followed your career and feel you're the man for the job. Are you interested? Before you answer, you should know that if you decline it won't be held against you."

Curley took a quick breath, curious about the assignment, then answered, "Yes, Sir. I'm interested."

"Good. Now here's the plan: Our English friends tell us the Germans are starting to rearm, in violation of the Treaty of Versailles, and are building their air force back up." The general leaned forward and said, "I've made arrangements with the RAF. Your mission, in an unofficial capacity, will be to travel into Germany and find out what you can. Bring back facts and figures. Report to no one but me when you return.

"While in England you will study German terrain and politics. Also, an instructor will teach you phrases and as much German language as you can absorb in ten days. Your unofficial duties will be as a civilian delivering a Vega

147

to Holland. You've been checked out on the 247. It's been equipped with extra gas tanks and fuel diverters. You'll be on the crew taking it to England tomorrow afternoon. Any questions?"

Besides the thrill of flying the big new 247, Curley had lots of questions. For one thing, he knew that a military man out of uniform and in civilian clothes sent into another country could be shot as a spy. But then, Germany was not an enemy. He asked, "What's my time period for this surveillance?"

"Take as long as you need, within reason. I expect you to use some of that ingenuity you displayed while you were a cadet."

By the glint of amusement in the general's eyes, Curley knew he meant the weekend air shows he participated in every chance he got. He nodded. "Yes, Sir."

That afternoon he visited the Post Exchange and bought slacks, a shirt, a jacket, and a suitcase to put them in. The next afternoon he stowed his duffel bag full of military clothes in the base locker. Wearing his flight suit, he carried his new suitcase filled with civilian clothes onto the big 247.

Chapter 3

Perched on the edge of her bed, Amanda frowned over her open suitcase, stuffed with so many clothes the lid wouldn't close. Victoria sat cross-legged, resting her back against the headboard, her white batiste night-gown stretched over her knees. The turmoil that had followed Amanda's announcement of her trip to Germany hadn't fazed Victoria; she was elated over Amanda's adventure.

Amanda, however, swallowed hard, bravely choosing clothes for the trip, while her heart was in chaos. She grieved at the rift between her and her father, but she felt a strong need to prove she was a person in her own right.

Victoria picked up a peach-colored sweater from a pile beside the suitcase. "I can see you strolling the deck, looking out over the ocean. A handsome man comes up." She caressed the soft wool with a faraway, dreamy look. "You shiver slightly, he whips off his jacket and puts it across your shoulders. You. . ."

Amanda rolled her eyes. "There's a full moon, a zillion stars, and the man looks like Clark Gable. Which movie did you see that in?"

Victoria dropped the sweater on the bed "No, silly, it's Delbert! He's as handsome as Gable!" She leaned forward and looked into Amanda's face. "Just think of it—this could be your honeymoon trip!" She sat back, grinning.

Amanda solemnly studied the clothes stacked in the suitcase. She slipped her hand between two skirts and carefully pulled one out. "The only men paying any attention to me will be the porter carrying these suitcases and the dining room waiter," she said, balancing the skirt on the discard pile.

Victoria expelled a long sigh and clasped her hands behind her head, lifting her hair. Blond curls bounced beside her sparkling eyes. "Delbert can put his arm around me anytime!"

"Victoria!"

"What? I'm sixteen, and I've been kissed. Lots of times."

Amanda paused with her hand on the suitcase. "Oh? When?"

Victoria looked at the ceiling and pursed her lips, as if trying to remember all of them. Amanda eyed her suspiciously, as the door opened and their mother came in, a worried expression chiseling a vertical line between her eyebrows.

Amanda's throat tightened at her mother's pained expression. Holding in her churning emotions, she turned and shut the suitcase with a click of finality.

"Amanda," her mother began. "Please. . ."

"Mom, it's all right." Leaning over the closed suitcase, she bit her upper lip to keep control. If she explained once more, would her mother understand? She touched her mother's shoulder and said, "Please believe me, Mom. This is something I have to do."

Her mother's eyes misted over. "But it's so sudden, and your father. . ."

"I know," Amanda said softly. "Dad doesn't understand; but I'll be fine. Really. I'll be with Aunt Esther and Uncle Jacob, and I'll write as soon as the ship docks in London."

Her mother still looked worried, but Amanda knew that she was looking forward to hearing firsthand news of her family.

Although her mother had left the Jewish faith when she married Amanda's father, the ties between the two families had remained strong through the years, and they had visited back and forth, the children spending summers together with one family or another. In fact, it was during one of those summers that Amanda's nanny, Miss Whitney, had taken Amanda and her cousin Martha with her to church, and both girls had accepted Christ as their Savior. Amanda smiled, remembering, and the tiny lines that puckered her mother's forehead disappeared. "Well," her mother said, "so long as you're with your aunt and uncle, I suppose you'll be all right."

★ ★ ★

The next morning Amanda, her mother, and sister rode to the pier in a taxi. Her father, unwilling to condone any part of her crazy notion, had said his good-byes at the front door. He'd given Amanda a stiff hug and slipped two fifty-dollar bills into her hand.

On board the ship, Victoria eyed each of the passengers, looking for celebrities; and quite a few male heads turned toward her youthful attractiveness.

At Amanda's cabin, they found suitcases on one bed and a cosmetic bag open with a turquoise scarf lying beside it on the dresser. Her mother agreed the cabin was "nice" but insisted that Amanda should have it to herself. "And you didn't bring enough clothes," she added.

"Mother, I have to carry both suitcases. What would I do with a trunk?"

"There are ways. Porters are everywhere."

Amanda put her arm across her mother's shoulders. "Look at it this way. At least Uncle Jacob won't think I'm moving in."

Her mother's eyes grew teary. Amanda hugged her and said, "I'll be all right, Mom. Really."

"I hope so," her mother said, dabbing at her eyes as she looked at Amanda sadly.

Victoria took Amanda's hand. "It's not too late for me to come along." Before Amanda could say anything, she continued, "I know I don't have clothes, but we could go shopping in London. Wouldn't that be a lark?"

Her mother smiled weakly and took Victoria's hand. "You're coming home with me. I'm not letting both my girls go away at once."

Amanda walked them to the ramp, and they said their last good-byes. A few minutes later the ship moved away from the shore. Amanda had been on many departing ships, but this time it seemed as though the ship sliding away from the shore was like fate, pulling her away from her family toward a new destiny. The shouts of the crowd faded away as they receded with the harbor, until her mother and sister were no longer distinguishable.

Swept along in the swarm of exhilarated passengers leaving the rail, she left them at the hallway to her cabin, while they headed for a party in the ballroom. The hallway was deserted except for a young mother holding the hand of a toddling little boy. They nodded and Amanda continued on.

Inside her cabin, the feeling of unreality was underscored by the ship's gentle swaying. Amanda sat on her bed, absorbing the almost monastic solitude. After a moment she reached inside her carryall bag for her notebook and pen. She'd really done it; she had asserted her independence and was bound for Germany.

She slowly rotated the top of the pen between her teeth, lost in thought. Her bravado had carried her through the past two days, strengthening her to stand up to her father's disapproval, disarm her mother's worry, and laugh off her sister's fantasies. Thoughts bombarded her in a crazy mixture of excitement and nervousness. She had to succeed. She couldn't go back without her "big story."

She had no intention of failing. This was her most important assignment, even if she had delegated herself; and she'd write the best story of her career.

She opened her notebook and wrote in bold letters at the top of the page: "GERMANY, THE REAL STORY," then underneath, "by Amanda Chase."

A few lines lower she wrote: "HITLER—LIBERATOR OR TYRANT?" Too strong. She had no proof of the vague rumors she'd heard. Besides, reports touted him for miraculously bringing order and justice to the chaotic German politics and economy.

She crossed that headline out, and wrote "GERMANY, A MODERN-DAY UTOPIA" and a subtitle, "Or Does a Secret Shame Mar the Image?" She smiled. For now, that would do. She imagined a front-page headline, with inches and inches of story and a photograph beneath her byline.

She hung up her clothes in the small closet and folded her underwear in the dresser. Her Bible went on the nightstand. Slipping her book, *Guide to Germany,* in her purse, she left. It was time to meet people and find her roommate. There must be Germans on board, and she intended to meet and interview them.

★ ★ ★

After seeing his wife and two daughters off, Amanda's father sat in his drawing room, drumming his fingers on the desk, thinking. Amanda had always been a dutiful, obedient daughter. Perhaps the philosophers were right—it wasn't a good idea to educate a girl too much. But she was bright, and he would have been wasteful to restrain her curious mind from exploring all the knowledge she craved.

He moved the inkwell a fraction of an inch, wondering if he should have introduced her to more young men; but he'd been proud when she devoured the business details of the galleries. If she'd been a son, she'd have followed in his footsteps and be running one of them now.

But she was a girl and, therefore, had led a sheltered life. She'd always traveled with the family and had no idea how dangerous traveling alone could be for a woman. He paced the room, grinding his teeth. *Should have forbidden the impetuous girl to go,* he thought. But he'd tried that, and she lifted her chin in defiance, stating she was free, grown-up, and was going.

He stared out the French doors. Reaching a decision, he strode back to his desk and picked up the phone.

★ ★ ★

Curley and the crew relaxed as the powerful Boeing 247 flew high over the Atlantic Ocean toward England. After the sun set behind them, the blackness was punctuated by stars above and a few weak lights from an occasional boat below.

Motioning to Jim Blake, his copilot, to take over, Curley pulled off his headphones and worked his way to the rear of the plane. He pulled a Coke from the ice cooler, popped off the cap, and took a long swallow. He glanced at his watch: 6:40 P.M. East Coast time. Smith, the other crew member, was stretched out across two of the airplane's seats, asleep.

Curley had been in the cockpit for hours and had no desire for more sitting, so he braced his arm above one of the windows and looked out. These same stars shone over California, where he'd be right now if his orders hadn't taken him east instead.

It had been almost two years since he'd been back West. He'd looked forward to surprising Johnny and Meredith when he flew his Moth onto their airstrip. But he'd have to wait.

A wispy cloud passed the window, disappearing like smoke. He dropped the empty Coke bottle into the box beside the ice chest and went to the other side to look out. Another gauzy cloud flew past, and he had to catch hold of the seat back to maintain his balance as the plane began to climb.

He made his way forward and got into his seat. Blake glanced at him. They were climbing through clouds, and the turbulence jabbed at the plane, rocking them in their seats. Curley motioned to Blake to continue taking her up over the problem, while he grabbed the swaying flight chart off its peg and checked the instruments. They were 522 miles east of Saint John's in Newfoundland.

The big plane bounced its way up, as if ascending stairs. For ten minutes both pilots fought to hold it steady. Suddenly a vicious blast of wind shoved them sideways, and the right wing dipped, dangerously threatening to send them into a stall.

"We can't climb out! Clouds too high," Curley yelled. "Let's take her down and see if it's better underneath."

They pushed the controls slowly forward, carefully maneuvering the plane down through the turbulence.

"Trouble on engine one," called Blake. Curley looked to his left. Through ice particles flying past, he saw small flames flickering behind the propellers.

"Hold on, baby," he murmured, and eased up on the throttles, enough to let the plane glide slightly, yet enough to maintain control. Smith had entered the cockpit and stood, bracing his hands on the ceiling, watching the struggle against the buffeting winds.

According to the altimeter, they were six hundred feet above water. "We'd better bottom out under this storm soon or we'll be in the drink," shouted Smith. With one last jolt as if they'd been spit out, they emerged from the cloud.

They turned southward, staying beneath the cloud, until they found its edge and rose again to higher altitude. Following their radio beacon, they were soon back on course.

All three sighed in relief and began checking the damage, especially to engine number one. Smith went to the rear, while Blake and Curley checked electrical and pressure gauges.

"Manifold pressure is down," said Curley. Blake nodded. "We can't land and fix her," he added, "so we'd better start lightening our load."

"There's not much cargo back there, Sir," said Blake, "but we can toss out seats and fixtures."

"You and Smith get on it, and I'll keep her steady."

"Yes, Sir." Jim Blake disengaged himself from his seat and left the cockpit.

Curley shut the traitorous engine down and feathered the propeller to keep the plane on a steady course with the one remaining engine. With over a thousand miles to go, even if they lightened the load, the chances of setting down in England were small. He considered turning back, but the chances of running into the storm behind them checked him.

He felt the surge of lightness as the crewmen reduced the load. When Blake and Smith returned he said, "One engine is damaged. The plane won't make it, not unless we lighten her load even more. Only two people are necessary to fly this baby, so as soon as we see a ship, one of us is going to book passage."

"I'm the heaviest," said Smith. "I volunteer."

Curley shook his head. "We're all checked out to fly her, so what we're going to do is draw straws to see who takes a cruise."

Blake pulled out three matches, broke one, and turned aside, arranging them in his fist. Smith pulled the first, a whole match, then Curley drew the short one. "But, Sir. . ."

"That's the deal, and there's nothing to say," said Curley. "Now, when you get to Sedley Field, report what happened; and tell them I'll report in as soon as possible. Now let's hope the first ship we come across is a seaworthy vessel heading east."

Handing the controls to Smith, he went aft to secure his suitcase near the cargo door and strapped on a parachute. He scanned the black water below, suddenly engulfed in the horrible image of water closing around him, crushing him. These disturbing anxieties surfaced occasionally, since the day his father's foreman had broken the news of his father's death in a collapsed Arizona cave. Curley was nine at the time. He shook off the gruesome vision, renewing his vow to avoid caves and dark underground chambers. Compared to that, jumping into the darkness below would be a breeze.

★ ★ ★

On deck, Amanda clutched the railing and hunched her shoulders against the cold wind. Ilsa, her redheaded Norwegian roommate, stood beside her. Ilsa had been curious about Amanda's ubiquitous notebook and pencil, and when she found out Amanda was a reporter, she appointed herself as her assistant. The same age as Victoria, Ilsa proved to be a cheerful companion.

"If my uncle Eric were here, he'd say the wind is charged with the feel of a coming storm," said Ilsa.

"It's whipping up the water." The slap of waves against the side of the boat almost drowned out Amanda's reply. In the four days they'd been collaborating, they had investigated the ship, its operation and crew, and some passengers.

"I followed those two big fellas to the lounge this morning. They spent a lot of time in there. I think they're gangsters."

Amanda moved her hands away from the warm spot they'd made on the railing, then moved them back. "We could interview them and ask them."

"But, they wouldn't tell us! I think we should. . ."

". . .give those two a wide berth," said Amanda. "I'm more interested in interviewing the Mexican acrobats who are going to entertain us tonight."

"Remember, you said I could come with you."

"Right. Now let's get back to our room and go over our list of questions."

That night, after the acrobats finished their show and two encores, Amanda and Ilsa interviewed them with the handsome purser there to translate. The father of the talented family spoke some English, giving Amanda good quotes for a story.

While she was asking the age of the youngest girl, an ensign rushed in and urgently tapped the purser on the shoulder, telling him the captain wanted him right away.

Sniffing a story, Amanda quickly thanked the Escobar family and followed the purser to the bridge. Captain McNally and several of his crew held receivers to their ears, listening with great concentration. Amanda's eyes darted from one to the other, trying to figure out whether another ship was in trouble, or if dire world news was coming over the radio waves.

"We hear you, N-C-niner-five-five. Go ahead," the captain spoke into the ship-to-ship communications system.

Ilsa tiptoed to the purser and put a light hand on his shoulder. "What's happening?" she asked.

He shook his head and lifted his shoulders, a bewildered look on his face.

"Cut the engines," barked the captain, squinting out into the darkness. "All hands on deck. And spread out."

Amanda stepped back to let them by, then she followed. As soon as they stepped outside, they heard the drone of an approaching airplane.

Chapter 4

Curley communicated to the ship's captain that they'd be overhead shortly. When they approached the ship, Smith said, "Good luck, Sir, and don't get wet."

Curley grinned and patted the suitcase tied to his parachute harness. "Hey, in my barnstorming days I could jump from a thousand feet and land on a nickel."

Smith opened the passenger door. The lights of the ship came closer, and Curley shouted, "See you at Sedley." He pushed himself into the night air and relished the brief silence.

"One thousand. . .two thousand. . .three thousand. . .*pull!*" His right arm reached across his chest, found the rip cord, and yanked. He felt the jerk and then the bobbling motion of the chute opening. He looked up in satisfaction at the white canopy overhead. Below, a ring of lights glowed on a cleared area near the ship's stern, and he settled into his harness, preparing for landing.

★ ★ ★

Sensing a good story, Amanda raced down to her cabin and snatched up her camera and flashbulbs. She was back on deck in time to see four crewmen setting up a fifteen-foot circle of lights on the promenade deckhouse roof. A crowd had gathered, murmuring baffled comments as they watched the sailors.

Amanda spotted Ilsa on the roof, waving at her and tugging on the purser's sleeves. He gestured to the men at the bottom of the steps holding back the crowd, and they let Amanda by.

She snapped pictures of crewmen standing around the lighted area looking up. A large plane roared overhead, and in a few seconds a chutist drifted toward them, his parachute a white dot in the dark sky. She focused on the man floating down. But he was still only a white dot in her lens.

"I hope he doesn't land in the water!" cried Ilsa.

"If he's good, and if the wind is right, he'll land right here," said the purser, quickly looking away from Ilsa's shining eyes.

Amanda hoped this man was as skilled as some of the experts she'd seen at air shows. She watched, fascinated, as the man skillfully maneuvered directly over the lighted circle. She snapped his picture. He came closer. She popped a bulb in the flash in time to snap his feet hitting the deck. She shot another as his parachute drifted down around him, and he quickly gathered it up. The crowd on the deck below applauded.

Amanda's finger froze on the shutter release. She lowered the camera to get a better look. Curley Cameron! It was really him! She pulled her gaze away, aware that she was gawking. With trembling fingers, she picked up the spent flashbulbs at her feet.

The crew had gathered around Curley, congratulating him as he loosed himself from the parachute harness. Ilsa pulled herself away from the purser and whispered to Amanda, "Oooh, would you look at him?!"

Amanda did look. She blushed, remembering back almost seven years. She had been seventeen. Her father had taken her to an air show near New York, where Curley Cameron was billed as "Curley the Kid—the young daredevil from the Wild West." He'd flown his plane in the most outrageous loops and madcap upside-down tricks, making her almost swoon with fright that he might crash, but afraid to tear her eyes away.

After the show, at a reception in her father's country club, she was introduced to him. He charmed her so thoroughly that later she haggled with a girl who'd bought his picture from a hawker and had brought it to the reception; Amanda finally persuaded her to trade the picture for Amanda's beaded purse. After that, she saved newspaper articles about him and pinned them up in her dormitory room when she returned to school in Paris a month later.

That had been so long ago, a silly schoolgirl crush. She thought she'd forgotten the appealing young man with the dimpled smile. Apparently she hadn't. She gazed at him for a moment, noticing that the years had been good to him; he looked more handsome and rugged than the eighteen-year-old she remembered.

He still had a friendly face with eyes that seemed to have a perpetual teasing light in them. His dark red hair was combed back and trimmed neatly over his ears. As if drawn by a magnet, his eyes looked directly at her. She could feel a pulse throbbing in her neck, and she raised a hand to her throat as if to still it. Then he looked away and the moment passed.

"Oh, Amanda! He looked right at me!" Ilsa grabbed Amanda's sleeve. "Come on! Let's get closer."

Amanda dropped the spent bulbs into a sack in her camera bag. He hadn't recognized her. *Of course, why should he?* she asked herself. But still, an odd twinge of disappointment nudged her. She shook it off, coming back to reality.

"Amanda!" Ilsa's urgent tugging amused Amanda, reminding her of Victoria's methods of coercion. "This is a scoop! A big story," she added. "Come on!"

Amanda snapped her camera bag shut and followed Ilsa through the shipmen surrounding Curley. He had taken off his parachute and knelt as he packed it neatly together. As there was nothing more for the crew to do, they drifted away, back to their work. The captain, purser, and an engineer remained, talking with Curley, their backs to Amanda and Ilsa.

Ilsa tapped the purser on his shoulder. "Where's he from?" she whispered.

"Looks American," he said.

". . .and I'll debark at your first port. . ." Curley's gaze slid past the captain to Ilsa, then Amanda. He stood up, the smile in his eyes revealing his delight at seeing them. "And what part of the crew are these lovely ladies?"

The captain stood back and nodded at Amanda. "This is Miss Amanda Chase, passenger and reporter." He nodded at Ilsa. "And this is Miss Ilsa Johnson, passenger and ambassador of cheer."

"Pleased to meet you both," he said, dipping his head slightly.

Amanda's jaw dropped in surprise for a second, before she could catch her breath. He was taller than she'd remembered, at least six-foot-three, somehow more athletic-looking, with wide shoulders looking as hard as granite beneath his flight suit.

The captain gestured with his hand to Curley. "And I'd like to introduce you to Curley Cameron, our newest passenger."

Ilsa eagerly reached out her hand, but instead of a formal handshake, Curley gave it a gentle squeeze. He glanced at Amanda for a second, then gave Ilsa a smile that made her grin and lift her shoulders in a childlike gesture of delight.

"No need to stand out here in the cold," said the captain, leading them toward the steps. Amanda clutched her sweater closer, realizing that the night wind had become chilly.

She couldn't think of a good reason to follow them, but she smelled a story too good to pass up. A few of the passengers who had lingered congratulated Curley as they walked toward the cabin-class promenade. One woman thanked the captain for the splendid show and asked why he hadn't announced it the day before so more passengers could enjoy it. Curley grinned and said he was glad she'd enjoyed it. As they walked on, he winked at Amanda and Ilsa, as though they shared a private joke.

Amanda boldly met his eyes, denying to herself the feeling that the temperature had just gone up ten degrees. She looked away, mentally concentrating on a headline: *The Man Who Dropped from the Sky*. Yes, that might do.

The ship shuddered as its great gears were engaged, moving forward again through the sea toward its first stop in France. Clutching the camera bag strap, Amanda braced her feet to steady herself. But there seemed no way to steady her mixed emotions.

Amanda and Ilsa stopped at the corridor to their cabin, and the men paused to wish them a good night.

"Mr. Cameron, I'd like to talk with you about your flying and parachuting adventures, if I may," said Amanda.

"It would be my pleasure," he answered.

They made arrangements to meet for breakfast the next morning before her ten o'clock interview with a baroness.

In the hallway back to their room, Ilsa danced in front of Amanda, skipping backward. "Let's go to the lounge. I'm too wound up to turn in!" she squeaked.

"You go on ahead. I have to plan my interview with the redoubtable Mr. Cameron."

"Plan? Don't be silly! Just ask whatever comes into your head."

"Goodness, no! I have to think of all the possible directions the interview could go and be prepared."

"Well, if you must," said Ilsa with her hands on her hips and shaking her head. "Go ahead, but at least come when you're through. I'll save a place for you."

Amanda sighed. "I might, but don't get your hopes up." Before Ilsa rounded the corner behind her, Amanda had pulled out her notepad and was scribbling: *What were you doing up there? Why did you parachute out? Did you have to? Why in the middle of the Atlantic Ocean? Was the plane in trouble?* By the time she got back to her room, she already had half a dozen questions.

She sat, looking out the porthole to the silver-lined clouds, reminding herself that she was grown-up now. After all these years, the great Curley Cameron held no more appeal. Besides, he had obviously changed. That thought took her in the dangerous direction of his more manly, stronger appearance that made him infinitely more handsome and desirable than ever. *Headline, headline,* she told herself. *Airline Passenger Prefers Ocean Liner Luxury.* Too long. She couldn't concentrate.

★ ★ ★

Curley settled himself in the small cabin on a lower deck and stowed his flight suit in the bottom of his suitcase. What a day! He'd have to write to Johnny and Meredith to tell them that their prayers were working. They never failed to mention they were praying for him. *Well,* he thought, *this was one time I really needed it. If the ship hadn't been right in our path, and if the storm had covered more area than we'd thought, or if—*

He shook his head free of the negative thoughts and looked around the cabin. One room with a bunk, a desk and chair, a small closet with a dresser inside it, and a rest room just big enough to turn around in. He wouldn't spend much time in here anyway, because on the other side of the door was one great big ship to explore. The purser had given him a chart of the accommodations.

He set his suitcase inside the closet, then picked up the chart and went out to find if there was somewhere to get a bite to eat at ten o'clock. He found a small bar on B deck, where passengers in "lesser accommodations" gathered to socialize.

He ordered a roast beef sandwich and a Coke and sat on a stool watching a young couple swaying together on the small dance floor. A plaintive song tinkled from the player piano in the corner. *This is probably their honeymoon voyage,* he thought.

He took a swig of Coke and narrowed his eyes, thinking. He'd have to get out of the interview with that reporter girl. The expression in her eyes when he looked up from his parachute startled him. He'd felt the strangest glimmer of recognition, something familiar about her he couldn't place. But that couldn't be. He'd never have forgotten a girl like her. But there was something, and it bothered him.

Too bad she was a reporter. A journalist was like a dog after a bone going for an interview. If she was reporting the story for some shipboard chronicle, it would be harmless, but if the story were to somehow get into the *real* newspapers, it could mean trouble for his mission. Since he couldn't dodge her forever, maybe he could invent some boring story that wouldn't capture her interest.

The piano stopped playing, and the young husband sauntered over to start a new tune. As Curley idly watched, he overheard a man speculating with the bartender why a man would parachute onto the ship. He had to reconsider letting the girl interview him, he realized; it would be too difficult to make his story boring.

★ ★ ★

Though she was tempted, Amanda decided that bringing Ilsa to her interview with Curley would be cowardly. He couldn't know that she'd idolized him, even if he did remember her. So, arriving alone at the twelve-foot-high double doors of the fashionable cabin-class dining saloon, she asked the steward to escort her to Curley's table. The aromas of coffee, freshly baked rolls, and eggs floated around Amanda, reminding her she was very hungry.

Curley held the chair for her, then sat across from her. "I'm starving. How about interviewing after we eat?"

His smile disarmed her nervousness, and she set her notebook and purse aside. "I wouldn't want to have to write the obituary of a man who starved to death giving an interview."

"Good." Curley glanced up into her eyes, entranced by the mixed shades of amber and green ringed by black lashes and felt another strange glimmer of recognition. Something in her manner was vaguely disturbing. *Why is she looking at me like that?*

The waiter poured coffee for them and took their order. She asked him about his work, and he told her about his love of flying. She told him about newspaper reporting.

He asked her where she was going, and she told him of her aunt and uncle in Eisenburg. She glanced at the tables nearby to be sure no one was eavesdropping. "Mr. Hitler is getting so much good publicity these days; it makes one wonder how much of it is true." She lowered her voice and leaned forward. "I have sources that indicate otherwise."

He leaned forward and matched her soft voice. "Sounds like a daring adventure!"

Amanda sat up stiffly, feeling she might have revealed too much. "Oh, no. I've gone all over to get a story—even some very scary places." She sipped her coffee to capture her composure and asked, "So, what's your business in Europe?"

"Are we officially starting the interview?" he asked.

"Might as well." She pulled a pencil from her purse and picked up her tablet. Flipping the cover to her page of questions, she read the first one: "What is your full name?"

"Curley Cameron, at your service, Ma'am."

She paused and looked up at him. "Is Curley the name on your birth certificate?"

"No, but I've been called Curley as long as I can remember, and it fits me better than the other, more proper names."

"Well, it'll do, I guess. So, Mr. Cameron. . ."

"Curley."

"So, Curley, where were you headed when you found yourself directly over this ocean liner?"

His eyes caught and held hers, which she found vaguely disturbing. "You're asking which direction I was going?"

"Yes."

"To Europe, same as you. How long have your aunt and uncle lived in Eisenburg?"

"I'm the one doing the interviewing."

He cocked his eyebrows and shrugged his shoulders. "Okeydokey."

His reaction amused her. "Aunt Esther and Uncle Jacob have been in Eisenburg for eight years while they've been operating my father's art gallery. Were you one of the flight crew on that plane?"

"In a manner of speaking."

"Please elaborate." She looked at him, waiting for his answer.

"Look," he said, "maybe I want to know where my story and picture are going to appear. Who do you work for?"

She nodded. "A fair question. I work for the *Boston Chronicle*. That's where I'll send the story."

"Hmm." His dark eyebrows slanted in a frown as he considered this. Suddenly, as if the sunshine overcame the darkening doubts, his lips turned up in a grin, and he nodded. "All right."

His appealing smile almost made her forget her questions. She stared at him, unable to say a word.

"How about if I just tell you what happened, and you can ask what you want when I'm through."

She nodded. "Fine. Begin."

"I was one of a crew of men bringing the new Boeing 247 to England, when we hit a storm north of here. One of our engines was damaged and we had to lighten the load. Finally, one of us had to abandon the plane. This vessel was the first one we contacted, and luckily it wasn't going west. We contacted the captain, and here I am."

Amanda listened and made notes. The story seemed too smooth somehow, too convenient. He was leaving something out. "Were there passengers aboard?"

"No. How long are you going to be in Eisenburg?" He watched her with great interest, and she had to fight an impulse to lean closer toward him. *What a frustrating man!* He was distracting her from probing further into his story.

She clenched her jaw and wrote the headline, "Abandon Plane!" circling it. Keeping her tone even, she asked, "Who do you work for?"

He stood. "I wouldn't want to make any bad publicity for my bosses, now would I?" He came around the table and stood behind her chair, ready to pull it out when she stood.

Amanda made no attempt to stand. She stubbornly held her notebook up with the pencil poised over it. He leaned over her shoulder and said softly, "We can continue out on the deck." Her cheek grew warm where his breath softly fanned it. She didn't dare turn her head; his face was too close to hers. She was more tempted than offended.

Snapping her notebook shut, she grabbed her purse and stood. He held the chair out for her, and with his hand under her elbow, guided her out of the elegant dining room.

I used to dream of being with him, she thought. *But in my dreams he was mellower, more agreeable. Reality is like having a wildcat by the tail.* She fought the impulse to walk away, yet she didn't want to lose a good story.

Chapter 5

The feel of Curley's hand on her arm warmed Amanda as they walked out into the sunshine. A fresh, salt-scented breeze fanned them as they made their way across the gently rolling deck, passing other passengers who didn't recognize Curley as the man who had parachuted from the sky the night before. In his dark pants, blue shirt, and pullover sweater, Amanda thought he looked more the college man than daredevil.

He steered her around a maid walking two little prancing dogs and said, "What drew you to newspaper writing?"

She looked away from his dimpled grin. "It's my way of helping people understand what's happening in this world."

"Ah, yes. The trip to Germany." They stepped close to the rail as a group of children trooped by, herded by a buxom young woman wearing sturdy shoes. She nodded to Amanda, glanced at Curley, and dropped her gaze, then shouted to the children to keep up with her. She was the ship's junior activity organizer. Amanda had interviewed her on her first day aboard. Though she looked like a girl, the young woman was twenty-nine years old.

"So, where were we?" asked Curley.

She opened her notebook to a blank page. "We were talking about careers. So, what made you decide to fly airplanes?" Her thoughts traveled back to his wild air-show escapades. It was on the tip of her tongue to tell him that she'd seen him then, but she decided not to. Maybe later, when she got to know him a little better.

He looked out over the sea, squinting at the billowy clouds on the horizon, and lifted his shoulders. "It's something I always knew I'd do." He turned and leaned back, resting his elbows on the railing. "Hung around airplanes 'til I was old enough to fly. I took to the air as naturally as I breathe."

She forced herself to look away from his dimpled smile and his hazel eyes that danced with life and mischief. "I know exactly what you mean," she said, jotting his statement in her notebook.

Curley watched her write, enjoying her nearness. Though he enjoyed women in general, this one intrigued him, with her hypnotic eyes the same green color as the sea. She was exquisitely beautiful, like a soft ribbon of moonlight glowing on the tops of clouds. He never forgot a face, and he knew he'd met her somewhere. It bothered him that he couldn't remember. He'd never had to resort to the old line of asking a girl if they'd met before. He was beginning to think this was the time.

They stood there for a few minutes, while he answered her questions and peppered the conversation with a few of his own.

Amanda's pulse was racing, and she bit her lip to force herself to concentrate on the interview. A middle-aged man in a bad mood and a suit too large asked if they'd seen the steward. They hadn't, so he grumbled and went to look for him.

She'd asked Curley all her questions, and there was nothing more to say. But she didn't want the interview to end. She looked at her watch and gasped. It was 9:45.

"What's the matter? Coaches don't turn into pumpkins until midnight," he said, devastating her with that smile again.

She snapped her notebook shut with the pencil inside and shoved it into her purse. "I have to interview a baroness in fifteen minutes."

"Time not only passes, it flies sometimes, doesn't it?"

Amanda smiled, feeling comfortable with him. "Definitely."

Curley drew in a deep, shaky breath and guided her across the white scrubbed boards, past the linoleum stairway, down to the second-class deck, to the elevators. Each elevator had a bas-relief motif signifying its destination. The library elevator had open books over the door; a smoking cigar noted the smoking lounge. The one to the swimming pool was adorned with mermaids and shells. She entered that one, and he held the door open.

He leaned inside. "I'd like to escort you to the banquet and ball tonight. What do you say?"

He looked like a hopeful teenager asking for his first date. "You haven't finished the interview," he added.

She felt a strange tugging on her heart. "All right. That would be nice."

Curley grinned and let the filigreed door shut. He liked a decisive woman. "I'll be at your cabin at eight," he said, raising his head to follow the elevator's upwards glide.

Her few words, "But you don't know my. . . ," were lost in her ascent. He stood, looking up with a happy grin on his face. "Don't worry. I'll find you." The library elevator landed with a thunk. Curley smiled and whistled a tune as he passed the opening door.

★ ★ ★

Amanda hurried to the heated pool, where the baroness and her personnel occupied the stern end of the pool. The water faintly lapped against the blue and gold mosaic tiles. At the other end, a waterfall cascaded over a series of lighted steps that made the water sparkle as it fell. A few swimmers were enjoying the pool, while some sat sipping champagne and showing off their French designer bathing suits.

Amanda took in the atmosphere and stored it in her memory for story background. She approached the baroness, who was as slim as a fashion model and attired in an elegant black cape over her silver bathing suit.

★ ★ ★

After the interview, Amanda went back to her room and raised the blinds the maid had shut. Ilsa had been there and changed clothes. What she'd worn at breakfast was carelessly tossed on her bed. Amanda smiled, thinking of Victoria, and sat at the writing desk to compose her notes and impressions before she forgot them. She gazed out at the darkening clouds and composed headlines. *Baroness Bares All.* . . No, maybe not; she giggled, thinking someone might get the wrong idea, and wrote a few more titles instead.

Soon it was time to meet Ilsa for tea. She folded her notes and put them in a large envelope and wrote "Baroness" on it, then freshened up in the bathroom and left.

In the Grand Lounge, Ilsa sat at a table near a bank of palm fronds. With her sat a tall, very handsome blond man dressed in white pants and striped shirt. He stood and pulled Amanda's chair out for her.

Ilsa's eyes sparked with delight as she introduced Nels Thordahl. His white eyelashes fringed sapphire blue eyes. "I am so glad to meet you," he replied with a Scandinavian accent, vigorously shaking her hand.

Ilsa could barely contain her excitement. "Nels won a tennis championship; next year he might play in Wimbledon; he's from Bergen, close to my hometown, and—"

Amanda had to laugh at the expression on Nels's face. He was nodding in agreement, and he didn't take his eyes off Ilsa.

Amanda declined the turtle soup the waiter offered, choosing cucumber sandwiches and a spoonful of cashew nuts instead. She glanced across the lounge but didn't see Curley. On the bandstand a clarinetist stood, performing his solo part as the small band played "Bye, Bye, Blackbird."

Ilsa and Nels continued to describe the beauties of Norway, and Amanda promised to visit someday.

Though happy for Ilsa, who'd said she wanted a shipboard romance, Amanda felt like an old-maid aunt at their party. A short, dainty woman in a shiny pink dress passed their table, followed by a middle-aged man with dark wavy hair. The woman's strappy shoes matched her dress. This woman would be a knockout at the Grand Ball. Amanda wondered which of her two evening dresses she should wear.

As if Ilsa had read her mind, she said, "Nels is going to be our escort to the ball tonight!"

Amanda smiled into their eager faces, and said, "How gallant! But I have an escort, thank you." A vision of Curley's boyish grin between the elevator doors brought a warm glow to her cheeks.

Ilsa sat straight up in her chair, almost knocking off the tray of hot scones, strawberry preserves, and clotted cream the waiter was placing on their table. "Who? Who? No! Let me guess!" She gazed upward and frowned thoughtfully, then beamed with delight. "The man from the sky! Right?"

"Right." Amanda glanced at her watch. "I have a lot of things to do between now and then, so I'll see you later, at the cabin." Nels quickly rose and moved her chair back for her.

★ ★ ★

Amanda chose her dusky rose satin dress with a ruffled collar that dipped low in the back. Ilsa wore black. They stood side by side before the green marble counter in their bathroom. Amanda patted loose powder on her nose, while Ilsa leaned forward to stroke pink lipstick on her pursed lips.

Pulling on her earlobe, Amanda winced. "I shouldn't have let you talk me into buying these earrings. This one pinches!"

"Here, let me fix it for you."

Amanda unclipped it, just as someone rapped on their door. She went to answer it while Ilsa concentrated on bending the earring wire to loosen it.

Amanda opened the door and gasped. Curley stood in the hallway, in a black tuxedo made of some soft-looking material, over a pleated white shirt with a black tie at his neck. Abruptly, she dropped her gaze, embarrassed to be caught staring, and invited him in. She caught the masculine scent of his cologne as he passed her.

Curley crossed the threshold into definite feminine territory and held out a white gardenia corsage. He breathed deeply. "It smells nice in here." The room smelled like a rose and lavender garden, mingled now with the scent of gardenia.

Ilsa came out from the bathroom with the earring. "Hello, again," she said to Curley.

"Hello." He gulped to quell the dizzy sensation racing through him as Amanda in her shimmery floor-length gown fastened the gardenia to her dress. Most of her thick dark hair was piled high on her head, with a cascade of curls laying against her creamy skin. He was entranced by the graceful way her hands moved as she tilted her head and clipped on the earring.

She picked up her beaded bag. Another visitor knocked on the door and Ilsa started toward it. She stopped, lifted her head in dignified control, and walked slowly to answer it.

The four of them stepped off the elevator into a chattering crowd in the Grand Lounge. Some of the gowns were elegant, some scandalously revealing, and all very expensive. Jewels glittered everywhere. One woman had a diamond necklace so large it lay over her bosom like a sparkling bib.

A deep gong echoed through the room, announcing that the banquet was served. Curley escorted Amanda into the first-class dining saloon. The diners' entrance was like a grand procession. The orchestra played a lush Jerome Kern melody, with cymbals and trumpets punctuating the violins. The baroness entered, looking regal in a slim evening gown of gold lace. Her retinue strode behind her, in the wake of her grandeur. She and one of her companions separated themselves from the group and went to the captain's table.

Ilsa and Nels found their table, then Curley guided Amanda to the captain's table, where he pulled out a chair for her. She nodded to acknowledge the baroness and sat down. The man across from her looked like an aging movie star. He dominated the conversation with a story about a recent safari in Africa.

After the appetizers were cleared away, the stewards scurried around the table with dove breasts in ginger-flavored aspic. The woman with the aging actor took up a lull in his conversation and leaned toward Curley. "I didn't catch your name?" she said. Her neckline dipped dangerously low.

Amanda turned her head to avoid the view, and Curley kept his eyes riveted on the woman's face. He nodded toward Amanda and said, "Amanda Chase. And I'm James Cameron."

"Sit back, Darling." The actor gently touched her bare shoulder, and she relaxed in her seat with a petulant frown on her pretty lips.

"What do you do, Mr. Cameron?" asked the man.

"Oh, a little of this and a little of that," shrugged Curley. "Nothing as exciting and courageous as your exploits."

The man leaned sideways slightly so the steward could remove one plate and place another before him. With a bored look he answered, "It gets tiresome sometimes, and one longs for home and hearth. You know?"

"Have you ever been to Poland?" asked Curley.

This set the man off on another story that lasted through the main course, sorbet, and into dessert.

Amanda longed to ask the man if he was an actor, but decided that if he was, she should know his name, and if he was nobility or a wealthy businessman, he'd be offended. She smiled at his lovely companion, who kept glancing at Curley with a hungry look. Curley nodded at the right places in the man's story and seemed interested, but the moment Amanda glanced at him, he winked at her and reached beneath the table to grasp her hand.

She took a deep breath to maintain her poise, but a stir of something deep in her heart pushed her emotions off balance. She looked down the table, catching the eye of the baroness, who raised her eyebrows inquisitively.

At last the dinner was over and the crowd made its way to the Grand Ballroom. Curley put his hand on Amanda's slim waist and guided her through the moving stream of people. When the guests turned right, he steered her to the left, toward a balcony-type landing with an arched window. A cool ocean breeze drifted in from the black sky and ocean.

He put his hands on her upper arms, and in the shadowy light his features softened. He looked too good to be true. *No wonder the woman across the table from us couldn't keep her eyes off him,* thought Amanda. He was one of those rare men who could dress up and look more masculine than ever.

"Why didn't you tell that man that you're a flier?" she asked. "Especially when he told the story about flying over the Yukon snows to hunt moose?"

Curley chuckled. "He was blowing smoke. You know, telling a yarn. Why rain on the guy's parade? Especially when he's the grand marshal!"

"You skillfully evaded my detailed questions about your flying. There's some reason you don't want to talk about it. You're not shy, are you?" She grimaced, reaching up to unclip her left earring, and rubbed her sore earlobe. He looked so concerned she smiled back at him. "New earrings," she explained.

He gazed so long at her, watching her closely, that she turned her head in embarrassment. He gently reached out, touched her chin, and turned her head toward him. "I know this may sound like a come-on, but I've met you somewhere before."

Her heart skipped a beat, and she wanted to turn her head away, but she continued to gaze back at him.

He looked past her, out to the black night. "Somewhere, I know it." His eyes focused back on her. "Or maybe it was only in my dreams."

His thumb slowly caressed her arm, and she tried to still her response to the tingling feeling racing through her. She licked her lips. "Actually, we, umm. . ."

His hand slid up to the back of her neck and he drew her toward him, murmuring, "Actually we're here right now, and. . ." His face drew nearer to hers. "And you're more beautiful than any dream I've ever had."

Amanda closed her eyes as the distance between them vanished, and he kissed her.

The warmth of his lips on hers sparked a response that surprised her. She started to raise her hands to lay them on the smooth white shirtfront, then stopped herself. As much as she wanted to resist, she found herself rising on her tiptoes, eagerly responding to the delicious sensations she was feeling.

She basked in the glow for a long moment, then realized he wasn't kissing her anymore. Her eyes flew open to see him gazing at her in wonder. He was close, so close she longed to reach up and pull his head down and continue what they'd started. Somewhere inside her a voice warned against letting her feelings control her.

As if sensing her reluctance, he drew back slightly, but he didn't stop staring down at her.

"You," he breathed. "It's so. . .I mean. . ." For once, Curley was at a loss for words. He couldn't tear his gaze away from the moist gentleness of her mouth, the large, soft eyes that showed too much what she was feeling. He'd kissed enough women to know she wanted him to kiss her again, but he was disturbed by the fierce desire that rose up in him to do exactly that.

He framed her face with both of his hands and said, "Are you real, or am

I dreaming?" She slowly closed her eyes, interrupting the strong force transmitted through their eyes.

Struggling for control, Amanda stood still, trying to make sense out of what had just happened. But wonderful warm waves of pleasure washing through her made it difficult to think clearly.

He grinned down at her and said, "It's pretty heady stuff out here. Would you like to go see how the other half is celebrating? There's a party on each level."

She nodded, not trusting herself to say a word.

"Come on, then." He held out his hand, and she laid hers in it, allowing him to lead her to the lower levels of the ship.

In the second-class salon, with its dark paneling showing off floral bouquets in lighted, window-size recessed frames, the passengers were slow dancing to soft music. Curley and Amanda found a table and ordered lemon-lime fizzes. A bowl of chocolate mints and peanuts sat beside a small candle lamp set in the middle of the pink linen tablecloth.

Curley leaned forward and put his hand over hers. "At last I've got you all to myself," he said. He raised his eyes. "Up there, too many people, too much distraction."

Amanda smiled, thinking that being on a real date with her hero, Curley Cameron, was a dream she'd given up ever coming true. But here she was, and it was happening. "I'll let you off the hook tonight," she said, removing the earrings that were still pinching. "But tomorrow we land in France, and it'll be a madhouse from then until we dock in London."

"I'll never be off your hook, Amanda Chase," said Curley. He picked up one of the chocolate mints and slowly held it up to her mouth. She laughed and called him silly, and he slipped the chocolate inside.

Amanda let the sweet dark flavor melt on her tongue for a moment, then said, "I'm going to the church service tomorrow morning. Let's finish the interview right after, all right?"

He smiled and it was as intimate as a caress. "No business tonight. Save a place for me in church. I'll meet you there, then we'll talk."

She studied him thoughtfully for a moment. "Are you a believer?"

"Yes!" he exclaimed, his face shining with glad memories. "I vaguely remember my mother praying, but then she died and my dad and I never went to church. When I was older I met up with some Christians who took me in, gave me a job, and," he shrugged, "God sort of snuck up on me." He shook his head. "No, He was always there, so trusting Him was the most natural thing in the world."

Amanda felt a warm glow settle over her.

Curley stood and grabbed her hand. She slipped her earrings into his tuxedo pocket and followed him.

They went deeper down to the third-class saloon. The air was thick with smoke, and passengers snaked through the room, stepping and swaying to some line dance. The revelers looked so silly to Amanda that she laughed, partly at the scene before her but mostly for the sheer joy of being with Curley.

They stood in the doorway, watching. Curley waved his hands before his face. "If I had a knife, I could cut a path through the smoke so we could enter." He glanced at her, enjoying the sparkle of her smile and her infectious laugh. He chuckled and, with his hand on her elbow, led her back into the hallway.

They climbed to the upper levels, passing a few people at a distance. He'd loosened his tie, and she clung to his arm while they strolled along the deck beside the rail, looking out over the water and talking. The musical hum of the engines and the gentle dip and roll of the deck cradled them in a special moment in time on the Atlantic waters. They told each other of their childhoods, their families, compared likes and dislikes, and found that they had a lot of attitudes and opinions in common.

Curley noticed that there were fewer and fewer people out on the deck, and the ship seemed to glide more quietly through the black swells. He'd never felt so comfortable with a woman, and he didn't want the moment to end. He saw her suppress small shivers, so he put his arm around her as they leaned out over the rail, watching the foam lap against the ship's wall. "Let's stay here and talk all night," he said. "I've never met anyone so easy to talk to."

Amanda watched a sliver of moon lifting from the black horizon. "Your childhood is truly fascinating. It's sad that you were orphaned at such a young age, but the way you followed your dream of flight, making a home in the hangars and eventually with a mechanic. . ." She looked at his strong profile watching the same moonrise. "It's like dime novel stories of a boy running away to join the circus."

He caught her gaze. "It wasn't all as exciting as it sounds." The corners of his mouth lifted in a slight smile. "But I did eventually perform in air circuses."

Amanda opened her mouth to tell him she'd seen him perform, but before she got the chance he said, "I wish you could have seen my aerobatics. But since the government cracked down on daredevils, we've had to find other ways to get our thrills in the sky."

"Like parachuting onto ships at sea?" Her eyes glowed with speculation in the pale moonlight, and Curley shook his head slowly.

"That's the business part, which we'll discuss later."

"Later," she agreed.

"Meanwhile, let's get you back to your cabin for a catnap so you don't fall asleep in church tomorrow."

They strolled slowly back to her cabin, neither one wanting the evening to end. Curley kept a protective arm over her shoulder. "You know," he said, "you're a courageous woman, and I admire that."

"Me? I'm merely working for what I feel is right."

"Not all women would go to such lengths to try to make sense of this crazy world. You're like a missionary."

They stopped at her cabin door. "My mission is to find the truth and reveal it to the world, so people can form their own opinions."

"Well said! If you ever run for president, I'll vote for you."

She loved the amusement that flickered in his eyes and the companionship they shared. As she watched, the amusement began to disappear and a contemplative look came into his hazel eyes.

She thought for a moment he was going to kiss her, but he said, "Be careful, Princess. Don't trust everything you see in Germany to be as it seems."

"But that's why I'm going!" she said with a smile.

He lifted his brows in acceptance, and said, "Just remember. Be careful."

"I'm always careful." She put her hand on the door handle. "Good night, then. And thanks for a wonderful evening."

He quickly brushed his lips over hers and came away with his eyes half closed. "Thank *you*," he said. She watched him walk away, then she slipped inside the dark cabin. She closed the door softly and leaned against it with a sigh.

★ ★ ★

Curley felt like skipping, but he settled for a fast trot back to his cabin. A note hastily stuck to his cabin door caught his attention. "Contact Captain McNally immediately." He stuck the note into his pocket and loped down the silent hallway.

A crewman ushered him into the bridge. "The captain has retired for the night, but he asked us to wake him when you arrived." He nodded to the crewman standing at the wheel. "I'll return shortly," he told him. Passing Curley on his way out, he said, "We tried to locate you, but. . ."

Curley locked his hands behind his waist and looked around. In contrast to a cockpit, the bridge seemed spacious. Rows of shiny dials lined one wall, and a gyrocompass and electric telegraph stood against the other.

The crewman at the wheel noted his interest and said, "The very latest equipment."

"She's a fine ship indeed," agreed Curley. He squinted at one dial. "This looks like a wind velocity indicator."

"Right. The latest in anemometers."

He was about to say more, but Captain McNally came in, followed by his crewman. The captain was in uniform and looked as if he were rested and ready to face the day. He reached into a drawer near his chair and pulled out a piece of paper. "This came over the telegraph at oh-one-hundred." He handed it to Curley.

"Captain James Lee Cameron. USN dispatching ship to intercept and retrieve. ETA 0400 hrs." He stared at it for a moment, trying to make sense of it. Why?

He planned to dock in France, find an airfield, then report to Sedley in England.

Captain McNally interrupted his musings. "Captain Cameron, you have exactly forty-two minutes to get your gear together and report back here."

Hurrying back to his cabin, Curley struggled to think of a way he could explain his leaving to Amanda. The retrieval ship was obviously coming at an hour which was meant to keep the rendezvous a secret from the passengers. What would she think when he didn't show up in church? He didn't have to guess. She'd think he was a playboy who was merely toying with her.

He yanked the few clothes from the hangers in the closet and stuffed them into his suitcase. What were his intentions toward Amanda? He shook his head in consternation. Maybe he'd never know. But he'd have liked to have known her better.

He glanced at his watch. He had about five minutes leeway to dash to Amanda's cabin and—and what? He couldn't tell her anything without arousing wild suspicions. And he didn't even have time to tell her he wouldn't be at church.

When he arrived back at the bridge a few minutes later, the navy ship's lights were approaching. He asked Captain McNally for a slip of paper and scribbled a short note. "Please see that Miss Amanda Chase in Cabin A-12 gets this message."

Chapter 6

Amanda awoke the next morning with the pleasant feeling of lingering, nice dreams. As she surfaced up through the sleepy fog, she realized that the images were real. She'd spent the most romantic evening of her life with the man of her young dreams.

Young dreams, she thought. A wonderful gift from her guardian angel. She inhaled deeply and opened her eyes. On the other bed, Ilsa lay curled beneath her covers, clutching her extra pillow to her chest.

Amanda turned to lie on her back and gaze up at the polished wooden ceiling. "Amanda's Idyllic Evening." It would make a good headline. She blocked out a full-page photo layout complete with captions describing the lovely scenes.

She allowed herself a few minutes of fantasizing, then got herself in hand. *You've daydreamed long enough. Time for reality!* She picked up her Bible and read for a few minutes but had difficulty concentrating. The small clock ticking away on the table between the two beds said only nine o'clock. She closed her eyes. *Last night was nice,* she told herself, *but a romantic, moonlit evening, partygoing aboard a gently rolling ship, and a charming, handsome escort are nothing to go gaga over.* Not enough to make a girl lose her objectivity.

Remember Lili, she told herself. A French girl at the Sorbonne, Lili had fallen in love aboard ship and spent the whole school term crying over a man who never contacted her again. *None of that for me,* vowed Amanda. *No man is going to tip my life into a morass of tears.*

She tossed off the covers, rejected the image of Curley's dimpled face smiling at her, threatening to unravel all her fine logic, and padded into the bathroom. She ran warm water into the bathtub, keeping busy to avoid daydreams.

At 10:30 a steward brought a silver service with coffee and flaky rolls. Amanda poured herself coffee and said, "I'm going to skip breakfast and have brunch later, after church." She didn't tell Ilsa that she was busy controlling the butterflies in her stomach and trying to quench the excitement of seeing Curley.

"Me, too," answered Ilsa, lying in bed until the last possible minute while Amanda sipped her coffee. Neither noticed the note slipped between the sugar and creamer.

They left the room, passing early morning deck strollers. The instant they turned the corner toward the Garden Lounge, Nels hurried toward them, a large toothy smile lighting up his face. He held out a hand to each of them, and Amanda couldn't help but smile in return, avoiding the urge to let her glance slide off him to search for a certain auburn-haired fellow.

"You ladies look lovely this morning," he said in his lilting Norwegian accent.

They thanked him, and Amanda allowed herself to glance around at the people arriving for church while Ilsa chattered, "It's hard to believe the voyage is almost over."

"Ya," agreed Nels. "We leave America Monday and come to France on Sunday. So fast a world!"

Two gentlemen in their gray morning coats and gray silk neckties nodded at them as they passed.

"Should we wait for Curley?" asked Ilsa.

"No, let's go on in. He'll find us," said Amanda, thinking that Curley could perhaps already be inside, saving them places.

Amanda sang the familiar hymns and tried to concentrate on the speaker without turning to look behind her to see if Curley had come in. She finally reached into her purse for her small notebook and forced herself to listen to the speaker by jotting down his main points. "Ambassadors for Christ" was the headline she gave his sermon. He reminded his listeners that no matter where they traveled, they'd always be God's ambassadors.

When she was thirteen years old, Amanda's nanny, Miss Whitney, took her regularly to church. Amanda had had the zeal of an ambassador then. But as she got busier with school and traveling, she attended less often, except when accompanying her parents to the cathedral's fashionable Christmas and Easter services. But in the last two years she'd gone back to church, seeking fellowship and stability.

After the closing hymn, Amanda, Ilsa, and Nels followed the crowd out onto the deck.

"I wonder where Curley is," said Ilsa, frowning and looking about.

"Must have had better things to do," said Amanda, forcing a smile. A high stack of cumulus clouds had risen and was approaching like a white and gray army.

"Well! It's quite rude!" Ilsa glared at the back of a man walking by, as if he were the guilty party. "It would be so lovely to explore Cherbourg together this afternoon."

Amanda looked out over the deck rail to the dark green cliffs in the distance. "Yes, it would be. You two go on ahead. I have a million things to do before I arrive in England tomorrow." Before they could urge her to join them for brunch, she added, "I have a couple more people to interview before we dock. See you two later!"

Amanda turned and escaped to the other side of the ship, spending the next two hours on a padded wooden deck chair in an out-of-the-way corner on A deck. *I must remember that this is not a pleasure trip,* she told herself and began jotting her thoughts on paper. *I can never allow myself to forget those small stories buried in the newspapers—skeptical stories of outrageous rumors too horrible to believe. One writer of such a story was forced to leave Germany. Persecution and cruelty were never the central theme of stories of Hitler's new regime. They mostly centered around the new orderly stability.*

She couldn't think of any more to add to her notes. She simply had to get there and assure herself that Aunt Esther, Uncle Jacob, and her cousins were all right.

Quick, confident steps approached; and her heart beat a little faster, thinking that Curley had found her. A smile locked itself on her mouth.

She blushed at her stupidity when a steward walked briskly past. *Captain Cameron means nothing to me,* she told herself. *But what if something came up, and he's looking for me right this moment? What if he's sick or he was waylaid by. . .*

She leapt up from the chair and stomped off the deck, down a linoleum stairway. *Sure. He was kidnapped by pirates. If Captain Curley Cameron,* or CCC, as she began thinking of him, *were really interested in you, he would have been where he said he'd be. So, face it!* she told herself.

Two long, majestic blasts of the ship's whistle drowned out her footsteps as she entered the second-class lounge. She found a table near the porthole and munched on cashew nuts, watching small boats bobbing in the distance as the big liner cruised into the harbor.

After the ship docked and those passengers who were going ashore left, Amanda made her way back to her cabin.

★ ★ ★

Curley couldn't stop the easy smile that lifted the corners of his mouth as he stripped off the tuxedo in the navy ship's bunk. Miss Amanda Chase was more than he'd expected. At first she'd seemed all business, then when he'd picked her up for the dinner and ball, she had that knockout gown on that shimmered softly over her curves. Coupled with the innocence in her eyes, it was a dangerous combination.

She apparently didn't know how she affected him. Maybe she merely went about knocking guys out in her own subtle way, taking it all in stride. No, he couldn't believe that. She seemed genuinely taken aback by his kiss. Her sweet surprise wasn't faked. He found that an unusual and intriguing quality.

He began folding the tux to put into his suitcase when Amanda's earrings tumbled out, sparkling as they bounced off his shoe and under the bunk. He picked them up, almost believing in fate. *Now I know I'll have to return these.* But the first thing on the agenda was to find Eisenburg on a map.

He wrapped the earrings in a handkerchief and put them in his trouser pocket. He closed the suitcase, thinking that he was glad he'd put the word "postponed" in his note to her. He'd find a way to see her again.

★ ★ ★

Amanda cabled her parents when she arrived in London. She exchanged addresses with Ilsa and said her good-byes in their cabin.

She stayed three days in London. Monday she shopped, buying a rose-colored cashmere sweater for her mother, a gold compact for Victoria, and soft kid gloves for her father, having the store ship the gifts directly to them. Tuesday and Wednesday she visited her father's gallery and used their typewriter to type some of the ship interviews and sent two articles to the *Chronicle*.

When she helped Mr. Seton, the gallery manager, write a report for her father, Amanda inserted her own note assuring him she was fine, hoping he'd come to terms with her plans. She telegraphed a message to Uncle Jacob that she was leaving for Eisenburg the next day.

Thursday morning Mr. and Mrs. Seton took her to the ferry to Calais. Gazing out over the water, her mind began to drift toward the idyllic evening with Curley. She quickly replaced the thoughts with story ideas. Peering past her reflection in the window at the water sliding past, she realized she'd have to write a library full of books to cover all the story starts she'd fabricated to stop thinking of him.

Maybe, she thought, *it would be easier not to make such an issue of what was merely a nice evening.* She should simply acknowledge the pleasant thoughts when they cropped up, agree that Curley was an interesting man, shrug her shoulders, and get on with life. She knew, though, it wouldn't work: Trying to ignore an evening more fabulous than any other in her life was futile.

In Calais she boarded a short train to Paris, remembering her school years and thinking that Victoria would have loved being with her. Her Thursday night in Paris was spent quietly in her hotel room, listening to the sounds on the street. The next afternoon she was on a train to Berlin.

Finally out of the city, the lovely eastern France countryside glided by, with cows standing silently on the rolling hills. She closed her eyes, letting the swaying, clacking train gently rock her. The train ground to a stop for a few moments, and when they got rolling again, they passed a mother and her small son carrying their bags into the small depot. Amanda sighed and looked out at the darkening hills and quaint cottages dotting the landscape.

Now that she realized she couldn't stop evading memories of Curley, they came flooding in, starting with the morning they had stood on the deck talking. She pursed her lips in consternation as she remembered. She considered herself an excellent interviewer, but he had easily deflected her questions. She didn't even have enough notes to fill two column inches.

But she'd had an interesting talk on board ship with an older German gentleman who was returning home. He'd told her that he remembered the terrible times before Adolf Hitler was elected, and that things were so much better now that Hitler had restored order. The wildly inflating money had stabilized, and peace and harmony were everywhere. Amanda sensed his words were too well chosen, sounding too much like they were memorized. When she tried to dig beneath their surface, he angrily cleared his throat and scoffed at exaggerated stories insinuating themselves into frivolous newspapers. He stared off into space, then informed her he had an urgent appointment.

Father, I pray that Uncle Jacob and Aunt Esther are all right. Amanda's eyes flew open as the shrill screech of brakes interrupted her prayer.

"Gelsenkirchen!" the conductor shouted, striding toward the rear of the car. They stopped briefly, then rolled on. She paged through her notebook, scanning the interview for anything of substance. The man was hiding something, but what?

Amanda made herself as comfortable as she could as the train sped through the night. Just after dawn, on the road beside the tracks a group of children waved as they passed. This was the land of Beethoven and Goethe. It looked so peaceful. Maybe the rumors were exaggerated. She'd think positively and look for the best.

When they reached Berlin at last, Amanda picked up her two suitcases and lugged them through the crowded depot. The noise of hundreds of travelers and the shouts of trains arriving and leaving bounced off the high ceiling, mingling into a cacophonous mush. The warmth of the day lingered in the station, making her uncomfortably hot in her wool coat.

Outside the station, she set the suitcases down for a moment and took off her coat. She hired a taxi to take her to Eisenburg and settled in for the ride. She was a child when she last visited Berlin, and this visit was like seeing the city for the first time. The old, narrow streets were clean; people moved quickly, as though they had important business, and Amanda noticed there were no destitute people in front of the well-preserved baroque buildings. She was glad they didn't suffer the same plight as out-of-work Americans dealing with the depression.

The taxi pulled up by the fence in front of Uncle Jacob's house. The driver unloaded her suitcases and she gave him a large tip. The house sat quietly behind its finely manicured lawn and garden. Looking up at the windows, she hoped to see a familiar face.

She pulled her suitcases inside the gate, left her coat draped over them, and walked to the front door. The house echoed the chime of the doorbell, as though a long silence had been broken. She had the odd feeling that something wasn't quite right. The house was too quiet. . .maybe the family was out. . .maybe they were at the train station looking for her. . .maybe—

The door opened and a man frowned out at her. *"Was begehren Sie?"*

Amanda stared at him for a moment. "Who. . .I mean, *Wo ist die Familie?"*

They continued speaking in German. "Where is what family?" asked the man.

"The family who lives here." Amanda glanced around, noting that the house had changed in subtle ways. It was too perfect, like a flawless model. Not like the happy home she remembered where a family lived.

"There is no family here," the man said, and closed the door a few inches, eyeing her suspiciously.

Suddenly, the rumors of persecutions came into sickening focus. If they were true, even her appearance at the house was dangerous, both to herself and her family, wherever they were. She forced a slight smile. *"Danke,"* she said, and stepped off the porch.

Back at the gate, she put her coat on to dispel the chill she felt. She picked up her suitcases and looked back at the house, feeling that she was being watched. Though she was exhausted, she raised her chin and set off in the direction of town. Uncle Jacob would be at the gallery, and he'd tell her what was going on.

Chapter 7

A breeze flicked Amanda's hair as she walked away from her aunt and uncle's house, wishing she'd asked the taxi to wait. The neighborhood was oddly silent for late afternoon. The houses looked deserted. It hadn't been that way years ago when she, Martha, and Tamara played tag in the front yard.

A small black car slowly approached, its tires snapping a rhythm over the brick road. The two men inside turned their heads, staring at her as they passed. The car glided into the house's driveway. *God, who are they, and what happened to my family?* she asked, turning the corner. The house had lost its friendly glow. She shivered, now thankful for her heavy coat.

Walking and lugging her suitcases made the streets back to town seem much longer. But, she reasoned, if Eisenburg was as large as Berlin, she would've had to ask the men at the house to call a taxi.

She recoiled at the thought, telling herself to be reasonable. Maybe they were very nice people, and she interrupted them at a bad time. Maybe they were just naturally grouchy. That sounded most logical. Had Uncle Jacob sold the house to them? Aunt Esther's last letter hadn't mentioned they were moving.

The slanting twilight sun glinted off Eisenburg's baroque buildings. The fragrance of sausage, baked bread, and cooking vegetables wafted past her. She set her suitcases down beside a shop with a large window open to the street. She ordered apple-peel tea and a buttered roll from a thin, mahogany-haired teenage girl who smiled brightly at her.

"*Bist du Eng-a-lishe?*" she asked.

"*Nein,*" answered Amanda in German. "I'm American."

The girl's eyes widened. She leaned over the wooden counter to peer at Amanda's clothes. "Ahh," she said with admiration.

They spoke of American music and fashions. Amanda told her she'd visited Eisenburg when she was very young. She sipped the last of her tea and asked for directions to Drehenstrasse. Pointing and speaking rapidly, the girl told her how to get there. Amanda thanked her and continued on her way.

She walked the three blocks down the main street and half a block down Drehenstrasse, resisting the feeling that something was wrong. An unnatural quiet breathed between the buildings. The gallery was dark, the windows boarded up, and the door had a heavy chain draped across it. A sign stuck inside the bottom of a window said, "*Geschlossen.*" Closed.

Amanda stared at the dried leaves blown in and crammed against the bottom of the door. Closed! When had this happened? A slight chill wove its tendrils around her heart.

It was almost dark now. The other stores on the street were closed, and two other stores looked as abandoned as Uncle's Jacob's gallery.

Walking away, she noticed someone had scrawled on one of the boarded-up shops the words *"Kauft nicht bei Juden."* Don't buy from Jews?

Two men in uniform walked smartly past her and she hurried to the more lighted main street. The rumors were true! To keep the fears for her family from overtaking her, she concentrated on headlines for her next story. *Jewish Businesses Boycotted in Hitler's Germany; Have Pogroms Really Been Discontinued?*

She sat down on a wooden bench under a dim streetlight and sighed. It was time to plan her next move. She would not panic or cause her father to worry until she knew more. *I'm like an actress in a foreign spy movie,* she thought. Her first duty was to find her family.

A few people, strolling after their dinner, passed her. A policeman on the corner fixed her with a bright blue-eyed gaze and approached her. He glanced at her suitcases, then asked if she needed directions.

She gripped the handles of one and started to stand. "No, thank you. I'll be on my way."

He took the suitcase from her. "Allow me, *Fraulein,*" he said. "Though it's safe to walk our streets after dark, I will accompany you. Where are you staying?" He smiled, waiting for her answer.

Amanda thought quickly. "The main hotel," she said, reaching into her purse. "I have its name here. . . ."

"Come," he said, picking up her other suitcase. "I know the place."

Walking beside him, she wondered briefly if he was the one who boarded up Uncle Jacob's gallery. After they'd gone one block, he turned and led her up the steps into the parlor of a three-story rooming house. He set her bags down and rang a silver bell he picked up from a small table beside the door.

A short, energetic woman appeared and warmly greeted them. She sat at the table, moved the bell, and opened a large registry book. "How long you stay?" she asked with a smile.

"A couple of days." Amanda produced her identification papers and paid the woman while the policeman stood near.

The woman, Frau Reinhardt, led them into the parlor. The policeman left them, pushing the door into the kitchen. Amanda and Frau Reinhardt climbed the stairs to the third floor and walked its carpeted length to the next-to-last room.

Frau Reinhardt adjusted a knob on the radiator beside the door and said, "The bathroom is the third door down the hall; the maid comes to clean at eleven A.M., and there will be no visitors and no music or loud noises after nine P.M."

Amanda nodded, glad she'd had the roll and tea, because her eyes felt heavy, and her head was beginning to pound. Frau Reinhardt left, and Amanda let out the breath she hadn't realized she was holding. She sank onto the faded yellow chenille bedspread, and with her toes pushed off each shoe by its heel.

On a bedside table sat a pitcher and washbasin. A closet door stood open on one wall. Curtains covered a window opposite the door. She was curious to look outside but too tired to. *In the morning,* she thought, lying back on the cool pillow.

Thoughts of Uncle Jacob and the family dodged in and out of her tired attempts to plan how she was going to find them. She started to doze, but a loud clang startled her as the radiator began heating the room.

She lay there, her eyes closed, adjusting to the noise, letting her mind relax. Curley Cameron's face flashed across her thoughts. His eyes looked deep into hers, a dimpled smile on his handsome face.

She tried to bring her mind back to the problem at hand, but it didn't work. All she could think of was Curley, the sparks, the warm sensations she felt when he kissed her. No man had ever affected her that way. Certainly not Delbert.

The few times Delbert had kissed her, his lips felt cold, and there was no excitement, no thrill. Afterward, her heart continued its steady beating as though nothing had happened. *Delbert's a nice enough fellow,* she thought. *Handsome, rich. But even if I was attracted to him, he still wouldn't be the right man for me, not when he doesn't understand my commitment to Christ. Some girl, though, will be thrilled to be the object of his attention—but not me.*

Curley, on the other hand, had not only thrilled her heart, but he shared her faith. Or had that been just a line? His expertise at kissing was probably all part of a charming act, too. Still, he'd seemed so tender when he drew her close and kissed her. She'd never forget the lingering look of wonder he'd had on his face when she finally opened her eyes.

She sat up abruptly, fighting for control. She pursed her lips, telling herself that she was being foolish, falling for a smooth line and a handsome face. *I refuse to think about a man who plays fast and loose with the ladies. Someday I want a man who will offer true love, if there is such a thing.*

Curley must know he'd affected her, since she'd almost shamelessly begged him to kiss her again. *Maybe that's why he didn't show up the next morning,* she decided sadly. These were futile thoughts because she'd probably never see him again.

She'd certainly never be the same naive teenager who'd had a crush on him. She rolled her eyes in relief that she'd stopped short from telling him they'd met before.

Yawning, she got out her pen and paper and recorded today's events in her journal and fell asleep while trying to concentrate on planning a search for her family tomorrow.

★ ★ ★

That same night while the other guys were celebrating in town, Curley stayed in the barracks. He'd worked hard all week, hoping to finish in nine days and be on a Monday flight to Salzburg.

★ ★ ★

The next morning Amanda rose early, refreshed from her long sleep. Sometime during the night she'd changed into her nightgown. Now, she opened the window and leaned out into the cool fresh air. Below was a narrow walkway between the rooming house and the building next door. She wondered if Frau Reinhardt tended the row of rosebushes lining the walk.

She shrugged into her robe and took the pitcher to the rest room. A tall, slim woman with circles under her eyes and hair so black it could have only come from a bottle, let her in. "Ach, what a morning!" she said, peering glumly into the mirror over the sink. She pulled the belt of her pink robe tighter around her waist.

"It's going to be a nice day." Amanda smiled at her. The bathroom was as large as her room. Behind a door slightly ajar sat the bathtub.

"You are new tenant?" asked the woman as Amanda washed her hands.

"Yes, I came in last night."

"You speak German with an accent. You are English?"

"No, American," answered Amanda, filling her pitcher with warm water. "Can you tell me where I can send a wire?" she asked.

"At the post office, on the park square. But not on Sunday."

"Thank you," said Amanda. Back in her room, she took a sponge bath standing on her towel in front of the dresser. She put on her gray skirt and orchid sweater and comfortable shoes. Taking her camera and notebook, she left the room.

She followed the fragrance of breakfast to the dining room where several guests were already seated. The long table supported plates of fried potatoes, sausage, eggs, ham, and several other entrees.

Frau Reinhardt, seated at the head of the table, welcomed Amanda, motioning to an empty chair on her left. A red-haired girl carried a pitcher of cream to the table, glancing covertly at Amanda.

Amanda chose a large piece of blueberry coffee cake with streusel topping and poured herself a cup of coffee. The other tenants kept their attention on their breakfasts, hardly noticing her until Frau Reinhardt asked how she liked her room. They nodded in satisfaction when she said it was fine.

The park square was in the middle of Eisenburg, and she easily found the building with "Postamt" chiseled into its exterior. The door was tightly closed and the window shades were drawn, giving the place a forbidding look.

Church bells pealed a somber welcome, and she followed the sound to a gray, ornately baroque building with a few folks climbing the old steps and entering a door that was at least fifteen feet high. The sanctuary was cold, but the majestic organ music was like being at a concert. The service was stately and dignified, with the reading of a whole chapter from Esther that went along with the short sermon.

Afterward, feeling a peaceful calm, Amanda walked away from the church, knowing that since it was Sunday, she'd not make much headway in finding her family. So she strolled around the quaint little town, snapping photos, then went back to the rooming house to write some letters and make notes for future articles.

★ ★ ★

Monday, Curley was a passenger on a flight into Austria, where he'd pick up a small plane hangared in a field outside of Salzburg. He'd been briefed to enter Germany from the southeast corner, delivering the plane to Holland. His flight would take him over a lot of German territory, giving him a good look at reported growing squadrons of airpower in Nuremberg, Munich, and Berlin.

Seated in the last seat of the plane, he looked out into the clear black night. The noise of the two engines changed slightly as the plane started its descent. The seven other passengers leaned toward the windows to look down. A row of landing lights glittered in the inky darkness below.

The plane touched down, bounced once, then with a roar slowed and turned around. They taxied to a stop beside a large hangar, and the passengers stood, grabbing suitcases and bundles.

He descended the steps behind the other passengers. Two crewmen stood looking up at the engines. He would have commented that she was a sweet ship, but keeping his anonymity, he didn't. He walked across the tarmac to the barn-like building. Over the door was a sign, *Flughafen von Salzburg*, between tall columns with winged cherubim sitting on them.

Curley followed his fellow passengers across the slate floor through the terminal. The blond girl and her chaperon were met by a middle-aged man in a gray overcoat. There were no passengers waiting to board the plane he'd just left, and the only people inside were a wireless operator, a clerk, and a stoop-shouldered man pushing a loading cart out the door.

In the chilly night air, Curley approached the closest of two taxis. A talkative, gray-haired driver with a large mustache assured Curley he knew the best place in Salzburg to find a room for the night. The clerk in the deserted lobby was so happy to see both him and the driver, Curley was sure they must be relatives.

He signed in, dropped his suitcase in the room, and went to find something to eat. Sitting alone at a linen-covered table waiting for his order, he suddenly wondered what Amanda was doing at that precise moment.

The thought of her made him smile, and he touched his shirt pocket, where he'd stashed her earrings. *I'll be returning these to you soon, Miss Amanda Chase.* He absently stared at the row of mugs on a shelf across the room, thinking of stories he'd heard of persecution and hardships imposed on innocent German citizens. If Amanda asked questions in the wrong places, she could get herself in trouble. He'd find Eisenburg on the map and fly in as soon as possible.

★ ★ ★

The next morning, just after dawn, Curley left the hotel, carrying his suitcase through the streets with their ornate wrought-iron signs leaning out over the sidewalks. The graceful old buildings glowed in the early morning light, as he kept the sun behind him. Several signs proudly bore the picture of Mozart, their most famous son.

Curley loped past a blue-domed cathedral and crossed the bridge over a meandering river. The crisp morning air magnified the twitter of waking birds. His steps slowed as he caught sight of a grand old building perched on a hill above groves of trees. It looked as though it had been there for hundreds of years. The dawn light gave the mountain behind it a peach glow, and the oval windows a golden liquid sheen.

At the end of the street, a cathedral thrust its ornate spires to the sky, and a group of angels graced the arch over its door, two of them holding slim trumpets between a coat of arms. Curley made a mental note to return and explore this beautiful Salzburg, tucked in the hills of Austria. The cottages became further apart, and soon he was in farm country, with wisps of smoke rising from their chimneys.

He found the airstrip easily, by simply walking west and scanning the vista for a wind sock. There it hung on a pole, limp in the quiet morning. He approached the hangar and found its doors open, the Vega's propeller shining in the sunlight.

A tall man in his thirties, with curly dark hair and blue eyes, walked toward Curley. "James Cameron?" he asked, smiling and wiping his hands on a red rag.

Curley nodded, and they shook hands. "Looks like a sweet little bird," he said.

The mechanic beamed, looking fondly at the plane as if he were a mother hen and this was his favorite chick. "You take Vega to Herr Schmidt in Amsterdam, *ja?*"

"That's right." His orders were to deliver the plane within ten days, while observing all he could on the way.

Curley checked it out from tail to nose and found it to be in excellent order. He wasn't surprised, because the hangar was clean and neat. Together they rolled the Vega out onto the grass field, and Curley climbed into the cockpit. Touching his fingers to his forehead in an informal salute, he started the engines.

In the air before 7:30 A.M., he headed northwest toward Munich.

★ ★ ★

That same day, early, Amanda went to the post office in the square. Inside, a row of boxes with numbered brass plates filled one wall, near a counter with a uniformed man standing behind it. Behind him sat a wireless telegraph machine.

She sent a message home, telling them she'd arrived, was fine, and would contact them later. She mentioned that Uncle Jacob and Aunt Esther had moved from their home. Dad might know that the gallery was closed, but until she knew more, Amanda wouldn't worry them unnecessarily.

Outside, in the park, a blond boy in knee britches bounced a ball toward her and she rolled it back to him. She strolled to the other side of the park, thinking. She couldn't simply ask anyone where the family had gone. She couldn't go to the police because she wasn't sure she could trust them yet.

First she had to see the gallery in the daylight. She turned around and headed in that direction. A young woman in a white apron and nurse's cap pushed a carriage past Amanda. Amanda looked inside the carriage fondly and smiled up at the woman, who stared straight ahead and resolutely pushed the buggy past.

Amanda slowed her steps, pondering the strange impression the town was giving. She'd met a few friendly people, but most of the others went about their business quietly, seeming to shun contact. The cold attitude was conspicuous in the midst of gracious buildings, a charming park squarely in the middle of town, and benches on the main street, made for sitting and chatting. But the people walked through this charming setting with reserved, uncommunicative faces.

The street looked different in the sunlight. On the corner, the music store window displayed a gleaming trumpet surrounded by sheet music with the swastika emblazoned on their covers. Amanda walked past a tobacco shop to the Chase Gallery.

It looked even more forlorn and neglected in the daylight. One of the windows had been broken, and someone had propped a board behind the hole. Scrawled on the board, which she had not seen last night, were the words *Deutshland erwache! Juden verecke.* "Germany awake! Jews perish." A ripple of fear jolted through Amanda. Did anyone take this slogan seriously?

Where had all the artwork gone? She shook her head. Where had her family gone! Backing away, she crossed the street to take a picture of the desecrated gallery.

Further down Drehenstrasse, the other two closed businesses were boarded up, one with a hateful slogan written on its door. She snapped a photo of them also, catching sight of a shopkeeper in his doorway with his hands clasped over his massive belly, watching her. When she caught his eye, he looked away and went back inside.

Something sinister was going on in this town, and a chill crept around Amanda's heart, but she recoiled from it, determined to find the truth. *Oh, God, who can I talk to?* she prayed. *Who's behind this outrage? And where is my family?*

Chapter 8

Amanda stared at the door behind which the shopkeeper had just escaped. Four-feet wide, painted gold wire-rimmed spectacles decorated the window, and the man's name was lettered below. She slipped her camera back into its case as she approached.

Inside, she found him concentrating on polishing a black, cylindrical device. Light from the window gilded two mahogany chairs standing before a glass-topped counter.

After a space of silence, he looked up. "May I help you?"

"I'm interested in the art gallery down the street," Amanda answered with a calmness she forced herself to show.

He shrugged and said, "I'm sure there are other art sellers in this town."

"I'd like to know what happened to the people who owned that one." She adjusted the strap over her shoulder to a more comfortable position.

"Why do you ask?"

"I know them, and I'd hoped to see them again." She chose her words carefully, avoiding the Jewish issue.

"They are gone. That's all there is to it." He set the black cylinder down and rubbed the cloth over it one more time.

"Could you tell me where they went?"

He put his hand to his forehead and looked at her reflectively. "You are very persistent in their whereabouts."

Amanda sucked in a deep breath, hoping she was right about him. He didn't seem sinister, just careful. "Mr. and Mrs. Goldstein are my aunt and uncle, and I'd really like to find them."

He stood still for an instant, as if he were frozen, then squinted at her again. He leaned on the counter that separated them and pulled a card from its depths. "You go talk to Herr Verendorf, here." He pointed to the name on the card. "He may be able to tell you something."

She took the card and slipped it into her pocket. "Thank you."

"Don't thank me. I didn't tell you anything. And don't tell anyone you talked to me." He looked past her out the window. "Now, I think you should go."

She looked over her shoulder but saw no one outside. She thanked him again and left. Before the door closed, he said softly, "Good luck, *Fraulein*."

★ ★ ★

Curley navigated the plane through bright blue skies, between snowcapped mountains to Munich, approximately fifty miles from Salzburg. Flying low, he scanned every possible airfield and building large enough to be hangars for airplanes. He circled and came back, over the city again, then headed on out to the countryside. Spotting a suitable road, he set up an approach and landed the airplane. He taxied off the road into a field and cut the engines. When he opened the door, the fragrance of harvested wheat rose up from yellow stubble.

He sat there for a few moments, letting time pass. Making too many passes overhead would look suspicious. He reached for his harmonica, then let it slip back inside his pocket. Making music would be redundant in this place.

He took Amanda's earrings from his other pocket. They twinkled in his palm. He pushed them with his finger, making them flash. She had looked so lovely that night on the ship, the earrings sparkling against her creamy skin.

He wasn't the kind of man to put stock in fairy-tale romances, but he'd felt a powerful pull on his soul when he kissed her.

Her green eyes, dark and fathomless, had looked up at him, begging him to kiss her again. *I should have done just that,* he thought. But something had stopped him. Maybe it was her innocent seductiveness combined with open trust. Maybe the intense emotion that hit him and rocked his world upside down just plain scared him.

Before that, when he first landed on the ship, he had felt her standing there, and his eyes were drawn to the one person in the crowd who mattered. There had been instant recognition; that was why he was sure he'd seen her before. He always remembered people he'd met, yet she eluded his memory.

He let out a deep breath and curled his fingers around the sparkling earrings. The whole event on board ship was probably due more to moonlight, ocean breezes, and a lovely woman in his arms than destiny. He slipped the earrings back into his pocket before his emotions could dispute that conclusion.

He pulled the door shut, admitting that he was looking forward to seeing Amanda again. A few minutes later he circled over Munich once more and spotted an airstrip with large hangars at one end of the field, and several planes lined up near them. He waited while one took off, then when the airspace was all clear, he landed.

As soon as he taxied to a stop, two German state soldiers approached him. *"Was machen Sie hier?"*

In his simplified German, he answered that he was there to check a noise he'd heard in his engine.

Another soldier approached the two standing beside him. Curley turned to open the plane's door and retrieve his toolbox.

"Halt!"

Curley stopped and slowly turned. The three soldiers glared at him.

"Your papers," they demanded. One moved his hand to the gun holstered at his waist.

Curley grinned. "Sure." He opened the plane's door and reached inside, retrieving his passport. While the soldier studied it, Curley glanced at the facilities surrounding the airstrip.

The soldier grunted, apparently satisfied, and handed the passport back. He told Curley to work on his plane but when finished, to be on his way. To assure that he complied, two left, leaving the third to stand near the plane, watching him.

Unruffled by their distrust, Curley couldn't help wondering if there was something they didn't want him to see. Unlatching the cowling, he glanced at the hangars and planes behind it. He memorized their number and placement.

When he was finished, he put his tools back into the toolbox and hefted it back inside the plane, anchoring it in its place behind the left seat. He grinned at the soldier guarding him and said, "Thanks for the company, Sir. I need to use your facilities, then I'll be on my way."

The soldier jerked his head toward the building behind them and led Curley in that direction.

Inside the metal building, thin wooden walls separated rooms, and behind wooden-bordered glass doors was the mess hall. The civilians sitting at tables looked out at them.

"A cup of coffee would sure be nice," said Curley. "Care to join me? I'm buying."

The guard scowled, following him.

"Come now. What harm can I do in the mess hall?" He pushed the door open, and the guard followed him. Curley ordered two coffees and joined a young couple at their table. The guard didn't seem to know if he should stand or sit. Finally, he sat, stiff-backed, in a position where he could observe and hear everything at the table.

"Nice day, isn't it?" Curley asked the couple.

"*Ja*, a good day for flying."

"Where are you folks from?"

Their eyes glowed with joy. They glanced at the guard, then the man leaned forward. "From here, but we have just been to Nuremberg to honor our *führer!*"

The woman rolled her eyes. "Such splendor! Thousands cheering, soldiers marching! Four brass bands!" She put her fist over her heart. "Herr Hitler is so wonderful! We cheered his speech for ten minutes!"

Curley nodded and took a sip of coffee. "Sounds like quite a spectacle."

The man beamed. "Our *führer* has unified the people, and things are going to be better. You should have seen the girls and boys marching! Germany will soon come into her glorious destiny. The future ahead is bright."

"So I've been told," said Curley, smiling. He finished his coffee and having no further reason to delay, he stood. So did the guard and the young couple.

The man said, "*Heil* Hitler!"

The guard hit his chest with his fist. "*Heil* Hitler!"

Back in the plane, Curley took off, craning his head toward the dark planes and large hangars. Two of the doors were opened, and he saw more planes inside. He banked over the buildings, counting eleven large hangars, each capable of housing six airplanes. He counted the planes tied down between the hangars and flew on, northward over the rolling hills.

He circled over Nuremberg, looking for airstrips and more planes, finally landing and inspecting an airstrip as he had in Munich.

He fueled up, left Nuremberg, arcing westward toward Frankfurt, and did the same search, eating a late lunch there. He lifted off, leaving the factories and industrial buildings of Frankfurt behind, and headed northeast toward Berlin. *What a joy to fly,* he thought as the Vega responded smoothly to his handling.

He approached Berlin from the south, looking down at the sprawling city. Three rivers converged, with dozens of bridges crossing them. He followed one river for awhile, then circled and crisscrossed over the city, observing three small airstrips. *Somewhere down there,* he thought, *is their glorious leader.* From what his trained eye had seen, Curley knew the *führer* was gathering the beginnings of a powerful air force.

At last he followed a narrow road due east, where the map told him Eisenburg, and Amanda, were. *A few miles more and I'll be in Poland,* he thought, as he saw the tiny town, seated in a shallow valley. One hill to the south sheltered the hamlet. There was no airstrip, so Curley found the flattest, most remote place he could, and set the plane down. He cut the engines, got out, and pushed the plane behind a bank of bushes.

★ ★ ★

Amanda stood outside the Verendorf cottage on the hillside south of town. It had taken her two hours to find the place, and her feet were tired. No one answered the door when she lifted and dropped the knocker. She'd gone around to the side of the house and saw a greenhouse in back, but no movement, and no one answered her calls.

Her hand holding Verendorf's card dropped to her side, and she sighed. The nearest house was a quarter of a mile ahead. She slipped the card into her pocket, took her camera out of its case, and started shooting. Satisfied that at least she'd get some good shots of the countryside, she walked up the hill to the next house.

A brown-haired boy with pale blue eyes answered the door. His mother told Amanda that Herr Verendorf had gone to the Nuremberg festival and wouldn't be back for another week. Amanda thanked her, grinned at the child, and walked back to town.

She trudged up the boardinghouse steps, realizing she hadn't taken time for lunch. Tired and hungry, she looked at her watch, glad to note she had a few minutes to rest before dinner.

"Amanda! There you are."

She stopped abruptly at the parlor door and stared. It was Delbert, approaching her with outstretched arms. "Delbert! What are you doing here?"

"Why, darling girl, I've come to rescue you, if you're in trouble, or to help you if you need assistance." He flashed her his dazzling smile.

"How did you know where to find me?"

He gestured to a parlor chair. "Let's not stand here in the doorway. Come sit, and we'll talk."

"I don't want to sit and chat. Please, how did you find me?"

He hesitated for a moment, then said, "Your father called me after you left. He's been unable to contact your uncle and felt you might need help. So, I dropped everything and here I am."

"I cabled my father I was all right," she said, turning her face away from him. Then, not to be unkind, she laid a hand on his shoulder and said, "Delbert, it was nice of you to come all this way, but I'm taking care of myself just fine. Go back to Boston and tell my father thank you."

"But—"

"I'm tired and I'm going upstairs." She turned from him and walked away.

In her room, she dropped her camera bag on the floor and plopped down on the bed with a long, exhausted sigh. Nothing had gone right. She pressed the heels of her hands over her eyes to soothe the burning sensation.

How would she find her family? She had no more leads. *They have to be somewhere! If they're in Eisenburg, I'll find them, even if I have to knock on every door and ask everyone in town.* The optometrist might know something more. Even though he seemed nervous about her visit, tomorrow she'd return to talk to him.

She lay back on the pillow and closed her eyes, thinking of her cousins. Were Martha and Tamara in danger? Something sinister was happening. The rumored beatings and tortures suddenly became all too possible. But how could that be in this modern day and age?

She was too tired to think of Delbert, but she appreciated her father's protectiveness. She'd have to keep her doubts and fears to herself. Delbert would approach the situation as a private eye on a federal case. She shuddered, thinking that he could endanger the family, turning their disappearance into an international incident.

At dinner, Delbert charmed Frau Reinhardt and the cook. They piled extra dollops of whipped cream on his dessert, and Amanda hoped they wouldn't credit her for his being there.

The policeman dropped in just in time for the cook to bring him a piece of apple strudel topped with whipped cream. Delbert chatted with him, praising Adolf Hitler for solving Germany's problems, claiming that Americans applauded his efforts to lead Germany into prosperity.

The policeman set down his fork and with shining eyes said, "I was in the crowds at his hotel last summer. There were thousands of us waving our swastika flags. 'We want our *führer!*' we all shouted. It was splendid." He scanned each face around the table to be sure they were listening. "He stood on the balcony for a moment. Women swooned, but men shouted '*Heil* Hitler!'"

He sat straighter in his chair and in hushed tones added, "The *führer* looked down, and I knew he was looking right at me. Then he spoke." The policeman slowly shook his head. "How wonderful were his words."

The rapt expression on the man's face baffled Amanda. He viewed Hitler as some kind of god. Did Hitler really inspire such devotion? It reminded her of her studies in Roman history. The caesars, proclaimed as gods, brutally eliminated dissenters. *What happened to Hitler's dissenters?* she wondered.

★ ★ ★

Darkness had settled over the town as Curley walked the road. Behind the western hills the sliver of moon shed weak light over the road, and a chilling wind pulled dry leaves off the trees. Eisenburg was eerily quiet, until a long, black car slid up beside Curley and stopped. A policeman got out and blocked his way. "Who are you, and where are you going?"

"Jim Cameron. I'm headed for Eisenburg."

The policeman's eyes narrowed as his gaze darted about. "How did you get *here?*"

"What?" Curley bought a few seconds to think quickly. He didn't want to mention the plane and risk an inspection.

"Herr Cameron, you did not walk from America, *ja?*"

The other policeman got out of the car and stood listening.

"Oh, no, I had a ride as far as a mile or so back."

"Do you have business in Eisenburg?"

Curley shrugged. "You fellows can tell by my accent that I'm an American. I've always wanted to visit your great country, and now seemed like a good time to do so, since Herr Hitler is bringing such prosperity."

The two officers glanced at each other. Curley hoped these men didn't patrol the countryside, though the plane was well hidden from the road.

The second officer opened the back door of the car. "You come with us. Eisenburg has a curfew, and you cannot be on the streets now."

Curley got into the car, setting his suitcase beside him, and they drove into town. He wondered if they were taking him to jail. But if he'd been in real trouble they would have asked to see his passport.

He looked at his watch—9:45. The streets were dark, and in the windows of the homes they passed, light filtered through thick curtains with a subtle glow. No one walked the streets, and corner lamps were dimmed.

"Nice town," he said, looking out the window.

He got no response, so he said no more. *God, I hope I'm not under arrest,* he thought, looking out at shops they were passing. *They can't have any idea who I am.* He'd flown over at least two hours earlier. They couldn't know the plane had landed, and even if they had, they couldn't connect him with it. Still, their militant attitude worried him.

When they stopped in front of an official-looking building and roughly pushed him inside, alarm bells began to go off in his brain.

Chapter 9

With the disdain of a man who had seen hundreds dragged into the station, a sour-faced guard wrote down Curley's name, took his suitcase, and told him to wait. Curley sat on a high-backed oak chair, trying to appear innocent of any violation they could pin on him. Knowing he wasn't didn't help.

There was a gun case full of rifles behind the guard and his desk, and a large painting of Adolf Hitler on the wall beside it. A red flag with a black swastika within a white circle hung from a pole in the corner.

Curley understood that each nation had its own identity and customs, including flags and pictures of its leaders, but this was somehow different, more aggressive. After withdrawing from the League of Nations, and then in August after the death of President Hindenburg, Germany had overwhelmingly voted Hitler as its *führer*. His promise to bring the people together as "one man" was probably behind the sense Curley had of a clan gathering itself for a confrontation. But with whom? They were just coming out of a depression after a long and bitter war.

Opening a door noisily, the guard who had picked him up and another officer with a bar of ribbons on his brown shirt marched into the room and ordered Curley to stand. They asked him for his passport, asked again what he was doing in Germany, and what his occupation was.

"I'm a mechanic," he said.

A flicker of suspicion glinted in the officer's eyes. "Explain."

Curley lifted one shoulder apologetically. "I do not speak German well. I fix automobiles." That was true; his Tin Lizzie kept him busy. He assured them he was in Germany as a tourist who was interested in the beauty of their land.

"Why are you walking at night into Eisenburg?"

"I explained that. I got a ride to the outskirts of town." The silence lengthened and he stood ramrod-stiff, waiting for them to decide he was harmless and let him go. The ticking of a large round clock on the wall pounded like a blacksmith's hammer.

The officer glared at Curley's passport, then thrust it at the guard. "We will keep this until tomorrow. Tonight you sleep at Frau Reinhardt's." He picked up Curley's suitcase, flipped it open, and moved the clothes and shaving kit around.

He snapped it shut and told the guard who had picked up Curley, "Frau Reinhardt has two rooms left. She will not refuse. Take him and tell her nothing." He handed Curley the suitcase.

Curley glanced at his passport on the guard's desk as he walked toward the door. He wasn't sure how good their spy system was, but if it was even mediocre, he could be in hot water very soon.

At Frau Reinhardt's, he stood in his third-floor room, listening to the guard's fading footsteps. The room was at the end of the hall with a fire escape outside the window. He climbed out and sat on the cold metal, thinking. They knew he wouldn't go anywhere without his passport. But if he didn't get it back soon, he'd have to leave anyway or face the firing squad as a spy. A light wind rustled the trees behind the building. If it continued, the wind would be a help in getting him and his plane out of here.

How was he going to find Amanda quickly? The town was small, and she was with her family. The police would be no help, but she'd told him her uncle ran one of her father's art galleries. That should narrow the search. He smiled and hunched back against the brick building, thinking of her. In his note he'd said he'd see her soon, but she'd be surprised it was this soon—and in Eisenburg.

The police could become a problem. *I should have waited until I was back in the States and contacted her then.* But he was so near, and he'd felt drawn to her, and. . .

A pebble hit a window about twelve feet away. *A lover's tryst,* he thought. He hadn't heard footsteps. Slowly leaning forward, moving barely a muscle except his eyes, he squinted down into the darkness below. Another pebble struck the window, then another. The window remained shut. Whoever was being hailed wasn't expecting it.

Then the window opened halfway, and a dark head peered out, looked down, then to both sides. Curley took a quick, sharp breath. Amanda! She looked past him, not seeing him in the darkness. From below came a soft whistle in four quick tones.

He couldn't see the person on the ground, but he heard a "Sh," and then a whispered, "Catch." Amanda held her hands out and caught something tossed up to her. She grasped it firmly, straining forward and peering down at the person below.

As Curley leaned forward to look down, the metal squeaked. He froze, but Amanda saw him.

★ ★ ★

Amanda couldn't believe what she was seeing. Curley Cameron here in Eisenburg, at this very boardinghouse? Impossible! She closed her eyes for a full three seconds, then opened them. He was still there.

He lifted a hand in silent greeting, touches of humor framing his mouth and eyes.

She grasped the rock in her hands so tightly it bit into her palm. She looked down, where her cousin Martha had stood seconds ago, and then she drew back inside her room, completely ignoring the apparition on the fire escape. She couldn't believe he was really there.

Reminding herself that after he'd not shown up at church aboard ship, she'd given up on him, taking him for a fast-talking playboy, she turned on the lamp beside the bed, adjusted the faded silk shade, and then unwrapped the note from the rock Martha had thrown to her. *Meet me in the park tomorrow at 6:45 A.M. Tell no one; trust no one.*

She put the small piece of paper on the table, smoothing out the wrinkles, reading it again. Why all the mystery? If Martha was playing a game, it could be fun, but this was no game; the need for secrecy was real.

Amanda folded the note into a tiny square and slipped it behind the mirror in her compact. She turned off the lamp and pressed the round, gold compact between her palms, praying that God would keep her family safe.

She went to the window and looked out. The breeze felt cold against her cheeks. Weak moonlight and shadows gave the walkway below a forlorn appearance. If she hadn't heard the secret whistle she and Martha had shared as children, and had she not held the note in her hand, she'd have thought the whole thing was a dream.

She turned her head slowly to the right. Curley still sat on the fire escape, knees up, forearms resting on them.

"Hello, Princess," he said softly.

"What are you doing here?" she whispered.

"Looking for you."

She stared at him incredulously.

"I told you I'd see you soon. Here I am."

"You're a little late, don't you think?" she said, instantly regretting her petulant tone.

"What?" His grin faded and his eyes probed hers.

"Never mind," she said. "Good night." She started to pull back into the room.

"Wait!" His loud whisper blended with the sound of the breeze. "We haven't finished the interview."

"Good night," she said, ducking back into the room and closing the window.

She climbed under the covers and forced her eyes closed, trying to go to sleep. She reached out and touched the sharp edges of the rock on the bedside table. She said another quick prayer for Martha, Tamara, Aunt Esther, and Uncle Jacob. She frowned. *First Delbert bursts in, just when I don't need him, then Curley shows up.*

She sighed and turned to her side, hugging her pillow. *I don't really care if he's here,* she told herself. Why was the first thing she said a rebuke for standing her up at church? All those years she'd daydreamed of him seemed so silly now that he was here, because the timing was all wrong. Four years ago if he'd appeared in the moonlight, she would have swooned.

She turned to her other side. *I shouldn't let him get to me.* She determined to ignore both Curley and Delbert and concentrate on finding out what was happening with her family. After all, that and the big story were her mission. *Girl Reporter Shuns Distractions to Follow Story—that's the headline for tomorrow's activities,* she thought.

★ ★ ★

Curley sat where he was for awhile, perplexed. Why had she brushed him off? *You're a little late, don't you think?* What did she mean by that? He put his hands into his jacket pocket, fingering her earrings. Who had thrown the item up to her just now? Such stealth was calculated. But why? And why was Amanda here and not with her family? He turned up his collar against the cold wind, pondering these things.

The next morning after a fitful sleep, Curley awoke as the sky turned pale gray. The wind had picked up, and gusts blew the tree limbs, making them scratch against the building. He had a very short time to find answers to his questions, get his passport back, and get back to England with his report.

He was the first person in the bathroom, where he washed up and shaved. Downstairs in the kitchen, the cook hadn't arrived yet, so he poured himself a glass of water and took it to the parlor. He switched on the lamp beside a rose-colored brocade couch. A magazine caught his attention. Pages of pictures showed Hitler and his officers at their headquarters with happy people gazing up with awe.

Curley sat and sipped his water, waiting for Amanda to come downstairs. The cook peeked around the doorway and offered him coffee. He eagerly traded his glass of water for it, making her smile.

Other tenants began making their way down to the dining room. Curley joined them for a huge breakfast of sausage, potatoes, rolls, and eggs. He was pouring another cup of coffee when Amanda came in.

He grinned and rose to greet her. The man across from him also stood and said, "Good morning, Honey." Curley composed himself quickly and sat down.

Amanda stood in the doorway, looking from Curley to Delbert. She shook her head slowly and took a seat at the end of the table, between them. She poured herself a cup of coffee and selected a sweet roll.

Curley sipped his coffee while observing the man across from him. *A real dandy,* he thought. His dark hair was slicked back in the latest style, and he wore a striped shirt and a pale blue cardigan sweater. His hands were immaculate, the long fingers lifting the cup almost daintily. His eyes, so dark they were almost black, glittered with intelligence. They also seemed drawn like a magnet to Amanda.

She ate her breakfast, conversing in German with the older redheaded woman seated beside her. She didn't look at either Curley or the man across from him. Curley finished his coffee and left. Amanda's glance locked with his as he was on his way out. He nodded. "Miss Chase," he said, and left.

Back in the parlor, he picked up the magazine, waiting for Amanda to finish her breakfast, so he could speak with her alone. He hadn't come all this way just to be brushed off. He'd find out what was going on, deliver her earrings, and get out of Germany. He'd hoped to make a date with her for when they both got back to the States, but she was acting so oddly, he wasn't sure how this meeting was going to turn out.

Suddenly Curley heard two people arguing in low tones. He recognized Amanda's voice saying, "I told you last night I don't need a baby-sitter."

"But, Honey, you know I. . ."

"Don't 'Honey' me! Go back and tell my father. . ." They entered the parlor and saw Curley. She stared at him, then shrugged her shoulders and walked out. Delbert grinned and said to Curley, "Women!" He watched Amanda but didn't move.

Curley did. He walked past Delbert and up the stairs behind Amanda. He knocked on her door and waited. She didn't answer. He knocked again. "Amanda? Please. I want to talk to you."

The door opened a crack and she said, "I can't talk now. Please go away." He didn't move. She looked at her watch. "Look. I'm busy right now, but we can talk later."

"How about one o'clock in the parlor?"

"One is fine." She shut the door but he didn't hear her walk away. After a moment, he went next door to his room. In less than a minute, he heard Amanda's door softly close. He opened his door a half inch and looked out. She was walking away, her camera bag hanging from one shoulder.

She moved quickly down the stairs. He followed her. Outside he saw a man fall into step behind her. The man crossed the street against the wind, still going in the same direction as Amanda.

She stopped at a corner. She looked back, and Curley sidestepped into a doorway. She crossed the street to the park. The man walking on the other side of the street crossed also and turned left. Amanda strolled into the park and seemed to be enjoying the sights. Curley stayed at the corner, knowing she'd spot him if he came any closer.

Amanda sauntered past a girl seated on a bench in the middle of the park. Then she stooped to pick up something, perhaps a rock. The man following her had circled the park and now stood on the opposite side, watching her.

★ ★ ★

Amanda sensed that she shouldn't approach Martha openly, and so she knelt, examining a pebble. "What's happened?" she asked in a low voice. "Have you moved? There were strange people at the house."

"The Nazis took our home and forced us to move into a Jewish neighborhood. They warned us that if we even came near the house we'd be killed."

A shudder coursed through Amanda, and she knew it wasn't because of the cold wind. She stood, brushing off her hand. "I can't believe it!"

"They took the gallery, too."

Amanda walked slowly past Martha. "No!"

"Don't look at me. Ignore me." Martha's pale blond hair was pulled up under a blue scarf tied beneath her chin.

Amanda stood a few feet away, her hands clenched at her side. "Tell me what this is all about." She reached for her camera and focused on a grove of trees and empty swings swaying in the wind.

"Jews are being rounded up into special neighborhoods. Father's business is gone. Tamara had a baby last week, and the circumcision ceremony is tomorrow. If we can find a *moyell* who is willing to come perform it. Everyone is afraid. We've heard awful stories of Jewish people being tortured, cut into pieces, and. . ." Amanda whirled to face her. "Look away. You don't know me!"

"I'm an American citizen, Martha. I came to see you. Where is this. . .special neighborhood?"

"You mustn't!"

"Martha, you know we can trust God to keep us safe. Don't you remember?"

Martha looked at her at last, and said, "It's all so mixed up in my mind. But you look good. I wish. . ." She sighed. "I wish God would help us."

Amanda circled the bench. "Where are you living? I want to come to the *bris*."

"We're at the east end of Domstrasse. Number 22. Tomorrow at nine o'clock. But be careful." Martha stood. Amanda didn't dare do more than glance her way. Martha's gray coat looked like warm armor as she walked with the wind at her back. She wore wool socks and sturdy shoes.

Out of the corner of her eye, Amanda saw a figure approaching from the opposite direction. It looked like one of the men who turned her away from her aunt and uncle's home. She ignored him, focusing her camera on a drinking fountain with a dried-up vine wrapped around it.

Curley watched the man approach the girls and tensed for action. The girl on the bench got up and left. He crossed the street, in case Amanda needed help. She didn't seem to notice the man; and he walked by, looking at her for a moment, then going on. His glance narrowed at Curley as he passed him.

Curley turned and gazed down the sidewalk after the girl in the gray coat. Amanda had hurried to this park, before seven A.M. The only reason could be that she was meeting the girl on the bench. Why? Who was she? The girl was now two blocks ahead. He hurried after her.

Chapter 10

Amanda trudged back, the wind pushing her toward Frau Reinhardt's. Something was terribly wrong. Martha's face was pinched and frightened, and her appeal for secrecy alarming.

Inside the boardinghouse, Delbert's happy voice grated on her ears. "You're out early!"

"Yes, I have a lot to do." She smiled weakly at him, trying to be polite.

"You didn't tell how the visit with your relatives went. By the way, I've asked around and was told there's a baroque cathedral in Eisenburg. We should go see it."

"What?" Thoughts of her family's plight whirling in her brain distracted her from what he was saying.

"I said there's a cathedral we should visit. Bach may have even played there."

Amanda winced. His bright smile was a mockery to the life-and-death situation going on with her family. They weren't in jail, though; or was Domstrasse Street some kind of prison?

Delbert touched her arm. "Amanda? Are you all right?"

"I'm fine. I just have some things to do. Go see the cathedral and tell me all about it later."

"But, Honey. . ."

She brought her arm close to her side, away from his touch. His endearment irritated her as much as misspelled words in a headline. "Later, Delbert," she said, heading up the stairs.

In her room she set the camera bag in the closet, beside her suitcase, and splashed water on her face. *First, I'll find a library and read some local newspapers. That may give me a clue to what's happening here. Lord, help me.*

★ ★ ★

Curley followed the girl in the gray coat. The ends of her scarf flapped in the wind as she kept her head down against its gusts. Passing a young woman sweeping the sidewalk, she took a wide course around her. The woman shook her broom at the girl and said something Curley could not hear.

The girl hurried on, and Curley passed the young woman who freed the dead leaves from the base of the building to fly off into the wind. She smiled at him. Her light blue eyes were framed by an oval face and shiny blond hair. Nodding politely, he wondered why she showed hostility toward the girl and not to him. He shrugged. Maybe it was some neighborhood conflict.

He followed the girl past a knot of people whom she avoided by crossing the street. Several blocks later the street ended by a barricade across the last few blocks. Guards with rifles slung over their shoulders marched in front of the open gate.

The girl stopped, pulled something from her coat pocket to show the guards, and darted inside.

Curley slowed his steps at the barrier, an ugly fence of rough-hewn brown boards. Both sides of the gate were swung inside. On the fence were signs proclaiming this a Jewish holding area with a Star of David and the word *Juden-Heim* beneath. A white-painted Star of David was scrawled near the signs.

Curley approached the guards. They marched back and forth, their high black boots almost to their knees. A third guard standing beside the gate watched him. Carley slowed his steps, looking up at the two-story building behind the wall.

"Was machen Sie hier?" One of the marching guards stopped and gestured by lifting his head.

They keep asking me that, thought Curley. *"Ich bin Amerikaner,"* he answered, looking up, as a tourist would, and told them he was just looking. Inside the gates, people were out on the sidewalks, apparently going about their business the same as those outside the gate.

"Hmm." The guard assessed him with skeptical eyes. A third guard came and told the other one to keep moving. He saluted, clicked his heels, and continued pacing before the open gates.

Curley shoved his fists into his pockets, smiled at the blond giant, and nodded at the sign. "What is this, uh, *Juden-Heim?*"

The guard took a deep breath, his chest swelling beneath his brown jacket. "This camp is protective custody for our Jewish citizens."

Curley's gaze followed the guards and scanned the fence. "Why do these citizens need protection?"

The man smiled, his blue eyes glittering fiercely. "There are those who look upon them as less than human, worthy only of extermination."

Curley's breath trembled in his throat, and he swallowed quickly. "And you protect them?" This man's feral attitude didn't seem that of a protector.

"We protect them," he snapped.

Curley ran a hand through his hair, smoothing it down in the wind. There wasn't much he could say after that. He took a deep breath, looked up at the rows of barbed wire above the fence. The two guards' boots smacked the sidewalk in front of the gates.

"Well, I guess I'll be getting back to town," he said.

"Ja, there are other pleasant sights to enjoy in Eisenburg." He turned and went to stand at his former post beside the in-swung gate.

Curley walked away, looking back once, with the feeling that the gate was more to confine than to protect the Jews from anything outside. What had the young girl done to sentence her to a life in this place? Was she a Jew? How was Amanda involved in this?

He had a lot of questions to answer before he met with Amanda at one. He had a lot to do in a short time.

★ ★ ★

Amanda slipped out the back door at the end of her hallway and down the back stairs of the fire escape. The wind howled between the buildings, trying to push her back as she made her way to the street. Gray, menacing clouds hung overhead.

She walked a couple of blocks before coming to the bakery where she'd had her first cup of tea. The window was closed against the strong wind, so Amanda went inside.

The mahogany-haired teenage girl smiled brightly when she saw Amanda. "Are you liking your stay in Eisenburg?" she asked.

"I certainly am," said Amanda, inhaling the fragrance of rolls, strudels, and pastries. She chose apple-peel tea and a couple of ginger cookies with thin lemon frosting.

Amanda sat on a high stool at the counter, and the girl brought her tea and cookies. "Have you seen the new movie starring Marlene Dietrich?" the girl asked with breathless eagerness.

Amanda sipped the tea and said, "No, I don't get to many movies."

"Oh! I go all the time—that is, I wish I could go more. I went to Berlin with a friend, and we stood in line for hours to see Mae West's movie." She rolled her eyes. "All I could see were the wonderful clothes she wore. I wish. . ." A clattering noise from the kitchen area startled her and she snapped her head toward the sound.

"Elisa!" A woman's voice called.

The girl raised her eyebrows and her shoulders. "That's me." She left Amanda and pushed back a gray cotton curtain in the doorway to the kitchen. "I'm coming, Grandmother."

Amanda nibbled on a cookie. She hadn't been able to get a word in edgewise. She'd have to ask somewhere else for what she needed. Thank goodness her tea wasn't boiling hot, so she could sip it quickly. She slipped one cookie into her pocket and drank the last of her tea.

She left some money on the table and was leaving when the girl returned, looking surprised and dismayed. "You're leaving? So soon?"

"I'm afraid so," answered Amanda. "I have business I have to take care of." With her hand on the doorknob, she smiled at the girl. "Would you tell me where the library is?"

"Oh, but Eisenburg doesn't have a library," the girl said.

Amanda frowned at the girl's words. "No library?"

"No, but when we need to look up something we go to the school." With pride she added, "*They* have a library!"

Amanda's grip on the doorknob eased, and she asked, "Where is this school?"

"I have to make a delivery, and I go right by there. I'll show you!" She ran back through the curtained doorway and returned, shrugging on her coat while carrying a wicker basket.

They walked down the windswept streets, Elisa chattering away about gowns and hairstyles. They rounded the corner past a church with a steeply sloping roof and decorative ironwork adorning the eaves. "I go to church here," announced Elisa. "Do you go to church? Are you a believer? What town are you from?"

"Yes, I'm a believer, and I go to church," said Amanda. "I'm from a town called Boston."

"Do they have Jews in Boston? My best friend was a Jew, but she's gone to America now. Well, it doesn't matter, I guess." She looked about guiltily and pointed up the street. "That's the school."

"Why do you ask me if there are Jews in Boston?" Amanda looked down into the hazel eyes that looked away quickly.

Elisa shrugged. "I'm not supposed to talk about it." She stopped. A sign over the door advertised an architecture firm. "This is as far as I go," she announced. "Come back soon to the bakery, Miss Boston."

The school, a three-story building, displayed a Nazi flag flapping in the wind on the flagpole. Windows every few feet lined themselves together on each floor. Above the door a huge photo of Hitler in uniform looked down on those who entered.

Inside, her footsteps echoed on the polished wooden floors. She passed a classroom full of children, with books propped in front of them on their wooden desks. On the wall was a picture of Hitler. In the library, racks of newspapers and magazines clustered beneath a portrait of Goethe. She chose several and spread them out on a wooden table.

As she began to read, her heart pounded. She could scarcely believe the hateful words she was reading. There was nothing subtle about the venom they spewed: Germany was at the mercy of Jews; they were behind every wicked scheme to destroy the country. They were physically repulsive, said one newspaper article; another said they were a lower form of life; "parasites plundering the nation without pity," said Hitler. Joseph Goebbels summed it up: "The Jews are to blame for everything." Cartoons showed ugly, slack-jowled Jews corrupting the morals of Germany as child molesters, enticing innocent children, seducers of Aryan young maidens, and responsible for every vile sin in the land.

Amanda's stomach knotted up and her blood ran cold. A chilly black fog seemed to fill the room. She sat stunned for a few moments, with strange, disquieting thoughts racing through her mind. This was too bizarre to be real! Why had none of this made headlines in the States? Rumors and innuendoes were all she'd heard; and they were denied. But they were true! More than that, the rumors were mild, compared to what she was reading.

Uncle Jacob and his family were in danger. She had to get them out of the country somehow. She paged through a few more papers, hoping to find some articles disputing the shocking reports she'd just read, but there were none. She closed the last paper on a drawing describing the unappealing physical and character traits of the Jew.

Amanda looked across the room at the window. It was merely a frame for the dull gray sky. She couldn't shake the feeling of unreality, as if she'd stepped onto the stage of some nightmarish, mad drama. Her fingers moved over the papers and magazines. It was all too real.

A wave of nausea swept over her. She struggled under a heavy darkness that had settled over her mind. Suddenly, the door at the end of the room opened, and a teacher led her classroom into the library. Amanda snatched up her purse and fled, willing herself to briskly walk and not run.

Outside, she took several deep breaths but was unable to calm herself. She walked aimlessly for a long time, thinking, worrying, hoping, planning. No wonder Martha looked so frightened. *I'm an American citizen,* she told herself. *They have no power over me. Or do they?* she wondered. *I am in their country— but still I'm an American.* Having been an American student in France, she knew there were limitations on the power a foreign government had on American visitors, but from what she'd just read, this country's policy was outside all rules of decency and order.

★ ★ ★

At noon, Amanda found herself back at the park where she'd met with Martha that morning. She sat on the same bench, her thoughts churning as fast as the wind shook the trees around her. *I need a plan of action. First, I must find 22 Domstrasse.*

Glad to have some direction at last, she went to the post office, looked at a map of the city, and found Domstrasse. She gasped when she saw the wall drawn on the map. Icy fear twisted around her heart, and she began to shake when she thought of the hate she'd read at the library. At one o'clock she pushed the door open at Frau Reinhardt's and started dully for the stairs.

★ ★ ★

Curley was anxiously waiting for Amanda. He heard the door open when she entered, and he saw her walk slowly by the parlor door. "Amanda. In here!" he called. She kept on walking. Something was wrong.

He leaped up and came into the hallway behind her. He touched her arm, and she turned. Her eyes were glazed and full of pain. "Princess! What's wrong?"

She flinched and kept on walking.

Stepping in front of her, he gripped both her arms. "What happened? You can tell me."

She shook her head. "I can't talk now, Curley. I just. . ."

He put his arm around her shoulder. "You look like a girl who could use a shoulder about now."

"I. . ." Her voice wavered and she hung her head.

"Come," he said, leading her up the stairs. He opened the door to his room and ushered her in. He sat her on the edge of the bed and pulled up a straight-backed wooden chair for himself. "Sweetheart, something happened. What was it?"

She licked her lips nervously. "My family. . .they. . ." She remembered Martha's note telling her to tell no one, trust no one. She sucked both lips between her teeth and hugged her arms to her chest. "I can't talk about it."

Curley watched her wretched sadness and understood that she couldn't talk now. In those seconds he was consumed with compassion, wishing he could take the pain and sadness from her.

He knelt before her and gently took her hand. It felt so cold. He covered it with his other hand. "Amanda, I don't want to cause you any more grief, but there are some things I think you should know."

Her eyes had a flat, faraway look in them that alarmed him. "Amanda! Tell me what happened." He looked steadily into her eyes, wishing he could discern her thoughts.

A tear rolled down her cheeks, and he melted. He moved to her side and put his arm around her. "I told you this shoulder is yours if you need it." He drew her head to his chest.

She sat quietly for a moment, then he felt her softly crying. He rubbed her back. "Shh. It's okay. I'm here." He would slay dragons or walk on fire for this woman, he realized with surprise.

He enjoyed her closeness for a few minutes more, until she drew back, sniffling. He reached into his chest pocket and drew out a handkerchief for her.

"I'm sorry," she said, patting the wet front of his shirt.

"It's fine," he assured her. "You needed someone, and I'm glad I was here for you."

"I must look a fright," she said, dabbing at her eyes.

"You look good to me," he said, lifting her chin with his curled index finger. She sniffed once more and turned her head.

"Did you have lunch?" he asked. She shook her head. "I found a quiet little place where we can talk. Let's go."

Amanda paused, as if she were going to refuse him.

"Remember, we have a one o'clock date," he reminded her.

She sighed and said, "I remember."

They sat in a booth of dark wood in a cozy restaurant. After they'd had a satisfying lunch of dumplings in a dark consommé, they shared small talk, until Amanda began to relax. He asked her what she meant when she'd first seen him on the fire escape. "You said I was a little late?"

Mentioning their date at the ship's church service, she shrugged as if it didn't matter.

"Didn't you get my note?" he asked.

"What note?"

He explained his hasty departure and apologized again. She closed her eyes, enjoying the way his words warmed her heart.

Over dessert, he leaned forward and said, "I told you earlier that I found out some things I think you should know."

Her eyes, like green polished jade, were fixed on him.

"Listen, I notice you're staying at Frau Reinhardt's and not with your relatives."

She opened her mouth to speak.

He held up his hand. "Let me finish." She nodded. "I've been around town, talking to various people, and I have heard some very disturbing things." He leaned forward and lowered his voice. "Hitler has special forces confiscating Jewish homes and businesses, sending Jews into restricted areas."

Amanda winced.

"You know about the wall?" he whispered.

She nodded. He understood now why she was so distressed. She set her spoon down and took a shaky breath.

"I took a look at it," he said. "It was horrible! Like an ugly scar stretching across the street." Curley took hold of her hand and squeezed. "Don't go near that wall. It's dangerous."

"I'll be careful."

"I'm serious. If you have family in there, have them come out to see you. But if you insist on going in, I'll go with you. Do not go there alone."

"How. . ." She clamped her mouth shut.

"How what? How did I find out about your family? That's unimportant for now. What counts is that you need to get away from here. You can work from the States to get your family out."

She shook her head. "You don't understand."

"I understand danger, and this is the real thing. Tell me, are your Jewish relatives believers in Jesus as their Messiah?"

Flexing the fingers of her hand that lay near his, she sighed. "My cousin Martha believed years ago, but I don't think she had the strength to talk openly about it at home."

"Believe me," he said, "the only way to get through something like this is to hang onto God with everything you've got."

Amanda nodded. "That's right. I must get in to see them and pray with them."

"I told you it's dangerous. We can pray together for them. I'm leaving tonight. Come with me."

"I can't do that," she answered, waving his concerns aside.

He admired her valiant determination, but the evil tide he saw building here would engulf her. "You must! There are things here that you don't understand."

"I'm a reporter, remember? I've done some fact-checking on my own, and I understand clearly what's happening here."

The waitress came to clear away their dishes, and they sat back silently, watching.

Amanda opened her purse and pulled out her compact. She flipped it open and turned her head from side to side, patting her hair. She snapped the compact shut and said, "I have to get back now." Her eyes darkened as they fastened on his. "Thanks so much for the shoulder," she said softly.

"Anytime." He stood as she slid out of the booth. He paid the waitress, and reaching into his pocket for change, his fingers brushed against Amanda's earrings.

All the way back to their rooming house, he tried to think of a way to tell her of the rumors he'd heard. She may have found out about the German takeover of Jewish businesses and homes, and even of the relocations, but he didn't think she knew that plans were afoot to march Jews out of Eisenburg to some unknown place.

He had been able to glean this information from sources she'd have no access to, by putting together a word here, a gesture there, whispered hints, and fearful constraint which spoke louder than accusations.

Curley stopped outside Frau Reinhardt's. Amanda looked up at him with questions in her eyes. Reaching for her hand, he curled her fingers around the earrings he'd taken from his pocket. "You left these in my care back on board the ship."

Amanda opened her hand and looked at them, then back at Curley.

It seemed perfectly natural to him to lift her hand and kiss the inside of her wrist. "I thought it was a dream," he murmured tenderly. Again, just as on board the ship, he had trouble tearing his gaze away from the moist softness of her mouth.

The door opened, and Delbert looked out, smiling. "Are you all right, Amanda?" He peered at her as she pulled her hand away from Curley. "Did you hurt your hand?"

"I'm fine, Delbert. Just fine." She smiled at them both and swept past Delbert into the rooming house.

You will listen to me, Curley thought, as soon as the door closed. *I'll not leave here without you,* he vowed. He hunched his shoulders against the wind and set out to take care of business. He was, after all, on a military mission.

Chapter 11

Amanda sat on her bed, with her coat on, yet she couldn't stop shivering. The soup she'd eaten hadn't warmed her at all. She slipped off her shoes and tucked her feet beneath her, to warm them. But nothing could warm the icy coldness that gripped her heart.

She needed a plan. But what? Germany had become too dangerous for Uncle Jacob's family. Did they have passports, or were they confiscated? Tomorrow she'd find out at the *bris* ceremony, and she would appeal to the American Embassy if necessary.

She bent the pillow and leaned back on it, pulling the blanket over her. *No one knows I'm related to anyone in Eisenburg—or at least no one except Delbert and Curley—and the optometrist.* Surely, none of them would betray her. Because Uncle Jacob was her mother's brother, their last names were not the same. The ghetto wall crouched at the edge of her thoughts. How could a country single out citizens and segregate them from society? An image of a headline she read today spooled through her memory. *Jews Open a Pandora's Box to Turn Loose Evil in the Land.*

She reached for her pad and pencil. After a moment's thought, she wrote, "Germany's Infamous Secret." Under that she wrote "Millions Suffer Persecution and Humiliation." This was the big story she'd come to find. But she felt no sense of accomplishment. Instead, she felt sick and frightened.

She flung off the cover and swung her legs over the side of the bed. With practiced speed, she wrote everything she'd seen and experienced since her arrival in Berlin, the neatly swept streets, the clean, main thoroughfares where tourists walked, and the darker side of the pristine image. She described her uncle's defaced gallery, the ghetto wall. . . She quit writing at last and gazed at the gray ceiling.

The guards! How would she get in tomorrow morning? She could say she was a nurse. But they might demand identification papers. They probably wouldn't allow a tourist in. What if she told them she hated Jews and was glad to see them segregated from the decent people of Eisenburg; would they consider her a sympathizer and let her in? She grimaced at the thought of even pretending to go along with their madness.

There must be a way in, otherwise Martha wouldn't have told her to come. Maybe it was easy to get in but difficult to get out?

Amanda began pacing the small room, from the window, past the bed, to the door and back. What if she got stuck behind that wall? *I'm an American citizen.* That carried some weight, didn't it? On the other hand, these people seemed callous enough to disregard such courtesy.

She picked up her notebook and sat on the bed again, continuing her notes. Clouds darkened the sky, and afternoon faded into dusk. A knock on the door jarred her, slashing the pencil across the page.

She turned on the lamp and opened the door. Delbert stood in the hallway, smiling down at her. Glancing over her shoulder, he commented, "Working hard, I see."

Amanda glanced back, to see her notebook open and the pencil beside it on the bed. Delbert's handsome face beamed at her. *What is he really doing here?* she wondered.

She felt better for having recorded her confused thoughts and impressions. Now it was time to deal with Delbert. She sighed. "What time is it?"

He pulled his gold watch from its pocket. "Five-fifteen. May I come in?"

Amanda stepped back and let him in. He sat on the wooden chair, hands on his knees. She stood beside the bed, her hand resting on the table, near the earrings Curley had just returned. "Why are you here, Delbert?"

"I'm glad you asked." Delbert leaned forward. "Maybe I was too bold offering you an engagement ring in front of the family." He flashed her his most brilliant grin. "But I meant it. I do want you to marry me."

"But we already discussed that, and you. . ."

He put up his hand to interrupt her. "I know, I know. I didn't realize how seriously you take your newspaper career. But when you turned me down and then left the country, I had to face it. I was slightly overbearing." He rubbed his chin slowly.

"Slightly! You called my work 'little newspaper stories.' You absolutely missed the whole point." Apparently her Christianity meant so little, he didn't even think it had any bearing on their relationship. Amanda picked up the earrings and rubbed her thumb across the flat facet of one of the jewels. "Look, Delbert. We don't need to go over this again. You still haven't answered my question. Why are you here?"

"That *is* the point, Honey. I see now how important your work is, and I'm here to show that I support you." He gestured toward her notebook. "Are you writing a story about the new government here? Let me help. I can talk to people and get information for you. We can work together!"

Amanda took a deep breath, trying to cover her annoyance.

"Before you say no, listen! While you were out today, I went to that cathedral and talked with some of the local people. The cathedral is magnificent. Bach didn't play there, but Brahms did. And I talked politics to the people. Adolf Hitler has unified the country. He's brought order to the chaos they were in and stabilized their money. Do you know their currency was so worthless some housewives used it to light fires in their stoves?" He sat back with a satisfied smile. "Between the two of us, we can send back interesting articles to the *Chronicle*."

"Quaint travel articles, telling how lovely it is here, and how happy everyone is?" she asked.

"Exactly. What do you say, Honey? Germany, from our point of view! We'd make a good team."

Amanda shook her head. "Thanks for the offer, but I need to do this by myself. And, Delbert, please don't call me Honey."

He hung his head sadly. "I'm sorry. You asked me before not to call you Honey. But it's merely an endearment."

The silence lengthened between them. A thunderclap shook the window, startling her. She looked out, seeing nothing but darkness.

"All right. I won't call you that anymore, but it'll be hard, because you're so sweet." He stood and stepped close to her. Putting his arm around her shoulders, he said, "Please reconsider about working together. We'd make a smashing team."

Amanda moved from under his arm. "Sorry." The room was so small, she had to slip between him and the bed, taking her stance in the center of the room. "So, are you going back home soon?" If she sounded anxious to be rid of him, he seemed not to notice.

"No, I'm going to escort you back when you're ready. Meanwhile I'll be here, helping until then." He crossed his arms over his chest in a self-satisfied gesture.

Amanda clenched her jaw and maintained an even tone. "That's nice of you, but I really don't need an escort."

Delbert raised his eyebrows. "You're aren't at your family's house. Why not?" Raindrops began pelting the window.

She looked away from him, unwilling to go into the story. She put her notebook and pen on the bedside table, then turned to him and said, "I'm famished! It must be dinnertime."

Delbert came forward with his hand outstretched. "I'd take you out to dinner, but it's beginning to rain. However, I'd be happy to escort you to Frau Reinhardt's table."

Amanda nodded. "All right, but I have to freshen up first. I'll see you down there later."

Delbert ran a hand over his slicked-down hair. "Good." His eyes grew serious as he stared down at her.

Amanda stepped back and said, "Later, then." She closed the door, relieved to be rid of him. A headline flew into her mind: *Gullible Delbert Benedict Approves of Nazi Tactics.*

★ ★ ★

Frau Reinhardt bustled happily around the tables, making sure her guests had plenty to eat. The aroma of meat, potatoes, and vegetables mingled with a spicy cinnamon smell. The good smell, combined with the rain pouring down and beating on the window, gave the room an aura of a cozy island in a cold, blustery world. Amanda and Delbert were seated at one of the smaller tables, set for six. The dining room was full. Most of the residents were there. Minus one. Curley was conspicuously absent.

Had he left without saying good-bye again? She sucked her lips between her teeth. He told her he was leaving, so she shouldn't be surprised or disappointed. *It's just as well,* she thought. She had no time for romantic notions. She had to concentrate on forming a plan to rescue her family from behind that awful wall.

Maybe sometime in the future she'd meet Curley again. He seemed the kind of man who attracted women, enjoyed them for awhile, then moved on. A man who might be a good friend but dangerous to become fond of. She didn't need complications right now. She bowed her head slightly and said a silent prayer of thanks for the food and also prayed for the safety of her family.

Delbert, speaking to the elderly lady with dyed red hair seated across from them, thanked her for recommending a visit to the cathedral. "A magnificent structure," he said.

"Did you also enjoy it?" the woman asked Amanda.

Amanda was on the verge of excusing herself. She had so much to plan and do before tomorrow, and this chitchat seemed irrelevant. "Enjoy? Oh, no, Ma'am. I didn't get there. But Delbert told me all about it."

The woman reached out and took Amanda's hand. "There is no substitute for being there. And you can call me Winnie," she said. Wrinkles fanned out from her big brown eyes as she smiled. "Tomorrow will be sunny. I will speak to the priest, and he will open the bell tower for you. Up there you can see for miles. It is a superlative view."

"Thank you. I'll certainly think about it and let you know."

The woman withdrew her hand with a smile.

Delbert turned to Amanda. "This is a marvelous start to our partnership! Let's do it."

Amanda quickly realized she'd have to leave the house at dawn in order to avoid Delbert, his questions, and perhaps even an attempt to follow her. Too much depended on her to risk being waylaid by nosey, helpful Delbert. "We'll discuss it later," she said.

Delbert turned back to his dinner with a pleased look.

Between the main course and dessert, Frau Reinhardt checked each table to be sure all was well. She laughed delightedly when Delbert said the meal was as appealing as her sparkling eyes.

She'd just gone back into the kitchen when the front door opened and a cold blast of air whooshed inside. All eyes turned in that direction.

★ ★ ★

Curley brushed the rain out of his eyes and stripped off his soaking jacket. He wished he was wearing his leather flying jacket with the fur-lined collar instead. The warm, fragrant entryway welcomed him.

Frau Reinhardt rushed to him, taking his jacket. "Come, warm your hands in the kitchen," she said, leading him. He walked gingerly, to keep his soggy shoes from squishing. Pausing at the kitchen door, his eyes were drawn across the room to Amanda. For a long moment she looked back at him, then he forced himself to turn and enter the kitchen.

Steam enveloped him with another warm welcome. Frau Reinhardt spread his jacket over three wooden hooks near the back door and placed a towel beneath to catch the drips. The cook moved a pot from one of the burners, and Curley warmed his hands. "This is just what I needed. Thank you." He grinned at Frau Reinhardt.

"A night good only for ducks and fish," observed Frau Reinhardt.

Curley rubbed his hands briskly. Though they were warming, his feet still felt frozen.

As if Frau Reinhardt read his mind, she said, "You have dry socks in your room, *ja?*" He nodded. "Go on, then. Warm your feet. Your dinner will be on the table when you come back down."

He touched his forehead in a mock salute. "Aye, aye, Captain."

Back in his room, Curley turned on the radiator and removed his shoes and wet socks. He tied his shoes together with the strings, removed the picture over the radiator, and hung them on its nail. The radiator clanked and ticked as it began heating. He draped a sock to hang from inside each shoe. A drop of water fell on the radiator with a hiss.

He removed his passport from his shirt pocket. The police had given it back with strict orders that he be gone by tomorrow noon. He'd strolled past the edge of town, then jogged out into the country to check on the plane. He found it just as he'd left it. He thanked God for the high winds and threat of rain that kept curious country folk inside.

It wouldn't be smart to take off in the storm, though this sweet little plane could do it, and Curley had the expertise to fly out, if necessary. Early would be the best time to leave, and if the storm eased up and the westerly wind continued, he'd make good time.

Back in the dining room, Frau Reinhardt directed him to sit next to the redheaded lady across from Delbert and Amanda. "You sit with your American friends. Relax."

He inclined his head to Amanda, Delbert, and the lady beside him. Giving quick thanks for the meal set before him, he felt a strange comfort at being so near Amanda.

She and Delbert had finished eating and had coffee cups at their places. Delbert laughed at something Winnie said. Amanda sipped her coffee, gazing distractedly into her cup. Long lashes lay against her cheeks. Curley flexed his fingers, longing to lift her chin and look into her clear, observant eyes.

Just as if he'd done so, she looked up with a burning, faraway look. He tilted his head and leaned forward. "Hello?" She focused her eyes, startling him with their soft emerald glow.

Delbert looked from Curley to Amanda. He laid his hand over hers, and Curley didn't miss the implication of possessiveness.

Amanda slid her hand out from under Delbert's and stood, excusing herself, and Curley and Delbert rose. Curley thought, *I have to talk to her alone and warn her of the danger out there.*

Back in her room, Amanda began her preparations. She wrote a letter to her parents, sealing it in two envelopes so that it would be difficult to hide any tampering.

She tapped her pencil on her chin, contemplating her next step, when her eyes caught sight of a small piece of paper lying on the worn burgundy linoleum just a few inches inside the door. It hadn't been there when she went down to dinner, and she must have pushed it aside when she'd come in just now.

She quickly unfolded it. Inside was a small yellow triangular patch. "Pin this, point up, on your chest, left side," was written on the paper, signed "M."

A chill zinged up her neck, and her gaze darted about the room. How did Martha get this message here? All day Amanda had wondered how Martha had known she was here, and now this.

The rain beat against the window, sliding down in watery rivulets. She fingered the patch, looking toward the rain-streaked window, trying to remember details she'd read at the library. Certain citizens were given a serial number and triangle. Red for politicals, green for criminals, purple and black for something she couldn't recall, pink for homosexuals, yellow for Jews. Holding the actual symbol made it all more terribly real.

A knock at the door startled her. She crammed the note and yellow triangle into her pocket and opened it.

★ ★ ★

Knocking on Amanda's door, Curley reminded himself to be patient. As a captain in the air corps, when he issued an order it was obeyed without question. He wasn't used to the art of persuasion. But persuade her he must.

The door opened slowly, and Amanda stood in a soft dark pink sweater and slim skirt, with the glow of the lamp behind her. She looked feminine and vulnerable, and he relaxed. Convincing her might not be as hard as he'd thought.

"Curley! Well, this is a surprise." She glanced at his stockinged feet. "You didn't even wait for your shoes to dry." She stepped back. "Come on in."

He entered, leaving the door slightly ajar behind him. The only evidence of her occupying the room was the tablet on her bed and a wet washcloth draped over the radiator pipe.

"Did you come to say good-bye?" she asked.

He leaned his shoulder against the door and crossed his ankles. "Yes. And I'm asking you once again to come with me."

She raised an eyebrow. "And why should I do that?"

He pushed himself away from the door and stood with his legs apart. "I told you, the situation here is much more dangerous than you realize."

"Thank you for your concern, but I *am* an American citizen and an observer, and I'm not going to do anything to draw attention to myself," she answered in a determined tone of voice.

He reached out and gripped her arms. She looked up at him with wide, surprised eyes. "American citizen or not, you'll be in danger if you stay," he said, more harshly than he intended.

She frowned, her eyes darkening. "I saw. I read the hideous lies and actions against certain citizens. But I see no danger to me."

Curley realized his hold on her was tightening. He let go of her arm. "Listen, and don't ask me how I know, but soon, maybe tomorrow, the police will take a group of its 'protected' citizens from behind the wall to some unknown place."

Amanda's mouth tightened a fraction. "Which group?" She reached for her tablet and pencil. He reached for her wrist.

"This is not to be written—yet. I don't know which group, but they will be Jews." Her raised chin of defiance irritated him. "Amanda, I'm telling you—leave now."

She looked away, not answering. Her wrist felt birdlike and fragile in his large hand. He moved his thumb and marveled at the velvet softness of her skin. He let go of her and she seemed to relax.

Gently rubbing her wrist, she said, "I can't leave right now, but I do thank you for the warning. I'll be careful."

He stared at her, wanting to shake sense into her, to tell her of the brutal look in the eyes of the guard at the wall. He couldn't explain the vicious ways of fighting men. She knew nothing of such things. "We need to pray," he said, unable to keep quiet. "Now." He reached for her hands.

She looked startled, but obediently she bowed her head.

"Father God," he began, "You have power over every evil in the world. I pray now for Amanda's safety, and for her family's, and. . ."

When he finished, he let go of her hands. "If you change your mind, you know where my room is. I'm leaving at dawn." He did have his orders to report soon.

She followed him to the door. "Thanks. And good-bye."

Curley gave in to the impulse to touch her shoulder. The lamp behind her

213

again surrounded her in a soft glow picked up by the sweater's fine wool. "I want to see you after we both get back. Will you give me your address and phone number?" He could feel the magnetism that pulled him when he was close to her.

"All right," she said almost in a whisper. Her gaze dropped from his, and she moved away to pick up her tablet and pencil. She wrote on the bottom corner of the page and tore it out. Handing it to him, she smiled and said, "Well, then, this is it. Good-bye, and Godspeed."

This isn't a final good-bye, he thought. He'd see her again. He'd walk through hell and high water if he had to.

An overwhelming need to hold her swept over him and he drew her to him. He held her in his arms for a long moment, simply enjoying the feel of her softness against him. She brought her arms around his waist and sighed. He dipped his head and kissed her cheek, her chin, then settled his mouth on her lips.

She raised herself on tiptoes and moved her arms to his chest, then slid them up around his neck. The warmth of her lips ignited a fire that flared through him. He pulled back briefly, then reclaimed her lips again. The delicious joy that resulted almost drugged his senses. He pulled back and crushed her to his chest.

He rocked back and forth a moment, then kissed her on the forehead. "May God take care of you." He looked into her eyes which were smoldering with embers of desire.

"You, too," she whispered. Before he gave in to his urge to stay there and kiss her all night, he reached behind him for the doorknob. She slid her hands from his neck and clasped them at her waist as he left.

Back in his room Curley sat on his bed, running his fingers through his hair. He had his orders to get that Vega to Holland. Of course, they'd given him plenty of time, but he'd already delayed his takeoff until tomorrow at dawn, hoping to take Amanda with him.

He remembered when his best friend Johnny met Meredith. Curley was only fifteen at the time, but he'd thought Johnny was foolish, even though Meredith was a special woman. Just last spring, Johnny had told him that someday he'd find a woman who could inspire him to walk through fire or flood for her, just as Meredith had inspired him. Curley had scoffed then.

Now he began to see that until Amanda came into his life, he'd led a lonely, single existence. It was as though he moved all alone among people who connected with each other, never allowing himself to think there was anything missing in his own life.

He placed his elbows on his knees, hands clasped behind his neck, remembering back ten years. When Meredith came into Johnny's life, Curley was sure that such a perfect match was something that only happened once every century.

Lately, though, he was beginning to feel the stir of something in the corner of his heart that had been locked away from the time he was four years old when his mother left. Amanda seemed to be able to reach past his defenses and touch the childlike hunger for love and acceptance.

Curley covered his face with both hands. Since Amanda had come into his life, nothing was the same—that thought alarmed him more than he wanted to admit. He took a deep breath and went to the closet for his suitcase. He had a mission, and the sooner he got his mind on that, the better off he'd be.

He packed everything, closed the suitcase, then lay on the bed, fully dressed. "God, take care of her. She doesn't know the danger she's in. But You do." He closed his eyes, drifting in and out of sleep until dawn's thin light crept into the room.

Chapter 12

After Curley left her room, Amanda leaned against the door for support. She had dreamed of being held in his arms, but his unexpected gentleness awakened a deep feeling of peace in her heart. She took a ragged breath, surprised at her swift and passionate reaction to him. She stroked her arm, conscious of the lingering feel of his arms holding her close to his warmth.

She touched her lower lip, still warm from his kiss, inspiring an intense desire for more. She forced herself to walk across the room, away from the door, afraid of her need to go after him. She stood watching rain streak the window, and she jammed her fists into her sweater pockets.

The yellow triangle bristled against her right knuckle, as if an iceberg were thrusting itself up through her warm, sensuous haze. She retrieved the note and angrily tore it to shreds. She opened the window a crack and let the storm grab the pieces.

She pushed back the closet curtain. Moving the clothes about, she finally pulled out a classic navy blue skirt, matching jacket, and white blouse. From her purse she got two safety pins and pinned the triangle to her overcoat lapel.

She longed for someone to confide in, but there was no one. Even Curley, who saw the danger, wouldn't understand her need to stay and help. She almost wished her father were here. She knew, however, that even if he were in the next room, she couldn't tell him. He'd tell her to stay in her room, then he'd take over and demand the release of his family.

But would that be the right thing to do? No. She'd done her research at the library, and she was well aware that this persecution ran deep. To face it head-on would only result in being crushed.

She stared down at her camera bag on the floor. She would take pictures of her new cousin and the rest of her family at the *bris*, but getting the camera past the guards would be tricky. She unlatched the flash attachment, took it apart, and laid the pieces, along with two new rolls of film, on the dresser. She slid her notebook inside her purse, glad now that she hadn't surrendered to the fashion rage for pert little clutches.

After washing her face and brushing her teeth, she put on her pajamas and climbed in between cold sheets. Hoping for a little sleep before dawn, she tried to push Curley and the Nazi problem from her mind. The tip-tap of the rain and the metallic noise of the radiator lulled her to sleep.

She woke with a start. The rain had eased, and the silence was heavy. She bit her lip, hoping she hadn't cried out. She'd been dreaming; she was in a large garden, fleeing from a menacing pursuer. She came to a pond and tried to go around it, but it grew to become an ocean. Waves crashed at her right, and her pursuer was closing to her left. She saw a bridge ahead and ran faster, but her legs felt as if they were running through glue.

Uncle Jacob, Aunt Esther, and the family were on the bridge, looking out to sea, unaware of her plight. She shouted a warning, but they smiled, waving at someone in the distance. She glanced over to see what the family was waving at. It was Curley, falling into the water from the sky. *No!*

Her heart was still pounding. She flicked on the lamp and looked at her watch. Three-thirty. She turned the lamp off and lay back on her pillow, wondering who was chasing her in her dream. What was her family doing there? She trembled at the vision of Curley falling from the sky. The sky was his milieu. She'd seen him perform breathtaking stunts when he was a teenager. He'd parachuted flawlessly onto the ship just two weeks ago. So why did she dream of him falling?

She understood the part about her family on a bridge, unaware of the peril; but the peril was theirs, not hers. She thanked God that He'd promised to walk with her, even through the valley of the shadow of death. *Lord, help me to speak up tomorrow, so they'll know they can trust You, no matter what the circumstances. Please provide an opportunity to show them the gospel.*

She turned to her side, puffed the pillow, and forced herself to relax, knowing she'd need to be alert tomorrow—actually, in just a few hours.

She drifted on the edge of sleep, and when the night lightened to pewter gray, she sat up and put her feet onto the area rug beside her bed, adjusting to the semidarkness.

She wrapped her robe around her and hurried to the bathroom. Then she heard a noise. Holding a damp washcloth in one hand, she opened the bathroom door with the other, then froze. The weak light showed Curley standing beside her bedroom door. With suitcase in hand, he paused there for a moment, as though listening, or making up his mind about something. Then he scowled and strode down the hall. She quietly pulled the door shut until he'd gone past and had plenty of time to get down the stairs.

Back in her room, she brushed her hair until it crackled, then gathered it in a clip at her neck. She finished dressing and slipped the flash attachment parts into her jacket pockets. Opening her blouse, she slipped in the camera, settling it uncomfortably above her waist. Over all of this she wore her overcoat.

She stole quietly through the house and slipped through the front door into the frigid morning. The sky had lightened to a silvery color. Breathing in the fresh scent of rainwashed pavement and wet bricks, she put on her scarf and gloves. The air chilled her cheeks. She checked her watch: 5:55.

At the corner she turned left for a few blocks, then proceeded down a street that paralleled Domstrasse, toward the barrier. As she got closer, she detoured another block, to Eisenburg's last street, in order to approach the wall as far from the guards as possible.

A block to her left was the wall's corner. She went around the corner, determined to walk all around the confine. How big was the walled-in area?

To her left were rows of fruit trees with their branches stripped by the wind. Amanda walked the path beside the wall for approximately five city blocks, tiptoeing in some places to keep her heels from sinking into the moist earth.

Wisps of smoke rose from behind the wall, and she could hear doors opening and the faraway murmur of voices. She thought she heard someone behind her and looked around quickly, but all she saw was an orange cat darting into the orchard. She folded her coat lapel with its yellow triangle to the inside and kept walking.

She followed the encircling wall to the front which faced Domstrasse. She checked her watch again: 6:45. She passed the only gate and walked on a few blocks down narrow streets, passing somber, unsmiling people.

How would they react if she turned her lapel out and they saw the yellow triangle? She didn't, reluctant to risk the sting of discrimination toward Jews. Was this in a small measure what her family lived with? The thought, even for a few minutes, was offensive, but how did a person live with it daily?

The aroma of coffee and sweets baking distracted and tempted her, but she didn't think her stomach could handle food. A middle-aged man seated at a table near the bakery window looked up from his newspaper and gave Amanda an appreciative glance, with a warm, friendly smile.

He looks like a nice person, she thought. Would he smile if she turned her lapel outward to show the yellow triangle? What would he say if she interviewed him about his country's policies toward Jews and other "inferior" groups? It was hard to believe that these seemingly normal, nice people would support such repulsive decrees.

The bakery door opened and someone came out. That's when she saw the sign, "No Jews Allowed." Her stomach knotted up and she turned back the way she'd come. *I've avoided this long enough*, she thought, pulling her lapel out to expose the yellow triangle. She was a fool to tell herself she was merely gathering information, learning more about the town, when the truth was she delaying going inside that hideous fence.

She took a deep breath, held her head high, approaching the gate where a guard stood at each side. She looked straight ahead and walked inside.

"Halt!"

Pushing back a surge of anxiety, she stopped. She took another quick breath and looked back. *"Ja bitte?"*

"Where have you been?" His eyes narrowed.

"On an errand," she answered as calmly as she could.

"I'd remember you," said the other guard with raised eyebrows. "You did not leave this morning."

Amanda looked him straight in the eye. "Maybe you were in the gatehouse."

The other guard adjusted the gun strap over his shoulder, eyeing her. At that moment, a truck full of soldiers roared up to the gate, distracting him. His gray eyes hardened at Amanda and he sneered, "Move on, Jewish whore!"

Amanda felt her cheeks burn as she turned and hurried inside. Her legs weak, she steeled herself to keep going and not look back. As she gritted her teeth, trying not to reveal her anger, she began noticing details. The street and buildings didn't look so different on this side of the wall, but there was a sense of despair in the few people who shuffled passed her. The light of hope gone from their eyes, they didn't speak to each other. Her footsteps echoed loudly in the quiet street.

An old man with a beard down his chest gave her a skeptical look, then he crossed the street as if to avoid her. A baby's cry from overhead pierced the silence. Amanda glanced up. The dark second-story windows all looked the same. She moved on, staying close to the building so she'd be less visible to the guard in case he was still watching her.

She turned a corner and continued walking the oddly silent but occupied streets. She encountered no guards. Apparently they didn't enter the confine; they simply guarded the gate.

She stopped at a stone wall, took out her notebook and pen, and jotted some notes. Her anger stirred as she wondered why there was no outrage, no reports of this monstrous assault on whole segments of a country's citizens.

That anger energized her as she went back to Domstrasse and found number 22. Carved figures sat upon ledges over the doors, and wrought-iron railings enclosed minuscule garden spaces, most filled with yellowing grass.

By now it was almost nine o'clock, so she mounted the steps and opened the door. Her eyes took a moment to adjust to the dark foyer. She stood in the dim hallway, confused for a minute, wondering how she'd find the right door. The foyer smelled of old wood, lemon oil, and mint.

She was searching for a list of the occupant's names when the door behind her opened. Her cousin Tamara, with a blanket-wrapped bundle in her arms, entered with a man. They squinted at the darkness.

"Tamara!" Amanda touched her cousin's shoulder. "It's me, Amanda."

"Amanda! I'm so glad you've come. But it's not safe."

"So everyone keeps telling me." She nodded at the man with Tamara. "You must be Nathan. I'm glad to meet you."

A door opened behind Nathan, and Tamara nodded at the old woman who looked out. "Hello, Mrs. Mandelbaun." The woman looked uneasily toward Amanda and shut her door without a word.

"Come on." Nathan motioned, leading them behind the stairs.

The door opened into a short hallway so narrow they had to walk single file into the tiny studio apartment. The room had one small window looking out onto another building.

Uncle Jacob approached them with hands outstretched. *"Mazeltov!* Enter! Enter!" He embraced Tamara, then gave Amanda a glowing smile and hugged her, too.

Amanda, so glad to see her uncle, tried to ignore the shock at seeing the family reduced to living in such cramped and shabby quarters. She hugged him back, and he kissed her on both cheeks.

Smiling broadly, Aunt Esther entered from the kitchen with a wooden spoon in her hand and Martha right on her heels.

"Amanda!" Martha anxiously waited for Aunt Esther to step back from hugging Amanda so she could hug her long and hard. She stepped back with a confused look. "What's this?" She felt the bulge at Amanda's waistline.

Amanda laughed. "My camera. I smuggled it in."

"It's good to see you still have your sense of humor. We're so glad to see you," said Aunt Esther, and added sadly, "but not in these circumstances."

Aunt Esther took Amanda's coat and said, "Have you seen our little David?"

Tamara had unwrapped the blanket and smoothed back the baby's dark hair so they could admire his ruddy-cheeked face. She looked up at her mother with a worried frown. "Are Rabbi Benjamin and the *moyell* coming?"

"They said they would."

Nathan shrugged. "They are afraid." The defeated words fell heavily into the silence.

Uncle Jacob waved toward the small sofa. "Sit and tell us what's happening in America. We don't get much news here."

Amanda sat, close enough to the edge to leave room for Martha. "Dad and Mom are doing fine. Business is good, since most of our investments are in foreign countries. You've probably heard there's a depression in America. But President Roosevelt has everything in hand. He's instituted programs to keep people busy earning a little money."

Aunt Esther called through the kitchen arch, "Talk loudly, so I can hear!"

"This place is so small, you'll hear us breathing," said Martha. She squeezed Amanda's hand and whispered, "There's so much I want to tell you."

Tamara and Uncle Jacob sat on wooden chairs, while Nathan stood behind Tamara, his hand on her shoulder. Amanda glanced around while she assembled her camera, wondering where they slept. There was the room they were in, a cramped kitchen, and probably a closet behind the fringed material hanging over a shallow doorway.

She didn't want to cause her uncle sadness, but she had to ask, "What happened to the house? I went there and found some very unfriendly men."

Uncle Jacob's eyes blazed. "Those. . ." He fumbled for a word. "Those poor excuses for human beings, they ordered us out of our own home."

Amanda stared at him, dumbfounded. "By what authority. . .how could they do that?"

"Just walked in and took over." Aunt Esther stood in the kitchen doorway, fists on her hips. "We had to scramble to gather together what we could carry out." Her accusing voice grew sharp. "Those worthless curs have our family china. They better not eat off it!" The thought of that seemed to incense her more, and she added, "I'll have to disinfect everything."

Amanda liked her aunt's feisty expression, and she took her picture. She lowered her camera. "You're going back? When?"

Uncle Jacob stroked his chin thoughtfully. "I expect we'll be back home before Hanukkah." The whistling teakettle got Aunt Esther's attention and she went back into the kitchen.

"Then you believe this displacement is temporary?" Amanda took a candid pose of Tamara, Nathan, and the baby.

"Most certainly," said Uncle Jacob. "It's a passing thing. The Nazi Party wants to show its strength, that's all. This will all blow over in a month at the most."

Amanda thought of the newspapers she'd read yesterday afternoon. "The gallery. . ."

Uncle Jacob's face blanched, his fists clenched. Aunt Esther saved the tense moment by entering the room, asking Amanda if she wanted her tea with sugar and apologizing that they had no cream.

There was a light tap on the door and Martha jumped up to answer. She ushered in a stout man wearing a heavy black coat, and a *yarmulke* on his head. He carried a small case in his hand and had the friendliest eyes Amanda had seen since she entered Germany.

Uncle Jacob and Nathan greeted him and clasped his hand. "*Rebbe* Stein. Welcome."

"*Rebbe* Benjamin sends his prayers for your family."

Uncle Jacob introduced him as the *moyell,* and Aunt Esther offered him a tray of scallop-shaped cookies pressed together with jam inside and powdered sugar sprinkled on top.

He took one, thanking her, and she handed him his tea. He sipped it and touched the baby in Tamara's arms, saying, "We must wake the little man and hurry with the ceremony. I am sorry, but I feel there is trouble brewing outside."

Amanda shuddered, remembering the nastiness of the guard and the soldiers arriving as she entered the gates. She shot a picture of all of her family, the baby in their midst.

Tamara prepared David while Rabbi Stein opened his black case. He said the ceremonial words, then circumcised the child, who began wailing.

Tamara hugged the crying baby to her breast, while Nathan thanked the rabbi.

He washed his hands, using a special cloth he'd brought, and repacked his case. He took a quick sip of tea, picked up a cookie, and apologized for having to leave so abruptly.

Tamara handed the baby to Aunt Esther and followed Nathan as he walked Rabbi Stein to the door. "We understand. Thank you," said Nathan, seeing him out.

Aunt Esther cooed softly to the baby and he stopped sobbing. Amanda picked up her teacup and asked Martha, "How did you know I was at Frau Reinhardt's?"

Martha smiled. "It was—"

Gunshots suddenly stabbed the air, popping over and over. Panic swept through Amanda. She set down her teacup with shaky hands. Aunt Esther's eyes widened in fear. The baby wailed again, and Tamara cried, "Oh, God, help us!"

The warm family gathering was shattered by a bullhorn. A roaring voice yelled, "Everyone out! Anyone left in this building in two minutes will be shot! Out! Now!"

Chapter 13

Amanda gaped at the furious activity. Aunt Esther scooped something golden and twinkling from a jar on her cupboard shelf; Uncle Jacob, with knees bent, reached deep into the closet; Nathan stood clutching the bawling baby while Tamara, with tears streaming down her face, stuffed his new booties and sweater into the diaper bag. Martha had her hands in an open box, pulling out warm woolen scarves, socks, and hats. Then she reached beneath the couch to retrieve a small notebook and pen.

It all happened so fast, Amanda stood as if in a dream, watching. Martha bundled the warm woolen items into a scarf and tossed Amanda's coat to her. "Hurry!"

Amanda woke from her shocked daze. She shrugged her coat on and quickly unscrewed the flash attachment from her camera, then stuffed all the pieces into her pockets. "What can I do? Can I carry something?" She looked about helplessly.

"You're an American!" shrieked Tamara wildly, thrusting her baby into Amanda's arms. "Say he's yours. Take him to America. He has no chance here!"

Amanda shook her head, startled and shaken. "But I. . ."

Nathan reached for his son and put an arm around his distraught wife. "This is temporary. We'll all go home when—"

"Come!" Uncle Jacob held the door open while they filed out. Martha carried the bundled scarf in one hand and took Amanda's hand with the other when they got out into the dark hallway. Footsteps hurried down the steps from the upper floor. The woman in the front apartment walked unsteadily out the front door, clutching a shawl to her neck. Tamara's baby had grown quiet, and the silence was broken only by the sniffling of a young boy holding his mother's hand as they walked out into the dim sunshine of an unknown future.

On the front steps of the building, Amanda could barely believe what she saw. German soldiers stood with rifles pointed menacingly. Some used them as prods to move people huddling in the middle of the street. It reminded her of pictures she'd seen of cattle drives. People were being rounded up in the street!

Those emerging from the building behind her streamed around her. "Come on!" urged Martha, "before they use force on us."

A soldier approached, glowering, and Amanda followed Martha into the street, to stand with her family. Fear and confusion threatened to erupt into hysteria as people looked from one to another for an explanation, a shred of hope or dignity, and found none.

All I have to do is show my passport, thought Amanda. She decided to wait, to endure what lay ahead with her family. Maybe the soldiers assembled the people to give new rules, or to frighten them by a show of strength. Amanda put an arm around Martha. Nathan had an arm around Tamara, supporting her while she cried softly.

Uncle Jacob turned his head from side to side, as though looking for a logical reason for this ousting of people from their temporary homes. Aunt Esther glared at the guard stomping through the crowd. Amanda had seen that look before, when she and Martha were children and had gotten into trouble. They always said that look could make a stone tremble. *These soldiers are harder than stone,* thought Amanda. *They won't tremble; they'll strike back.*

Amanda reached out to touch Aunt Esther, when all of a sudden they heard a wail from the building across the street. A soldier emerged from the doorway, behind an old man who was clutching his hip and limping. *"Schnell!"* shouted the soldier and whacked the man across his shoulders, sending him sprawling down the steps.

Reacting quickly, Amanda dashed to the old man's side and helped him to his feet.

"Leave him!" snarled the soldier.

Amanda looked up and muttered, "He's hurt."

The icy gray eyes filled with contempt, sending a chill down her spine. "Vermin have no feelings."

She bit back an angry retort as the old man struggled to his feet.

The soldiers began pushing and urging the crowd to the gate. Faces near her looked about in panic. There were no explanations, only shouts and prodding. No one dared question the soldiers, but a raw, primitive dread shot through the group.

A suffocating tension gripped Amanda's throat. She grimly noted every nuance and action. *Outrage in Eisenburg* would be her next headline.

Curley had warned her of this. She suddenly longed for his strength. She looked up; was he up there in the skies, gone from this madness? And Delbert. What would he do? He hadn't been able to sense any trouble was brewing. Visiting tourist attractions, he might never know this atrocity was happening. *When I get out of here, everyone will know,* thought Amanda. *I'll tell them!*

"This is outrageous!" Amanda said to Martha, almost choking on her anger. She ripped the yellow triangle from her coat and threw it to the ground.

Martha squeezed her hand. "They want to humiliate us. They can do their worst, but they can't crush our hearts."

"You're right. We have to keep our faith in God."

Children, sensing their parents' fear, were crying. "Faith?" Martha cried. "You need to rethink this 'faith.' Look around you."

"Martha! What are you saying? Remember back when Miss Whitney took us to church, and we gave our hearts to Jesus?"

Martha drew in a breath of cold air and looked up into the leaden skies.

Walking sideways, Amanda stared into Martha's face. Her light blue eyes wavered. Amanda repeated fiercely, her voice barely above a whisper, "Remember?"

Martha's face showed her pain. "I remember," she said, and looked away. "It was so long ago. I've tried to stay close to Christ since then. But where is He now?"

"He's here. He said He'd be."

A man in his thirties moved up in the crowd and put a hand on Uncle Jacob's shoulder. "Where are they taking us?" he asked, his dark eyes darting from face to face, averting his eyes from the guards hustling them through the gate.

Uncle Jacob turned a serious face to the man. "Why do you ask me? I don't know." The man shook his head, seeking answers in the faces around him, finding none.

As the Jewish group was herded through the streets of their own town, their silent fear turned to restless murmurs. Their former neighbors hung back in doorways, the younger ones watching curiously, some insolently, from the sidewalks.

Amanda glanced at Tamara; she was just starting her family, but what was her future? She hadn't had time to retrieve a thing from her home. Amanda's first article would focus on this new family, and what these forced moves were doing to them.

The guards made the people hurry through town. They reached the outskirts of the small town in a few minutes. A black car slid up beside them, and an officer got out. He barked an order to the guards, who nudged the people forward. Those who balked were prodded and kicked. Terror and outrage, combined with the pushing, caused a crush of people in the narrow street.

Amanda shouldered through the crowd to approach the officer, but one of the guards pushed her back. Sick with their cruelty, she glared at him and said, "Where are you taking these people?"

With a brutal stare, he pushed her back again.

"I am an American citizen! I demand to know where you're taking us."

"Pah! You are no American. You are with this trash, so you march with the rest of them."

Refusing to turn away, she pointed to the officer. "I will speak with him!" She opened her purse and reached inside.

"Get back!" he roared. The officer glanced at the disturbance.

Amanda held her passport up, waving it. "I am an American citizen! I refuse to be treated like this." She fought to keep her voice calm and authoritative.

The officer approached. "What is going on here?"

Amanda shot the guard a cold look while he saluted. Before he could speak, she said, "Yes, what *is* going on here? I am an American citizen, and I find myself rounded up, shoved about like an animal." She looked behind her. "And what have these people done? Where are you taking them?"

The officer stared from under the black brim of his hat, then he took her passport. He calmly opened it and flipped the pages, his lips thin with contempt. He gave her a measuring look, then put her passport in his pocket as if it were too filthy to look at.

Amanda took a deep breath to quell the panic welling in her throat.

"I will keep this and check your story. Now, get on the truck."

The guard grinned and gave her an extrahard shove. Amanda searched through the crowd. She spied Martha's blond head and went to her. "Where is Uncle Jacob and the rest of the family?" she asked.

Martha's eyes were bleak as she pointed through the crowd, and then they heard a cry. Everyone turned to see a pillar of smoke rising from the other side of Eisenburg. "They're burning our homes!"

★ ★ ★

Curley checked the instruments for the tenth time in as many minutes. The view outside hadn't changed. Low, flat clouds below, with glimpses of land between. All engine gauges were in the green. The airspeed indicator showed 120 mph; the engine sounded good; this sweet plane was performing beautifully.

But something was wrong. He knew it. He'd learned to trust his sixth sense when flying; it had saved his life more than once, especially on the stunt-flying circuit. Now, on his way to Holland, he felt more and more uncomfortable. Something was not right. Another check of the instrument panel and the steady drone of the engine confirmed that the problem was not in the plane. Then what?

Taking his mind off the plane's performance, he looked at the landmarks below. A bridge, a large stretch of water ahead. He'd just passed Hamburg. He stared out over the horizon. *Amanda.* He shook his head. She was on his mind too much. When this mission was over, he'd contact her and see where he stood. He didn't believe Delbert's statement that they were engaged.

He slipped the plane to the left to get a good view behind him and saw nothing but the sun rising. No German planes on his tail. His mission was safe, and he had an easy trip ahead. He reached behind his seat and took a candy bar from his flight bag. He peeled down the wrapper, telling himself there was no reason for this sense of uneasiness.

He bit off some chocolate and thought of Amanda again. He checked the map on his lap, putting a finger on his present location to note his progress. It didn't work. Amanda's face filled his mind. Coupled with the uneasiness he couldn't shake, he began to wonder if he should turn back.

If what he heard was true, and there were to be an uprooting of the Jews behind the wall, where would she be? Not anywhere near; not if she was smart and heeded his warning. No, she was all right. He smiled, thinking that at this minute she probably had her family with her at Frau Reinhardt's, eating strudel.

He finished his candy and flew on toward Holland. *Go back.* He turned his head sharply. He'd heard the words as surely as if someone were sitting beside him. Even the engine throbbed: *Go back. Go back. Go back.* He frowned, as a vision of Amanda's face floated across his mind again.

Pressing the left rudder pedal and turning the control wheel, he made a 180-degree turn, retracing his progress. The closer he came, the more the urgency pulled at him. *Remember, God; I asked You to take care of her.*

After passing over the gray haze from Berlin's factories, he squinted at a column of smoke ahead. He hoped it was merely some farmer burning the chaff from his fields, but the smoke was billowing too high to be a burning field.

When he flew through the thin clouds low over Eisenburg, his suspicion was confirmed. The ghetto was on fire.

Curley knew he had to be careful; his mission, his very life could be in jeopardy, but he would have taxied down the main street, if it were wide enough, and rescued Amanda if she needed it. He knew now the strong urge to return was because somehow she was in trouble. And, he grudgingly noted, the only trouble was in the ghetto where Amanda's family resided. He knew her—nosey reporter, stubborn champion of her family. She'd be right in the thick of things, trying to help.

He brought the plane down as close to town as he dared, making sure it was well hidden in the trees. He ran, parallel to the road about fifteen feet away, to avoid being seen.

Entering town from a side street, he pulled up his collar against the damp air, concealing his face, and made his way to Frau Reinhardt's. *Lord, let them be there in the parlor, away from the trouble. It will be so easy,* he thought, *to get Amanda—and her family, too, if they want—back to the plane and out of the country.*

He arrived at 11:15 A.M. Winnie, the elderly, red-haired woman, looked up as he stood at the parlor doorway. Her hand held a pen, poised over a journal. Smiling brightly, she said, "Hello there! We missed you at breakfast!"

"Thank you!" She was alone in the parlor. Curley pushed back his disappointment and smiled at her. Behind him he heard low voices and the rattle of dishes as the kitchen help set out the noon meal.

He was about to ask, when Winnie volunteered that Amanda hadn't been at breakfast, either. "Her friend said the two of you most likely went out to see the sunrise." She craned her head to peer behind him. "She's not with you? Ah, well, perhaps she's still in her room." She touched her chin with the top of the pen thoughtfully and said, "I hope she's feeling well."

"Thank you," said Curley and nodded to her. "Good day." He hurried up the stairs and knocked on Amanda's door.

A maid came from a room across the hall. "Miss Chase isn't in." She clutched a bundle of rolled-up sheets in her arms.

Curley looked briefly over his shoulder at her. *"Danke."* He went down the stairs, two at a time, the hair at his nape prickling. *Where is she? How will I find her?* He stood at the front door, rubbing his chin, when Delbert entered.

"Hello, old man!" he said, with a bright smile. "So, you're back. Did you and Amanda do some early sight-seeing?" He pulled at the white muffler around his neck, unwinding it. "It's chilly out there."

"I saw smoke. What was burning?" asked Curley, ignoring Delbert's question.

Pulling off his gloves, Delbert answered. "Oh, that. I heard that some apartments were burning. They wouldn't let anyone near; said it wasn't safe. The police escorted the poor folks who lived there through town, probably to a shelter."

"Which direction did they go?" asked Curley.

Delbert slapped the gloves across one hand and peered into the parlor. "What? Oh, south. Down that street by the park, the one with the shop that sells baroque figurines and paintings. Where's my dear fiancee, Amanda?"

Fiancee! He wouldn't believe Delbert's arrogant boasts. "Don't know. Excuse me." He reached past Delbert and pulled the door open. Looking both ways, he hurried away. He skirted the park, away from a policeman who stood with feet apart and hands clasped behind his back, watching the area.

He followed the street for a few blocks and, nearing the edge of town, saw nothing in the distance. If they had walked this street, it would have been over an hour ago at least. Keeping a low profile and walking quickly, but not so fast as to catch attention, he left town. As soon as he was back in the meadows, he ran to the plane.

Back in the air, he followed the winding road south of town. After a few minutes he saw them—a knot of about thirty people walking, with a black car behind them. He tipped the left wing and squinted at the group, but he wasn't close enough to pick out Amanda if she was in the crowd.

He followed the road, not daring to fly too low. The road curved its way south between low hills. He saw a bulky warehouse beside a railroad track. Three trucks and a black car were parked between the warehouse and a smaller building.

Curley flew on, scouring the area for a safe place to land and investigate. Orchards filled the hillsides, making it difficult to find a clear landing place, but the houses were few and far between, which made concealment easier.

Finally, he found a dirt road between rows of trees. Throttling back, he set the plane down, hoping the road was long enough for a takeoff later.

He tightened the wobbly tail wheel and was putting his wrench in the tool sack when he heard the crunch of footsteps. He froze for an instant, then stood slowly and turned to face whoever was approaching.

Chapter 14

Grimly, Amanda marched with the Jews, passing hills with orchards rising on both sides of the road. The guards ordered them to walk in silence. Martha's remarks echoed in her mind. Why *had* God allowed their home to be taken, and now this?

A plane flew overhead, and she thought of Curley. *If only I'd believed all of what he said and got my family away. I saw the evidence in the library, but I couldn't believe the Germans would brazenly evict the ghetto residents in broad daylight.*

Where was Curley? Probably in England by now, she figured, wondering if she'd ever see him again. The memory of how he'd held her and kissed her last night rippled warmly through her. She glanced at Martha, attempting to divert her thoughts of Curley.

Amanda shivered in the weak sunlight as a chill wind stirred. She jammed her fists into her coat pocket, longing to get her notebook and pencil from her purse and take notes as she walked. Headlines flashed in her mind. *The Reich's Evil Side*, or *Hitler: Leader or Despot?* How she'd expose the cruelties going on here! First, she'd have to get out; and how would she do that? The ruthless officer had her passport in his pocket.

She remembered a Sunday school teacher saying God always provided a way out of trouble. *God, we need Your help now!*

Amanda and Martha were at the rear of the plodding group. Near the front, a young child suddenly stumbled. His mother, who held a toddler in her arms, stopped and encouraged him to stand. He whimpered as the guards told them to keep moving. Amanda scooped up the boy in her arms to avoid falling behind and incurring the guard's wrath. "Don't lose hope," she told the mother. "God will help us."

"Where are they taking us?" wailed the little boy.

"I don't know." Amanda hugged him close to her. "But as long as we have each other, we'll be all right."

When Amanda's steps slowed from the extra weight of the child, Martha carried him. They grew tired and thirsty, moving more laboriously as the day progressed into afternoon.

★ ★ ★

Curley tensed as the man approached him. He was tall, well over six feet, thin as a prop blade, wearing a black short coat and faded black beret. The blue eyes that peered out from his wrinkled face were keen and observant.

230

His gaze flicked to the plane, scanning it from prop to tail wheel. *"Schones Flugzeug,"* he breathed, then narrowed his gaze back to Curley. *"Aber was machen Sie hier?"* His clear eyes held no hint of malice or suspicion, merely a bright curiosity.

What should Curley tell him? He wouldn't lie, but he didn't need to spill the details of his mission. "My girlfriend is with a group of people walking the road over there." He gestured down the hill. "And I'm here to pick her up."

The man's eyes narrowed as he studied a thin straggle of grass which he nudged with his toe. After a moment he said, "You're American, aren't you?"

"Yes, I am." Curley bent to pick up his tool sack. Putting the wrench into it, he said, "I won't be here long, Sir, and I'll pay you something for the bother."

The man looked up with a troubled expression. "No. No need to pay. This is bad business," he said, shaking his head.

Curley wondered what he meant, until he added, "Good and true citizens separated out, and for what? Where will it end?" He looked Curley square in the eye and said, "I will do all I can to help you." He shaded his eyes, looked down the row of trees, and whistled twice. "My grandson will help us."

Then he motioned Curley toward the plane. "Let's pull her back to a more secluded space, good for a quick takeoff."

A young man loped toward them, his eyes widening with surprised admiration when he saw the plane. The older man held out his hand to Curley. "My name is Horst Friedrich, and this is my grandson, Rutger."

Curley took his hand. "James Cameron. Thanks for the help," he said, shaking the young man's hand, also.

Together they pulled the plane into a small grove, kicking aside some underbrush to make a clear path out. Walking down the hill together, Horst Friedrich told Curley he'd enlisted in 1914 as a pilot in the kaiser's war. He talked of the plane he had flown, and they talked of Curley's Vega.

When they arrived at the farmhouse, Herr Friedrich offered Curley his truck. "It's a relic, like me, but reliable," he said. He waved aside Curley's protests. "Don't worry; I know you'll be back—your plane is here."

Rutger begged to go along, but his grandfather said no. Curley suspected the man wasn't sure Curley could successfully rescue his girlfriend and return the truck.

He quickly caught up with the group struggling to keep ahead of the two black cars behind them. He pushed the pad in the middle of the round steering wheel, and a baritone bark came from the truck's horn. The black cars ignored it.

Curley pulled the truck off the road and got out. He ran to one of the cars and tapped on its window, walking to keep up. The guard pretended not to see him, then finally rolled the window down a few inches and ordered him to get away.

"Stop! I need to talk with you. *Bitte*." His German was minimal, and he hoped adding the word "please" would help.

The guard rolled the window up and stared straight ahead. The car continued moving, with Curley persistently tapping on the window again and again.

Finally, the guard ordered the driver to stop, and opened the door, almost knocking Curley over. "What is this? You are interrupting state business. Get out of here." The guard rested his hand on his holster to reinforce his demand.

The group huddled in the cold, their shoulders heaving with exhaustion. "One of your. . .group does not belong here. My friend, Amanda Chase. She is a visiting American citizen."

The guard's eyes narrowed. "What lies are these you tell? These criminals are none of your business."

Curley bit back his anger to keep from asking the man what crime the small children had done. Another officer, from the other car, approached and asked what caused the delay.

They commanded Curley to go, but he refused to leave unless Amanda was with him. He took a chance that they were not ready to risk exposing their present activity. They threatened to arrest him. He told them he had friends waiting for him to bring Amanda back.

Amanda approached them, and Curley smiled, calling her to join them. The other guards kept the people in the middle of the road, moving them to one side when a car passed.

"Hello, Amanda," said Curley with a smile. "What are you doing here?"

"That's what I'd like to know!" She put her hands on her hips and glared at the guard who had her passport. "I told you," she said to him. "I'm an American citizen and I want to go home."

The guard arched an eyebrow, and patted his pocket. "We'll check your passport." He folded his arms across his chest. "And if you really are an American citizen, then you may go."

"Listen." Curley curbed his temper. "I sympathize with your efforts to relocate so many families devastated by fire, but I'm a businessman and don't have time for passport checking and other tedious delays." He clenched his fists. "Let the girl go."

Amanda stepped closer to Curley and touched his arm. "Thanks for coming back." To the guard she said, "Please believe me; I'm not one of these people. If you keep me, you could get into great trouble with your superiors. My father is an influential man who knows President Roosevelt, and he would not rest until I was released."

"Lies!" screamed the guard. "Get back in the group."

"I will not." Amanda brought her face close to his. "Shoot me now, because I won't walk in your stupid parade anymore." She kept her voice low to keep it from wavering. She longed to demand her passport back but feared pressing this guard too far.

After an awkward moment, the guard jerked his head toward the car, ordering the others back inside and the driver to move along. "Move, you vermin scum!" he yelled to the people huddled in the cold road.

Martha, holding the child in her arms, approached. "Amanda, what's happening?"

The guard shoved her, and she fell, clutching the child so he wouldn't be hurt. Amanda started forward, but Curley pulled her back. "Come on. You can't help her now."

He was right. She couldn't help Martha by being arrested, but as a free person she might help. She walked away but shouted back to Martha, "I won't leave you here!"

With tears distorting her vision, she pulled at her coat buttons. By the time they got to the old truck, she had her coat and jacket open and the lenses out of her pockets.

Curley opened the door for her. "What are you doing?"

"Documenting," she muttered. By the time he climbed in behind the steering wheel, she was fastening the lens on her camera. "Drive as close as you can," she said.

"They have guns, remember," Curley warned. "If I see one drawn, we're making a hasty exit." He turned the truck in a wide circle, almost miring it in the soft dirt on the side of the road as he jockeyed them into position for perfect photos. "Be quick. We can't make another pass."

Amanda wiped her eyes and blinked back the tears, then snapped the heartrending scene. As they sped away, she leaned out of the truck for one more shot.

When they were too far away for more pictures, she drew her head in out of the biting wind, set the camera on the seat, and rolled up the window. *"Brrr. Does this truck have a heater?"* With cold fingers she buttoned her jacket, then her coat.

Curley reached beneath his seat and drew out a pair of stiff gardening gloves. "I kicked these under the seat when I got in. They'll soften up once you get them on."

Amanda pulled on the cold gloves, then wrapped her coat closer around her ankles. Looking at the confident set of Curley's shoulders, the strong lines of his profile, she felt his strength as he drove them away from danger. "How. . .where did you get this truck? I thought you left this morning. How did you know where to find me?"

He used the grin that was always there on the edge of his mouth, as he said, "Hey, one at a time!" His movements were swift and graceful as he shifted the gears and steered the truck expertly down the country road.

She relaxed back against the seat, relief flooding her to be in his presence.

"Right. A good reporter asks one question at a time." The gloves were beginning to warm her hands.

"I did leave this morning," he said, leaning slightly to look out the rear-view mirror. "But something made me return—don't ask me what. If I had to guess, I'd say it was the Holy Spirit. All I know for certain is I just knew I had to come back. The truck belongs to a local farmer, and we're returning it as soon as I make a quick trip into town."

Amanda twisted in the seat, looking back, worry etching her brow. Doubt ate at her; had she been right to leave her family behind? Maybe she could have somehow brought them with her. Or maybe she should have stayed with them, no matter what the cost. Tears blurred her eyes. "Stop the truck!" she cried suddenly, reaching for the door handle. "I won't leave my family to those butchers!"

"Hey! Calm yourself," said Curley. The road had turned, and the group behind them was no longer visible. He pulled the truck over to the side of the road, keeping the motor idling.

Bracing his left elbow on the steering wheel, he reached over and took her hand from the handle. "Think. Alone you can't stop them. You could get yourself hurt, or share whatever fate the Nazis have in store for their captives."

"But. . ." She looked back in anguish.

Curley squeezed her hand. "I know. We can't leave them there." He reached up and cupped her chin, turning her face to his. "I have a plan, which I hope will free them all from whatever those thugs have planned."

"How? What can we do?"

His fingers lingered against the softness of her cheek. The shine in her eyes which a moment ago threatened to overflow into tears now regained the intellectual curiosity he'd first noticed about her. A memory flashed through his mind from many years ago, of a much younger girl with the same curiosity mixed with intelligence, looking up at him with admiration.

He slid his hand down, pulling her collar closer around her neck. "First I have to make a quick trip into town to discover for sure where they are taking them." He turned back toward the steering wheel, put the truck in gear, and started forward.

Amanda leaned toward him, peering into his face. "Who would tell you *that?*"

The truck swayed as he steered it back onto the roadway. "Trust me," he said. "We don't have much time, so I'll drop you off at Frau Reinhardt's. Gather up your things while I find out what we need to know. Then we'll make a mad dash back here to put my plan into action."

"What plan? Tell me!"

He rubbed his thumb on the steering wheel, thinking, and finally decided to tell her. "First," he said, "if I'm right, we have to wait until it's dark and very late."

He sketched the highlights of a plan and, in response to her concerns, promised to tell it in detail later.

Soon the old truck chugged up to Frau Reinhardt's rooming house. Amanda slipped off the gardening gloves and laid them on the seat. "See you in five minutes," she said.

Curley was already turning the corner as she entered the foyer. She ran up the stairs and down the hall to her room, thankful for Curley's intervention into this sordid situation.

Quickly entering the room, she breathed a quick prayer. *God, help us. We're against evil forces here that I don't understand. Without Your help we could ruin everything.* She threw one of her suitcases on the bed and snapped it open. She yanked her warmest clothes off their hangers and stuffed them in, along with her cosmetics, which were hastily thrown into their satin-lined drawstring bag. The suitcase refused to latch. She pulled her tweed jacket from the jumble of clothes. *Someone will get a lot of use from this,* she thought, laying it across the pillows.

She forced the suitcase shut and slung her purse strap over her shoulder. Reaching into the closet, she grabbed the camera case, then picked up the suitcase. At the door she took one last look before leaving. The room was as it was when she arrived, except for the jacket lying on the pillows and the clothes that still hung in the closet.

Downstairs, she was almost out the door when Delbert rose from a chair in the parlor and eyed her suitcase. With a wave of his elegant fingers, he gestured toward it. A shocked petulance crept into his voice as he asked, "Honey— oh, sorry. Amanda, my dear. What does this mean? Are you leaving?"

Amanda set the suitcase down, seeing him clearly for the first time. After all their years as friends, she felt she had never really known him. Yet, somehow he believed she would someday become his wife. He stood before her, his pretty-boy face lit from within with selfish ambition.

"Amanda?" He cleared his throat, and she realized she was still staring at him.

"I've found my family," she said, "and I'm going to them." She reached into her purse and drew out some money. "I'm paid up with Frau Reinhardt, but would you be a pal and give her this? And could you take care of the rest of my stuff that's up in my room? Have it shipped home for me?"

"Of course I will." He brought his hand back to his chest. "But I'll take care of your bill."

She pressed the money into his sweater pocket. "Really, Delbert, I insist." She pulled the door open, and he grabbed her suitcase before she could and went out with her.

"Where can I reach you?" He took her arm and turned her to face him. "After all, Amanda, I came here to be with you, to assist you however I could."

When she pulled away from him, he added, "Remember, your father entrusted me with your care."

Amanda wished the old truck would appear. "So you said, and I said I was grateful for your concern. If you'll remember, I also told you I don't need a baby-sitter."

"Now see here—"

"No. *You* see here. I don't need you, Delbert. Go back to Boston." At his look of shock at her uncharacteristic outburst, she softened somewhat and added, "Please!"

As if on cue, the truck chugged around the corner and slid to a stop in front of them. Amanda opened the door before Delbert could do it for her. She slung the suitcase on the floor, put the camera case on the seat, and climbed in. Curley leaned around her and nodded to Delbert.

Pulling the door shut, she looked straight ahead and said, "Let's go!" Curley gave her a curious look, stepped on the clutch, put the truck in gear, and they sped away.

Chapter 15

Curley skillfully sped down the narrow streets, braking suddenly in front of the bakery shop. "Stay here. I'll be right back." Shifting the truck into neutral, he flung open the door and jumped out, leaving the motor running. Amanda's stomach rumbled, reminding her she hadn't eaten anything since the cup of tea and cookie at Aunt Esther's that morning. So much had happened that the morning's events seemed ages ago.

In less than a minute, Curley came out with two full gunnysacks. He slung them into the back of the truck and went back for more. Finished, he jumped back into the truck and scanned the street ahead, then checked the rearview mirror, put the truck in gear, and pulled away. Soon Eisenburg faded into the twilight behind them.

"What's in the bags?" asked Amanda.

Solemnly watching the road ahead, Curley answered, "Apples, bread, rolls, jelly—whatever the baker could assemble in a hurry."

Amanda pressed her stomach to keep it from feeling too empty and nodded. "Good idea. The soldiers certainly won't feed those poor people." She busied herself by putting the camera and pieces back into its case.

Curley's jaw muscle flexed as he clenched his teeth. "No doubt about it," he said.

Surprised by the stern tone of his voice, Amanda glanced at him. He wasn't just a pretty flyboy. Suddenly, his boyishly handsome profile showed an inherent strength and power she hadn't noticed before. He gripped the steering wheel tighter and stepped hard on the gas pedal, urging the truck to move faster.

"How are you going to get this food to the people?"

He glanced at her. "Part of the plan."

She felt the shock of power blazing from his hazel eyes, and she knew that nothing would stop him from taking food to the Jews.

He switched the lights on, and in a few minutes he turned off the road, into a long dirt driveway. He stopped behind a white peak-roofed house.

A tall older gentleman and a younger similar-looking man stepped out of the porch shadows and approached the truck. The older gentleman leaned down and looked past Curley to Amanda. "I see you got her, *mein Herr.*"

The young man's eyes widened as he caught sight of Amanda. "Oohh," he breathed, then hastily rubbed his chin and turned nonchalantly as if seeing a beautiful woman was nothing new.

Curley turned off the motor and lights, plunging them into almost total darkness. He got out of the truck, and Amanda reached for her door handle, but the young man suddenly appeared and opened it for her.

She pulled her coat collar up against the biting cold as Curley introduced the older gentleman as Horst and the younger as Rutger Friedrich. They shook hands and exchanged smiles before walking into the lamplit kitchen. Coal embers glowed brightly in an iron stove against one wall, warming the room somewhat. Washed dishes were neatly stacked beside the sink, and a dark wood table sat against the outside wall.

"Rutger and I are alone for a few days while my wife is away at her sister's." Herr Friedrich pulled two more cups from the cupboard. "So, you will be taking off soon?" Rutger brought them each a cup of hot tea. Amanda brought in some dark bread from the truck.

Curley took a sip of the hot brew and shook his head. "No. Not while those people are captives."

Amanda curled her hands around the cup, warming them for a moment, darting him a grateful look. "How are we going to free them?"

"It's going to be dangerous. You must wait in the plane while I go."

"You don't know my uncle and aunt. I have to go with you."

Curley shook his head. "I saw you with your cousin, so that's not a problem." He leaned toward Herr Friedrich, relying on Amanda for German phrases, and laid out his plan.

After intense discussion, they determined that Rutger would go along to distract the guards while Curley did his part. Herr Friedrich nodded his assent and said, "We do nothing but we ask God to go with us. You have no objection to that?"

Curley smiled. "Not at all. He's with me everywhere I go."

"How about you, Miss?" Herr Friedrich asked Amanda, looking at her keenly.

"No. It's fine." She glanced at Curley, impressed by his faith. *That must be why he has such a calm attitude about all this,* she thought, remembering with chagrin that she didn't always remember to trust in God, knowing the serene feeling that He had everything in control.

After a prayer that lifted her courage, they hugged each other. Rutger smiled and said, "God's been saving His people for generations. This isn't exactly the Red Sea, but He'll do something great tonight. Wait and see!"

They all laughed, then solemnly prepared for the night ahead.

Outside, a cold, silvery full moon hung over the bare branches of trees silhouetted on the hillside. Horst and Rutger went to work on the truck while Amanda followed Curley along a path up the hill behind the house. He carried her suitcase and a flashlight to illuminate the path ahead, while she shouldered her purse and camera case, carefully stepping over the uneven ground.

As soon as they reached the top of the hill, she grabbed Curley's arm, and he turned to face her. She steadied her camera case to stop it from swinging and glared at him. "You can't leave me behind. I need to go with you."

He set the suitcase down, taking her hand in his. He smiled. This was his feisty Amanda, ready to jump into the fray. He'd been worried by her earlier silence in the kitchen. "You can't. They'd recognize you in an instant."

"I'll stay in the shadows. They won't even see me."

"We can't risk it. You stay in the plane; I go to the rescue."

She stared at him, unable to look away. She'd never met a man like this. So gentle and loving at times, yet so hardheaded as he was now. She admired his boldness and had no doubts that he'd do exactly as he planned. But her mind was made up. "You'll have to tie me down to make me stay here."

Curley dragged his gaze away from hers to keep from faltering. "If you want to fly out of here with me, you'll go with my plan." He dropped her hand and continued walking.

She stood in the silent darkness, stunned for an instant. Then she ran after him. "Listen, Mister, I'm not some dainty little woman who'll faint at the first sign of trouble."

He looked back at her, arching one brow. "No?" He shook his head, leading her through shoulder-high bushes to the plane. He opened the cargo door, placing her suitcase inside, then opened the passenger door.

Amanda slung her camera case and purse up behind the copilot seat and turned to Curley with a sigh. "Listen, I didn't mean to sound flippant. But I. . . I need to go. This is my family!" She liked his decisiveness, but there must be some way to convince him of her need to be involved.

Curley made the mistake of gazing down at her, watching the play of emotions on her face. He suppressed a sigh. She had, after all, gone right into the ghetto in search of her family. He imagined her stalking dark Boston streets, searching for a story, and knew she was right. She needed to go.

He turned away from her and ran a hand through his hair, not sure if her foray into the ghetto had been bravery or foolishness. "You heard the plan. The guards have guns. People could get hurt if something goes wrong."

She looked up at him. "I know," she said softly. "But remember, we prayed, and God will protect us."

Curley lightly touched his fingertips to her chin and then leaned down, swiftly kissing her mouth. Then he turned abruptly and went to the other side of the plane where he opened the door and retrieved a flare, a can of gasoline, and a few small tools. He pulled the plane forward a few feet so it faced a makeshift runway for a quick, clear takeoff.

★ ★ ★

With Rutger driving, soon they were turning onto the roadway and heading south on the road she'd walked earlier. After about five miles, Rutger turned off the lights. He slowed enough to peer carefully at the moonlit stretch of road.

"It's there, on our left," he whispered, pointing. Curley and Amanda bent their heads to their knees, so Rutger would seem to be driving alone.

Curley slowly opened the door a fraction of an inch. "Remember, if I don't get back right away, go on without me. I'll make my way back somehow. But don't wait!" Rutger nodded, driving past the turnoff. He turned the truck around and came back, pulling off the road.

Rutger hopped out and reached into the truck bed, grabbing one of the sacks. Shouldering it, he walked down the gravel road toward two small buildings. Lights glowed from within one of them. The other stood dark. He grinned. The German guards would love the treats he was bringing.

Once Rutger had disappeared into the shadows, Amanda and Curley quietly pushed the open door and slipped out of the truck. Curley grabbed his flare and gasoline and a sack of bakery goods from the truck bed. Amanda took another sack, and they tiptoed toward the large warehouse straight ahead and down an incline.

They stayed close to the bushes, away from gravel that would crunch loudly with each step. They reached the warehouse and moved stealthily along the wall nearest the road, looking for windows or some kind of opening. They found steps leading down to a metal door. Curley descended to investigate. The door was rusty, looking as if it hadn't been used in years. Amanda stood straining her ears, listening for sounds of movement. It was eerily quiet. Curley ascended the stairs, and they continued to the corner of the building and scrutinized the next wall. A small vent lay open a few inches off the ground.

On the other side of the building, facing the railroad tracks, they found a loading dock. The faint light from a smaller building illuminated the area.

Curley ducked back. "This is a good place to leave the sacks," he whispered to Amanda. "Stay put while I check out the other side of this building."

Amanda nodded, but after a few moments she crawled back to the spot where they'd seen the vent. She bent down, finally lying on the ground to get closer. She heard a sniffling noise and a groan. She'd found them! She picked up a pebble and tapped lightly on the wire screen. She waited, but she didn't receive an answer. Pulling her pencil out of her pocket, she stuck it inside, making contact with something.

She poked again, hoping it wasn't merely a sack of grain. The object moved. *Please don't be a rat or a cat.* She pushed her pencil in again, startled when it was drawn out of her hand.

"Hello!" she whispered as loudly as she dared. "Is someone there?"

Something or someone shifted on the other side of the wall.

"Hello. Is someone there?" A frightened child's voice came from the square hole.

Amanda breathed a sigh of relief. *Thank God.* "Shhh. Get your father or mother quickly." She heard scuffling, and then another voice came through the wires. "Who's there?"

Amanda told the person who she was and asked him to get Uncle Jacob. Soon he was there, head to the floor, talking to her. She told him of the escape plan, the bread beside the loading door, and asked him to keep the people calm and quiet.

★ ★ ★

Curley hid in the shadows, hugging the wall on the other side of the building. He found a boarded window with an open slot large enough to talk through. His message was the same as Amanda's to her uncle. When he finished, he crept silently back to where he'd left Amanda. There was a moment of pure panic when he couldn't find her. He finally spotted her; she lay unmoving in the shadows. He advanced slowly toward her, relieved to hear her faint whispers and an answering voice.

He motioned to her to be ready to run back to the truck, and he slowly made his way to the loading dock wall. There, he unlatched the loading door's bolt and slid it from its rings. Then he crawled across the loading dock and pried the bolt loose, sliding it from its rings slowly so as to minimize the noise. He glanced up at the light over the door of the guards' building, wishing he had some way to put it out. The weak light was just enough to be dangerous.

He froze as a guard opened the door and walked out of the small building. The guard turned to speak to someone inside, and Curley slipped around the corner into the shadows. A second guard came out, followed by another and Rutger.

"*Ja,* you tell the baker we liked his gift," one of the guards said as he adjusted his holster strap, preparing to make his rounds.

"I will." Rutger held the empty gunnysack in his hand, walking after them. "I could come tomorrow and bring more."

They shook their heads. "We will not be here tomorrow. You go now."

Rutger slowly walked up the road. He looked about casually, not wanting to appear nosey, but obviously wondering where Amanda and Curley were.

Curley waited until the guards walked behind the building. He closed his eyes, praying that Amanda had gotten out of the way. Then he moved around the supply shed, dripping gas down the walls, and along its base. When he finished, he moved behind the warehouse and lit the flare.

A guard rounded the building. "Halt!" he shouted, and started running toward Curley, who tossed the flare and dived to the ground. With a *whoosh* and flash of heat, the supply shed was instantly engulfed in flames. Guards shouted. More came running out of the office building. They pointed their guns into the darkness, momentarily confused. Then a voice rose above the others, giving orders.

On his belly, Curley used his elbows to ease himself forward. He worked his way along the ground beside the building, rolling into the underground doorway. Jumping to his feet, he pushed the door with all his strength. It groaned and scraped loudly, but the sounds were lost in the roar of the fire and the shouts of the scattering guards.

★ ★ ★

When Amanda heard the guards talking to Rutger, she slid the two gunny-sacks of breadstuff toward the door which someone inside had pushed up a few inches. The bags were slowly pulled inside. She crawled through the bushes and made her way along the road to the truck. She spotted Rutger but didn't dare call out to him. He reached the vehicle first, spying her at the same time the supply shed went up in flames. Amanda dashed the last few feet to the truck, praying for Curley's safety. The Germans sprinted about, shouting orders, moving cars, and throwing pails of water on the fire.

Amanda and Rutger could do nothing more but wait for Curley. Minutes passed. Rutger paced impatiently. Finally he turned to her, frowning. "They know I'm here, so I'll go tell them I want to help," he said. "I'll find out what happened to Curley."

"No! Don't! What if they think you're the one who set the fire?" Her plea fell into the darkness. She was alone.

The blazing building lit up the area, and Amanda knew she had to keep down, but it was agony not to look. She caught her breath, heaving a mental sigh of relief when first one, then another car drove by the truck and sped down the road. "Come on! Come on!" she whispered, clenching her fists. "God, help them!"

She heard a light tapping and, lying across the seat, she opened the driver's door. A familiar face greeted her. "Uncle Jacob!"

Her uncle huddled beside the truck, his arm leaning on the running board. His eyes were wild and frightened. Amanda stretched the door open a few more inches. "Are you all here?" she asked.

He nodded. "In the bushes."

"Good." She glanced nervously up the road. "As soon as Curley and Rutger get here, climb in the back."

He nodded. "But we must hurry!" Then he slipped away, back into the bushes.

Less than two minutes later, Rutger climbed into the truck, frowning. "Where's Curley?"

"I couldn't find him! I'm sorry, Amanda. He has disappeared."

Amanda peeked out the window. Seeing no one, she looked frantically up and down the road. "They'll be back any minute, with help."

"I know," Rutger agreed. "We have to go."

"We can't leave him!" cried Amanda.

"It's what he told us to do," Rutger insisted.

"But—"

"I don't want to leave him, either, but if anyone can get himself out of this jam and back to his plane, Curley can."

Turning the trees into black skeletons, the flames leaped into the sky with a sickly orange vengeance. Amanda looked back at the bushes and saw her aunt peering out at her. "You're right. We have to trust Curley to make it." She motioned to Aunt Esther, and in a few seconds they'd all scrambled from the bushes onto the back of the truck.

Rutger started the truck, hesitated a moment, looking at the burning buildings. Now the warehouse was in flames. He didn't see Curley. He put the truck in gear. It lurched forward, and soon they were on their way back to the farmhouse.

Amanda looked back, hoping to see Curley, but there was nothing but the surging flames. She saw two people dash across the road, and she wished them well. In the truck bed, all that remained visible were blankets and burlap bags covering lumps of supposed farm products.

★ ★ ★

When Curley closed the metal door, darkness engulfed him. He pointed his flashlight at the wall and pushed its button. Nothing happened. He tried again. Nothing. His fingers explored the metal cylinder and found the glass and bulb broken. The darkness grew oppressive and ominous with its silence. He struck a match, looking around, quickly assessing his surroundings. He was in a small vaultlike room, about ten feet square. Two shelves along one wall held several boxes of musty papers and a few cans that were so rusted he couldn't make out their labels.

He checked his watch. Eleven-twenty. The match died out. He stood in the darkness, waiting, knowing he couldn't go out yet. He heard muffled footsteps above, sounds of prisoners escaping. Hours seemed to pass before all he could hear was his own breathing and the slight movement of his feet on the dusty floor.

A cold, clammy feeling crept up from his belly to encompass him. He felt powerless to stop it. He stared straight ahead, straining to see something, anything, but there was nothing. Only a loathsome opacity. Fragments from old nightmares floated into his mind. The pain that started when his mother died. He was four years old. He didn't remember much about her but the aching sadness. He and his father had been close.

Then his father's death in the mine shaft, a freak accident of boulders and crushing debris. Curley's terrible dreams about it were coming true.

He had learned to hide his grief with nonchalance and an exaggerated sense of independence. Deciding never to need anyone, since no one would be there anyway, he'd gotten by, living where he could, finally ending up in

Johnny Westmore's hangar. Johnny had taken him under his wing, literally, taught him to fly, and to trust God to be with him always. Johnny had become the closest thing to family Curley had.

He shook himself and pulled out another match. *I'm not alone,* he thought, *I'll get through this just like I always have. By my wits and with God's help.* He forced himself to put the match back without lighting it and face the darkness. He didn't need a crutch, not even the match. This might be the worst predicament of his life, but he'd manage.

He felt the darkness closing around him, suffocating like a vise of black death. He squeezed his eyes shut, imagining the free feeling of soaring over the clouds in an open cockpit. He was an eagle, far above problems on the ground, strong, needing no one. The image faded, pushed out by the oppressive blackness, leaving him gasping and groping for the door.

He clenched his fists, fighting off the feeling of being nine years old again, of hearing the imaginary sounds of men screaming as a mine shaft fell in on them, of fearing he heard his father's screams. "Oh, God!" he breathed. The oppression loosened a little. Curley closed his eyes and said into the darkness, "Yea, though I walk through the valley of the shadow of death, I will fear no evil." His shoulders relaxed.

Johnny used to tell him there was no shame in admitting a need for God's help. *I know I'm no lone eagle, needing no one. I know You're there, God. Thank You.*

He took a deep breath and stood for a moment, savoring the feeling of peace. Then he once more took out a match and struck it, checking the time. Eleven forty-two. Twenty-two minutes had elapsed since he'd shut himself in this musty vault. It seemed like twenty-two hours. The air was getting thicker and warmer by the minute. He wondered if Amanda, her family, and Rutger were all right. He hoped they hadn't waited for him.

He smiled. Amanda was no frail female. He couldn't think of any other girl who he'd even consider letting come with him into this situation; and she'd done it with such aplomb. A glow of determination in her eyes, courage in that thrust-forward little chin, strength to tread where angels feared, and beauty. *She's the real article,* he told himself. Suddenly, he couldn't wait to get to her and get his arms around her.

The door handle felt warm. Carefully, he pulled the door open a fraction of an inch. A flame curled downward, blocking his escape. Pulling at his jacket sleeve, he wrapped it around his hand and pushed the rapidly heating metal door. The coast was clear, so he dashed out through the flames and up the steps.

He stepped right into the path of a German guard carrying an empty bucket in each hand.

Chapter 16

The guard stumbled as Curley ran into him. He dropped the buckets and slapped at Curley's shoulder. Raising a fist to strike back, Curley suddenly realized the fierce burning he felt on his shoulder was his smoldering jacket. Together he and the guard put it out.

An acrid gray smoke drifted up from the burning leather. Someone dashed past them with pails of sloshing water. Before the guard could question him, Curley gestured wildly down the steps he'd just come up, then picked up the discarded pails.

His eyes darted from side to side, assessing the area. The truck had gone with Amanda, Rutger, and—he hoped—her family. Though adrenaline and tension fueled his alertness, he was relieved that Amanda was out of harm's way. He worried about her getting into another dilemma. Their safe escape depended on his getting out of here soon.

He ran with the pails to the water tower. Orange flames crept up the building where the prisoners had been kept, sending sparks flying out the narrow upper windows.

A truck skidded down the road, off the highway, the people in the back jumping out before it stopped. Curley pushed the pails under the waterspout, filling them. He was relieved that others were so intent on getting water to the fire there was no conversation.

He rushed to the track side of the warehouse and sloshed water up the wall. The door was open and there was no sign of the Jews. Thank God, they'd escaped. The guards, plus volunteers, were getting the fire under control. A middle-aged man ran past him, toward the building, smothering the fire with a sack full of sand. Curley handed him the pails and ran toward the guards' small hut.

There was no fire here. No guards, either. They were directing volunteers and dousing bushes and the warehouse. Their motorcycles sat next to the building. The black car was gone.

From the dark bushes behind the hut, Curley scanned the scene. Twenty or more people ran to and from the water tower. Others beat the bushes with blankets and burlap bags to choke the fire. The supply shed smoldered from its burned, blackened stubble, a pocket of water seeping from its foundation.

He heard voices near and froze. The captain came toward the guard hut, gazing from the fiery pandemonium to the bushes behind him, where Curley crouched. *"Der Amerikaner ist hier."*

Curley couldn't hear every word, but he caught the meaning. The guard was told to bring the American to his captain. As soon as the soldiers left, he sneaked toward the motorcycles and chose one without a sidecar. He guided it quietly on a well-worn footpath around the back, behind the bushfire. The flickering flames gave enough light to get the motorcycle up to the road.

He stood on the crank three times, but the machine didn't catch. He was raising it a fourth time when an oncoming motorcycle's light shined on him. Behind him, a guard ran toward him, shouting and gesturing.

Suddenly, the oncoming motorcycle turned sharply and pulled up beside him. Curley shoved the kickstand down and turned, ready to fight for his life, if necessary. But it was Rutger's cheerful face smiling at him.

Rutger slapped the fender behind him. "Get on!"

Guards down the hill were wheeling their motorcycles away from the guard hut. Curley hopped on the back and held onto Rutger's seat. "Step on it, Boy!"

Rutger tore off down the road as fast as the cycle would go. Curley looked back and spotted headlights behind them. At first he thought it was a car, but the lights moved independently, and he knew there were two motorcycles following him. He and Rutger leaned into the wind, keeping the accelerator wide open.

About a hundred yards before Friedrich's driveway, Rutger slowed and turned off the road onto an overgrown lane. A minute later he turned off the lights, but he kept a steady pace as he twisted and wound along the dirt road.

The cloudy moonlight was barely enough for him to see to steer between the bushes. The guards' motorcycles thundered past the turnoff.

Rutger rounded a bend, flicked the lights on, and gunned the engine again. They bounced through the orchard, and he cut the engine and coasted into the clearing where the plane sat.

They had only minutes before the guards doubled back, found the side road, and caught up with them. Curley vaulted off the motorcycle and grabbed the handlebars from Rutger. One of the motorcycles rumbling toward them sputtered and whined, sounding as if it had slid off the path into the dirt. The other one bore down on them.

Rutger glanced uneasily behind them toward the approaching roar. Curley took his arm and pushed him back into the shadows. "Go home. I don't want you involved in this. Get back!"

"Yes, Sir." Rutger slipped silently into the shadows, saying over his shoulder, "Everyone is in the plane, waiting for you."

"Good job! Now you must go. *Go!*" The moon had gone behind a cloud, and Curley stood, facing the oncoming guard, then straightened his shoulders and watched the light loom brighter. "Lord, help me," he muttered. "And keep Amanda in the plane."

★ ★ ★

Amanda watched Curley face the motorcycle leaping into the clearing. In the surrounding darkness, the scene looked as if it were a stage play unfolding before her. But this was no act.

"What's happening? What is it?" Aunt Esther's voice rose to an hysterical pitch.

"It's all right," said Amanda softly, failing to keep the fear from her voice. "Mr. Cameron is here to fly us out. Sit back, and. . ."

"But I—"

"Now, now, Mother. Come, lean against me," soothed Uncle Jacob. Aunt Esther allowed him to pull her into his arms, while Tamara, Nathan, and the baby huddled together in the rear of the plane. Martha's head touched Amanda's as they peered out the small window.

"What's he going to do?" asked Martha, reaching for Amanda's hand and clutching it tightly.

"Shh!" Amanda chose her words carefully to cover her own growing alarm. "He'll be all right. Just keep our passengers quiet. Please."

She could tell by the guard's slow, deliberate motions as he stood his motorcycle on its stand that he felt he was in total control. He left the light on, pointed his pistol at Curley, and motioned toward the plane. Amanda ducked down, even though she couldn't be seen. When she looked again, Curley had edged away from the plane. He and the guard faced off, looking as motionless as chess pieces.

She touched her forehead to the cool window and said a quick prayer for all of them.

"Explain yourself! *Wer sind Sie?* Who are you? Why is this plane here?" The guard motioned to the plane with his Luger.

"*Etwas langsammer, bitte,*" said Curley after a long, tension-filled minute. "I speak very little German." He assumed a relaxed pose, but every sense was on alert.

The guard backed up to his motorcycle, all the time keeping the gun on Curley. His stare lingered as he pulled a flashlight from the saddlebag and snapped the light on. "I will inspect the plane before I escort you back to my captain."

In a voice of authority, Curley said, "That plane is RAF property and off limits."

"You are on German soil! You will do as I say." He shone his light from the propeller to the tail of the plane, stepping closer to it.

A sweat broke out on Curley's neck. Time was running out. The guard's momentary attention on the plane gave him an opening. He leaped at the man, but the guard turned, raising his gun. Curley grabbed the wrist holding the weapon.

Amanda could scarcely breathe as she watched Curley move with incredible lightning speed. He and the guard scuffled, the flashlight beam darting crazily about until Curley forced the guard to the ground. They rolled in the dirt, struggling for the gun. She watched in horror as the guard pinned Curley beneath him. The flashlight's beam shone uselessly into the trees.

Curley seemed to relax and give up for an instant, then he surged up, threw the guard off him, and knocked the gun from his hand. It skittered across the dirt under the plane's wing. The guard lunged and Curley slugged him. He staggered back, then lowered his head and charged Curley.

"I've got to help," said Amanda, reaching for the door handle.

"No!" Martha grabbed her sleeve.

Amanda gently pulled her hand away. "Keep calm! I'll be all right." She opened the door and slid into the cold darkness.

The gun glinted dully beneath the plane's wing. She picked it up. It felt like a piece of ice in her hand.

Holding it in both hands, she pointed it toward the guard. In German she said, "The only thing I know about guns is that if I pull this trigger, it shoots. So don't move, or you'll make me nervous, and you could get hurt." She breathed deeply, stilling the fear tensing her chest.

Curley moved to her side, his eyes on her face. "You surprise me, Sweetheart."

The German snarled an obnoxious epithet, and Curley leveled a sudden, icy glare at him. "The lady means business. Keep quiet."

Anger faded from the guard's red face as he watched Amanda's hands shaking. She stood, arms outstretched, pointing the gun at him. To Curley she said, "I'll keep him here until the plane is ready to go. Hurry!" Curley picked up the flashlight and set it on the guard's motorcycle seat, so that it spotlighted him.

The guard's eyes flickered as he watched Curley leave the circle of light.

Amanda moved the gun slightly. "Don't try anything," she warned. She moved her eyes as far to the right as she could, following Curley, but he had ducked beneath the plane. She heard the door close and fought down her fear.

The guard glared at her, tensing as if for a leap in her direction. Heavy, almost clumsy footsteps heading in their direction made him smile.

Amanda kept the gun pointed on him. The man's smile faded as Rutger walked into the light. "Who are you?" the man demanded, his voice rising to a shriek.

"I am a fellow countryman, looking for my motorcycle." Rutger looked from the guard to the plane. "Why is that here?"

"You idiot! This is not *Der Führer*'s plane!"

"Then what—"

"Both of you keep quiet," said Amanda.

Rutger peered toward Amanda. "Who's that?" A cloud drifted in front of the moon, casting unearthly shadows. The guard stood in eerie light, and Rutger, half in shadow, half in the light.

"Stop asking questions!" screeched the guard.

"You sound like the guard at the roadside. He is injured," said Rutger, glancing meaningfully toward Amanda.

She pulled in a deep, shaky breath, her arms beginning to ache. *Oh, please, Curley, start the plane!* She hadn't known there was a second guard who might come upon them at any second.

"Hey, lady," said Rutger, approaching her, "did you see who took my motorcycle?"

"Keep back!" warned Amanda.

"She has a gun, you stupid boy," snarled the guard.

"She—"

The plane's engine coughed and began to rumble. Amanda backed up carefully. As soon as she was beneath the wing, the engine was roaring. The propeller's wind whipped her coat around her ankles. Her head touched the strut, and the plane's door opened. Martha shouted, "Get in!"

Amanda threw the gun as far as she could into the darkness and scrambled up into the plane, pulling the door shut.

Curley glanced at her and grinned. "My little gun moll," he said, flipping a switch on the panel and squinting into the darkness. "Come on, moon! Come out and give us a little light."

The baby's wails, combined with the engine's roar, pounded into Amanda's head. They couldn't take off into the dreadful darkness outside.

Curley inched the plane forward slowly, then stopped, shaking his head. "We need more light!" The engine throbbed idly.

"God, help us!" cried Aunt Esther.

Suddenly Amanda's door was flung open, and the guard's hand reached for her. "No!" she screamed, kicking at him. He grabbed her ankle. She felt herself being pulled down.

Her terror turning to fury, she beat her fists on his head, but he held on.

Slowly, the moon slipped out from behind the cloud, and the plane edged forward. Amanda clutched her seat with all her strength. Curley wagged the plane slightly, sending the guard off balance for a second, long enough for Amanda to kick his shoulder and send him sprawling. She slammed the door shut, and the plane rumbled and bounced between the trees.

Suddenly they were aloft. Amanda closed her eyes and concentrated on calming her racing heartbeat. She was shaking like a twig in a windstorm and her ankle hurt.

Curley squeezed her hand. "You can open your eyes now."

She did so. He had a pleased, contented look on his face. One curly lock separated itself from the others. She longed to smooth it down but held her hand nervously in her lap.

She turned to check the group behind her. Aunt Esther lay against Uncle Jacob, her eyes squeezed tightly shut. Nathan looked out the window, while Tamara soothed the baby, whose wails had turned to a mewling cry. Martha's eyes glittered with excitement. "We made it!"

Uncle Jacob's face glowed as he said loud enough for them all to hear, *"Baruch atoh adnoy, elohaynu melech ho-lom shee-osoh li nays bamokm hazeh.* You are blessed, Lord our God, King of the universe, who performed a miracle for me in this place."

They were all quiet for a moment, their faces registering the awesome realization that God had indeed just performed a miracle for them.

"Amen," said Curley.

"I hope the others escaped, too," said Nathan.

"They were all gone by the time I got to the scene," said Curley, loud enough for them to hear over the engine's rumble. "So were the packages of bread."

"Where are we going?" asked Uncle Jacob.

"You're going tc England," replied Curley, looking back at his passengers. Nathan nodded and went back to his window view.

"Speaking of bread," said Martha, "have some." She opened the sack and handed out bread sticks. "How did you find us?" she asked.

Amanda and Curley related their stories, marveling at how the rescue had happened, as if guided by an unseen hand.

"I prayed we'd get out of there somehow," said Martha, a look of wonder on her face. They talked for awhile longer, until Martha sighed and relaxed in her seat, closing her eyes.

Amanda looked out at the silver-crested clouds. The vista ahead was majestic. Chewing on the crusty bread, she could think of no appropriate headline to describe it. Poetry seemed more appropriate. "It's beautiful up here!"

Curley seemed pleased that she thought so. "Look down," he said, pointing to a space between the clouds. "We're over Holland." A pleased smile curved his mouth.

As she looked down at the colorful toy-sized roofs below, Amanda wondered if he was aware of how appealing his smile was. She sighed and stretched her back. "Rutger certainly had that guard flustered."

"Rutger!" Curley glanced sideways in surprise. "I told him to keep out of it."

"He must have been watching, because he came to help me," she said. "Actually, he made himself seem like a bumbling, innocent kid only looking for his motorcycle."

"Tell me what he said and did."

When Amanda finished telling Curley exactly what happened, his expression grew still. "Hmm," he said. "He may have saved his grandparents from a lot of suspicion. Even though the plane was far from their home, there is still a chance they'll be suspect. We owe him for defusing a potential bombshell."

"I wonder what will happen to the Jews." Amanda rubbed her sore ankle, thinking of the disturbing newspaper and magazine articles she'd read in the Eisenburg school library.

Curley looked grave. "We can only pray that somehow God's presence will be with them." He shook his head. "Now, you should get some rest. We'll be in England in a couple of hours."

Chapter 17

Curley flew them into the night, toward the moon that was setting below the clouds. He shuddered. Being trapped beneath the earth like his father was his most hideous nightmare. Shrugging off the feeling, he gazed out over the miles and miles of freedom before him. For him, freedom was soaring anywhere he pleased. Why had he returned? What drew him back? He shook his head, knowing the truth. It had to be God.

Amanda's eyes were closed, her long, dark lashes lying on her cheeks. Shifting moonlight and shadows played on her lovely face. Her hands lay open in her lap, giving her a vulnerable appearance. Gently reaching out, he brushed a soft wisp of hair that strayed toward him.

Every moment he spent with her made him want her more, and he wasn't used to that. It usually happened the other way: Women wanted him. Unlike the others, though, Amanda hadn't pursued him. She'd simply been herself, and that was enough.

When did he start caring? It hadn't come all at once, like a bolt from the blue. That sense of familiarity he'd felt from the first moment he'd seen her. . . a memory of a long-ago air show, her eyes looking up at him, burst full-blown into his mind; and at last he remembered where and when he'd seen her before. He nearly laughed aloud, for he realized his feelings had had a logical progression after all. The seed had been planted at the air show years ago, lying dormant until her eyes caught his across the ship's deck. Then it was nurtured with his admiration for her zeal-like dedication to her work, and it had blossomed when he recognized the sweetness and purity radiating from within her. He loved her courage to meet her cousin in the park; he loved her loyalty when she marched beside her family through the town. He loved her tears welling in her eyes at the plight of Hitler's innocent victims.

She had broken through his barrier against commitment. He ran a hand through his hair and frowned. Somehow she'd made him want her and her alone. All he could see was Amanda's face.

What would happen after they landed? He couldn't imagine her married to Delbert. It was wrong. Maybe it wasn't true. He'd ask her soon.

If it were true, he'd have to get over her. He'd miss her smiles, her bright eyes as the idea for the "big story" illuminated her imagination. The idea of getting over a girl was another new experience. He'd blithely gone through adolescence and adulthood enjoying the company of women, their adoration and devotion, but moving on when one began to stir his fancy. After all, like the planes he flew, he was not made to be tied down, but like an eagle, to freely soar.

"Even an eagle has a nest." The thought zinged through his brain. *Where did that come from?* he wondered. *"Behold, I make all things new."*

Curley knew that voice. He glanced at Amanda again. He wanted to hold and protect her. *Lord, she may be promised to someone else. Are You telling me this feeling I have for her is just to teach me what it's going to be like when I find the right woman?* Or was this retribution? Letting him know how it felt to be unlucky in love?

Love? Where did that word come from? But the idea of loving someone other than Amanda was suddenly distasteful.

He pulled out his clipboard, looked at the lights below, and studied the map. To keep his errant thoughts from straying back to Amanda, he concentrated on the terrain and the list of German airfields and number of planes he'd observed. Something was up. Who would be the target of all those planes Hitler was gathering?

★ ★ ★

Amanda awoke, realizing the sound of the engine had changed and they were descending. She hunched her shoulders and stretched her arms straight over her lap, then raked her hair back into place.

Curley lifted one eyebrow and grinned at her. "Feel better?"

"Yes. How long did I sleep?"

"About two hours. We're over the east English coast."

The first piercing rays of dawn touched the tips of trees and houses below, turning them to liquid gold. A vast amount of water on her side was changing from gray to blue even as she watched.

"They call that the Wash," said Curley, leaning over her and looking down into the bay. He banked the plane to the left, glancing at the land below and back to the map.

Amanda looked back at her family with compassion. Martha lay scrunched up around the armrests on two seats, Aunt Esther still lay against Uncle Jacob, his jacket over her, and he leaned against the wall. Nathan sprawled straight in his seat, legs thrust beneath Martha's seat, head back, sound asleep. Tamara had just finished diapering the baby on her lap. She gave Amanda a sad smile and pulled the baby's bunting down over his feet.

Amanda smiled back, then turned to look ahead. Rosy-hued, gold-tipped spires stood like sentinels among lower-roofed buildings. They loomed closer as the plane dipped lower.

By the time the wheels touched the ground, the passengers were awake. Aunt Esther straightened her clothes, Uncle Jacob pulled the sleeves of his jacket down over his wrists, and Martha ran a comb through her pale hair. Nathan bent forward, tying his shoes, while Tamara held the baby to her shoulder, gently patting his back.

Four jeeps drew close the minute Curley cut the engine. "Wait here," he said and climbed out. He saluted to the approaching officer. "Captain Cameron reporting, Sir. I wasn't able to complete my mission. Civilians are on board in need of assistance."

The officer looked up at faces crowded in the plane's window. "Explain."

Later, as the family sipped coffee in the barracks, Amanda cabled her parents, then she and Curley slipped outside. He tucked her hand in the crook of his elbow and they walked in the nippy morning air. Small bushes swept down the hillsides, blanketing the landscape in autumn gold and green.

"I have to leave soon," he said. The thought of her marrying Delbert haunted him. He raked his fingers through his hair. How could he ask her about it without seeming nosey or jealous?

"Where are you going?" she asked.

"Back to the States to report to my commanding officer. I was supposed to take the Vega to Holland. But my orders have been changed."

"We'll always be grateful to you," she said.

The heartrending tenderness in her gaze drew a wave of love over his heart. Confused, he shrugged. "I was glad I was there for you." They found a gate, and he pushed it open.

"Don't be modest. You're a knight in shining armor." They strolled along a path, between a line of elms, stopping at an arbor. Amanda sat on the stone bench, and Curley stood facing her with one foot on the bench beside her, bracing his right forearm on his thigh. "We have to talk," he said impatiently. "I heard you'll be marrying Delbert when you get back and—"

"Delbert?" Amanda's nose wrinkled. "I'm not marrying him!"

"But he said—"

"I don't care what he said." Amanda stood and poked Curley's chest. His foot came down, and he leaned back slightly. "Men! I'm so sick of men deciding where I'll be going, with whom, when, and how! And Delbert can go jump in a lake."

"Hold on! You're not classifying me in with the rest of those men, are you?" He gripped both of her shoulders. "I'm not trying to talk you into doing anything. I want a companion, an equal, not a slave." He hesitated, then added, "That is, if I ever decide to. . ." He dropped his hands from her shoulders, disgusted at himself for sounding like a bumbling adolescent.

"Curley?" Hearing his name on her lips almost stole his breath away.

Amanda reached up and put her hand on his cheek. Dark green specks glowed in the artless gaze she fixed on him. "If you ever want a companion, a friend, I'll be there."

That promise filled him with intense happiness. All his excuses to keep from getting tied down by some wily female were going down in flames. The cynical, reckless bachelor, the lone eagle persona, suddenly no longer suited him. He had thought falling in love was being caught in a trap, but it wasn't like that at all. Instead, he felt a soaring freedom, as if a dozen invisible restraints had just been broken.

For a long moment they simply stood there, looking at each other. *She's not marrying Delbert!* A breeze moved through the trees, a finch whistled a lilting tune, and his heart sang along. She seemed to be waiting for him to say something.

"Marry me, Amanda." Another finch answered the first one.

She stared at him, her green eyes misting. Romantic cliches sprang to mind. She took a shaky breath. "This is rather sudden, don't you think?"

"No. On the plane I suddenly remembered seeing you years ago at an air show. I knew then there was something special about you. Then from the moment I landed on that ship and took another look, I knew I loved you."

"You what?"

He looked down at her for a second, then groaned and hugged her to him. "I love you, Amanda. I didn't realize it until I almost lost you to those Germans. Or to Delbert."

"Oh, Curley," she sighed. "You were right. If I'd listened to you, I wouldn't have been captured." Then she lifted her chin. "But we wouldn't have rescued my family, either. I would never have known what had happened to them if I hadn't been captured along with them."

He cupped her face in his hands, marveling at the petal softness of her skin. "God and I will always take care of you. Can you believe that?"

Amanda nodded, brushing a tear from her eye. Ever since she met him at that air show, she'd wanted him. This was one request she hadn't dared make to God, but He'd known. "I love you, too," she said. "I've loved you since I was seventeen years old."

Suddenly, Curley dropped to one knee, took her hand, and brought it to his chest. She felt his warmth beneath his jacket. He looked up at her with a mixture of boyish exuberance and earnestness that made her knees weak.

"Amanda Chase, will you marry me?"

She smiled down into his eyes, blissful happiness flowing over her like a warm wave.

Before she could answer, he went on, "First, there's something you must know: I don't want you to stop doing what you love. Chasing down stories and reporting is in your blood, and it's one of your lovable charms. Of course, if you want to quit and settle down—"

"Yes."

"Yes?"

"Yes, James Cameron. I'll marry you." He rose in one fluid motion. She flung her arms around him, burying her face in his shoulder.

He talked about his duty to the army, she of her excitement for writing the truth about what was happening in Germany. He told her of the air race of the century starting that week, in Middlesex, with aces in their souped-up planes racing for Australia. "I'll pull some strings and get you a special press pass. Watch the Comet," he said. "It's the fastest thing with wings—next to my little Moth," he added, grinning modestly.

They made plans to meet and announce their engagement as soon as she arrived back in the States. Amanda felt peace, like a comforting aroma, enveloping them. She sighed. "This is a fairy tale and I'm the girl who got the prince."

He laughed and pulled her away with him. "Come on, Princess. Let's go live happily ever after!"

Epilogue

G od delivered Cousin Joseph's grandparents, but others were not so fortunate," said Curley to his youngest grandson, Sam. They were leaving the Yad Vashem, memorial of the Holocaust.

"Were you there?" Sam spoke softly, matching their respectful mood.

"We almost were," said Amanda, putting a hand on his slender shoulder. "But your grandpa rescued us in his airplane."

The boy looked up at them, excitement shining in his eyes. "Did you shoot 'em out of the sky?"

"No, Grandma knocked him flat on his back before we even took off." Curley caught Amanda's eye and winked.

"Wow! How did you do that, Grandma?"

"Hold still," said Amanda, removing the temporary *yarmulke* he had to wear to enter the memorial. Sunshine glinted off his curly auburn hair. "I'll tell you all about it this afternoon when we get back to Cousin Martha's house."

Sam walked ahead of them, shuffling through the postcards they'd bought. Amanda shuddered, and Curley hugged her to his side. "Are you okay?"

"Yes." She looked back at the monument. "When I think that Uncle Jacob almost went back—"

He stopped and put both hands on her waist. Their eyes on each other, he said, "Think back. No one in 1934 could have seen the horror that was coming. Many thought it was temporary and they'd get their homes and lives back. I know you feel sad; so do I, but we both had the satisfaction of helping put a stop to that madman. You with your words, and me with the air corps."

She glanced back at the building again. "But so many! Millions, each one with hopes, dreams, memories, a different story for each life."

Sam tugged at her sleeve. "Please, can I have my candy now, Grandma?"

Amanda took the postcards, put them into her purse, and drew out a candy bar. Sam walked beside them, tearing the paper off.

Hand in hand, Amanda and Curley walked down the sidewalk to their car. "I can hardly bear to think of the Holocaust," said Amanda. "Thank God for this memorial."

Curley squeezed her hand. "God willing, the world won't forget—so that it will never happen again."

JANE LAMUNYON

Jane lives in California with her husband and designates much of her time to writing and the business of writing. She is the author of *Me God, You Jane,* her autobiography, and two **Heartsong Presents** novels, *Fly Away Home* and *Escape on the Wind.* She has written short stories for adults and children, how-tos on a wide range of topics, and a stage play. Her work has encompassed many genres, including newspaper stories, book reviews, corporate newsletters, technical manuals, and prize-winning poetry. She is a speaker and workshop leader in many different areas.

The Rising Son

Darlene Mindrup

To Michelle Finklea,
my most avid fan (besides my husband and mom).
And to those Japanese Americans who loved this country
enough to stand by it even when it didn't stand by them.

Chapter 1

March 1941

K eiko lifted the last item from the depths of the huge box, gently unwrapping the tissue paper from around it. She smiled at the Japanese
daruma, its one colored eye giving it a somewhat strange appearance.
Lifting the doll to place it on the shelf among the others of her collection,
she was careful to select a place of prominence. Settling back on her heels, she
stroked her hands down her silk kimono, studying each doll's position.

Although Keiko considered herself a rather traditional American, she still
loved to celebrate many of the Japanese holidays. *Hinamatsuri,* or the Doll's
Festival, was her favorite.

She stared at the *Bodhidharma* doll. It had no arms, no legs, and only one
eye. Reaching up, she gently pushed the doll over, watching as it returned to
its upright position. Her thoughts went back to the day her mother had told
her of its meaning.

"Mama-san, why does this doll have no legs or arms? And why is only
one eye painted?" Six-year-old Keiko frowned up at her mother, her brown
almond eyes filled with curiosity.

Her mother reached down, gently stroking the frown from her face. "Don't
frown so, Keiko-chan. It will give you wrinkles." Lifting the little girl onto her lap,
Keiko's mother's voice took on the singsong quality she used when telling a story.

"Long ago, a man—Bodhidharma was his name—traveled to China. He
wanted to see the great Buddha. He waited and waited, sitting in the Zen
posture that Buddha likes to sit in. He waited so long that eventually he lost
his arms and legs."

Keiko stared up at her mother, her mouth open. "Is this true?"

Her mother's brown eyes twinkled back at her. Hugging her close, her
mother whispered in her ear. "No, my little Keiko-chan. It is just a story. But
the doll is cute, do you not think so?"

Keiko's eyes went back to the doll. She tried hard not to frown, but it was
a losing battle. "But it only has one eye. It looks. . .it looks. . ." She frowned
again, unable to explain how the doll made her feel.

"When a girl receives a Bodhidharma doll," her mother explained, "she
makes a wish, so to speak, and colors in one eye. When her wish is fulfilled, or
her endeavor is completed, she colors in the other eye."

Little Keiko took the doll into her hand, stroking one finger softly over the painted eye. Glancing back up at her mother, her eyes asked the question that her lips refused to utter.

"That colored eye represents you and Kenji," her mother told her quietly. "I prayed for children, and God has blessed me with two fine, beautiful angels."

Keiko looked back at the doll, her forehead puckering. "But there are two eyes and two of us."

Her mother smiled, hugging her close again. "Yes, Keiko-chan. But my one wish was for children who would come to love and serve Jesus. When that happens, then I will color in the other eye."

That had been almost twelve years ago. Keiko's eyes filled with sadness that her mother had not realized the fulfillment of her wish. Although Keiko knew and loved the Lord, her mother died before Keiko accepted Jesus as her Savior.

The back screen door slammed, and Keiko frowned. Without turning around, she knew who was behind her. It was always the same. Kenji, so alive with energy, so volatile in his emotions.

"Hey, Sis." He stopped dead, his eyes going over her from the top of her head with its Japanese-style bun to the cork geta on her feet. His eyes darkened with anger, but he refrained from comment. Kenji hated anything that even remotely resembled Japan or Japanese ways. He considered himself only an American and wished to be treated as such, whereas Keiko was proud of her Japanese heritage.

Kenji took in the assortment of dolls lined on the shelves around the living room. Suddenly, his eyes softened. Walking over, he took a doll gently into his hands, studying it intently. Keiko saw the sheen in his eyes.

"Remember when she bought this one?" His voice was husky with suppressed tears.

Keiko nodded. "When we took our first plane trip to Oregon to visit Obā-san." Their aunt had smiled tolerantly while their mother had purchased the small doll at the airport. Mama-san had always tried to purchase dolls for her collection that would hold memories for her in the years to come.

Kenji set the doll back on the shelf and turned away. "I have baseball practice today, so I'll be late. Jason invited me for supper."

Jason and Kenji had become close friends since attending the university together. But Papa-san was not happy with their relationship. He blamed Jason for much of Kenji's anti-Japanese feelings.

Keiko bit her lip. Papa-san would not be pleased, but it would do no good to remind Kenji of this. Keiko's heart thumped hard. She should say something, but she knew from past experience it would only make Kenji angry, and then he might not come home for days.

Kenji slammed back out the door, and Keiko's eyes went back to the Bodhidharma doll. No, it looked like her mother's wish would never be fulfilled and the poor little doll would forever remain without one eye. Keiko felt the tears gathering in her throat. Where had it all gone wrong? Had it started with her mother's death six years ago? Everything seemed to have changed after that.

It amazed Keiko that her mother's strong Christian beliefs had had so little impact on her father and her brother. How could they not see? How could they not believe?

When her mother had come to America in 1920, she had been only seventeen. A picture bride. Even then she had been a Christian, taught by the missionaries in Japan. But her father still practiced the Shinto religion. Keiko shook her head. Never would she ally herself with a non-Christian. Watching her mother's heart break little by little had hardened her own resolve. No, she would never marry a non-Christian.

She got to her feet, studying each doll as she did so. Most of the dolls were her mother's, but Keiko had added several of her own. As with her mother's dolls, each of her own dolls held memories for Keiko.

She grinned at the little Kewpie doll that looked so out of place among the others with its bright red topknot. She had purchased it at the fair last year when she and her best friend, Sumiko, had gone. It had been so much fun.

She sobered, remembering how so many boys had followed Sumiko around. Even white boys were drawn to Sumiko's ethereal beauty.

The same could not be said of herself. She knew she wasn't ugly, exactly, but neither was she pretty. If she had to describe herself in one word, that word would be "ordinary." Except for one thing: By some accident of genetics, she was taller than most Japanese women. Compared to Sumiko, she felt like an amazon. And her nose tilted up on the end ever so slightly. Pushing a finger against the offending appendage, Keiko shrugged her shoulders. Oh, well, there was nothing she could do about her height or her nose.

She made her way to the kitchen, trying to decide what to make for supper that night. Sudden inspiration brought a sparkle to her eyes. Since Kenji would not be home, she would prepare her father a traditional Japanese meal and serve it to him in her kimono.

She grinned slightly. The kimono was not meant for comfort, but one day would not hurt anything. Besides, it gave her father pleasure to be treated in the old ways. She knew he didn't expect it of her, but it pleased him when she did.

Keiko picked up a porcelain teapot and turned to fill it. The screen door stood somewhat ajar from its last encounter with Kenji. Shaking her head, she reached over to latch it as she passed to the sink. She jumped back when a face suddenly appeared in her line of vision. The teapot shattered into tiny porcelain pieces as it fell at her feet.

She stared down in dismay, her heart slowing to a more reasonable pace. Glancing angrily at the man standing at her back door, she forgot to be afraid.

"Haven't you ever heard of using the front door? Now look what you've made me do!"

Brown almond eyes crinkled back at her. Although the stranger's lips twitched, his face remained serious.

"I apologize," he told her in flawless Japanese. "I already tried the front door, but I think that the bell is not working."

Undaunted, she continued to glare at him. "You could have knocked." Her sudden switch from Japanese to English seemed to surprise him. He pulled himself to his full height, which was considerable for an Oriental, and his narrowed eyes surveyed her from head to foot. Unlike Kenji, the stranger seemed to approve of what he saw.

"I did," he told her, his English as perfect as his Japanese had been.

Since Keiko had been in the kitchen, in all probability he was telling the truth. She couldn't have heard him if he had knocked softly.

Embarrassed, Keiko continued to stare at the stranger. She had never seen an Oriental so tall. And his hair curled softly around his head instead of hanging straight. It occurred to her then that he must be of mixed parentage.

"I am looking for Tochigi-san. Is this his house?"

"Hai." Instead of the short, staccato syllable, the affirmation came out in a soft drawn-out sigh. Color flamed into her cheeks, and her eyes went to the floor.

"He is my father," she informed him. "But he will not be home until later."

"My name is Shoji Ibaragi. I think your father is expecting me. Will you tell him I have been here and that I will return at. . ." He glanced at his watch. "Tell him I will return at six."

Remembering her manners, Keiko suddenly blurted out, "Come for supper."

He hesitated. "Are you sure? I do not wish to be any trouble."

"Hai." This time her voice was firm.

Bowing from the waist, he turned to go. Suddenly, he turned back. *"Onamae wa?"*

Keiko dropped her eyes, the color once again blooming in her cheeks. "Keiko."

She wondered at the light that suddenly entered his eyes and the intense scrutiny to which he subjected her, but he turned away too quickly for her to be sure of what she had seen. Relief?

"Sayonara." His voice drifted back to her as he rounded the house.

The rest of the day, Keiko wavered between having a traditional meal as she had planned or making something more appropriate for company, like roast.

Did Mr. Ibaragi like traditional Japanese food? Picturing him in her mind was easy. She could remember every detail about him, from his purely Western clothes to his flawless Japanese. She was dying to know more about him, but that would have to wait until Papa-san came home.

Finally, Keiko decided on *sukiyaki* for supper, and she saw no reason to change her plans where her father's guest was concerned. Probably she would never see Mr. Ibaragi again after tonight, so she might as well continue with her plans to please her father. Perhaps, in the back of her mind, was the thought that by pleasing him, he would not be so hard on Kenji.

Keiko could feel herself tense when her father came through the front door. He dropped the basket he used to carry vegetables to the market on the table by the door. She watched patiently as he took off his shoes and placed them in their cubbyhole in the *getabako*.

When he raised up, he noticed Keiko standing in the living room. His eyes gleamed when he saw her bright pink kimono. A small smile tilted his lips at the corner.

"Keiko-chan," he told her softly. "You are as lovely as your mother."

She knew that was not true. Her mother had been a beautiful woman, but she understood what he meant, and she was glad she had made the attempt to please him.

"Come, Papa-san," she told him, taking his arm and urging him to his favorite chair. "I have fixed some hot *ocha* for you."

She quickly retrieved the tea she had left in the kitchen on a tray. The old teapot reminded her of Mr. Ibaragi's visit.

"Papa-san, there was a man who called to see you. His name was Ibaragi. Shoji Ibaragi."

Her head was bent over the teapot, so she missed seeing her father's head shoot up and the color drain from his face.

"He was here?"

"Hai."

Keiko was alarmed at her father's sudden pallor.

"Did he say he would return?"

"Hai." Again her agreement was slow and drawn out. "I. . .I invited him for supper."

Her father's eyes grew wider. "Did he accept?"

"Hai. He said you were expecting him." It sounded more like a question.

Her father rubbed his face with his hands, his shoulders slumping. *"Hai,"* he told her. "But I did not expect him so soon."

"Is there something wrong, Papa-san? Should I not have invited him?"

Slowly he shook his head. "No, nothing." Apparently forcing a smile, he studied her with loving eyes. "Sometimes I forget that you are growing up."

Frowning, Keiko wondered what that had to do with anything. She noticed how tired her father looked. How frail. Sometimes she forgot that he was getting older too.

"Drink your tea, Papa-san. Mr. Ibaragi will be here at six."

Although Keiko had prepared a traditional Japanese meal, she set out the porcelain dishes on the dining table. She lay the chopsticks next to each place, wondering as she did so if Mr. Ibaragi would object to using them as Kenji would.

Her father had been so upset over the news of his arrival, Keiko had forgotten in her concern for her father to question him about the man. She remembered how Mr. Ibaragi's shirt and tie had accentuated his strong physique. Again she wondered about the size of him. He had towered over her.

When a knock sounded on the front door at precisely six o'clock, Keiko felt her heart lurch, and her pulse begin to race. Her eyes went to her father, who was calmly walking toward the door. Nothing about him suggested anything other than casual interest.

Keiko waited in the entryway behind her father, but she couldn't see around the door her father held open. Her father was bowing low in the way only a true Japanese could do. His murmured greeting was too low for her ears.

Mr. Ibaragi stepped through the door and bowed as low as her father had. "Tochigi-san, *konban wa.*"

His "good evening" held a wealth of respect, as had his bow. Keiko's eyes widened at the sight of him in his jeans mixed with the *happi* coat of the workingman. On him the garment looked wonderful and not the least out of place. His tunic was tucked neatly in at the waist with a tie belt, the black silk highlighting the darkness of his skin.

Without being told to, Shoji leaned down and removed the shoes from his feet. When Keiko reached for them, his eyes met hers. Again there was something in their depths she didn't understand.

She followed them into the living room, watching as her father offered his guest the best seat in the house.

"Ibaragi-san, I had not expected you so soon," her father told him.

The young man bent forward, wrapping one hand around the other, draping them casually between his legs. His eyes were focused on the floor. When he finally looked up, there was such pain in his eyes that Keiko almost cried out to him.

"Tochigi-san, my father recently passed from this life. His final wish was that I come to you."

Keiko saw understanding in her father's eyes and sympathy as well. "I did not know. I am sorry to hear of this." He sighed gently. "We have much to discuss, Ibaragi-san, but for now, let us share a meal. Come; Keiko is a fine cook."

Keiko looked at her father in surprise. It wasn't polite to brag on one's children, and her father rarely broke with decorum.

"Please, call me Shoji." His smile reached out from one to the other, and Keiko felt her heart give a thump so loud she was sure he must have heard it. Her face colored with confusion. Lifting her eyes to Shoji's, she found amusement lurking in their depths.

What was it about this man that could have such an impact on both her and her father? Her brow drew down in a frown. The man was a definite enigma.

She watched discreetly as Shoji used his chopsticks proficiently. Her father gave her a broad smile, and his eyes gleamed when she placed the dessert of hot apple cobbler in front of him. They exchanged smiles before Keiko handed Shoji his own serving.

"I hope you like apple cobbler, Shoji-san."

He smiled, his eyes warm. "It is one of my favorites, Tochigi-san."

Before she had time to answer, they could hear the back door slam open. Kenji entered the room, his nose sniffing.

"Is that apple cobbler I smell?"

Keiko felt her father's frown before she saw it.

Rising quickly from her seat, she pushed her brother into his. "It is. Sit down, and I'll get you some."

When she returned to the table, the tension in the room was thick enough to cut with a knife. Glancing at Shoji, Keiko found him watching father and son, a slight frown marring his features.

They finished dessert in silence. Keiko almost choked on her own. Why, oh, why couldn't Kenji and her father get along? Why couldn't her father see that he was driving Kenji away with his constant demands? And why couldn't Kenji see that her father only wanted his son's respect?

Kenji rose from the table, throwing his napkin on his plate. "I got homework to do!"

Her father's frown increased. "Kenji-san, we have things to discuss."

"Look, Pop, I don't have time. I have an English lit test tomorrow."

"What I have to say will not take long. I need to speak with you both."

Kenji started to protest, but Shoji rose gracefully to his feet. "Perhaps I should leave."

Her father shook his head. "No, Shoji-san, this includes you, also."

Both Keiko and Kenji looked at the young man in surprise.

"Who is this guy?" Kenji demanded. "Whatta ya mean it involves him too? What's he got to do with me?"

Instead of answering, her father turned and went into the living room, a clear indication that he didn't wish to discuss whatever it was in the kitchen.

Keiko followed her father with Kenji close behind. Shoji brought up the rear.

She sat down next to her father, her worried eyes begging her brother for tolerance. If there was one thing Keiko hated, it was conflict.

Shoji remained standing, arms folded across his chest, his face an inscrutable mask. Keiko finally understood what the term "inscrutable" really meant. There was no indication of embarrassment or anger or any emotion on his face. She had to admire his stoic countenance as she sat trembling from head to foot.

Keiko's eyes came back to her father when he cleared his throat. "Many years ago," he started, "I made a contract with a man I knew from Japan."

He stopped, unable to go on for a moment.

"What kind of contract?" Kenji demanded, glaring at Shoji. The inscrutable look never wavered.

Her father cleared his throat again. "Ibaragi-san was a good friend. We knew each other in Japan. We went to school together, until. . .until he went to the mission school. He later came to America and. . ."

Kenji began to fidget. "What kind of contract?" he asked again.

"A marriage contract between his first son and my first daughter, or my first son and his first daughter, whichever came first."

Kenji was on his feet in an instant. "Are you outta your mind? You must be if you think I'm marrying a girl I've never even met!" He shoved his hand through his slicked-back hair. "I can't believe even you would do such a thing!"

Keiko's eyes were on Shoji. He looked her way, and for an instant, his poise melted. His eyes were almost pleading. Only a moment, then the closed look returned to his face.

"He doesn't mean you, Kenji—do you?" she asked her father quietly, her eyes fixed on Shoji's. "Mr. Ibaragi has come for me, hasn't he?"

Kenji's eyes flew to Shoji's face. The truth was there for all to see.

"Get out!" Kenji hissed. "Get out before I throw you out!"

"Kenji!"

Never had Keiko heard her father's voice filled with such authority. Kenji was silenced, but she knew it wouldn't be for long.

"You will not disgrace me before a guest in my home."

Keiko watched her brother's face contort with rage. "Me disgrace you! That's a laugh! You brought this disgrace on yourself!" Jerking his jacket from the coatrack in the hall, he headed for the door. "I'm outta here."

"Kenji!"

Ignoring his father's outraged voice, Kenji slammed the door behind him.

Still shaking, Keiko rose from her seat. "Father," she told him, using the title she so rarely used, "this is impossible, and you know it."

"Keiko," he pleaded. "I have given my word."

Turning to Shoji, she asked, "And what of you? Do you accept this arrangement?"

He hesitated only a moment. "I am willing to consider it. For my father's sake."

Keiko's eyes grew dark with suppressed fury. He may be an American, but obviously he had been raised in the old ways in Japan. It was bad enough to be considered as a wife for his father's sake, but to be told in so many words that she was being a disobedient daughter was more than she was willing to take from this man. Drawing herself up to her full height, she pinned him with a glare.

"Go back to Japan, Mr. Ibaragi, where you belong. I'm sure you will find a woman to accommodate you there."

She would have fled the room, but her father grasped her arm. "Please, Keiko, can we not discuss this?"

"No, Papa-san," she told him, hating the hurt look in his eye. "There is nothing more to discuss."

His shoulders slumped in defeat. Letting go of her arm, he took two steps before clutching his chest and suddenly pitching forward.

Chapter 2

Shoji handed a cup of hot coffee to Keiko, who lifted tear-filled eyes to his face. She curled her fingers around the warm mug. She felt cold all over. Shoji stared back at her, wordlessly offering her sympathy and comfort. Between the two of them, they had managed to get her father into the farm truck and to the hospital.

Even if they had a telephone, it was unlikely an ambulance would have come that far, especially for a Japanese. Keiko was grateful that she had not been alone with her father since she did not know how to drive. If not for Shoji, Keiko wasn't sure what she would have done. But this would not have happened if he hadn't come.

Rage filled her like none she had ever known before. She turned away from his intense scrutiny, pretending to study the cold, stark hospital waiting room.

The hardback chairs with their orange vinyl covers were something less than restful. The cold white walls made her shiver.

"Did you find Kenji?"

She jerked around, facing Shoji again. The anger bubbled just below the surface, waiting for an opening to allow an explosion. The only thing that kept her from lashing out at him was the remembrance of how gentle he had been with her father.

"No," she told him, looking away. "I left messages with all of his friends. That's all I can do for right now."

Nodding, Shoji sat down beside her. She pulled herself away as much as the seat would allow.

"Keiko, we have to talk."

She jumped to her feet, going to the room's only window.

"Can you not see that now is not the time?" In her agitation, she lapsed into Japanese.

Getting up, he crossed the room to her side. "I only wish to help," he returned, also in Japanese.

She rounded on him furiously. "Help! If not for you, none of this would have happened."

"I think you know that is not true."

At his soft-spoken words, she felt the air go out of her. It was true what he said. She had noticed her father looking haggard over the last few months.

269

She knew it had to do with the fact that the United States didn't allow *issei* to own property, since they were not American citizens.

Any property they "owned" had to be leased from nominees, and sometimes the nominees charged twice the going rate to rent the land. She knew that their landlord, Mr. Dalrimple, was not an honest man. But what could they do? Kenji wouldn't be twenty-one for another two years. When that happened, everything could be put in Kenji's name since he was a *nisei*, the American-born son of Japanese immigrants. But until that happened, they simply had to bide their time.

She knew the hard work and stress were taking a toll on her father, little by little. That and the fact that he and Kenji were constantly locked in conflict. Now. . .

A nurse walked into the room, breaking the silence that had lengthened to several minutes. Her eyes raked over Keiko's kimono, a curious glitter appearing in their frosty blue depths.

"The doctor will see you in a moment."

She left before Keiko could ask her any questions. Keiko and Shoji exchanged glances, returning to their silence.

Keiko moved away from the window and retreated to the safety of the only orange chair in the corner. The potted rubber tree somewhat obscured her from view. Being too close to Shoji made her very uncomfortable.

She watched him stare out the window, tall, strong, and totally in charge of his emotions. She, on the other hand, was a bundle of nerves.

When the doctor entered the room, Keiko was the first at his side. Her worried brown eyes searched his face for some clue to her father's condition. Unlike the nurse, the doctor was gently sympathetic.

"I'm sorry," he told her softly, and Keiko felt her heart drop.

"Your father is in a coma."

Keiko's eyes went wide. "You mean, he's still. . .he's alive?"

When the doctor nodded, she took a deep breath. *Thank You, God! Oh, thank You!*

"He's had a heart attack, as I'm sure you've surmised." He hesitated. "His condition is not good. Physically, we've done all we can for him, but. . ."

Shoji spoke for the first time. "But what, Doctor?"

"It's almost as though he has no will to live." He looked from one to the other, as if hoping they could enlighten him.

Keiko sucked on her bottom lip as she eyed Shoji. Could her father not face his "shame"? To an *issei*, a debt of honor would be a matter of life or death—not something to be taken lightly by one's children. Keiko had never understood the *issei* rigidity when it came to matters of principle. Or was it even more than that?

"May I see him?"

The doctor hesitated. His look went from one to the other. Sighing, he crossed his arms. "Yes, but only for a minute."

Keiko looked down at her father lying so still and small against the starched white sheets. She flinched at the intravenous drip attached to his arm.

She stroked a hand gently across her father's forehead, bent, and kissed him gently. The tears began again.

"Can I stay with him tonight?"

The doctor shook his head. "I'm afraid not. It's against hospital policy. Besides, there's nothing more you can do for him tonight. I don't foresee him awakening from this coma for some time, if—"

He bit off the last word, but Keiko knew what he meant to say. If ever.

"You need to get some rest yourself," he told her gently.

Shoji took the coat from her arms and held it out for her. When she slipped her arms through the sleeves, he held onto her shoulders, squeezing gently.

Angrily, she pulled herself away, hurrying across the room and down the hallway. She knew Shoji was right behind her, but she didn't really care. Suddenly she was weary beyond endurance. She wanted to crawl into her own bed and cry the tears that were threatening release.

She was waiting in the truck when Shoji slid into the driver's seat. He looked at her a long moment before starting the truck. The truck growled as he shifted the tired gears and pulled out of the hospital parking lot onto the desolate road out of town.

Over the rumble of the engine, Keiko sensed the waves of anger and frustration emanating from Shoji, and she swallowed hard. It suddenly occurred to her that she was alone with a man who thought she was his future bride.

Glancing his way, she found his dark almond eyes glittering at her in the darkness. His jaws clenched tightly as he turned his gaze back to the road.

When they pulled up in front of her house, Keiko reached for the door, anxious to escape. Shoji's hand came down over hers.

"Wait."

He eased his tall frame from the truck, walked around the front, and opened her door. He reached a hand up to help her from the vehicle, but when she placed her hand into his, she was unprepared for the jolt of excitement that flashed through her.

Jerking her hand away, she quickly headed for the house. When she turned around, he was right behind her.

"Thank you for bringing me home and for helping with my father." His eyes never left her face as she stammered to a halt.

"Keiko," he admonished softly, "I told you we needed to talk."

"I'm too tired," she snapped. "And too upset."

He sighed. "You are not making this easy," he told her.

Shoving back the hair that had fallen from its bun, she continued to glare at him. "I have nothing to say to you. Any conversation you have will have to be with my father."

There was a strange gleam in his eyes that she didn't understand, but she took a quick step backward.

"Fine," he agreed. "Where do I sleep?"

"Excuse me?" Her eyes searched his features for some sign of understanding. *"Gomen nasai?"* she repeated in Japanese.

His lips twitched slightly. "Your father invited me to stay here."

Her eyes rounded in alarm. "You can't stay here! We're. . .we're. . ."

"Alone. I know," he finished for her. "But I can't walk back to town now. It's too late."

"Walk?" Her eyes searched the yard, but there was no sign of a vehicle anywhere.

"You walked?" she asked him incredulously.

"Hai."

She ground her teeth in frustration. "Is that all you can say?"

"Iie." His grin was infuriating. "No," he repeated as though she couldn't understand Japanese. "Keiko," he implored patiently, "may we go inside and talk about this?"

"Iie!" she snapped back at him. "You can't stay here. Neither my brother nor my father are here. We can't stay here alone."

"We are engaged," he told her softly. At the instant flash of fire in her eyes, he sighed again. "I didn't mean it like that."

"Well, however you meant it, you're not staying here."

Shoji rubbed his forehead with his hands, dropping them lamely to his sides. "May I sleep in the truck?"

Keiko stared at him in surprise. "What?"

His eyes held hers for a long time. "The truck. May I sleep in the truck? That way I will be here to drive you to town in the morning. You do wish to go to the hospital?"

Keiko would have denied him if she could have. Biting the corner of her lip, she wavered back and forth in her mind the advisability of doing as he asked. Surely Kenji would come home before morning. But what if he didn't? She simply had to get into town and see her father. *I have got to learn to drive.*

"Okay," she told him and saw his shoulders slump with relief. "Wait here, and I will get you some bedding."

When she returned, she saw that he hadn't moved from the same spot she had left him in. He turned to her, taking the pillow and blankets from her hands. When he looked back at her face, his brown eyes were velvety soft in the moonlight.

"Oyasumi nasai," he told her softly.

"Good night," she repeated and watched him walk back to the truck and climb in the front. She shivered slightly, pulling her coat tightly around her. Maybe she should have let him stay in Papa-san's room. She knew without a doubt that her father would be mortified if he knew how she had treated his honored guest.

Sighing, she went inside and shut the door. It was cold tonight. March in southern California was still a little cool for camping out in trucks.

Gritting her teeth, she pushed such thoughts from her mind. He could very well look after himself. Anyone who would walk fifteen miles—no, wait, forty-five miles—well, he could look after himself, that's all.

When she finally lay in her bed, she could no longer keep the thoughts at bay. *Lord, what do I do now?*

Was she the cause of her father's attack? She knew how traditional he was. Had her refusal to honor his contract made him lose face to such an extent that his heart couldn't take the strain? It was ridiculous, and yet. . .

God, help me. Tell me what to do. But the only words that kept coming to her mind were from the book of Ephesians. *"Children, obey your parents in the Lord: for this is right."*

She pressed her palms tightly against her temples in an attempt to ward off any more thoughts. Groaning, she rolled to her side.

I don't even know if he's a Christian, Lord. He's kibei. *Born in America but raised in Japan.*

Since she hadn't bothered to ask, she knew she was being unfair. He had tried to talk to her.

Finally, exhaustion took its toll, and she fell into a deep, dreamless sleep.

★ ★ ★

The sound of Otomodachi crowing brought Keiko back from the dreamless realms of sleepland. She smiled slightly, remembering her father bringing the red bantam home.

"If you do your duty and wake me in the morning, then you will be my friend," he told the cock. So his name had become Otomodachi, because he had done just what was expected of him and her father considered him a trustworthy friend.

But was she doing what was expected of her? All the events of the night before came rushing back at her.

Flinging her quilt aside, she hurriedly dressed. How had Shoji fared the night? Guilty pangs of conscience followed her everywhere.

When she opened the front screen door, she found him sitting on the porch.

"*Ohayo gozaimasu,*" he greeted her, his eyes wandering over her, taking in her changed appearance. There was nothing in their inscrutable brown depths to tell her whether he approved of the change or not.

273

Her dress was typically American. It flowed past her knees from a gathered waist cinched by a black patent leather belt. The apple-blossom-pink material accentuated her complexion, and the white Peter Pan collar brought out the brightness in her dark amber eyes, which were highlighted by the dark bangs across her forehead. Her black hair hung straight and silky down her back.

Shoji had removed his *happi* coat, leaving only the black turtleneck beneath. The material hugged his body, allowing Keiko to see the muscles that were so evident. Again Keiko marveled that an Oriental could be so large.

"Good morning," she returned his greeting. "Would you like some breakfast?"

"If it is no trouble."

"Iie, it is no trouble. Come inside."

Shoji followed Keiko into the kitchen, wondering at the change in her. From traditional Japanese to typical American. Which was the real Keiko? It was important for him to find out.

"I like the dress," he told her and hid a smile at her evident embarrassment. "But I like the one you had on last night as well."

She glanced at him briefly as she filled their plates. "I only wear my kimono on special occasions. I much prefer the comfort of American clothes."

One eyebrow quirked upward, but he said nothing. He wondered if the inference meant that she would not live in Japan. Keiko laid a plate of eggs and toast in front of him.

"I'm sorry it's not more, but I'm rather anxious to get to the hospital."

"It is enough. *Arigato.*"

"You're welcome."

Shoji bowed his head in thanks. *Father, bless this food and let it strengthen Keiko in this difficult time.* When he looked up, he saw Keiko's eyes widen in surprise.

"It is good," he told her, and her face flushed as she dropped her eyes to her own plate.

Shoji watched Keiko push her food around on her plate. He knew she must be desperate to know if her father was all right.

"You need to eat," Shoji admonished. "We have no idea what to expect, but you should do it on a full stomach."

Keiko choked down as much as she could, but in the end, she left most of it on her plate.

★ ★ ★

The hospital was more crowded than it had been the night before. People hurried to visit their family members, mindless of anything else.

Keiko was no different. She hurried to the nurse's desk to find out her father's condition and where they had bedded him. The nurse pointed them in the right direction but asked them to wait until she could summon the doctor.

When the doctor arrived, Keiko was distressed to find it was not the same man as last night. His eyes were colder, and his attitude was one of impatience.

"Miss Tochigi?"

"Yes. My father. . ."

He stopped her with an impatient jerk of his head. Motioning to the waiting room, he frowned down at her. "Could we speak in here?"

Keiko was comforted by Shoji's presence standing so near. For some reason, this doctor frightened her. When Shoji put a large hand against her back, she made no objection.

"Your father is still in a coma," the doctor told her bluntly. "At this point, we have no idea when he will come out of it, or even if he will."

The cold statement left her speechless.

"Where is he?"

Although Keiko could detect no change in Shoji's demeanor, she could hear the anger laced through his voice. Her eyes went to his, but they were as fathomless as ever.

Obviously, the doctor sensed the same thing, for his attitude altered slightly. "I'll show you the way," he told them stiffly.

When Keiko entered the room, she saw her father as she had seen him the night before, only looking more frail than ever. The doctor last night said that they had done all they could medically, but that her father seemed to want to die. Could this be true?

He couldn't die! He just couldn't! He didn't know the Lord. He wasn't ready.

She knelt by the edge of the bed, taking his small hand into her own. Bowing her head, she began to frantically petition the Lord on his behalf. A hand on her shoulder brought her eyes around.

"I will leave you alone with him. If you need me, I will be in the waiting room."

She should be grateful for his support, but instead she was aggravated by it. He had no right to be here. This had nothing to do with him. But, wait. Didn't it? Maybe she didn't think so, but she knew that being raised in Japan, he would have a whole different concept of honor. He would abide by his father's wishes no matter what his feelings in the matter.

A kibei! *Oh, Lord, I can't marry a* kibei. *I would be nothing but a slave.*

She could feel her father's weak heartbeat through her fingers. She didn't know how long she knelt there praying and petitioning, but she finally came to terms with herself. She knew what she had to do. She couldn't let her father die.

"Papa-san," she whispered softly. "Papa-san, can you hear me? Please, Papa-san, come back to me. I need you." His breathing remained shallow, but she thought she detected a slight movement of his eyelashes.

"Papa-san, if you come back to me, I will honor your contract and marry Shoji."

Was she daring to tell a lie? No! She would marry Shoji. She just hadn't mentioned when. Maybe in fifteen years or so.

Guilt washed through her. No matter how hard she tried to justify it, she knew she was trying to be deceitful. Groaning, she dropped her head to the sheets beside her father's hand.

"I will marry him, Papa-san. I will," she whispered softly.

She jerked in surprise when she felt a hand on her shoulder. Shoji. It unnerved her the way he moved around so silently. She never heard him approaching; he just appeared. Had he heard her declaration? She looked into his eyes and realized that he had. For the first time, their fathomless depths were alive with his feelings, but she could not interpret them.

He lifted her from the floor. She wanted to protest, but she was just too tired.

"Kenji-san is in the waiting room," he told her softly. Her heart dropped at the announcement. She didn't think she was up to handling a confrontation now.

"How long has he been here?"

"About an hour."

Her eyes widened in surprise. "Why didn't you tell me sooner?"

He shrugged his broad shoulders. "We had a long talk."

"About what?"

"Things," he told her, making her grit her teeth in frustration. "He wants to see his father."

Keiko glared back at him in response. "No! I won't allow him to upset Papa-san."

"Keiko-san, he has as much right as you to see his father."

"I didn't run out on him!"

"Keiko-chan."

The soft croak from the bed brought her whirling to encounter the tired, pale face of her father. Although he was pale and drawn, there was a sparkle in his eyes. Tears filled her eyes.

"Papa-san, oh, Papa-san!" She flung herself to her knees, cradling his hand against her cheek. "You have come back. Thank God." The relief that washed through Keiko was palpable.

Her father's small brown eyes went from one face to the other. A slow smile spread across his features. Holding out his other hand, he took Shoji's hand and joined it with Keiko's, his own hands closing around their clasped ones. There was joy in the look he bestowed upon them.

Keiko felt her heart still, then thunder on. Had her father heard her declaration after all? Was it possible that was what had rallied him? It couldn't be possible! Not so quickly.

"I wish to see Kenji-san," he told them weakly.

"*Hai*, Papa-san," she answered him softly.

Shoji again helped her to her feet, but her eyes refused to meet his.

"I think we should tell the doctor first," he told her, his voice little more than a whisper.

When Keiko agreed, Shoji went from the room to inform the doctor of her father's changed condition and to bring Kenji.

Kenji was the first to arrive, his face white and pinched. His eyes met Keiko's.

"I only found out this morning."

She bit back the comment she wanted to make. Now was not the time.

Kenji went to the bed, taking a closer look at his father. If anything, his face became paler.

"Papa-san, I am sorry," he told him in halting Japanese.

Their father's eyes twinkled back at him. "That is what I wished to tell you," he said. "I have been wrong, Kenji-san."

He stopped, frowning back at his son. "I mean, Ken."

Keiko could tell how much it had cost him to call Kenji by the shortened American version of his name that he preferred. It had been a battle between them since Kenji had been about fifteen.

Kenji bit his lip, taking his father's hand into his own. "No, Papa-san. I am the one who is sorry. I have not been a very good son. If we had lost you now. . ."

Keiko felt her tears come again as she watched her brother struggle with his.

"For you, and only you, I will always be Kenji."

Their father's tired smile was reward enough. A minor battle won by compromise. Perhaps there was hope for their future after all.

A look passed between Kenji and Shoji, who had entered the room in time to hear this last bit of conversation. Keiko frowned. What had happened between the two that they seemed to suddenly be bosom buddies?

After the doctor examined their father, he looked from one to the other. "I don't know how to explain it. I really hadn't expected him to recover."

Keiko was appalled at the doctor's insensitivity, and again she could sense Shoji's anger, though there was no visible sign.

"Perhaps we have more faith than you," Shoji told the doctor, and Keiko's eyes widened at the thread of steel in his normally soft voice.

The doctor looked uncomfortable. "Yes, well, I have other patients to see."

They waited until he exited the room, and they all began to talk at once. Mr. Tochigi lay weakly back against the pillow, smiling tiredly at his children. All three of them.

Chapter 3

Keiko stared out over the garden, her thoughts in turmoil in contrast to her peaceful surroundings. Basically, she had agreed to marry Shoji Ibaragi. She closed her eyes tightly, feeling helpless.

Although her father was doing better, he was still not out of danger. He had suffered some minor spells of irregular heartbeat, and the doctors were keeping him under close watch.

He had insisted that Shoji have his room until his return, hopefully in a few days. In return, Shoji agreed to help Kenji run the farm until their father came home from the hospital.

When Shoji appeared at her side, she was unsurprised. She had expected him.

"I always promised myself that I would marry a Christian," she told him quietly.

She chanced a glance at him and found his inscrutable almond eyes staring solemnly back at her.

"What makes you believe that I am not a Christian?"

She stared at him in surprise. "Are you?"

He leaned on the porch rail, his eyes focused on the pagoda-roofed *kasuga* lantern in the far corner of the garden.

"I am."

Keiko frowned. "That doesn't make sense. A Christian wouldn't force someone to marry them."

He snorted softly, turning to her. There was an angry sparkle in his normally mysterious brown eyes.

"No one is forcing you, Keiko. I came here willing to fulfill my father's contract to your father, but I had no intentions of forcing you to do the same. That choice is yours."

She wanted to think about what he said, but he continued.

"Frankly, I am pleased with what I have found. I was unsure what kind of girl I would find."

The trepidation in his voice brought a sudden grin to her face. "What did you expect?"

He shrugged, for the first time looking uncomfortable. Keiko thought that he wasn't going to answer, but his voice came back to her, even and low.

"I had this vision of a girl with bobbed hair, thick makeup, and a tight-fitting dress."

Keiko laughed out loud. "And instead you found a rather dull-looking girl in a bright pink kimono."

His look was curious. "There's nothing dull about you. Why do you belittle yourself?"

Keiko flushed. In fact, she had been picturing Sumiko, her best friend. She was everything Shoji had just described, and yet she had beauty that Keiko would die for.

"I have seen for myself that you would make a fine wife." Her face colored crimson at the compliment, but he ignored her embarrassment and continued. "I think we can learn to. . .to care for each other."

"Like my parents," she answered him softly, refusing to look him in the face.

"*Hai,*" he agreed. "I am willing to give you time. . .to give us time to get to know each other. Is this agreeable to you?"

When she didn't answer him, he lifted one of her hands into his. "Look at me, Keiko."

Slowly, hesitantly, she turned to him.

"Is there someone else?" he wanted to know.

Keiko would have laughed, but it wasn't funny. The only time men wanted to get close to her was when they wanted to be introduced to Sumiko.

"No; there is no one."

"Then will you agree to be engaged to me?"

If he had said the word "wife" she would have turned him down flat, but somehow the thought of being a fiancée was not as disturbing. It seemed less final somehow. Besides, what choice did she have?

"*Hai.*" Her throat was tight with tears. When she turned away, he pulled her gently back. His hands curled softly around her upper arms.

"Keiko."

The command in his voice brought her eyes swiftly to his.

"We can make this work," he told her, pulling her inexorably closer. She read the intent in his eyes and felt a little thrill of fear. She would have turned away, but it was already too late. His lips closed over hers, warm and purposeful.

Frozen in time, Keiko felt a small flicker of response that suddenly burst into flame. She returned his kiss with a passion that surprised her.

Shoji slowly released her lips, pulling back from her slightly. Keiko saw the frown on his face and felt her own crimson with embarrassment and shame. She had been too forward. It was not like her. Sumiko might perhaps get away with acting that way, but it was not like Keiko. What had gotten into her anyway?

Turning, she fled. This time Shoji didn't try to stop her.

Shoji slid one hand behind his neck, leaned back, and exhaled slowly. That was certainly unexpected. Actually, he wasn't sure just what he had expected to happen, but it certainly wasn't Keiko warm and responsive in his arms. He had meant the kiss to comfort her, to help her see that they would be a good match.

Confused, he slowly dropped his hands to his side. Who was this girl anyway? She had so many faces to her, he couldn't begin to understand the real Keiko. If he wasn't careful, he could wind up doing something they both would regret.

He sauntered down the steps, taking the path to the corner of the garden where a small pond was fed by a little waterfall. He crossed the bridge that led across it and seated himself on the stone bench next to the Japanese lantern.

For a time he watched the koi fish darting to and fro, their orange and white bodies bright against their dark background. Trapped. The creatures didn't even know that they were. Like him.

He watched the fish longer and began to realize something. They were quite content with their little world. They were well fed, well tended, and had a place of their own.

Leaning his head back against the wooden fence, he closed his eyes. Shouldn't he be content, also? Didn't the apostle Paul say to be content in all circumstances?

Keiko was a wonderful girl, a Christian even. She would honor and respect him all the days of their married life. What more could he desire?

Love. No matter how much he tried to push it away, the thought kept returning to him. He had always dreamed of having a marriage like his parents had shared for over twenty-seven years—loving and devoted. He yearned for such a relationship.

"Papa-san, how could you do this to me?" The whispered words drifted upward to where he knew his father resided.

It didn't make sense. His father had loved the Lord, loved his mother, loved his marriage. How then could he have arranged a loveless marriage for his only son and expected Shoji to abide by it?

No matter how he looked at it, it still didn't make sense. He didn't think it would be hard to love Keiko, but that was beside the point.

He went back into the house, passing Keiko doing the dishes in the kitchen.

"Do you need some help?"

Her eyes opened wide, and Shoji smiled.

"I may be *kibei*, but I have a thoroughly American mother. I assure you, I do not think women are here merely to serve me. If I was taught that way, my mother would have disabused me of that notion very quickly."

At her curious look, he grinned. "Of course, it seems a perfectly good way to me if you should choose to believe in it."

She gave an unladylike snort. "Don't hold your breath."

Laughing, Shoji picked up a dish towel and started to dry the plates. "You are a very good cook," he told her. "Did your mother teach you?"

She shrugged. "Mostly, although I learned a lot in Home Ec in high school."

"Such as?"

"How to care for the home, mostly. Sew. Things like that."

"A most worthwhile occupation," he told her, testing the subject.

She ignored the bait. "What of you? What occupation do you hope to attain?"

"For right now, I am a farmer."

Before she could comment, he laid the towel aside. "I think I will go to bed now. Good night."

When he reached the doorway, she called his name. He turned back to her, one eyebrow raised in enquiry.

"Father's room is comfortable for you?"

He grinned. *"Hai.* I have slept on a futon for years."

She shook her head disparagingly. "The rest of the house has mainly American furniture, but Papa-san had to have his room like the old land. He feels more at home in that room than in any room in this house."

Shoji glanced around. "I am impressed with the way you manage to combine the two cultures in your decorating."

He smiled slightly and left.

Keiko finished the dishes and turned out the light. Climbing the stairs, she made her way to her room in the dark. She was reaching for the lamp beside her bed when she heard a car coming down the road to the farm. It seemed to be coming at a high speed, spitting gravel as it came.

Her first thought was that something had happened to her father, but then she realized that was foolish. No one from the hospital would come racing out here and especially not at this time of night—unless it was Kenji.

Racing down the stairs, she flung open the front door and hurried down the porch steps to stand in the yard. Her heart was pounding.

The car pulled to a stop almost twenty feet away, its headlights blazing into her eyes. Keiko cupped a hand across her eyes, peering into the darkness.

"Kenji?"

Ribald laughter met her call, and Keiko realized that the people in the car were not friends. She thought she recognized the driver from her high school, but she couldn't be sure.

"Hey, *geisha* girl," one drunken voice shouted. "Why don't you go back to Japan where you belong?"

Hoots of laughter greeted this statement. The driver's door opened.

"Better yet," the boy stumbling from the vehicle called, "whyn't ya show me what you *geisha* girls can do?"

Yells of encouragement followed him from the car. Keiko felt real fear as she watched the boy stumbling toward her. She should have run, but her feet were frozen to the spot.

When the boy was less than ten feet away, Keiko saw a form blocking her view.

"Go inside," Shoji commanded.

"But. . ."

"Now!"

Keiko fled to the porch but stopped there. When she turned back, Shoji was face-to-face with the boy from the car. In the headlights of the car, she could see the boy's stupefied expression.

He had to look a long way up to see Shoji's face. Obviously unprepared for such an encounter, he began to back away.

"Who're you? You're not Kenji."

"If you don't turn around and leave, I'm going to become your worst nightmare."

Keiko realized i. was no idle threat. It seemed the boy must have realized it too, because he began to slowly back up, his eyes never leaving Shoji's face. The boy was probably seeing double, and one angry Shoji was frightening enough.

The boy climbed back into the car, throwing it into gear. The tires spun, throwing more dirt and gravel as he backed up.

"Go home, Tojo."

With that parting shot, he sped back down the dirt road. Keiko came slowly down the steps, coming to stand at Shoji's side. He was still staring after the car, his face once again an inscrutable mask.

"Has this happened before?" he asked her.

She shook her head, wrapping her arms tightly around her waist. "No. Never."

His eyes came to rest on her frightened face. He watched her a moment before he pulled her into his arms, giving her some of his body heat. She stayed there a minute, letting her legs regain some of their stability. Realizing that Shoji was standing there with nothing but his jeans on, she pulled away.

"You will catch your death out here. Come back inside."

He followed her back into the house. They seemed to have one mind, realizing that there would be no sleep for either of them until Kenji returned.

"I'll make us some tea."

When she reached the kitchen, she collapsed against the counter. She knew there was a lot of dislike for the Japanese, especially since they had invaded China and were helping Hitler. But she had not experienced very much herself. At least only what she considered normal. Usually, the Japanese were excluded from school functions, or the ones they were allowed to attend were routinely divided.

She felt the stirrings of anger at the injustice of it all. *I am an American citizen just like they are.* She even had the best scores in her class. When it came to scholastics, no one was superior to her. Yet they were still treated like outcasts. No matter what they did, how they dressed, how they acted, they would never be accepted.

★ ★ ★

She was still burning with anger four days later when they brought her father home from the hospital. Although many of the nurses were kind, there was still that attitude of superiority.

Sumiko was waiting on the porch when they pulled Kenji's car into the drive. She grinned, waving excitedly.

"Welcome home, Papa-san."

Keiko smiled. Long ago, Sumiko and her father had adopted each other. When she turned to introduce Shoji, she found him staring at her friend, his enigmatic eyes giving away nothing of his feelings.

"This is Sumiko Shimura. Sue, this is Shoji, my. . .a friend of the family."

Shoji's gaze came to bear on Keiko's flushed countenance, thereby missing Sumiko's look of awe. Kenji hadn't missed it, though, and his lips turned down in a frown.

Shoji's look seemed to say, "That's what I was expecting of an American girl."

Keiko hid a grin. Sumiko's hair was bobbed close to her scalp, little pieces curling becomingly on her cheeks. Eyeliner added to the slant of her eyes, a touch of blue shadow brightening her dark brown orbs. Full red lips stretched into a flirtatious smile as she held her hand out to Shoji.

"Nice to meet you."

Without accepting the hand, Shoji bowed down low in front of her. *"Hajimemashite."*

A quick frown replaced her fulsome smile. She stared from one to the other, before giving him a slight bow. Her perplexed look rested on Keiko. Taking pity on her friend, Keiko turned to Shoji. "Sumiko speaks very little Japanese."

Shoji's eyebrows flew up in surprise, his eyes traveling once more over Sumiko's form.

"I'm sorry," he told her in perfect English. "I am pleased to meet you."

The smile returned to her face. "And I am pleased to meet you." Curling her arm around his, Sumiko tried to lead him inside. He gently disentangled himself and turned to help Keiko's father.

"Tochigi-san, allow me."

Her proud father waved him away. "Surely you would rather spend your time with a pretty girl."

Keiko should have been amused, but instead she was aggravated by Sumiko's questioning expression.

"Oh, Papa-san. I am so sorry. Here, let me help you inside," Sumiko said.

Brushing away Kenji's and Shoji's hands, Sumiko helped Mr. Tochigi into the house. She brought him tea from the kitchen, knowing that Keiko would have it ready.

Smiling, Sumiko made sure Mr. Tochigi was situated before she turned to Keiko. "May I speak with you a moment?"

Keiko hesitated, but her father waved her away. "Go on. I am fine. Kenji-san and Shoji-san will keep me company."

Following her friend up to her bedroom, Keiko shut the door behind her. For some reason, she was reluctant to hear what Sumiko had to say.

Sumiko threw herself down on Keiko's bed. "I need your help," she told her without preamble.

Keiko's sense of dread increased. "What do you need?"

"I need to ask you a favor, but first, who's that hunk of Japanese manhood?"

Biting her lip to keep from grinning, Keiko tried to sound nonchalant. "I told you. He's a friend of the family."

"Girl, why didn't you tell me you had a friend like that? Ooh, won't the other girls be as jealous as sin!"

Keiko frowned. "What do you mean?"

"Sister, you have yourself one of the best-looking jocks I've ever seen."

"I didn't say he was mine!"

"Well, if he's not, you'd better do something about that."

Shaking her head, Keiko smiled wryly. "You're incorrigible. What was the favor you wanted?"

Sumiko threw herself to her knees, her hands folded together in front of her. She looked like a cherub kneeling there in the middle of Keiko's bed.

"I want you to ask Kenji to take me to the school prom."

"What?" Keiko stared at her friend as though she had grown two heads. "Kenji?"

"Please, please, please, please, please."

Keiko giggled, shaking her head. "You're nuts; do you know that? Why can't you ask him?"

She snorted softly. "Like I would."

"If he knew you wanted to go, I'm sure he'd take you. He loves you like a sister."

Sumiko's smile vanished. She turned her face away, picking at the chenille bedspread.

"What is it, Sue?" Keiko asked softly.

"I don't want Ken to love me like a sister."

Keiko sunk slowly to the bed. "Oh, Sue. I didn't know."

She laughed without mirth. "I've loved Ken since we were six years old, when he punched that bully in the face for calling me a name."

Twisting her hands together, Keiko studied her friend. "What can I do?"

Sumiko turned her look back to Keiko, a serious glitter in her dark brown eyes. "This prom is my last chance, Kay. If I can't get him to see me as a woman, I'll be gone and it will be too late."

"Gone?"

"My father is sending me to San Diego to go to the university there. I leave next fall."

Keiko stared at her friend in disbelief. She couldn't remember a time when Sumiko hadn't been a part of their lives. She couldn't imagine not having Sumiko in her life.

"It's murder growing up!" Sumiko declared vehemently.

Silently, Keiko agreed. Everyone was growing older, including her father. Keiko pressed a hand to her forehead and gently started kneading it.

"I'll try," she told Sumiko. "But I can't guarantee anything."

"If he knows you're coming too, he'll come. If for no other reason than to protect you."

It was true, Keiko knew. But she was almost equally sure Kenji would go to protect Sumiko. But, since Sumiko was not about to ask him, or anyone else for that matter, Keiko felt pushed against a wall.

Sumiko leaned forward excitedly. "I know. Ask Shoji."

"What?"

"You said he was a friend of the family. Surely if you ask, he'll go." Sumiko saw the hesitation on Keiko's face. "Please! I'll be your friend for life!"

She threw herself from the bed, kneeling at Keiko's feet. "Please! I'm begging you!"

Keiko started laughing, pulling her hand from Sumiko's grasp. "Oh, get up, for heaven's sake."

Sumiko continued to stare at her with those pleading brown eyes. *Heaven help my brother if he ever falls in love with this girl*, Keiko decided. No one could resist those eyes. She would be spoiled rotten. No wonder her parents doted on her.

Keiko rolled her eyes to the ceiling, heaving a great sigh. "Oh, all right. I'll try."

Squealing, Sumiko threw her arms around Keiko's neck. "I love you; I really do!"

"Yeah, right." Still, it felt good to make her friend so happy.

She would have to set Shoji straight in case he thought she was asking him to the prom for herself.

Chapter 4

The brightly-spinning ball in the center of the room reflected the lights of a thousand tiny prisms. As usual, Japanese Americans were on one side of the room, white Americans on the other.

Keiko's eyes went to Shoji. She felt again the thrill she had experienced when she had first seen him in the black tuxedo, white shirt, and black silk cummerbund. He was so compellingly handsome, yet it was not his looks so much as his air of aloofness that made him seem so alluring.

A dark curl from his hair dipped tantalizingly across his forehead. Keiko's hand ached to push it back for him, but she hadn't the courage. Frowning, she mentally chastised herself.

She had seen the same look of awe in Sumiko's face that had been there the first time she and Shoji had met. The message in her eyes was clear. *You better nab this guy before someone else does.* If she only knew!

Kenji stood beside Sumiko, one hand possessively at the small of her back. Sumiko's triumphant look brought a small smile to Keiko's face. It seemed Sumiko had her wish. From the moment Kenji had laid eyes on Sumiko in her sleek, gold silk dress, something subtle had changed in their relationship.

Sumiko's dress hugged her curvaceous figure like a second skin. It made Keiko uncomfortable. As a Christian, she could never countenance such an unlikely outfit. It seemed to have one purpose, and that was to shout to the world, "Here I am."

Her own chiffon dress flowed around her in soft, billowing folds. Its pale blue color added a soft radiance to her face that she was unaware of.

Keiko tried not to notice Shoji's eyes as they followed her and the look of silent wonder in their dark brown depths.

"Sumiko."

The four of them turned at the sound of a slightly slurred voice behind them. Keiko almost dropped her glass of punch when she was confronted by the youth who had accosted her in their driveway just a few weeks before.

She glanced at her friend, wondering at their relationship. Sumiko's eyes had gone suddenly cold, her face becoming a haughty mask.

When Keiko turned to Shoji, she realized that he had recognized the boy, also. As he was the last time, so he was now—drunk, though not as far gone as that night.

Shoji's eyes darkened to obsidian as the boy's eyes roved boldly over

Sumiko before turning to Keiko.

"Hey! It's the *geisha* girl!"

"Why, you. . ."

Keiko grabbed her brother's arm. "Not here, Kenji."

The boy only grinned, his cold blue gaze going from the top of Kenji's head to the polished toes of his shoes.

"Anytime, anyplace, Kenji boy."

Sumiko pushed herself between them, one hand on each of their chests. Keiko had never seen her friend's eyes so cold.

"Go back to your girlfriend, John Parker. She's waiting for you."

The girl in question hovered uncertainly on the edges of the crowd that was forming.

"Let her wait." Embarrassed, the girl turned and fled at his belligerent response. John Parker's eyes grew serious, though his voice was still slightly slurred. "I wanted to talk to you," he told Sumiko, his voice taking on an irritating whine. "Why haven't you returned my calls?"

Kenji's eyes flew to Sumiko's face. She stared helplessly back at him, shrugging her shoulders.

"It's not what you think."

Before Kenji could make any kind of response, John's friends joined him, their cold glances surveying the small group.

"Come on, John. Come back to the party."

John looked at Sumiko. "I'm not going anywhere until I have my dance with Sue."

"Over my dead body," Kenji raged. "You're drunk as a skunk, and you're not fit company for anyone, much less a lady."

John ignored him, his eyes still on Sumiko's face. It was obvious that he intended to have his way. As the only child of the town's banker, John was hopelessly spoiled, believing himself above even the law. That much was obvious by his intoxicated state.

"Stay here," Sumiko commanded John, pulling Kenji to the side. They were at once embroiled in a heated debate that left Kenji smoldering, while Sumiko returned to John.

"One dance, John, and that's it."

Kenji stormed off, and Keiko watched him go with worried eyes. She turned a pleading look on Shoji.

"Will you go with him?"

Shoji's eyes had already followed Kenji's progress across the room. He shook his head.

"No, I will not leave you alone."

Her brows drew down in irritation. "I'll be okay. It's Kenji I'm worried about."

Taking her by the arm, he headed in the direction they had seen Kenji disappear. "Fine, then you can come with me."

They found Kenji sulking in the corner of the hallway outside the gymnasium doors. Dropping her arm, Shoji strode over to him, glaring at the younger boy.

"You would just leave your date?"

Kenji glared back at him. "What would you have me to do? She made her choice."

Snorting softly, Keiko pinned her brother with frosty brown eyes. "She was trying to stop trouble before it started. You know that. What's one dance?"

Surging off of the wall, he gave her glare for glare. "I could have taken care of John Parker."

"Right! And how would you have done that? Fight?" Her scathing look caused him to flinch. "And where would that have gotten us? Think! For once in your life, let your brain rule over your emotions."

She turned to stalk away, only to encounter Shoji's amused expression. Gritting her teeth, she pushed her way past him and back into the gym.

It was only moments later that Shoji and Kenji followed her back. Keiko didn't know what Shoji had said, but it obviously affected her brother. Although he was sullen, he seemed more amenable.

The soft sounds of the Glenn Miller orchestra filled the auditorium through the speaker system. Without realizing it, Keiko began to sway slightly to the music. She loved his songs.

"Dance?"

Surprised, Keiko turned to Shoji. "You know how?"

Smiling, he took her into his arms and began to drift around the gym. Keiko's expression amused him. Bending down, he began to hum the music into her ear. She pulled back, her look eloquent.

"I think there's a lot about you that I don't know."

His smile turned into a full grin. "That makes two of us. I didn't know you had claws."

She knew he was referring to her encounter with Kenji.

"Remind me never to make you mad at me," he told her softly, pulling her closer in his arms.

Keiko closed her eyes and gave herself up to the pleasures of the music and, admittedly, to Shoji's company. Shoji was an excellent dancer. Where had he learned to dance? His mother? Keiko was becoming increasingly curious about the woman who had raised such a son.

When the music ended, Sumiko returned to Kenji. Keiko could tell there had been no pleasure for Sumiko in dancing with her antagonist. John could tell that too. His brooding eyes followed Sumiko as she took her place on the floor with Kenji.

At first, they were stiff in each other's arms, Kenji holding Sumiko at arm's length, but before long, the soothing music helped ease the tension between them. Keiko saw them relax. When Sumiko smiled up at Kenji with those soulful brown eyes of hers, Kenji hadn't a chance.

Shoji followed her look, a grin forming on his handsome face. "Kenji will have his hands full with that one."

Keiko arched an eyebrow at him. "Oh?"

He slanted her a sideways look, one eyebrow cocked. "You know it's true. Aren't women the same anywhere? They pretend to submit, when all the time they make a man dance to their tune."

She was flabbergasted at his totally un-Japanese assessment of women. "Is that what you really think?"

"Keiko-san," he answered her softly, "I have already said more than I should have. I think it is time to dance." He grinned at what he had just said. "No pun intended."

As he pulled her onto the floor with him, Keiko lifted exasperated eyes to his. She opened her mouth to continue the argument, but he smiled down at her, causing her stomach to do flip-flops.

"Shhh," he told her, effectively ending the conversation.

Keiko was confused. Shoji was unlike any *kibei* she had ever known. No *nisei* girl of her acquaintance would willingly align herself with one. They were too Japanese in their treatment of women. Everyone knew that American-born Japanese boys raised in Japan soon forgot their American heritage. How had Shoji been immune? Was it his mother's influence again?

To her way of thinking, it was much better to be *nisei*, a second-generation Japanese born and raised in America.

The *kibei* were more Japanese than American, and when they returned to America, they expected the Japanese here to be the same.

All of the *nisei* girls that Keiko knew would be horrified if they knew that Shoji was *kibei*, not to mention that she was engaged to him due to their fathers' contract. Even Sumiko didn't know. As a *nisei* herself, Sumiko had been raised totally American. Unlike most *issei*, Sumiko's father had left Japanese ways entirely behind.

It had been Keiko's experience that most of the *issei* clung tenaciously to a way of life they knew. That's what caused so much resentment among the Americans, even to the point of denying them citizenship.

Keiko's chest swelled. Well, she was as American as anyone else. She had been born here in California, and she had been raised here in California.

Through a gap in the crowd, she spotted John Parker standing on the other side of the gym. He was deep in discussion with his two buddies, but his eyes followed Sumiko wherever she went.

John's father was part of the Oriental Exclusion League, which probably accounted for much of John's antipathy toward the Japanese. Keiko wondered what John's father would say if he knew that John was in love with one.

Keiko could tell by Sumiko's rapturous expression that she was totally unaware of anyone except Kenji. For tonight, Sumiko was living her dream.

"You're very quiet."

Startled, Keiko turned her face up to Shoji. She had to look such a long way up. How tall was he? Six-four? Six-five?

"I wanted to thank you for coming with me."

One dark brow winged upward. "You didn't think I would allow my fiancée to come alone, did you?"

There was almost an aggressive note in his voice that caused Keiko's friendliness to slowly evaporate. She hated being reminded of the situation between them. If not for that, maybe they could have become friends, but as it was, every move was suspect to her. It was always in her mind that he was doing it because it was his duty, and he would fulfill that duty to the best of his abilities.

A scuffle at the other end of the room brought them to a standstill. Kenji and John were in a heated argument, Sumiko trying her best to intervene.

Keiko tried to pull away, but Shoji held her still. "No, you stay put."

She rounded on him. "I will not! There's three against one!"

His eyes were fierce when he looked at her, and Keiko felt a tingle of alarm. It was at times like this that Shoji was all *kibei*, and Keiko was more than a little afraid of him.

"I said, stay put." Although his voice was soft, there was that in it that had the effect of freezing Keiko to the spot.

She watched him cross the room to where Kenji was surrounded by John and his two friends. He moved with such grace and quiet that the group never heard him approach.

John was the first to spot him. Keiko could hear his angry voice even from her position halfway across the gym.

"Get outta here, Tojo. This is none of your business."

Keiko couldn't hear Shoji's quiet response, but it must have held the same quality he had used with her because the crowd around them began to pull back.

Though Shoji was slightly taller than John's friends, it wasn't his height that was so frightening. It was that air of leashed violence that surrounded him at times. Keiko shivered, but not from being cold. That the others were frightened was obvious, though they made a show of being brave.

John shoved Shoji, but his body never moved. His feet were firmly planted. Keiko would have given all she owned to see his face at that moment. Were his eyes as inscrutable as they usually were?

When John threw a punch, Shoji lifted a hand so quickly he was able to catch John's fist with it. He continued to hold it as John struggled for release.

The whole time Shoji continued to speak to them.

Keiko envied Sumiko for her location next to the scene. Her eyes were wide with the awe she revealed every time she looked at Shoji.

Kenji continued to argue heatedly. One look from Shoji and he was silenced. It was clear that Shoji was trying to avoid a fight. Perhaps if John's bravery hadn't had a little boost from alcohol, he would have heeded the message. As it was, he continued with his hostile tirade.

When one of John's friends grabbed Shoji from behind, Keiko felt herself loosed from the power of his influence. She was across the floor in seconds, but before she reached their position, she saw Shoji flip the boy across his shoulders. John and the other boy jumped to help, but they found themselves flat on their backs.

Keiko reached Shoji's side, her eyes going from one boy to the other. They got slowly to their feet, losing some of their belligerence.

The largest of the boys lunged at Shoji again, but he stepped aside. The momentum carried the boy forward, and he found himself once again on the floor.

"That's enough." Mr. Collins, the school principal, descended on the group, his angry gaze fixing on Shoji. "What's going on here?" he demanded.

John brushed off his tuxedo without looking at the principal. "This guy attacked me. Mark, Stan, and I weren't doing anything when Kenji started a fight."

"That's a lie!" Sumiko's angry form planted itself in front of Mr. Collins. "John started it. He wouldn't leave me alone."

Mr. Collins stared at them all with disgust. His eyes came back to Kenji. "What are you doing here, Kenji? You graduated over a year ago."

Sumiko answered for him. "He's my date."

"And you?" He looked rather uncomfortable when faced with Shoji's mysterious dark stare.

"He's my date," Keiko told him.

"I see." He looked from one to the other before turning back to Sumiko. "I think you and your dates had better leave."

"That's not fair!" Sumiko fumed. "Why should we have to leave when we didn't do anything?"

Mr. Collins's eyes became black in their intensity. "Would you rather be expelled?"

Sumiko's face drained of color. She and Keiko were only two weeks away from graduation.

"We'll go," Keiko told him, taking Kenji and Shoji by the arms.

Sumiko struggled with the desire to say more. Prudence won out, and she turned away, but not before fixing John with such a look of loathing his eyes went wide.

Shoji helped Keiko into the backseat of Kenji's roadster, climbing in beside her. His look was thoughtful as he continued to stare at her.

Keiko felt herself squirm under his perusal. What was he thinking? As for herself, she had a lot to think about. How could she possibly marry a man who could frighten her half to death?

Shoji could be so gentle and kind, but there was always this air of ferocity that surrounded him. What would it be like if he ever became really angry? Her toes curled into her shoes at the thought. Heaven forbid.

Shoji opened his mouth to say something, but Kenji interrupted, his voice full of enthusiasm.

"Man! That was great! Can you teach me to fight like that? Was that judo?"

Keiko saw the closed expression come to Shoji's face even in the dark. The moon highlighted his features, making them seem cast in bronze.

"Yes, it was judo, and no, I will not teach you."

Kenji took his eyes off the road, turning to Shoji in surprise. "Why not?"

"It would take too long to explain. I'd rather not go into it now."

"But. . ."

"I said, not now."

Silence filled the car. What had started out as such a promising evening had turned into a fiasco. Keiko looked at Sumiko and noticed the tears slowly coursing down her cheeks.

When they reached the house, Keiko and Shoji got out of the car. Keiko squeezed her friend's shoulder before Kenji roared away. She was watching the car disappear down the road when she felt Shoji take her arm. Flinching, she pulled herself away.

His look was as inscrutable as ever. He followed Keiko into the house, but she went immediately to her room, closing the door firmly behind her.

Shoji sighed heavily as he heard Keiko's door close. When would he ever learn? Fighting was not an answer to anything. True, he hadn't provoked the fight, but it had given him great pleasure to end it. It would have given him even more pleasure to have beaten those three thugs to a pulp.

Shoving the anger down inside, Shoji went to the kitchen and poured himself a glass of milk. He closed his eyes as he thought of that day so long ago.

A schoolmate had called him a name, and though they were all taught judo, Shoji's size gave him the extra edge he needed to conquer even the hardiest of school chums. That and his constant anger.

When Kenzo had attacked him verbally, Shoji had attacked him physically. Groaning, Shoji placed the glass back on the counter. He had wound up putting Kenzo in the hospital. A fourteen-year-old boy, and he had almost lost his life.

That's when it had been decided that Shoji needed extra guidance, and he had been placed under the tutelage of a Chinese monk. Boy, how his mother had reacted to that one.

Still, Master Wong had taught him the art of self-control. At least to an extent. Never again did Shoji wish to do what he had done to Kenzo. Until tonight.

Shoji's father had told him that he was much like Jesus. Power under control. That's what his father had said was the true definition of meekness. It didn't mean being a doormat. It meant you knew you had the power to destroy and yet you controlled it.

Jesus' destruction of the temple and driving out of the money changers was nothing compared to what He could have done. Isn't that what He tried to show His disciples when He had cursed the fig tree? Only a word from His mouth, and it was forever destroyed.

Jesus witnessed many injustices, but He held His wrath. That was for His Father to handle; that was not His purpose.

Just as it was not Shoji's purpose to punish those who hurt the people close to him. Judo was meant for defense and defense alone. Even the word itself meant "the way of gentleness."

Shoji rubbed his face with his hands. He had to get a handle on his temper. Even twelve years in Japan had not been much help.

Throwing back his head, he closed his eyes. The look on Keiko's face. He would never forget it. Such fear. How could he possibly undo the damage he had inflicted tonight? And what was worse, he was pretty sure there would be retribution from John Parker and his friends.

★ ★ ★

Two months after the prom, it took all of Shoji's willpower to keep from throttling Keiko Tochigi. He gritted his teeth now thinking about it.

She was avoiding him as much as possible. When he entered a room, if she was alone, she quickly left. He tried to get her by herself several times, but she was adept at outmaneuvering him.

So far, he had been unable to apologize for that night. He sighed, slamming the shovel into the ground in his aggravation. This was definitely not what he had meant when he said they needed to get to know each other.

When he looked up, Keiko was coming across the field with a glass of lemonade. It was obvious from her face that it was not her own idea. She pulled up next to him and held out the glass.

Taking off his gloves, he reached for the drink, his eyes never leaving her face. She looked everywhere but at him. When he took the glass, she turned to leave, but he reached out a hand and took her by the arm.

She didn't flinch away from him like he expected. She merely stood with her head bent down.

"Arigato."

"You're welcome."

He continued to hold her arm, watching her face for some sign of the friendliness they had shared before. He knew she didn't hide her feelings well.

"Keiko, I want to apologize for the night of your prom."

Her head remained bent, her eyes focused on the ground. "You have nothing to apologize for. You only did what I wanted to."

When her eyes looked into his, he saw a contriteness he hadn't expected. "I'm sorry for the way I have been acting." She turned her face away again. "It's not easy for me to apologize. I have a rather stubborn nature."

Surprised, he set the glass on the ground. Taking her by the arms, he turned her to face him.

"You want to apologize to me?"

She nodded. "I have been very inhospitable. Even my father has noticed it."

He leaned back, still not releasing her. "Ah. So this was your father's doing."

"I. . .I wanted to apologize. I mean I. . ." She stopped, biting her lip. Her eyes clashed with his. "You frighten me, Shoji. There's something so. . .so. . . intense about you. You're so. . .unreadable."

He released her, but she didn't move away. "That comes from years of practice. If you want to know what I'm thinking, ask me."

She ducked her head again. "Maybe if I knew you better."

Shoji was careful to keep accusation out of his voice. "It has not been my fault that we still know so little about each other."

"I know." She smiled timidly up at him. "May we try again?"

He lifted the empty glass from the ground and handed it to her. He returned her smile. "I would like that."

Nodding, Keiko turned and left him standing there, remembering how she looked the night of the prom. He watched her cross the yard before turning back to his work.

★ ★ ★

August turned into September. October saw the end of the summer harvest. When November rolled through with its chilly winds, Keiko planned a special Thanksgiving.

There was much to be thankful for, though anti-Japanese sentiment was growing progressively. Since her graduation, she had spent very little time in town.

When Sumiko went off to college, she was wearing Kenji's ring. This was one of Keiko's major reasons for thanks. Her father's health was improved, and the crops had been good. There was quite a bit of money in the bank.

Shoji was planning on taking Keiko to see his mother before Christmas. Just the thought of it sent fear spiraling through Keiko's midsection.

Although Keiko and Shoji had resumed their friendship, there had been very little time to get to know each other until now. She was unsure if she wanted their relationship to change. There was still that little niggle of fear that surfaced from time to time when she saw Shoji in one of his rare moods—usually when he returned from town with Kenji, whose face would be as black as a thundercloud.

Sundays were special days for Keiko, when she and Shoji would go together to church. Even Kenji had been cajoled into going a time or two.

On this particular Sunday morning, Shoji had borrowed Kenji's roadster, and Keiko was feeling euphoric after listening to a wonderful sermon by Mr. Kosugi. She tied a red silk scarf to her head, trying her best to keep the cold wind from whipping her hair into a frenzied mess.

Smiling, Keiko reached to turn on the radio. The strains of a Glenn Miller song drifted out to them, reminding Keiko of that night so long ago. She was about to turn it off when an announcer broke into the music with a special message.

"The Japanese have attacked Pearl Harbor. I repeat, the Japanese have attacked Pearl Harbor."

Keiko froze with her hand outstretched. "It can't be," she whispered.

Shoji pulled to the side of the road, and together they listened to the message. Death and destruction and untold damage to the U.S. fleet.

Shoji looked at her, his eyes unreadable. What must he be feeling? She didn't think now would be the time to ask.

"Let's go home." His voice was deathly quiet.

She nodded to let him know she agreed.

Surely this meant that now the United States would declare war on Japan. *Dear God! Dear God!*

Chapter 5

For the rest of the day, Keiko, Shoji, Kenji, and Mr. Tochigi huddled around the radio. The radio's continuation of its regular programming seemed oddly out of place against its periodic messages of devastation.

"I still can't believe it," Kenji declared in a tight voice.

"What will it mean for us?" Keiko wanted to know.

Her father shrugged. "We will have to wait and see."

Keiko wasn't worried for herself and Kenji. They were American citizens. It was her father that concerned her. She glanced over at Shoji. His eyes were focused on the radio, but she could tell he wasn't listening. He got up from his seat.

"I have some things to do."

Keiko watched him leave, realizing that he was in one of his dark moods. Swallowing hard, she followed him from the room. She found him in the garden pulling dead weeds from the flower beds. Kneeling down beside him, she began to methodically help.

"You're. . .you seem. . ." She didn't know how to continue and was a little afraid to do so.

Heaving a deep sigh, he turned to look at her. His eyes moved over her face, coming to rest on her lips, then back to her eyes. His were so fathomless she had no hope of reading into them.

"I told you all you had to do was ask."

She studied him intently. "I'm asking."

He sat down on the ground, wrapping his arms around his legs. Resting his chin on his knees, he seemed to be trying to get his thoughts in order.

"I have no idea of who I am! Never have, and I'm not sure I ever will." His gaze focused on a bird in the pine tree in the center of the garden. "In Japan, I was an American. In America, I'm Japanese. But not really."

Keiko nodded understanding. As a *nisei,* she understood all too clearly the implications of dual nationality. His look returned to her.

"It's not the same with you and Kenji. You have been raised as an American, so at least you understand Americans. I, on the other hand, have been raised for the last twelve years in Japan. I understand their ways more than the American ways, yet not fully."

Keiko remained silent, knowing that he hadn't finished. She could tell he was trying to find the right words to say.

"At least you and Kenji are full-blooded Japanese. I am mixed Japanese and white. I love my parents, but at times I have been so angry with them, I wanted nothing more than to never have anything to do with them. In Japan I was treated as less than nothing. In America I am treated much the same. I know what the *nisei* think of the *kibei*."

Eyes turned away, Keiko knew she couldn't deny it. Hadn't she thought much the same herself? For some reason, it hurt her to hear the pain in his voice.

"So you carry your anger around with you like a shield."

He pursed his lips, not looking at her. "I suppose."

Deciding to risk his wrath, she sat down close to him. "And what has Jesus done for you, Shoji?"

He smiled wryly at her. "I know what you are trying to say. It's something I have grappled with for many years. I love the Lord. I try to serve Him. But I can't seem to let go of the anger. I feel like a nobody."

Keiko's lips tilted at the corners. "Perhaps I should introduce you to my friend Anna."

"Anna?"

Keiko looked into his eyes, willing him to understand her. "Anna is a Christian too."

His eyes narrowed, not following her.

"Her parents are Jews."

He leaned back, understanding written across his features. "And how does Anna deal with this?" he wanted to know.

Keiko smiled, throwing a weed on the pile that had been growing as they spoke.

"Anna says it doesn't matter to her. She is an alien no matter where she goes. Her citizenship is in heaven. So, she tries to help as many people as possible attain that citizenship too."

"She sounds like a nice girl," Shoji commented softly.

"She is. But her parents have disowned her."

He frowned. "What does she do then? Who takes care of her?"

"She lives with a Christian family and works at their store. She keeps hoping and praying that someday she can win her parents to the Lord."

"Like you."

Keiko looked at him. Shrugging, she got up from the ground. "I have to fix supper."

"Thanks for taking the time to ask."

"Thanks for talking to me."

Keiko fixed supper, but no one was interested in eating. They had heard on the radio that towns along the western seaboard were preparing for an invasion. There was a blackout restriction as of seven o'clock.

With each broadcast, Keiko felt her heart grow heavier. It was evident that war was imminent. She watched her father, afraid the stress would cause another attack. Instead, he calmly rocked in his favorite chair, seemingly oblivious to the raging tide around them.

"Keiko-chan," he addressed her. "I would like to hear you read from your mother's Bible."

She jerked her head up in surprise, studying his face. Her brows creased with concern. Her father had never shown any interest in the Bible before. What was running through his mind? And why her mother's Bible?

She found out a few minutes later. Lifting her mother's Bible from the chest where it was kept for safekeeping, Keiko carried it carefully back to where her father sat. Although her father understood a lot of English, he had never learned to read it.

"Read any notes from your mother that you see."

The Book flipped open to Ephesians, seemingly of its own accord. Her father nodded solemnly as she read about unity in the body of Christ and living as children of light.

She had never read her mother's Bible before and hadn't realized how many notes she had written. The familiar handwriting brought tears to her throat.

When she read the part about wives submitting to their husbands, her voice faltered, then stopped.

"What is wrong, Keiko-chan?"

"Nothing, Papa-san. There is a note in the margin from Mama-san."

She hadn't realized that Kenji had been drawn into the reading until his husky voice penetrated her own musings.

"Read it," he commanded quietly.

Keiko hesitated. "It says. . .it says that a Japanese wife is taught this from birth."

Her father's eyes took on a decided twinkle. "There had to be more."

Keiko smiled wryly. "Yes. It also says that if Japanese men were taught the rest of those verses, marriage would be a heavenly thing."

Mr. Tochigi laughed aloud. "I knew she would have something to say on the matter."

He got up from his seat. "It is time for me to go to bed. It has been a long day. *Oyasumi nasai.*"

Keiko smiled softly at him, her heart overflowing with love. "Good night, Papa-san."

Kenji rose to follow his father. "I think I will turn in also. Good night."

Keiko and Shoji each added their good nights and watched her brother walk from the room.

"Keiko." Shoji's voice was soft but compelling.

"Hai?"

"I do not wish for you to go into town for awhile. At least not until this blows over."

The seriousness of his expression warned her that he was in earnest. She was about to argue with him, then thought better of it. The only reason she wanted to argue was that she hated being told what to do. This was no time to be stubborn.

"*Hai,*" she answered him softly.

He got up from the sofa, stopping when he reached her side. His hand extended, he stroked a finger across her cheek. Bending, he touched his lips lightly against her cheek.

"*Oyasumi nasai,* Keiko-chan."

Her eyes flew to his at the unexpected title of endearment. Keiko-san was a title of respect. Keiko-chan was used for someone dear. Her heart fluttered at the brooding intensity of his look.

"Good night." She didn't recognize the croak as her own voice.

That night when Keiko said her prayers, she included her country. What a mess men made of this planet. Why couldn't people learn to get along, especially the different races?

She knew the answer to that one. Sin. If not for that first sin, they would even now be living in a perfect world.

Angrily, she thumped her pillow into a ball, burying her head into its soft down. "Thanks a lot, Eve," she mumbled into the darkness.

★ ★ ★

The doorbell rang early the next morning, and Keiko hurried to answer it. She opened the door to a woman, not young but neither was she old. She had what Keiko had always called "class," her auburn hair beautifully coiffed and curled.

She smiled at Keiko. "Is this the Tochigi residence?"

"Yes." Surprised, Keiko temporarily forgot her manners.

"May I come in?"

Flustered, Keiko opened the screen door. "Of course. I'm sorry; please come in."

The woman moved inside, her glance carefully surveying the room. When she turned to Keiko, her beautiful blue eyes smiled warmly, though there was a hint of reserve behind their obvious friendliness. There was something vaguely familiar about the woman.

"What a lovely home."

"Thank you." More confused than ever, Keiko asked the woman to be seated.

She continued to look around with interest before her eyes returned to Keiko's face. Her smile was genuine, and Keiko felt herself relax slightly. There was something about this woman she liked.

"I suppose you're wondering who I am."

299

Before Keiko could reply, the door opened, and Shoji and Kenji came in. They were brushing hay from their pants, laughing at some joke they had shared.

Shoji looked up, and the smile froze on his face.

"Mother!"

The woman rose gracefully to her feet. "David, how are you?"

"David?" Kenji and Keiko questioned at the same time.

Shoji frowned. "Mother, what are you doing here?"

"David, where are your manners? I haven't been introduced."

Sighing heavily, Shoji turned to Keiko. "Keiko Tochigi, Kenji Tochigi. My mother, Mrs. Ibaragi."

"How do you do?" The woman's gracious smile was lost on Kenji. "David?"

His mother looked perplexed. Shoji motioned for her to be seated.

"I haven't gone by David in years, Mother, and you know it."

"I don't understand." Keiko's puzzled glance went from one to the other.

"David Shoji Ibaragi," his mother intoned, her sweet smile resting on her son. "After King David, don't you know."

Shoji must have decided to use his middle name when he lived in Japan, Keiko decided. It made sense. He would be less likely to stand out as an American.

"You haven't been in touch with me since you arrived back in the States," Mrs. Ibaragi told her son, a decided edge to her voice.

He looked away. "I know. I would have called you soon."

"Be that as it may, after what happened yesterday, I wanted to make sure you were all right."

"Well, as you can see, I am." Keiko couldn't understand Shoji's reluctance to see his mother. She seemed like a wonderful person.

There was a strained silence in the room until Mr. Tochigi came in. Introductions had to be made all over again, and Keiko watched in surprise as her father became animated in his discussion with Mrs. Ibaragi. Of course it helped that she spoke fluent Japanese.

Shoji looked decidedly ill at ease, even tense.

"Shoji-san will make a fine husband for my daughter," Keiko's father told Mrs. Ibaragi, and the room grew uncomfortably quiet.

Without looking at her son, Mrs. Ibaragi gently encouraged Keiko's father. "Do go on, Tochigi-san. You were saying?"

Shoji rose to his feet, intent on intervening. A hand sliced his way by his mother had the effect of bringing him to silence. Keiko was amazed.

When Mr. Tochigi finished extolling the virtues of both his daughter and future son-in-law, Mrs. Ibaragi turned an icy glare on her son.

"Well, I really must be leaving. I have to get back to town before dark.

I'm staying at a hotel there." She fixed her son with an eloquent look. "Why don't you accompany me and see me situated?"

Keiko's father hastily agreed. "That is a good idea, Shoji-san. Take your time."

Keiko saw a swift glance at his mother tell Shoji that was exactly what he was going to do.

After they left, Keiko exchanged a look with her brother.

"David! Can you imagine? Why would he want to be called Shoji?"

Keiko shrugged, going to the screen door and looking down the road. Either name sounded fine to her, but she thought she preferred Shoji. He looked more like a Shoji than a David to her.

★ ★ ★

As Keiko was washing the supper dishes, she could hear a car barreling down the road to their house. She grinned. Shoji must be in one fine temper.

But it wasn't Shoji that pulled into her drive. It was Cindy Masters, a friend from school. Surprised, Keiko went out to meet her on the porch.

"Cindy, what are you doing way out here this late?" she asked in surprise.

Cindy's face was filled with panic. "I have to see Kenji. Is he here?"

Frowning, Keiko nodded, pushing open the screen door. "Come in."

She shook her head quickly. "I can't. If I could just see Kenji?"

"Just a moment; I'll get him."

Keiko followed Kenji down the stairs and out onto the porch, where Cindy was still waiting. She twisted her driving gloves anxiously as she paced up and down. Turning in relief, she smiled at Kenji.

"Oh, Kenji. Am I glad I found you at home!"

"What's going on, Cindy?" Kenji frowned at the girl, and Keiko found herself holding her breath, waiting for the girl's explanation.

"You don't have a telephone, so no one could reach you. Mr. Shimura was taken away by the FBI."

The color drained from Kenji's face. "When?"

"Just this evening," she told him, twisting her hands together. "Mrs. Shimura wanted me to let you know."

"Has anyone contacted Sumiko?"

The other girl nodded. "She's getting ready to come home now. She plans to take the train, and she'll be here by morning."

Kenji was already headed off the porch. "Since Shoji has my car, I'm taking the truck."

Keiko nodded. "What are you going to do?"

"Someone needs to be with Mrs. Shimura. I don't know when I'll be back."

"Be careful."

Cindy followed him. "I can't stay, either." She turned back to Keiko. "They're picking up Japanese men all over the place. I'm sorry, Keiko."

301

"Thank you, Cindy." Keiko hurried back inside. What about her own father? Would they come for him too? Suddenly, she wished Shoji were here.

★ ★ ★

Shoji twisted his face into a wry grimace as his mother's tirade continued. Rolling his eyes to the ceiling, he clenched his hands at his sides. Well, at least he knew one thing for certain. His mother had known nothing of his marriage contract.

"I can't believe you're going to go through with this!"

"Mother," he told her softly, "it was Father's last wish."

She stared at him in surprise. "I don't believe it. And besides, I could care less. An arranged marriage, of all things."

She threw herself into the overstuffed chair of the penthouse suite. "David, this is quite impossible."

Before he had gone to Japan, he and his mother had a very close relationship. Now Shoji felt himself holding back from her. Was it because he was no longer a boy? Or was it because of his Japanese teaching? He found it hard to reconcile the way he was taught with the value system in America.

"Mother, I know this is hard for you to understand, but I intend to fulfill this contract."

"We'll get a lawyer."

"I don't want a lawyer." The cold anger in his voice brought his mother to silence. She watched him warily.

"Mother, this is a matter of honor."

"Honor, my foot." His darkening look only increased her own anger. "How can you stand there and calmly agree to such an arrangement? Of all the preposterous ideas!"

Shoji sighed heavily. "It's not a preposterous idea. It was Father's last wish."

"How do you know that? Who told you such a thing?"

"He did." The poignant tremor in his voice stilled her. There was no denying the truth of the statement.

"When?"

"When he was dying. I came to see him because he asked me to."

The color drained from her face. "You came to see your father and you didn't come to see me?"

He looked away. "I couldn't. I knew what you would say."

"You mean to tell me you are seriously considering marriage to a girl you hardly know?"

A soft look entered his eyes, bringing her up short. "I know her. She is not beautiful like the *geisha*. Even among the Japanese she would be considered ordinary to look at but for her eyes."

His own eyes seemed to burn with a strange intensity.

"Whereas the other Japanese girls I know have such calm, vacant eyes,

302

Keiko's glow with a mysterious inner fire. As though she has hidden depths and secrets it would take an eternity to unravel."

Mrs. Ibaragi's eyes went wide at her son's uncharacteristic eloquence. A sudden glow entered their depths as she stared at her son, a slow smile spreading across her face.

There was nothing to worry about where Shoji's marriage was concerned, she decided. Nothing at all.

★ ★ ★

Keiko paced the floor. She was a nervous wreck. Where were Shoji and Kenji? It had been hours since Cindy had come and gone.

"Keiko-chan, come and read to me."

Keiko knew that her father was only trying to ease her mind, but she was afraid nothing would help. Sighing, she decided that reading the Bible couldn't hurt, either.

Flipping through the pages, she came to the account in John, chapter seventeen, where Jesus was praying in the garden. Her father's eyes were soft with sympathy as she read His petition for all believers, those at that time, and those to come. In verse twenty her mother had erased the words "them also" and replaced it with her own name, Yuki Tochigi.

Going back, she reread the verse again, inserting her own name. Such peace filled her as the realization came to her that Jesus had prayed for her long before she was ever born. She closed her eyes, imagining Him in the garden talking to their Father on her behalf. He seemed to say, *I know what you are going to go through, Keiko, and I am here with you. If I am with you now, I will be with you then.*

"Keiko-chan." Her father's soft voice ended her peaceful reflections. "Read it now with my name."

Keiko gladly complied, and she saw the tears come to her father's eyes. "This Jesus was a remarkable man."

"Hai. Very remarkable."

A car coming down the drive sent Keiko scurrying to the door. In the dusky twilight, she could just make out the form of the roadster. Shoji.

He came into the house, his look going from one to the other. "What's wrong?"

"Sumiko's father was picked up by the FBI."

His eyes narrowed. "When?"

"This evening."

He studied her thoughtfully before going to the living room and seating himself beside Mr. Tochigi. He tucked his lips together, watching Keiko as she slowly seated herself.

"Tochigi-san," he began. "I think it is time for Keiko and I to be married."

Chapter 6

Keiko turned over in her bed, thumping her pillow angrily. Of all the nerve! Shoji had merely marched in and stated his demands. Keiko gritted her teeth. To be fair, that was not totally accurate. He and Papa-san had sat for a long time discussing things, while Keiko sat silently seething.

She didn't dare defy them right now. Her father's health was still too fragile to consider an open confrontation. Biting her lip, she rolled onto her back, covering her eyes with one arm.

How could Shoji even consider such a thing right now? Out of the clear blue sky! What was he thinking?

She heard the truck returning and hurriedly climbed out of bed, throwing on a flannel robe as she quickly went down the stairs. She stopped when she heard Kenji's angry voice.

"Someone told the authorities that Mr. Shimura was dealing with enemy agents overseas."

"I'll give you one guess who it was," Shoji offered.

There was silence for several seconds before Kenji answered. "John Parker."

Keiko gasped. Surely even John Parker wouldn't do something so despicable. And even if he had, surely the authorities wouldn't believe him.

Eyes swiftly scanning the living room, Keiko soon realized that her father must have retired for the night. She sighed with relief. This was one more thing he didn't need to worry about.

Unsure why she did so, Keiko remained out of sight of the two young men. She felt slightly guilty for eavesdropping, but she couldn't help herself. It was the only way she knew of to find out what was truly going on. Both Shoji and Kenji seemed to think she needed to be protected from all the madness going on around them.

"What are you going to do?" Shoji asked.

Keiko could see her brother's face pinched with concern. His shoulders sagged with weariness.

"I came back to pick up a few things for the night, then I'll go back and stay with Mrs. Shimura. Sumiko will arrive sometime in the morning, and I'll pick her up at the train station. But I'm worried about Papa-san."

Shoji heaved a sigh. "Don't worry about things here. I'll take care of everything until you get back."

Keiko heard Kenji moving across the room, and she hastily scrambled around the corner into the kitchen. She leaned back against the door, listening as Kenji mounted the stairs. Straining her ears, she listened for some sound to indicate Shoji's whereabouts. What was he doing anyway?

"You can come out now."

She jumped slightly at the whispered voice from the other side of the door. Feeling like a child caught with her hand in the cookie jar, Keiko slowly pushed open the door.

Shoji took in her embarrassed face, a small smile tilting the corners of his mouth.

"How did you know I was there?"

He grinned fully. "Keiko-chan, I could find you anywhere. You have a soft scent that is purely your own. Besides, I heard you."

Not sure whether to be offended or pleased, she settled for not commenting. Biting her lip, she glanced up the stairs.

"I hope he will be all right."

"Kenji can take care of himself." He silently stared at her, his look serious. "We need to try to keep as much as we can from your father. You agree?"

When she turned her look on him, there was fire in her eyes. "As long as you don't do the same to me."

He pursed his lips, returning her look full force. "Agreed. Keiko. . ."

She was almost sure she knew what he was about to say.

"I'm tired. I'll see you in the morning," Keiko said as she turned away.

He let her go, watching her make her way back up the stairs. When Keiko reached her door, she knew he was still watching her.

★ ★ ★

They didn't hear from Kenji for three days. Keiko was frantic with worry, but she tried to hide it from her father. She busied herself around the house as much as possible.

Friday morning they heard Kenji's car, its roar unmistakable. Keiko flew out to the porch to meet him, her eyes going wide when she saw Sumiko sitting beside him.

Keiko had never seen her friend anything other than immaculate. The dispirited, disheveled girl who climbed from the car barely resembled the girl Keiko had always known. Sumiko's tired face was devoid of makeup, but that did nothing to detract from her beauty. If anything, she looked lovelier than before.

Sumiko had tied a kerchief around her head, knotting it at the back. Her dress was still the epitome of fashion, though, causing Keiko's lips to quirk slightly.

Running down the steps, Keiko took her friend into her arms.

"Oh, Sue. I'm so sorry. Have you heard anything?" Her eyes went to her brother.

He sighed heavily. "We just heard last night. They've taken Mr. Shimura to Missoula, Montana."

Keiko was surprised, to say the least. "Montana! Whatever for?"

Kenji went to Sumiko, placing a gentle arm around her waist. "Let's go inside, Kay. Sue needs to sit down."

"Of course. I'm sorry; I should have thought."

After Kenji had helped Sumiko into a chair, he turned to Keiko. "Where's Shoji? I need to talk to him."

"He's out in the field digging up rocks."

Keiko knew her brother was keeping something from her, but she wasn't sure what. Hopefully, Shoji would share whatever Kenji had to say.

"Would you like some tea, Sue?" she asked absently, her look following her brother out the door.

"Please. I need something to calm my nerves."

Keiko brought the tea from the kitchen, setting the tray on the table beside Sumiko.

"What's going on, Sue? How long are they going to keep your father?"

Burying her face in her hands, Sumiko burst into tears. "We don't know. They won't tell us anything, except that he and some others are being held for questioning."

Keiko knelt in front of her, taking Sumiko's cold, trembling hands into her own. She didn't know what to say, so she offered silent sympathy.

"This is all so crazy," the distraught girl continued. "My father has always been a loyal American. He loves this country. He wouldn't do anything to harm it."

"I know, Sue. And they'll realize it too. We just have to have patience."

Sumiko snorted. "Not one of my strong suits."

Keiko grinned. "Mine, either."

By the time the men returned, Sumiko had managed to gain control. Her face was still tight with worry, and Keiko noticed that she clung to Kenji.

"I'm going to be staying with Sue and her mother for awhile," Kenji told them.

"But what about us? What about Papa-san?"

His eyes found Shoji's, and Keiko noticed the look they exchanged. "Shoji is here. If I'm needed, you know where to reach me."

"Kenji." Keiko placed a hand on his arm to detain him. "Why did you take so long to tell us?"

His lips pressed into a tight line. "The FBI wouldn't let any of us leave Mrs. Shimura's house. An agent stayed the whole time to make sure no one came in or went out."

"He even answered our phone and refused to accept any calls," Sumiko stated heatedly.

"Why did they let you in?"

"I told them I was Sumiko's fiancé. I think they knew that they couldn't keep me out without trouble. Regardless of his actions, the agent seemed friendly enough."

Keiko watched them leave, a horrible feeling in the pit of her stomach. What next? Would they come for her father too? If John Parker had been instrumental in causing Sumiko's father to be taken, wouldn't he have a much bigger grudge against Shoji and Kenji? This waiting was killing her.

Shoji curled his hands around her shoulders, pulling her back against his chest. His voice came softly against her cheek, stirring the strands of her long, dark hair that she had left hanging.

"It will be all right, Keiko. Everything will be all right."

But in the end, it wasn't. Anti-Japanese sentiment was growing every day. Even the Chinese consul had gone so far as to make the Chinese wear special badges to differentiate between them and the Japanese. Keiko felt as thought the world were spinning out of control. How much longer could this go on?

★ ★ ★

January first arrived, cold and unusually wet. Keiko shivered as she prepared the vegetables for the *ozoni*, a thick chicken stew made with carrots, bamboo sprouts, *daikon*, and taro roots. Kenji hated the dish, but since he would not be here, Keiko prepared it anyway, knowing her father would be pleased.

Every year it was the same thing. Papa-san was determined to celebrate New Year's in the traditional Japanese way. First Keiko would fix his favorite buckwheat pancakes for breakfast, then Papa-san would pay off all his creditors, then came the traditional Japanese supper of *ozoni* and *mochi*—little rice dumplings served with the stew.

Fortunately for Keiko, Papa-san restricted his observance of the holiday to only the one day. She rolled her tired shoulders, closing her eyes against her tiredness. She had been busily cleaning the house from top to bottom, another Japanese custom for New Year's.

Actually, she hadn't minded all the extra work. It had helped to keep her mind off other things. Kenji came by from time to time, usually bringing Sumiko with him. One day he brought Mrs. Shimura and called a family conference.

In the end, it had been agreed upon by both parents that it would be all right for Kenji and Sumiko to marry. Keiko was surprised, but there was little she could do about it. Besides, she had always wished for Sumiko to be her sister. She just wished it could have been under more joyful circumstances.

Her eyes found Shoji's, and she could read his unspoken message. Although he had refrained from saying anything since the night he had talked to her father, Keiko knew that he was biding his time. It unnerved her.

When Shoji asked Keiko to go into town with him, Keiko agreed, mainly because her father had asked her to pay their creditors, the usual Japanese practice on New Year's.

They drove several miles in silence. Finally Shoji glanced at her briefly, his eyes typically inscrutable.

"How do you feel about Kenji and Sumiko?"

She squirmed on her seat. Surely he wouldn't bring up the subject of their marriage now.

"I'm pleased. I only wish it could be during a happier time."

Shoji sighed heavily, as though preparing himself for a big battle. "Keiko, Kenji tells me that the government is talking about moving the Japanese out of California."

"What?"

His eyes roved her surprised face before returning to the road. He nodded. "It's probably true. There is so much jealousy here by the *hakujin* who own the land that they will probably afford themselves of this opportunity to get rid of the 'yellow peril.'"

Keiko grinned at his Japanese term for white people. If the situation were not so serious, she would have laughed.

He glanced at her, noting her amusement. "They are talking about sending all Japanese back to Japan, including American citizens."

"You can't be serious! I've never been to Japan in my life. I have no desire to go to Japan!"

He cocked a brow at her. "You needn't get so irate. It's a beautiful country."

She was appalled. "Are you seriously suggesting that I consider it?"

Shoji shook his head, his eyes going back to the road. "No. What I'm suggesting is that with everything that is happening, it's entirely possible that families and friends will become separated. I can't allow that. You're going to have to accept the fact that we need to be married soon."

She opened her mouth to protest, but his look silenced her. "Kenji has already realized this," he told her.

Keiko curled down into her seat to think about what he had just said. If Kenji was separated from Papa-san and her, what would become of them? Especially with Papa-san's delicate health.

She looked at Shoji, his attention focused on the road. He would stay with them, she was sure. She hadn't realized just how much she had come to depend on him over the last several months. But was dependency enough reason to get married?

She turned back to the view from the truck's window. At least he shared her faith in the Lord.

★ ★ ★

Shoji dropped her off at Mr. Anson's store.

"I'll park in front of the telegraph office," he told her. "I want to send a message to my mother, then I need to pick up some things from the hardware store. I'll meet you there."

Nodding her head in agreement, she climbed from the truck. When she went inside, she wasn't sure what to expect. She hadn't been to town since the bombing of Pearl Harbor. All she knew was that anti-Japanese sentiment was growing everywhere. She was more than a little frightened.

"Keiko! How nice to see you." Mr. Anson's cheerful voice caused her to relax. Mr. Anson had been a friend of the family for many years, and it seemed he hadn't changed.

"Come to pay your bill?"

Keiko grinned, shrugging her shoulders. "It is January first."

He laughed. "I know. I've been expecting you. I have it all made out."

He pulled the register from under the counter, pulling out a slip of paper. He handed it to Keiko, and she smiled at the bold red words stamped across it: PAID IN FULL.

Keiko smiled when she handed him the money. "Thanks, Mr. Anson."

"Anytime. How's your father, by the way?"

"He's doing better, but we still have to be careful with him."

"Well, you tell him I said 'hello,' okay?"

"I will."

Turning, Keiko left the store, stopping a moment to admire a pale blue dress that was hanging in the shop window next door. Keiko had never been able to afford purchasing a garment from Mrs. Saxon, but she admired the woman's abilities. Although Keiko could sew, she couldn't match Mrs. Saxon, even though Mrs. Saxon had been the one to teach Keiko's Home Ec class sewing.

"Keiko! Hello."

Keiko smiled at the small gray-haired woman. "Hello, Mrs. Saxon. I was just admiring the blue dress in your window."

Mrs. Saxon glanced at the garment mentioned. "It is pretty, isn't it? It's a new fabric from Paris."

They chatted for a few minutes before Keiko went on her way. As she was passing the alley next to the telegraph office, someone reached out a hand, snatching her into the darkened void.

Keiko opened her mouth to scream, but a hand shoved hard against her mouth. She was effectively pinned against the wall, and John Parker's angry eyes glittered menacingly down at her.

"Hello, *geisha* girl," he whispered, and Keiko flinched at his breath so close to her face, reeking of alcohol.

Glancing from the sides of her eyes, she saw Mark Jeffries watching the street in case anyone came by. On her other side, she found Stan Marcus leaning against the wall, his malicious grin sending shivers of apprehension sliding down her spine.

John moved his face in closer, and Keiko tried to turn her face aside. It was no use. He was much too strong for her.

He uncovered her mouth long enough to replace his hand with his lips. She tried to squirm free, but this only seemed to incense him further. His teeth scraped against her lip, cutting it slightly, his fingers bruising her arms.

When he finally released her lips, his hand shot up to once again cover her mouth.

"I have a message for your boyfriend," he whispered. "Tell him I'm waiting for him. You give him the message, hear? But just to be sure."

Keiko heard a rip and felt the sleeve of her blouse give way. Her eyes widened in alarm, and she began to squirm in earnest.

"Remember, *geisha* girl. It's your word against mine. Just give your boyfriend the message."

He shoved her slightly toward the entrance to the alley, and she stumbled, clinging to the wall. Her legs were like jelly beneath her, but she managed to make it to the truck and crawled inside. Her body was shaking all over, and tears ran in rivulets down her cheeks. She brushed them away with an impatient hand.

Inspecting the damage to her blouse, she was relieved that it was the right sleeve. At least she could keep it away from Shoji's sight. She knew she would never tell him. She couldn't. Not with the volatile temper he had.

When Shoji returned to the truck, Keiko continued to stare out the side window, not really seeing anything. One hand clutched her blouse at the shoulder as she tried to make it seem as if nothing was out of the ordinary.

Shoji did nothing toward starting the vehicle, and Keiko realized he sensed something was wrong.

"Keiko?"

Keiko bit hard into her bottom lip to keep from sobbing out loud. She felt Shoji move closer in the seat.

"Keiko, what's wrong?"

She felt his hands on her shoulders as he turned her toward him. A confused frown puckered his brows as his eyes roved over her face searching for some clue to her unusual behavior.

Her blouse fell apart under his fingers, and his eyes went wide. His gaze rested on her lips, where a trickle of blood ran down the side. His face became like granite, his eyes glittering dangerously. "Who did this to you?"

Keiko tried to turn her face away, but he pulled her back, his fingers unusually gentle against her chin.

"Keiko." The hard, determined voice demanded an answer.

"Let it go," she told him softly, her voice wobbling with the effort.

Without him realizing it, Shoji's fingers bit into her chin. When she flinched, he jerked his hands away, clenching them on the steering wheel. He knew that Keiko had a stubborn streak a mile wide, and if she had decided not to tell him, he doubted there was anything he could do to make her.

Rage bubbled inside him unlike anything he had ever known before. He felt he could easily kill someone. *"If any man hates his brother, he has committed murder already in his thoughts."*

Frustrated, he glared at Keiko. She watched him warily, gnawing on her bottom lip. The blood was still there. Grinding his teeth together, he looked away from her out the back window of the truck.

When he saw John Parker leaning nonchalantly against the telegraph office, a cigarette dangling from his mouth, he thought he had his answer. When John crossed one foot over the other, tipping him a one-fingered salute, he was sure of it. His two buddies flanked him on either side.

Keiko followed his gaze, her eyes flying back to Shoji's face. She opened her mouth to protest, but it died on her lips at the look on his face.

Keiko laid a hand on his arm and felt the tenseness of his muscles beneath her fingers. His body was shaking with a violent rage that terrified her.

When he looked at her, Keiko felt her own body start to tremble. This must be what it was like to look death in the face. There was that about Shoji that told her he was beyond control and that someone was going to pay dearly.

When he spun to the edge of the seat reaching for the door, Keiko grabbed his black turtleneck sweater, clinging tightly with both hands.

"Shoji, no!"

He tried to shake her off, but she clung more tenaciously.

"No, Shoji!" she begged. "Please. He didn't do anything!"

Tears were once more streaming down her face.

"Listen to me! He didn't do anything. Nothing happened. Don't you see? If you hurt him, they'll put you in jail. They'll say you're a murdering Jap, and they'll kill you." She shook him to make him see reason. "Please, Shoji. Papa-san needs you. I need you!"

She felt his body go still, his look returning to her face. Some of the anger began to drain from him, but Keiko could tell that it wouldn't take much to fan it to life.

His fingers gently cupped her cheek, his thumb sliding softly across her lips. He bent, kissing the corner of her mouth where the blood had congealed on her cut.

Without looking around, he started the truck. Shifting into gear, he peeled out, leaving a burning black mark on the pavement. He never even looked around, but Keiko did.

There stood John Parker, his fists clenching and unclenching at his sides.

Chapter 7

Keiko stood on the porch of her home, gazing at the fields around her. Already there were signs of spring. Everything looked the same, yet everything was different.

When she saw a car in the distance, she thought it might be Kenji and Sumiko, but she soon realized that the gray sedan was not her brother. When the car pulled to a stop, Keiko's face grew grim. Mr. Dalrimple. What could he possibly want with them?

Mr. Dalrimple's burly form emerged from the car, a feigned smile upon his lips.

"Keiko! How are you?"

"I'm fine, Mr. Dalrimple. Is there something you wanted to see us about?"

The cigar that hung from the side of his mouth suddenly switched to the other side. "Well, yeah, but it's your father I need to see."

Keiko felt her heart drop. "He's inside. Come with me, please."

Keiko opened the door and led him inside to the living room. Her father was dozing in his favorite chair, and she was reluctant to disturb him. Before she had the chance, he opened his birdlike eyes and stared up at them. Rising to his feet, he bowed low before Mr. Dalrimple.

"Dalrimple-san, how are you?"

The big man seemed slightly uncomfortable. "I'm, uh, fine, Tochigi-san. But I'm afraid I have some bad news for you."

Keiko moved to her father's side, unconsciously offering him her support.

"Please, sit down," her father offered.

Mr. Dalrimple glanced around him, shifting uncomfortably from one foot to the other. "No. I can't stay. I just wanted to let you know that this land has been sold."

Keiko's eyes widened. "You can't do that! This is our land! We bought it!"

Mr. Dalrimple snickered nervously. "Not technically. Technically, it's my land."

Keiko felt rage rise like bile in her throat. "We gave you the money to purchase it for us! You didn't buy this land. You didn't sweat over it!"

"Keiko-san!"

Keiko glared at her father. "He can't do this!"

The cigar switched to the other side of the mouth. "Look, Girlie, legally

312

I can. I'm letting you know right now that you can stay here until the sale is final, but then you gotta go."

Keiko's father dropped into his chair, his face pinched white. Keiko flew to his side, dropping to her knees beside him. She glared up at the man standing beside her, so confidently sure of having his way.

"Get out!"

"Now, look here."

"You heard the lady. Get out."

Mr. Dalrimple turned at Shoji's quiet voice. "Who're you?"

Keiko rose to her feet. "He's my fiancé. Now get out. I don't know what I can do legally, but I'll find something."

After Mr. Dalrimple was gone, Papa-san rose to his feet. "I think I would like to lie down for a bit."

Keiko searched his face worriedly, noting his unusual pallor. Her worried eyes found Shoji's.

"That's a good idea, Tochigi-san. We'll call you when supper is ready," Shoji told him.

As he walked slowly from the room, Keiko noticed how old he looked. She looked back at Shoji, who was studying her intently. She hadn't spoken to him much since the occurrence with John Parker several weeks ago.

"I have to go into town for awhile," he told her, and Keiko panicked.

"I don't think that's a good idea."

His eyebrows rose to his forehead, and Keiko gritted her teeth at his arrogant look. "I won't be long. But I need to talk to Papa-san for a minute before I leave."

"Let me go with you."

"And Tochigi-san?"

Keiko slumped onto the couch. She couldn't leave her father. Not now. "Promise me you won't fight with John Parker."

His lip curled up at the corner. "I will not fight with John Parker if he will not fight with me."

With that she had to be satisfied. Moments later he left the house.

★ ★ ★

When Shoji returned, Kenji was following him. Sumiko was with Kenji along with Mrs. Shimura. Behind them another car pulled to a stop, and Mr. Kosugi, the minister, climbed out.

Surprised, Keiko invited everyone inside.

"Well, Keiko," Mr. Kosugi smiled. "After watching you grow up and baptizing you so many years ago, I now get to marry you."

His grin went from ear to ear. Kenji was studying Keiko seriously. He laid a hand on her shoulder.

"I'm happy for you, Sis. I don't think you could find a finer man."

Sumiko grinned at her. "You sly old dog. Imagine not telling your best friend."

Keiko couldn't say anything. Her throat was dry, and she was too stunned to do more than nod her head at everyone's congratulations.

Shoji followed her father as he entered the room. Her father bowed low before Mr. Kosugi.

Mr. Kosugi returned his bow deferentially. "Tochigi-san, you must be very happy for your daughter."

Her father bowed again. "I am. Shoji will make a fine son."

Keiko moved as though in a dream. Mr. Kosugi performed the typical American wedding ceremony, his droning voice lulling Keiko into an apathetic acceptance of everything that was happening. Papa-san seemed to accept the ceremony, even though it was not a traditional Japanese one. Keiko had to be thankful for that at least.

When Shoji's lips closed over hers in the conventional sealing of the vows, Keiko found her knees buckling beneath her. Shoji supported her with his arms, but there was no disguising the fear in her eyes. She had just agreed to live with this man for the rest of her life. She didn't know much about him, and what little she did know frightened her half to death.

No, that wasn't exactly true. She knew he could be extremely gentle and kind, and for the most part he was. It was only when the demons of his past came back to haunt him that she was afraid. His inscrutable almond eyes stared down into hers, and she felt some of her fears subside.

Later, Keiko sat in the garden next to the pool, trailing her fingers in the water. Her unfocused gaze rested on the koi fish darting to and fro. She didn't hear Shoji come up behind her and jumped when he sat down next to her.

They were quiet for a long time, neither knowing what to say. Finally, Keiko turned to face him.

"What kind of marriage do you want?"

He didn't pretend to misunderstand her. Taking one of her hands into his, he began to stroke it tenderly without looking her in the face.

"I want a real marriage."

Only then did his eyes come back to hers. There was a softness in his eyes she had never seen before. When he leaned forward, she didn't draw back. When his lips touched hers tentatively, she kissed him back. She still didn't know how she felt about him, but she knew he attracted her and now they were husband and wife.

He deepened the kiss, pulling her fully into his embrace. When he lifted his head, there was a glow in his eyes that was more intense than anything she had ever seen before. Her heart began to hammer furiously in her chest.

"Let's go to bed," he told her quietly, lifting her gently into his arms and carrying her inside.

★ ★ ★

Three days later Kenji returned. His set face let Keiko and Shoji know something was wrong. Fortunately for them, Papa-san was taking a nap.

"There's nothing we can do about the land," he told them without preamble. "The same story is being played over and over all over California and other states besides."

Keiko sighed. "What now?"

"That's the least of our worries," he told them. "Word just came down that President Roosevelt has issued Executive Order 9066."

"What does that mean?" Keiko asked, fearful of the answer.

"It means that the president has just given the government the authority to declare the Japanese in this country 'hostile aliens.' "

"Even us?"

Kenji shook his head. "Not yet, though we're to be treated as such. There's word coming down that the Japanese are going to be sent to internment camps."

Keiko sat down on the steps. *Dear Lord, how can You let this happen?*

"Mass evacuations are about to begin. I came to tell you that and to invite you to Sumiko's and my wedding."

Keiko was stunned, though she knew she shouldn't have been. Shoji was pleased, pumping Kenji's hand up and down.

"When?" he wanted to know.

"Tomorrow morning at ten o'clock at the Japanese Community Church. You'll come?"

"Nothing could keep us away," Keiko remonstrated.

"I'll let you tell Papa-san. I gotta get back."

Shoji placed an arm around Keiko's waist, and they watched Kenji disappear from sight. Three days of being married, and she still wasn't accustomed to his touch. Would she ever be? Could she truly learn to love him someday, like her mother had her father?

Pulling away, she retreated to the safety of the house. She knew he wouldn't follow her; he had too much to do in the fields.

For some reason, she was shy with him during the day. But at night. . . Her face crimsoned as she remembered the past three nights. Could she possibly respond to a man the way she did Shoji if she didn't care? It was something to ponder.

★ ★ ★

Sumiko's wedding was as unlike Keiko's as it could have been. There were flowers and candles everywhere. The church was decorated fully, and Keiko wondered how Sumiko had managed to do it in such a short time.

"Kay!" Sumiko rushed forward, grabbing Keiko by the hand. "Come on! I thought you'd never get here!"

"Why aren't you dressed?" Keiko demanded, her eyes going over Sumiko's plain housedress.

"I will, but I had to see that you got dressed first." Sumiko shoved her into one of the small classrooms. "Put that on."

Keiko's eyes widened at the beautiful blue dress that had been hanging in Mrs. Saxon's shop window. It completely took her breath away. Sumiko grinned, pleased with her surprise.

"Well, you didn't think I could have my matron of honor dressed in anything but the best, did you?"

Perplexed, Keiko could only stare at her friend. "But how did you manage this? They've frozen everyone's bank accounts. How did you get the money for all this?"

Sumiko giggled. "Daddy has a hidden safe in the house. That's where he keeps a large portion of our money. He doesn't exactly trust banks."

Keiko knew that Mr. Shimura was a wealthy man, but she hadn't known exactly how wealthy.

"Hurry up, for goodness' sake." Sumiko quickly pulled her own dress from a mannequin in the corner. Keiko gasped at its beauty, the pearls on the bodice shimmering in the sunlight.

"Isn't it a pip?" Sumiko asked, her eyes dreamy. "Of course, Mrs. Saxon made it, and anything she makes is bound to be beautiful."

When Keiko preceded Sumiko down the aisle, her throat was choked with tears. This was how a wedding should be. Beautiful flowers, a beautiful church, and a bride and groom whose eyes glowed when they looked at each other.

★ ★ ★

When they went to bed that night, Shoji leaned over her, tracing a finger across her forehead. In the moonlight she could see his broad-shouldered physique. There was nothing about him that wasn't physically perfect.

"I'm sorry, Keiko-chan." His soft voice sent shivers of awareness tingling up her spine.

"For what?" she asked curiously.

"I know how much beautiful weddings mean to women. I would have done the same for you if I had had time."

Her eyes studied his, and she could see that he was sincere.

"It's no matter," she told him and suddenly realized that it wasn't. It wasn't the wedding; it was the marriage that counted. Her mother had given everything to her marriage, and her father had fallen hopelessly in love with her.

Keiko smiled as she thought of doing the same. She knew if she wasn't already in love with her husband she was halfway there. She remembered her mother telling her once, "Love is not a feeling, Keiko-chan. It is a decision."

Deciding right then and there that she would make this the best marriage possible, Keiko tried to pull Shoji's lips down to hers. He held back, questioning with his eyes.

Keiko smiled softly, her eyes glowing; and whatever had been bothering Shoji must have been put to rest, for his lips met hers eagerly in the dark.

★ ★ ★

By the middle of March, Lieutenant General John L. DeWitt was ready to carry out President Roosevelt's executive order. He did it with such enthusiasm, no one was left in doubt as to his feelings for the Japanese.

Since early in March, a curfew had been imposed on Japanese Americans. No one was allowed on the streets past six o'clock, and no one was allowed to travel more than five miles from their home.

This presented a problem for Keiko since she lived fifteen miles from town. Keiko fumed, wondering how the government expected them to arrange for supplies with no phone. Her dilemma was solved a few days later when she saw Mr. Anson's black truck coming toward their house.

He jumped out of the truck, and although there was a smile on his face, Keiko could sense his anger. She watched him go to the back of the truck and pull out a large cardboard box. Marching over to her, he demanded, "Where do you want this?"

Puzzled, she looked to Mr. Anson for some explanation.

He stared belligerently back at her. "This stupid government might keep you from coming to me, but they can't keep me from coming to you. You tell me if there's anything else you need, and I'll see that you get it."

"But. . .but I can't pay you. Our bank account has been frozen."

He waved his hands. "I know all that. It doesn't matter. You've always been a good customer, and I know you'll pay when this crazy government comes to its senses and begins to treat you like human beings again."

Tears welled up in Keiko's eyes though she tried to prevent it. She knew Mr. Anson was already uncomfortable. His kindness and generosity were what made him such a special man, and she somehow knew that he wouldn't appreciate her profuse thanks.

Shoji appeared at her side, his eyes on the store owner.

"Mr. Anson has brought us some supplies," she told him.

Face red with embarrassment, Mr. Anson turned back to his truck. Reaching inside, he pulled out another box. "I told Keiko you can pay me back whenever."

Laying the box at Keiko's feet, Mr. Anson smiled. "You've done business with my store so long, I reckon I pretty much got it figured what you need. Oh, and congratulations on your marriage."

Glancing over the supplies, Keiko realized he was right.

"Thank you, Mr. Anson," she told him quietly, and the deferential tone of her voice conveyed her full meaning to him. She was very thankful, and she appreciated his kindness.

Relaxing, he grinned back at her. "I'll come out this way every Friday until this stupid restriction is lifted. You just let me know what you need."

Climbing back into his truck, he smiled at them both before turning and heading back the way he had just come.

"People like him more than make up for the people like John Parker," Shoji told her softly, his eyes still on the truck.

"*Hai.*"

Shoji smiled at her, giving her a quick kiss on the lips. "I've still got work to do."

"Shoji?"

"*Hai?*" He halfway turned back to her.

"Why are you bothering with the field when it's no longer ours?"

He looked as if he were about to say something, when suddenly he shrugged his shoulders. "What would you suggest I do? Sit in the house all day?"

Knowing what a physical person he was, Keiko understood his problem. He could never just sit around and do nothing. She watched him go, a feeling of pride washing over her. She would never need to worry as long as she had Shoji.

The rest of the week, neighbors continually made a path to their door. All of them were white, since it was beyond the five-mile limit of the other Japanese in the area.

Keiko hadn't realized just how many friends they had. Her heart warmed with appreciation for them all. Everyone brought something with them.

Mrs. Ames brought her famous sourdough bread; Mrs. Simpson brought an apple pie; Mr. Pierce brought some tools he thought Shoji could use. Keiko watched her father become once more the man she remembered, and she knew that he was growing on love.

One night Keiko heard the front screen door open quietly while they were in bed. She was about to go and check it out when Shoji pinned her to the mattress.

"Stay here," he whispered, and she found that she had no desire to disobey him. He moved with such stealth that he was out of the room before she knew it.

A strangled cry brought her from her bed, sending her flying down the stairs. Funny, she had no fear for Shoji, but she could just picture John Parker lying on the floor in a pool of his own blood. There was no doubt in her mind that Shoji could be lethal if he needed to be.

Flicking on the light, she stood on the bottom stair. Her brother dangled from Shoji's hands. Keiko covered her mouth to keep from laughing at the surprised expression on her brother's face, then realized that something must be terribly wrong for Kenji to break the curfew. The smile fell from her face, and she rushed to his side.

Shoji was already apologizing, but Kenji brushed his concern aside, straightening the collar on his shirt. "It's okay; it's okay! I'm thankful my sister and father are so well protected. But couldn't you give a guy some notice?"

Keiko grabbed his arm. "What's wrong? Why are you here?"

They all sat down in the living room, and Kenji leaned forward, his face serious. "I don't know if you've heard yet, but they've begun the mass evacuation. They started at Terminal Island today after giving the people just three days' notice."

Shoji sucked in his breath. "It's finally come."

"I came to tell you so that you can be prepared. They're only allowing people to take what they can carry."

Shoji sat with his elbow draped on the arm of the chair, his lips pushed between his thumb and forefinger. He was so silent Kenji shifted uncomfortably.

"I can't stay any longer. I have to get back."

"How did you get here?" Keiko asked. "I didn't hear your car."

"I didn't want to chance using it. The noise would give me away. I walked."

"You walked?" Keiko's voice rose a full octave.

Remembering his own sojourn, Shoji grinned. "It can be done."

Shoji pulled Keiko to her feet, and they walked with Kenji to the door.

"Be careful, Kenji!" Keiko implored her brother.

Kenji smiled at his sister before shaking hands with Shoji. "Take care of our girl."

"I will."

Keiko watched as her brother's form was swallowed up by the darkness, a lump forming in her throat. Shoji wrapped his arms around her from behind.

"He'll be okay," he told her, his voice husky against her ear.

Nodding, she said nothing.

"Come back to bed."

Keiko followed him up the stairs, her heart aching for what was happening to them all. Never had she felt so victimized, not even when John Parker had assaulted her. She could understand his hatred. But the whole country?

Remembering her path of visitors, she shook her head. No, not the whole country.

She curled into Shoji's arms, knowing that come what may, she would be safe with her husband and her Lord. With both of them looking out for her, she knew she had nothing to fear. But deep down inside, there was still that little niggle of worry.

★ ★ ★

Keiko stood at the sink washing dishes the next morning when it occurred to her that it had been a little over a year since Shoji had first come into their lives. Sadly, she had missed putting out her dolls for Hinamatsuri, but Shoji had felt it best that they remain packed away just in case they received notification to evacuate.

Keiko still had a hard time believing it could actually happen. It was appalling to believe that their government could so haphazardly disregard the Constitution's protection of its citizens.

So much had changed in just a year, not the least of which was that she was now Shoji's wife. Had anyone told her a year ago that this would be so, she would have laughed in their face. But then, had anyone told her that she would be forced to leave her home just because she was Japanese, she would have scorned that, also.

When she heard a car coming down the road, she hastily wiped her hands on the kitchen towel and went to the front door. She didn't recognize the man who stepped from the car. His black coat reached to his feet, and she could see a black pin-striped suit underneath.

He removed his hat, creasing the gray felt brim between his fingers. "I'm looking for a Mr. Tochigi or a Mr. Ibaragi."

He turned as Shoji came from the side of the house. As usual, Keiko hadn't even heard him arrive.

"I'm Ibaragi," he told the man, and Keiko realized the inscrutable mask was hiding his anger. She was beginning to know her husband's moods.

The man handed Shoji a paper. Shoji glanced at it, his face going white.

"What is it?" Keiko asked him, coming to peer over his shoulder.

"Our evacuation orders," he told her, no inflection in his voice. He handed the paper to Keiko, his eyes focused on the man before him. "We have ten days to report to the Tulare Assembly Center."

"Ten days! But that's not enough time." Keiko directed an accusing glare at the man.

"I'm sorry, but it's all the time you have." He looked at Shoji. "The male head of each house needs to register. You need to report to the Civil Control Station being set up at the Japanese Community Church."

Placing his hat back on his head, he climbed back into his car and sped away.

Shoji stood staring after the man a long time. "Well, at least we know the restriction has been lifted."

A short while later, Keiko watched Shoji follow the same path as their visitor in her father's truck. Burying her face in her hands, she tried to pray, but suddenly she found she had nothing to say.

Chapter 8

There was an air of abandonment that surrounded the house, its insidious presence moving among the rooms as each was quickly emptied of its residents. The only furniture left in the house was the mattresses they still slept on and a small table in the corner of the living room that housed a lone occupant.

The small bonsai tree had resided in the same spot for as long as Keiko could remember living in this house. It had been given to her father the day he was born, and now, fifty-six years later, it was not much larger than when it had been given to him. Her father tended it lovingly, believing that if the tree died, he would also die.

The gentle sadness on his face caused her heart to constrict within her.

"What is troubling you, Papa-san?"

Startled, he turned quickly at her voice. His hands moved softly over the needles of the pine. He heaved a huge sigh.

"I cannot take my tree with me. We are allowed only what we can carry, and there are too many things we need for me to worry about my tree."

Shoji came in the door in time to hear his last words. Dropping the dusty suitcase he had retrieved from the storage shed, he went and laid a hand on the old man's shoulder.

"You carry the tree, Tochigi-san, and let me worry about the rest."

Keiko agreed, but her father was already shaking his head.

"No. I must do my part, also. We need to take many things with us, and there are only the three of us to do it."

"Mr. Anson has agreed to store our things for us," Keiko told him. "At least we don't need to worry about that."

Shoji nodded. "And your tree will go with us if I have to carry it in my teeth."

Keiko's heart swelled with appreciation. If anyone would understand her father's need for his tree, it was Shoji. She smiled warmly at him, her eyes glowing with her feelings.

Shoji turned away, checking over the bags Keiko had packed. He smiled slightly, realizing that she had packed sparingly, hoping to relieve him of some of the weight he would need to carry.

"Keiko, where is the hot plate?"

Looking down, her face filled with color as she realized he had figured out what she had tried to do. "I thought perhaps we would not need it since the government will provide us with meals."

Shoji went to the kitchen, returning with the aforementioned article in his hands. Shifting things in the duffel bag, he placed the hot plate inside.

"I think perhaps the government probably has a different idea of what constitutes a meal than you and I. Besides, Papa-san will want his tea."

"But, Shoji, we already have too much to carry as it is."

"Keiko," he told her softly, "let me worry about carrying our bags, and you worry about making sure we have what we'll need."

Heaving a sigh of acquiescence, she turned to her father. "I still have some things I need to go through in my bedroom. Is there anything I can help you with?"

Her father shook his head. *"Iie.* You go do what you need to do."

Shoji found her an hour later sitting cross-legged in the middle of her bedroom. She glanced up as he came in, answering his unspoken question.

"Mementos," she told him, and her voice was thick with the tears she was trying hard to suppress.

He came and sat beside her, leaning forward to investigate the small box she was digging in. Reaching in, he pulled out a dried arrangement of flowers twined together with a faded royal blue ribbon.

"Aren't these the flowers I gave you for the prom?"

Looking down at her lap, Keiko's cheeks filled with fiery color. *"Hai."*

When she dared a look at his face, she found him watching her, his brown almond eyes unfathomable. Frowning, she wondered what was going on behind that inscrutable mask now.

Gently, he placed the corsage back in the box. When his eyes again found her face, they were no longer mysterious but filled with a strange longing. Keiko sucked in a breath, not releasing it until he lifted one hand and softly stroked her cheek.

It had been eight days since Shoji had last touched her. Eight long days, and eight even longer nights. She leaned her cheek against his palm, smiling slightly.

For some reason he was tense. It communicated itself to her through his very touch. He seemed to be fighting a battle within himself, but for what reason she had no idea.

Growling softly, he leaned forward and kissed her. When she readily responded, he pulled her tightly into his embrace, taking her down to the floor beneath him.

Keiko wrapped her arms around his neck, trying to pull him further toward the vortex of emotions she was experiencing. When he suddenly pulled away, she was confused.

Shoji rose quickly to his feet, brushing a hand through his hair. His emotions were once again hidden behind his dark eyes, but Keiko knew that he had been just as affected as she by their encounter.

"Keep your mementos, Keiko. Perhaps they will remind you of a happier time."

Keiko watched him leave the room, more confused than ever. What made Shoji draw away from her? Was it possible that he held her partially accountable for the situation they were in? Did he resent her country for what it was doing to them?

Standing, she moved to the window and saw Shoji heading for his favorite spot in the garden. What would happen to that garden when they left? An aching sadness left her depressed. Nothing would ever be the same again. Shoji was right. She should keep her mementos because they might very well be the only thing she had left to remember of her life in this country.

Several hours later, they were ready to leave. It had been decided that they would spend the night with Kenji and Sumiko tonight since they lived in town, thereby saving themselves the embarrassment of being picked up by an army truck in the morning.

Shoji checked the bags one more time to be sure they had their family identification number on them. They were no longer the Tochigi or Ibaragi family. Now they were Family 73896. That little ticket with that little number seemed such a betrayal of everything Keiko had been taught to believe as an American.

That the government could so forget itself as to call American citizens "aliens" and refuse them due process of law in the name of the "protection" of that government was more ludicrous than anything she had as yet experienced. The pain of that rejection was almost overwhelming.

They made the trip into town in silence, each busy with their own thoughts.

Keiko sat between her husband and her father feeling lonelier than she had ever felt, even lonelier than when her mother had died. She had a father on one side of her, too frail in health to be worrying with her own morbid thoughts, and a husband on the other side of her that had suddenly become more of a stranger than when she had first married him.

Kenji was waiting for them when they pulled into the Shimura driveway. The huge structure inspired the same feeling of wonder in Keiko that she had felt as a child. Mr. Shimura was a very wealthy man, and that was probably the very reason he found himself in Missoula, Montana. Many in the vicinity were jealous of Mr. Shimura's wealth.

Sumiko showed Keiko and Shoji to their room, while Kenji showed Papa-san his. Mrs. Shimura was already in bed even though it was still very early in the evening.

"Mama had to be given tranquilizers," Sumiko told them. "This is more than she can take."

"What of your father?" Keiko asked her.

Turning away, Sumiko bit her lip. "We hear from him often by telegraph. I think he is more worried about us than we are about him." A tear dripped slowly down her cheek. "No, that's not true. He can't be any more worried than we are about him. We've heard that some of the men in Montana might be moved."

"Where?" Shoji asked.

Sumiko shrugged. "We don't know. Rumor has it that some are believed to be spies for Japan."

Keiko was filled with a righteous wrath. "That's the most ridiculous thing I've ever heard!"

"Is it?" Kenji walked up and put his arm around his wife. "We know that, but do you remember Mr. Ito?"

Keiko did. The man was positively Japanese through and through. They had always wondered why he had come to America in the first place when it was so obvious that Japan was the country that he loved.

"There are others like him, Keiko, and though they are probably as harmless as you or I, you can't blame the country for its doubts at a time like this."

"Can't I?" The angry sparkle in Keiko's eyes warned her brother that it was time to change the subject.

"We have to meet at the Japanese Community Church first thing in the morning. We'd better get some sleep."

That night, Keiko lay in the still darkness listening to the even breathing of her husband. Again, he had turned away from her as soon as they had climbed into bed. Was it something she had done? Was he tired of her already?

She curled into a small ball, biting the knuckles of her hand to stop the tears that threatened to come. Her quiet sniffles were muffled in the soft feather pillow that she clutched as though it were a lifeline.

With a groan Shoji rolled over, pulling Keiko roughly into his arms.

"Don't cry, Keiko-chan."

Instead of helping, the endearment made her cry all the harder. She burrowed against his shoulder, allowing the tears she had been holding back for days to work their healing balm on her scarred soul.

"Shhh. Don't cry, little one."

"I can't help it," she gulped. "Everything is gone. Everyone is gone!"

"That's not true, and you know it," Shoji admonished softly. "You still have Kenji, Papa-san, Sumiko, and I."

She looked up at his face in the dark. "What if they send Kenji somewhere else? What if they take Papa-san to Montana? What if you. . ." She stopped, unable to complete the thought.

"What if I what? They won't separate us, Keiko, you know that. We are both American citizens. Husband and wife. They won't separate us."

He sounded so sure of himself, yet hadn't he left her in a way already?

"Shoji, do you love me?"

She felt him stiffen against her. He started to pull away, but she clung to him.

"Answer me. Do you?"

He tried to pry her fingers loose from their grip against his shoulders. "Keiko, now is not the time to discuss this."

"Why? Why can't you just admit that the only reason you married me was for some honor-bound duty you felt justified in performing?"

He seemed as surprised at her anger as she was. Suddenly, she let go of him and rolled to the edge of the bed. Before she could get up, Shoji pulled her back.

She could see his eyes glittering down at her in the moonlight. She could sense his anger and was suddenly afraid.

"Let me go," she commanded, but he ignored her.

"Are you suddenly unsure of my feelings for you because I no longer make love to you?"

Hot color flooded her cheeks. One thing about Shoji, he had an uncanny knack for reading her mind. She struggled again, embarrassed to even be having this conversation.

He shook her none too gently. "Listen to me. I will not have a child born into captivity like some animal at the zoo."

She stilled at his declaration, her eyes roving his features. The shadows gave him a grim, unsmiling appearance.

"I know that you aren't already with child." Again Keiko felt the hot color flood her cheeks. "And I intend to make sure it stays that way."

Releasing her, he rose to his feet. She could see his broad-shouldered silhouette in the moonlight that was slanting through the window and across the floor.

"Go to sleep, Keiko," he commanded harshly. She watched him pull on his clothes in preparation for leaving.

"Where are you going?"

The trepidation in her voice brought a long sigh from him. He crossed to her and sat beside her on the bed.

"I have some things to do. Here. In the house. I'm not going outside, okay? Now go to sleep."

He pulled the covers gently up against her neck. Bending, he kissed her briefly on the lips. "I'm not sure what I feel right now. Things are all mixed up. In here." He pointed to his head. "But you can be sure of one thing. I will always be here for you. Understand?"

Keiko knew she would have to be satisfied with that for the time being.

She could better understand his reasoning now. She had never thought about becoming pregnant. Instead of making her afraid, the thought warmed her.

But Shoji was right. Now was not the time. But someday. Someday.

★ ★ ★

The sidewalks were crowded with the milling throngs of Japanese. Many Keiko recognized, but many she did not.

Everyone clung to their luggage, chattering to others around them. The church was offering them sandwiches and drinks, but most were too distraught to partake of the friendly repast.

Keiko watched a young mother of two struggling with her children. She was obviously very pregnant and very frazzled. Where was her husband?

As she watched, a young man hurried to her side. Taking the youngest child from her arms, he lifted a huge suitcase with one hand and told her to follow him.

Keiko jumped when Kenji dropped an arm across her shoulders. He smiled wryly down at her upturned face. "It's only me."

They watched the progress of the young couple together.

"The children, Kenji. What of the children? What harm could they possibly do?"

The smile left his face, and he straightened his shoulders. "None, but do you think they would really want to be separated from their families?"

"I guess not." Keiko was thinking of their own upcoming separation. She had found out this morning that Kenji would be going to Tanforan Assembly Center, while Keiko, Shoji, and Papa-san would be going to Tulare. Only the United States government had any idea why.

Turning, Keiko hugged her brother tightly. His arms tightened around her, and there was a suspicious huskiness in his voice when he finally managed to speak.

"Keiko, I don't know what's going to happen, but I want you to know that I thank God Shoji is here to take care of you."

She nodded into his chest without speaking. Already, tears were pouring from her eyes, and she had the distinct feeling it was going to be a long flowing river.

Shoji joined them, giving them time together just by being silent. Finally, Kenji handed Keiko over to her husband.

"I have to get back to Sumiko and Mrs. Shimura." His eyes found Shoji's and held. "Take care of them."

Shoji nodded briefly, sharing Kenji's pain. There was no doubt that Kenji loved his father and sister, and his brother-in-law, if Keiko read him right. It was all too evident in the repressed tears he fought to control. After shaking hands, the two men parted, and Kenji strode away.

Struggling with her own tears, Keiko leaned back against Shoji when he

326

curled his hands around her shoulders. Everywhere people were calling good-byes. Keiko soon realized that she wasn't the only one having a good cry.

Armed security guards roamed among the Japanese, their rifles loaded, their bayonets at the ready. Just their presence made Keiko go cold all over. Suddenly, she felt like a woman without a country, like she had no place to call home.

"It's time to go," Shoji told her, turning her to where she knew her father was waiting.

He sat resolutely, guarding his precious bonsai tree. Keiko grinned through her tears. What a major battle that had been. Keiko soon found out that steel had met tide when it came to the forces of will of her parent and husband. She was only now beginning to realize how inflexible such a soft person as her husband could be.

Slowly they made their way to the buses. Shoji carried the major load of luggage, but Keiko had insisted on doing her part. Between them, they had convinced Papa-san that he would best serve their purpose if he could carry his tree and help navigate them through the crowd.

It seemed hours before the buses were finally ready to roll—not that Keiko was in any particular hurry.

Almost as though the Lord was feeling their sorrow, a gentle rain began to fall, turning suddenly into a torrent. The sun refused to show its face, and Keiko blessed its seeming sensitivity. Surely the Lord was looking down on this atrocity and feeling her pain.

She knew without a doubt that most of her fellow passengers were either Buddhist or of the Shinto faith, but the Lord was with her.

Her father sat beside her, staring silently out the window. Keiko felt a pang of alarm. What would this do to her father's frail heart? To lose everything, including his only son. Almost as though he could read her thoughts, he turned to her.

"At least I have you, Keiko-chan, and Shoji."

Keiko turned to watch her husband, who was standing at the rear of the bus. Yes, at least they had Shoji. Strong, dependable Shoji.

When she studied her father's face more closely, she could see the tired lines that radiated out from his eyes. Their dark amber-colored irises blinked back at Keiko sedately, and she wondered at his calm.

Keiko felt the tears threatening again as she watched their little town slowly receding in the distance. Her home, gone. Her brother, gone. All her memories. No, they weren't gone. They could never be taken away. Would she ever see her home again?

She was surprised when her father took her hand into his own leathery one and began to absently stroke it. When he spoke, his voice seemed to come from far away.

"At least your mother was not here to see this."

Keiko gnawed on her bottom lip. "Do you think she knows what's happening to us? Do you think she can see us now?"

He turned surprised eyes to her. "Does not your Bible say that there are no tears in heaven?"

"Hai."

He turned back to the window. "Then she does not know what is happening, because she would surely be crying right now."

Keiko felt humbled. Here she had thought to comfort her father and instead he was trying to comfort her. Somehow his words were not as comforting as they should have been. She had always wanted to believe that her mother was watching over her, smiling with her triumphs, crying over her hurts.

She realized then that she had allowed her mother to take the place of God. He was the One who rejoiced with her victories and hurt when she hurt. He was the One who watched over her, took care of her. Even Shoji could not replace Him.

Bowing her head, she prayed silently as the miles rolled past. She gave herself into His care and turned her anger and bitterness over to Him to deal with. It wasn't the Americans or the Japanese who were the real enemy. It was Satan, and she realized how in control he was. But God was sovereign. Nothing could happen without His will. With that thought, peace descended.

The peace stayed with her even when she opened her eyes and saw the looming grandstand of Tulare. Dusk was falling and it was hard to see, but the darkness did nothing to hide the bleakness, the barrenness of their new home. The converted racetrack loomed ominously against the darkening sky.

Barbed-wire fences gave Keiko the feeling that she was some horrible criminal. She felt a tightness in her chest. Is this what it felt like to walk through a prison door knowing you might never come back out?

Faces peered at them from the semidarkness, almond eyes searching for family and friends.

As the bus drove through the gates, Keiko heard them clang shut behind them. Shivering, she turned to find her husband's eyes watching her. The strength that flowed from him seemed to reach through the fog of her fear, and she felt her peace restored.

God had sent her Shoji to be the arms that she needed to wrap securely around her in her most trying times. At first it had been her mother, then her father, and now, Shoji. His was the physical love she needed just as God was the spiritual.

They were unloaded from the bus and directed to an area where they filled out registration papers. Soldiers inspected their baggage for contraband items. Keiko felt her anger rise when one woman was relieved of her Japanese Bible, but she kept silent.

Everyone had to go through a cursory medical examination, and Keiko wondered what they would say about her father's heart condition. Did they realize they could very well be sentencing him to death?

Surprisingly, they said nothing, allowing Papa-san to pass through the inspection line. Shoji took their suitcases and prepared to leave. The rest of their luggage would be delivered later when the bus was unloaded.

Keiko followed her husband and her father through ankle-deep mud to some buildings toward the rear of the center. She was so tired that all she wanted was a place to lay her head and go to sleep.

They stopped outside what appeared to be a stable, and Keiko wondered how much longer it would be before they reached their final destination.

"Well, this is it," Shoji told them. "C-5."

He opened a small door and went inside. Keiko blinked at his disappearing form. Surely he had to be kidding. This was a horse stable, for goodness' sake.

Suddenly a light illuminated the entryway. Shoji returned to the door, motioning them inside.

Keiko followed her father up the one step, stopping in the doorway. Her eyes went wide. In this ten-foot-by-ten-foot space, three army cots drooped lazily against the floor. An attempt had been made to whitewash the walls, but not before any insect species had been removed. Little white bodies clung to the walls.

Keiko could smell the still-lingering aroma of the horses that had so recently made their homes here. Other evidences of their occupation were the teeth marks in the stall doors and particles of straw that littered the floor.

Shoji stood watching her from below the one lone lightbulb that hung suspended from the center of the ceiling.

"Is this it?" she wanted to know.

His lips twisted crookedly. "I'm afraid so."

That was the last thing Keiko remembered before darkness descended.

Chapter 9

When Keiko slowly opened her eyes again, her mind was still foggy. She had been dreaming a wonderful dream in which her mother was chasing her through a field of flowers, her long dark hair streaming out behind her. Picking a daisy from the millions around her, she handed it to her mother, whose radiant smile brought an answering response from Keiko.

"You are my little angel, Keiko-chan."

Keiko smiled her little girl smile, reaching up a hand to touch her mother's soft features. Suddenly the smile left her mother's face.

"I am not your God, Keiko. Remember that. I love you, but I am not your God."

She took one of Keiko's hands into her own, stroking it softly. "Do you hear me, Keiko?"

"I hear you, Mama," she answered softly.

Slowly, the image faded and the eyes peering down at her so intently were not her mother's. They had been replaced by eyes the color of mahogany, alive with worry.

"Keiko, can you hear me?"

Finally, the scenery came into focus, and Keiko found herself staring up into Shoji's anxious gaze. Beyond his shoulder, her father had an equally anxious expression.

Shoji was rubbing her hand vigorously, not softly at all.

"Shoji? What happened?"

Shoji couldn't hide the relief that swept his features. Laying her hand down, he began to stroke her forehead softly, gently pushing the hair from her face.

"You fainted."

Frowning, Keiko tried to sit up, realizing as she did so that she was on one of the now set-up cots. Shoji supported her, and she leaned her weight against him gratefully. Rubbing her forehead with one hand, she tiredly tried to get her mind to focus. She still felt groggy and reluctant to return to the real world when the dream one had been so beautiful.

Returning consciousness brought returning anguish. Her eyes inspected the cubicle they were now supposed to call home. Shivering, she turned back to the two men in her life. No use crying over spilled milk. What was done, was done, and nothing would change it now.

Her father's tired features brought her to her feet, where she had to pause as a wave of dizziness assailed her. Shoji wrapped a strong arm around her waist.

"Take it easy. We don't want to pick you up off the floor again."

Keiko studied the area mentioned and decided with distaste that she had no desire to be there again, either. Shrugging out of Shoji's hold, she rubbed her hands briskly together.

"So. Now what?" Wrinkling her nose with distaste, she studied the small apartment. "First things first. We need some way to clean this place."

Shoji felt a thrill of pride in his wife. She was stronger than she seemed, although he had wondered when he picked her up from the floor. His heart was just now slowing from its thundering pace that was a result of the terror he felt when he saw Keiko slump into unconsciousness.

Still, days of going without sleep and irregular meals that were rarely eaten had left a mark on all of them. Her body had finally succumbed to its need for respite.

Keiko went to her father, squeezing his shoulder reassuringly. "It's almost like camping out. Remember when Kenji and I put up a tent in the backyard?"

As she spoke, Keiko watched her father's face relax. *"Hai.* You were worried about the bugs, if I remember correctly."

Keiko grinned. "That wasn't the half of it. I was just as concerned with four-legged critters as with six-legged ones."

When she turned to her husband, Keiko found him smiling. "Have you ever been camping?" she asked him.

Suddenly his eyes went blank. He turned away before answering. "Many years ago. When I was a boy and still living with my parents."

He began to unload a large bag that he had insisted Keiko keep with her at all times. Pulling out several shirts, he then produced several apples, a bag of peanuts, a box of tea, and several other food items.

Keiko's mouth dropped open in surprise. She hadn't even realized until now that she was hungry. When she knelt beside Shoji, he handed her a soft bundle, which, when she unwrapped it, happened to be a loaf of bread.

"What else do you have in there?" she asked curiously, trying to peer past him into the bag.

Instead of answering, he handed her another bundle. This time when she unrolled the shirt, several bills of different denominations fell into her lap.

Keiko's eyes went wide with surprise, and she almost choked. "Where did you get this? Our bank account has been frozen for months now."

He shrugged, continuing to unload the sack.

"Shoji!" She was peeved at the way he continually refused to explain things to her.

When he turned his dark eyes her way, anger glittered just below the surface. Was he angry at her for asking? Well, that was just too bad. She had a right to know.

"My mother sent it to me."

"Oh."

Silence echoed around the room but was suddenly broken by the loud chattering of returning people.

"I'm afraid we missed supper," Shoji told her. His lips curled into a wry smile. "It seems we had other things on our minds."

An elderly woman peeked her head in their door, her little birdlike eyes taking in the occupants of the room. *"Konban wa."*

Both Shoji and her father rose to their feet. *"Hajimemashite,"* they answered her in unison, both bowing from their waists.

The little woman entered their apartment, her eyes roving over its barren desolation.

"I have cleaning supplies you can use," she told them. Keiko could have hugged her. "I get them for you now."

When she returned, she was carrying a bucket, mop, and broom. She handed them over to Keiko, who took them thankfully.

"Arigato," Keiko told her, and she saw the first hint of a smile on the old woman's face.

Nodding, she turned to Shoji. "There still a little wood and nails laying around if you think you can use. You must hurry before more people come."

Shoji's eyes went from the old woman to Keiko. Bowing, he turned to leave the room. Papa-san started to follow him. Both Keiko and Shoji tried to dissuade him, but he was resolute.

"I would only be in the way here," he told Keiko. "Perhaps I can be of some use to Shoji."

Since he was right, they didn't argue. The old woman watched them curiously, her bright eyes full of wisdom. Keiko had felt immediately drawn to her. She turned back to Keiko when the men had finally departed.

"You *nisei*. You speak Japanese?"

Keiko nodded. *"Hai."*

The old woman pursed her lips together. "Still, it better, I think, if we speak American. You agree?"

Keiko could understand her reasoning. These were perilous times, and they were part of an obviously paranoid country. Better to conform. Something in her rebelled at the thought.

"Onamae wa?" she asked, and the lady's eyes crinkled merrily back at her.

"My name Benko Kosugi. Everyone call me Obāsan."

The smile Keiko returned to her was full of warmth. She looked like a grandmother. "Well, Obāsan, I am Keiko Ibaragi."

Grinning, the old woman handed her the broom. "Make yourself useful, Keiko-san, and I see about getting a bucket of water."

She returned a short time later laden with an overflowing bucket. Keiko had already swept the compartment as clean as she possibly could, but it still looked dirty.

As Obāsan and Keiko worked, they got to know each other. The time flew, and by the time the men returned, Keiko knew that Obāsan was a widow now living with her son and his family. Keiko also had a pretty accurate picture of Obāsan's background, from her homeland in Japan to her son's occupation. She also found out that Obāsan's family lived just next door.

"My son, the American citizen," she told Keiko scornfully, then colored hotly when an angry voice rebuked her from the next cubicle.

"That's enough, Mama-san."

Keiko looked up at the top of the partition, which extended down from the ceiling by at least twelve inches. She had expected to see a face there, but Obāsan's son obviously considered his verbal chastisement enough. It was soon apparent that there would be very little privacy afforded them in these tiny quarters.

After Obāsan left, Keiko helped Shoji and her father set up the other two cots. After that, there was nothing left to do but wait for their other things to arrive.

Shoji handed Papa-san and Keiko each a slice of bread spread lavishly with jam. As they munched on their supper, Keiko couldn't help but wonder what would happen to them now. She had to be strong for her father's sake, if not for Shoji's. Sighing deeply, she turned to find her husband watching her.

"You are tired. Why don't you lay down for awhile?" He turned to her father. "You too, Papa-san."

Keiko frowned when her father did as he was bid without argument. His tired shoulders drooped dispiritedly. Keiko watched as his eyes slowly closed and his breathing became deep and even.

She turned her eyes back to her husband. "I couldn't sleep if I tried. I'm too keyed up."

Shoji shrugged his shoulders and walked to the corner, where he had dropped some wood.

"What are you going to do with that? And where did you ever get it?"

He bent to his task, answering her as he worked. "There were pieces left lying around from the construction they did here. The nails Papa-san and I found in the dirt. Hopefully there will be enough."

"For what?"

His look was enigmatic. "A table of some sort."

Since he had no hammer, he proceeded to pound together the boards with a large rock he had found. Keiko watched the way his muscles rippled with each blow of the rock. His strength, both physical and spiritual, was his greatest asset. She couldn't help but admire him.

A loud beeping outside sent Keiko scurrying to the door. A young

Japanese boy climbed from the passenger side of an old army truck and began hauling out bundles. He smiled at Keiko. "Ibaragi?" he asked.

She could feel Shoji's presence behind her. *"Hai,"* she answered him.

Nodding, he began lifting their luggage up the one step. Shoji reached around her to relieve the boy of his burden. When the last of the bundles had been unloaded, the boy tipped them a cheerful salute and climbed back in the truck, which roared off to its next rendezvous point.

Since she was thirsty for some tea, Keiko began by unloading the duffel bag. She lifted out the hot plate, thankful for Shoji's insistence on bringing it. Setting the plate aside, she looked around for some place to plug it in. There was nothing except the bulb hanging from the ceiling.

"I'll be finished in a minute," Shoji told her. "Then you can set the plate on the table and plug it into the light receptacle."

★ ★ ★

Their first morning found them standing in line waiting to get into the mess hall, or cafeteria, as the government preferred to call it. There seemed to be little food, and what there was had so many additives to spread it around that it was hardly recognizable.

Thankfully, the government had sent them letters warning them to bring eating utensils and plates. Each person stood clutching their dishes and flatware, stoically biding their time until they could get inside to eat.

Over the next few months, they would grow used to standing in long lines, but for now Keiko was growing impatient. She tapped her plate against her leg restlessly.

"Be still, Keiko-chan," her father admonished quietly, and again Keiko marveled at his serene countenance. Why was he so composed when she felt like she was walking on needles?

When they finally were inside, Keiko wondered just why she had been so anxious. The huge cavernous building reverberated with the din of hundreds of people talking and eating.

A spoonful of scrambled eggs was dumped on her plate, along with half a piece of bread and two Vienna sausages. There was no butter, no jam, nothing to make the dry bread more palatable.

After finishing her meal, such as it was, Keiko was still hungry. She had already found out that there were no seconds. Many of the people that were supposed to eat in this hall would go hungry or try another mess hall.

Keiko felt guilty for having eaten herself, although the flour that had been mixed in with the eggs to make them go further still clung to the roof of her mouth.

Shoji dumped his eggs on her plate. She glanced up at him in surprise. "I'm not that hungry," he told her, but Keiko knew he was lying.

She pressed her lips together tightly. "Christians don't lie, Shoji." Pushing her plate toward him, she fixed him with a steely eye. "Now eat."

He was shaking his head, his chin set stubbornly. "No. You need it more."

Rising swiftly to her feet, Keiko placed her fists on her hips. "Then leave it," she told him implacably, "because I refuse to eat your food."

With that she turned and stalked toward the exit. He caught up with her before she could reach the door. Taking her by the arm, he pulled her to a stop. "Come back to the table. I'll eat the sorry mess."

Her eyes went past him to her father, who was grinning with amusement. Reaching up, she touched Shoji's cheek with her fingertips.

"Go back and finish your meal. Someone else needs my seat. I'll just go back to the apartment and see about getting our dirty clothes together."

Shoji quickly surveyed the room. Every possible seat at the wooden picnic tables was occupied, and still people were standing around waiting for a seat. Nodding his head sharply, he let her go.

Since Keiko had unpacked their bedding the night before, there was little for her to do. She gathered their laundry together and headed for the laundry room.

The lines here were as long as at the mess hall. Sighing, Keiko laid her bundle at her feet and waited for the next available tub.

Four hours later, she was still waiting. Impatience had turned to aggravation, then to a seething anger. The stoic features of the older *issei* women only exasperated her all the more. How could they accept their fate with so much aplomb?

Finally, Keiko reached the washhouse only to find that they were expected to wash their clothes by hand. This didn't bother her as much as it obviously did some of the other *nisei* since she had always washed her clothes by hand, but it irritated her nonetheless, especially since all the hot water was long gone.

After scrubbing her clothes and rinsing them, she took them back to the apartment to dry them. Obāsan had already told her that she could use her clothing lines anytime she chose.

She hung the clothes outside, watching the sky for any sign of rain. Dark clouds were once again forming across the horizon, causing Keiko to throw up a little word of prayer.

When she went inside, she found her father tending his bonsai tree. She glanced around. "Where's Shoji?"

"They gave him a job working at the mess hall," he informed her without looking up.

Surprised, Keiko crossed to the cot where he sat and seated herself beside him. She watched as he lovingly removed dead needles and trimmed some of the larger branches.

"Will he be gone all day?"

"Hai."

Keiko blew out her breath. Now what? What was she to do all day? Realizing she had missed lunch, she scrounged in the bag of food they had with them and found an apple.

"Do you want one, Papa-san?"

"Tie." Laying his scissors next to the small tree, he rose to his feet, rubbing his back with his hands. "I am meeting with a few of the men. I will be back later, but I am not sure when. Do not worry about me, Keiko-chan. Understand?"

She dropped her eyes in the old way. *"Hai,"* she agreed, though she knew she wouldn't obey. How could she help but worry?

Taking the kettle, Keiko went to the washroom to fill it with water. When she returned, Benko was waiting for her.

"Would you like some tea, Obāsan?"

The little lady smiled warmly back at her. "That would be nice, Keiko-san."

Benko handed Keiko a small bundle. Keiko looked at her questioningly as she slowly unwrapped it.

"Some material I do not need. Perhaps you can make use of it."

Keiko's eyes filled with tears and she hugged the woman unabashedly. Benko would know that there was no privacy to be had at the bathhouses nor at the latrines. Keiko had already suffered once from embarrassment as she realized that she would have to use the bathroom with no doors on the stalls. She had been pondering what to do when she noticed some of the women had taken either paper or swatches of material to put up when they used either. Since she had neither, she had merely been thankful for the cover of darkness to hide her humiliation.

Shoji came home looking tired and grim. He told her that although there was a menu for each meal and that a truck delivered food for each meal, there was never enough and rarely what was on the menu.

"I watched the cook try to carve six hundred sixty pieces from one side of bacon."

Keiko could see that he was deep in thought. He left moments later, returning after about an hour without telling her where he had been.

★ ★ ★

Their days became routine after that. Shoji would be paid twelve dollars a month for helping at the mess hall, but what good was money if you had no way to spend it?

Keiko later learned that things could be ordered from Sears & Roebuck or Montgomery Ward. Using some of their money, she ordered things to make their stall look more like a home. Although some people ordered linoleum and furniture, Shoji could see no sense in that when he knew their quarters were only temporary until the government had permanent locations built.

Still, Keiko ordered things that would give comfort to her father and help alleviate Shoji of some of his worry.

Thankfully, the weather was not too much of a concern. Although it seemed hot as the summer progressed, it was not unbearably so.

July came in with a lightning display that would rival any fireworks. Many of the families had arranged for their children to perform in a Fourth of July parade, so they were thankful that the day dawned warm and bright. How ironic that they could celebrate their freedom from the depths of a concentration camp.

The food situation had resolved itself after many weeks, especially when many people brought food to their friends in the camp.

Shoji's mother had shown up to bring food with her, as well. Keiko hadn't even known Mrs. Ibaragi had been and gone until she found the boxes in her apartment. She had been furious with Shoji for not telling her and allowing her to visit with the older Mrs. Ibaragi. Keiko genuinely liked Shoji's mother.

For his part, Shoji could not tell Keiko that his mother had arranged for freedom for Keiko and himself but had not been able to manage it for Tochigi-san. He knew Keiko would never agree, and since coming here he had watched Keiko's bitterness toward the American government grow.

Sure, she had the right, but it was doing no one any good, least of all Keiko.

★ ★ ★

Toward the end of August, word came that they would soon be moved. No one knew where, and no one knew exactly when.

For three days it rained, and by the time it stopped, Keiko had a cold that left her feeling miserable. She stayed in her cot most of the day. When Shoji came home, he fixed her some canned soup.

Squatting on his haunches beside her cot, he gently brushed the damp hair away from her face. "At least your fever is gone," he told her softly. She tried to smile, but he could see it was just too much effort.

Shoji kissed her lightly on her lips, hoping that when her sickness left, so would her lethargy. She had been so unlike herself the past few weeks he was really beginning to worry.

Sitting on the floor beside her, he pulled his Bible from the table and began to read out loud. After reading a few verses, he turned to find her gently snoring. Smiling, he laid the Bible aside.

When Keiko awoke, the apartment was empty. Her father was once more with the other men, trying to beautify the grounds. That they were somewhat successful was a testament to their grit and determination.

She supposed Shoji was helping. He often did when he wasn't at the mess hall. Getting up, Keiko went to the door, throwing it wide. Sitting on the step, she watched the hustle and bustle around her.

Women were washing their clothes and tending their children. Men were busy working at whatever their hands could find to do. It was no wonder the place had begun to look less like a racetrack and more like a community.

With something of a shock, Keiko realized that she had done nothing toward making this so. For weeks now, she had been busy feeling sorry for herself.

Even Papa-san had made the best of the situation, and he was the one she thought would be least likely to survive the ordeal. His strength came from within and was not dependent on circumstance.

Overcome with guilt, Keiko threw her head back, staring at the vibrant blue sky. "I haven't done very well, have I, Lord?" she asked, her voice rising up into the heavens. "Forgive me, Lord," she whispered. "I'll try to do better. Help me to think less of myself."

Keiko soon realized that the men worked not because it was necessary, but because they wanted to. They wanted to make this place the best that they could for their family and loved ones.

★ ★ ★

Word came that they would soon be uprooted. They had only a few days to prepare, but what was there to prepare?

Many had more to take out than what they had brought in, including Keiko, but somehow things seemed different. There was no longer the fear of what they would have to withstand, but instead a fear of the future.

When it came time to leave, they were loaded on a train just a block from the racetrack. The windows were nailed shut, as were the shutters.

Keiko huddled against her husband, the dusky interior of the train leaving her feeling gloomy and morose. A guard moved purposefully up and down the cars. It was obvious to everyone that they were not considered a threat, or there would have been more military.

The *issei* attitude of *shikata ga nai*, nothing can be done, had nearly driven Keiko crazy at first. Now she realized that it was that very perspective that helped them to survive.

As the train rattled its way along the track, Keiko felt that her teeth would surely be rattled from her head any minute. The old train had obviously seen better days.

Hour after hour passed with little relief from the horrible monotony. Children whined fretfully at their forced inactivity. Keiko leaned back and gave her mind over to its thoughts. Would Obāsan be coming later to wherever it was they were being sent? She had not been sent on this train, so Keiko had no idea.

Shoji curled an arm around her shoulder, pulling her head down to his shoulder. "Why don't you try to get some sleep?"

Keiko hid a grin. He had to be kidding. But when she looked at her father, she found his head drooping to the side, and he was sound asleep.

Deciding to humor her husband, she closed her eyes, but sleep would not come. Instead she let her thoughts roam freely. What would they find at the end of this trip? More importantly, where were they going?

The farther they traveled, the more the heat intensified until the train seemed like a traveling sweatbox. There was a distinguishable difference in the sound of the train moving across the tracks, but Keiko's untutored mind could not tell what it was.

"We're crossing the Colorado," the guard told them, and for the first time they had an inkling of which direction they were headed. East.

Several hours later the train began to slow, then pulled to a stop. As they disembarked, Keiko's eyes hurt from trying to adjust to the intensity of the sun after the dark interior of the train. And the heat. Roiling waves of it seemed to billow all around them. Sweat poured from their bodies, making Keiko long for a cool drink.

"Where are we?" she asked Shoji, and he motioned to an old water tower in the distance. Across its silver surface, Keiko could read the faded black letters: CASA GRANDE, ARIZONA.

Chapter 10

Shoji picked the last of the cotton in the row, then stood stiffly to his feet. Although he was in good physical condition, picking cotton was back-breaking work. How must the older men be feeling if he was stiff and sore?

He stood for a moment, watching the others. For the most part, they moved swiftly and efficiently. Only a few straggled behind. Even the older men worked diligently not far in back of him. It was rare for Shoji not to receive the extra three dollars incentive money for the most cotton picked in a day, not because he particularly needed it, but because his energy drove him relentlessly on.

Shoji wondered how Keiko was managing. His lips curled up at the edges, and his eyes took on a decided glow.

She had certainly surprised him. Somehow she had mysteriously transformed from a shy, quiet girl to a forceful, determined young woman. The change both mystified and delighted him.

When they had arrived, Keiko had immediately jumped in to help turn this barren desert into a remarkable community. Although many buildings had not been completed when they arrived, and still weren't for that matter, Keiko and Papa-san had tried to rally their block in the relocation center into a living, thriving community.

Already, many noticeable changes had been accomplished in the short time they had been here. Two long months. He glared at the sky. *How long, Lord? How much longer?*

In the beginning, he had worked in the mess hall, but when the surrounding farmers had asked for volunteers to pick cotton, he had jumped at the chance. When he was picking cotton, he was on the outside. It was amazing how confining even such a large area as Gila River, or Butte Camp, as others called it, could feel.

Imagine. A concentration camp, and it was still the third largest city in Arizona. Shoji grinned wryly. He would be willing to wager a lot that the good people of Arizona weren't exactly thrilled with the news.

A throbbing drone in the distance brought his eyes swiveling around. His lips set grimly. Often they could see the B-17 bombers practicing in the distance, dropping their bombs of flour on the surrounding fields.

Shoji knew it shouldn't bother him, but it did. Someday those planes would fly over Japan and kill many people, some of them possibly friends whom he'd gone to school with.

He knew Keiko would be appalled at his thoughts. She would consider them un-American. Perhaps they were. He didn't wish America to lose the war; he only wished his friends and his father's family not to, either. That part of him that was Japanese cried for the country of his father's birth—a beautiful land with a mostly gentle race of people.

But he knew also the stubborn dedication of that people. They would not give up their quest easily.

How had this war come about, anyway? He still wasn't sure. All he knew was that the Japanese were suffering, both here and abroad.

When he handed in his pickings, he wasn't surprised to find that he again had earned an extra three dollars. Smiling slightly, he pocketed the money in his jeans, thinking of what Keiko would do with the money.

Since they still had the money he had brought with them when they went to Tulare, they didn't really need much. The government provided food, and that had certainly improved over what they had received at Tulare. Many things were different and better here than they had been there.

Keiko had asked him if they might share the money he earned with others in their block who had larger families and less income. He had been surprised, but he had readily agreed. The warm smile she had given him had made him warm all over. Even now, thinking about it brought a new rush of feeling.

He had been right. Keiko had been easy to love. There was no denying it. He was hopelessly, irrevocably, crazily in love with his wife. He looked forward to returning to her each evening, and although they had army bunks and didn't sleep together, he still felt her presence keenly.

As usual, it was late when he returned. Supper was long past, but Shoji knew Keiko would have something prepared for him. His mother was continually sending them packages of food and items she thought they could use. That, added to the fact that Gila was an agricultural center, made it relatively easy to procure food.

Some of the Japanese even traded with the Pima Indians. He could still remember Keiko's face when a friend had shared his tamales with them. Shoji grinned to himself. He thought for sure Keiko's eyes would pop from her head. Since Shoji was used to the spices of Japan, the tamales had seemed mild to him, but Keiko was not used to such heat. Ever since, whenever their friend shared his tamales, Keiko saved them for Papa-san and himself.

He climbed the porch step to their door and went inside. A happy feeling washed over him at the warm interior. Already, fall was sending its freezing temperatures to the desert at night. The contrast between days and nights was remarkable.

Keiko came from behind the blanket they had put up as a curtain to separate their living quarters from their sleeping quarters. She stopped, surprised to see him.

"I didn't hear you come in."

He dropped his lunch sack on the table he had built from the excess lumber lying around the facility. Although others had taken lumber from the stacks piled up for buildings, he had limited himself to the scraps he found.

It had taken time, but eventually he had managed to build a table, three chairs, a cupboard each for Papa-san and he and Keiko's clothes, shelves for the walls, and a storage cabinet. His furniture was not nearly as elaborate as some had made, but it was well built and sturdy.

Keiko went to the little oil stove the army had provided and lifted a pot from its surface. She dished the stew onto a plate, and Shoji's mouth watered appreciatively.

"Smells good."

Keiko grinned. "I'm afraid it's just fish stew. Little Ishimi caught some catfish in the canal." She lowered her voice to a whisper. "Don't tell anyone."

Shoji frowned. "He could get in big trouble if he's caught."

Shrugging, Keiko laid the bowl in front of him. "They're not as strict with the security around here as they used to be. I think most people realize that the Japanese are no threat to them."

After washing his hands in the washbowl Keiko provided, Shoji sat down at the table and began to hungrily devour the food. It had been a long time since lunch.

"Where's Papa-san?"

Keiko handed him a bowl of rice and some bread. "He went to a block manager's meeting. He may be late."

Shoji stopped chewing, his brows coming together. "Not later than ten?"

Keiko placed her fists on her hips. "You know Papa-san wouldn't miss curfew. What's bothering you?"

Shoji resumed eating. How could he answer such a question? How could he tell her that every time he saw the B-17s practicing their bombing runs he felt unsettled?

"It's nothing," he finally told her. "I just worry; that's all."

Keiko slid into the chair opposite him, eager to share her day. This was Shoji's favorite time of the evening. He loved listening to her tales of the people and the situations they could get themselves into.

"So what else did little Ishimi get himself into today?"

Wrinkling her nose, Keiko proceeded to tell him how the little boy had thought perhaps Keiko would like to have a lizard for a pet. Shoji grinned.

"And how did you get yourself out of that one?"

"I told him the poor thing would probably miss his mama so much he would just up and die."

Shoji's grin turned to laughter. "Leave it to you."

Keiko watched her husband and felt a spiral of warmth work its way throughout her body. She loved Shoji's laugh. When he laughed, he forgot to be inscrutable, and his mahogany eyes grew bright with his feelings.

She was so intent on her thoughts she didn't realize that Shoji had asked her a question. Color flooded her cheeks.

"What did you say?"

An eyebrow winged its way upward, and a small smile tilted the corner of his lips. "It's not important."

Coming around the table, Shoji lifted Keiko to her feet and into his arms. He grinned down at her surprised face before settling his lips across hers in a soft kiss.

Keiko was so surprised that for a moment she hung limp in his arms. Surprise gave way to desire, and Keiko found herself kissing Shoji back in a way they hadn't shared for a long time.

When Shoji felt Keiko's response, his lips became more demanding. Sliding his hands across Keiko's back, he found himself wanting to pull her closer and even closer still. He couldn't seem to get enough of her.

Just when reason was about to leave him, Shoji heard a sound at their door. Pulling back, he set Keiko away from him and returned to his seat at the table.

Keiko sank gratefully into her own chair, her legs like noodles beneath her. The pupils of her eyes were still dilated with desire, and it took her a moment to compose herself.

Papa-san came in the door, his eyes going from one to the other.

"How did you do in the fields today, Shoji-san?"

Shoji looked up in surprise as if he had almost forgotten. Pulling the money from his pockets, he threw it on the table.

Keiko looked at the three dollars and shook her head. "You had the most again today?"

"Hai." Shoji nodded to the money. "It's yours. Do with it what you wish."

Her warm eyes sought his. "Is there nothing you need?"

His intense look brought color flooding to her cheeks. "Nothing that money can buy."

Papa-san coughed softly. "If you will excuse me, I think I will go to bed now."

"It's only six o'clock, Papa-san," Keiko admonished him. "You can't possibly be tired."

"I am, actually," he told her, and for the first time Keiko noticed the tired lines fanning out from his eyes. There were times when she forgot that he was still recovering from a heart attack.

Noticing her distress, Tochigi-san waved a hand airily in her direction. "Now do not start worrying about me. I think I may be catching a cold, that's all."

Keiko said nothing, but she determined to watch her father carefully for the next few days. How she would get him to behave himself was beyond her, but she would manage it somehow.

When they were all in bed that night, Keiko was painfully aware of the distance that separated her from her husband. Only a few feet, but it may as well have been miles. What would have happened if her father had not arrived when he did?

Shoji had told her he didn't want to take the chance of conceiving a child in a concentration camp. Had he perhaps changed his mind? Her heart raced faster at the prospect. One was never sure where Shoji was concerned.

The next day the linoleum arrived. Keiko was thrilled. Already many of her neighbors had procured the flooring, but she had waited, choosing to spend her money on other things.

Since the camp had been built with mostly green pine, as it dried, huge cracks formed between the slats, leaving gaping holes that just begged the dust to come in. It wouldn't have been so bad if it hadn't been for the dust storms.

Dust blew in from every direction, getting in everything and everywhere. The linoleum helped some, but when the wind blew, nothing stopped the sand in its relentless march.

Keiko moved the furniture and unrolled the flooring. It gave her immense satisfaction when she was finished. Slapping her hands together, she smiled widely.

"There. Now let's see the dust come up through the cracks."

One thing she was heartily thankful for was the fact that the weather had finally cooled off and the thunderstorms from the summer monsoon had subsided. If the heat didn't kill you, the humidity would. Now temperatures continued to drop, and the air was long past dry.

At night the temperatures dropped so low that water would freeze in the buckets. Fortunately, they had an oil stove to keep them warm.

A letter arrived from Sumiko, and Keiko eagerly tore it open.

November 11, 1942

Dear Kay,

How's the weather out there? Is there anything worse than a desert? Boy, how I miss the green fields of California.

The food here is awful, the living conditions primitive, and the facilities inadequate. Other than that, things are great.

Did you hear about John Parker? He was drafted and sent to Europe somewhere. France, I think. His dad tried everything he could to get him out of it, but I guess he didn't have enough clout.

Now for the good news. You're going to be an aunt. Isn't that wonderful? Ken is so excited.

Imagine. Me, a mother, I can hardly wait. I know you'll tell Papa-san for us. Let me know what he says.

I guess I'd better go for now. I have to get ready for school. I'm help-ing to teach second grade. The kids are great but mischievous. They don't like Mrs. Carson, who is the main teacher. I don't know why. She's a nice enough lady. I think maybe it's because she's white.

Give that hunk of Japanese manhood a big kiss for me, and Papa-san, too.

Love ya,
Sue

When Keiko finished the letter, there were tears in her eyes. Oh, how she missed Sumiko and Kenji. Papa-san would be thrilled, she knew, but what would Shoji have to say? If Kenji was excited about the baby, would that per-haps make Shoji reconsider his position? If there was one thing Keiko wanted more than anything, it was Shoji's baby.

She wasn't sure how it had come about, or when, but she knew now with-out a doubt that she loved her husband.

She found out later that evening what his reaction would be. If anything, Shoji's eyes became once again enigmatic, and he seemed to draw even fur-ther away from her.

Papa-san, on the other hand, was ecstatic. He couldn't wait to share the news with his friends that he was about to become an *ojiisan*. His pride knew no bounds, but the looks he threw at Keiko and Shoji were speculative, to say the least.

The weather grew progressively cooler until temperatures were cold both day and night. Keiko used the four-dollar allowance she received for each of them to order winter clothes from the Sears catalog.

A box arrived from Shoji's mother, only Mrs. Ibaragi brought it herself. Shoji stared in surprise at his mother waiting in the administration office.

"What are you doing here?"

She looked around, before arching an eyebrow. "Is there somewhere we can go to talk?"

Picking up the box, Shoji led the way along the barracks until they reached Barracks Forty. The door to apartment C was closed firmly against the cold temperatures. Leading his mother inside, Shoji watched as she studied her sur-roundings. When she turned to him, there were tears in her eyes.

"How can you stand it?"

His lips pressed tightly together. Setting the box on the floor, he straight-ened and went to the stove to light it.

"What are you doing here, Mother?"

Without being asked, Mrs. Ibaragi pulled out one of the seats from the table. Lowering herself against the sunny yellow seat cushion that Keiko had made, she settled her purse on the table.

"I want to get you out of here. You and Keiko." Seeing the look in her son's eyes, she rushed on. "I know Keiko doesn't want to leave her father, and I still haven't managed to arrange for his leave. But if we can make Keiko understand her chances of getting her father out will be better if she is on the outside. . ."

The anger in Shoji's eyes communicated itself to his mother. "None of this makes any sense," he told her. "Did you know that here in Arizona many Japanese were never sent to camps? They're still free. While others. . .others lose everything. It just doesn't make sense."

"I know. In Hawaii, where there are more Japanese than anywhere else, and where they would have the most cause for such actions, most of the Japanese haven't been relocated."

Shoji brushed a hand in agitation through his hair. "It has to be because of the land in California." He gritted his teeth. "Did you do as I asked about the farm?"

She got to her feet. "Yes, I purchased the farm for you. Does Keiko know?"

He turned on her. "No, and I don't want her to. If Keiko learns to love me, I want it to be without obligations."

Mrs. Ibaragi pl..ced a hand on her son's arm. "And what about leaving here? Your grandfather pulled a lot of strings to get you and Keiko set free."

Shoji looked less than pleased. "Tell him thanks, but no thanks. Keiko and I will stay here."

"Shoji. . . ," she implored, using the name he preferred.

"Forget it, Mother," he snapped. "If Papa-san cannot go, then neither do we."

Sighing, she pressed her lips tightly together. "You're as stubborn as your father."

He opened his mouth to answer her, but the door opened and Keiko came in. Her eyes lit up when she saw Mrs. Ibaragi.

"Mrs. Ibaragi! What are you doing here?"

Receiving a speaking look from her son, Mrs. Ibaragi went and took Keiko in her arms.

"I came to see if everything is all right with you two."

Keiko smiled softly. "We are well, as you can see." Keiko's eyes went to her husband. "You are not in the fields today?"

He shook his head. "No. There is no more cotton to be picked. I will be starting to work at the model factory tomorrow."

"Model factory?" Shoji's mother retreated to her previous chair, while Keiko set about fixing them some tea.

Keiko nodded. *"Hai.* They make models of ships and planes that the military use in their operations."

Mrs. Ibaragi turned to her son. "You should like that. You've always like working with wood.

"Maybe." Shoji's noncommittal answer hid the real reason for his reluctance. True, he knew he would enjoy the work, but those models represented ships and planes that might very well hold a friend. Of course, the same could be said of the American models. Sighing, he turned away. Whichever way this war went, someone he loved would suffer.

Shoji's mother left but not before arguing again with her son. He walked her back to the administration building where her rented car was parked. Kissing her, he closed the door firmly behind her, not sure that he was doing the right thing for Keiko.

★ ★ ★

Shoji's mother showed up again for Thanksgiving. Having received a permit to do so, she took Keiko, Shoji, and Papa-san to Phoenix to have dinner in one of the hotels.

For Keiko the experience was bittersweet. It had been so long since she had had turkey, she almost forgot what it tasted like. The bitter came in knowing that no matter what the atmosphere in the restaurant, they had to return to Camp Butte.

They could just as easily walk out the door and never return, but what would that accomplish? Only when this crazy war ended would life make any sense again. Maybe not then. Who knew what would happen to them after the war?

Mrs. Ibaragi told them that she wouldn't be able to come for Christmas, but she sent them all Christmas presents anyway.

★ ★ ★

Keiko was wearing her new dress when Shoji came in from outside. His eyes swept over her in a brief appraisal before his lashes swept down to hide his eyes.

Keiko knew that the pink chiffon was becoming. She was irritated that Shoji said nothing.

"We got a card from Kenji and Sumiko," she told him.

"How are they doing?"

Keiko began to set the table with the new dishes Mrs. Ibaragi had sent.

"Sumiko said it's really cold there in Utah. She said the government provided stoves, but they didn't install them. They are sitting outside beside the door, but no one is supposed to install them. They're supposed to wait for the government engineers to do it."

Shoji snorted. "That could very well be after the war ends. What are they doing for heat?"

"Sumiko said that Kenji installed it anyway. It seems they have a harder time getting food than we do too."

Shoji took the plates from her hands and set them on the table. He took her hands into his own, kissing each one softly. Keiko felt her heart drop to her feet.

"Don't worry, Keiko-chan. They'll be okay," he told her softly. "There's nothing you can do. They can order things, just like we can. They get money just like we do. They'll be okay."

Sucking in her breath, she nodded her head. "I suppose you're right. But I think I'll do some heavy praying nonetheless."

"I'll join you," he told her—and did.

January 1943 rolled around, and Keiko tried to celebrate it for her father's sake. They had no bills to pay, and the apartment was only twenty feet by twenty feet, but Keiko cleaned it thoroughly anyway.

She managed to find the fixings for the *ozoni* and *mochi*, but the buckwheat pancakes were beyond her. At least Butte Camp had plenty of agriculture to allow them vegetables. Even *daikon* was grown here to be shipped to all nine of the other relocation camps.

When spring came, it came softly to the desert. Keiko was amazed that a barren land could suddenly be so filled with color. Even the birds returned to the region full of vibrancy and vitality. Keiko envied them for their freedom.

April brought with it shower upon shower. Keiko hadn't seen so much rain since last summer's monsoon. She didn't mind, because it helped the lawns the families had planted between the barracks. Since Gila River was used for farming, there was plenty of water to supply the camp's needs; however, the rain was an added blessing. Except for all the mud that was a result.

Keiko wandered to the mess hall for lunch. Shoji was again in the fields, and Keiko felt the desire for some company. Her father was constantly busy with friends his own age. They were *issei*. They understood each other.

Shaking her head, Keiko grinned wryly. She was glad somebody understood them.

After receiving her food, she looked for an empty place to sit. Amazingly, she found an empty table, but she knew it wouldn't be empty for long.

There was a commotion over by the doors, but Keiko ignored it. She was busy trying to find one of her friends to talk to. Suddenly, someone was standing next to her elbow.

"May I sit here?"

Keiko looked up at the white-haired woman standing next to her, and the many men surrounding her. Her shrewd eyes studied Keiko thoughtfully.

Rising quickly to her feet, Keiko almost spilled her plate.

"Mrs. Roosevelt."

The woman smiled slightly. "That I am. May I sit with you?"

Flustered, Keiko looked from her to her companions and back again. "Of course. Please. Have a seat."

Mrs. Roosevelt sat down across from Keiko, ignoring her traveling companions. Her bright eyes appraised Keiko slowly.

"Have you been here long?" she wanted to know.

"Long enough," Keiko answered her stiffly.

The woman wasn't the least embarrassed. Nodding her head, she began to eat.

"These are sad times for our country."

Keiko snorted. "For some more than others."

Mrs. Roosevelt's birdlike eyes twinkled back at her. "You surely have reason to be bitter. I know that I would."

"Would you?"

The old woman's eyes flashed at the question. "There are many things in this life that aren't fair. Life is not fair. But life is what you make it. It can defeat you, or you can defeat it."

Realizing that she had offended the president's wife, Keiko dropped her eyes. When she looked back up, she had her feelings under control.

"Mrs. Roosevelt, God is in control of this world. Mr. Hirohito may think he is. Mr. Hitler may think that he is. Mr. Roosevelt may think that he is. But they aren't. You're right, Mrs. Roosevelt. Life is not fair. Only God is."

Rising swiftly to her feet, Keiko left the woman sitting with her mouth slightly open.

Chapter 11

For the next several days, Keiko continually berated herself for losing her temper with the president's wife. What had she accomplished by her actions? Nothing! If only she had held her bitterness and temper in check, she might have been able to better help those from Gila River who needed it.

Dropping her knitting on the table, she got to her feet and began to pace. Everything was so unsettled, not the least of which was her relationship with her husband. At times she felt as though she were on a whirling merry-go-round.

Going back to the table, she reached for the baby blanket she was knitting for Sumiko. Her fingers trailed gently across the soft material, her eyes taking on a faraway look.

How long could this war go on? She hoped not much longer, because she longed with every fiber of her being to begin a family. But as for now, Shoji wouldn't hear of it.

She had to get out of here for awhile. The very walls seemed to be closing in on her. Leaving a note for her father, she hastened outside and headed in the direction of Barracks Fifty-nine.

Benko Kosugi had arrived shortly after Keiko, and although she lived a considerable distance away, Keiko and the old woman spent much time together.

When Keiko knocked on the door of apartment 6B, the door was flung open by a young girl. Keiko recognized Obāsan's granddaughter and smiled.

"Hello, Mayumi. Is Obāsan here?"

The girl's eyes brightened. "Hi, Keiko. Sure, come on in." Turning, Mayumi yelled over her shoulder. "Obāsan! Keiko's here."

Benko came from the rear, tut-tutting at her granddaughter. "Such manners, Mayumi."

The girl's eyes met Keiko's. Rolling them, she shrugged her shoulders, passing Keiko on her way out.

When Keiko was sitting across from Benko with a cup of tea in front of her, she didn't really know what to say. What had brought her here in such a hurry anyway?

"So, Keiko-san. How is Shoji-san?"

"Fine, Obāsan," she answered the old woman absently.

"And your father?"

Perhaps that was the crux of the matter. For days now, her father had been listless. Pale. Keiko's eyes probed Obāsan's.

"Your son is a doctor."

Benko nodded, her wise eyes flittering across Keiko's face. "You wish him to look at Tochigi-san?"

Keiko blew air from her lips, causing the bangs on her forehead to stir. "I don't think Papa-san would allow it."

Obāsan leaned back, understanding filling her expression. "Ah. You wish him do it without your father's knowledge."

Tracing a pattern on the tablecloth with her fingers, Keiko couldn't meet Obāsan's eyes. She knew that being *issei* herself she would think it untoward that the daughter should try to rule the father.

Benko reached a hand across the table, folding Keiko's fingers into her own. "I will ask him, Keiko-san. We see what we can do."

Relieved, Keiko got to her feet. *"Arigato,* Obāsan. *Arigato."*

Keiko left the old woman standing on her little porch. She had as much love for Benko as if she were her real grandmother.

Stopping by the post office, Keiko found another letter from Sumiko. Her eyes sparkled as she hurried home to read it. Only this time, the mood of the letter was much more somber.

May 7, 1943

Dear Kay,

I am pleased that Papa-san was so happy with our news. Now I have some bad news to share with you.

Ken has decided to join the army and go overseas. I was angry at first. Why should he fight for a country that would deny its people their due process of law and force them to be interned in such awful conditions?

But Ken explained to me that even when your government does something stupid, you don't stop loving your country. If that were the case, no one would ever serve their country, because the government is always making stupid mistakes.

I didn't want him to go, especially now with the baby coming, but I understand his need to give something back to the country that has given us so much.

Look out, Hirohito! My Kenji is coming.

Look out, Mr. Hitler, the Americans are coming to pay you a visit.

Take care of yourself. We love you.
Sue and Ken

P.S. Do you have any news for me yet? Hmmm?

351

Keiko crushed the letter in her hand, her face as white as the proverbial sheet. *Not Kenji! Dear God, not Kenji!*

★ ★ ★

When Shoji arrived home that night, he found his wife distraught and distant. There were traces of tears on her cheeks. Frowning, he tried to take her in his arms, but she pulled away from him.

"Keiko, what's wrong?"

She threw a piece of paper at him. "Here. Read this."

He watched her piddle about the apartment, straightening things that didn't need to be straightened, cleaning a table that was already clean.

Sumiko's letters were always short, but they always packed a wallop. Grimacing, he dropped the crumpled sheet on the storage cabinet. He didn't say anything. What was there to say? He admired Kenji his noble sentiments and was proud of his courage, but there was nothing he could do, nothing he would want to do. Except perhaps comfort Keiko.

Why had she pushed him away? What thoughts were going through her head now? Every time he thought he was making headway with her, something happened to set them back in their relationship.

★ ★ ★

When they went to the mess hall that evening, the atmosphere in the building was tense. Keiko noticed many glances thrown their way. Papa-san seemed to see nothing amiss, enjoying his meal with a relish he hadn't shown in a long time.

A young man came to their table, bowing slightly from the waist. "Tochigi-san. We have received word from Mr. Dillon Myer, the director of the War Relocation Authority, that some evacuees are to be sent to Tule Lake in California. Is this true?"

At the mention of what was considered the Japanese correctional facility, Papa-san's face became more inscrutable than Keiko had ever seen Shoji's. His eyes darkened in anger.

"Am I not to be allowed to eat my meal in peace? Must you take this opportunity to question me on such matters?"

The young man flushed scarlet. "I am sorry, but you are the block manager."

Tochigi-san fixed him with a steely eye. "Then be at the block meeting tonight. We will discuss it then."

Looking from Keiko to Shoji and back to Papa-san, the young man nodded his head and turned to go. When Papa-san glanced up, he caught Shoji's eye. A message flashed between them, and Keiko felt a little thrill of fear.

"What's going on?" she demanded.

Her father continued to eat his meal. "Eat your food, Keiko, before it gets cold."

She turned to her husband. "Shoji?"

He looked down at his own plate. "Nothing you need to worry about."

Angry, Keiko rose slowly to her feet. She dumped the contents of her plate onto Shoji's. "When will you ever start to treat me as something other than a child?" She glared at his bent head. "Fine. Enjoy your meal. But I will be at that block meeting tonight also."

Shoji watched her walk away with a great deal of irritation. Why couldn't Keiko trust him to do what was best for both of them? For all of them?

His eyes came back to Papa-san's, and he saw the sympathy there. "She never has liked to be managed."

"I wonder where she gets that from?"

Papa-san cackled gleefully, and Shoji grinned as he rose to his feet.

"I have no doubt that you can control her," Papa-san told him.

The smile left Shoji's face. "I don't want to control her. I want a partner in my marriage, not a slave."

The gray eyebrows lifted upward, and Shoji felt himself color hotly. If what he said was true, then why hadn't he talked with Keiko when she had wanted him to? Seeking to right the wrong he had just committed, Shoji bowed and quickly left his father-in-law.

He found Keiko getting ready to go out the door of their apartment.

"I want to talk to you," he told her softly.

She fixed him with a scathing look. "I don't have time. I promised Obāsan I would stop by and see her, so I need to go now to be back in time for the block meeting."

"You're not going to any block meeting," he told her, but for once his words had no effect whatsoever on Keiko. She tried to push past him, but he gripped her arm in a hold that was gentle, but nonetheless unyielding.

"I want to talk to you," he repeated.

She looked from his hand holding her arm back to his face. Her look was eloquent.

Letting go of her arm, Shoji pulled out a chair at the table for her. She settled herself against it, her eyes going to Shoji's face.

"You already know that the government came to our camp in February and March to offer us enlistment in the army."

She nodded.

"Well, many of the young men refused to sign up. There was a form that needed to be filled out. Question twenty-seven asked if we would be willing to serve in the army, and question twenty-eight asked if we would renounce all loyalty to Japan and swear allegiance to the United States of America."

He glanced at her to see if she was following him so far. Her intelligent brown eyes stared back at him.

"And what did you say?"

Here it came; he just knew it. The explosion to end all explosions. "I answered no to the first, and yes to the second."

Keiko swallowed hard. "And just exactly what does that mean?"

"We have been separated into groups. The yes-yes, no-no, and yes-no."

"You mean some actually refused to swear allegiance to America?"

"*Hai.* Mainly the *kibei* and *issei.* But others who are loyal to America still refuse to serve in her armed services. They want no part of a country that would treat them like criminals just because of their race."

"Like Sumiko."

Nodding, Shoji took her hand, hoping he could make her understand. "Keiko, I refused to serve in the armed services not because of loyalty to Japan, but because I cannot bear the thought that I might be responsible for the death of a friend or loved one. I have many friends and family in Japan. Can you understand?"

She studied him for a long time, and he felt his mouth go dry. Sliding her hand from beneath his, she rose to her feet, looking down at him.

"I understand," she told him softly. "It must be hard for you. But let me ask you something, Shoji. What happens if the Japanese win this war? What then?"

She went quickly from the room and didn't look back. For the first time, Shoji actually considered what the United States losing this war would mean. The thought was a chilling one.

★ ★ ★

Keiko walked across the roads that connected the barracks, oblivious to where she was going. The air around her grew warmer, and perspiration began to run in rivulets down her back.

When the wind started to blow slightly, she was thankful for the breeze. Lifting her long dark hair from her shoulders, she balled it into a bun on top of her head, twisting it so that it would stay.

She should be thankful that Shoji wasn't going to be sent to Europe. Thankful that he wouldn't be killed on a foreign battlefield, fighting an enemy he considered no enemy at all.

Her path took her away from the barracks and toward the front gate. Guard towers stood sentry, but the soldier on duty was not concerned with her. His eyes were focused across the barren desert toward the mountains in the distance.

Following his gaze, Keiko could see a brown column of dust rising into the air for as far as the eye could see. Her heart dropped. A dust storm. They came suddenly, attacked fiercely, and receded just as quickly. From its rapid advancement, she could tell she probably wouldn't have time to make it back to their apartment.

Glancing quickly around, she tried to decide her best course of action. Already the wind was picking up, and the air was starting to cool.

If the storm was followed by rain, flash floods would more than likely occur in the vicinity. She stared harder, but she couldn't tell if this storm had rain behind it.

Before she could decide, Keiko saw little Ishimi struggling against the wind, which was growing stronger by the minute. She hurried to his side, kneeling beside him.

"Ishimi, what are you doing so far from home?"

Relief flashed momentarily in his eyes. He held one arm up, and Keiko could see the string of catfish the boy had caught in the canal.

"We have to get you home." Already Keiko had to yell to be heard above the wind. They were still a long way from the nearest barracks, and the first traces of sand were stinging against their skin.

"Hurry, Ishimi."

Taking the boy by the hand, Keiko tried to hasten them in the general direction of where she knew the barracks to be. If only they could get to the barracks, someone would give them shelter.

In moments vision was impossible. Sand swirled angrily about them, refusing to allow them to turn in any direction. Keiko couldn't tell which direction was which. She clung to Ishimi, afraid that she would lose him.

The wind was so strong, pieces of debris scuttled across the compound around them. Fearing for their safety, Keiko pulled the little boy closer, trying to protect him as much as possible.

Ishimi clung to her legs. "I can't see!" He hollered, rubbing his eyes with the backs of his fist.

"I know," Keiko yelled back. "Hang on to me tight, Ishimi. Don't let go, whatever you do."

Fighting her way against the wind, Keiko pushed forward, hoping she was going in the right direction. She would hate to find herself out in the middle of the desert when this was all over.

What seemed like hours later, she bumped into a structure, hugging it in her relief. Shuffling her hands along its surface, Keiko soon found herself in front of the administration building. She struggled with the door, but it was already locked.

Of course. It was after five o'clock. The warehouse buildings next door would be closed too. Trying not to panic, Keiko stopped, willing herself to remain calm.

For a moment the storm seemed to abate, and in that moment Keiko thought she heard her name being called. Lifting her head, she listened harder. She could faintly hear a voice being blown away from her in the distance.

"Here! We're over here!" she screamed back. Could they hear her? What was more, could anyone ever hope to find them in this chaos?

What seemed like an eternity later, a body appeared at her side. Strong arms wrapped securely around her, and Keiko sagged with relief.

"Shoji! Thank God you found us."

"Us?"

Keiko pulled Ishimi into the safety of their embrace. Without warning, the sand stopped blowing only to be followed a moment later by a torrent of water, drenching them within seconds.

"There's no time to get to a barracks. Get down."

Shoving both Keiko and Ishimi toward the ground, Shoji tried to get them as far under the building as possible. Flashes of lightning lit up the sky, followed by resounding booms of thunder.

Since the buildings were built somewhat on supports, there was a small space to crawl beneath. Ishimi fit his body almost entirely under the building, whereas Keiko and Shoji could only get halfway.

Shoji tried to shield Keiko's and Ishimi's bodies as much as possible from the elements. Previous encounters with dust storms convinced him that hail wasn't far behind.

Half-inch balls of ice began to pelt the ground around them. Shoji grimaced as they hit his back like little shots of fire. Keiko gasped when a pellet found tender skin.

Before long the hail stopped, but the rain continued. Water was rapidly filling the areas beneath the buildings.

"Ishimi, come out."

The boy hurried to obey. Keiko couldn't tell if there were tears mixed with the water on his face. Funny, he didn't seem frightened. And although she had been terrified in the beginning, now that Shoji was here she felt safe once again. Foolish perhaps, since they were standing in the middle of an Arizona thunderstorm.

Bolts of lightning continued to light up the darkening landscape. It amazed Keiko that it had grown so dark so quickly.

Shoji took her by the hand, grabbing Ishimi with his other. "We have to hurry."

Keiko tried to keep up with Shoji's long footsteps. For every one of his, she had to take three. What must it be like for little Ishimi? Shoji finally seemed to realize the situation. He hoisted the boy into his arms and continued striding along.

Before long they reached Barracks Fifty-four. Keiko didn't think she knew anyone here, but she knew they would be taken in.

The first door he knocked on brought a response for Shoji. The elderly man who answered his knock stared in surprise before quickly ushering them inside.

His wife hovered around them, her hands flailing helplessly about her. She reminded Keiko of a little hen, her clucking somehow soothing. Ishimi clung to Keiko's wet skirt, his almond eyes wide with the uncertainty of the situation.

They declined the couple's offer of dry clothes, knowing that the storm was already beginning to subside. The rumbles of thunder became farther and farther apart until they were an echo in the distance.

Thanking the couple for their hospitality, Shoji picked the now-exhausted Ishimi up in his arms. He followed Keiko to the barracks where he knew the little boy's mother would be frantic with worry.

"Did your mother know where you were going?" he asked Ishimi.

When the boy ducked his head without answering, Shoji had his answer.

"You should never leave without telling your mother where you are going. Never! Do you hear me?"

Ishimi's small voice returned to him from the depths of his shirtfront. "Yes, Shoji. I won't do it again."

"You better not, because if I find out you do, I will personally spank your backside."

Even in the dark Keiko could read his look. He meant the same for her, and she had no doubt that he would do just that. It had been childish of her to go so far in her fit of pique.

Ishimi's small voice brought Shoji's head closer to the little boy. "I lost my fish," he sniffed.

Keiko caught her breath at the tender look Shoji bestowed on the small child. His eyes were filled with a warmth she had rarely seen. He would make such a wonderful father.

"We will get you some more. You and I together. *Hai?*"

Eyes sparkling with delight, Ishimi nodded his head.

Moments later, Shoji handed Ishimi over to his grateful mother. Her worried tears brought forth a response from her now-repentant son. Keiko was fairly certain the boy would never wander off by himself again.

When they got back to their own apartment, they had to slush their way through the mud to their small porch. Keiko was thankful that Shoji had built the small structure now. At least they could remove their shoes before going into their apartment.

They both stripped their sodden clothes from their bodies. Standing in her slip, Keiko was shivering from reaction and cold. How could it be 110 degrees one minute and nearly freezing the next? California was nothing like this.

When Keiko turned to pick up her dry shirt, she found Shoji watching her. Butterflies started tumbling about in her stomach, and she couldn't take her eyes from his.

When he walked across the small space and took her shirt from her lifeless fingers, Keiko did nothing to protest. He wrapped his arms about her, pulling her into his warm embrace. Sliding her hands up his bare arms, she willed him to continue.

His eyes darkened in response, and Keiko knew with a certainty that the time of her waiting had come to an end. Inevitably, his lips found hers, and Keiko sighed with pleasure. She gave herself up willingly to the fiery pleasure surrounding her.

The heat from their passion soon had Keiko warm all over. For the time being, she could forget Shoji's still sodden jeans that pressed against her. Nothing mattered to her at this moment except the pleasure she felt in her husband's embrace. She had missed their shared passion, for it was at these times that she felt most loved.

When she heard a soft pounding, it seemed to come from far away. At first, she thought it must be the thundering of Shoji's heart so close to her face. When Shoji pulled reluctantly away from her, she realized it was not.

"The door," he told her wryly, and Keiko became aware that the sound she had heard was someone's thunderous knocking against their apartment door.

Keiko watched Shoji disappear around the blanket and heard him open the door. An agitated voice drifted clearly back to her from the opening.

"Shoji-san, you come! Tochigi-san, he in hospital. Heart. Not good. Not good. You come."

Chapter 12

Benko set a cup of tea in front of Keiko, but Keiko wasn't aware of it. Papa-san was gone. Dead. Her mind refused to acknowledge the fact. What would she ever do without Papa-san?

Throwing her head on her arms, Keiko let the grief wash over her in waves. She hadn't felt such agony since her mother had passed from this life.

The tears refused to come. It was as though she were made of ice, as though every part of her were frozen and would never thaw again.

She ached to have Shoji take her in his arms and soothe away the pain. She wanted him to be with her, but she knew he was making arrangements for the burial of her father.

Time passed slowly. Nighttime turned to dawn, then into a full-fledged day. Still Shoji didn't come.

At one point in time Keiko slept. When she awakened, she was more tired than if she had not slept at all. Her dreams had been sweet; she knew that, but she couldn't remember them.

"Keiko-san," Benko pled, "please lay down on the cot. You can use mine."

Keiko lifted sorrow-filled eyes and stared at her blankly. The effort to move proved to be too much for Keiko. Shaking her head, she lay it back down on her crossed arms.

"I'm okay, Obāsan. I will be fine."

Benko frowned at the lifeless voice, but she kept her own counsel. What Keiko needed most right now was the healing hand of time.

★ ★ ★

It was after two o'clock in the afternoon before Shoji knocked on the door. When Benko let him in, his eyebrows rose in question.

Benko shook her head, motioning to Keiko's form bent over the table. Shoji went to her, his hands gently massaging her shoulders.

"Keiko, it is time to go home now."

Her tired voice drifted back over her shoulder. "Someone needs to tell Kenji."

Shoji's eyes found Benko's. A look of understanding passed between them.

"I will come stay with her tomorrow," Benko told Shoji softly, and he nodded in agreement.

Shoji bent to his haunches beside Keiko. "I have already sent word to Kenji."

Keiko turned lackluster eyes to his face. "Thank you."

Shoji studied her weary face a moment before rising to his feet. Reaching down, he lifted Keiko into his arms. Instead of protesting, she hung limply against his chest, burrowing her head in his shoulder. Benko held the door open for him, patting his shoulder sympathetically as he passed her.

When they reached the apartment, Shoji placed Keiko on one of the cots, pulling a sheet over her even though it was past a hundred degrees. He had felt her shivering against him and knew she was suffering from shock.

Keiko lay quietly, while Shoji moved about the apartment doing things that needed to be done. He worried that her mind refused to focus on anything except Papa-san.

Although Tochigi-san had continued to have Keiko read from her mother's Bible in the evenings, and although he often attended the Christian church here in camp, still he had never made it known to her whether he accepted Christ as his Savior. Now, it was too late. Shoji knew that she suffered from the guilt of not knowing. . .not making sure.

Keiko slept so soundly that she didn't stir at Benko arriving and Shoji leaving. Nor did she waken when Shoji returned two hours later. It was as though she were sleeping the sleep of the dead.

Shoji fixed a can of soup and sat eating it alone, watching and worrying about his wife. He was even more worried about what would happen when she found out that Kenji had gone to France and was now missing in action.

Sighing, he leaned his tired face into his palms. Where was it all going to end? Keiko was already on the verge of snapping. What would happen if she lost Kenji too?

Pushing his half-empty bowl aside, Shoji went and hunkered down next to Keiko's cot. He brushed the tendrils of damp hair from her cheeks, placing his lips where his fingers had been.

She looked so angelic laying there. Dark lashes fanned across light brown skin that had deepened in color due to the Arizona sun. Her lips worked softly in her sleep, almost like a baby's.

His own eyes darkened with tenderness. He would be less than alive if anything happened to her, and he knew it. She had woven her way into his heart so tightly that it would be impossible to remove her. Did she feel the same about him? She responded to his kisses in a most gratifying manner, but that was not love. Or was it? Surely a girl like Keiko would not share such passion with a man she had no feelings for.

Kissing her again, he returned to his now-cold lunch. Closing his eyes, he began to pray.

★ ★ ★

For the next two days, Shoji watched Keiko move as though in a dream. She had understood that they would be unable to attend her father's funeral because

Shoji had arranged for the body to be sent back to California to be laid to rest next to her mother. It angered her that she couldn't go, but she said she was thankful that her father wouldn't be buried in the pauper's cemetery in Phoenix.

Shoji saw Keiko's responses improve but still worried. So at last he told her about his purchase of her father's farm. He could not bear to see her without hope for the future, even if it meant he would never know if she would love him without obligation.

When Keiko questioned Shoji about his keeping the information from her, he gave her a noncommittal answer.

That day, Shoji's mother arrived again. He was grateful for her compassion and sympathy for Keiko, and he was relieved to find Keiko sobbing into his mother's arms after two days of stoically enduring her grief. But he ached to be the one to comfort her. Ever at a loss before tears, Shoji left the apartment and wandered through the camp.

Already many barracks were losing people. Some Japanese had been allowed to return to Japan in fulfillment of their desires. Many others had found sponsors and jobs outside the encampments and had moved away—some as far away as New York, Chicago, and parts of Florida. "Repatriation," they called it. Shoji snorted. Imagine repatriating American citizens.

When Shoji returned to the apartment, Keiko and his mother were sitting at the table having the inevitable cup of tea. He pulled a cup from the storage cabinet and poured himself a cup of the brew before turning to his mother.

"How did you get here so quickly, Mother? Fly?"

She nodded her head. "I came as soon as I got your telegram."

Shoji barely heard her. He was studying Keiko's face, sighing with relief when he noticed that some of the color had returned to her features. Although the eyes she turned his way were still filled with pain, they now glowed with fresh life. It had been good for his mother to come. Keiko missed a woman's presence in her life. That was probably why she loved Obāsan so much.

"Sit down, David. I have something to discuss with you."

Shoji frowned at his mother. He would rather not discuss things in front of Keiko right now, not until he was sure she could handle it.

Ignoring his look, Mrs. Ibaragi turned to Keiko. "I told David several months ago that I could get you and him out of this camp. He refused because I couldn't arrange things for your father. Now, however, things are a little different."

Flinching at his mother's lack of couth, Shoji went to stand beside Keiko. His hand rested protectively on her shoulder.

When Mrs. Ibaragi fixed her eyes on her son, they were dark with some unnamed emotion. "David, I can no longer get you out of here."

Shoji sat down in surprise. "Why? If anything, I would think it was easier."

"Not since you answered no to question twenty-seven."

Shoji hadn't realized he was so tense until he felt himself relax. Pressing his lips together, he sighed heavily.

"I see."

"I'm still working on it, but so far I haven't had any luck. Your grandfather is less than pleased."

Shoji leaped to his feet and began pacing the floor. "My grandfather be hanged!"

Both Keiko and Mrs. Ibaragi stared at him in surprise, their mouths hanging open.

Snapping her lips together, Mrs. Ibaragi rose to her feet, fixing her son with a steely glare. "I have arranged to stay with one of the Anglo schoolteachers here. I don't wish to inconvenience you, and I know Keiko doesn't need the added burden right now." She began gathering her things together. "I'll see you sometime tomorrow."

Filled with remorse, Shoji met her at the door. His anger at his grandfather had reflected itself upon his mother for years now. Why had she allowed his father to send him away when they had been such a close family? Knowing his mother, she could have done something to prevent it. But she hadn't. Studying her face, he suddenly realized how old she looked. She was still a beautiful woman, but hidden beneath her carefully applied makeup, time was creeping up on her. "I'm sorry, Mother."

Unexpectedly, she smiled at him. "I know, Son. It's not easy being the grandson of Andrew McConnell. Trust me; I understand. If you think being his grandson is tough, you should try being his daughter."

After she left, Keiko raised questioning eyes to her husband. "Andrew McConnell, of McConnell Aeronautics?"

He rubbed his neck tiredly before turning to her. His eyes were an unfathomable dark brown.

"The same."

Keiko nodded in understanding. "That makes a lot of things clear."

Shoji refused to talk about it, but Keiko continued as though he had encouraged her to.

"I remember hearing about Andrew McConnell's daughter giving up her wealth and going to Japan to be a missionary. Her father disinherited her."

Shoji snorted. "Until he realized he wouldn't have any other children. And it wasn't because she went to Japan to be a missionary that he disowned her. It was because she married a Japanese."

"I'm sorry."

"Why? What do you have to be sorry for? Since I was the only child that would ever be a grandchild of his, he decided to acknowledge his daughter after all. But he never did my father."

"You sound as though you hate him."

Leaning his palms against the storage bureau, Shoji glared up at the ceiling.

"I don't hate him. At least I don't think I do. I just resent his always trying to run my mother's and my life." His face twisted with anger when he turned to her. "I want nothing to do with him. I just want him to leave me alone. That's why I wouldn't accept my mother's offer to get us out of here."

He looked at her apologetically. "And because I knew we couldn't leave Papa-san."

Keiko sighed heavily, rising and taking the cups to the basin of water she kept in the corner.

"What now?" she asked him.

He sat back down in his seat. "I don't know. We'll have to wait and see."

She picked up her knitting from a chair in the corner that his mother had brought with her on one of her earlier visits. The overstuffed armchair seemed to fit right into its new home. Keiko sat down and began to knit furiously. Shoji had no idea if she knew what she was doing, or whether she would have to take everything out and start again.

"What about Kenji?"

Shoji's eyes flew to her down-bent head. Was she suspicious, or had someone already told her that he was missing?

"What about him?"

She looked at him in surprise. "Will he be able to go to Papa-san's funeral?"

Taking a deep breath, Shoji bit his bottom lip. He had to tell her something. "Keiko, Kenji has been sent overseas. France, I think."

She dropped the knitting, her hands visibly shaking. "Then there's no way he could have gotten the message yet."

Shoji avoided her eyes. "Probably not."

"Poor Sumiko."

When she rose from the chair, Shoji followed her with his eyes. "What are you going to do?"

She began pulling paper from the bureau drawer. "I'm going to write Sumiko."

Deciding that it couldn't hurt, Shoji said nothing. By the time Sumiko could answer, he would have told Keiko the truth about Kenji anyway.

That night they lay in separate bunks thinking separate thoughts. Shoji had dealt with his own grief in his own way. He had no idea how to help Keiko. Surely it affected women differently than men. He was unaware of his *kibei* training in such thoughts.

Keiko slept fitfully, her dreams not so pleasant this time. She was trying to find Kenji, only he was surrounded by fire. Every time she thought she would reach him, flames would leap into her way. She knew she was his only hope of survival, but she couldn't get to him.

Whenever she thought she was about to reach him, Shoji would appear, pulling her inexorably away from her brother. His smiling face did nothing to dispel her fears.

Suddenly, the whole scene burst into flames, and Kenji was swallowed up by the conflagration. Screaming, she tried to fight her way to his side, but Shoji held her back. She fought against his iron grip, but she couldn't free herself. She screamed. "Kenji! No!"

A slap across the face brought Keiko fully awake. Tears were streaming down her face, and she stared at her husband uncomprehendingly.

He looked as shaken as she felt. "I'm sorry," he told her apologetically, his voice hoarse with emotion. "I couldn't get you to wake up."

Her glazed look roamed across Shoji's face, and she began to moan. "You wouldn't let me save him!" Rolling her head from side to side, she tried to push Shoji's hands from her shoulder. "You wouldn't let me save Kenji."

A chill raced down Shoji's spine at her words. Had he somehow been responsible for this nightmare? Had Keiko discerned the situation with Kenji even though he had said nothing?

"It's just a dream, Keiko," he crooned. "Just a dream."

Her level gaze held his. "What's happened to Kenji?"

Shoji rose slowly to his feet, his eyes going everywhere but near Keiko. She gripped his arm with her fingers.

"Shoji?"

He fought with himself several minutes before he finally breathed out harshly, focusing his gaze on his wife. She had risen on one elbow, reclining against the bed. He carefully sat down next to her.

Taking her hands in his, he told her what she wanted to know. She took the news calmly, and Shoji felt relief. She didn't say much, laying back against the cot.

"I'm sorry I didn't tell you," he told her softly.

"This time I understand."

They exchanged a long look that left Keiko feeling as though the sun were surely about to rise. Since it was only a little past three in the morning, she had to smile at her own foolish thinking.

"Get some sleep," Shoji commanded quietly.

Nodding, Keiko watched as he went back to his own cot. She turned her look to the window above her bed. The stars were shimmering brightly against the dark Arizona sky. Somewhere, those same stars were shining down on her brother. Closing her eyes, she began to pray. Her last waking thought was of her brother, but she no longer feared for him. Somehow she knew God was watching out for him. She felt the peace of God enter her soul and wash away all her anxieties.

★ ★ ★

Shoji stared at the slip of paper in his hands. A buddy of Kenji's had decided to write to let them know more about Kenji's disappearance.

Shoji felt a thrill of pride that his brother-in-law was a member of the famed 442nd. Entirely Japanese, they were fast becoming the most decorated unit in the whole United States Army.

While their unit was fighting a severe battle on the outskirts of Italy, Kenji had somehow become separated from them. One soldier had found Kenji's canteen on the banks of a small river, but there was no other sign of him. It was believed that Kenji must have been wounded and possibly slipped into the river. Since it flowed behind enemy lines, there was no way they could follow its course to find out if their theory was correct.

It was just possible, the soldier's letter went on, that Kenji would be picked up by the French or Italian underground. Shoji prayed that would be the case.

Crumpling the paper in his hand, Shoji stared out the window at the surrounding desert. He would have to tell Keiko. He had promised. But he sure didn't relish the idea. All he wanted was to spare her more pain than she had already endured.

He glared at the sky overhead. *How long, God? How much more can she take?*

Immediately, he was filled with a sense of shame. What a foolish assumption to believe he knew more about Keiko than the One who had created her. How arrogant.

Closing his eyes, he whispered a prayer for Keiko and another one for Kenji. His pride in both knew no bounds. They had become the family he had craved for years now. Even Papa-san.

Shoji felt renewed pain at their loss. He couldn't have loved Keiko's father more if the old man had been his own father. No wonder the two men had been such good friends. They were much alike.

Closing the post office door behind him, he quickly made his way across the compound.

Chapter 13

Keiko stared at the wall calendar. December seventh. Had it already been two years since that fateful day when the Japanese had sent their bombers to Pearl Harbor and changed Keiko's world forever? In many ways it seemed much longer.

Shortly after the news of Kenji's disappearance, Sumiko had gone into labor. Keiko fretted until word came that Sumiko had delivered a healthy baby girl. With the arrival of Kenji's and her daughter, Sumiko had something positive to occupy her thoughts and time.

Pulling herself from her reflections, Keiko lifted her coat from the chair and slid her arms into the sleeves. She would have to hurry if she wanted to make it to the barracks that housed the Christian church before noon.

As Keiko walked along, she noticed many of the older *issei* working on their barrack homes even though the temperatures were barely above freezing. Whoever heard of freezing temperatures in a desert?

Many people were stuffing newspapers in the half-inch cracks between the wall boards, trying to help keep the cold winds from penetrating to the less-than-warm interiors.

Some of the barracks boasted Christmas wreaths on their doors, but there were very few. The main religion in the camp was Buddhism, although there were still quite a few Christians.

Keiko smiled at the tumbleweed snowman sitting at the corner of the church barracks. Someone had taken the time to spray-paint it white, adding bits of vegetables for the eyes and nose. The resourcefulness of the Japanese people continually amazed her. There was very little thrown away, and what was trash to one was something needed to another. Everything that might have been discarded seemed to have been reused and made into something useful.

Even Shoji had used pieces of leftover pipe and cord to create a wind chime that was the envy of everyone in their block. Of course, Shoji being Shoji, he then set about making one for each family who requested one.

Keiko entered the building, thankful for the stove that warmed it to at least tolerable temperatures. Unbuttoning her jacket, she searched the building for the minister, Mr. Takai. No one else seemed to be around, so she began pulling out decorations for the play the children were to perform on Christmas Eve.

Before long, she heard sounds from outside, laughter mingled with excited chatter. Children began filing into the room, their bright eyes sparkling with the joy of the season.

Ishimi ran across the room, flinging himself to his knees beside Keiko. "Hi, Keiko."

She returned his smile. "Hello, Ishimi. Are you ready to practice?"

He solemnly nodded his head, and Keiko hid a smile at Ishimi's seriousness over the part of playing Joseph, the father of Jesus.

Mr. Takai followed the children into the room, taking off his glasses, which had frosted over. His short, rotund body made Keiko think of him as a sort of Japanese Santa Claus. When he donned a white beard for the occasion, his transformation would be complete.

He grinned at Keiko. "Hello, Keiko. Will Shoji be coming later?"

"Yes, Mr. Takai. He has to work until two o'clock, then he will come help with the scenery."

The minister nodded his head absently as he flipped through the sheets of dialogue in his hands. Today would be spent practicing scenes because the parts had been decided long ago.

Rounding up the chattering children, Keiko had them practice taking their positions on the small stage that Shoji had built just for the occasion.

For weeks now, Keiko had been helping the minister with his Christmas program. It was something she needed as much as he had need of her, for she found herself without much to do and too much time to think. The children were a joy to her and kept her busy making costumes, practicing scenes, making scenery. And once again she felt useful, a feeling that had been lacking since Papa-san had died.

She found Ishimi's eyes going to the door as often as Keiko's. The boy's feeling for Shoji had developed into a hero worship that caused Keiko's lips to twitch with amusement. He had lately become Shoji's shadow. Shoji didn't seem to mind; in fact, he somewhat encouraged it, knowing that Ishimi had no father figure in his life except an uncle who was a devout Buddhist.

Keiko had been studying the Bible with Iku Sawado, Ishimi's mother, and Iku had accepted Christ months ago. Now she struggled with her family's obvious disapproval. It would be a battle for her, that much was for sure; but Iku was a very determined young woman. It was sad that she was a widow so young and with a small child to care for without his father's influence.

Shoji and Keiko tried to help her in any way they could, but the biggest help seemed to come from the boy's devotion to Shoji. Keiko felt a tightness in her chest as she thought again about what a good father Shoji would make.

The door opened, and Mrs. Tsushima blew in with the wind. It was the only way to describe Mrs. Tsushima. She was young, not much older than Keiko, yet she had experienced more in her life than Keiko imagined she would probably ever experience in hers.

She breezed over to Keiko, her voice preceding her. "Keiko, I'm so glad you're here. Could you possibly take little Marie for awhile? Honestly, the child is teething, and she's an absolute terror about it."

The loving look Mrs. Tsushima bestowed on her baby girl gave lie to her words. She handed the baby to Keiko, gently unwrapping her daughter from the confines of the blankets she had carried her in.

Keiko eagerly took the little girl into her arms, smiling down at Marie's cherubic features. Marie waved chubby brown fists at Keiko, gurgling happily. Her bright almond eyes and dark hair were very similar to those of the woman smiling down at her.

As Keiko played with Marie, she couldn't help but wish for a child of her own. It had become almost an obsession with her. Since the night of her father's death, Shoji had taken great pains to avoid being alone with her. She knew he was again avoiding any chance of conceiving children of their own, and her own heart ached. Not only with the knowledge that she wouldn't have a child of her own anytime soon, but also with the pain of separation from the one man she loved most in the world.

Although he was with her in the evenings, he was still distant, forcing her to reconcile herself to the fact that his stubbornness far exceeded her own. The realization that he suffered as much as she did, did nothing to alleviate her own pain.

As usual, thoughts of babies brought Sumiko to mind. Kenji was still missing, and hope was growing dim that he would be found alive. After five months, the odds were against it.

Keiko hugged Marie tighter, bringing forth a protesting yelp from the small baby. Would Sumiko wind up like Iku, a young widow with a child that would never know its father? *Dear God, please don't let it be so.*

When Shoji came, the children seemed to settle down, and rehearsals went more smoothly. Even the younger girls responded to Shoji's magnetism and tried to outdo each other in a bid for his attention and a word of praise.

Keiko watched him, her heart in her eyes. When his eyes met hers, his were caught and held by the intensity of emotion he witnessed there. Only for a moment did they find themselves in seeming isolation before Ishimi latched onto Shoji's knees and drew his attention away.

Later that evening, when Keiko and Shoji were at the mess hall, Shoji told Keiko that he had arranged for her to visit Sumiko for Christmas.

She began making plans for their trip, but Shoji placed his large hand over her smaller one.

"Not me, Keiko-chan. I could only arrange for you to go."

Keiko's brows puckered into a frown. "I can't go without you. It's Christmas. I can't just leave you here." Her voice began to rise. "I won't do it."

"Shhh. Lower your voice." Shoji's eyes went around the room and came back to her. "I think Sumiko would like to see you. I think she needs to see you."

Keiko struggled with the desire to go and the need to remain. Sumiko had her mother, father, and baby Esther. Shoji had only her. She began shaking her head again.

"If you're worried about me being alone, don't be. My mother is coming to stay for a few weeks."

Somewhat relieved, Keiko still hesitated. This would be little Esther's first Christmas, and Keiko would love to be there for that, but still, could she just leave?

He was finally able to convince her, and Keiko would be eternally grateful for that.

★ ★ ★

The time she spent with Sumiko was good for both of them. They gained strength from each other, both sure in their knowledge that Kenji would be okay.

Before she left, Keiko studied Esther thoroughly, trying to memorize each little detail as a picture in the memory book of her mind.

Keiko hadn't realized just how much she would miss Shoji, and although part of her longed to remain with Sumiko, nothing could have induced her to stay; so when the bus left Topaz Relocation Center, she was on it.

The day she arrived back at Butte Camp, Shoji met Keiko with the news that Kenji had been found alive. Word had reached Shoji while Keiko was still en route. Kenji would be returning to the States soon. Both Keiko and Shoji went to their knees to thank God for His goodness and to ask His continuing protection over them all.

★ ★ ★

As the months passed, Keiko found little jobs at the school and at the church to keep her occupied. Shoji still worked at the model ship factory, but he refused to even consider Keiko doing the same.

"I don't want you to work. If you want to help one of the teachers or teach a class on origami or something, that's fine, but I don't want you working."

Although she felt his attitude was a little archaic, still she bowed to his headship of their family. Actually, she was rather pleased, because in truth she had no desire to be anything other than a wife and mother. The problem was, Shoji was gone all day, and she couldn't foresee motherhood in the near future the way things were going. Deciding to do the next best thing, Keiko volunteered at the day nursery.

Early in 1944, word came that Butte Camp would be closing by the next year. Since Italy had secretly surrendered in September 1943, hope was high that an end to the war was in sight. Only the battle with Japan and Germany was still being waged, but it seemed that Germany was fast losing steam. Japan was another matter.

Keiko continued to pray because although Kenji had returned home and was still recuperating, if the war continued he could still be recalled. His letters to her were full of news of his little girl, and Keiko rejoiced at his fatherly love. She also sympathized with his chafing at the delay in getting them out of camp and into a normal home.

Many of the Japanese were being allowed to leave, but the West Coast was still off-limits. Still, they were finding new homes and new lives in other parts of the country. Mrs. Roosevelt had stated that this was a good brought about by the war, and perhaps it was; but Keiko was still angered by the way in which it was accomplished.

Since no official word had come yet about the center closing—only the rumors that ran rampant among their facility—Shoji maintained his stubbornness in refusing to take a chance on starting a family. Keiko marveled at his self-control. Many times they had come to the brink of forgetting, but Shoji would always pull back.

June arrived with its scorching temperatures. Using his ingenuity, Shoji devised a sort of evaporative cooling system. They could have purchased a real evaporative cooler like some people did, but Shoji felt better using his own devices.

Keiko was thankful for the relief from the oppressive heat when she was in her own apartment. Often she had company: people trying to avoid the hot part of the day. Fans proved almost less than useful, though they were better than nothing.

Shoji came in from work that evening nearly exhausted from the hot temperatures. He laid his head back against the overstuffed chair, rubbing his hands tiredly across his face. Keiko could sense trouble, though Shoji had said nothing.

She brought him a glass of tea that she had been cooling by wrapping it with wet cloths and letting the air from the fan blow on it. It was amazing just how cool this could make things, even in the soaring temperatures.

He thanked her, chugging down the drink without pause.

"Is something wrong?" she asked him, sitting on the arm of the chair.

His eyes met hers as he handed her back the glass. "The Allies invaded Normandy two days ago. Thousands of Americans are dead."

A cold numbness entered her body, raising the flesh on her skin into tiny bumps. *Thousands*, he had said.

He pulled her down onto his lap, and she buried her head against his chest. How much longer? How much longer would this insanity go on? How many more people had to die?

He held her a long time before rousing himself to the time. "They'll be serving supper soon."

Keiko shook her head. "I'm not hungry. You go ahead."

"I'm not hungry, either, but I want to see if there's any more news. Sure you don't want to come?"

Deciding that she preferred his company to her own, she went with him. The noise level in the mess hall was louder than usual, making Keiko believe that word was spreading rapidly of recent developments.

Keiko listened in fascination as the men discussed the hows and wherefores of the invasion of Normandy's coast. Closing her eyes, she could see bodies floating en masse in the waters of the English Channel. Shivering, she got up and fled back to her apartment.

On July 18, the shocking news came that Japan's Prime Minister Tojo had resigned. Ripples of feeling regarding this action spread throughout the camp. Was Japan beginning to crumble?

In that same month, an attempt was made on Hitler's life. Perhaps it was unchristian of her to feel it, but Keiko was sorry that the attempt had failed. She considered the man a monster, and she struggled daily with her own evil thoughts regarding the man.

Fall was fast approaching, and Keiko dreaded spending another Christmas in Butte Camp. Last year, Mr. Takai had done much to make Christmas at the camp seem homelike and reminded them constantly of the purpose for the season. Still, Keiko wanted to be in her own home, planning her own Christmas dinner, and putting up a tree with lights.

More and more, the rumors spread of a possible end to the war. Keiko began to have hope that her wish might come true.

In October, Keiko received another letter from Sumiko, this time telling her that Kenji was returning to his unit. Keiko felt as though the bottom had dropped out of her world. The one good thing that Sumiko had to tell her was that Sumiko's father had been offered a job in San Antonio, Texas, and that her parents would be leaving immediately to take it. Sumiko and Esther would be going with them.

Keiko told Shoji when he came home that evening.

"Thank God!" was all he said.

Not many nights later, Shoji came home from work, and Keiko could tell he had something on his mind. He took Keiko in his arms, kissing her long and hard.

Surprised, Keiko searched his face for some clue to his mood. Finding none, she leaned back against his arm, a tentative smile forming on her lips.

"Okay, what have you been up to?"

He returned her smile with one of this own. His eyes took on a gleam as they roved over her face. "We're leaving here."

The smile deserted Keiko. "What? When? How?"

Shoji sat down, pulling her down with him. "I've been offered a job in Palm Beach."

Thoroughly confused, Keiko waited for him to continue.

"My grandfather owns the plane manufacturing plant there. He used his influence and pulled some strings, and there you have it."

Confusing emotions skittered around inside Keiko. She was thrilled to be leaving Butte Camp, but the thought of all the friends she would leave behind caused her a pang of loss. What would she ever do without Obāsan's love and guidance? And Ishimi! What would happen to him without Shoji there to lead the way?

Her eyes found Shoji's. The very inscrutableness of his look told her more than he would say.

"You don't want to go, do you?"

His feigned look of surprise didn't fool her. He opened his mouth to deny it, but Keiko covered his lips with her hand.

"I know how you feel about your grandfather. I know you don't want to be beholden to him for anything."

His eyes softened. Kissing her fingers, he removed them from his mouth. "I love you more than my pride. I know how badly you want to start a family, and I refuse to consider it under these circumstances. I want a family too. But more than that, I want to hold you in my arms again the way I did before this whole war came about."

Keiko knew how much it had cost him to lower his pride, and she felt an overwhelming flood of love for him.

"I can't let you do that."

His eyes took on that steely look that she had come to recognize as his desire to have his own way. Placing her lips against his, she hushed him with a kiss.

"Listen to me for a change. This war can't last much longer. You said so yourself. With everything that's happened, surely the end must be in sight. Why else are the rumors growing stronger every day that this camp will be closed soon?" She searched his eyes with her own. "We've waited this long; we can wait a little longer."

He smiled wryly. "I'm not so sure I can."

She blushed at his inference, but her eyes glowed with love. "If nothing changes by the end of this year. . .well, then we'll consider your grandfather's offer."

Shoji sighed heavily. "Two months is an awfully long time."

"So is two years," she admonished him gently.

His eyes twinkled back at her. "You have no idea!"

"Haven't I?"

Swallowing hard, Shoji gently pushed Keiko from his lap. "Okay," he told her, his voice raw with emotion. "But if nothing changes by the end of this year, then I will accept my grandfather's offer."

"Hai," she told him softly. She knew how painful it would be for her husband to submit to someone who so obviously disliked his father. Keiko decided

it would be best to pray for a quick end to this war—not that she hadn't been doing so for nearly three years.

On December 17, 1944, official word came down that Butte Camp would close the following year. For the first time in three years, there was hope that the end of the war was imminent.

Immediately, families were encouraged to seek employment outside of the camp. Anyone who had a job lined up was given clearance to leave, but the West Coast was still a forbidden zone.

Since Keiko and Shoji's farm was in California, they knew they would have to bide their time, hoping against hope that California would be freed from restriction soon.

The official date for Butte Camp to close was set for November 15, 1945, over eleven months away. Since the war with Germany and Japan was still being waged, this seemed a premature presumption that the United States would win. Still, the euphoric feelings were running high.

For many of the *issei* and *kibei,* this was a sad time. The death toll on both sides was high, and many of the Japanese wondered about their families still in Japan. Shoji was one of them. There was no way to get word to or from family and friends.

With the beginnings of closure of the camp, Shoji and Keiko decided to stay and help their friends with their relocation. Shoji helped Benko and her family load their goods onto a truck, while Keiko cried in the older woman's arms.

"I will miss you, Obāsan," Keiko told her.

"And I you. But someday we will meet again. You taught me this."

Keiko realized that Obāsan was referring to her recent conversion to Christianity. She and Keiko had studied for months together, and Benko had decided that the Christian religion "made sense," as she put it.

"I hope we don't have to wait for heaven, Obāsan," Keiko told her. The old woman merely smiled before climbing into the army truck.

Keiko listlessly prepared a meal for Shoji and herself since they had missed the five o'clock meal. Her heart was heavy from the loss of her friends, but she was thankful that they were finally resuming a normal life.

When Keiko pushed through the curtain that separated their sleeping quarters from their living quarters, she stopped dead in surprise. There, sitting in the middle of the room, was a double bed with mattress and box springs.

Shoji put his arms around her from behind, nuzzling his lips against her neck. She turned her head slightly, her eyes full of questions.

"Benko's son said he didn't need it. I bought it from him."

She turned in his arms, a happy glow filling her eyes. Drawing his lips down to hers, Keiko told him without words just how happy he had made her. Shoji lifted her in his arms and carried her to the bed.

Epilogue

Keiko lifted the doll from the box beside her, smiling at the gift from Shoji. Her very own Bodhidharma doll stared sightlessly back at her. Picking up the small paintbrush sitting on the table beside her, Keiko carefully colored in one tiny eye. Smiling, she set the doll on the shelf to dry.

She reached into the bassinet beside her, stroking the soft, dark hair on her son's tiny head. "I will fill in the other eye when you accept Christ as your Savior," she told him softly. His sleep was undisturbed, and Keiko continued to watch him, finding it hard to get her fill of just looking at the little wonder that was part of both Shoji and herself. What a tiny miracle!

The back door slammed open, and Keiko had a sense of déjà vu. Lifting her eyes, she almost expected to see Kenji enter the room. Instead, her husband peeked his head around the corner.

Shoji came fully into the room, eyeing the dolls on the shelves much like the first time he had visited this house. He smiled at the new Bodhidharma doll he had ordered for Keiko from Japan and gently stroked the cheek of his son. It was hard to believe that the war was over and trade with Japan continued as though it had never been interrupted.

Many years had passed—some of them good, some of them not so good. For Shoji, there was a feeling of coming home. His anger, his feelings of nonentity, had finally been put to rest with the birth of his son. He now knew just where he belonged, where God had intended him to be from the beginning. He was Keiko's, and she was his, and wherever they were together was home.

In April 1945 Hitler had committed suicide, and seven days later Germany had surrendered. For all intents and purposes, the war had ended. Only Japan had refused to give in.

Even an atomic bomb dropped on Hiroshima in August hadn't budged them. It was only after a second one was dropped on Nagasaki that they had finally sued for peace in September. Had it really only been six months ago?

Shoji knelt beside his wife and son. His eyes were tender when they finally connected with Keiko's.

"I see you've colored in your first eye."

"Hai," she answered softly, bending forward and swiftly kissing his lips. "Now I will begin to pray for the fulfillment of my endeavor."

Shoji watched as Keiko lifted her mother's *Bodhidharma* doll from its box. The one eye stared grotesquely back at her, much like the new one.

Lifting the paintbrush again, Keiko carefully colored in the other eye of her mother's doll. Her own eyes were filled with tears as she set the doll on the shelf next to the new one.

"I never thought I would be thankful for a war," she told Shoji. "But if not for this war, I'm not sure my brother would ever have accepted Christ."

Shoji reached for Keiko's chin, turning her face toward him. "Only God knows."

Keiko realized that was true. And only God knew how all of this would end. Someday, maybe this country would finally grant citizenship to the *issei* who had remained faithful and loyal to a country that had betrayed them.

For now, life went on much as it had before the war. She had the farm, but instead of Papa-san, she had Shoji. Instead of Kenji, she had her son, Andrew Shinichi Ibaragi.

Shoji had asked her why she wanted to name him Andrew. Keiko realized that Shoji wanted his son to have a Japanese heritage as well as an American one, except instead of forcing it on him like his own father had, Shoji hoped to teach his son by example.

She told him that Andrew was her favorite apostle because in every instance recorded in the Bible where Andrew was mentioned, he was bringing someone to Christ. Keiko hoped that her own son would do the same someday. And she chose the name Shinichi after her own father.

Shoji rose to his feet, pulling Keiko up beside him. Placing an arm around her waist, he led her outside to the porch. Together they watched the sun begin its descent below the horizon. Already the fields were ripe with the harvest.

On a hill in the distance, the shadow of two tombstones could be clearly seen against the flaming sky. Keiko hoped that her father was with her mother. She would never know until that day when she would join them, but until then, life went on.

Shoji smiled at her, and Keiko felt for the first time in her life like she really belonged. This was where she wanted to be. Now and forever.

DARLENE MINDRUP

Darlene is a full-time homemaker and home-school teacher. A "radical feminist" turned "radical Christian," she lives in Arizona with her husband and son. Darlene has written several novels for Barbour Publishing's **Heartsong Presents** line. She has a talent for bringing ancient settings like the early church in the Roman Empire and medieval times to life with clarity. Darlene believes "romance is for everyone, not just the young and beautiful."

Candleshine

Colleen L. Reece

In memory of my good friend Al Smith,
whose knowledge and experiences of World War II enriched this book.
Special thanks go to Ron Wanttaja for his technical advice on airplanes.

Chapter 1

Twin rows of stiffly starched, white-uniformed young women wearing white caps with the cherished black band—the result of three long years of hard work—lined the long hall. Of the original fifty who had enrolled in January 1939 at the Mercy Hospital School of Nursing in Seattle, Washington, thirty-six would complete the course. Behind the soon-to-be graduates stood gray-clad, white-bibbed underclassmen, their aprons, collars, cuffs, and unadorned caps spotless. Beginning probationers in blue breathlessly admired the thirty-six and dreamed of the day they would replace the senior nurses.

Three years. . .a moment, a lifetime. Candace Thatcher, nicknamed Candleshine by family and friends, glanced at the nurse beside her. A wave of emotion rushed through her. What did the war-torn future hold for Connie Imoto, her best friend from the first day they entered training? Would the sadness that had lived in Connie's expressive eyes ever since the Japanese attack on Pearl Harbor—aptly described as "a date that will live in infamy" by President Franklin Delano Roosevelt—ever disappear?

For one cowardly moment, she wished she had never left Cedar Ridge, Washington, her home. The peaceful mountain hamlet seemed far removed from war. Why should Tojo, Hitler, and Mussolini add to the pain and suffering nurses worked so hard to overcome?

She drew her slim body to its five-foot, six-inch height, exactly six inches taller than Connie. If ever the rigid discipline and training of the past years must be practiced, that time was now. Her short, fair hair that turned up at the ends had been secured neatly under her cap; her blue eyes, normally lively with fun, had darkened with uncertainty. Only slightly out of line were the few tiny freckles that made her pink and white skin look like wild strawberries. In short, it was a face scrubbed and pleasant but not beautiful.

A slight ripple of movement heralded the slow procession into the large auditorium. Connie smiled tremulously and faced front as did Candleshine. Yet even this final walk seemed to fade when Candleshine confronted a multitude of searing, significant memories. . . .

★ ★ ★

"Hold him still!" yelled Bruce Thatcher to his pigtailed cousin.

"How do you hold a squirming cat still?" shot back Candleshine as she tightened her hold on the big yellow cat, protecting herself from his claws with layers of her cotton skirt.

Bruce carefully swabbed the long cut on the cat's back. "Now, whatever you do, don't let him go. This salve may sting, but it will make him well."

Five minutes later, the indignant but well-doctored tom escaped to the barn loft, muttering under his breath. Candleshine grinned. "By the time *you* get to medical school, you'll be teaching *your* instructors."

Bruce's brown hair stood on end, and his blue eyes laughed. "Don't forget you're going to be a nurse."

"I won't." She leaned back on the grass and stared up through the dappled shade of a big maple. "Bruce, I wish we were the same age and could go away together."

His laughter died. "I do too, but since I'm more than five years older than you, we can't. I can just see you entering a school of nursing when you're thirteen!"

She smirked, and her flaxen pigtails spilled to both sides of her head. "When I *do* get there, they'll say, 'Why, Miss Thatcher, you already know so much about the medical field we're going to give you your diploma. The world is just waiting for you, and there's really no reason for you to spend three years repeating what you already know.' "

"So what *do* you know that so highly qualifies you, Smarty?"

She sat up and ticked off on her fingers. "I know the name and location of every bone in the body. I—"

"You don't!"

"Do too. Think I could hear you say them over and over and not remember?" A little puff of exasperation colored her expressive face.

"Say them." The cousin who had adored Candleshine since she was born couldn't help teasing.

Candleshine adjusted imaginary glasses, took on the pompous air of a lecturer, and began. "Ladies and gentlemen, there are two hundred bones, exclusive of teeth, in the human body." In rapid-fire order she named them, accurately identifying their locations until Bruce interrupted her monotonous recital.

"Stop, stop; I'm convinced."

"Let that be a lesson to you," his companion admonished. She abandoned her pose and became pensive. "I wonder if I can stand to leave all this, even to be a nurse?"

Bruce's gaze followed her gesture. From the slight rise above the Thatcher home, once a one-room schoolhouse where Candleshine's mother, Trinity, taught all eight grades at a time, tall firs, rounded hills, and sharply rearing mountains basked in the late afternoon sunlight.

Bruce caught her mood. Not often did the reserved young man open his heart, even to his cousin and best friend. "I think that knowing it—and your folks and mine—will always be here to come back to makes it easier for me to go and learn. Remember how your mother always quotes her grandmother about each person carrying a torch for God? And passing it on to the next generation? Besides, she even named you Candace because it means glittering, flowing white."

"I know." The girl's sunny nature didn't allow time for prolonged sadness. "White for a nurse's uniform. White for a bride."

"Bride! Better concentrate on being a nurse first." Bruce sighed and stood, brushing off his old pants and shirt. "I have to get home and finish the chores." As he strode away with long steps he called over his shoulder, "Thanks for helping with the cat."

"Any time." Her contentment pealed out in a final, mocking laugh. Yet when the tall figure got smaller and smaller, then vanished into the grove of trees that separated Will Thatcher's and Jamie Thatcher's land, she frowned. Some of the goldenness of the afternoon went with him. How tall Bruce had grown in the last few years! How strong and caring, even more than when she had been small.

"He's better than any brother could be," she told a dandelion puff, then watched it fly into the still air. A feeling that someday she and Bruce would be tossed and torn apart the same way made her shiver. "Silly me. Nothing can change Bruce." Her smile returned, and her blue eyes shone. Of course she'd miss her pal, but time would go by rapidly, and he'd be home for vacations. Mother and Dad had promised to take her to Seattle sometimes too so they could see the boy who had practically grown up in their home after his mother died.

Candleshine kept that smile all through his leaving and the years that followed. She also studied hard and graduated as valedictorian of her class. As her valedictory address she chose the subject, "Hold High the Torch," and triumphantly ended with a challenge to her fifteen classmates—and herself.

"We can refuse to carry on all that is good and worthwhile." Her voice rang. "Yet dare we?" She paused before continuing. "King David, a man of great wisdom, once said, 'For thou wilt light my candle: the Lord my God will enlighten my darkness' (Psalm 18:28). While we rejoice on the completion of our high school days this beautiful May 1938 afternoon, dictators are rending China, Spain, Austria, and many other countries. The darkness of war cannot help but touch us in many ways, and only the lighted candles of our lives can help lift the smothering blackness creeping over the world.

"I will be eighteen in December. In January I begin training to become a nurse. I intend to follow Florence Nightingale's bright example. It doesn't matter *how* we keep our torches burning, but that we do. Together, we can create an everlasting flame." She stumbled back to her place amid loud cheering and the satisfied, proud looks she received from her parents and Bruce, who had somehow wangled time off from his studies and hard work to attend this milestone in her life.

Summer, a busy time for all, seemed to fly. Candleshine took over complete charge of household duties so her mother could return to Bellingham for summer school before going back to teaching after so many years. Candleshine sang as she cooked, secretly delighted at her father's eager acceptance of meals and help with haying.

Fall became a waiting time to be put to rest by a joyous celebration on the twentieth of December. A combination eighteenth birthday and farewell party left Candleshine understanding how a wishbone must feel when pulled two ways. Through teary eyes she thanked family and friends and assured them her body would be in Seattle but much of her heart would always be in Cedar Ridge.

In the first week of January 1939, Candace Thatcher presented herself to the Mercy Hospital School training office and discovered Superintendent of Nurses Miss Genevieve Grey. Her shiny, steel-drill eyes, which perfectly matched her equally efficient hair, saw right through probationers. Candleshine shivered as she recalled Bruce telling her some classmates would be weeded out in the first three probationary months before being accepted as student nurses. Common sense came to her rescue. No one could be better prepared, and again she silently thanked God and Bruce for their help. She also determined she would *not* be dismissed. Bolstered, she met the keen gray gaze and found compassion, fairness, and even a twitch of humor in Miss Grey's stoic face.

After a jumble of corridors that might be harder to learn than bones, Candleshine stumbled through the covered passage that led from the School of Nursing to Hunter Hall, the two-story red brick nurses' residence that matched the various hospital buildings sprawled on a hill above Seattle.

"Probationers and first-year students on the first floor; second year, seniors, and graduates on the second." Dark-haired, dark-eyed Winona Allen, who proudly admitted junior status, took Candleshine upstairs before showing the newcomer her own room.

"Why?"

Winona stared. Although Candace had to look down a few inches at her guide, she felt dwarfed until a mischievous look led to a whisper.

"Don't let it get around but it's so probies and first years won't sneak out. No one gets past good ol' housemom." She grinned. "Juniors and seniors are supposed to be past all that. Besides, when we have night duty it's quieter upstairs."

This time Candleshine bit her lip and didn't blurt out another stupid question. As she meekly followed Winona to her own room on the first floor, Winona announced she looked forward to being the Cedar Ridge girl's Big Sister. Although it little resembled her wallpapered, comfortable bedroom at home, Candleshine rejoiced that her spotless window framed a view of Puget Sound.

"I lived in this room last year," Winona said. "You get some spectacular sunsets over the water."

Excitement blended with shyness. "I–I'm glad you're my Big Sister."

"So am I. If you ever need a shoulder to cry on—and you will, we all do—I'll be here." An unexpectedly sweet smile replaced the elfish grin. "Welcome, Candace Thatcher, or is it Candy?"

She hesitated. Would Winona think her nickname silly?

"It's—Candleshine."

"That's lovely, and how fitting for a nurse! Just don't let your light go out when you drop a bedpan or a doctor yells." For a moment doubt crossed her face. "You're really strong, aren't you? Nurses have to be."

"Strong enough to lift hay bales and drive a tractor."

"Good!" Winona glanced at her watch. "Oh, you have an hour before dinner. Better study the thou-shalt-nots."

"I beg your pardon?"

"Those." Winona nodded toward the list of rules conspicuously posted on the inside of the door. "And that." She indicated a framed motto next to it. "Probationers' supper is at six-thirty. Someone will be in the living room here to take you over. See you later; I have to go." She left the door open when she went out. "Friendlier this way."

How lucky to have this vivacious nurse for her Big Sister! "Thank You, God," she prayed before examining the forbidding list.

None was unfamiliar. Bruce had already warned her of the rules in "his" hospital—no jewelry, no eating on wards, no accepting invitations from doctors, no visiting wards except when on duty or sent by a superior, and one must always rise for doctors or higher ranking nurses.

"Yes, Doctor Thatcher." Candleshine bobbed an absurd curtsy and came upright to face a slight, smiling girl who stood giggling in the hall.

"Hello!" Candleshine stepped aside. "Won't you come in? I'm Candace Thatcher, but everyone calls me Candleshine. Are you new too?" she added hopefully.

"Very. I'm Constance Imoto, Connie to you. I came yesterday."

"I see you survived Miss Grey."

Candleshine clapped her hand to her mouth but relaxed when Connie laughed and said, "Barely!"

By the time they were escorted to supper, Candleshine knew God had sent a friend. Afterward when they strolled on the parklike grounds in the unusually warm January evening and Connie gazed at the lights of Seattle and whispered, "I thank God I am able to come here," Candleshine rejoiced. Imagine finding a fellow Christian the first day of training! Connie said her Japanese-American family had been shocked when she'd accepted Jesus after a high school friend witnessed of God's love. Now she prayed for her Shinto* family.

Connie was born of *nisei* Japanese parents, that is, children of immigrants born or educated in the United States. "I look Japanese and think American," she shared. She never tired of hearing stories about Cedar Ridge and how Will and Trinity took one look at one another and fell in love. By the end of the week, both girls looked forward to visiting the other's home if they could have time off together.

They also served to inspire each other's best. Candleshine's knowledge of anatomy complemented Connie's deft bedmaking, and together they shared honors in physiology. Connie hated bandaging and Candleshine secretly rejoiced in the times she'd worked with Bruce on the ranch when animals got hurt. Connie acted a little awed that her new friend was a cousin of the much-respected Doctor Thatcher, who sent ripples through the entire student nurse population!

As juniors and seniors, the girls participated in the wide variety of training necessary before taking state exams and earning their coveted RN (Registered Nurse) status. They also made mistakes. None tragic, but a few disheartening enough for Candleshine to seek out faithful Winona until she graduated with honors.

Suddenly, the hectic pace increased even more. Decisions had to be made on what type of nursing to do when they graduated. Dr. Bruce Thatcher and a team of specially selected nurses, including Winona, won the chance to work and learn in a hospital in Manila, the Philippines. Now thousands of miles would separate Bruce and Candleshine, yet through the rest of her training his parting admonition to always keep her light shining for their God steadied her. The year-long assignment would fly, then Bruce would return. Winona wasn't so certain of her future. After the peacetime draft in September 1940, the dedicated nurse's childhood sweetheart enlisted and later was stationed in Hawaii with the U.S. Pacific Fleet.

When Winona told the girls good-bye, her snappy dark eyes glistened. "I must be crazy. The Philippines are even farther from Hawaii than Seattle." She shrugged. "Oh, well, maybe one of us can get leave. It's been months since I saw him."

"I think it's exciting," Candleshine told her. "If you weren't already engaged, I'd love to have you for a cousin-in-law."

"If I weren't already 'spoken for,' as my grandmother persists in calling it, I wouldn't mind at all," Winona shot back.

Weeks grew into months until just a short time remained until graduation.

———————————

*A principal religion of Japan based on the worship of nature and of ancestors.

Candleshine and Connie still hadn't settled on how and where they could best use their skills, although both had prayed fervently. When Candleshine had a long weekend in early December, Will Thatcher came for his daughter and proudly escorted her to the car. Trinity had elected to have dinner ready for a family she knew from experience would be starving after the long drive from Seattle to Cedar Ridge.

Saturday offered total relaxation, a dusting of snow, and more peace and quiet than Candleshine could ask. She had a long talk with her parents that evening, discussing Bruce and her future. She needed an island of rest before the final, hard pull to shore that marked the end of her training.

The next day the world exploded, made even more horrible by the contrast with the calm such a few hours earlier. Japanese planes had bombed Pearl Harbor at the same time Japanese ambassadors were meeting with Secretary of State Cordell Hull. The world sat stunned, except for Candleshine.

"Mother, Dad, I must go back." Every tiny freckle stood out against her pale skin. "I'll be needed, especially by Connie. Oh, how could this evil thing happen?"

Millions of people asked the same question. The next day President Roosevelt officially declared war on Japan. So did Canada and Great Britain. On December 9, China declared war on the Rome-Berlin-Tokyo Axis. Germany and Italy retaliated on December 11 by declaring war on the United States. Christmas 1941, in the midst of World War II—truly a global conflict—would be bleak.

Now Candleshine fought unspeakable battles. Not against sickness and death but against the sidelong glances, sneers, and unfriendly comments a few of her classmates directed at both Connie and herself. "How can they?" she cried one day when she and Connie discovered signs on the doors of their Hunter Hall rooms. Connie's read, "TRAITOR," while Candleshine's read, "JAP-LOVER."

Candleshine ripped the signs down and tore them to bits while dissolving into angry tears the way she hadn't done since childhood. "You're an American, more loyal than anyone I know. So are your parents." She thought of the gracious Imotos and the way they had welcomed her. She thought of Connie's older brother who had raced to enlist the moment he heard news of the attack.

"Some people will always be afraid of what is different," Connie said quietly. "They do not know God is color-blind."

Trust and faith shone in the smaller woman's face, and Connie wordlessly gripped Candleshine's hands, then entered her own room and shut the door.

A dozen times Candleshine walked by little knots of nurses who looked down when she passed, especially if Connie was with her. Gradually, the hostile atmosphere depressed even the brave Japanese American. "I won't quit after I've come so far," she said as she fingered a package Candleshine had wrapped for home. "Perhaps the Christmas spirit of peace will help."

Both women were on duty Christmas Eve. Candleshine swallowed back her disappointment. She hadn't been home for Christmas since before entering training. Neither had Connie. They had put aside their own longings and volunteered to work and relieve nurses with families.

For the third time they joined the serpentine procession of white-clad nurses who marched through the halls carrying candles and singing timeless carols of hope and joy and peace. Candleshine saw those blessings in Connie's face and gave thanks, although her vision blurred until the many flames dimmed. . . .

★ ★ ★

The long line of seniors, juniors, and probationers reached the end of the hall separating the graduates from training and duty. Candleshine returned to the present from a past that blended faith and fear, joy and love, and tragedy.

Again she looked at Connie who walked beside her in friendship and faith, more serious than ever before.

Candleshine shivered. The day they had so eagerly anticipated had dawned, but to scowling, dark skies that prophesied an uncertain future.

Chapter 2

T hree years ago, Connie Imoto's appearance in the hall outside Candleshine's room interrupted the Cedar Ridge probie's study of the thou-shalt-nots and turned her attention from the framed motto beside it. Yet during those years both girls had memorized the motto.

Nursing is an art; and if it is to be made an art, it requires as exclusive a devotion, as hard a preparation, as any painter's or sculptor's work; for what is the having to do with dead canvas or cold marble, compared with having to do with the living body—the temple of God's spirit? It is one of the Fine Arts. I had almost said, the finest of the Fine Arts.

FLORENCE NIGHTINGALE

Now at graduation the framed charge graced one side of the large room. On the other hung the beautiful Florence Nightingale Pledge. At the end of graduation, the nurses rose as a body and repeated the timeless vow. Never had Candleshine felt so strongly about her chosen profession as when hushed voices in the room lit only by symbolically lighted lamps promised before God and those assembled to pass their lives in purity, practice their profession faithfully, and dedicate themselves.

Candleshine choked and fought back tears. She could see wet faces around her. Even the most irresponsible young women who had barely made it through training obviously grasped the significance of the moment.

Miss Grey, spotless as usual, dismissed the assembly in a ragged voice far from her usual disciplined timbre. "Sister Elizabeth Kinney said it far better than I when she spoke in truth and beauty the words, 'There is no profession that so closely follows in the footsteps of Christ, than the work of healing.' Go. Serve. And make Mercy Hospital and Training School proud to name you as our own."

A mighty wave of applause accompanied the dignified superintendent's hasty exit from the platform, but not before those gathered saw her twisted face and glistening eyes.

Candleshine felt her heart swell with pride and pain. The petty irritations at classmates and staff and even the strenuous work faded into bonds that would hold no matter what came. She felt Connie's small but strong fingers dig into her arm and knew her friend felt the same way.

"I wonder—a year from now—where will we be?" Connie whispered.

"I'll be overseas." Candleshine set her lips in a grim line that aged her face. "I've already asked Miss Grey to let me stay on in the casualty ward. It will be good training." She looked deep into her friend's dark eyes. "What about you?"

"I too will stay here for the present." Connie's lips trembled, and a curious paleness flooded her smooth skin.

Candleshine impulsively hugged her friend. "No matter how far apart we may be, it won't make a difference. Out hearts will stay close."

"Always." Connie drew in an unsteady breath. "I have thanked God every day since I came for your friendship and love."

Too filled with emotion to speak, Candleshine nodded and quickly turned from the pain in Connie's face. "Dad, Mom—are you proud?"

Trinity seized her daughter, and Will beamed on both girls impartially.

"Glad I became a nurse?"

Will cocked his head to one side, and his blue eyes sparkled with fun. "Well, seems I remember you two moaning that until you passed state exams you wouldn't really be nurses."

"We intend to pass them with honors," his daughter boasted, but her blue eyes darkened. "It's more important now than ever." She ran one hand over her misty gaze. "I just wish Bruce and Winona could be here. Who knows what is happening in Manila?"

"Now that General MacArthur's forces have abandoned Manila and withdrawn to the Bataan Peninsula, communications will be terrible," said Will impassively, yet his worry for the boy closer than a son was etched in crisscross lines on his face.

"Bruce and Winona will never leave unless they're ordered out," Candleshine said. Visions of her laughing cousin and Big Sister who had guided her through early training days engulfed her. An urge to smash through the helplessness brought an agonized cry. "Oh, if there were only something we could do!"

"Our job is to pass our tests, become registered nurses, and wait," Connie reminded. "And pray."

"I know." She slowly unclenched her fingers.

"Think of Winona," Connie continued, her eyes enormous in her small face. "Her fiancé was stationed in Hawaii. He may have been killed."

"Connie's right." Trinity's blue eyes so like her daughter's did more to calm Candleshine than anything. "The same God we trusted before all this is still in control." She even managed a little smile. "Our part is simply to do the work we are given and, as Connie says, pray." She glanced at Will.

Candleshine caught the look. Would she one day look at a special man with the same love and trust in her mother's face? Her mouth set in a straight, unnatural line. Not until this hellish war ended. She could barely stand knowing Bruce was in danger. If she had a husband or fiancé off fighting. . .she refused to finish the thought. Not even for the precious love she had been privileged to witness in her home would she risk the certain torture of love in wartime.

To their surprise, the next afternoon Connie and Candleshine both received summonses to Miss Grey's office. The superintendent had little of the starch associated with her demeanor except for her pressed uniform and ever-present cap. The steel-drill eyes looked liquid gray, and compassion flowed from her. "Candace, I have bad news for you." She hesitated and added, "That's why I asked Constance to come with you."

"Bruce?" Candleshine felt the blood drain from her face. She stared at Miss Grey, a tower of strength in a shaking world.

"We do not know that either Dr. Thatcher or Winona Allen have been harmed," Miss Grey continued. "We do know Manila has fallen. On January second, Japanese forces took control of the city."

"The hospital? The staff?"

"No word is yet available, Candace." Miss Grey leaned forward, and some of the steel returned to her eyes. "If Dr. Thatcher could send you a message right now, it would be to not let this news keep you from doing your duty."

"Duty!" Candleshine didn't know whether to laugh or cry.

"Yes, duty. You once told me Dr. Thatcher's dream was for you to become a nurse. Nothing must interfere with that. *Nothing.*" Only Miss Grey's tightly clasped hands betrayed the woman behind the dedicated administrator.

"I—I don't know if I can."

"You must and you will. Constance, see that Candleshine gets a brisk afternoon walk. I've arranged for you to have the rest of the day off. Walk her until she can barely stumble back, then eat and get her to bed." She turned and gazed out the window into a Seattle sky as gray as her eyes. "I find that prescription works when I falter." She stood and added, "You may go."

Only later did the young women remember that for the first of a very few times Miss Grey used Nurse Thatcher's nickname.

With the spunk of her pioneering ancestors, Candleshine obeyed Miss Grey. When the clouds of war hovered, she forced herself to ignore them and rejoiced when every single class member passed the state exams. Many, like the two friends, elected to get extra training until accepted by the army, navy, or Red Cross. Never had the work been more grueling for those remaining of the class of '42. Grim-lipped but with a forced cheerfulness—not only for the patients' sake but for what their skilled hands would someday be required to do—the nurses bonded and served.

One good thing came from the long hours: The prejudice against Connie

Imoto dwindled. No one could see the way she drove herself and not respect her. She would need every ounce of her strength and endurance to withstand what lay ahead.

★ ★ ★

In mid-February, Miss Grey called the two nurses in again. She sat with her head in her hands for a time before speaking. Finally she raised a haggard face. "Nurse Imoto, Constance—" She spread her hands helplessly. "Dear God. . ." Not a curse, but a prayer.

Connie clutched Candleshine's arm until the taller nurse wanted to scream with pain. "Is it my parents?"

Her terror penetrated Miss Grey's abstraction. "No, no, child. Not your brother, either." She wordlessly pointed to a message on her desk. "President Roosevelt has signed the Japanese Relocation Order."

"But what does that have to do with Connie?" Candleshine burst out, for once unafraid of her superior's attitude. "Connie and her parents are *Americans!*"

"I know." Miss Grey's control gradually returned. "In times of war fear dictates strange happenings."

"What is it?" Connie whispered.

"In simple terms, West Coast Japanese persons will be sent to designated military relocation centers to avoid any possibility of espionage."

"Espionage? Connie?" Candleshine wanted to laugh. "Who in his right mind would think Connie or her parents could be spies?"

"It is also for the protection of Japanese and Japanese Americans," Miss Grey said soberly. "There have already been a few incidents of rock throwing, and the Ku Klux Klan is said to be burning crosses and threatening people. These are isolated incidents, probably by individual fanatics rather than organized groups, but enough to cause concern."

Connie moistened her dry lips. "Wh—where will we be sent?"

"It's too soon to tell," Miss Grey said.

"Can't you do anything?" Candleshine pleaded.

"I will do everything in my power," Miss Grey promised. "But Constance, I doubt that even the strongest recommendations on the part of Mercy Hospital will prevent your relocation."

Youth died in her face. She stood erect, her shoulders squared. The woman within spoke proudly. "I would not accept anything else. I must go with my family."

Candleshine made a muffled, hurting sound, and Connie turned to her.

"Please don't. Didn't we vow to serve wherever we might be? Think of the need I will find in a camp. Sickness knows no boundaries." Pity for her friend drowned out possible fear and anguish. "One day the war will end. Until then—" She gallantly raised her head and smiled. "I will serve in the place my God has allowed me to be."

Connie slowly walked across the room, opened the door, and slipped through.

Candleshine made a move to follow her, awed by the radiance in Connie's whole body.

"No, Candace. Let her pride remain intact. Only God can see your friend through the next moments. Let Him work before you go to her."

By night every person at Mercy Hospital and Training School knew the situation. Almost unanimously they agreed to approach their department heads, supervisors, and even the hospital board of directors. Not once did Candleshine see a glimmer of triumph or gladness over Connie's misfortune.

"I can take that with me," Connie told her when she left the hospital. In a few days she and her family and hundreds of others would be transported to a relocation center, perhaps Tule Lake in northern California or Minidoka in Idaho. How could she face the barbed wire and guards Candleshine heard surrounded the barren camps?

"My brother is fighting somewhere far worse than where I will be," Connie said immediately. "We don't even know where, just that he's been shipped out. We won't be mistreated or starved. Candleshine, there are many ways to fight and win a war. Our United States of America *will* fight. We *will* win. That's what I hang onto."

Candleshine never mentioned it again.

Connie's absence from Mercy Hospital left a gaping hole. Yet the increased tempo since December 7 kept even Candleshine from more than temporary mourning. She volunteered for extra duty; she worked as if the entire outcome of the war rested on her slim but capable shoulders. She prayed constantly and often sang small patients to sleep when all the formal care and medications in the world could not soothe. From casualty to surgery, pediatrics to medical she went, rejoicing in the splendid strength God had given her to serve beyond her own capacity. Little by little, doctors, patients, and even Miss Grey dropped the more formal "Candace" or "Nurse Thatcher" and called her by her well-chosen nickname. One usually grumpy surgeon said all that Thatcher woman had to do was walk on a ward and patients brightened up.

At times the war seemed far away. When President Roosevelt ordered General MacArthur to Australia from Bataan in March after three heartsick months of repelling the Japanese despite malnutrition and disease, a new feeling of dread was sparked. MacArthur's promise to the Filipinos, "I shall return," gained instant notoriety and enlisted sympathy for the cause.

Candleshine went on with her home-front battle against sickness and accidents. Not one word had been heard from either Bruce or Winona since before Christmas. The name of Winona's fiancé had appeared in the "killed in action" lists from the attack on Pearl Harbor.

Newspapers faithfully followed the war's progress, and no amount of pretense could keep patients from getting copies. Candleshine learned to know in those endless weeks how things were going by the morale on her wards when she arrived. The staff looked the other way when excited patients on the less serious wards pulled tricks after any bit of good news. Bad news brought an even greater measure of tenderness toward those with "boys over there."

Candleshine heard herself reassure many a faded mother, "God can care for your boy in the Pacific theater as well as here at home." How many quiet prayers did she offer when gnarled hands or burly, ashamed shoulders shook with agony?

The morning of April 9, 1942, Candleshine awoke to a feeling of foreboding reinforced by total exhaustion. She had been on an extra-long duty the night before. She discovered the courageous 75,000 worn-out troops had finally surrendered Bataan to the Japanese. Stories hit the press of a sixty-five-mile march—American prisoners of war forced to march to Japanese prison camps—with many deaths on the way due to disease and mistreatment.

Had Bruce been part of the so-called Bataan Death March? Had Winona? Candleshine shuddered and called on God for courage before going back on duty.

Japan would not be safe for long. On April 18, 1942, Lieutenant Colonel James "Jimmy" Doolittle led sixteen Bruce-25 bombers from the flight deck of the aircraft carrier *Hornet* more than six hundred miles and raided Tokyo and other Japanese cities. Although the attack did little damage, the shock value reverberated in the hearts of a waiting people and rocked Japanese confidence. The expression, "We did it once—we can do it again," rang through Mercy Hospital.

And still Candleshine waited. Her parents trembled when she took her stand and said she'd go overseas as soon as she could. But even as Will and Trinity shared sleepless nights praying for their daughter and Bruce, Winona, Connie, and all the other young men and women caught in the war, they clung to each other and to their God.

"We cannot order her what to do," Will said brokenly. Yet pride streaked his face.

Not even the miscarriage of their first child had brought suffering to match Trinity's exquisite pain, a pain evident in the new white gracefully blended into her dark locks. First Bruce, then Candleshine. Yet on the few occasions she and Will had to see Candleshine, Trinity kept things light except for that final, penetrating look that said more than she could speak.

Weeks droned by until May when the Battle of the Coral Sea—in which neither side ever saw the other's ships but fought only by planes sent from aircraft carriers—halted the threat to Australia.

When the first of the returning wounded began to arrive, Candleshine requested exclusive duty on the wards now set apart for them. Grizzled and middle-aged men, boys scarcely out of their teens—together their indomitable spirits pulled them through against incredible odds. Deeds of bravery and reports of trivial incidents mingled. But all the men had one thing in common: They wanted to rest, heal, see their families, *and go back.*

One normally profane sergeant who successfully curbed his tongue in the presence of the nurses said it all in one sentence: "The job ain't done and 'til it is, I gotta be there." In vain Candleshine tried to convince him he'd given all that was required, including three fingers of his left hand when a grenade misfired.

"Little gal, you an' others like you won't never be safe while Tojo-devils are runnin' loose," he said, patting her hand with his good right one. "I still have two good legs and one good hand, don't I?"

She didn't have the heart to tell him she doubted he'd be sent back to the Pacific theater with a disabled left hand. The day new orders came and she ripped them open for him, Candleshine admired this rough man more than ever. A black shade dropped over his face. He swallowed hard, lifted his chin, and stared into her eyes as if daring her to disagree with him.

"Guess what, Nurse! They're gonna give me a medal an' take advantage of all my smarts. Soon as you let me out of here, I've got me a new job right here in the good old U.S. of A. I get to herd new, ignorant guys around at Fort Lewis an' show them how to be real soldiers."

"Good for you. No one can do it better," she flashed back at him, and the entire ward cheered.

But that night long after low groans betrayed troubled dreams, Candleshine's quick ears caught a muffled sobbing. She hurried to the tough sergeant's bed and without a word, gripped his good hand with her own. He hung on for dear life. The sobs dwindled, then stopped.

"Think I'm a baby?" The shamed, broken whisper pierced Candleshine's soul. It could be Bruce lying in the darkness, hiding his feelings from others.

"No, Sergeant." Her low voice stilled him, and he let go of her hand. "Remember, things always look brighter in the morning." She deliberately switched from comforter to efficient nurse, smoothed his pillow, bathed his hot face, and brought fresh water. "God bless."

"An' you." A final, convulsive sound told her the storm had ended.

A few days later he moved on, one of an endless line of soldiers, sailors, and fliers who claimed Candleshine's attention and care for a season before continuing on the human conveyor belt to fight again, some back overseas, many at home.

In early June, America again rejoiced, this time over the first major Allied victory in the Battle of Midway. By taking out four of Japan's nine aircraft carriers, the enemy's naval power was crippled. Slowly, the terrible tide of aggression had begun to turn. Yet America fell to its knees again when a few days later Japan seized two islands at its own back door, at the tip of the Alaskan Aleutian chain.

One summer evening, Candleshine turned from sickness and war news to the solace of a warm, inviting evening overlooking Puget Sound. Gold-touched waves from a setting sun lapped the beach clearly visible from the weary nurse's window. The forested slopes of Bainbridge Island brought a homesick longing for Cedar Ridge. Would their family ever be intact there again?

Candleshine threw wide the window, unwilling to be separated from the evening even by a single pane of glass. All the heartache, worry, and struggles loosened their bindings for a single moment.

A feeling this could be one of the last times she stood at the window touched her. Not a premonition, but a thought. God had left her at Mercy Hospital to learn many lessons. Now she believed the time to move on loomed near, even as the ferryboat coming across the Sound grew larger.

She suddenly remembered what Bruce said long ago when she held the squirming yellow cat for "Dr. Thatcher's" bandaging.

"Knowing this—and your folks and mine—will always be here to come back to makes it easier for me to go. . . ."

"God, may this peaceful, beautiful part of Your creation continue free," she prayed. The last ray of daylight hovered on the horizon as one star appeared. Comforted, Candleshine watched the velvet night descend and cherished the moment.

Chapter 3

While Candleshine drove herself and chafed at the waiting, a world away, Bruce Thatcher and Winona Allen struggled against unspeakable odds to practice their skills. The tall brown-haired doctor and the petite, bubbly nurse worked as smoothly together as two blades on a pair of shears. A warm friendship based on mutual love for Candleshine and home sprang up between them. In addition, Bruce offered the solid security of his personality and position: After only a few weeks at Manila Hospital, the quality of Bruce's work was evident.

The bombing of Pearl Harbor and the landing of the first Japanese troops in the Philippines three days later presented a grave problem for the medical team from the States. Should they stay or ask to be evacuated?

"If we wait, we may not get out later," Bruce warned his fellow workers. "Winona, what about you?"

Her dark eyes flashed while her short black curls bobbed in a defiant gesture. "I stay." ●

"And I."

"Same here."

Not one of the team agreed to leave, even when an influx of wounded sent the entire hospital scrambling to provide care. Supplies ran low. Although red-eyed from lack of sleep, the only thing that kept the staff going was the knowledge that they made a difference.

More and more, Winona turned to Bruce for strength. The first time a badly hurt Japanese soldier lay helplessly waiting for the aid she could offer, Winona cringed. While she proceeded to give the best care she could, an half-hour later Dr. Thatcher found her crying in a linen closet.

"How can I take care of those—those—" She broke off, but her anger, despair, and guilt still raged within.

Bruce didn't say a word. He just gathered the small nurse into his strong, brotherly arms and waited.

"I—I keep th—thinking that maybe a b—brother or c—cousin was one of those at P—Pearl Harbor," she sobbed. "One who helped b—bomb our fleet a—and. . ."

Before she could pronounce her deepest fears involving her fiancé, Bruce said, "I feel the same way."

She jerked away from him, stunned by his quiet words. "Then h—how c—can you—?"

Bruce's poignant blue eyes looked deep into Winona's. "'Inasmuch as ye have done it unto one of the least of these my brethren, ye have done it unto me'" (Matthew 25:40). Bruce's jaw was set. "I repeat this over and over." He smiled at Winona. "I can't say I don't still rebel, but it helps me put aside my own feelings to see a hurting human being instead of a fallen enemy."

Chastened and humbled, Winona murmured, "I wish I had your faith."

"I've seen you do things only Christ could do as far as compassion," Bruce told her huskily. "You told me you accepted Him long ago."

"I did." Winona groped for a handkerchief and blew her nose. "Maybe I'm just so filled with anger at all this unnecessary dying and misery I can't concentrate on Jesus." Her unsinkable spirits rose. "Thanks, Pal, I mean, Dr. Thatcher. I can go on now."

That evening Bruce saw Winona bending over a dying Japanese soldier no older than herself. Every trace of hatred had vanished, and her worn face shone like a flower in the overcrowded ward.

A few days later when Manila's capture was imminent, Bruce, Winona, and the others were taken to the Bataan Peninsula. Common sense had driven them away over protests. Winona would never forget the midnight trip in a small boat painted black against detection. Incredible as it seemed, they got through, due to the skill of the Filipino fisherman who knew the waters as well as he knew himself.

The beginning of 1942 saw the team in a hastily constructed tent hospital. The anguish a few days later when news came that Manila had fallen left Winona feeling the world had turned upside down. To a nurse born in Seattle where winter rains and snow now fell, January in Bataan with its mild temperatures, continual enemy attacks, and privation added to her confusion. Too tired to do more than grimace, she went on with her work.

Malnutrition and disease added to the general misery. "It's bad enough just trying to care for the wounded," Winona told Bruce. "But *this!*" Their encampment, camouflaged as much as possible against the enemy, provided little defense against hunger and sickness.

"Are you taking your Atabrine? Every day?" he demanded. "The last thing we need is for you—or any of us—to come down with malaria."

"I take it." The corners of her mouth turned down. "Can't you tell by my beautiful yellow complexion?"

He managed a tired grin. "Better than malaria."

"Barely." But she reluctantly responded to his teasing. Not often did humor touch any of their lives these days. And she faithfully continued with her Atabrine. She might joke about malaria but the thought of it left her weak. Every pair of able hands must be available to work.

At times, Winona and Bruce felt time meant nothing: a few hours sleep, then back to duty, with insufficient food hastily wolfed down when time permitted, and always the threat of attack. Weeks limped by. Late in March the commander of the camp called the United States team aside.

"We can't hold out much longer. We've beaten back Japanese attacks for three months, but we can't go on. Too much sickness, not enough food and manpower." He wiped his sweaty face. "You have to go." He ignored the wave of protest. "You'll be taken to Corregidor—tonight. It's all arranged."

They stared. Corregidor, the rocky, fortified island at the entrance of Manila Bay on the island of Luzon, held large caves. United States and Filipino troops had dug in and continued to defend it.

The weary commander silenced their protests. "It's my hope they can hold out on Corregidor longer than we can here, at least long enough to get you away."

"But there's no guarantee." Steel laced Bruce's statement.

"None."

"Then why should we go?" Winona exploded. "I won't. Even with everything every one of us can do, we can't begin to handle the ocean of patients pouring in. How can you expect to get by without us?" Her clear voice rang in the suddenly silent room. "Every one of us pledged to serve where needed, as do military personnel." Her voice broke for a moment, the way it had done when they finally received word her fiancé had been killed at Pearl Harbor. The next instant she proudly finished. "Excuse me, Commander, but if our meeting is over I have work to do on the ward. May I go?"

Winona held her breath. Had she gone too far in making her point? Doubt clutched her throat. Maybe they should go to Corregidor. Those rock caves promised at least temporary security.

No. If the God she had grown close to in this continuing fight against death wanted her to live, nothing could happen. If not—she shrugged. She had seen too much dying to fear it, especially when she knew with all her heart physical death would not be the end for her or Bruce or any who believed in the saving power of their Lord.

Perhaps something of her inner acceptance showed in her face. The commander peremptorily waved toward the door. "Dismissed, Nurse Allen. What about the rest of you?"

Before she got to the door, Winona heard her team's unanimous promise to stick together no matter what happened.

If some team members later regretted the decision, only God knew. They doubled and tripled their efforts until one fateful day when Winona fell asleep on her feet and dropped a precious bottle of medicine.

"That's it," Bruce ordered, his heart torn by his friend's stubborn refusal to quit. He seized her by the shoulders and faced her toward the ward door. "Go to bed and stay there until you wake up naturally."

She managed a feeble grin, a shadow of her former smile. "Okay, Boss.

We can't afford to lose any more medicine." She shook her head to clear it for the short walk to a nearby tent that housed the nurses after an enemy bomb leveled their former quarters. Too tired to get out of her disheveled, soiled uniform, she fell on her hard cot, pulled a rough blanket over her head to diminish the sounds of bombing in the distance, and slept.

Hours later she awakened to Bruce's fierce shake and chilling orders. "Get up. We have to get out!" He shook her again, hard, his medical bag in his other hand.

Refreshed by sleep, Winona's body and mind responded to the urgency in his voice. "What is it?"

"Our troops have surrendered. They had no choice." Bruce's haggard face showed no surprise but an acceptance of the inevitable. "We're going to make a break and see if we can get to Corregidor. Don't wait to take anything; just come!"

If the midnight trip to Bataan had been a nightmare, their flight to Corregidor made it seem like a Sunday school picnic. Still wearing her messy uniform and clinging to Bruce's strong arm, Winona stumbled with her protector, glad for her renewed strength. She and Bruce raced through shell-pocked ground until both gasped for breath. Once Bruce stopped, clutched Winona's hand, and whispered, "We've done all we can, God. Now we're in Your hands."

From the prayer came endurance beyond belief that lent courage to go on long past human will.

Of those who fled to Corregidor, only a few made it. A dozen times Winona's heart leaped until she felt smothered. Only silent prayers and the nearness of Bruce Thatcher kept her huddled and quiet. Even when they drifted to an apparently uninhabited bit of Corregidor shore and ran for cover after intently scanning the terrain, Winona crouched beneath Bruce's protective arm, too numb with shock to realize they had actually slipped past enemy territory. Hours later, the Bataan refugees made contact with a nearby Allied unit. To Winona, the dirty and unshaven U.S. and Filipino soldiers looked like a platoon of angels.

"Begging your pardon, but we've a place for you," a kindly soldier told her. He led her deep into a cool cave and pointed to a corner. In the brief time since the newcomers' arrival, someone had hung a frayed army blanket so she could have privacy.

All the tears Winona had held back so long rose inside her at such incongruous thoughtfulness in the middle of war. She blinked hard. "You have wounded. Where can I help most?"

"Dr. Thatcher says you're to rest first." The gruff order left no room for argument. "Sorry we can't offer you the Waldorf, but then, you look like you haven't been staying there lately anyway." His weathered lips split into a grin.

He disappeared and a little later came back with a small basin of water, a canteen, and some food. "No hot and cold running water." He looked her up and down. "Hmmmm. Pretty dirty."

Again her self-appointed guardian vanished. Winona covered her mouth with her hand to keep from giggling when she heard his bellowing voice to his comrades.

"Hey, you guys, cough up some clothes for our visitor. She can't keep wearing that imported frock camouflaged as a uniform."

A loud cheer arose, and a few minutes later the soldier came back in with a khaki shirt and pants that, if not clean, were an improvement over her current clothing. "You'll have to roll up the sleeves and pant legs; even Shorty's a lot bigger than you."

"They'll be fine. Thank you and thank the men."

"We're honored."

American chivalry at its best, Winona thought. She bathed simply, ate the unappetizing but necessary food, and, with the help of a belt someone had considerately punched more holes in, dressed in her new apparel. A pallet in the corner invited. She'd sleep for just a few moments, then. . .

Winona awoke to discover a comb, a toothbrush that smelled as if it had been dipped in some kind of disinfectant, and two pairs of socks more holey than righteous.

Once more tears crowded behind her eyelids but she ignored them, thanked God, and prepared to burst into the society of her new neighborhood.

The first person she met stared, then couldn't help exclaiming, "Haw, haw!"

Winona's lips turned up in sympathy. "I know. Isn't it awful?" In the dim light in her cave corner she couldn't see what she was doing. Now she surveyed her deeply turned-up pant legs, one leg hanging down four inches longer than the other, and the bunched waist of the donated khakis. For the first time in weeks, her laugh rang out. It brought instant response from the soldiers who quickly gathered around her.

"Better than a tonic," one yelled. "That's what we've been needing around here. Some real, live, fashion model!"

Healing laughter echoed throughout the cave, and Winona's spirits lifted.

"Do you feel ready to help me?" Bruce asked from the cave entrance.

Winona noted he had also been given fresh clothing, only his shirt didn't quite meet in front. Its donor must be much slimmer. "I'm ready." She trotted after him.

The pattern began that lasted for almost a month. Bruce beckoned; she followed. She learned to know and love the patients who eagerly turned to her, some even younger than herself. Her respect for Bruce deepened. How could he accomplish so much under such conditions?

One harrowing night, Bruce literally saved a young Filipino soldier's life by performing a tracheotomy by flashlight. Afterward Winona thought of how many times Candleshine had talked about holding high a torch. Would she and Bruce ever see her again?

To the young nurse's surprise, she discovered that although guns boomed and reverberated, fear waited to pounce, and death surrounded her, "the peace that passeth understanding" never left her. Along with her deepening faith and devoted service, something else crept into Winona's life. Memory of her lost fiancé dulled with the passage of events she'd lived through and the daily necessity to go on. She realized one day while she'd never forget her first young love, she had the capacity to love again.

Sweeny, who doggedly claimed her as his girl " 'cause he took care of her when she first came" staked his claim. "Remember, guys. Hands off. When we get outta this dump and back home, I'm going to come calling on Miss Winona Allen. When I wear my best blue serge, who can resist me?"

"You dumb guy, I bet Doc Thatcher will have something to say about that," someone called.

Sweeny spun toward the doctor. His eyes rounded and he exaggerated the awe in his voice. "That right, Doc?"

Winona felt red creep from her open shirt collar up into her face. *How will Bruce handle such joking? Maybe he'll be uncomfortable.*

Bruce didn't hesitate even for a heartbeat. He simply turned his blue gaze first on Winona's red face then toward Sweeny. "Sorry, Buddy. When we get outta this dump—" He mimicked Sweeny perfectly. "I'm going to come calling on Winona wearing my best white doctor's outfit." His grin lit up his thin face. "What nurse can resist a doctor?"

"Aw, Doc." Sweeny's face fell. "There ain't no way I can compete with you. Hey, short stuff, do you have any sisters?"

She escaped to her corner, her face flaming. For hours she wondered why her long-frozen heart felt as if Bruce had indeed lighted a candle in its depths that left her warmed all over.

By May 5 the valiant Corregidor holdouts knew, in spite of everything they could do, the end lurked in the shadows. Bruce talked over with Winona what lay ahead.

"We'll be taken prisoner. I'm not sure where the Japanese will send us. Probably either to Santo Tomás internment camp or Bilibid prison. It's not going to be easy, Winona."

She knew the fear in his eyes was for her, not for himself. She sighed. "At least we missed the Bataan Death March." She shuddered, remembering the news gathered in bits and pieces through the limited contact with the outside world.

"The only way I can see that we may be spared at least a few of the indignities is to make much of our medical skills," Bruce said. "I wouldn't do it for myself." His lip curled. "For you—"

The poignant light that sometimes touched his blue eyes now filled them. Bruce gently took her hands. "Winona, I know it's too soon after Pearl Harbor and all that happened, but I meant what I told Sweeny. If—no—*when* we get home, would you open your door if a certain spiffed-up doctor knocked on it?"

A rush of emotion left her speechless. She could only nod.

Bruce left it at that. He squeezed her hands and whispered a broken, "Try to rest" before leaving her alone with teary eyes and a hope that could never be extinguished.

The next day Japan claimed victory on Corregidor, and the organized Allied resistance in the Philippines died.

Only Winona's faith in God and growing realization of her love for Bruce kept her from sheer insanity in the weeks and months that followed. True to Bruce's predictions, conditions in the internment camp proved sickening. His fervent pleas for the humane treatment guaranteed to prisoners of war under the Geneva Convention went unheeded. Treatment and care of the sick and wounded that was provided for in the Convention remained nonexistent. So did protection for civilians. Prisoners suffered from lack of food and existed on one small bowl of rice a day with now and then a few scraps of meat that Winona refused to identify for fear she could not get it down. As winter came, a lack of blankets and adequate covering against the tropical rains left many dead.

Winona fared slightly better only because Bruce proved of immeasurable value with his medical knowledge. Not that the guards cared for their prisoners. They treasured Dr. Thatcher's skills for the sake of themselves, but even that didn't help him escape all cruelty. When the men and women were separated into filthy barracks, Winona learned through the unstoppable line of communication how Bruce faced death.

The uniformed officers spotted the small caducean pin Bruce had managed to keep and proudly wore on his collar. "What is that?" they demanded.

"A symbol of my profession. I am a doctor."

"Silence!" One backhanded him and brought blood from his lips. "You are an American spy, sent to betray Japan."

"I am a doctor."

The soldier hit him again. "You are a spy."

Battered until almost senseless, Bruce knew he must convince them if he were to help Winona. His swollen lips continued to proclaim his profession until the guard threw him in a cell and left him there, evidently convinced this strong man spoke the truth.

A few days later, the same guard jerked open the cell door, pulling Bruce out of a restless, troubled sleep, and ordered him to follow. Bruce stumbled back into the same room where he had been beaten.

"If you are a doctor, fix him." The officer in charge pointed to a fellow officer on a cot in the corner who lay groaning and clutching his right side. Three minutes later, Bruce knew he had one hot appendix to deal with—fast.

"I need help," he told the officer. "Bring Nurse Allen here."

"Impossible!" The officer glared and his thin eyebrows met in a scowl.

"Are you prepared to assist me?" Bruce's voice cut like a polished scalpel.

The officer on the cot wavered, then ordered the guard, "Bring this nurse here."

Bruce lived a lifetime waiting for Winona. At least he would see her and know for himself how she fared. He would see in her eyes if she'd been mistreated.

Thank God, his heart cried when she came in, her eyes enormous with being summoned but untouched by horrors he'd imagined.

Less than an hour later, Bruce and Winona had scrubbed in surprisingly hot water that had never made its way to the prisoners, and Bruce made the incision.

Great beads of sweat stood on his forehead. If the appendix had burst or if peritonitis had set in, it meant his and Winona's deaths as well as the Japanese officer's. "Easy, now," he breathed, grateful for the small, skillful hands that had not lost their touch in the months of hardship.

"Now." He finished preliminary duties and with a lightning, trained motion removed the swollen, diseased appendix.

It burst in the pan.

"Sutures." Bruce stitched the wound as carefully as a woman sews her wedding dress and breathed a sigh of relief. He caught Winona's matching sigh with keen ears and whispered, "Praises be."

"No whispers. Guard, take the nurse away," the officer ordered.

"Thank you, Nurse Allen." Bruce's eyes said much more, but her demure reply successfully hid from their persecutors how clearly she had received his message.

"Good night, Dr. Thatcher."

Her soft and eloquent look remained with Bruce long after he again lay in the wretched space allotted to him.

Chapter 4

"Nurse Thatcher?" A probationer still in her teens lightly tapped on Candleshine's open door.

"Yes?" Candleshine finished securing her cap and smiled at the hesitant young woman. How long it seemed since she had been a probie approaching her Big Sister's door. "Come in, Sally. How are you getting along?"

Sally Monroe stepped inside but shook her head when the older nurse motioned her to a chair. Her unruly red curls threatened to dislodge from the hairpins that restrained them. "Everything is fine, so far," she said. "Miss Grey would like to see you." Her brown eyes looked enormous. "Is it as scary to get called to her office when you're a real nurse as when you're a probie?"

Candleshine laughed, a joyous burst that relaxed Sally. "Almost." Her blue eyes twinkled. "Don't let Miss Grey frighten you, Sally. She's one of the grandest women I've ever been privileged to know."

"I agree." Sally clasped her hands in earnestness, and her entire face glowed. "It's just that when I see her I feel I must have done something wrong even when I know I didn't, if that makes any sense."

"It does. That's her way of getting the best from you." Candleshine hesitated, then impulsively confessed, "Don't let it turn your head, but Miss Grey thinks you show the most promise of anyone in your class."

"Oh, Miss Thatcher!" Red swept into the attractive face.

"That also means she will be harder on you than any other woman in your class," Candleshine warned.

"Think I care about that?" Sally squared her shoulders. "Thanks a trillion!" She swooped across the room, quickly kissed Candleshine's cheek, then fled, happy tears flowing.

"Was I ever that young?" Candleshine marveled then shrugged. "Probably, and far less sure of myself than Sally." She hastened downstairs, wrapped her cape close against the crisp winter air, and rapidly walked through the covered passage from Hunter Hall to the hospital and Miss Grey's office. Before entering, she idly fingered the letters SUPERINTENDENT OF NURSES on the door. Could Miss Grey have the news that Candleshine had waited on for so long, that would send her overseas? She breathed deeply and opened the door.

The first thing she noticed was Miss Grey's smile. The second, a soldier who leaned on a crutch and awkwardly got to his feet. She stifled the urge to tell him not to stand. Months ago, she'd learned how much wounded soldiers resented being babied about their disabilities.

"Candace, this is Sergeant Sweeny." Miss Grey stood with a rustle of starched skirts and walked toward the door. "You may use my office for as long as you wish."

"Grand old dame, ain't she?" Sweeny commented almost before the door closed behind Miss Grey.

"I wouldn't exactly use those words, but yes, she's an excellent nurse and friend." Candleshine couldn't help laughing at the kindly but blunt sergeant. "How can I help you?"

"Sit down so I can." He settled back in his chair after she dropped to one nearby. "You're Bruce Thatcher's cousin, aren't you?"

Excitement washed through Candleshine and brought her out of her chair to kneel at Sweeny's side. "How do you know? Where's Bruce? Is he all right? And Winona—Nurse Allen?"

Sergeant Sweeny grinned his crooked grin, and his eyes shone, then shadowed. "How long has it been since you heard from either of them?"

"Not since the fall of Manila."

Sweeny grunted in satisfaction. "Well, as of the sixth of May when Corregidor fell, your cousin and friend were alive and as well as could be expected, considering all things."

"Thank God!" Bright drops gathered, but her hard-won discipline held them back. She blindly groped for Sweeny's hardened hand. "Tell me everything, please."

In brief sentences that allowed her to read far more between the lines than what he actually said, Sergeant Sweeny described the welcome arrival of "Doc" Thatcher and Nurse Winona. Candleshine laughed at his description of her short friend in khakis several sizes too large and rejoiced over the good the medical duo did on Corregidor. She held her breath when Sweeny continued.

"I know both of them were okay when we reached our new vacation hotel internment camp," Sweeny assured her. But his face wrinkled and he scowled. "Some dump." He hurried on, obviously unwilling to go into details about the camp.

"Oh, Doc got in good with the head honchos by performing a neat little operation and saving one of them whose appendix went haywire. Your nurse friend helped." He threw back his head and laughed. "Can you believe I actually got down on my knees and gave thanks for that appendix?"

Candleshine couldn't even move. Her mind whirled. Bruce and Winona, incarcerated in a prison camp and still doing their medical best!

Sweeny's laughter died. "See, Doc traded on what he'd done and kept reminding the officers. Finally, probably to shut him up, they let him and Nurse Allen look after the worst hurt of the prisoners. They couldn't do a lot, but boy, they did a whole lot more than anyone could believe. Just having that pint-sized nurse walk into a filthy cell and grin that grin of hers shot morale out of the mud."

"How long ago was this?"

Sweeny scratched his head and stared out the window at the Seattle dusk. "Months."

"Sorry," he added, when Candleshine's head drooped. "Hey, they're going to be all right. That God of theirs won't let it be any other way."

So Bruce and Winona offer more than physical help, she thought.

"How did you get out?"

"Dug, at night. Thought we'd never make it." He licked his lips, and Candleshine wished she hadn't asked.

"Five of us started. The guards got all but me." Anguish aged him. "I did all the things I learned as a kid. Waded when I could. Climbed trees. Finally, I made it to the middle of nowhere, and they quit looking, I guess."

"What happened to your leg?"

"Took a bullet at Corregidor." A spasm of pain crossed his face. "If the Japanese hadn't finally let Doc look at it, I'd be missing my left leg. It kinda slowed me down when I got out, but my buddies waited until I could walk pretty good." He shifted the leg. "Anyway, I hid out, pretty near starved, and met up with some Filipinos who'd escaped and hid in the hills. They took care of me." He closed his eyes and swallowed hard. "Say, if I hadn't believed in miracles before, I do now."

Candleshine tingled at his reverent voice and tightened her grip on the big man's hand.

"I wouldn't have thought an eel could get out of there, but two Filipinos I'm proud to call brothers snaked me through the jungle, stole a Japanese boat, knifed three guards, and appropriated their uniforms. I knew every inch of ocean we traveled would be our last."

His sudden raucous laugh almost curled Candleshine's eyelashes. "We had enough trouble with the Japanese, but when we got to where we had a chance of meeting up with our own troops, those darned prison uniforms near got us killed! I jerked off my T-shirt and waved it like a flag, then started singing 'The Star-Spangled Banner' at the top of my lungs. It worked."

His breathless listener could almost see the vivid scene.

"Well, as soon as they could they got me picked up and taken to Australia. I spent some time in a hospital there—man, but those nurses are hardworking and pretty. One of them reminded me of your friend. . . ."

Disappointment filled Candleshine, but she forced a bright smile. "I am so glad you came." Her lips quivered. "At least we can have hope for Bruce and Winona."

Sergeant Sweeny's face spread into a grin. Mischief danced in his eyes. "Think two people as much in love as those two need proper food and all that stuff? Didn't you ever hear about living on love?"

"Really? Are they really in love?"

Sweeny drew his mouth down in a fake frown. "Doc up and told me his intentions in front of everyone when I said I'd be calling on our little nurse after the war."

"What did Winona say?"

"Nothing. She just turned pink as the roses that climb into my window back home and headed for her own private bood-wahr in the corner of the cave." He looked wise. "They deserve each other. Besides, I've got someone writing to me and waiting until this mess is over. If her letters mean anything."

"I'm sure they do, Sergeant," Candleshine softly told him. "I will never stop being thankful that you came."

He freed his hand and struggled to his feet. "My train's leaving in an hour so I have to go. Soon as I quit hobbling around I'm going back. Me and General MacArthur aim to return." Once more Sweeny smiled at the girl who had risen when he did. "Before that, though, I'm heading home to see my girl and folks."

"God bless you." Candleshine kissed his leathery cheek.

He swung out, leaning a bit on his crutch, then made the universal V-for-Victory sign with his right hand and gallantly saluted. She watched him out of sight, the embodiment of the spirit of America, and silently prayed for his safety.

★ ★ ★

"Will you be home for Christmas?" Trinity asked on a rare visit from Candleshine when she had been given a little time off from her ever-increasing duties.

"No; the government has asked civilians not to travel so there will be more plane and train space for servicemen. Besides, I can do so much good with the homesick GIs who can't go home."

"We've been saving our gasoline, just in case," Will put in. He, as well as Trinity, showed the effects of war and worry. Silver streaks mingled with brown in his curly hair. "Suppose we come down and find a restaurant for an early holiday."

"I'd love it." Candleshine sighed. "Mom, Dad, if only I could do more! Why don't I get approval so I can go overseas?"

"When that's what God wants you to do, it will happen," Will quietly reminded her.

Her blue eyes looked almost black in her thin face. "I know, but waiting must be even worse than actually being in the middle of things."

"When you grow impatient, think of Bruce and Winona, how they must feel. And Connie."

Candleshine had never felt so selfish in her life. She was fed as well as rationing would allow at the hospital and even better at home where her parents raised almost everything. Thousands of miles away, Bruce and Winona existed on scraps. She couldn't even envision the hardship that surrounded them.

Candleshine remembered the latest of the few letters she had received from Connie. Although she sounded cheerful, describing how the relocated people refused to become bitter against their country, how they ordered things from catalogs to brighten their existence, she felt the underlying mood. The worst thing about communal living was the lack of privacy. Connie and her family had taught Candleshine how important the individual family unit's privacy was to their lifestyle. How did the Imotos survive in the same quarters, with little chance to be alone? Shame erased her impatience. With so much need before her right at Mercy Hospital, longing for new pastures in which to serve was inexcusable.

The war years created a lifestyle and mood not to be duplicated again. War bonds. Rationing. Frozen jobs. Women flocked to factories by the thousands to meet the demand for planes and ships. Parachute packers, whose skill would mean life or death for those who used them, worked tirelessly. Trinity Thatcher struggled to interest children in history, yet their minds flew with the planes that sometimes zoomed above isolated Cedar Ridge. Even while logging and farming, Will Thatcher and his family were always alert to the war news.

The year 1942 stumbled into 1943 and still the holocaust continued. Sometimes Candleshine wondered if even her faith in God could keep her going. Mercy Hospital's staff had changed drastically. Younger doctors vanished monthly, needed in the war efforts. Older doctors came out of retirement and gave their best. Candleshine's nursing class had dispersed literally to the ends of the earth. When word came that one of her own classmates had been killed while serving in Germany, the staff wept and relentlessly went on serving.

Countless wounded men fell in love with Candleshine and the other nurses. Sally, a junior now, came to Candleshine's room one evening. "I know you aren't really my Big Sister," she said. "I mean, you're a graduate, not another student. But you're always there when I need you." Despondency marred her usually vivid face. "Candleshine—I'm glad you said I could call you that—I have a terrible problem."

"Miss Grey again?"

"No—Jim." A flood of tears erupted.

"The young man you've dated since high school."

"He's been working in a defense factory until he could gain enough weight to enlist," she whispered. "Now he wants us to get married before he goes. He's on furlough after basic training."

Candleshine felt old enough to be Sally's mother. She bit her lip to keep from crying out, "Don't!" Instead she quietly asked, "How do you feel about it?"

Sally wiped her tears with the handkerchief Candleshine offered. Her honest brown eyes held doubt. "I don't know. I love Jim and I always will. Shouldn't I do this for him? He might not come back. But if I marry, it means giving up my training. I couldn't just keep still and live a lie."

The words hung in the night air. Candleshine desperately prayed inside to know how to respond. Sally and Jim faced one of the major crossroads of their lives. How they chose to act would color their entire futures.

"Have you told Jim exactly how you feel and why?"

Sally's head drooped. "Not yet. He just mentioned it last night and wouldn't let me answer. He said I had to think about it but that he would be able to face anything in the world if I married him before he goes in the service."

"Sally, talk with him. Tell him how important your studies are to you. Your Jim may not even have considered how far-reaching the results of a war marriage can be."

Sally's muffled voice came from behind the handkerchief. "I—I don't know how to begin. I've prayed about it, but somehow with all the problems in the world God must be too busy to answer right away."

"Anything that concerns you is big enough for His attention," Candleshine told her.

Sally raised her head. "It's not like he's just asking me to go away for a weekend," she said proudly. "Jim would never do that and neither would I. I told one of my girlfriends that when she bought a phony ring at the dime store. She said a girl should sacrifice something for her country. That's nuts. Our brave men are fighting so America will remain the upstanding country it is."

"You are very wise." Candleshine sighed. "A few years ago the big question in the advice columns was, 'Should I let him kiss me good night on the first date?' Now this war has turned the world so upside down even nice people are shifting their values and accepting false ones!"

Sally smoothed her crumpled uniform and raised her head. "Thanks for listening. I'll see Jim as soon as I have time off." Her sensitive lips quivered. "I'm not exactly sure what's going to happen, but talking with you helped—a lot."

Later Candleshine pondered Sally's problem. Suppose she were in Sally's shoes, in love with a worthy young man, as Jim appeared to be. Would she have the strength to resist a hasty marriage and a few days together that might be all they would ever have? Would Sally, wise but deeply in love, make the right decision?

A week later Sally brought her Jim to meet Candleshine. She glowed with happiness and something more. "Jim didn't know I couldn't finish training if we married," she said.

"It's what she's wanted since she wore rompers," the steady-faced young man said. "I guess I went haywire when I suggested getting married."

"Not haywire," said Candleshine, and she impulsively laid her hand on the arm of the brand-new khaki sleeve that signified Jim had finished basic training.

"Take care of her, will you, Miss Thatcher? I mean, as long as you're here. Sally told me you're waiting for marching orders yourself."

"You are making a wise decision," Candleshine said. "I honestly believe that putting aside your own desires for the good of the country is for the best. Nurses are desperately needed, more now than ever before in history."

The look Jim gave Sally sent a lump to Candleshine's throat. "When I come home—" His voice underscored each word with absolute certainty. "When I come home we'll do it the right way. Church wedding, white dress, all the trimmings—not a quick ceremony in a stuffy little office."

Sally's eyes looked as if a small piece of heaven had dropped into her lap, and Candleshine quietly left them alone with their deferred plans.

The experience brought Sally even closer to her mentor. Letters from Jim nearly always contained warm greetings to Candleshine. Sally bore up proudly, even when the message—*shipping out, destination unknown*—arrived. She studied harder, used every iota of training she had, and won the admiration of the formidable Miss Grey. Somehow the superintendent had gotten wind of the proposed elopement and final decision and had called Sally in to congratulate her. The student nurse floated around Mercy Hospital for a good week.

"Haven't you ever been in love?" Sally blurted out one day when she and Candleshine were assigned to the same ward and met in the linen room.

"What makes you ask?" Candleshine felt more astonished than angry.

"Just about every GI you take care of is either gone or at least half-gone on you." Sally peeked out from behind a stack of precariously balanced clean sheets.

"Here, let me help." Candleshine quickly shifted the mountain. "You know these men are just homesick and missing their own girls. They fall in and out of love with all the nurses. It's our job not to take them seriously."

"How can you help it?" Sally rolled her brown eyes. "Some of the officers are so dreamy. If I didn't already have the greatest guy God ever created in the twentieth century, I'd have no willpower at all!" She giggled. "I guess maybe with you it isn't willpower but *won't*power. You won't let any of the guys get beyond a patient-nurse relationship."

You don't know the half of it, Candleshine thought even while she nodded. The hospital grapevine had it that Candleshine didn't even give a good-night kiss to the few *doctors* she occasionally dated!

"Can't help it," she muttered when Sally disappeared with her sheets. "If I don't care about a man, I'm not going to let him think I do." She finished her work and shut the linen room door behind her with a little bang. "Someday, when skies smile and the world is free, I'll meet the person God already knows I will marry. Until then, forget it. Period."

The ring of a bell that signaled someone needed her drove errant thoughts away, and Nurse Thatcher responded on swift and silent feet.

Chapter 5

Lieutenant Jeffrey Fairfax knelt and laid a sheaf of wild roses between the new twin mounds in the tiny western Montana cemetery. His unseeing deep blue eyes, so dark they looked black in times of emotion, barely registered the distant, snowcapped peaks and gentle breeze that relieved the dry heat. Slowly-waving hemlocks and cedars forever stood sentinel over the dead.

If I had been home, would Dad and Mom still be alive?

He bared his head, and the sympathetic sun sent blue shadows dancing in his black hair. He would never know. Heartsore and numb, he muttered, "What a way to come home."

A little shiver went through his six-foot muscular frame. Darkly tanned hands clasped around one knee, and he remained kneeling, his head bowed.

A callused hand fell on his shoulder as a ragged voice brought him back to life. "Jeff, Boy, you couldn't have done a thing. Your daddy and mother would still have rushed to Kalispell when the call came about your aunt being sick." John Carson, foreman of the Laughing X Ranch for thirty years, shook a bent forefinger at the uniformed man, then cleared his throat. "So long as there's trains, there's gonna be wrecks. Doc said your folks were killed instantly. They didn't have to suffer." Carson's hand dropped as he made circles in the earth with a dusty-toed boot.

Jeff stood no taller than the white-haired foreman and no stronger, despite the difference between twenty-five and fifty-five years. Carson represented the last of the trail-hardened Western breed who actually made a living running cattle and horses. By shrewdly adding new, improved methods to his wealth of knowledge, Carson's keen blue eyes could usually see trouble coming and handle it before it got to the ranch—*but not this time.*

"Well, Boy," said Carson, shoving his battered Stetson to the back of his head, "what next?" He followed Jeff's rapid stride down the knoll and toward the ranch house that gleamed as white as the day the first pioneering Fairfax built it for his wife. More at home in the saddle than on foot, Carson surprisingly kept up with his pensive friend.

Once inside the comfortable house, Jeff prowled the length and width of the worn but attractive living room. Polished wood floors and bright Indian blankets, harmoniously blended with good furniture and a few choice paintings, gave the room Old West charm. A rock fireplace that could accommodate a Bunyan-sized log now housed only dead ashes.

Carson's uncanny ability to understand Jeff became evident once again. "The way I see it, the good Lord did it right. Can you imagine if just one of them had been taken?"

"No," Jeff muttered softly. Their eyes met and held in wordless recognition of the unusual bond of love between Jeff's parents.

Carson's face softened. "I know it's a rotten homecomin' for you. No two folks ever had more pride than what they felt about you, Boy."

Jeff squirmed as he remembered a few best-hidden things in his life Dad and Mom never knew.

"Why, it seems like just last week when you up and said you weren't goin' to college, and your daddy reckoned you were." A reminiscent light shone in the faithful foreman's eyes. "I recollect him standing right there at the corner of the fireplace, his face set hard as the rocks that made it, saying, 'You're going, Jeff. Once you're done you can come back and take over the ranch, and your mother and I will give thanks and rejoice forever.' He wanted you to marry a good girl and fill this old ranch house with pattering feet and laughter. But first, he knew you had to know a whole lot more than even a range-trained high school boy. Learn about the rest of the world. 'You may think the Laughing X is the nearest place to heaven that God ever put on this earth,' he used to say. But he knew once you learned what's on the other side of those mountains, you'd understand that we live in troubled times."

Carson took a deep breath, and Jeff stayed nailed to the spot. He remembered that conversation as easily as Carson.

"Your daddy wanted you to go out, learn what you could about life, and come back, a full partner in the Laughing X."

Carson abruptly changed the subject. "When all's been said, just remember your folks believed dyin' wasn't all that different than ridin' out of sight to new territory across the mountains."

"What do you believe?" Jeff demanded.

"Me?" Carson's brows rose. "I reckon they were right." His blue gaze sharpened. "You'd better too what with all this fightin' you'll be in, and soon, I'd say. You'd have been in it a lot sooner if the good old U.S. didn't need our cattle so much they up and ordered you to stay home." Carson cackled. "Thought I'd never see so much letter writin' as you did to convince them you should go when the way I hear it, there are those who are writin' a passel of letters to get out of the service!"

"Dirty slackers." The little smile Jeff wore had faded. "We had them when Dad fought in World War I. Now we've got them again."

Carson sighed. "I won't say it's gonna be easy here with all our boys joinin' up." He snorted. "The bunch of pilgrims I'm able to hire these days shoulda stayed in the old folks home. I ain't complainin', though, at least not much. I aim to help win this war by raisin' the best beef in Montana so our boys can eat right." His leathered face cracked into a grin. "Just look at that." He pointed toward the open window that framed prime steers, each with the Laughing X brand on its flank.

"Wonder how long it will take to whip our enemies so I can get back here?" Jeff mused.

Carson's satisfaction died. "I think we're in for a long, hard war, Boy." He stood and stretched, then froze, his hands still in the air. "Uh-oh. Here's trouble."

Jeff's sharp ears caught the whine of a car motor he'd learned to dread in the week he'd been home. "What's she doing here, anyway?" he said furiously.

"Well, she sure didn't come to see me," said Carson, chuckling. "You've faced wild steers and mountain lions, coyotes and wolves. I reckon you can handle one little bitty city gal." He hurried across the room and out the back door.

Jeff muttered something more descriptive than elegant and strode to the wide-roofed porch. Right now he'd take one of each of the animals Carson had mentioned rather than meet Lillian Grover!

He dispassionately surveyed the small woman whose platinum hair and delicate makeup were her trademark. A lovely face, no, a lovely *mask*, like those worn at fancy balls. Why in thunder had he ever been polite to her when introduced by a friend at college? She must be in her early thirties, although she didn't look it.

Jeff sighed. Fairfax hospitality demanded at least a lukewarm reception. He walked down the steps to the graveled half-circle driveway. "Hello, Lillian; what brings you out here?"

"Oh, Jeff!" Suddenly the ingénue, she clapped her hands and ran to him on tiny spiked heels. A wave of cloying perfume polluted the fresh Montana air, and the rustle of silk seemed out of place against the rustic Laughing X terrain.

"I have the most wonderful news," she bubbled after Jeff seated her in a big porch chair and haughtily brought ice-cold lemonade instead of the drink she demanded. When he told her no one on the Laughing X drank—or didn't remain on the ranch if they did—Lillian didn't seem fazed at all.

"You know my father's in big with the powers that be," she reminded him, as she had before on the few occasions he'd seen her. "Well, it's the same as arranged. All you have to do is sign the final papers and you have a total deferment." She beamed, and her pale blue eyes wore an unusual sparkle.

"*What?*" Jeff sloshed his lemonade until it spilled on his pants. His eyes narrowed, and the tiny wrinkles caused by the sun and hours of watching long distances increased.

"It's a surprise. I didn't say anything until Father got approval. You're to be his top advisory assistant in his plant. You know he's making munitions now instead of cars."

For the first time in his life, Jeffrey Fairfax lost all power of speech. How dare she interfere in his life? What right did Lillian Grover have to arrange his future? Most importantly, just what game was she playing? She certainly didn't think he cared about her, did she? Jeff wanted to laugh. Even if he hadn't been too busy with college to be interested in young women other than as casual dates, Lillian or any woman like her would be the last type he'd admire.

"Just what's the idea?" he asked ominously.

Lillian slowly sipped her lemonade and lowered the dark eyelashes so strangely out of place with her silvery hair. She glanced up through them with a look Jeff recognized and found unappealing. "We—I—you, Jeff." Her hands played with the small handbag in her skirted lap. "From the time we met, I felt an immediate flow between us. When you talked about the Laughing X, it sounded heavenly." She turned toward the rolling reaches of the Fairfax spread, and her eyes glistened.

Good heavens, this woman must think I'm rich! Knowledge struck Jeff like a lightning bolt. He quickly said, "It's nothing like heaven when northers rip through and the summer sun beats down. A woman like you would freeze or shrivel out here."

Storm signals came to the pale blue eyes. "I'm tougher than I look, Jeff."

I'll just bet you are. Jeff smothered a grin.

"Besides, we—a person wouldn't have to live out here all the time. You have competent hired hands, don't you?"

Jeff almost choked. He could just see Carson if he ever heard little Miss Silk-and-Ruffles dismissing his position in that offhand voice!

"Lillian, I hate to be inhospitable," said Jeff, deliberately glancing at the lowering sun. "But it's a long way back to the city, and frankly, this isn't a good time to visit. I came home when Dad and Mom died in a train accident, and—"

"I know." Sympathy dripped from her voice. "Why, the very minute I heard the news I knew you'd be back, so I canceled a dozen engagements and came as soon as I could."

Fury crept into Jeff's heart. This silly but determined woman had obviously kept track of his movements! How long had her surveillance been in effect? All through the time he remained on the ranch waiting for orders?

"I really think you'd better go." He shed his former courtesy, wondering if later he'd regret being the first Fairfax ever to dismiss a guest from the Laughing X. "Carson and I have much to discuss, and I won't be home long. Thank you for taking the trouble to look up such a casual acquaintance." He stood.

If his dart found its mark, Lillian didn't let it show. She merely smiled. "Sit back down, Jeff. I'm not finished."

"Oh?" He cocked an eyebrow, and again his eyes turned midnight blue. "Excuse me if I didn't say I am not interested in working in the munitions factory. I have a job to do, and I will be overseas as soon as I can get things squared away here."

"Don't be stubborn. You're too important to become cannon fodder."

"I won't be facing cannons. I'll be flying. Dad and Mom encouraged me to take lessons years ago; they thought maybe someday we'd be able to have a small plane. Things didn't work out, though. We never had the money. On the other hand, now I can use my flying skills to serve my country." He looked at her curiously. "With every American desperately needed, how are *you* going to serve, Lillian? As a nurse, or maybe in the women's armed forces?"

"Heavens, no!" She shuddered. "My nerves are far too delicate for that. I'm doing a really *important* job, getting up all kinds of morale-boosting entertainment for the servicemen, recruiting attractive girls to work in the USO. Daddy's working on my getting sent to Washington, D.C." She slanted a glance at him. "That's not far from his munitions plant, you know."

"How did you ever happen to go to college in Montana?" he asked irrelevantly, wishing she'd go.

Lillian laughed. "I didn't have the grades for a big-name Eastern school. Besides, Daddy wants to get into politics, and being a big toad in a small state like Montana could be a first step. He thought my attending school out here would give him some good publicity. You know, 'daughter of important Montana-born millionaire chooses home state' kind of thing."

With an eel-like movement, she slipped from her chair and stood next to him. "That uniform looks good on you, Jeff. Too bad you won't be wearing it at the plant. Or—" She considered for a moment. "I could have Daddy do some wangling and get you a Washington assignment. It's too bad for you to have to go back in civvies."

"I won't be." He smiled as he thought of sending her flying down the steps, out of sight and back where she belonged. "Thanks again for coming, but I have work to do."

Lillian's pretty face turned mutinous.

"Carson?" Jeff called.

The lively foreman appeared faster than you could say Laughing X Ranch. "Right here."

"Miss Grover's ready to go now so we can get back to our ways and means committee of two. I'll be in by the time you get a pot of coffee going. We'll delay supper for a time and get at our problems."

"Drive carefully," Carson told Lillian before disappearing into the ranch house.

Jeffrey piloted her to her expensive car, talking all the way to stop the protest he knew trembled on her painted lips. He ended with a firm handshake. "I know you're busy and so am I, so I'll just say good-bye now. If you see any of the college crowd, give them my greetings. Maybe someday after this war ends we can have a reunion."

Silenced by a determination that overshadowed her own, Lillian angrily jerked her car into gear and shot out of the driveway after calling, "I'll be in touch about the post in Washington!"

"Good riddance." Jeff stalked up the steps, across the porch, and inside the sprawling home.

"Reminds me of a filly that needs to be broke," Carson reflected. "Pretty as paint but too much paint to suit me." He glanced at the large, framed photograph of Jeff's parents that hung over the mantel. An unaccustomed mist clouded his old blue eyes and Jeff saw his hands clench, then relax. "Boy, if ever you bring home a gal, get one like your mother."

"I will. . . ." Jeff's voice trailed off, and the work he'd called pressing seemed to dim. "Are there any more like her? I'm old-fashioned, I guess, but I can't stomach women like Lillian Grover—and since this blamed war started, I'm seeing a lot of them!"

"She shoulda been turned over her pa's knee when she was small."

"How come you never slipped into a double harness?" Jeff asked Carson.

"I'm a one-woman man, and besides, she married someone else," Carson said quietly, causing Jeff to regret the question.

That woman was Mom, Jeff suddenly knew, but he didn't let on. Carson's well-hidden secret would remain his own unless he chose to tell it.

Instead, Carson turned from the photograph to Jeff and said, "Let's get down to facts and figures."

As much as Jeff loved the Laughing X, demands and all, he chafed under the necessary restrictions that kept him in Montana and not on his way overseas. He agreed with Carson that everything must be left in the best possible condition to raise the best beef in Montana for the troops. From dawn to dusk, Jeff, Carson, and the hands Carson called "pilgrims" rode hills and valleys, rounded up strays, and counted cattle and horses.

"I don't hire aliens," Jeff curtly told three men one afternoon. "If a man's not willing to take out citizenship papers, then there's no place for him here."

Carson's eyes flashed. "You didn't have to tell me that."

"I know." Jeff's steady gaze simmered down his irascible foreman. "You can run this place with both hands tied and one foot missing. At least I don't have that to worry about." His brows knitted into a clean, black line. "Wish I could say the same about other things."

"Such as how to duck outta sight when Miss Grover shows?" Carson's teeth gleamed in a wolfish smile. "Say, want me to get rid of her for you?"

"Yeah, if you can without nailing her hide to the barn door."

Carson's eyes beamed with satisfaction. "Next time that little ol' auto of hers comes bouncin' in, leave it to me. But if you want to have some fun, stick close enough to hear."

A few days later Carson got his chance. Puffs of dust on the valley road heralded Lillian's approach. This time, instead of flinging himself on a barebacked horse, Jeff crouched just inside the big casement window off the front porch, fervently praying Lillian wouldn't suddenly find a reason to come inside.

"Where's Jeff, Carson?" Lillian's crisp voice little resembled the tone she used for her quarry.

"I saw him ride off earlier," Carson said truthfully and failed to add he'd also seen him return. "Miss Grover, may I be so bold as to get your advice, about Jeff, I mean?"

"Why, of course." She came up the steps and sat down, while Jeff stuffed his fist in his mouth to keep from betraying his presence.

"It's like this. A long time ago the Laughing X made money. Then came the Depression and now with the war—"

Jeff couldn't resist raising his head and peeking through the window to where Carson sat on the porch rail facing Lillian and the house, his face bland and eyes innocent.

"You mean it's not a paying proposition anymore?" The small woman's incisive voice cut through Carson's hesitation.

"Let's just say we're not sellin' beef the way we used to."

Jeff was in agony. Wily Carson, who scorned to tell a lie but only told part of the truth. Of course they weren't selling beef just now, and they wouldn't until roundup a few weeks off!

"I was wonderin'—your daddy's got a lot of money and all. Think he'd be willin' to give Jeff a helpin' hand?"

A cold chill slid down Jeff's spine. Had Carson overplayed his little scene? He felt sure of it when Lillian spoke.

"He'd help but only to get Jeff in his factory or behind a desk in Washington, Carson. I don't plan to marry a rancher, especially if he's running a downhill place."

"Marry?" Carson's hand stroking his unshaven chin sounded like a buzz saw. "You're right, Miss Grover. A rancher's the worst kind of man to tie to, specially one like Jeff. Why, he'd expect you to come right out here and take charge of the house. Our cook's been mutterin' about askin' for his time—say, can you cook and clean and milk cows?"

Lillian's gasp reached Jeff's ears. She hastily rose. "Carson, I want a straight answer. How tied to the Laughing X is Jeff? I'm getting discouraged trying to get him to agree to leave it."

Carson stood and swept off his stained Stetson. His poignant blue eyes shone like mountain lakes. "Miss Grover, this place, such as it is, why, it's Jeff's *life*. Never under God's blue sky will Jeffrey Fairfax live anywhere else. Now if you're willin' to accept that and come make a home for him—"

"Never." She exhaled loudly before running down the steps.

Heedless of giving himself away, Jeff peered out the window and saw the defeat in Lillian's face.

"I'd just as soon you didn't mention our little talk to Jeff." She saucily blew Carson a kiss. "Thanks for letting me know how things are. Oh, tell Jeff I've gone to Washington. Daddy's been wanting me to come back." Her racy car left dust whirls as she fled from the idea of ranch life.

"I think I'll give you a raise," Jeff said, stepping onto the porch. Their laughter rang across the ranch, and Carson slowly nodded.

A week later Jeff's orders came for overseas duty.

Chapter 6

Miss Grey shuffled papers in front of her and let her hands rest on them. The same clear, gray gaze that had once terrified Candleshine now looked deeply into her top nurse's sparkling eyes. "You'll be leaving us soon. Your orders have come through. Your country needs you even more than we here at Mercy Hospital, if that's possible." A little sigh escaped the superintendent's lips.

How tired and old she looks, Candleshine thought before she said, "I'm glad the waiting is over."

"Someday, when this insanity is over, you'll come back to us?" Miss Grey's voice actually trembled, and concern spilled into the room.

"If I can, or if Bruce doesn't need me elsewhere."

A hundred feelings rose within Candleshine: relief; sadness at leaving the hospital and Hunter Hall, her home for years; excitement and fear of the future; inadequacy. Would everything she had learned here, the hundreds of hours of training and ward work be enough to sustain her and save lives?

"Miss Grey, am I ready?" Her impulsive question burst out like a grenade.

Her supervisor's head shot up. Her eyes steeled, and once more she became the dreadnought of Candleshine's early training days. "Of course you're ready, Miss Thatcher!" She rose in the magnificent motion that signaled the end of the interview. "No nurse trained by Mercy Hospital and kept on afterward will fail in duty, *whatever that duty may be.*"

Candleshine relaxed and let an impish grin curl her lips upward as she stood and started for the door.

"Here are your orders. You'll be transported on the troopship *Fortitude.*" Miss Grey swept the papers into a bunch and handed them over.

Candleshine barely glanced at them, but she caught one word. "Australia?"

"Your skills will be desperately in demand. The nurses there have performed magnificently, but human flesh can only carry on so long." All pretense between them fell for a telling moment. "Candleshine, Child, go with God's blessing, and mine."

The younger nurse swallowed hard. "Th–thank you, Miss Grey. I'll try to be a credit to Mercy Hospital." *And to you,* she mentally added, knowing by the softness in Miss Grey's eyes those unspoken words came through clearly.

Candleshine felt she had left part of herself behind when she finally stowed the last of her possessions in the family car and Will headed for Cedar

Ridge. "I'm glad for the days I have in between," she quietly said. "It's like changing from one life to another. Home is the neutral zone, my security."

Trinity clenched her hands tight in her lap and nodded. Will's hands tightened on the steering wheel.

"Mom, Dad, I'm going to be all right," Candleshine continued. "You know for years I've felt God wanted me to go. You've taught me He will be there with me the same way He went with me to training school."

Will cleared his throat. "It's a mite farther to Australia than to Seattle, Honey. Like you said, though, God's everywhere." He took a deep breath. "Wait 'til you see what Trinity's done to the house since you were home last."

Successfully sidetracked, Candleshine turned toward her mother. "What this time?" She smiled, remembering childhood days when one of "Mom's decorating spells" left their house in confusion for days and ended with newly papered walls or fresh paint on cupboards and furniture.

"You'll see soon enough." Trinity smiled mysteriously.

A few hours later the ecstatic girl viewed her redecorated bedroom. White walls and ceilings brightened and lightened the big, square room. Chintz curtains with sprigs of lilacs matched the bedspread. New lilac dressing table appointments tied the room together and a leaf green floor covering gave the feeling of being in the middle of a Cedar Ridge spring.

"It's gorgeous," she cried. "I suppose you made the long curtains?"

"Of course. Yardage is less expensive than finished curtains. Besides, I wanted to add a few extra touches." Trinity fingered the crisp material.

"Was any girl ever luckier or more blessed with better parents?" Candleshine dropped to the soft bed and let its familiar contours erase the tension that had built ever since her long-awaited orders came.

"We think we were pretty lucky *and* blessed to have such a daughter," Will observed from the doorway where he lounged against the jamb.

"You'll write, won't you?" The full meaning of thousands of miles of looming ocean rose in the young nurse's mind.

"Haven't we always?" her father demanded in mock indignation.

"Where do you get the *we?*" Candleshine teased. "Mom writes and writes. I'm lucky to get a postscript from you."

Will's round blue eyes took on a look of aggrieved innocence. "Now, what's the use of my repeating all the news your mother already has said?"

"You fraud!" She sent him a smile that said more loudly than words that she saw through him and loved him because of it.

Candleshine hadn't known how much she needed her neutral zone. The first few days passed in a blur of memories. She knew the time just before leaving would be one of looking ahead. The precious middle days would restore her sorely-tried strength and peace of mind and free her from past turmoil. She walked, visited relatives and friends, and rode horseback. She climbed, and she ate like a harvest hand. She slept in the still, black, untroubled nights better than she had done in years, clinging to her oasis in the middle of the world's shifting sands.

There had been no news of Bruce or Winona. A few straggly letters from Connie continued to speak of the incredible way those in the relocation camp kept up morale and waited. How far away it seemed from Candleshine's and Connie's struggling training days! A letter from Sally Monroe allowed Candleshine a glimpse into the younger girl's heart. "If I can ever be half the nurse you are, I will have fulfilled God's calling to me," Sally wrote. "Now that you're gone, I'm trying to be to some of the beginning students what you were, rather *are*, to me." Sally finished on a touching note. "I'm holding the torch high, Candleshine." Below the signature Sally added, "P.S. I hope the war is over before I graduate. If it isn't, I'm joining up with either the army or navy and help win it myself!"

"She'll do it too," Candleshine told her folks, her eyes shining. "That girl has the ability to be one of the greatest nurses ever. Her heart and head and hands work in perfect balance."

The next day she wrote back to her self-appointed protégée. "Whatever field of nursing you choose will be fortunate to have you, Sally. I am a better person because of your faith in me." She licked the envelope, then hastily reopened it and scribbled on the bottom of her letter, "Take care of Miss Grey, if you can. She bears such a heavy load. She won't accept sympathy or much outward friendship, but just doing your work plus a little more and encouraging others to do the same can make a real difference." Relieved by the knowledge Sally would follow instructions to the letter, as she had in her training and ward work, Candleshine quickly stamped the envelope and raced to the mailbox so the rural carrier would pick it up on her rounds.

★ ★ ★

Years earlier, Candleshine had found the buildings in Seattle enormous to her rural eyes. When she and other nurses boarded the *Fortitude,* she felt much the same way. The troopship that carried hundreds of persons, food, medicine, and supplies to keep it self-sustaining was in many ways a floating city! It didn't take long for her to recognize the determination of everyone aboard. Most of the nurses had already seen battle, but not one of the older women made Candleshine feel unwelcome or without value. Rather, they greeted her with enthusiasm and warmth. Every pair of trained hands meant relief to the wounded and respite to the overworked nurses in Australia.

Before the *Fortitude* ever reached its destination, Candleshine found her skills in demand. She proved to be a surprisingly good sailor, even when a storm the ship's commander identified as "just this side of a typhoon" tossed the staunch troopship high one moment and sucked it deep between waves the next. The crowded quarters didn't help, either. Candleshine did all she could to relieve those of her cabinmates who succumbed to seasickness, then volunteered to the ship's doctor and spent long hours working with those in sick bay.

One husky soldier eyed her suspiciously. "How come a gal like you trots around brighter than a July day and us poor slobs that're s'posed to be the stronger sex wind up being the patients?"

"I honestly don't know," she confessed. The young nurse's candor brought a laugh from everyone who heard, and many passed on the remark.

Other than in her official duties, Candleshine had little contact with the troops. The nurses' quarters remained off-limits. Even when she went topside after the storms abated, the men respectfully kept their distance except to smile, nod, or give a brief greeting.

The crossing of the equator changed everything.

"Wait 'til you see the initiation," one of the veteran nurses told Candleshine.

"Initiation? For what?"

The older woman's eyes twinkled. "For the troops who are crossing the equator for the first time. We'll keep back out of sight, but you don't want to miss it."

Something in her voice put Candleshine on alert. When the crossing time came, she hid herself in a well-screened corner and stuffed her hands in her mouth as raw eggs squashed on unsuspecting heads in the traditional equator initiation. Someday, when her letters would not fall under the censor's stamp due to possible detection of the *Fortitude* and its movements, she would write home. How Dad would howl at this grotesque comedy in the middle of a war!

The stories that floated around the ship had begun to make Candleshine feel at home. While she expertly wrapped a staff sergeant's sprained ankle after a doctor's examination, there was this exchange.

"Hey, Nurse Thatcher, I must be living right."

"I hope so," she told him and kept on wrapping.

"No, really." His sunburned face lit up like a Cedar Ridge full moon. "I got wise to the initiation and ducked out." He grimaced as her gentle fingers touched a tender spot.

"Really? I thought everyone had to participate." She eyed him suspiciously.

"Oh, I got three days of latrine duty for not showing," he admitted. "That's the best part of the whole thing."

"First time I've heard that latrine duty's so welcome." Candleshine's blue eyes snapped with fun.

The staff sergeant dropped his joking. "It gave me a chance to talk tactics with some second lieutenants just out of officer candidate school." His keen gaze penetrated her doubts. "The more I know about such things, the better I can do my own job. Those second lieutenants are a whole lot smarter than some give them credit for. You watch and see—the so-called ninety-day wonders will turn out okay in spite of what some of the noncoms think."

Time crawled by. One night Candleshine slipped topside, feeling crowded by her small, shared quarters. Even in Hunter Hall she had been in a single room. Learning to live day after uncertain day surrounded by people at all times left her longing for freedom. She knew the necessary peace she required lay over the *Fortitude's* rail. The Pacific Ocean in its newly settled state offered wide vistas to relax tired eyes and spirits.

She sank on a pile of rope neatly coiled and closed her eyes for a moment as she whispered a prayer. When she opened her eyes again, she gasped. Never in all the days at Cedar Ridge had she seen such a gorgeous sight.

The clear night spread like an inverted bowl above her. Dark blue velvet canopied the sky and hosted stars that looked close enough to gather. Yet even their grandeur faded when she turned her head a bit to one side.

The Southern Cross constellation she had read of in geography books hung above her as if suspended on a string. Its perfect crossbar of space shimmered in the heavens, a symbol of hope to the weary even as the cross of Calvary offered hope and salvation. The four glittering stars lighting the Southern Hemisphere were steady and sublime, never to be forgotten by any who saw with hearts as well as eyes.

Candleshine felt warm drops slide onto her clasped hands. Oh, that she were a poet to describe this night! Who could see such indescribable beauty and deny the existence of a Creator?

"When I consider thy heavens, the work of thy fingers, the moon and the stars, which thou hast ordained; what is man, that thou art mindful of him? and the son of man, that thou visitest him? (Psalm 8:3–4).

Candleshine trembled. Had someone spoken? No, the night remained still, the ocean in surrender. The memory verse she had learned years before echoed in her heart. Drawn closer to her heavenly Father by the night glory, at last she reluctantly left her post and slipped below deck. Yet the glowing Southern Cross and the feeling that she had seen the hand of God remained with her.

★ ★ ★

The first time Candleshine heard firing in the distance and saw the sky torn apart and aglow with wicked light, it took all her ancestral courage to keep from hiding in her bunk. Closer and closer the ship drew to the actual fighting, sliding through the dangerous waters like an avenging angel. Nerves were pitched to the breaking point. News grew nonexistent with the need for increased security, and even most of the scuttlebutt died.

The air attacks intensified. How could the *Fortitude* escape? Candleshine hid her fears and continued caring for those who needed her, praying continuously.

One black night she awoke when a violent jolt threw her from her bunk. Incredibly, she had learned to sleep in the middle of noise and tumult. The cries from her cabinmates, the warning gong of the ship's bell that signaled all hands to deck, and the chilling words, "We're hit" brought her scrambling into her clothes as best she could. Minutes later, the deserted cabin held a wealth of discarded clothes. Each nurse had grabbed her medical bag and the single already-packed bag of necessities and hurried topside.

Even as the Southern Cross defied description, so did the scene of horror that awaited them. Candleshine felt chilled to the bone despite the heat from flames on the starboard side of the ship. "Big trouble," a black-faced, half-dressed soldier called. His teeth bared, he reassured the nurses. "We aren't sinking or anything like that. But just in case that Zero comes back, get your life jackets on."

Would she awake to find this only one more nightmare? Candleshine wondered. She pinched herself, hard. This was no dream but the real thing.

"Is anyone hurt?" an older nurse demanded.

"Yeah. Over there."

"Come on; no time to loiter now." The speaker took command. "Thatcher, move it."

The order freed Candleshine. She obediently ran after the other nurse. After what seemed an eternity of caring for burned and bleeding men, word came to the crew and nurses the fire had been stopped. Unfortunately, one of the engines had been affected. The *Fortitude* could continue sailing, but a turgid flow of oil was staining the ocean waters.

The ship's commander ordered everyone on deck. "We're going to change course. We'll never make it to our original destination. We're in no danger at the present time." His sardonic face broke into a sour smile. "At least, no more than we have been. We do have to get somewhere and lay over for repairs, though. Keep ready. There's no written-in-blood guarantee we won't take another hit."

Candleshine barely heard him. Now that the immediate danger had lessened, a multitude of men who had shrugged off burns and wounds as nothing so they could fight the fire needed her attention.

"Where will we go?" In consternation, she looked at the same staff sergeant she'd cared for earlier. "I'm sorry. I know I shouldn't have asked that."

His massive, sweaty shoulders shrugged, and he didn't even flinch when she dressed an angry red burn that ran from shoulder to wrist. In a low voice he told her, "Keep it under your hat, and I may be wrong, but I'd guess we'll head for Guadalcanal in the Solomons. The Japanese evacuated it in February after a vicious six-month battle. Admiral Halsey's working his way up the islands." He grinned at her. "Of course, I could be wrong. I have been once or twice."

"At least you admit it." Candleshine smiled back.

"Say, if we get parked on Guadalcanal for repairs, you'll see something. It's 2,500 square miles, has a 7,000- or 8,000-foot mountain range in the middle, and a sharp drop to the sea on one side, a gentle one on the other. Coconuts, pineapples, bananas, and tropical forests—they're all there. The Japanese were building an air base so they could attack our ships, but we surprised them."

"You're better than a tour guide," Candleshine told him.

"Listen, when I knew I might get sent somewhere out here, I made sure I got some smarts about things." His grim voice made her feel ashamed for twitting him, but his ready smile flashed again. "The Melanesians—they're the dark-skinned people who live on Guadal—build their houses on stilts. Keeps them cooler. If things were different, it'd be one great place for a vacation. Temperatures between 70 and 90 degrees all the time, and lots of rain to keep things green. Course I don't know how much greenery's left after the fighting. It may be pretty bleak."

"How long do you think it will take to get the *Fortitude* patched up?" Candleshine couldn't resist asking. She snipped off the end of the gauze with her curved bandage scissors and tucked it in.

Her friendly informant grunted. "No way to tell. What's the matter? Don't you want a Guadalcanal vacation?" His teasing smile put things back in proportion.

The *Fortitude* limped toward Guadalcanal, leaving behind inerasable oily evidence. The few times Candleshine chanced to see the ship's commander, he appeared a decade older, and his stern face sent shivers through her. She felt without asking that he feared another attack that would make arrival on Guadalcanal impossible. The nurses slept lightly, ever on the alert for the inevitable.

Like a swarm of angry bees, Japanese fighter pilots did discover and attack the *Fortitude*, miraculously avoiding the answering antiaircraft that had begun firing immediately when the fighter planes appeared. Yet the boom of the ship's cannon and the belching shells from the long-barreled antiaircraft guns sent the enemies on their way.

Hope of reaching Guadalcanal died an instant death. In a subdued but undefeated voice, the commanding officer ordered the evacuation of the *Fortitude*. As the survivors of the night attack huddled in lifeboats and wondered what lay ahead, only the moans of the badly wounded mingled with the ocean's roar in an eerie duet.

Chapter 7

For three days, the lifeboats from the sunken *Fortitude* battled a malicious storm determined to defeat them. Candleshine and the one other nurse on her lifeboat did all they could to help the wounded. A hundred times Miss Grey's crisp statement, *No nurse trained by Mercy Hospital will fail in duty, whatever that duty may be,* bolstered Candleshine's sagging spirits. She set her lips and went on, hampered by lack of shelter against the beating rain and lack of proper space to allow those in the boat to lie down and rest.

Twice during those three days Japanese fighter planes appeared in the leaden skies, once in the distance and once swooping toward them only to be intercepted by Allied planes that drove them away. Too numb from heat and exposure to care, Candleshine continued cleansing wounds, wiping sweaty faces, and whispering encouragement. Once when her charges restlessly tossed with the never-ending motion of the waves, she hummed an old hymn. An uneasy peace settled over her patients.

"Sing the words," a soldier still in his teens asked through fever-parched lips, his eyes blinking back drops.

Candleshine dampened a handkerchief and wiped his face again as she sang, " 'Jesus is calling! Oh, hear Him today, calling for you, calling for you.' " When she came to the chorus, one bass voice joined in, then another.

Calling for you; calling for you!
Hear Him today; do not turn Him away!
Jesus is calling for you.

Even the sullen storm could not withstand the surge of renewed hope that swept over the little group. The only other lifeboat that had remained in sight through the driving rain echoed the song.

Jesus is calling! He stands at the door. . . .

Suddenly Candleshine could sing no longer. These gallant comrades were defying the forces of nature in unfamiliar waters with the immortal words of a hymn many had learned at their mothers' knees. Nothing so far threatened to shake her as this had done.

"More," someone pleaded.

Until voices grew so hoarse they could no longer utter the words, the castaways drifted from song to song and ended with "Amazing Grace." On the third stanza, all the hidden fear and homesickness spilled out.

> *Through many dangers, toils, and snares*
> *I have already come;*
> *'Tis grace has brought me safe thus far,*
> *And grace will lead me home.*

No one could go on with the last verse. The word *home* conjured up scenes too powerful to deny.

A feverish hand clutched Candleshine's. "Nurse, are we going to die?"

"I don't know." Candleshine silently called on God for strength and wisdom. This young soldier, so badly hurt, needed far more than she could give on her own.

"Are you afraid?"

"Horribly." She knew every pair of ears had tuned in to the conversation. "I want to live and serve and go back home to my family." She took a deep and ragged breath, then laid her free hand on the seeking one. "But if God doesn't choose to spare me, I know I will live forever in a wonderful world where war and dying and hatred can never live. I know my God cared so much for me and you and everyone that He sent His Son to die so we might live."

"I've done some pretty bad things," the soldier continued, averting his gaze and nervously plucking at his uniform.

"Christ didn't come to save those who are righteous. He came to save sinners, and that means all of us."

"I used to know Him."

"He has always known and loved you." She smiled into the worried face. "Do you know the story of the lost sheep?"*

"I did when I was a kid."

Totally oblivious to the others and caught up in her desire to help this one soldier, Candleshine's voice lowered. The rain slackened, and a watery shaft of light hovered.

"Jesus told a parable of a shepherd who had a hundred sheep. One got lost; we don't know how. Perhaps it strayed from the flock looking for a tempting place to graze. Maybe it got caught in a thornbush. Anyway, the shepherd left the ninety-nine safely penned up and went out to find his lost sheep. He may have faced storms or danger, black nights or rough trails. The important thing is that he didn't stop searching until he found his lost sheep.

*From Luke 15.

He carried it home on his shoulders and called his friends and neighbors and told them to rejoice with him.

"Jesus went on to say that there is more joy in heaven over one sinner that repents than over ninety-nine just persons."

Silence greeted the story, broken by the young soldier's whispered thanks. "Look!"

Candleshine's gaze followed the pointing finger. Off to their left lay a small island.

With renewed strength, men whose blistered fingers had attempted to guide the lifeboat through the storm grabbed oars. After a guarded call to the second lifeboat, the two craft headed for shore.

"Will it be occupied?" Candleshine whispered to the other nurse.

"Who knows?" Her face set in grim lines. "We don't have much choice. Even if it is, we can't stay out here any longer. One more bad storm or another attack and. . ."

Candleshine could guess the rest.

Slowly and cautiously, the lifeboats approached the small island. Its tropical foliage could hide enemy forces. Candleshine saw coconuts and bananas and thought of the staff sergeant who had given her information on the Solomon Islands and Guadalcanal. Had he escaped death on the *Fortitude?* This island couldn't be Guadalcanal or one of the Solomon's; they hadn't been that close.

"Not a sound," one of the rowers whispered. His haggard, unshaven face and taut shoulders showed his tension. *"What's that?"*

Candleshine quickly turned to the narrow coast. Her cry of joy joined the growing excitement and relief that filled the lifeboat. American soldiers stood on shore hauling three beached lifeboats out of the water. Under the cover of heavy vegetation that came almost down to the ocean, her staff sergeant was in the lead.

"Thank God! We have it to ourselves, at least for now." A few mighty strokes of the oars brought their boat into shallow water.

"Everyone out and fast," someone yelled from shore. "The Japanese have been flying low. They haven't spotted us, but they act like they're suspicious."

Before he finished speaking, the distant drone of unseen planes assaulted Candleshine's ears. She leaped into the waist-deep water, ordered those who could walk to help those who couldn't, and before the fighter planes came into sight the entire company of early arrivals and newcomers had managed to put themselves and the lifeboats out of sight. The staff sergeant and several others had even whacked off giant branches and swept clean from the sand evidence of the landing.

They crouched beneath the flimsy but interwoven green protection, while the planes circled, flew away, turned, and came back again and again. From her uncomfortable position on the ground, Candleshine didn't dare look up. She kept her face buried in her folded arms, wondering why the fighter pilots didn't hear the loud pounding of her heart.

Much later, the staff sergeant gathered his little band. "Anyone here of higher rank than I am?" he demanded.

"Second lieutenant here," a wounded man said. He tried to sit up and fell back, his face contorted. "I'm in no condition to command."

"Anyone else?" No one answered. "Okay, if our second lieutenant can't take charge, I guess I'm it. My name's Magee, and I don't want any guff about it." His eyes bored into the bedraggled crew. "The way I see it, we have to hole up here until we can make contact and be evacuated." His grimy hands nested on his wrinkled, stained khaki pants. "We hope it may be soon, but it may be later, a lot later." His far-seeing eyes scanned the horizon. "At that, we're a lot luckier than the rest of the *Fortitude* crew."

Candleshine thought of the small number on the island compared with all those who had been on the doomed ship.

"We've got rations and lots of fruit," he said, pausing to grin at Candleshine. "Coconuts and bananas and pineapples. The ocean's full of fish. We won't starve. But it's going to take every one of us working together to stay out of sight of the Japanese during our little vacation here."

His grin soon faded. "First thing we have to do is rig up a place so our nurses can take care of the wounded. Did we luck out and wind up with a doctor? No? Too bad, but we've got one, two, three nurses."

"I know some first aid," one soldier volunteered.

"Same here," another put in.

Magee stared at the two. "Your job's to do whatever you're told, okay?" He didn't wait for an answer. "The rest of you will do whatever's needed; the same as me—dig latrines, find clean water for drinking, put up some kind of shelter against the rain, collect food, and stand guard. How many weapons in the bunch?"

A show of hardware brought a pleased grunt. "We can use the tallest trees for lookout posts. Oh, there ain't anyone else on this island. Looks like the natives fled when things got hot. So we have it all nice and cozy to ourselves."

Before night, willing hands had erected a crude, thatched shelter that Magee tagged "No-Name Island Hospital." The dozen or more wounded soldiers lay on hastily constructed pallets formed by piling leafy branches on the ground covered with blankets from the lifeboats. To Candleshine and her fellow nurses' delight, only the young soldier and the second lieutenant had serious wounds. If the rest could avoid tropical disease, they'd be at least temporarily all right.

Staff Sergeant Magee triumphantly produced bolts of mosquito netting from the lifeboats' lockers, and soon every sleeping place and the crude kitchen stood draped with netting. Mosquitoes and other insects beat against it furiously but to no avail.

"We need to set up a schedule as long as we have critically ill patients," said Elizabeth, the older nurse from Candleshine's lifeboat who automatically took charge. "Any preference?"

The third nurse, who said her name was Jane, confessed, "I hated night duty every time I had it. I just can't keep awake."

"I'll take it," Candleshine volunteered.

Elizabeth's face lost some of its grimness. "Why don't we do it like this? Jane can have six A.M. to two P.M., I'll take two to ten P.M., and you'll work ten to six, at least for now. Later, when our criticals get better, we'll see about time off. Those two soldiers who know first aid will spell us."

The strangest period of Candleshine's nursing career thus far began at ten that night. Candleshine had managed to nap in the hot afternoon, thankful for the "quarters" the men eagerly made for them with available materials. At first, the unfamiliar bed of branches kept her awake, but her ward training and the breathing exercises she knew relaxed her body. Refreshed, she began her first shift at No-Name Hospital.

What would Bruce and her family think if they could see her now, separated from the night by only a thin mosquito netting? For the first time in days she had time to think. Fragments filled her mind, keeping her awake and alert. Would she ever forget the way her brave companions sang in the lifeboats? Or how eagerly the young soldier's eyes turned to her when she recounted the story of the lost sheep?

Never! Every experience she faced must become part of her and help her hold high that torch from generations who had gone before, fighting for freedom.

Candleshine smiled. Little had she known when she began nurses' training that her torch would actually be a flashlight! Dimmed with a handkerchief, the flashlight gave her just enough light to keep an eagle eye on patients in the makeshift hospital.

A little after midnight the mosquito netting swayed, and Staff Sergeant Magee stepped in. He stood with hands on hips, a now-familiar posture, then walked between the two rows of sleeping men, his step far lighter than Candleshine would have expected.

"Everything all right?" he whispered.

"Yes." She touched his arm, and they stepped outside so her low voice wouldn't disturb the patients. "We have a problem in caring for the men because they're so close to the ground. It means kneeling every time we give aid. Can you and the others make some kind of cots?"

"No problem." Magee cocked his head and glanced at the surrounding foliage. Bamboo stems as thick as his wrist showed in the pale moonlight.

"You know the health of our whole company depends on you three nurses. Anything you want that I can get for you, just holler and it's yours."

"Thank you, Sergeant Magee."

A slight sound behind her sent Candleshine back through the mosquito netting. The young soldier needed a drink of water and someone to talk with.

"I've been thinking about what you said," he whispered after downing the water.

The smile that had won patients' and doctors' hearts alike back in Mercy Hospital encouraged the boy. "It's worth thinking about."

"I told Him I wished I'd stayed straight instead of going my own way," the boy said, his face flushed. "I never did anything really terrible, but Mom wouldn't like knowing some things. When I get well, I'm going to start telling other people how important God is." He stirred restlessly. "I'm not just saying it because I'm down-and-out, either. I really mean it, Nurse."

"I believe you." Her low voice brought a new flush to his cheeks but this time one of pleasure.

"Good night, Soldier." She patted his hand and smiled again.

"Good night, Nurse." He closed his eyes. A few moments later his steady breathing showed that he slept untroubled by what tomorrow might bring.

"How do you keep your faith so strong?"

Candleshine whipped around at the whisper. The second lieutenant lay prone and stared at her with unreadable eyes.

She glanced the length of her little domain, saw that all was well, and knelt beside the speaker. "As far back as I can remember, I knew God was my best friend and that He cared about me." For a moment she saw herself as the small girl who confidently trotted into the presence of God eagerly spilling her childish prayers. *Please, God, make my kitty get well. . . . Please, God, help me be a good girl.* Memories stung her eyelids.

"You've done a fine thing for that boy," the lieutenant said, as he nodded toward the sleeping soldier. "Is he going to make it?"

"He is if there's anything I can do about it."

"I suppose that includes praying."

Candleshine heard the wistfulness behind the statement and responded to it with her whole heart. "Lieutenant, if I didn't add prayer to the care I give, I wouldn't be giving my best."

A strong hand gripped her wrist. "You might add a second lieutenant to your list."

"I will." Her face shone in the moonlight that sneaked through the mosquito netting.

"Thanks. Good night, Nurse." He turned to one side. She felt the tremor of his body from the slight effort. It would take the skill of all three nurses plus mighty prayer to pull him through. She smoothed his hair from his hot forehead, whispered, "Good night," and went back to her lonely vigil.

Uneasy hours passed, broken only by a few snores or someone asking for water. Candleshine faithfully made her rounds, as she had under far different circumstances a hundred times. Tonight Connie and Bruce and Winona seemed very close, closer than they had in weeks. Was it because she practiced her skills under primitive conditions and knew they did the same?

"God, help us all," she prayed in a quiet moment.

In the darkest hour after the moon had set and before the day began, Candleshine found herself fighting sleep. Every man in her care lay sleeping. She paced the short length of aisle between the pallets, checking and rechecking, especially her two criticals. From training days, she knew the human body sank to its lowest ebb at this time period. Patient after patient failed to pass the test, and too often even those who appeared to be on the mend slipped away in the early morning hours. It was then that Candleshine prayed the hardest: for those whose lives hung on the care they received; for friends and family; for all the Sally Monroes and Miss Greys who even at this moment might also be keeping watch by night.

A fuller understanding of what it meant to be a nurse slowly came to her. Crumpled by kneeling, sustained by prayer, Candleshine experienced the humility known by all who serve their Master. When Jane came in at six to relieve her, she found Candleshine smiling, with a look in her eyes never to be forgotten.

"They're all well so far. Our two criticals got some sleep, and their temperatures are down," Candleshine exulted. She squared her shoulders and rubbed her neck. "All that kneeling gets to you, but Sergeant Magee's going to see what he can do about it."

"Good." Jane, a few years older, beamed at her. "Anything special I need to know?"

"Just that all is well."

"That's the only thing that really matters," Jane said softly. "If I can help save someone, the way I wish my young brother could have been saved, it's all I ask."

Candleshine's quick sympathy rose as she wordlessly squeezed Jane's arm. Then Jane's clear voice rang out. "All right, men, up and at 'em. We've got faces and hands to wash before breakfast!"

A few days later, Candleshine discovered Elizabeth also served because of loss—her husband, in the early days of Manila. Elizabeth expressed much the same sentiments as Jane. "I couldn't live with myself if I didn't do what I could to help win this war. It's what Tom would expect of me." The next moment her usual brusque self returned, wasting little time in what couldn't be changed when so much needed to be done now.

Thanks to Sergeant Magee, two neat lines of bamboo cots with tautly stretched thatch and blankets soon replaced the ground-level pallets. Candleshine rejoiced when she arrived for night duty and found that Elizabeth had dismissed two soldiers to regular quarters. Another proudly boasted, "A couple more days and I'll be good as new," when he hobbled back from the closest latrine on a freshly-made crutch. "Hey, we musta had a visit from Santa Claus!"

Candleshine eyed the enormous stalks of bananas Sergeant Magee had thoughtfully ordered delivered to the ward. "Help yourself. There's a lot of energy in a banana." She peeled one and ate it, although supper had been filling.

Morale raised every day. Outside of one new patient who had cut his foot on sharp coral while fishing, the camp remained healthy. Sergeant Magee announced he had men working to rig up some kind of communication with the rest of the world, and in the meantime, everyone was to "eat all they could, sleep all they could, and in general, take it easy 'cause who knew where'd they go from here."

Yet the threat of detection kept Candleshine and the others from following orders to the letter. Again and again, Japanese fighter planes hovered above No-Name Island while its inhabitants froze beneath their camouflage and waited for the sound of bombs that must inevitably come.

Chapter 8

Nothing in Jeffrey Fairfax's twenty-five years had prepared him for life aboard an aircraft carrier in the South Pacific. His superb strength and fighting spirit nurtured by ranch work and college football, then by the rigorous U.S. Marine Corps training, had failed to make ready his mind. Dying held no fear for him. Possible capture, torture, and the niggling uncertainty as to how much he could endure without showing cowardice kept him awake when he needed sleep. Could any man withstand the atrocities of war?

In the darkest hours Jeff bared his soul, faced himself, and set his course. With God's help he would do a job he hated but must be done. When or if he came home—he shrugged. Thinking of the Laughing X now would make him soft when he could least afford it.

He thought of his intensive training. He remembered the way his stomach dropped while watching parachute practice and the involuntary tightening of his muscles when he breathlessly watched the chutes billow white against the sky and safely bring the men back to the earth. He fervently hoped he'd never have to jump. Flying was one thing; leaving the safety of the plane and leaping into thin air was something else.

Jeff's prior training with planes made him a perfect candidate for overseas duty. The weary-looking superior officer who called him in introduced him to the captain with whom he'd fly.

"I wish we had thousands with your health and training," he said, then slammed a meaty fist onto the desk. "I'd go myself but the brass say I can do more here."

"I'll do my best, Sir."

The heavy features relaxed in a comradely grin. "At ease, Marine. That's all any man can give."

Jeff and his senior pilot captain worked together as easily as Jeff worked with Carson back in Montana. Mission after successful mission they flew, growing close in their shared tasks until Jeff loved his captain as a brother.

Weeks passed in a blur of fighting and driving the enemy back. One night when a hammered sliver moon made grotesque shadows on land and sea, orders came for another attack.

"We're on mission to intercept southbound Japanese planes," the captain said. "It's going to be one grand ball, men. Choose your partners and hang on."

Jeff's skin crawled when they got underway. The smell of dying vegetation in the windless night crept through the open side window. The crash of sixteen-inch naval guns reached him even over the noise of their own engines. Death filled the air. Below, fleets of small boats left foamy, white wakes. Tracers streaked toward shore. Smoke and high-flung earth and falling palm trees combined in a lurid haze. Nothing seemed real to Jeff except the quiet control of his aircraft commander. If he lived long enough to fly the countless missions his captain had flown, would he ever become so much a part of his plane?

Jeff looked down again and shuddered. The scene offered a foretaste of the prophesied biblical blaze of fire. How could any man see this and still refuse to acknowledge the might and power of the living God?

"Captain, break left!" Jeff yelled when a Zero dove toward them. *Closer, closer.*

The commander dove, but the Japanese fighter stayed with them. Jeff felt cold sweat on his forehead. The plane shuddered when their gunners fired back. He heard the rattle of machine guns and knew the rest of the squadron was desperately trying to get the attacker.

Glass shattered. Splinters fell on Jeff's braced knees. The plane went into a crazy spin after a jolt that threatened to tear it apart.

The captain slumped, then straightened, and with a mighty effort righted the plane.

The intercom crackled. "We're hit, Sir. Our tail's on fire," a disembodied voice warned. Acrid fumes filled the plane.

"How bad? Can you put it out?" Jeff yelled.

"We're trying."

The plane shuddered again. Jeff saw blood seep down his commander's face. "Sir, are you all right?"

"Fine," the grim-faced captain barked. "Our boys got him." He nodded toward the spiraling Zero that flamed down into the sea.

The intercom crackled again. "We can't stop it, Sir. It's spreading, and the enemy got our bombardier."

"We'll have to ditch." The commander wasted no time. "But we'll get away from here first." He swung the crippled plane away from the land invasion and back out to sea. Only when the intercom informed him the fire had gone out of control did he order, "Ditching stations!"

Down, down they fell, through a night gone strangely calm, in sharp contrast with the horrifying red light on land. Jeff's mind went blank.

"If I don't make it, you're in command," the captain said. His weak voice alerted his copilot that only sheer guts and willpower had kept him going until the plane hit the water. Jeff snapped back to reality. What the Japanese hadn't done the tossing waves could do. The succession of events was bathed in confusion: throwing out the life raft, the crash into icy water, hoarse screaming, realizing his captain was beyond help, and dragging three of his crew members from the water to the life raft.

Praying as he had never done before, Jeff eyed the moon, wishing it would disappear. With its silver sheen the life raft made a grand target for any lone Japanese fighter plane that might have trailed them.

"And here he comes," Jeff muttered. "Hit the water. Stay under or float facedown like you're dead."

The Zero swooped low but evidently failed to see movement and, to the survivors' amazement, went on without raining bullets into their frail hope, the life raft.

"*Curse this rotten war!*" Jeff yelled after the departing Zero once it got nearly out of sight. Anger, grief, and saltwater poured from his face. "God help those who gave their lives—and us."

Exhausted, the four marines huddled in the life raft, easy prey for the enemy and the elements. Two of those Jeff rescued died the second day. Dan Black, the radioman, and Jeff drifted, silent and thirsty in the middle of unlimited water.

For a week, they drifted without compass or even one Allied plane to mark their plight. With his tongue thick and swollen and lips cracked, reality and fantasy merged until at times Jeff didn't remember where he was. His companion suffered more from wounds he had received in the water. At the height of his delirium, his ramblings sent cold shudders down Jeff's spine.

In late afternoon of the eighth day, Jeff awoke from a dream of home. He'd been riding with Carson with the scent of pines and sage filling his lungs. "You can do it, Boy," Carson kept encouraging him.

Do what? Why did Carson keep telling him that? And why did his own voice repeat over and over, "Too late, too late"?

Jeff's conscious state returned. His reddened eyes widened. Laughter that barely cackled in his dry throat rose, and he shook his barely conscious buddy. "Wake up, Fella, we're somewhere." His gaze never left the narrow beach toward which the life raft floated.

He got no response, only the feverish mutterings that showed how seriously ill the other man was.

"What shall I do?" he wondered in a voice too parched to carry. A dozen ideas came and fled. What new dangers lurked on the island ahead? How could he get there? Dehydrated and weak, could he swim if the tides turned against them? If he swam, what about the life raft and its precious cargo? Should he take a chance and shout? Should he just let the life raft drift in and make a run for it? If he stayed to help the wounded marine, would it mean capture for both of them?

The moment he had dreaded for weeks and months stared him in the face.

Jeff's soul swelled. No matter what the risk, he would not desert the only other survivor. The captain had put him in command. Well, he'd be the kind of commander the U.S. Marine Corps expected. Whatever lay ahead must come to both of them—or neither.

The capricious fate that had left them adrift in the ocean suddenly turned kind. Rocking waves brought them closer and closer to the island. Jeff squared his shoulders, sat erect, and waited.

Closer and closer, until only a few hundred yards remained between the life raft and the island. A hundred. Fifty. Thirty.

Out of an empty sky came the whine of planes. *Friend or enemy?* Jeff's keen, trained ears suspected the worst.

"Dear God, no!" His despairing prayer generated a bolt of energy beyond human strength. He leaped into the surf and cradled his companion with arms of steel. A lifetime ago and a world away he had been noted for his speed on the field. Now he ran with his heavy, mercifully unconscious burden, slowed by water to his waist but determined to go on fighting, head down.

Straight across the narrow beach he ran, to the dense growth ahead. Shouts reached his ears. Had he run into the arms of the enemy? Something exploded in his head. So the enemy had gotten him after all. He felt himself stumble and automatically threw out his arms. His buddy must fall clear or be crushed under Jeff's weight.

"Missed the touchdown," he whispered. "Someone tackled me." In a last convulsive effort, he felt a thrusting pain in his left side and crumpled to the ground.

★ ★ ★

Candleshine, Jane, Elizabeth, Magee, and the others settled into their routine. Days passed, and communication still hadn't been established. Hopes of an early rescue faded. The soldiers chafed at the inactivity, wanting revenge for loss of the *Fortitude*. "How long are we gonna have to sit out here on this vacation spot?" they grumbled.

Magee responded by putting them to work improving living conditions. "If you guys don't start counting your blessings—like us not having neighbors and so far keeping out of sight and alive—I'm going to knock some heads together."

"Aw, Sarge, you know you're just as eager to get out of here and where we're needed as the rest of us."

"Yeah."

Candleshine heard the fighting spirit in his reply. The next instant he spoiled it by ordering, "Any man who gripes can do double watch duty." A loud groan followed.

Gradually the patients improved, even the young soldier and the second lieutenant. Candleshine and the others rejoiced. Magee offered to turn over command of No-Name Island, but the nurses nixed the idea. "He's in no shape to do anything but get completely well," Elizabeth advised strongly.

Jane and Candleshine backed her up. Sergeant Magee held the reins.

Never had Candleshine been treated so well. The men's appreciation and respect remained unlimited. They could fight and make a home on the abandoned island, but the three women represented healing. As soon as the last of the criticals won convalescent status, the two soldiers who had assisted in the first aid spelled the women.

Life was far better than Candleshine could have dreamed possible on the day they drifted in from the luckless *Fortitude*. Magee and his men found a secluded pool some distance from camp, cleared a trail, cleaned it out, and provided a bathing place. "Ladies when they want it; the rest of us other times," he ordered, scowling. "And if I catch any man around that pool when one of our nurses is there, I'll shoot him on sight."

A wave of protest rang through the assembly. "What kind of guys do you think we are?" someone yelled. "Anyone bothers our nurses, he'll wish the Japanese had got him!" Loud cheers followed.

Magee grinned. "See that you remember it. Dismissed."

Every day the nurses slipped away and bathed. The single change of clothing they'd been able to bring in the lifeboats could be washed, dried in the hot breezes, and worn the next day.

With more free time they could explore the tiny island. The men had already beaten down the brush and made rough paths that resembled tunnels beneath a green canopy.

Candleshine's favorite spot lay on the highest point of their little kingdom. Although it meant a climb, she loved the rocky knoll that overlooked the entire island.

"Make sure you keep outta sight if you ever see or hear a plane," Magee warned. A heavy crease between his eyebrows left no doubt of the seriousness of his concern. "It's not just your safety, but all of ours." He scratched his head and grunted. "So far we've been okay, but I just don't know how long it will last."

"I'll be careful," she promised.

Sometimes Candleshine climbed with Jane or Elizabeth. Although soldiers begged to accompany her, most often she went alone. Something about the spot filled her need for solitude, a trait born and bred in her from Cedar Ridge. To draw apart for a time restored and freshened her. Once Magee teased, "If I didn't know better, I'd think you rendezvoused with your fella up there. You come back bright and shiny and full of ginger."

She laughed at the crusty sergeant's teasing. They'd become great friends since they landed, and she knew all about his wife and kids at home who waited and prayed for him to come back.

One afternoon after she and the other nurses straightened their quarters and left their two helpers in charge of the little hospital, Jane flopped to her bed. "My idea of heaven right now is a long, long nap and a good meal." She crossed her arms beneath her head. "I wonder if it will be fish and fruit or fruit and fish?"

"Who cares?" Elizabeth took off her shoes and placed them side by side in the precise way she did everything else. "I'm with you." She yawned. "Wonder when we all get home if we'll ever again be able to sleep without gunfire in the distance?" She lay back on her cot.

"I hope so. I don't intend to spend the rest of my life living next to a firing range," Jane sputtered. She glanced at their roommate. "Candleshine, are you taking a nap?"

She turned from the netting-clad opening and smiled. "No; I'm restless today. I'll walk up to the lookout point."

"Again?" Jane smothered a yawn.

"I really love it up there." She retied her shoes, and her blue eyes sparkled in her tanned face. "Have a good nap."

Mock snores followed her, and she headed up the trail. Past the bathing pool the terrain became more steep. By the time she reached the tall trees used for lookouts, she felt sweaty and hot but merely waved at the sentry who called to her and kept going. She'd have a swim and bath when she returned. Even her fair hair felt dirty and damp. She giggled and told a brilliantly plumed bird, "I never really thought Sergeant Magee could cut my hair with his knife, but he did a pretty good job. Something to tell my grandkids!"

The thought sobered her, and a few minutes later she sat down on the island's topknot. "Dear God, will I ever get married and have kids and grandkids? Sometimes it feels we've been here forever." Her unseeing eyes gazed at the beauty around her, but her mind didn't register it as usual. From meditation to blankness she let herself drift. The afternoon waned, and she reluctantly stood, stretched, and started back down.

When she reached the sentry tree, she couldn't believe what she saw. A half-dozen soldiers had gathered and stood staring out to sea. "What is it?"

"Look!" The speaker kept his voice low.

Candleshine had to strain her eyes to make out something low floating toward shore.

"It's a life raft," the sentry told them. "Can't tell—yes—there's something or someone in it. One of you guys go tell Magee, and move it! The rest of you get your weapons, just in case. It could be a trap."

Candleshine's feet moved of their own accord. She raced down the path and past the beckoning pool that had lost its lure. Her heart pounded. She heard herself panting as she burst into camp. Jane stuck her head out of the tent, her eyes filled with sleep.

"Not one of you is to show himself—herself," Magee bellowed. "Until we know what that is, this is just a nice little deserted island, got it? But be prepared." He snapped a look at Candleshine and Jane. "Whatever happens, *stay down.* We don't want stray bullets picking off our nurses. Where's the other one?"

"Sound asleep." Jane giggled nervously. "She said she was so tired it would take a cannon to wake her."

"Let her sleep then. *Now get down!*"

The nurses obeyed but picked a spot where they could see the water clearly. On both sides of them and in front, the men crouched and lay low. Each carried whatever weapon he had, and in a few cases, that weapon was merely a heavy club.

Candleshine could see clearly now. A dark figure sat upright on the floating raft, and something long and blanketed stayed motionless at his feet.

"I think he's one of ours, but we can't be sure," someone whispered and earned a black scowl from Magee.

In the distance, the sound of planes preceded the life raft. Jane's nails dug into Candleshine's arm. Tiny drops of sweat beaded on her nose.

A second later, the seated figure scrambled from the life raft, snatched the inert burden, and ran toward the hidden island inhabitants. Head down, still his height showed clearly.

"That ain't no Jap," Magee shouted. "Watch it, Buddy!"

His warning came too late. In a effort to find cover before the enemy discovered them, the runner had plowed head-on into the jungle foliage. A heavy branch, dislodged by the impact, snapped forward and struck his head.

"Help him, men! Get that raft under cover and blot out the traces." Magee and the others, spurred by danger of discovery and death for all, leaped to their feet.

So did the nurses. Before they could take a single step forward, the soaked, unshaven man in a marine uniform faltered. To Candleshine's horrified, fascinated gaze, the way he thrust his burden ahead of him, then buckled resembled slow motion. She saw the pain in his face. His lips moved. He twisted, and another spasm of agony crossed his thin face before he lay still.

Candleshine jerked free of Jane's painful grip and pelted toward the two downed men. "Get Elizabeth," she cried, "and our aides." Twice she caught her foot in roots and almost fell but reached the newcomers before either moved. All her experience rose in a hasty examination of the blanketed man. When her trained fingers discovered the crudely bandaged wounds, she ordered, "Get him to the hospital," glad for Magee's ingenuity that had prepared for disaster by making stretchers of bamboo stems and blankets.

The runner lay as he had fallen. Candleshine stanched the flow of blood from his head with pressure from the heel of her hand. "Turn him toward me, but be careful," she instructed Magee. "Head wounds always bleed a lot."

"He must have fallen on something sharp," Magee said when they got the marine turned. He jerked open the dirty shirt. A gaping hole oozed blood.

"It isn't as bad as it looks," Candleshine rejoiced and directed Magee how to stop the blood. "He's going to have one big headache from that lump, and we'll have to watch his side, but he should be all right."

Did the prone man hear her voice? He stirred, struggled against their restraining hands, and at last opened his eyes. Staring straight into Candleshine's face, etched against the fading sunlight, he licked his salty, cracked lips.

"Am I dead? Are you an angel?" He tried to sit up but flinched and fell back into unconsciousness.

Chapter 9

Candleshine had cared for hundreds of patients during her career, and dozens of them had fallen in love with her. A few had stirred a faint interest inside her, but that was always driven away by her desire not to care about any man until the war ended.

Now one glimpse of eyes so dark she thought they were black but later discovered were clear, deep blue, and the whispered words, "Am I dead? Are you an angel?" lighted a tiny flame in her heart. Fear shot through her when the pallid marine fell back unconscious. "Get him to the hospital," she ordered and ran ahead to whisk a blanket onto one of the cots, vacant now that her other patients had healed.

Elizabeth, refreshed from her afternoon nap, greeted them. Never had Candleshine been more thankful for the older nurse's advanced skills. Elizabeth stitched wounds as carefully as the finest doctor. Her firm, gentle hands sought and bathed the jagged gash on the man whose dog tag identified as Lieutenant Jeffrey Fairfax.

"Nice name. When he heals and gets over the effects of exposure, he will be as good-looking as ever." Elizabeth cast a sharp glance at Candleshine, who hovered near. "I don't like that goose egg on his head so I want you to watch him." She washed her hands in hot water and disinfectant. "Now for the other poor devil dog."

Candleshine remained by Lieutenant Fairfax's cot but heard Jane's quickly muffled gasp when Elizabeth exposed the second marine's chest.

"It's going to take a lot more than time and good food to restore this one," Elizabeth muttered matter-of-factly. "Fairfax did all he could and probably saved his buddy's life, but we've got to reopen the wounds so they'll heal from the inside out. Thank God both of them stayed unconscious until we could do our jobs."

An hour later she straightened. "That will do it. The warm air can help heal."

Time off for the three nurses vanished. Lieutenant Fairfax and his radioman, Dan Black, tossed and turned and relived the events preceding their watery plunge. From parched lips and fevered brains, Magee and the nurses got the whole story and marveled that any man from the ditched plane had survived. Candleshine spent most of her night shift trotting between Fairfax and Black. If her gaze lingered longer on the lieutenant than on the radioman, only the mosquitoes knew.

For two days and nights Black's life hung by a cobweb. Jane forgot her dislike of night duty and specialed the young marine, forcing water between his tightly clenched lips when she could and sponging away the rivers of sweat. "Don't be alarmed when he sweats hard," Elizabeth had warned. "It helps get the poison out of his system, and the fever itself burns up infection."

Candleshine stayed with Fairfax, who alternated between growing periods of consciousness and restless sleep. One night he violently jerked from her ministering hands. "No, Lillian! Just leave me alone."

"All right." Candleshine used the low but penetrating voice she employed to penetrate mental confusion.

"I won't do it. Uncle Sam says come. Think I'd leave the Laughing X for a desk job?" He strained to sit up, and Candleshine gently pressed him back.

"You don't have to, Jeffrey." The name felt good on her lips the first time she used it. "No one will make you."

He grunted. His lean face twisted, and his eyes opened. "You—you're not Lillian." Some of the fever receded, and recognition filled his eyes. "You're the angel. You won't let her—"

"Don't try to talk," she ordered and reached for a cloth. She dipped it in cool water and bathed his face.

"Where am I, anyway?" Jeffrey Fairfax slowly turned his head, surveyed the dimly lit ward, and picked at the light blanket with nervous fingers. "I didn't know they had bananas in heaven."

Candleshine started, then realized his wandering gaze had lighted on the eternal bunch of bananas Magee kept on hand for quick energy for the nurses. "No bananas in heaven," she told him. "We'll talk about it tomorrow."

"Okay, Angel." The tall body relaxed, and a little later Candleshine noted with satisfaction his deep and evidently dreamless sleep so in contrast with the frenzied periods of unconsciousness.

"Lieutenant Fairfax is much better," she reported to Elizabeth the next morning. A lilt in her voice matched the sparkle in her blue eyes.

"Good. Get some breakfast and sleep as long as you can," she advised. "You too," she told a weary Jane. The nurses could barely stay awake long enough to eat. But before they went to their quarters, they trudged to the bathing pool and came back with lifted spirits.

"Dan is improving but I just don't know." Jane's somber face showed her concern. "I wish we could get off this island and to Australia or Guadalcanal or anywhere!" Unaccustomed tears spilled, and she impatiently brushed them away. "I know," she told Candleshine. "We're not supposed to get emotionally involved with our patients. I don't. Ever. But Dan is so much like the brother I lost. . . ." Her lips quivered.

"Would you like to trade patients?" Candleshine offered, wondering why a little disappointment filled her at the idea.

"If it's all right with Elizabeth." Jane flung herself to her cot. Moments later she slept, more emotionally than physically exhausted in spite of the drain of strength used in caring for the late arrivals.

Elizabeth readily agreed to the switch when Candleshine privately explained, and that night the nurses changed places in the little ward. Candleshine looked at the wasted form of Dan Black and echoed Jane's prayer. How could they take care of him here when he needed the best possible attention? Limited by dwindling medical supplies and crude conditions, Candleshine turned to her heavenly Father in prayer, asking for mercy and guidance.

Once that night Lieutenant Fairfax whispered, "Where's the angel?"

Jane looked astonished but told him, "Right over there taking care of your radioman."

The answer seemed to satisfy him, and he fell back asleep, but Jane sent an impish grin across the barely lighted ward and raised one eyebrow. Candleshine felt rich color creep from her collar into her face.

A week later Lieutenant Fairfax had regained full control of his mental state and voracious appetite and, except for a sore head and side, had mended to the point of examining the encampment. He praised Magee, declined to take command at this time, and never let Nurse Thatcher out of sight when he could help it.

How much broken memory was real? He vaguely remembered her cool hands doing their healing work, her attractive face close when she cared for him. Once he asked, "Did I mumble?"

A wide smile lighted Candleshine's face. "Oh, yes." She couldn't help but tease a little even though something in his eyes caught her breath.

"What did I say?" He watched her capable hands mending a rip in one of the men's khaki shirts.

"You called for Lillian."

"Never!" His eyes flashed. His lips thinned. For a moment his face lost its peaceful look and turned dark.

"You talked about a laughing X and a desk job," she informed him.

His shout of laughter brought color to her face, and the quick gaze of every person in sight. Jeff settled more comfortably against the tree trunk where he'd found Candleshine working. "It's not *a* laughing x but *the* Laughing X. A cattle ranch in western Montana."

"Really?" The mending dropped to Candleshine's lap in a forgotten pile. "A real, live cattle ranch with horses and roundups and—"

"—and bunkhouse and ranch house and corrals," he added solemnly.

She bit her lip. "You're laughing at me."

"Not really. You just sounded so surprised."

His keen gaze confused her. "Well, what would you think? Here a marine lieutenant comes calling; we bring him back to health, and it turns out he's really a cowboy!"

Jeff's boyish grin contrasted sharply with the tiny patches of silver that hadn't graced his dark hair a few weeks earlier. "Rancher too. I own the place. If we ever get out of this hole and back home, would you like to visit the Laughing X? The other nurses too," he hastily added.

She liked him for that addition. "I'd love to," she said in the simple, honest way that left no room for misunderstanding. "We live in a beautiful part of the country. Cedar Ridge in the mountains of Washington State can't be beat. But I've always been crazy about Western history." Excitement made her blue eyes even bluer.

"I can show you a lot when you come," he told her.

Again she felt color steal into her face. He hadn't said *if* but *when*. The very thought made her heart beat faster.

Jeff half-closed his eyes and started talking. "The wide spaces, the smell of pine and sage, the mountains in the distance—sometimes I'd give everything I own to be back. Even the hard work and isolation in bad winters are worth it. My foreman Carson's back there right now raising beef for the government. He's fighting his battles, too, trying to get enough riders to do the job and hampered by the lack of skill." His lips curved reminiscently. "We don't hire any man who won't start the naturalization process."

"I don't blame you." Candleshine bent her head and went back to her mending. *How much this marine resembles Dad in character and outlook!*

"Just where is this Cedar Ridge? I have to confess I've never heard of it."

Candleshine's fingers stilled. "Forty miles east of Bellingham. Cedar Ridge is in a valley between mountains, like the bottom of a teacup." A flood of memories roughened her voice.

"How did you end up a million miles from it?"

In brief, revealing sentences, she shared how she and her cousin had vowed to make a team. She told him about Mercy Hospital and Training School, Hunter Hall, Bruce and Winona and Connie, Miss Grey, Sally, and the others. She lightly touched on her determination to carry the torch her great-grandmother had passed down and that she would faithfully keep lighted.

"It isn't easy sometimes," she said in a voice so low Jeff had to lean close to hear. "I—I'm not a very brave person." She hesitated. Could she tell him about her faith in God and how only that helped her get through the rough times?

Before she could continue, Jeff said, "My parents felt the same way. Their motto for living was that everyone owed the world the best they could give."

In the change of conversation, Candleshine's opportunity to witness slipped by.

Gradually, and to the chagrin of the other island inhabitants who vied for her attentions, Candleshine spent more and more of her free time with Jeff. Long before she knew he had fallen in love with her, she lay awake when she should have been sleeping and thought of him. Somewhere along the way, her solid determination never to allow herself to care for any man in wartime had melted.

"He isn't just *any* man," she whispered brokenly when at last she honestly admitted to herself the love in her heart. Next to God, Lieutenant Jeffrey Fairfax possessed her love.

A little frown crossed her face, and she shifted uneasily. They had so little uninterrupted time! Each time she had gathered her courage to ask how he felt about God and if he knew Jesus, something happened to stop the words on her lips.

Deteriorating conditions on the island added to her troubled state. Japanese planes patrolled daily. Had they seen something? No one knew for sure, but when bombs fell Magee called the entire company together and laid everything before them. Every trace of his good nature had fled in the face of necessity.

"We're running short of food, believe it or not. We still have some fruit and fish when we can catch them, but we can't hold out forever. The Japanese have to be suspicious or they wouldn't be wasting time and bombs. From now on, either sleep in your helmets or have them next to your cots. Hit the trenches every time you hear planes. The one good thing is that we've been able to make contact. Our people know we're here, but they're a little busy and can't be running a shuttle service to Guadal." He glared at the innocent-looking waves playing on the beach. "Keep out of sight even when you don't think there's any reason. Dismissed."

Candleshine took a deep breath, more from what he'd left unsaid than his actual orders. If they were invaded it meant capture and who knew what?

Yet in the momentous, waiting days even fear could not dampen her growing love for Jeff. A hundred times she glanced up and met his poignant gaze. She saw the longing in his face to speak and the rigid self-discipline that kept him silent. Did he feel as she often did that love born in the middle of fear could not survive? That it was too soon, too fast?

One early evening she climbed with him to the rocky point on top of the island. Mindful of Magee's orders, they didn't step into the open but observed their world from cover provided by the heavy growth.

"I never seriously cared for any girl," Jeff said out of the blue. "I was always too busy. . .until now."

Had she really heard the almost inaudible words? Candleshine felt herself blush as she had long ago the first time a boy sat with her in the little Cedar Ridge church. She turned toward Jeff.

"I love you, Candleshine Thatcher. Will you marry me?" His blue eyes looked black with emotion. "I wasn't going to say anything. It didn't seem fair. But with the Japanese getting closer all the time. . ."

She couldn't bear the pain in his face. "I—"

Jeff gripped her hands until they ached. His look burned into her soul. "Just knowing you love me, that you'll be my wife; you can't know what a difference it will make!" He drew her close and pressed her cheek against his shoulder then kissed her.

Candleshine's hands crept up his shoulders and clasped behind his head. She returned his kiss with all the love that had stormed and seized her heart in spite of everything she could do to lock it. "I'll marry you, Jeff."

"When?"

"Why, as soon as we can."

He kissed her again, this time joyously. When he released her and held her at arm's length, all signs of stress had flown. His dark blue eyes laughed into her own, and his white teeth gleamed in his bronzed face. "The minute we get to Guadalcanal or to wherever we can find someone with authority, we'll hunt him up." A shadow crossed his face. "That is, if we can get permission." Doubt sponged some of his gladness before the same indomitable will that kept him and Dan Black alive against impossible odds came to his rescue again. "They'll have to give it!" He pulled her back into his arms and sealed his promises with a tender kiss. "Shall we tell everyone?"

The first twinge of alarm sounded deep in Candleshine's brain. Released from the security of Jeff's strong arms Candleshine felt dazed.

"On second thought," he suggested, observing her confused stare, "let's just keep it to ourselves. It's too precious to share just now."

Relief filled her and the feeling she'd been given a reprieve. Yet cradled against his shoulder Candleshine found it hard to think beyond the moment and savored the sweetness that had so unexpectedly fallen.

Before they reached camp Jeff stopped her and held her close. "I'll never stop giving thanks for your love." The next instant he decorously followed her along the well-trod path. He saluted smartly for the benefit of curious eyes. "Thank you for the walk, Nurse Thatcher."

"You're welcome, Lieutenant." She blindly watched him stride away, every inch the trained marine and somehow not quite the Jeff who had opened his heart on top of the island.

That night when Candleshine had done everything she could for Dan Black and found time dragging, she brought out in the quiet ward every image of the afternoon engraved into her soul. She paced back and forth until at last she sank onto an empty cot and buried her face in her arms.

Dear God, what have I done? Promised to marry a man, to live as his wife— forever. A man I have only known a few weeks, one I'm not sure believes in God, though little comments of his could mean otherwise.

"I can't do it," she breathed, feeling great drops of perspiration spring to her forehead.

Yet how can I back down? The cruelest thing on earth would be to go back on her word. She imagined Jeff's face if she told him how she felt. She could picture his scorn and disgust for a girl who committed herself, then weaseled out with a lame excuse.

Torn, hurting, Candleshine sat for hours. A dozen ideas came and went, discarded as impossible. Never had she endured such a night. "Better to come forward than destroy two lives with a hasty marriage," she tried to tell herself, but her mind and heart went black.

When Jane came to relieve her early the next morning, she found Candleshine staring into the distance, unresponsive to Jane's greetings. The last thought Candleshine had before she finally fell asleep in her quarters haunted her dreams: *What should I do?*

She awakened to the roar of planes and the exploding of bombs. She snatched her helmet and zigzagged across to the nearest trench. Dirt erupted in little geysers on both sides of her. She saw running figures. Some fell. The instant the planes left she raced to the downed soldiers, selfishly glad Jeff hadn't been hit but ashamed at her relief. The hospital stood intact, and although several men had been injured, none had been killed. Candleshine, Elizabeth, and Jane probed, bandaged, and beat back death.

Four hours later Magee burst into the ward. "We're getting out of here. Now. Get your men on stretchers—a couple of PT boats are on their way. It's risky but better than staying here like sitting ducks." His grim expression did nothing to reassure the nurses.

They made their way to the narrow beach by starlight, thankful for the dark phase of the moon. "Keep under cover until I tell you," Magee ordered in a low voice.

"Where are the lieutenants?" Candleshine clutched his arm.

"They and a few others are covering our rear," Magee snapped. "Fine time for them to take command." Anger laced his hoarse whisper. "I should be the guy staying behind."

"What do you mean?" Candleshine felt sick.

"Somebody's got to do it. They'll run for the PT boats at the last minute, after everyone else is on." He dismissed the others in concern for the wounded. "Are you ready when I give the signal?"

"Yes." Elizabeth stood close, and Jane protectively patted Dan Black's hand. He had come back from the edge of death but needed more time to heal totally.

"Shhh. Here they come." Magee loomed big in the semidarkness and peered into the ocean.

Candleshine's gaze followed. Would any of them be spared? A surprise attack was always a possibility, either while they boarded or in the open water between No-Name Island and Guadalcanal.

Her heart lifted in prayer, she crouched next to the stretcher patients and strained her eyes toward the oncoming PT boats, desperately longing for Jeff and the others to appear.

Chapter 10

Why did *two* PT boats come?" Candleshine whispered, muscles tense. She was ready to run. "There aren't enough of us to crowd just one." "Probably as cover," Elizabeth murmured in her ear. "If one is hit, as least some of us will get out alive, we hope." She pressed Candleshine's hand, then Jane's. "Just in case we don't all survive, you're the finest nurses I've ever worked beside."

Candleshine couldn't have answered if she'd had time. Such high praise from this veteran nurse meant so much. In the heartbeat between Elizabeth's whisper and Magee's order to run for the PT boats, the young nurse cringed inwardly and wondered. What would Elizabeth say if she knew Candleshine had promised to marry Lieutenant Fairfax and now quivered with cowardice and shame?

The long-awaited and dreaded evacuation took fifteen minutes. Magee separated the group, and Candleshine shuddered, remembering what Elizabeth had said. The older nurse ordered Jane and Candleshine to go together and calmly saw to the loading of the stretcher patients. The rear guard joined the evacuees after satisfying themselves that so far no Japanese fighter planes had discovered the unusual activity on the beach. Lieutenant Fairfax gave a final sweeping to the narrow strip to cover their activity.

Candleshine's fears subsided when he boarded the PT boat and came to where she knelt by a wounded soldier. At least he'd be close if the evacuation turned into a nightmare.

Elizabeth called guardedly from the other PT boat, "See you in Guadalcanal!" Their last sight of the gallant woman was a wave in the starlight before the PT boat swung back toward open water. Candleshine looked back at No-Name Island only once. Dark and silent, from their position it looked as untouched as it had so long ago when the weary survivors from the *Fortitude* sought its shelter. The stripped fruit trees and a deserted camp would be the only indications of a human refuge.

"This little mosquito boat can sting the enemy—it's deadly in the dark," Magee told the nurses in barely discernible tones. "We may just get out of here yet."

For a time his prophecy proved true. No familiar hum that grew into the ugly whine of enemy planes marred the still darkness. No enemy warships loomed. Candleshine dared to breathe normally, until an explosion ahead shot bursts of orange flame into the velvet night.

"Dear God!" Jeff grabbed Candleshine and hid her face against his chest but not before the fiery scene was engraved in her mind.

She clung to him. "The other boat?"

"Torpedoed." His arms tightened around her. "I thought all the Japanese subs in this area had been detected and destroyed. One must have sneaked past our surveillance."

Candleshine tore free from his protective hold. "Why are we changing course? Why, we're running away!" Her voice rose to a shriek and anger burned out fear. "Why aren't we going to help, to pick up survivors? Elizabeth—the others—"

"There are no survivors." His burning eyes penetrated deep into hers. Yet her protests could not be quelled.

"You don't know that!" she cried wildly. "Magee, tell him." She licked dry lips. *"We can't just leave."*

Magee said hoarsely, "PT boats carry 5,000 pounds of explosives."

His defeated face sent red-hot pokers of pain into her, but she took a deep breath, held it, and submitted to a dull acceptance.

In a wild series of maneuvers, the PT boat fled, leaving part of Candleshine buried in the waters between No-Name Island and Guadalcanal. Even Jeff's reassurance that Allied planes would get the sub now that it had been located didn't penetrate the numbness that settled on her like a rain-soaked tarpaulin. Candleshine never knew how long it took to reach Guadalcanal. She barely responded to the welcoming cheers of the military personnel who held the reclaimed island. Only the needs of the men she cared for kept her going. She had seen men die in war and in civilian life. But to witness what she had had drained her magnificent strength.

For a full week Jeff observed her, knowing only too well her pain and the wall she erected to keep out more hurt. In a bold effort to smash the threat to her mental health, he drew her aside one day. "Candleshine, there's a chaplain here. You promised to marry me. If I can get permission, will you? Here? Now? Who knows what the future will allow?"

She came out of her fog and despair. Why not take what happiness she could when it could be all there was? Why let hesitation and thoughts of the future stop them? What if she didn't know him well? Having his strength to draw from helped her go on.

A fine, white line circled Jeff's lips. His midnight blue eyes searched hers. "I'm almost well. I'll be sent back to active duty soon." He cleared the huskiness from his voice. "At least we'd have a few days of heaven first."

She closed her eyes and remembered the security of his arms that night in the PT boat. Tomorrow and the next day dimmed. A single nod of her head would give them today.

"Nurse Thatcher," Magee's voice separated them. "You're needed." His stocky body followed his voice. "Oh, sorry, Lieutenant."

Jeff just grunted before turning glowing eyes on Candleshine. "Don't forget what I said."

As if she could! *God, help me,* she prayed. *I'm too tired to fight any longer.* She watched Jeff walk away, wondering if his meeting with a superior officer at the edge of the compound meant anything. Or the way his radioman Dan Black joined them.

Magee motioned for Candleshine and Jane to step to one side. His troubled gaze moved from one to the other. "I need one of you to accompany a patient to Australia," he said bluntly. "The medics say one of our boys who got hit in that last little episode on No-Name Island has to have better care than we can give him here. A medic can't be spared, so one of you is it."

Candleshine's heart raced. Could this be God's way of answering her prayer by giving her time away to think? She looked at Jane. "Do you want me to go?"

"It may be dangerous." Jane bit her lip. "I can go." Yet the look she cast in Dan Black's direction gave away her longing to stay.

"The way I see it," Magee began as he had done so many times before, "there's no real safety guaranteed here or anywhere." He scratched his head, and Candleshine felt a tide of friendship for the big, rough staff sergeant.

"I'll go. How soon do I need to be ready?"

"Four hours ago." Magee grimaced. "Grab what you can and meet me back here in fifteen minutes." He saluted them, marched off, and came back five minutes later to find Candleshine almost ready. "You're going too," he told Jane. "Orders from headquarters."

She stared, then set her jaw and started packing. Suddenly she stopped. "I have to see someone before I go."

"So do I." Candleshine crammed the rest of her stuff together.

"You've got five minutes," Magee warned. "Hurry up the good-byes."

Dan Black stood nearby, and Jane rushed to him. Candleshine raced after her. "Lieutenant Fairfax—where is he?"

Dan jerked his head toward the far side of the compound. His kind eyes looked sad and aware. "High-powered meeting with the brass."

"But I must see him!"

"Sorry, Nurse Thatcher. No one interrupts such meetings unless it's life or death." Pity softened his face. "I'll deliver a message when I can."

Half sobbing, Candleshine hurried back and found paper and pencil. Tears stained the page, and she barely got it into an envelope before Magee called, "Time's up."

Dan and Jane had crossed to them, their hands linked. Jane grabbed her things, and Candleshine pressed the envelope in Dan's outstretched hand.

"Tell him. . .tell him. . ." She couldn't go on.

For the sake of those they served, the nurses held back their own feelings. As Magee had said, this was war. Partings, fear, and service were all part of the deadly hide-and-seek game between those who sought to destroy and those who maintained freedom.

Candleshine thought of her hastily scribbled message. When would Jeff get it? How would he feel? She couldn't think about it. She must carry on, even as he would carry on. Something in Dan Black's eyes had warned how important the high-powered meeting would be to his future and Jeff's. Perhaps even now the two men were throwing things together as the nurses had done, preparing to leave on new flying assignments. Would Jeff understand the real meaning behind her words? Or would he see them for what they were, a desperate grab for a life raft of escape from marriage to him?

I've been ordered to Australia with the wounded. It will give me time to think. God bless and keep you.

Candleshine

★ ★ ★

Weeks later, Candleshine lay as a patient in the same Australian hospital she, Jane, and the others had reached after leaving Guadalcanal. Instead of caring for others, she chafed at her own inactivity.

"You're going home," Jane announced one day.

"What?" Candleshine started to sit up, but Jane grimly pushed her back down.

"Heavens, what terrible patients nurses make! I said that you're going home. No use arguing. The doctor says you're a victim of battle fatigue on top of malaria." Jane scowled. "How could you have forgotten to take your Atabrine?"

Candleshine felt tears of weakness slide down her nose. "If you remember correctly, we were involved in some pretty hectic times." Her voice trembled, and she turned her head away.

"I'm sorry," Jane quickly said. She smoothed the younger nurse's pillow. "Don't you see, though, unless you're able to help care for others you—"

"—I'm just an added burden," Candleshine finished bitterly. "What a way to end up my war efforts, flat on my back when you and every other nurse here is run off her feet!"

"Just be glad we got here," Jane quietly reminded. She sighed and cocked her head to one side. The grin that made her so popular among her patients crept out. "Frankly, I'd give a month's pay to trade places with you now that the chills and fever are over. I could use the rest." She yawned.

"Jane, have you heard anything from Dan Black?"

"No." The word hung between them. "If things work out, someday, well, he knows where to find me." She brushed aside personal concerns and stretched

451

tired muscles. "I have work to do." She patted Candleshine's hand. "I keep believing he's all right." She sighed again, and a faraway look touched her eyes. "It's all I—or any girl who loves a marine—can do." Jane slipped out of sight.

Candleshine repeated to herself what Jane had said. She closed her eyes. Love that made her ache filled her heart and mind, but guilt had the last word. Not only had she run from a promise, she had failed to witness of her Lord to a man who faced death every time he went out on a mission.

Did Jeff know God? Had he accepted Jesus? Candleshine couldn't be sure. She only knew that the precious moments they had spent talking of themselves, their love, and their dreams had failed to include the most important topic of all. If Jeff were killed in action, she would never know whether he'd been a Christian. Could she bear the cross of uncertainty?

★ ★ ★

Will and Trinity Thatcher openly rejoiced when they learned their only daughter had been ordered home. Surely Cedar Ridge would help erase whatever she had experienced in the long months overseas. Yet, when they picked her up in Seattle, pale, aloof, and strangely haunted, Trinity could barely stand to look at her. The imprint of her service had left an indelible mark. Where had Candleshine gone? Who was this stranger that sat between them and gazed out the window with eyes that neither saw nor cared? Physically run-down, the light that once made Candleshine far more attractive than her features had flickered so low Trinity wondered if it still existed.

Months passed. Candleshine's superb health slowly returned. Regardless of the weather, she spent as much time outside as possible, reveling in the crispness of a world away from tropical heat. Yet a shadow remained in her eyes, and her parents worried and prayed harder than ever.

Five times she traveled to Mercy Hospital in Seattle and begged Miss Grey to put her back to work. Five times Miss Grey sighed over how badly she needed Candleshine and denied the request. "Not until *I* feel you are ready," she said through lips made even grimmer by the war years.

"How will you—or I—know?"

"I'll know." Miss Grey's lips relaxed. "So will you."

In late fall 1944, Candleshine climbed to the spot where she and Bruce had dreamed and planned a lifetime before. A growing fever inside her demanded action, not this silly recuperating business everyone insisted she have. How much time off did Jane or Miss Grey, Connie, Bruce, or Winona have? Or Jeff. . . ?

Her blue eyes darkened. Sometimes Jeff and their love seemed like a dream or from such a shrouded past that it slipped away in the mists. Was he still alive? Did he remember the woman who promised to marry him? The dagger in her soul turned and pierced her to the core.

"Dear God, if I could only feel free." The desire for relief from her heavy burden welled inside her and spilled into the late autumn day. Time after time, Will and Trinity had given her the opportunity to speak, but something inside Candleshine froze the words.

Now she cried, "Dear heavenly Father, give me strength to tell them what happened over there and to rid myself of this specter. My skills are needed but my torch has burned so low I can't serve. Please, God, help me."

An hour later she stood, walked back to her home, and took a deep breath. "I have a story to tell you."

She began with her early fears about turning coward in the face of disaster. She relived the panic of fleeing from the sinking *Fortitude* and spared no detail concerning the time that followed: the drifting; sighting the island and wondering if the Japanese held it; living under a cloud of perpetual vigilance lest they be discovered.

Strangely enough, when it came to the arrival of Lieutenant Fairfax and his radioman, she said little except that they needed care. Something inside her shrank from exposing even to these two how she felt. If Jeff ever came home, it would be time to share.

With clenched hands and glazed eyes, she again boarded the PT boat. Even when she told how the Japanese submarine made a direct torpedo hit on the other boat she didn't flinch.

Once Trinity stirred in protest, appalled at the look in her daughter's face. Will's warning glance riveted her to her chair and silenced her. She sank back, suffering with Candleshine, but realized it must all come out before healing could occur.

Dinner forgotten, Candleshine talked until her voice came out in a croak and evening gloom crept into the living room. She stopped, emptied.

"My darling girl!" Trinity could stand no more. She reached out both arms.

Like a sleepwalker coming out of a long period of unconsciousness, Candleshine stumbled across the room and fell to her knees with her head in her mother's lap. Great tearing sobs came, washing away the painful remembrances of an unimaginable past.

"Steady, little girl," Will's broken voice said. "It's all over now. You're here and you're safe."

Except for the one, long splinter in her heart—her love for Jeff—Candleshine felt remade.

Two days later she stood in Miss Grey's office, impeccable in her Mercy Hospital white uniform and black-banded cap. "I'm ready for orders."

A lightning glance from the famous gray eyes, a slow smile, and warm handshake were evidence her time again had come. Miss Grey said, "We need you in rehabilitation. Can you handle it?"

"Yes."

"Thank God." Miss Grey rose, not in the old way that reduced her probationers to quivering jelly, but awkwardly, with weariness in every motion. "Welcome home, Candleshine."

Tested and found to be pure gold in the fires of war, Candleshine brought to the droves of soldiers necessary physical rehabilitation and the gentle firmness that encouraged them beyond themselves. Someone had told them her story, and the servicemen took her to their hearts. Anyone who had been under fire in the Pacific theater knew about nightmares, and that tears did not always mean weakness. To make up for the months of recuperation when she had nothing to give, Candleshine now worked long hours uncomplainingly and never failed to let the nurses she supervised know how valuable they were.

Sally Monroe had gone overseas as she predicted. New faces filled the wards and halls. Yet Mercy Hospital and Training School continued, an important cog in winning the war on the home front.

Although Candleshine never neglected a patient or gave one more care than another, she found herself especially drawn to those coming home from the Pacific. Wherever opportunities arose, she quietly asked, "Did you ever run across a marine lieutenant named Jeffrey Fairfax?" Yet after many weeks the only response was "Sorry." She also asked after Dan Black, but the answer remained the same, each time leaving her empty but determined to do all she could to locate Jeff. Even if he despised her for running away, she owed him an explanation, and her witness of Christ.

★ ★ ★

Early in 1945, encouraging war news drifted back to them. The United States and the Allied forces had liberated island after island from the Japanese. The New Guinea and Central Pacific campaigns had brought the Allies within striking distance of the Philippines several months earlier. In late October 1944, General MacArthur kept his pledge to return, but only after more than two years of costly fighting. The battle for Leyte Gulf in late October ended in a major victory for the Allies. The remaining Japanese navy no longer posed a threat.

Yet the continuing battle for Leyte that ran through 1944 brought perhaps the most chilling weapon Japan offered—the *kamikaze*. These "suicide pilots" crashed planes filled with explosives into Allied warships, unless shot down before they crashed. Candleshine set her lips, prayed the madness would end, and continued her own work, always hoping of news about Jeff. *How long could it go on?* she wondered. The very word *kamikaze*, which means "divine wind," stilled even the most talkative patients. How much the world needed Christ, with His message of unconditional love! Why couldn't Japan see they had no chance of winning?

In early March, news came that Manila had been retaken by the Allies. A burly soldier due to be released caught Candleshine around the waist and swung her off her feet into a wild victory dance. All her protests meant nothing.

The whole rehabilitation ward chanted, "Manila's ours, Manila's ours," until Candleshine pressed her hands over her ears. Even the doctor couldn't dim the spirit of hope that had built from early January when the Allies landed on Luzon.

"Sure, and it's about over," the burly soldier shouted. "They can't last much longer!"

Their contagious joy fired Candleshine's heart. Her torch indeed flared bright. God willing, the long, dark months would end and brightness would return. In the meantime, her body and soul must continue in service; more men would come home and many would need her skills.

She adjusted her cap and went back to work.

Chapter 11

C aptain Fairfax?"

"Yes, Sir?" Jeff stood with pantherlike grace and saluted.

"First, congratulations on your new rank. From what I hear, you've earned it. At ease," the hatchet-faced major barked. "Have a chair."

Jeff relaxed as much as the straight-backed office chair permitted. "Thanks." He eyed his superior officer.

"I understand you're due for leave." Keen eyes bored into Jeff's brain, but the younger marine's lips thinned.

"Due, but I don't want it, Sir. We've been flying successful missions, and we have the Japanese on the run. I need every pilot who can handle a plane." Jeff laughed. "Why am I telling you this, Sir? You know more about it than I do."

"I do."

Jeff's mouth twitched. The major sounded like a participant in a wedding, a thought that made Jeff's heart lurch.

The major leaned forward from behind his battered desk. "Manila is in rubble. Our massive incendiary raid has destroyed the heart of Tokyo." The gruff major cleared his throat. "Approximately 25,000 of our marines died or were wounded in taking Iwo Jima. Our B-29 bombers have been pounding Japan's industries and our subs sinking the supplies they need so badly. We've got them on the run but at a terrible cost." A gray shade dropped like a visor over his lean face. "Okinawa, 50,000 Allied casualties."

Jeff's heart went out to the major. "Yes, Sir. But every one of those men believed in what he did."

"It's the only thing that helps me stay sane." The major's eyes flamed. "Captain, if the world doesn't learn this time that war is more than a deadly game, I don't know what will happen. What lies ahead is worse than the past. If the Allies invade Japan itself, we could lose a million Americans alone! But I didn't call you in to discuss strategy. We have enough generals and colonels for that. Do I understand correctly that you are officially turning down the leave I was ordered to offer?"

"Yes, Sir."

The major rose. "I'd do the same." He stretched a surprisingly strong hand out, and the man behind the officer smiled. "Carry on, and thank you. Dismissed."

Jeff's eyes stung. He returned the grip and saluted, then turned smartly on his heel and marched out. All the heroes weren't on the front lines. Without being told, Jeff knew his major would give everything to be in the cockpit of an attacking plane instead of ordering others to go from behind a desk.

What would this summer of 1945 bring? More death and destruction? So far he had been spared, but how many more times could he get back to base when other planes in his squadron spiraled into flames? Jeff brushed his hand over his eyes to blot out those memories.

War stories raced like wildfire through his mind. When the army mop-up boys landed at Subic Bay, unloaded arms, and prepared to put the finishing touches on Japanese resistance, even aerial support couldn't suppress the danger. Nether did the support artillery that laid a ring of steel around them. Holding a position could be a nightmare. Every shadow or movement demanded attention from men so fatigued night came as an enemy instead of a time to rest. One soldier on watch saw two unknown entities "creeping up" the trail. He put a bullet in each. They turned out to be trees.

Another soldier whose weight had gone down to 160 pounds staggered under the weight of his apron, two mortar shells in front and two behind, plus a rifle and bandoliers of ammunition. Crossing a creek he fell and filled the bag with water.

Entering Iba, eerie silence had greeted the troops, one of the strangest experiences they encountered. Not a soul awaited them. Then Filipinos, who had fled to the mountains to escape imprisonment, came in from the hills just behind the soldiers, freed from their exile at last. The Japanese left the bridge at Iba ready to blow, but a Filipino soldier sneaked in and pulled off the wires.

Jeff's appreciation for every branch of the military increased with each tale. The ground crews who had the dirty mop-up job deserved high respect, living in trenches, following the rough trails made by carabao-drawn carts, fighting underbrush, prickly heat, and mud during the monsoon season, as well as the enemy. Unless they were fortunate enough to find a well with a pitcher pump installed by the Americans who had dug them early in the occupation of the Philippines, they had to push bamboo in a bank so water would come out. They would then drop halogen tablets in their canteens to purify the water, never drinking from a creek until it had been checked by the medics. If the person designated to bring food didn't reach them, it meant doing without. Sometimes they drank water from the water-cooled machine guns they carried.

Peril threatened the ships, from sky and sea alike. Earlier, a ship safely passed through a narrow entrance into a body of water with an island in the middle, located near New Guinea. It sailed around the buoy and swung back and forth on anchor with the tide, broadside to the inlet. According to scuttlebutt, when the crew went to breakfast they heard an explosion. A Japanese sub had thrown three torpedoes, one to each side and the third down the middle.

The outside ones missed. The third, which should have hit the Allied ship dead center, hit the buoy!

Jeff's next mission would come soon, and his body cried out for rest. Yet sleep evaded him, and for the first time in months he allowed Candleshine to creep into his thoughts. Familiar anger that had hit like a howitzer shell when he read her note and done nearly as much damage to his emotions was offset by the image of her honest blue eyes. But time and the necessity of concentrating on his job had dulled his outrage. He remembered her sweetness, the trust and lack of pretense she had shown when his arms encircled her on the PT boat.

His jaw set. How ironic that if Candleshine had stayed a few more minutes she'd have learned marriage was out. He'd been ordered back to immediate duty and left with Dan Black a bare hour after the nurses and their patient headed for Australia.

He shifted his position, willed himself to sleep, and failed. Perhaps his talk with the major had triggered his rebellion. This ungodly mess had to end soon. When it did. . .

A little smile curved his mobile lips and brightened his spirits. "Cedar Ridge, Washington," he murmured. "Go to sleep, Fairfax. The sooner this war ends, the sooner you can follow the gleam to Cedar Ridge." He smothered a laugh at his poetic flight, yawned, and fell into deep sleep.

Hours later, he awakened to the now-familiar summons. Alert and determined, Jeff headed out for yet another mission. Sometimes it seemed he had never existed except here fighting, retreating, fighting again. Carson and the Laughing X might have existed in someone else's lifetime. It didn't seem possible that somewhere peace lay over the land. A wave of nostalgia for home and his horses, for Carson and the ranch house, and for distant mountains that stretched to the sky beyond the cedar-darkened foothills left him grinning. "Almost, I'd even be glad to see Lillian." He immediately shook his head. He must be getting dotty.

Without warning, the plane shuddered beneath his guiding hands. Bullets ripped into the cockpit. A quick glance showed him that American planes had already pounced like hawks on mice and dispersed the enemy fighters. Funny, his left leg felt numb. He glanced down. Wet patches showed he'd been hit.

The crazy antics of his plane warned of more trouble. "Hand me the first-aid kit," Jeff told his copilot. He pressed the heel of his hand against his bleeding leg and applied pressure. "See if everyone else is okay."

"Copilot to crew. Everyone okay back there?"

"Yeah, but the plane ain't," came through the intercom. "We can't make it like this. We'll have to turn back."

"Just as well. Cap's hit." The copilot flicked off the intercom.

Jeff eased the plane in a wide arc. The numbness in his leg held but the initial shock wore off before they reached home base, and he gritted his teeth in order to finish the course.

"Fire off a red flare," the copilot ordered when they arrived. "We're going to need an ambulance."

They landed. Jeff swung out on his right leg, dragged the left over, and crumpled. His brain felt fuzzy as it seemed a million devils were hammering into his leg. Finally he felt himself being lifted and carried into the twilight.

Jeff awakened to find the hatchet-faced major looming above him. The major grinned sourly. "If you wanted leave why didn't you just say so instead of going out and getting shot up?"

Jeff's gaze snapped to his heavily bandaged left leg. "Sir, how am I supposed to fly with that thing?" Disgust filled him.

"You won't be flying for some time. That leg of yours needs more attention than it can get here. So do you." The major's eyebrows met in a frown. "You bled bucketfuls, and if it had been just a little farther coming back you wouldn't be here now. It's home for you, and I pray to God we'll all be right on your heels getting there. There's a feeling in the air something climactic is about to happen. Don't ask me what; I don't know. I do know you've done more than your share."

"Thank you, Sir. I'd rather stay. This little problem can't be that bad."

"You're under orders, Captain, and those orders are for you to be sent home." His wintry grin stilled Jeff's protests. "This time you have no choice."

After he'd gone Jeff stared at the doorway and felt like a slacker. What right had he to leave when he was needed? Grimly determined, he started to get out of bed and got the shock of a lifetime. The same crazy head-spinning he'd experienced after the accident left him as weak as the newborn calves he'd helped deliver back in Montana. Still ashamed but finally convinced, he sank back on the hard cot, glad for its support.

Dan Black came in once before Jeff left. "You're going by way of Australia?"

"Yeah, the scenic route," Jeff grumbled.

"Uh, mind doing me a favor, Sir?"

"Can the 'sir.' What do you want?"

Dan's steady eyes never left his captain's face. "Would you see if Jane's still at the hospital, and if she is, tell her nothing has changed?"

"That's all?" Jeff stared.

"She'll know what it means."

Understanding flowed through Jeff. *Nothing has changed.* If he and Dan were in opposite places with Candleshine in Australia, wouldn't his message be the same? He should never have pressured her. No wonder she seized the chance to get away and think! A rueful grin stretched his lips. War did strange things to people. If anyone had told him a few years earlier he'd fall in love, propose, and insist on marrying a girl he barely knew, he'd have laughed until his sides hurt.

"I'll tell her if she's there. When you get home, if you ever want an outdoor job—hard work and moderate pay—come to the Laughing X."

"I just may, if Jane likes Montana cattle ranches. We didn't have time to make real plans." Dan set his jaw. "I really don't know the things she loves. At first, I represented her brother. When I told her I cared and found out she did too. . ." His voice died.

"It's tough on everyone," Jeff quietly said, impressed with the truth in his radioman's simple statement, *We didn't have time*. God willing, there would be time, for them and thousands of other anxious couples.

An unexpected development hindered Jeff's going home. In the Australian hospital his wounded leg acted up. Infection fought against medication and delayed the healing process. Concerned doctors dressed his leg daily and finally quelled his complaints. "All your fretting is hindering our efforts. If you want to keep that leg, start working with us instead of against us by wanting to get back in the middle of things. Granted, top pilots are needed, but do you honestly think you're the only pilot in the U.S. Marines who can lick the Japanese?"

Jeff subsided, feeling the way he had when his second grade teacher stood him in the corner for fighting the class bully.

The minute he reached the hospital he had inquired about Jane. Not until he faithfully repeated Dan Black's message did he notice how pretty the nurse from No-Name Island had become. Or did the radiance in her eyes account for it?

She stopped in and visited when she could, but her busy schedule left little time.

Once he hesitated and asked, "Have you heard from Nurse Thatcher at all?"

"Twice, Sir. She spent a lot of time in Cedar Ridge getting over the effects of the malaria and—"

"Malaria?"

"Yes; we kept her here for a time. Anyway, the last letter came just a few months ago. She's back at Mercy Hospital in Seattle supervising the rehabilitation ward." After a moment she added, "And waiting with the rest of us for the war to end." Softness touched her eyes. "She asked about you, Sir."

How ridiculous for his heart to drum against his ribs! "Oh?"

"She just wondered if I had ever seen or heard about you or Dan or Magee."

"Oh." Jeff felt let down in spite of the good news. Just his luck to have her fall in love with one of those on-the-spot men in her ward. The next minute he laughed and told Jane good-bye in case he got out before she had time to come again. Candleshine was not the type to jump from sweetheart to sweetheart. He'd known when he kissed her the very first time that she embodied purity and untouched love. She also possessed valor and an overdeveloped sense of fair play. He bet she'd never let her heart get involved until she finished things up with a certain marine flyer. That thought alone made it easier to await his return to the States.

★ ★ ★

Jeff did not wait alone. The world also waited, for what they dared not conjecture. Every Allied victory, each setback sent waves around the globe. Stories leaked out confirming that the new developments in antimalarial therapy and drugs, the availability of blood derivatives, and the heroism and ingenuity of the medical corpsmen accounted for the saving of countless lives that other wars would have claimed. The world also watched as the upstart American vice president assumed the reins of the presidency in April 1945. Could Harry S. Truman, even though he had worked with FDR until his death, succeed at the tremendous task he faced?

The answer came in early August. The U.S., Great Britain, and China warned Japan to surrender unconditionally or be destroyed. Japan continued to fight.

August sixth rocked the world.

An American B-29 bomber, the *Enola Gay*, carried and dropped the world's first atomic bomb to be used in war on Hiroshima. It destroyed five square miles and killed 80,000 to 100,000 people.

The world again waited.

Japan went on fighting.

On August ninth, the U.S. dropped a second atomic bomb, this time on Nagasaki, killing approximately 40,000.

Unable to withstand such whole-scale destruction, Emperor Hirohito stepped into politics, despite the traditional hands-off policy of Japanese emperors. On August fourteenth Japan surrendered, but some of their leading military leaders committed suicide rather than accept the defeat of their dreams to control the world.

Japanese representatives and those from every Allied nation gathered on September second on the U.S.S. battleship *Missouri*, anchored in Tokyo Bay. When Japan signed the official surrender papers on what President Truman designated as V-J Day (Victory over Japan Day), World War II ended. Millions had died in a conflict based on greed and the desire for power.

American boys and men came home, old beyond their years. Some carried physical scars, but all brought emotional wounds with them. Candleshine doubled her efforts, then tripled them, demanding the best of herself and her staff. With the overseas fighting behind them, many still had long, painful fights ahead.

Yet in the quiet nights and busy days, hope never left Candleshine.

Japanese internment camps were disgorging their long-held prisoners. She prayed Bruce and Winona would be among them, survivors of mistreatment and unspeakable conditions, but alive.

She also prayed for Connie. What kind of world would her friend face after imprisonment in her own country?

A hasty note from Jane bore the good news that she'd be shipping out for America soon, and that *her husband* Dan Black would accompany her! They'd been married shortly after V-J Day.

> *We're seriously considering accepting Captain Jeffrey Fairfax's offer and settling on the Laughing X. Dan says after all the action, he can never go back to a desk job. He wants to be free, and whatever he wants will make me happy.*
>
> *Captain Fairfax is already there. We finally licked the infection in his left leg, and he won't lose it as we feared. As I mentioned when I wrote before, touch and go best described his situation. He seemed pleased that you had asked about him.*

The letter fell from Candleshine's nerveless fingers. *Jeff hurt, so seriously they thought he'd lose a leg? Jane mentioned a letter. Why didn't it come through?*

"Thank God he's all right," she whispered. A vision of Jeff as she last saw him danced in her mind—tall, commanding, his eyes aglow with the prospect of their marriage.

She clasped both hands around her knees. "Dear God, I failed him once," she cried in a broken voice. "More by not telling him of You than breaking my promise to become his wife. No matter how hard it is, when I see him again I will share my faith."

A few weeks later Candleshine received a summons on the ward to report to Miss Grey's office immediately. Her knees turned to pudding as she quietly gave orders to the nurse who substituted for her.

"Miss Grey may have new patients coming in," she scolded herself on the interminable walk down the halls and to the Supervisor of Nurses' office. Breathing deeply, she tapped.

"Come in," a male voice invited.

Candleshine stepped inside, stopped, then stared. With a glad cry she hurled herself at the tall, emaciated figure whose eyes glowed with light in an otherwise dead face.

Dr. Bruce Thatcher had come home.

Chapter 12

Candleshine clung to the beloved cousin she had feared dead in spite of her faith. An eternity later she voiced a remaining fear. "Winona?"

Bruce's deep voice did more to reassure her than anything else in the world. "Thin, nerves shattered, but alive and home."

Candleshine's head jerked up. "When can I see her?"

"Soon, but first let her family have her. She also needs rest. As soon as her parents agree, I'm taking her to Cedar Ridge to heal."

"As your wife?"

"How did you know?" Surprise punctuated each word.

"Sweeny stopped by a lifetime ago." Candleshine bit her quivering lips. "He told me what you said."

"Someday I intend to marry Winona, but not until she can put the horror behind her."

Candleshine shivered at the somber look in his eyes. "Can you talk about it?"

His blue gaze returned to her. "I can, but I won't. Whatever you heard from Sweeny, plus any other accounts, is about a hundredth of what happened. The sooner those of us who survived forget it, the better." He grinned, and a trace of the old Bruce surfaced. "Mind if we sit down? It's going to take awhile to get enough decent food in me to get back my energy." He glanced around the office, longing in his face. "I can hardly wait to be back here working amid order, cleanliness, and supplies. Candleshine, one of the worst parts of the last years is feeling helpless to save people who should be alive now and who would have, given proper conditions."

She felt the anger behind his bitter tirade. "You're home, Dear. As soon as you're ready, your work is waiting."

"I know." He stared directly into her face, but Candleshine had the feeling his thoughts lay across the ocean in a distant land.

Sensing his awkward pause, he clumsily patted her shining short hair. "I guess Cedar Ridge is planning some kind of blowout in honor of the boys coming home, including me, although I wasn't actually in the military. Can you come?"

"I wouldn't miss it." She smiled, a rainbow after rain. "If Winona feels like it, maybe she can come too."

"Don't push her in any way," Bruce warned. "So much happened in such a short time, I'm not sure she ever had the time to deal with her fiancé's death at Pearl. If she wants to talk, let her. If she doesn't—" He lifted his shoulders expressively.

Candleshine walked out to the street with him. In a few hours he'd be in Cedar Ridge. She wished she were free of hospital duties and could go with him, but she knew his father and stepmother and Will and Trinity deserved time with him. Her heart ached at how gaunt his body had become. Yet as she took in the squared shoulders and the head held high, bared to the hazy autumn sun, she realized he was a man among men. A cousin to be proud of for all her life.

Remembering Bruce's admonition not to push, Candleshine took the precaution of calling the Allens before attempting to see them. Mrs. Allen said Winona was sleeping, but she'd tell her Candleshine had called when she awakened. Some of her fears as a mother spilled out. "She's terribly changed, of course. The worst thing is the dullness in her eyes. I think so often how they snapped with mischief and fun. Candleshine, do you think my daughter will ever come back to me? To us?"

Candleshine's hand tightened on the telephone. "Yes, but she won't ever be the same person who went away." She took a deep breath. "Mrs. Allen, I didn't experience anything like what Winona lived through, but it took me a long time to heal or even to talk about it."

"What should I do? How did your parents handle it for you?" Mrs. Allen asked anxiously.

A big lump formed in Candleshine's throat. "They simply loved me, didn't ask questions, and waited. They also prayed—a lot."

"Thank you so much." Candleshine could hear Winona's mother crying softly. "I'll tell her as soon as she's awake. Right now all she wants to do is sleep. The doctor says it's the best thing for her as she probably didn't get one single good night's rest the entire time she was held prisoner." She thanked Candleshine again and broke the connection.

Early that evening Winona returned the call. When Candleshine picked up the phone, the first words she heard were, "Little Sister?" Yet Winona's voice sounded flat and lifeless, unlike the vivacious, bubbling voice that could turn serious with concern over a younger nurse's problems.

Dear God, what shall I say? Candleshine silently prayed, but Winona spared her the need for small talk.

"When do you have time off? Not just an hour but an afternoon or day? Candleshine, I really want to see you."

The unspoken appeal released her tongue. "I'm scheduled for time off Friday, but maybe I can get it changed." Surely Miss Grey would rearrange duties when she learned of Winona's need.

"Call me if you can."

"I will," Candleshine promised. She hesitated then added, "You must already know there's no one in the world I'd rather welcome as my new cousin than you when the time comes."

A little choking sound told her the ice jam around Winona had begun to crack. So did the quick "Bless you" before her friend hung up.

Miss Grey immediately rescheduled the nurses on the rehabilitation ward when Candleshine explained why she'd like time off earlier. "Tell Winona I expect her back here the minute she's ready, not one minute sooner or one minute later."

How true to form Miss Grey ran! Those were the same words she had used when Candleshine approached her about returning to Mercy Hospital.

Although the few days at home hadn't overcome the telltale signs of imprisonment, Winona had regained a tiny bit of sparkle by the time Candleshine visited her. By silent mutual agreement, they avoided talking about the war. Candleshine did tell how Sergeant Sweeny stopped by on his way home to recuperate. Winona laughed out loud at his calling Miss Grey a "grand old dame," and Candleshine caught the look of gratitude on Mrs. Allen's face.

"Sweeny made our stay on Corregidor a lot easier," Winona said before the familiar shadow fell back over her eyes.

"You and Bruce must have witnessed to him," Candleshine quickly said and was rewarded with a lifting of the shadow and a show of interest. She repeated the things Sweeny said and finished by saying, "I think Sweeny was well on his way to becoming a Christian, if not already there."

"I'm glad," Winona said softly. She reached a thin hand toward her friend, and a poignant light made her finely drawn features beautiful. "A very few good things came out of being over there, and my learning to rely on God for every minute of every day is number one." She added with a flash of the old Winona, "Bruce is number two!"

Candleshine just hugged her, too filled to speak. So all the prayers had borne fruit. Yet hadn't she always known Bruce could never join his life with anyone who didn't believe and serve his God? A little tremor went through her. One by one things fell into place. First Bruce and Winona were home; soon Connie Imoto would return. Yet until Lieutenant—no—Captain Jeffrey Fairfax came back, the ragtag ends of the war would not be secured for her.

In the next few weeks, Candleshine spent as much time as possible with Winona. Little by little, the thin, pale cheeks filled out. The dark shadows lurking in the black eyes slowly receded. Although quieter, in many ways Winona reverted back to the former beloved Big Sister with Candleshine, except now the two nurses shared a more equal friendship due to experiences and passing years.

Connie Imoto came home before Thanksgiving. She called Candleshine immediately and arranged a meeting. Not in the lovely home that had been the Imotos' for years but in a small place they had found in a Seattle suburb. It would take years to get established again after their heavy losses due to relocation.

Candleshine almost dreaded the meeting, but relief flooded her the moment she saw her tiny friend. Without being told, she knew Connie had kept her torch of faith in God and others burning.

Connie seemed reluctant to speak of the past except to share wonderful news. During the long weeks, months, and years of communal living, crowded into barracks, she had been able to minister both medically and spiritually. Her own refusal to harbor hate or resentment, and her firm belief that America would win the war and become the grand country that offered opportunity to all, had influenced those about her.

"My parents have left the worship of the old gods," she rejoiced. "They accepted Christ just a few months ago. Candleshine, God's promise to bring good from evil came true in the camp, especially for the Imotos."

She sat quietly and lowered her voice to a whisper. "All of us agree; everything we lost, the freedom taken from us, is nothing compared with the priceless gift we now have. And God has spared my brother! He fought valiantly, earned the Purple Heart, and is nearly ready to work again."

"Are you coming back to Mercy?" Candleshine asked.

"Oh, yes. Miss Grey has an opening in pediatrics the first of January. That gives me time to get ready."

"Winona will be back too, but I don't know when. Her family has agreed to lend her for a few weeks." Candleshine laughed. "Bruce is chomping at the bit waiting. He can't wait to show her Cedar Ridge in winter."

Sadness touched Connie's face. "I'd like to see her, if she's willing."

"Why wouldn't she be?" Honestly surprised, Candleshine blinked.

Connie glanced down at her interwoven fingers. "There are those who see me as the enemy."

Candleshine felt horror swim over her. "You don't mean you have had people treat you badly, after all you went through?"

Connie shook her shining dark head. "Not me, but friends have awakened to a cross burning in their yard and hooded figures chanting hate messages." The sadness spread, and Connie raised her head. "For some, the war will not end. Ever."

Again, Candleshine felt shame that people could treat fellow Americans who had suffered and fought, bled and died, so outrageously.

She never forgot the meeting between Connie and Winona. The look that passed between the two shut her out. Although they had been thousands of miles apart, her two friends had shared similar experiences. When their hands met in sincere friendship, Candleshine felt like crying. The symbolism of the mutual reaching out spoke volumes.

Winona left for Cedar Ridge. Candleshine made flying trips home when days off permitted the journey. The small town outdid itself welcoming back its war heroes. Thanksgiving 1945 mingled fervent blessings and mourning for those who no longer filled the empty chairs around family tables. Winona's stay in Cedar Ridge restored her health miraculously. She could go back to work in January and start planning for a June wedding.

In the midst of the excitement, and the idea that Bruce and all three women would again be serving at Mercy Hospital, Candleshine found herself restless. Jeff had been home for months during which she had expected a letter or a telephone call or visit. Instead, she heard nothing. She hesitated between wanting to take the initiative and letting things ride. What if she wrote and discovered he had found someone else?

That doesn't dismiss your promise to witness, her conscience reminded her. Sometimes she considered asking for a leave of absence and simply showing up on his doorstep! He had asked her to visit, hadn't he? Would she be welcome? Or would a stern-faced man look at her as if she were a pesky tumbleweed blown in where it didn't belong?

"I'll hear at Christmas," she assured herself. "Then I can go from there." Deep inside, she knew the real reason she could not contact Jeff lay in her relationship with her heavenly Father. Her love for Jeff, born on a tropical island, had never died. At times dormant and hazy, now that she saw the trust and love between Bruce and Winona, her own feelings demanded recognition. She loved Jeff Fairfax and always would, but first her allegiance belonged to God. As Christmas drew near, Candleshine inwardly fought the greatest battle of her life.

★ ★ ★

Two states away, Captain Jeffrey Fairfax struggled to become rancher Jeff Fairfax again. All of Carson's efforts hadn't kept the Laughing X up to prewar standards. The weathered foreman welcomed Jeff home with expressions of gratitude to God but abject apologies.

"I just couldn't get the right kind of help," he admitted as he beat dust from his faded Stetson. "Never hired an alien, though, just citizens and naturalized citizens or those who were workin' on becomin' Americans."

"So just where do we stand?" Jeff leaned back in his easy chair, stared at the fireplace, and shifted his left leg. Eager to ride and hike and see everything, now he paid for it. The jagged scars had healed, but every doctor he'd consulted said he had to give the muscles time to strengthen after their forced inactivity from the infected shrapnel wounds.

"You may carry a slight limp," one doctor warned. His tired face relaxed into a grin. "A small price compared with the possible loss of your leg."

Yet Jeff sighed. Someday he planned to visit Cedar Ridge and a family named Thatcher. Would Candleshine welcome a lame civilian when she'd fallen in love with a slightly-worse-for-wear-but-whole marine? He just bet she would, if she welcomed him at all. He scowled, and Carson's dry comment roused him.

"No need to get black in the face like some thundercloud. We ain't that bad off." He proceeded painstakingly to relate how he'd sold stock to the armed forces. "Prime steers," he announced proudly. "The buyers said they didn't get any better than ours."

"So what we have is smaller herds, fewer men, and no way to go but up?"

Carson cackled. "Beats me how a college feller like you can boil things down to practically nothin'. That's about it. Say, that new man of yours, Black, he's a tenderfoot but he sure is willin'." Carson snorted like a horse at a water trough. "I'll take one like him over a half-dozen know-it-alls like some that came and went while you were gone. I reckon they didn't like the workin' conditions."

Noticing Carson's smirk, Jeff mentally reckoned they didn't, either. Anyone who didn't pull his weight on the Laughing X incurred Carson's legendary wrath. If a cowboy got a second chance and failed, Carson fed him his time and pointed him off the ranch.

"That little wife of Black's a mighty fine gal too," Carson approved. "She up an' baked me an apple pie the other day that makes Cookie's stuff taste like sawdust."

"I'm glad they're working out," Jeff told him. "It's a long way from being a radioman to herding cattle."

"No longer than from being a pilot, I'd say." Carson swelled up like a pouter pigeon. "Jeff, are you goin' to be satisfied here on the ranch after all the fuss an' feathers an' excitement you saw?"

"I'll be content to spend the rest of my life right here in Montana." Jeff's quiet words spilled out more of what he'd gone through than anything he'd said since he got home. He amended the quick statement. "Sure, sometime I'll want to do some traveling when I can get away, but within the borders of the good old U.S. of A." He leaned forward, poked at the fire, and stared into the leaping flames.

"Know what, Carson? All the time I was overseas, I thought how I'd never really taken the time or trouble to get to know the country I was fighting for. Oh, I studied history and geography and all that stuff in school, but I want to go see Gettysburg and Washington, D.C., and Boston, all the places where our ancestors worked and fought so we could be free. It's a lot more important to me now that I know how high a price tag that freedom carries."

"Anytime you want to go, it's fine with me," Carson approved. "I kept the place goin' through a war. Seems like I should be able to keep it goin' while you gallivant around the country." His twinkling eyes showed he understood.

A little pool of silence fell, and Jeff stretched. Hard to believe that just months before he lay in an Australian hospital wondering if he'd lose a leg. God had been good.

Carson cleared his throat. His bright eyes peered out from beneath his thatch of white hair. "Say, Jeff, that Grover woman showed up once after you left."

"*What?*" Jeff grimaced when his sudden movement sent a thrust of pain through his leg. "I thought you'd tied a can to her when you told her I'd never be anything than a rancher."

"Me too, but she up and said she'd been thinkin' things over. This was after the papers got hold of your dunk into the ocean an' wrote up how our local hee-ro saved his radioman."

Jeff waved it aside. He hated being called a hero for doing what any decent man would do in the same circumstances. "So?"

"So I gently but firmly reminded her nothin' had changed an' you couldn't wait to get home and start punchin' cows again." Carson's grin failed to hide his satisfaction. "She sorta sighed like she wished things were different, but she didn't come back. A little later I read in the paper about the marriage of Miss Lillian Grover to Major Somebody or Other."

"Glad to hear it." Jeff grinned back. "How come some women try and put their brand on a guy when he isn't willing?"

"Human nature, I guess." Carson stood and straightened to full height. His persuasive voice sent color to Jeff's hair. "How come you didn't find yourself a girl as nice as Jane while you were gone? Or was she the only one around and Black beat you to it?" His keen eyes narrowed. "Or maybe you did?"

Jeff dropped his head to keep from blurting out that he had found someone far above the practical, devoted Jane. If he told Carson, would his old foreman understand? Had Jane said anything that had made Carson suspicious?

While he hesitated, his foreman's work-worn hand fell on his shoulder. "Boy, once we agreed you have to pick someone like her." He nodded toward the treasured picture of Jeff's parents. "When you do, fetch her home. Don't let anythin' stop you." He tightened his hold, then quietly walked out, leaving Jeff to watch the dying embers in the fireplace. If he could "fetch" Candleshine to the Laughing X, he'd never let her go.

Chapter 13

Sadness pervaded Mercy Hospital when Bruce received word that Sweeny had been killed in action. Candleshine grieved on her own account, remembering the cheerful sergeant who brought her word of Bruce and Winona. Yet she rejoiced that they had been able to witness to Sweeny and felt sure from what he'd said to her that the brusque soldier knew the Lord.

A subdued but ecstatic Sally Monroe came home and asked Candleshine to be her bridesmaid in the spring. Her Jim had come through unscathed. Sally's face glowed. "We're sure now, but it's been so long we want to get reacquainted.

"Besides," she added practically, "with the rest of our lives to be married, there's no hurry."

Candleshine stifled a sigh. Jim and Sally. Bruce and Winona. Even Connie Imoto shyly confessed interest in a friend her brother had met in the service. Sometimes Candleshine felt excluded from the small circles of love within her big circle of family and friends. *Does Jeff ever think of me?* she wondered wistfully. If so, had time cushioned the shock and left pleasant memories? Many times each day, she lifted her gaze from her work and thought of his lean face, his laughing eyes that held tenderness, and his white smile..

Four days before Christmas, Miss Grey again summoned Candleshine from her ward work. Breathless, the student nurse who came for her just missed breaking the hospital and training school rule of no running except in a dire emergency. "Miss Grey wants you *now*," she blurted out.

In spite of the dozens of times she'd been called to Miss Grey's office, Candleshine's heart never failed to skip a beat. Today proved no exception. As usual, she took deep breaths and slowly released them.

"A long-distance call came for you, and I asked them to call back in ten minutes," Miss Grey said. Her eyes looked apprehensive, something Candleshine had never seen before. "The operator said it was an emergency."

The phone on her desk shrilled, and she snatched it. "Yes? She's here. Just a moment, please." She put her hand over the receiver. "Shall I stay?"

"Please." Candleshine reached for the phone. "Candace Thatcher speaking."

"Candleshine, it's Jane, Jane Black."

Candleshine gripped the phone more tightly. "Yes, Jane, what's wrong?" She clearly heard the intake of breath before Jane faltered.

"Jeff Fairfax is badly hurt. He's delirious and calling for you. Can you come?"

The universe spun, but Miss Grey's discipline held, although Candleshine felt the blood drain from her face. "What happened?"

"He thought his leg had healed, but it evidently hadn't. He and Dan rode out this morning to check on the stock. Jeff's horse stumbled in a gopher hole. He tried to kick free of the stirrup, but his bad leg got caught. He was thrown and dragged."

"I'll be there as soon as I can," Candleshine promised.

"Dan will meet you in Missoula. That's where they took Jeff." Jane's voice broke. "Candleshine, please hurry."

"I will." She cradled the phone and whirled toward Miss Grey. "I have to leave for Montana immediately. The officer I met while in the Pacific, he's hurt again. He needs me now." A little glow softened some of the ice inside her. Once—no—twice, she had failed Jeff. She would not fail him this time.

"Go pack what you need for an indefinite stay," Miss Grey ordered. "I'll check on transportation." By the time Candleshine reached the door, the Superintendent of Nurses had dialed. She looked up while waiting for her number to ring. "I'll page Dr. Thatcher, and you can see him before you go."

Candleshine boarded a small, chartered plane arranged for by Miss Grey and Bruce when they discovered no commercial airline flew east for several hours. Bruce wisely asked for no explanations but hugged his cousin, who looked up at him with intense, blue, hurting eyes. "We'll be praying."

Comforted, she climbed into the charter plane and watched the pilot's skillful hands maneuver the controls.

Jane met her at the Missoula landing field. Every freckle stood out, and the strain she couldn't hide made Candleshine's heart plummet. "He's about the same," Jane answered her friend's unspoken demand. "His body took terrible punishment before Dan could stop the horse and free Jeff."

"Just how bad is it?" She had to know.

"He almost wrecked his left leg, and the doctors suspect his skull is fractured."

Candleshine bit her lower lip until she tasted blood. "What are his chances?"

Jane hesitated, her eyes troubled.

"Jane, *what are his chances?*"

"Not good," the other nurse whispered. "I overheard two doctors discussing him, and they're not sure he can stand surgery but without it—" Her silence finished the sentence.

From deep within came strength and peace. Candleshine drew herself up to her full height. Her eyes blazed. "Jeffrey Fairfax is going to lick what odds the doctors give him. He's going to get well. He can't die. I won't let him, and I don't believe God will, either."

"Then tell him so," Jane whispered. She guided her friend out into the beginning of an old-fashioned Montana blizzard, drove the ranch Jeep to the hospital, and waited while Candleshine hurriedly changed to one of the uniforms she brought with her. "It's all arranged that you'll special him," Jane said. "They're always shorthanded, like any hospital. I've even come in from the Laughing X and helped out a few times." She glanced outside and looked worried. "Good thing you got here when you did. No small plane could make it through what Carson says is ahead."

"Carson?" She tried to remember what Jeff had said about him.

"The ranch foreman and a godsend." Jane's lips quivered. "He has the same faith you do and refuses to believe anything but that 'the boy,' as he calls Jeff, will heal." She led Candleshine down the hall. Outside a private room a weather-beaten, white-haired man with the keenest eyes Candleshine had ever faced stopped pacing and shook the nurse's hand. Without a word, Candleshine knew Carson could be depended on in what lay ahead. She gratefully clung to his hand, instantly bonding with the man Jeff loved next to his own father.

"Nurse Thatcher?" A kind-faced woman several years older than the two women beckoned from the open door. She made no effort to whisper but kept a normal voice that stilled the hard beating of Candleshine's heart. "Captain Fairfax—we still think of him like that—has been asking for you. We don't know how much he can hear at the moment, but I know he'll be glad you've come."

Candleshine stepped close to the hospital bed, welcoming yet dreading the moment. She gasped. How little Jeff had changed from the time she cared for him in No-Name Hospital! A little white in the dark hair escaped the bandages near his temples, but otherwise he looked the same. A few new lines had been graven in his haggard face that hadn't been there when they laughed and fell in love.

"Go ahead and speak to him," the older nurse said. She slipped back out into the hall, and Candleshine heard her talking with Jane and Carson.

"Jeff?" She knelt by his bed and cradled his limp hand in hers. "It's Candleshine. I'm here."

Over and over she repeated the words. Sometimes she thought they penetrated the dim recesses of his unconsciousness. At other times she wondered if he'd ever be alert enough to hear her. A strange time began for her, one that demanded her finest skills. Spelled by Jane so the regular nurses could care for the increased patient load from the blizzard, the hospital room and the small room nearby where she and Jane rested became her whole world. A thousand prayers rose and fell when Jeff sank so low the doctors scheduled surgery in spite of his weakened condition. A simple, "Thy will be done," became the hardest prayer Candleshine had ever offered.

Because of her emotional involvement, the surgeon absolutely refused to allow Candleshine to assist. Never had hours dragged as did those in which the surgeon "patched Jeff's head," as Carson said. Yet the presence of the foreman who for once in his life had turned over the handling of the Laughing X to his cowboys and who stayed at the hospital day and night meant comfort for Candleshine.

"The way I figure it," he told her when for the dozenth time she paced the waiting room floor, "it's like this. If the good Lord's wantin' Jeff for some special work up there with Him, why, He knows Jeff will be willin'. If not—"

Candleshine's soul snatched the words. "Jeff will be willing? You mean he's a *Christian?*"

Carson's eyes rounded. "Of course. His daddy an' mother taught him from the Bible from the time he could sit on a pony. When they died in the train accident, Jeff went through a spell of doubtin', which is natural-like." Carson's eyes took on a faraway look. "I don't see that God holds that against us." He smiled and wiped years from his face. "Anyway, since he got back from overseas there's been a big change in him."

Candleshine stiffened.

"He's quieter, but when he talks it shows without him sayin' that somehow, somewhere out there in the Pacific, the boy made his peace with his Master an' those doubts disappeared. Would you be knowin' about that? Jane mentioned, real casual-like, that you were on that tropical island with them."

All this time I've wondered and worried for nothing. Candleshine felt dazed. *Why, Jeff must have taken for granted from things he let drop that I knew he loved the Lord. What have I done?*

Candleshine helplessly sank to a chair and hitched it closer to Carson's. "If you don't mind, I want to tell you a story. . . ." She faltered.

"Does it have a happy ending?" the old foreman asked quietly.

She twisted her fingers in her lap. "I—I don't know." She fumbled for words and at last told him everything from the time Jeff arrived on No-Name Island carrying his badly-wounded radioman and friend Dan Black. If Jane had shared some or all of what she knew, Carson didn't betray it with even a blink. He just listened, and when Candleshine finished, he patted her hand. "Don't you s'pose God knows all about it, Girl? You couldn't help bein' sent to Australia any more than Jeff could help leavin' Guadalcanal just after you went."

For the first time she pieced together what happened that critical day so long ago. In a few well-chosen words, Carson made her see what she'd been unable to comprehend on her own.

"I still don't understand," she whispered. "When he got home, after all this time, he must have known I wanted to see him."

Carson's eyebrows drew together in a straight line. "The boy's proud. As long as he limped so much, do you think he'd come knockin' at your door?

Not Captain Jeffrey Fairfax. He'd want to march up as straight an' tall as he was after you nursed him back to health out there in the Pacific theater." Carson scowled. "Now that he's busted up that leg even more, it may take some convincin' before he sees it doesn't matter."

"How could it?" Candleshine cried. "The only thing that ever held me back was feeling I'd promised to marry a man I barely knew and who might not be a Christian. As if a limp mattered!"

"Tell the boy that, when he's better." Carson grabbed a handkerchief from his pocket and blew his nose loudly. "Best medicine he could get."

"I will." But Candleshine silently added, *if I get the chance*. At least part of her prayer had been answered. Even if Jeff never regained consciousness, never knew she had come to him, he belonged to the Lord, now and forever. She bowed her head and gave thanks.

An exultant voice cut into her mind. "Well, that boy of yours is one tough nut, Carson." The beaming surgeon strode toward them. "Came through fine, and unless complications arise he's going to make it." The next moment the speechless surgeon found himself encircled in the arms of a laughing, crying nurse. "Why, Nurse Thatcher!" Yet he couldn't help grinning when she mumbled, "Thank you!" and fled.

The hours after the surgery passed almost as slowly as those before and during it. To Candleshine's disappointment, Jeff's doctors ordered her to call Jane and turn her patient over to her the moment he stirred.

"I understand it's been some time since he saw you," one explained. "Even joy can bring shock, and that's the last thing he needs at this stage." He must have noticed her drooping shoulders and downturned mouth. "You want what's best for him, don't you?"

"Of course." She put away her feelings and lifted her chin.

"It shouldn't be for long. In the meanwhile, why don't you go see the Laughing X? The storm's let up, and Carson says he has to go check on Black and the others." His grin showed he knew and understood Carson perfectly.

"Why, maybe I will, since I'm about to be fired from my job," she said smiling.

"Anytime you want a job here, it's yours," the doctor retorted. "Any chance you might be moving to Montana in the near future?"

She felt soft color steal up from her uniform collar. "I might."

"I thought so." He grunted. "Remember, you've got a job when you want it."

Candleshine had never thought she'd find a place so lovely in winter as Cedar Ridge. Yet the Laughing X, sleeping under its white blanket, did strange things to her. She ignored Carson's dry comment when they reached the ranch house that her first trip across the threshold should have been as a bride and reveled in the homey, warm atmosphere. The photograph of Jeff's parents drew her like a magnet. "It's like coming home," she murmured.

Carson crossed his arms and looked pleased. "Say, instead of lettin' Jeff know you're here, why don't you just stay with us until he comes home?"

Candleshine whipped around. "You mean be here in his own home when he arrives? I wouldn't dare!"

"Why not? Jane will be back in a few days, an' until then you'll have the house to yourself. I have my own place."

Her eyes darkened. "But what if he doesn't want me?"

Carson didn't move a muscle. "He will."

Her eyes sparkled. "All right, I'll stay, but it's on your head if Jeff throws me out when he gets here!"

For a week, Candleshine stayed at the Laughing X. She had long ago written her parents the story of her romance, and Christmas had flown by during the time of extreme concern over Jeff. January began, and she knew both Winona and Connie were back nursing at Mercy Hospital. A little pang filled her. If she and Jeff married, when would she see them again? Or Cedar Ridge? Yet western Montana and western Washington weren't really so far apart. The Scripture about leaving others and cleaving together came to her. With Jeff she could be happy anywhere. And to think she'd spent weeks, months, and even years miserable and waiting!

On a brilliant late January day, Jeff came home, after pestering his doctors for more than a week. "Look, I'm too hardheaded to let a fall keep me down," he told them. "So what if my leg's going to be in a cast for awhile? Carson can play nursemaid, can't he?" He scowled at the cast, then relaxed. "At least it will be gone by spring." He stretched. "Can't wait to get back outdoors."

"You're hopeless," his doctor told him.

"Yeah," Jeff agreed amiably. "How about it?"

"Well, since you'll have a nurse right there on the ranch I guess it will be all right." The doctor fixed a stern gaze on his unwilling patient. "You've got to promise me you'll do exactly what she says."

"Sure. Jane knows her stuff."

"Jane?" The doctor coughed. "Oh, yes, Nurse Black. Funny how I'm never good at names." He laughed his way out of the room, to Jeff's astonishment.

Left alone, he wrinkled his forehead and tried to remember. Fever and delirium did odd things to a person. He'd have sworn he heard Candleshine speaking to him when he was down and almost out. He shook his head and looked at the blue and white day outside the window. Just when he'd been almost over that limp he had to pull the fool stunt of falling off a horse. A wry grin tilted his lips. "Man comes through a world war and gets hurt worse right in his own backyard!" How long would it take to stand straight?

"Lord, am I wrong? Is it pride that's keeping me from contacting her?" he prayed. "Thank You for bringing me through all this and help me do Your will."

He felt better but the wheels of his mind began to turn in giant circles.

By the next day, he admitted that until he saw or heard from Candleshine, he'd never get his life completely back to normal. That afternoon he begged paper and pen from a nurse and wrote a letter to Cedar Ridge, Washington. *We have some unfinished business,* he began.

Jeff wrote until his hand cramped. He poured out all his anger, then the frowning realization of how much he had asked from Candleshine. *Too much, too soon.* The words haunted him even after he licked the envelope.

Carson showed up a few minutes later, and Jeff thrust the letter at him before he changed his mind. "Mind mailing this for me?"

Carson glanced at the address.

"Hey, Old-timer, you look like you just saw a ghost."

Keen eyes bored into the patient. "Maybe I did, Boy." Carson chuckled, obviously over whatever ailed him for a moment. "Yes, Sir, I'll see this gets delivered right an' proper!" He only stayed a little while and went out, still chuckling.

"What's so funny about this place, anyway?" Jeff demanded of the empty room. "Or is it me?" He twitched and paid for it. "Ouch! If people around here were in my position, they wouldn't find things so all-fired funny!"

The next day the doctor released him. Jeff felt better than he had since he returned from overseas. At least he had taken the first step toward straightening things out with Candleshine. If she had found someone else, or if she couldn't care for a man with a bad leg, so be it. If not—Jeff felt his heart pound. How she'd love the Laughing X as he now saw it! Even her beloved Cedar Ridge couldn't beat this scenery. One of these days he'd find out for himself. This cast wouldn't be around forever. By spring, depending on how she answered, he'd be in fit condition to take a little trip to Cedar Ridge and Seattle to see a certain nurse with short, fluffy fair hair and wildflower-blue eyes.

Suddenly aware of the way Carson fidgeted when they got to the ranch, Jeff demanded, "What's wrong with you?"

"Uh, I was just wonderin' if it's better to prepare a person for a surprise or just to let it happen."

"Surprise!" Jeff glared. "Don't tell me the boys are up to some big welcome home something. You know I hate a fuss."

"I wouldn't exactly say the boys are up to somethin'." But Carson's chuckle did little to soothe Jeff. It would be just like him to arrange a party when all Jeff wanted was to rest. He carefully hoisted himself out of the Jeep, leaned a little on Carson, and hopped to the house, favoring the leg in the cast. By the time he got inside and settled on the couch in front of the fire, he'd had it. "Carson, how about a cup of coffee?"

A slight rustle and light fragrance warned him. Surely Lillian hadn't barged in again. Married or not, it would be just like her! Probably Jane had come to make sure he followed doctors' orders.

He glanced around, stared, and rubbed his eyes and stared again. Had his fever returned? *"You? Here?"*

"For always if you want me." Candleshine ran to the couch, her eyes glowing in the firelight. "Jeff, can you forgive me?" All the time of bittersweet memories crashed in on her. "I didn't know you were a Christian. I couldn't face marrying someone I'd only known a short time and—"

"But my letter," he said hoarsely. "I just wrote yesterday. How did you get here so fast?"

She drew the letter from her uniform pocket. "I've been here since the day you got hurt."

"Then it *was* you! You stayed with me and talked to me. Candleshine, Beloved, you'll never leave me again, will you? Once I asked too much." He pulled back from her reaching arms, caught her by the shoulders, and looked deep into her eyes. "I'll always limp. Does it matter?"

Not a flicker of doubt shadowed her clear eyes. "I'd love you if you had no legs, Jeff."

Warm drops on his hands convinced him more than words.

"You'll be my wife as soon as I get better?"

A flood of color rushed through her fair skin. "I'm going to be your wife as soon as my family can come," she told him. "We can't very well ask Jane to stay with us and play chaperone while you mend, can we?"

Jeff's inarticulate cry answered her question. The same strong arms that had protected her on the PT boat reached and gathered her close. In the tawny firelight, Candleshine saw the love in Jeff's eyes that matched her own.

The war at last was over, and Candleshine's torch burned bright and clear.

COLLEEN L. REECE

Colleen, born in a small, western Washington logging town, describes herself as "an ordinary person with an extraordinary God." As a child learning to read beneath the rays of a kerosene lamp, she dreamed of someday making a difference with her writing. Yet she never dreamed she would one day see 135 of her "Books You Can Trust" (motto) in print with more than three million copies sold.

Several of Colleen's earlier inspirational titles have been reissued in Large Print Library Editions. She is deeply grateful for the many new readers who will be exposed to the message of God's love woven into her stories. In addition to writing, Colleen teaches and encourages at conferences and through mentoring friendships. She loves to travel and is always on the lookout for fresh, new story settings, but she continues to live just a few hours' drive from her beloved hometown.